THE BILL

THE BILL 1

THE BILL 2

THE BILL 3

John Burke

CHANCELLOR PRESS

The Bill first published in Great Britain 1985 by Methuen London
Novel copyright © 1985 John Burke
Television scripts © 1984 and 1985 Geoff McQueen and Barry Appleton
The Bill 2 first published in Great Britain 1987 by Methuen London
Novel copyright © 1987 John Burke
Television scripts © 1986 Geoff McQueen, Barry Appleton, Ginnie Hole,
Christopher Russell and Lionel Goldstein
The Bill 3 first published in Great Britain 1989 by Mandarin Paperbacks
in association with Thames Television International Ltd
Novel copyright © 1989 John Burke
Television scripts © 1987 Geoff McQueen, Christopher Russell,
Al Hunter and Nicholas McInerney

First published in omnibus format 1992
by Mandarin Paperbacks

This edition published by Chancellor Press
an imprint of Reed Consumer Books Ltd
Michelin House, 81 Fulham Road, London SW3 6RB
and Auckland, Melbourne, Singapore and Toronto

ISBN 1 85152 609 9

A CIP catalogue record for this title
is available from the British Library

Printed in the UK by Bath Press, Avon

CONTENTS

THE BILL

1

One

The voice on the car radio babbled on, pouring out a whole load of cheerful garbage. All right for him, tucked away in his cosy studio with his turntable and his tea and biscuits, nicely sheltered from the tough old real old world outside. Nobody ought to be that cheerful at half past five in the morning. Even the sunlight, pale and shifty along the edge of the railway viaduct and on rusty sheets of corrugated iron dangling from a derelict warehouse, knew better than to look cheerful.

Sergeant Bob Cryer stopped for a red light and looked both ways. It was a waste of time really, with not another car in sight; but policemen had to set a good example. All nice and quiet at the moment. A bit too early for today's crop of villains to be out on the streets, and a bit too late for whatever some of them might have been up to last night. It all looked nice and innocent and tranquil. Not much chance of it staying that way for long.

Cryer crossed the junction and swung into the covered yard of Sun Hill police station; slowed, swerved; and swore.

Trouble showed signs of starting already. An ambulance with its rear doors open was backed up to the ramp. As Cryer pulled into a vacant parking slot, two ambulance men emerged from the building and edged a stretcher smoothly between the doors. The police surgeon stood in the station doorway and watched. His face was drawn with tiredness and something else, something more sombre.

'Morning, doc.' Cryer made his way across the yard.

'What's all this, then?'

'Drink drive case.'

'Messed himself up?'

'No.'

'What's with the ambulance, then?'

Dr Grimshaw's lips were tight. 'Threw a fit in his cell. Epilepsy.'

'Oh, great. How is he now?'

'Not too good, I'm afraid.'

Grimshaw followed on into the ambulance, and the doors swung shut. Cryer sighed and turned along the clattering, echoing corridor into the nick to face whatever the day might bring. A flurry of good-mornings, the usual chatter of somebody having an argument halfway up the concrete staircase, and then the duty sergeant was saying, 'Am I glad to see you!'

Obviously it had been one of those nights: which often meant it was going to be one of those days as well.

Cryer flicked over a leaf of the night book. 'What's the score?'

'Three in the men's cell and one in the women's. No, sorry: two in the men's. We just had one carted away to hospital.'

'Yeah, I just saw the wagon pull out. The quack was looking well worried.'

'Dropped a right clanger, didn't he.' It was a statement, not a question.

The sergeant went on to explain, curtly and wasting no time. There never was time to waste on a lot of talk in here.

Two men on the beat had found an odd type parked up on the pavement in High Street at three in the morning. He was slumped over the wheel, with the engine still running. When Hollis and Burton opened the door, the smell of drink nigh took their helmets off. The chap was dead to the world so they brought him in. The duty sergeant hadn't liked the look of him and called out the doctor, who was none too pleased to be dragged out of bed. After giving the man the once-over he said he was just drunk. The usual routine: leave him in a cell to cool off until morning.

'Then about twenty minutes ago the guy throws a wobbler. Ain't never seen nothing like it.'

'No comebacks on us?' asked Cryer sharply.

'No. All done by the book. The doc might have some explaining to do, though.'

Cryer thought that was all too likely. Grimshaw had looked pretty sick.

He turned his attention to sorting out parade sheets. Even at first glance a familiar pattern emerged, carrying over from yesterday and from last week and the week before that . . . and on its way, you could bet, into the far distant future.

In the parade room he made a quick appraisal of the faces he knew as well as he knew the streets and alleys and doorways of Wapping. It was a tough manor, and if you weakened it could get right on top of you. But after twenty years Bob Cryer was still a fighter, trained the hard way and proud of it. He wanted his team to be fighters, too – but skilful fighters, knowing when to punch and when to shadow box and when to back away and play it very, very clever. It was from not being clever enough that he had once, long ago, had his own nose smashed in, and then had it repaired to look like the beak of an aggressive parrot. Not many people risked making comments on that, though.

PC Litten looked fagged out, even though the day was only just beginning. Maybe he had been up half the night chasing some bird; or maybe swotting for the next step in his hoped-for transfer to CID. The lad was getting just a bit too pushy in that direction: too much elbow and not enough know-how.

One of the girls looked unhappy – WPC Ackland, still in a state over some messed-up love affair. With Litten, Cryer suspected. Now he had other interests. She'd learn.

Young Carver's smooth, scrubbed face was bright and wide awake. But was he going to be tough enough? Some of these youngsters from the police college at Hendon were keen on the job and smart on the theory, but often lacked that real instinct – call it killer instinct, call it just plain bloody stamina, call it what you liked – the boil-up of intuition and slogging persistence that led you in the right direction and kept you moving. On the whole he thought Carver would make it. Not right away, but he'd go through the mill and in the end he'd make it.

'Right,' said Cryer.

Two of the men cleared their throats. The girls looked earnest and attentive. Duplicated sheets rustled as they were turned over and studied. At the side of the room, Detective Inspector Galloway propped his feet on the rung of a neighbouring chair and yawned ostentatiously. Roy Galloway always made a big act of letting the uniform branch know what he thought of them.

Ignoring him, Cryer briskly outlined the main duties for the day. A faint moan drifted back to him when he dragged up the old trouble, the disease they all knew about but could never quite cure. It was like a plague, transmitted from one street to another, checked in one back alley only to break out again halfway across the manor. Pickpockets were out in force again. Everyone with beats covering or crossing the High Street had to keep a beady eye out. There was every indication that the firm was the same as one operating on this patch about three months ago. Descriptions were sketchy, but there seemed to be at least three in the regular team: the usual pusher, the catcher, and of course the dipper. Also there were hints that one of the team was a blonde, good-looking woman who specialized in the pushing when the chosen victim was a male.

'Showing lots of cleavage, eh?' offered PC Edwards hopefully.

Cryer glared. 'Keep your attention on wandering hands, not the other bits. And now, sheet 4. Theft from vehicles. Figures are up again this month. Maybe now that the kids are going back to school there'll be a bit of a drop. Just the same, I want you on your toes. Pull anyone you see acting a bit sussy around the various car parks. But be careful. I don't want a stack of complaints from the public about over-zealous policing, understand?'

They nodded and murmured. Galloway's shoes scraped restlessly on the chair rung.

'OK, then.' Cryer glanced at the clock. 'Now, the last item on page 8. Crime Watch – which means breaking and entering. It's a month since this operation has been in effect, and I can tell you now that figures for last month are lower.' He allowed himself a faint smile. They waited for it like puppies grateful for a stroke and words of encouragement. 'However' – the rasp came back into his voice – 'I'd point out it's still early days. Too early for us to be patting ourselves

11

on the back. Right. Before you hit the streets, Inspector Galloway from CID is here. He'd like a few words on the subject.'

Shoulders slumped as Roy Galloway unhitched himself from his chair and sauntered forward. His sandy hair and high complexion seemed drained of colour this morning, like someone who had spent a sleepless night – and not for any fun he got out of it. One thumb went automatically into the waistband of his trousers. His nose wrinkled as if it hurt him to be here.

'Thank you, sergeant.' The word sounded like an insult. 'Now. You should all have a copy of my memo on a particular kind of screw-in, break-in, MO, yes?' As the papers rustled yet again, he snapped out: 'You all know what an MO is, eh? Edwards?'

Taffy Edwards smiled up guilelessly. 'Medical orderly, sir?'

'Modus operandi,' snarled Galloway. 'Latin.'

'Oh.' Taffy looked as if it would have made little difference even if it had been in Welsh.

'Make a mental note of this particular MO. Pay special attention to recent double-glazed properties with no sign of forced entry.' Cryer noticed that PC Litten was hanging on every word, staring attentively at Galloway, advertising himself as real on-the-ball CID material. It turned your stomach. 'If you get called out to a screw-in and it bears a close resemblance,' said Galloway, 'I want to know. And double-quick. Get straight on the wire to your guv'nor, then after that don't touch a thing. Stay on the scene until my team arrive. Got it?'

Cryer said: 'Thank you, inspector. All right, that's it. On your bikes.'

As they squeezed out into the corridor and their footsteps rattled off in different directions, Roy Galloway stood beside the doorway watching the dispersal with a curl of the lip. The skinny little sod knew at least ten different ways of twisting his face into expressions of scorn, thought Cryer.

'Didn't have to sit through all that lot really, did I, Robert? Didn't really expect quite such a production.'

'Listen,' said Cryer slowly and deliberately. 'I brief my officers in a tried and tested fashion. If you think I'm going to turn it arse about face just to please you, you have another thing coming.'

'Thanks for nothing.'

'And another thing. Don't come in here treating my lot like they're a bunch of schoolkids, right?'

'Yes, headmaster.'

Cryer brushed past him and stamped along to the front office. The switchboard was buzzing into life. All you had to do was wait, and it would all happen: kids would go missing, goods would go missing, someone would clobber his wife and someone else would clobber half the punters in the park, the complaints would come screeching in . . . and out there his boys and girls would spread out, hunt, call in or be called in, keep on the move for as many hours as the day had in it. They were like healthy corpuscles, he had once thought

12

after a compulsory lecture by some visiting expert from Forensic, rushing about on the alert through a very murky bloodstream.

Most of the time, though, Cryer didn't think in any such terms. He just tackled what came, on its own merits: if merits was the right word, which it very rarely was.

He glanced at the calendar. His next leave was a long way off. And his wife said he was a misery and a fidget when he was away from the nick for more than a couple of days, anyway.

From the switchboard June Ackland said: 'Sarge . . .'

The day was getting under way.

Two

Early shoppers were making erratic lunges over zebra crossings, blundering into men on their way to and from the riverside wharves and warehouses. The inevitable idlers shuffled from one shop front to another or lounged in the doorways of snack bars and newsagents, squeezing empty Coke tins into distorted shapes. Why, Jimmy Carver wondered, did folk like that come out at this time of the morning when there was nothing to do once they had got here?

Heads turned as the two constables plodded past. A group of youths in jeans and studded jackets allowed themselves a knowing sneer: contemptuous, but not *too* contemptuous. Then the heads turned the other way as a girl with puce hair wriggled her way towards an office block with a faded sign offering two upper floors to let. Carver watched her bottom as it disappeared up a brief flight of steps. At least it was doing something to brighten up the morning.

Taffy Edwards laughed. 'You know what, Jimbo? I reckon June Ackland quite fancies you.'

'Come off it.'

'I been watching her. In the parade room, the way she keeps giving you the eye.'

'Get away. You're winding me up.'

'It's not a wind-up, honest. You ought to get in there, you'll score first time.'

Carver felt himself going pink. All that sort of talk round the station, and the ribbing in the canteen, it was all harmless enough, but still he didn't go for it. All right, so once or twice during morning briefings he had glanced at June Ackland's profile, and rather liked the line of her neck below that crisp

13

blonde hair. And once or twice when she had been bending forward over the switchboard and had caught his eye she had half smiled: but it was a pitying sort of smile, the opposite of a come-on, half telling him he'd never be lively enough and half telling him to stop gawping. Anyway, she was still getting over some kind of bust-up with Dave Litten, and Jimmy Carver was none too sure he fancied one of Litten's leftovers.

No, that was pushing it too far. There was more to her than that. Maybe the thing had bust up because she didn't fancy anyone that crude. Good for her. Maybe when it had all blown over she'd smile in a different way, and they'd both be good and ready, and he, Jimmy Carver, with a lot more experience under his belt . . .

Hastily he said: 'I wouldn't get involved with anyone in the job. So scrub round it.'

'Oh, very commendable, Jimbo. Very professional.' Taffy grinned. 'Come on, I'll treat you to a bit of breakfast.'

'Breakfast? But we've only been on for half an hour.'

He found himself talking to Taffy's retreating back, and had to quicken his pace to catch up.

They turned down a narrow alley with a rich complement of dustbins, empty boxes, cardboard cartons, and a stench that had been around for a long time and was unlikely to go away in a hurry. A hot breath of bacon and chips belched out of an extractor in the wall. Taffy reached a grimy back door, and opened it with a dramatic flourish.

'This'll put some lead in your pencil, boyo.'

The draught of warm air and breakfast odours enveloped them. A girl in a flimsy blue dress was poised above a table in the act of laying two plates of sausages and beans in front of a couple of workmen. Quite an act it was, too. The men were more interested in a page of racing tips than in the girl. Carver wouldn't have been if he had been sitting where they were. The girl's dress was cut low, and for two very good reasons.

Taffy nudged him. 'See what I mean?'

Jimmy Carver saw.

Then the girl looked up and said, 'Cor, look what the tide's just washed up,' but smiled, and then got a good look at Carver and smiled a bit more.

Something came between them. It was a large woman who had long since given up wearing skimpy, low-cut little dresses.

'You're a bit early this morning,' she said to Taffy Edwards, and then, questioningly: 'A new face, eh?'

'Annie, meet Jimbo. But watch him. Quite an eye for the ladies, young Jimbo. Jimbo, meet Annie – does the best breakfast in the whole of London.'

Carver fumbled the helmet off his head and took the opportunity of edging to one side. This way the view was a whole lot better. Gathering up a pile of dirty plates and swinging towards the counter flap, the girl paused and let her dress slip, writhing one shoulder so that it slithered just so many inches and then was miraculously stopped.

Annie folded her arms across a bosom which was ample but no longer alluring. 'Carol, where'd you hide them tins of beans what came in yesterday?'

'D'yer look in the back?' Carol's voice was not as sleek and inviting as the rest of her. Carver flinched as the volume was turned up. 'Course you didn't.'

She stormed on through the open flap.

Jimmy Carver had already eaten before leaving his digs this morning, as he always did. He made do with a cup of tea while Taffy chomped his way through two bacon rolls. It was another chunk of experience – learning about a café like this, and watching his mate's lips begin to glisten with bacon fat. Taffy's mouth was in fact good and full when his radio crackled into life and WPC Ackland's voice came over. 'Uniform Oscar to one-oh-one. Over.' Taffy gulped, tucked a wedge of bacon and crust behind his upper molars, and acknowledged. 'Proceed to rear car park, supermarket, the High Street, tunnel end,' came the instruction. 'Report of suspicious person tampering with parked vehicles.'

Taffy pushed the plate away, washed the last mouthful down with tea, and was on his feet. 'Come on, Jimbo. Just down the road.'

They burst out of the back door into the alley as Carver struggled to get his helmet on straight.

The car park was on a rough patch of ground which was beaten hard in summer but like a marsh on a wet wintry day. Drivers who got here first made use of arches in the high building which cast a shadow over the site – arches which had once been wine cellars before the upper storeys facing out on to the main road had been expanded into a supermarket and shopping precinct. Others stayed outside and by the end of each day accumulated rust-red smears of soot and oily smut over their roofs and bonnets. Carver and Edwards paused at the head of the shallow slope down on to the main parking lot, and surveyed the bumpy surface. Nothing moved. Cautiously they went down and split up, Carver circling round to the west end and making his way back beside a row of cars close to the towering brick wall. Taffy reported arrival into his PR, cut off, and carefully closed in from the opposite end.

Carver reached the darkly gaping mouth of one of the arches. Something glinted and then was gone as he took another step or two.

He eased in under the overhang and tried to adjust his eyes to the sudden twilight.

It came into focus: a car radio below the partly open door of a pricey little coupé, and, half kicked under the car, a briefcase and a camera.

Someone had been interrupted by their arrival. Whoever he was, he couldn't be far away.

Carver stooped for a closer examination, then swiftly straightened up. Not ten feet away, from between a Rover and a rusty Ford Granada, a man broke cover and began to leg it across the car park towards the exit.

'Taffy!'

They scrambled between two lines of cars, found an open patch, converged between two more ranks and saw their quarry racing up the ramp. Carver's breath rasped in his throat. His first bit of luck, his first big chance: he couldn't fluff it, wasn't going to, *couldn't*.

'Stop – police!'

The man, going like the clappers, knew without looking round that they were gaining on him. He swerved away from the exit, went over the low wall, and sprinted like a mad thing across the road and towards the alley behind Annie's café.

Carver could hear him whimpering. Well out of condition, this one. He wasted none of his own breath, not even on another shout. He was gaining, and Taffy was close behind. He aimed to crowd the man, forcing him over towards the line of dustbins and teetering boxes.

Right. Now. Carver braced himself to make a long, wild leap on to the fugitive's back.

The door of the café opened: opened outwards.

There was no way either of them could stop. The man went head-on into the edge of the door and was flung aside. Carver took the full force of the rebound, and the two of them piled up in a thrashing heap on the rubbish bins, while the door thudded back to the accompaniment of a loud crash and a scream of rage from inside.

'Jimbo.' Taffy came panting to a halt. 'Jimbo, you all right? Like a bloody greyhound, I couldn't . . .'

His voice trailed away. He heaved Carver to his feet, then stood back. A yellow mess began to drip from Carver's shoulder down the front of his tunic. Taffy seemed happier to risk tackling their quarry; but the man had had enough. 'Awright, awright.' He waved a weary hand in defeat, and let Taffy prop him against the wall.

The door opened again, more cautiously this time. Annie's head came round it.

'What the bloody hell's going on?'

'It's all right, Annie. It's us. You all right then, love?'

'You put the fear of God up our Carol. Miracle she ain't broke her neck, the way that door slammed shut.'

Carol forced her way past, out into the alley. She was plastered from head to foot in what had presumably started life as three large helpings of beans, sausages and tomatoes in a great deal of juice – not to mention a liberal helping of brown sauce which had appeared from somewhere.

'I'll bloody kill whoever . . . I'm telling you, I'll kill 'em . . . I'll . . .'

Carver risked a friendly smile.

Annie contemplated the crumpled crates and one of the dustbins which had been knocked sideways.

16

'I told you. Them bins should have been emptied two days ago, not left here like this. And them eggs . . . I told you they was rotten, don't say I didn't tell you.'

Carver did not need to be told. His own nose had already settled that point. Helplessly he dabbed at the sticky mess on his uniform. Taffy kept his distance, beginning to smile; could not help the smile broadening; and Annie was cackling, doubling up, wiping her eyes with the hem of her none too savoury apron.

Dripping and demoralized, Carver stared beseechingly at Carol.

Bang went that daydream, anyway. Short and sweet. Only not what you'd call sweet. He had heard of having egg on your face, but had never thought of what the real thing would be like. Fat chance of even a cup of tea on these premises from now on.

A flash of colour slid to a halt across the end of the alley. One of the mobile patrols, alerted by June Ackland, had arrived to help, or at least to pick up the pieces. When they saw the pieces, the two men tried to nod sympathetically. The gesture was spoilt when they began to look and then snigger like Taffy Edwards.

'Well,' said the driver heartlessly as he carted them all away, 'you can't make an omelette without breaking something or other. A pity it had to be such a ripe vintage, though.'

Sergeant Cryer was waiting for them to return. His eyes welcomed them; his nose had second thoughts; his mouth twitched, and he turned away.

The duty sergeant took the arrested man and his two captors into the charge room. Whatever he thought about the grade or condition of the eggs adorning PC Carver's uniform, he said nothing. What he did say something about was the abject, sly little creep sitting behind the table. He said it loud and clear and kept hammering on about it, because it was too obvious that the little rat was getting his nerve back and deciding to play it all cocky and clever.

'I wanna see the CID.' The expression was smug enough to make Carver and Edwards uneasy. What did the grubby little crook know? *Who* did he know? It had to be a con, said Carver fervently to himself. 'A DI,' whined the man, his right eye beginning to twitch and blink. 'Or a DCI. No one lower.'

'You what? You got some chances, pal. You,' said Sergeant Penny weightily, 'are in dead lumber.'

At this moment Sergeant Cryer chose to join them. He winked approvingly at Carver, who ought to have felt flattered but was in no mood to wink, even respectfully, at anyone.

Penny said: 'Bob, this rubbish won't give his name, and is now demanding – demanding, mark you – to see someone from CID.'

'Let me make one phone call, and I'll front up me name.' The twitching eyes were bleary but knowing.

'Games ain't going to do you no good, son. Now, what's your name?'

'I've told you – '

'That's right. Go on telling me. *Name?*'

There was a pause, then: 'Mickey.'

'Now we're being sensible.' Sergeant Penny scribbled on the sheet before him. 'Michael . . .?'

'Mouse. Mickey Mouse.'

Penny went faintly mauve around his ear lobes. Cryer loomed behind him and said: 'Now look –'

'I gotta talk to CID. Leave it out, will yer? You just don't know, but *they* do. Tell the CID.'

'Belt up.' Cryer stepped forward, found himself too close to Carver, and winced. 'Honest, you pen an' ink, son. Go get yourself cleaned up.'

Jimmy Carver was only too glad to make his escape. In the locker room he showered and changed into a clean shirt, rinsing the old one and flicking water towards Taffy Edwards.

Taffy shook his head tolerantly. 'I remember my first collar. Great feeling, right?'

'Just doing our job.'

'Hark at Mr Modest! Don't try and con me, boyo. I was there, remember? I saw your face after it was all done. Pleased as punch you were.'

Carver felt the warmth glowing up inside him. All right, it was true. He had to admit it: he felt well chuffed. There had been panic for a moment, a moment that had seemed a ruddy lifetime, a moment, or ten minutes, or fifty flaming years, when he had thought the bastard might get away. But he'd done it. Got him.

'My,' said Taffy, 'but you can run. I'll say that for you.' Carver flung more water at him. Taffy twisted a tap on, put his thumb under it, and directed a jet back.

'Have we done?' It was Sergeant Cryer. 'There's an empty beat out there just yearning for two young coppers. Any offers?'

'Right, sarge, on our way.'

As they passed him, tugging their clothes into shape and groping for the buttons that he'd curse at if they didn't get them done up fast, he muttered to himself, but loudly enough to thrum through the washroom: 'Bleedin' woodentops!'

A man was standing at the counter as they went through the outer office. 'Detective Inspector Galloway, please. The name's Langley. Harold Langley.'

He looked glum and tense. Lots of people who got drawn into Galloway's net looked glum. Better to be out on the streets, thought Carver: even when contaminated with rotten eggs – human or the other kind – there was fresher air in the streets than in the DI's troublesome mind and troublesome office.

'What's the chance of two in one day, d'you reckon?' he said blithely to Taffy Edwards.

'Oh, got the taste, have you?'

They fell companionably into step. Everything was set fair for a quiet hour or two, keeping the peace – most of all their own.

A transit van skidded to the kerb beside them. 'Come on, that team of dippers are at it again. Two WPCs hit the wire.' As they were scrambling into the back, the driver shouted over his shoulder: 'Might flush 'em out this time. High Street, one of the big stores. Hold on.' They swung sharp left, slowed, veered, and shot ahead.

Roy Galloway watched Bob Cryer approaching past the glass partition. He looked cheerful. Galloway gritted his teeth. If Cryer looked cheerful it often meant he had something up his sleeve.

'Roy, want some good news? PC Litten's just attended a break-and-enter. Sounds like the MO you're interested in. Scenes of Crime are on their way. I've told Litten to stay put and touch nothing.'

'That was bloody quick,' Galloway had to admit. 'Double-glazed, this drum?'

'The usual bloody mess inside. Bloody vandals. But no sign of entry. And according to Litten, yes, it's double-glazed.'

'That's my little firm.' The phone rang. Galloway answered it and felt his lips curl with pleasure; could almost feel himself getting his teeth into something at last. 'Spot on time. just the right visitor. Three months of hard graft and it's paying off. Thanks, Bob.'

'Sometimes, Roy – only sometimes, mind – you can be quite human.'

'Get stuffed.'

The atmosphere was as normal. Healthy and normal.

Harold Langley was shown in. Galloway had had his questions pretty well lined up in advance. Now, with this latest news, he was ready to fire them all off at one hell of a rate. He didn't need to explain double glazing principles to Mr Langley, whose firm advertised its expertise in that field very widely in the area. Galloway knew the techniques and had piled up quite a few hunches about the men who worked on them. He could see from Langley's face that the boss of the firm was beginning to see what was coming: seeing it and fearing it.

'These fitters of yours,' said Galloway. 'Same team working on all your installations?'

'Small firm, inspector. Can't afford half a dozen different squads all over the place.'

'How long have these men worked for your company?'

'I'm not absolutely sure. You know how it is. I could get my people to check.'

'Roughly.'

Langley's dark, dour expression and the pout of his thick lips showed that he was more used to chatting up customers and overriding them with convincing patter than to answering hard, factual questions. 'Two years,' he ventured. 'Two and a half, give or take a few months.'

19

'Same routine, most days, most jobs? The fitters pick up their work sheets, I'd imagine, from your office – '

'Then go round to the factory and pick up the windows and doors required. They then go to the client's house and proceed with the installation. Straight-forward.'

Galloway looked at his notepad and at a sketch he had had done by one of the lab boys on the last but three of successive break-ins. 'These doors. I presume they come complete?'

'Double-glazed doors in a hardwood frame.'

'Locks . . . keys?'

Langley looked worried but honest. 'Each door has a standard Yale-type lock and a mortice dead-bolt. Keys are taped to the doors to avoid getting mixed up.'

'So,' said Galloway, feeling it all click into place the way one of those keys would click so neatly into place, 'it would be a simple task for dishonest fitters to have a spare pair of keys cut? Fit all the doors and windows, and then call back three months later, even six months later, and walk straight into the house?'

'I suppose it would.'

'And right at this moment, Mr Langley, it happens that we have another break-and-enter. Same pattern. Front door double-glazed, the lot. And it could just be your firm that fitted it. Think I'll have a car brought round so I can go and have a look. And those two fitters who do most of your work – on an installation right now, are they?'

It came out as a resigned whisper. 'I'll get on to my office for the address.'

'Do that, Mr Langley.'

He had no doubts about the conclusion. His only doubts were about PC Litten, when he got to the scene and had the lad fawning all over him. Litten was too big and brawny to fawn on anyone. But at least he had done everything he'd been ordered to do, and the fingerprint and photo-graphic boys had got here in double-quick time. Hard not to give him an encouraging nod.

The thing was as good as wrapped up, there was no doubt about that. Galloway was in an expansive mood when he got back to Sun Hill. Sergeant Cryer was in much the same frame of mind. Quite a day, one way and another: their two main concerns both neatly wrapped up, with two double-glazing fit-ters being carted into custody, and two teams of dippers rounded up in one fell swoop. It was definitely a day for smiling.

Trust Bob Cryer to find a way of wiping the smile off anyone's face.

'You've got a visitor.'

'Sorry to be so popular, Bob.'

'Not the sort I'd want to be popular with, this one. Knew him way back. How Operation Countryman never dug him out of the dirt I'll never know.'

20

Cryer puffed out an accusing breath and added sourly: 'One of *your* lot. A DS, name of Burnside.'

'Can't say I know him. What's he after, do you know?'

'At an educated guess I'd say he wants one of his snouts dropped out. Young Carver nicked a face earlier. We let him have one phone call, and he rang this Burnside. Shouting for a get-out, if you ask me. Only a guess, mind you. But it has that sort of stink about it.'

'Right, let's see the guy.'

As Galloway reached the foot of the stairs, Cryer said: 'He's too late, Roy. Mind you tell him that. The guy's nicked and charged.'

'That's what I like to see, Bob – co-operation.'

'Bloody superstars.'

Galloway stumped into his office. The man waiting for him was on his feet, with the sort of vague and guileless expression that made it clear he had been nosing through papers on the desk. He was a hulking six-footer with the jaw of a born bruiser, just as likely to have enjoyed being a criminal as being a police officer.

'Hello, sunshine, what can I do for you?'

'Burnside, guv. Hello. Well, guv, my guv'nor said I should pop over and speak to you. DI Hungerford. I think you know him.'

Yes, Roy Galloway knew Hungerford. But he wondered instinctively whether Hungerford had sent this Burnside character over here, or whether Burnside was in a spot and trying to get out of it under his own steam.

'Right. What's your problem?'

Burnside glanced meaningly at the chair facing the desk. Galloway waved him into it and sprawled back in his own chair. He didn't like the bloke's face or his manner.

'The thing is, guv, my best snout's gone and got himself lifted.'

'I just heard it might be that. So what?'

'Can you help, guv? You know how we need them. Specially when something's building up on our manor.'

Galloway knew all right. They all had to rely on greasy little villains to shop bigger villains. Never mind about the grease coming off on your own hands: there were times when a case simply could not be cracked unless you found the right little two-timer, the right snout.

'You're too late, son,' he said.

'He's done me some good in the past, and he's on to a big one for us right now. Real big number. You know how it is.'

'He's in the system. Already charged.'

'Oh, shit.' Burnside shook his head. 'My guv'nor won't be pleased, know what I mean?'

Galloway glared. 'A pox on your guv'nor. Don't you try that old number on me, toe rag.'

'Sorry, guv, I didn't mean . . . I mean, straight, I was only . . . look, guv, it's just that I need that body back out on the street. Need it bad. Was about due for a right result.'

Galloway tugged a lower desk drawer out with the toe of his shoe, and propped his foot on it. He stared at his foot rather than at Burnside. A nasty piece of work, almost as nasty as the people he was supposed to be fighting. But his story was likely enough, and the little rat downstairs wasn't going to be of any use tucked away in a cell.

'Yeah, well. I might just be able to swing that. But remember, the guy's still on to a nicking.'

'You can have him back in a few days, guv,' said Burnside eagerly. 'All I need is a few days.'

'I'll see what I can do.'

'And while you're at it, maybe I could have a few words with him?'

'See what I can do,' said Galloway again.

He hoisted himself to his feet. Burnside blundered up beside him, following him towards the door and down the stairs, trying to be matey, talking and rattling on. Galloway paid no attention.

Sergeant Cryer, at the foot of the stairs, watched them coming down. He wasn't offering them much in the way of a welcome.

Galloway said: 'Bob, could I have a word with you in my office?'

'I'll be . . .'

Cryer was interrupted by PC Hollis, hurrying through from the front office.

'Sarge, we've got a right pair at the desk. Fellow wants to log a citizen's arrest.'

'A what?'

'That's what he says. And there's a lot of blood about. I think we need the doctor.'

Cryer was on his way, calling back: 'Let me sort this out, Roy, and I'll be right with you.'

Three

Hollis had not exaggerated. There was indeed a fine old amount of blood around. The bigger man of the two was dripping it through the end of his shirt sleeve, torn and clutched to his fingers. Behind him, a dapper little man in his

22

middle forties was still triumphantly twisting his captive's arm up behind his back.

'Dr Grimshaw's on the premises, sarge. Having a word with the super upstairs.'

'Thank God for that. Ask him to come down, will you?' Cryer urged the two men into the interview room and said: 'Please, sir, I think you can let the gentleman go now.'

'Not taking any chances, sergeant.'

'Please release your hold.'

Reluctantly the smaller man did so. The other stumbled ahead of him, crouching over the mess of his hand. Sergeant Cryer indicated two chairs. Behind him, Sergeant Penny came in, wondering what new freakishness the public were playing on them this time.

Cryer wondered the same.

'Now, sir . . . ?'

'My name is Skene, sergeant. Wilfred Skene. Simply doing my duty as a law-abiding citizen.'

'I'm sure, sir. Can you tell us exactly what happened?'

'This creature tried to pick my pocket. My inside pocket.' Skene sounded genuinely outraged, as if attempts on an inside pocket were ten times worse than a simple dip into an outer jacket pocket.

'And you made a citizen's arrest.' Cryer and Penny looked disbelievingly at the bloodstained fingers and shred of what had once been a white shirt.

'That is so. His friends, I'm afraid, got away.'

'Not for long, I'm sure,' said Cryer reassuringly. He beamed at the slumped, shuddering man beside Skene. 'I bet that shocked you, eh? . . . *Fingers!*'

Skene, with mock diffidence, opened his jacket to display the inner pocket. Sewn along the lip of the pocket was a neat line of fish-hooks.

'An old trick I picked up whilst living in Hong Kong, sergeant.'

'That was quite a catch, sir.' Penny's comment combined admiration with uncertainty.

Cryer felt the same uncertainty. He was none too sure it was legal to go around fitted out like that, even to trap pickpockets. But what sort of charge could you bring? Possession of an offensive weapon. possession of an offensive pocket . . . ?

There was a tap at the door. Cryer, the nearest, opened it.

Dr Grimshaw said: 'I'm told you have a casualty for me.'

'That's right, doc. A man with injured fingers. Right in here.' As Grimshaw went on into the room, he added: 'By the way, how's the chap who had that fit? Pull round all right, did he?'

Grimshaw stopped, not looking round.

'Oh. Sorry, doc.' Cryer waved at Sergeant Penny. 'Can you take over and start the paperwork, Tom? Better go and see what Galloway's got in mind.'

23

He would have liked to say something consoling to Dr Grimshaw, but it wasn't his place to do so. And it wouldn't have done any good. A man had died. No use telling a doctor – least of all one usually as conscientious as Grimshaw – that you couldn't win 'em all, that we all made mistakes, that it was a rough old life and folk were dropping dead every second of the day.

It was going to haunt Grimshaw, that one error: he was that sort of man.

Cryer went upstairs and into Roy Galloway's office.

Galloway said: 'You told me porkies, Bob. You told me the snout had been processed and charged.'

'Well – '

'I just checked. He hasn't been charged, has he, my old son?'

'He will be as soon as we get the bit from CRO.'

'But he hasn't been charged yet,' said the detective inspector inexorably.

'All right, not yet. But I'm not dropping him out, Roy, no way.'

'Who said I wanted him dropped out?'

'Well, that's what Burnside's after, isn't it? Why else am I here?'

'All I'm asking for is – '

'He ain't walking, Roy, and that's it. He was caught fair and square. It's PC Carver's first collar, and you know what that means to a kid. And all that apart, you don't need telling my feelings about these silly games.'

'No, I don't need telling.' Galloway battered on: 'All I'm asking for is a couple of days. Don't charge him now. Bail him out to attend this station at a later date.'

'On what grounds?'

'In order that further inquiries be made regarding the property found in his possession. It can all be official. No problem.'

Cryer looked down his nose. There was a lot of it to be looked down. 'My, but you've got all the answers, ain't you, Roy?'

'I try, Bob. I try.'

Cryer turned and went out.

Galloway gave him time to get clear, then went down to see how Burnside was getting on with his pet squeaker. As he opened the door, Burnside was saying:

'You're a pain in the arse, Lennie. Caused me a right lot of aggravation. And you know what I can be like when I get naused.'

The cowering little thing on the other side of the table twitched his ferrety nose uncontrollably. 'I'm sorry, Mr Burnside, really. Straight up. I had to do a bit, I needed the poppy real bad. Had to have some, you know how it is.'

'You should have come to me, then, shouldn't you? You're rubbish, Lennie. Bleeding rubbish.'

His hand was raised, and Lennie was cringing, when they both became aware of Galloway in the doorway.

Burnside smirked. 'All right, guv?'

'You've got half a result, right? Just the way you suggested it. Understood?'

The snout looked questioningly from one to the other.

'What's that mean, Mr Burnside? Half a result. Look, I'm clear, ain't I? It's all right. You wouldn't let me down, not you, Mr Burnside.'

Burnside put a hand on his collar and lifted him to his feet. Galloway shrugged and turned away, leaving them to their happy reunion; but a few words drifted back along the echoing corridor as Burnside hustled Lennie away to the outside world.

'Just one thing, you. I gotta bring you back in about a week's time. Don't worry, no aggro. The guv'nor back there just wants to have a little chat, that's all.'

'You're sure, Mr Burnside? Nuffing heavy?'

'Lennie, would I wet up your leg, son?'

The outer door above the car park swung shut behind the two of them.

In the distance Bob Cryer was calling: 'Carver? You up there? Just nip along to the parade room, will you?'

Jimmy Carver had taken more than his share of ribbing. What with Taffy going on and on about his speed – 'Wouldn't stand a chance of bringing him down at Cardiff Arms Park, not any of them, I'm telling you' – and Dave Litten asking how Carol at the café had taken it and what else was she hoping to get in the near future and then going into details about his own thoughts regarding Carol and that dress of hers and the bits not altogether covered by her dress, he was almost glad to be summoned by Sergeant Cryer.

'What you been up to, then?' Litten was in no mood to give up the joshing. 'Sounds like aggro.'

'Just a pat on the back,' said Taffy. 'Don't worry, Jimbo.'

'A pat on the back – from *him*?' Litten raised his gaze despairingly to the ceiling. 'You've got to be joking.'

Carver made his way to the parade room with no idea what to expect.

When the door had clicked shut, the sergeant looked past him, somehow avoiding his eyes. A vein pulsed in his neck. He looked angry, all tightened up. Carver wondered what on earth had gone wrong.

Cryer said: 'Just thought I'd bring you up to date, son. Wouldn't want you to hear it from anyone else. That was a nice collar you made today. Nobody's going to take that away from you. But just for the record, we're not charging him today.'

That made no sense. Carver stared. 'Not charging him, sarge?'

'You didn't listen, son.' Cryer was still taut and fuming, but not at Carver. 'I didn't say we're not charging him. I said we're not charging him today.'

'Why, sarge? Did I do something wrong? I did everything the way I thought – '

'No, son. You did all right.' Cryer let out a snort of disgust. 'Look, from time to time we have to play silly buggers. Bend the rules slightly. None of us like it but it has to be done when there's bigger fish to catch.'

'But he will *be* charged?' Carver persisted.

'Of course he will. He's . . . he's just being released pending further inquiries on the property found in his possession.'

'Released? But – '

'You heard, lad.'

Carver drew himself up and waited for Sergeant Cryer to leave the room. He paused, trying to keep his hands steady.

He wanted to lash out and take a poke at the wall, for all the good that would have done.

He went out into the corridor.

'All right, Jimbo?' Taffy came out of the shadow of the staircase. 'No problem?'

'No.'

'You don't look very happy, boyo.'

'Forget it.'

'Come on, what's up?'

'Nothing. I've told you, forget it.'

They checked their buttons, tugged their tunics straight, and went to the main entrance.

A car turned out of the car park, gathering speed. Burnside was driving. Beside him, Lennie leaned out and jabbed two fingers derisively in the air as the car passed the two constables.

Behind Carver, Galloway said in a wry tone: 'Funny ol' business is cops and robbers, son. Very funny indeed.'

Four

There was often a fair old racket in the station canteen, and a good deal of leg-pulling. Today there was even more noise than usual, but no leg-pulling. Today things were deadly serious.

Tables had been pushed back against the wall out of the way, except for one behind which Chief Superintendent Brownlow sat, flanked by Detective Inspector Galloway. Brownlow's pouchy, bulldog features were heavy with the need for self-control as he faced the angry audience sitting on hastily assembled rows of chairs, or pushing themselves upright, shouting, arguing, talking over the deep, level voice of their own spokesman.

They were in no mood to listen. They had come here to make themselves heard and let their tempers run wild. You couldn't blame them for their anger. Clayview council estate looked new and smart enough, with its flats in well-organized blocks instead of high-rise monsters; the patches of green and a scattering of trees made it a desirable area, quite a credit to the local planners. But below its brightness there was dark menace. There were about two hundred youngsters living there – and out of that two hundred, thirty were known heroin addicts. Two had died of drugs overdoses: one found in a public lavatory, the other dumped at the hospital gates. There would be more to come. The men and women venting their rage on the two police officers were parents, scared out of their wits, wanting to take it all out on somebody.

'Let's have some action, instead of just sitting there like – '

'Never nick any of 'em unless they park on a double yellow line, will yer?'

'Quiet, please.' Tombo Robinson had been pushed forward to speak for them. A tall, handsome Trinidadian with a resonant voice, he was trying to keep things calm. 'You're not helping us. You're not helping me. But Mr Brownlow, Mr Galloway, you just gotta realize – '

'They're not going to do anything. You've only got to look at their faces.'

'They don't want to know.'

A woman with a taped-up pair of National Health glasses put her head out from behind Robinson's imposing bulk. 'You wanna come and see my lad. Sixteen, that's all, and just a bloody cabbage. That's all he frigging well is. Thanks to them drug peddlers. And no thanks to you layabouts for – '

'Do you want me to put our views forward in a proper manner, yes or no?' demanded Robinson.

'Take the law into our own hands, that's the only way.'

'String the bastards up . . . '

Brownlow put his hands on the table and pushed himself slowly to his feet. He was deliberately taking it calmly, playing it slow and heavy and unruffled. Galloway fidgeted. Never patient at the best of times, he wanted some plain talking, not low-temperature soothing stuff.

'We are as concerned as you are about the increase in heroin abuse,' said the chief superintendent. 'But let me say right away that you, as parents, also have a responsibility. A responsibility to speak out – '

'What the 'ell d'you suppose we've been doing?'

'To speak out and keep us informed, all the way along the line. Responsibility to others, as well. This war isn't restricted to your estate. It's a national epidemic. A world-wide one. We shall only succeed if – '

'It's our estate we're talking about, right here and now. Not bloody China.'

Brownlow took up a sheet of paper and read the figures out loud. Over the past three months there had been twenty-three arrests for possession of heroin, and sixteen for supplying. That success had been achieved as a direct result of criminal intelligence, and interpretation of such information as had been put forward through the tenants' association. It wasn't a bad achievement. But they had to keep working away at it, all of them.

'But these users you keep nicking,' protested a man at the back of the room, 'they're our kids, that's who – not the pushers. Don't you understand what we're getting at?'

Robinson said earnestly: 'What we are saying to you, Mr Brownlow, is that we have done our best to furnish you with names and addresses, but these same people are still walking the estate. Still supplying drugs!'

'Simply because the heroin found in their possession is of a small quantity, never enough to back up the charge of largescale supplying. That weakens the evidence submitted in court.'

'You just let 'em slip through your fingers. You don't bloody care.'

Roy Galloway could hold back no longer. When he rose to his feet it was not slowly and portentously. He got up fast, and kicked his chair back.

'I'm sorry, but I've listened to this long enough. You've been carrying on plenty about us not doing our job, not nicking the pushers. But it's *your kids*! Face up to it, that's what we're talking about. Most of your own kids are doing the pushing, financing their own addiction. We can run 'em in all right – and you'll be the first to scream blue bloody murder. The people we need are the big ones, the scum who are supplying those kids.' He slammed his fist down on the table. 'I'll bet some of you sitting there even know who the real dealers are.'

'Now wait a minute – '

'You know where that heroin's coming from, and I still say a couple of you, maybe more, have an idea who the dealers are. Perhaps you're too frightened to say. All I can say is we'll get nowhere if you're too scared to speak out. Get together. Confide in each other. Let us know, then we can really do something about this problem. Only don't leave it too late, because every hour that goes by, another kid gets hooked. You know what I'm talking about?'

There was a silence. The parents viewed him with wary respect.

Brownlow cleared his throat. 'Yes, well . . . I think perhaps this is an opportune moment to break for tea and biscuits.'

While the tenants queued up by the urn and munched biscuits, some still arguing with their mouths full, the two officers and Tombo Robinson drew away into a corner.

'I'm sorry if they got unruly at times,' said Robinson, 'but it's understandable, Mr Brownlow. They're worried parents. Very worried.'

'It's a pity we couldn't all have got together earlier. Now we've started, we've got to follow it up. As Inspector Galloway said, every hour that goes by, somewhere another youngster will be introduced to heroin.'

'I think you made that point. Oh, yes. And I think we'll be giving you the names of some pushers. Bit by bit, you understand? Where they live, where they hang out.' Robinson glanced cautiously at Galloway. 'They may not be the top people, but we have to start somewhere. You know, if there's any more I can do you've only got to ask.'

It was the chance Galloway had been waiting for. He was not going to risk consulting Brownlow. With sudden forcefulness, his finger prodding threateningly, he said: 'Listen, Tombo. You and I have a pretty good idea where the pushers get their "smack" from. Stop giving us the runaround. If you're scared, say so. But if you're not, let's be hearing from you.'

'If I knew, don't you think I'd be telling you?'

Brownlow turned his back on the rest of the room, keeping his voice down but putting some weight behind it. 'Please, gentlemen, not too much noise. And you're out of order, Inspector Galloway.'

'Out of order, am I? Well, let me tell you, sir, with respect . . . I'm the only one who seems to know what's going on, on this manor. All right! You want me to tell you where the heroin's coming from? Decker's Club. How about that?'

'Decker's?' said Robinson sceptically.

'The old cinema?' Brownlow was equally unimpressed. 'You've never mentioned that before, Roy. I know it was an illegal drinking club way back, but we put an end to that. Raided it so many times they packed up and disappeared.'

'Well, they've started up again. Nice and quiet and respectable. Only this time they're into drugs.'

'Decker's?' said Robinson again. 'Harry Decker back in town? I can't believe it.'

'You'd better, my old son, because that's where the action is.'

'If it's true,' fretted Brownlow, 'we'll have one hell of a job getting in there. The place is like a maze. Some of those raids we tried in the past were disastrous.'

'Not if we had an inside man.'

The two of them exchanged glances and then turned to stare at Robinson. He took a step back. 'Oh, no! I haven't been mixed up with that firm for years.'

'You'd be just the man,' said Galloway.

'You can't ask me. I've got a family. They'd cut my throat!'

'I understand, Mr Robinson,' Brownlow soothed him.

'Inspector Galloway shouldn't have asked you.'

'You were once a member,' said Galloway remorselessly. 'You're the ideal man.'

'I don't mix with those people any more. Don't mix with those kind of people. Don't you understand?'

'Look, Tombo. If you want to stop those people poisoning your kids, then you get me and my men into Decker's and this time we'll cut off the supply. It'll give us the chance we need. Come on, what d'you say?'

Robinson took a deep breath. In the background the others began to clatter their teacups noisily back on to the table as a signal that they were ready to get back to the argument.

Robinson muttered: 'Nobody to know except you and Mr Brownlow?'

'Got yourself a deal, Tombo.'

The chief superintendent's office was quieter than the canteen. On the other hand, Brownlow was looking more fierce than he had allowed himself to be in front of their visitors.

'You shouldn't have done it, Roy. I can see all kinds of complications. What if he gets sussed out, beaten up – or even worse? You put me in an awkward position, Roy.'

Galloway said nothing.

'And Decker's of all places!' Brownlow exploded. 'Why in hell didn't you come to me in the first place? Give *me* the information? It makes me look as if I don't know what's going on in my own division.' He dragged open a drawer, took out a bottle of whisky and two glasses, poured drinks and handed one to the detective inspector, with the air of one offering a draught of poison rather than a sociable drink. 'How long have you held back this information, Roy?'

Galloway took a warming gulp before risking the answer. 'I haven't.'

'What do you mean, you haven't?'

'It's . . . well, an educated guess, that's all.'

'Am I hearing right?'

'Only heard today that Decker's had been started up again.' Galloway tried to keep it airy and light-hearted. 'Illegal drinking, ponces, pimps, that kind of thing. Up to their old games. Only I bet you find this recent increase in heroin started about the same time Decker's turned up on the manor again. As I said, it's an educated guess.'

'And you've put in an inexperienced undercover man – an amateur, one of the great general public – on an educated guess?'

'Tombo will be all right. Once he's eased himself into Decker's, he'll come up with something. I know him. He'll find *something*.'

'I don't like it. When will he get in touch?'

'When he's got something to show. It'll take time. He can't just walk in there and wrap it all up in twenty-four hours. He'll ring me, we'll meet. We'll play it clever.'

'You'd better. I hope for your sake this doesn't go wrong, Roy.' Brownlow emptied his glass and began riffling through papers on his desk. 'Now, while you're here, there's something else.'

In this job there was always something else. Galloway sighed. 'Yes, guv?'

'Statistics.' Brownlow selected one sheet of paper and flapped it in the air. 'Statistics and more statistics.'

'Not quite my line, guv.'

'Trouble is it has to be everybody's line nowadays. All for the benefit of the Home Office. Now, these . . . um . . . bomb hoaxes.'

Galloway snorted. 'Those phone calls to restaurants? Been hearing about them, yes. All pranks, if you ask me.'

'The trouble is that when the Home Office match up our statistics with others in the Met, they're coming up with a different story.'

'There've only been three on our patch. Surely that doesn't constitute a problem?'

'Two of those were Jewish restaurants.'

'Perhaps somebody doesn't like salt beef.'

Brownlow scowled. 'Not what I call a very constructive remark. Let me tell you, Roy, the Home Office is breathing down the Commissioner's neck, and I'm getting some of the draught.'

Galloway restrained himself from making a further snide remark. It was really too crazy. Racial hoaxes? Arabs . . . terrorists? He said: 'This is just stupid pranks.'

'I won't beat about the bush. I want you to take over the investigation. And wrap it up fast.'

'Now, hang on, sir. I mean, Sergeant Cryer's dealing with that. I don't think I should interfere.'

'I've got the greatest respect for Sergeant Cryer, but his work load's been heavy over the last two weeks. On top of that he's got another graduate attached to him: PC Higgins. Unfortunately I don't have any other sergeants with his experience free at the moment.'

Galloway said levelly: 'You mean, on top of the heroin hurry-up I've got to work miracles on the restaurant lark as well, all overnight?'

'You've said yourself that it'll take a little while for Robinson to ease himself into that place. While you're waiting, you can tackle this one. If you're right and it's a prank, then I want it cleared up and out of the way. Just liaise with Sergeant Cryer, get the details from him, and take over.' Before Galloway could raise any further objections, the chief superintendent said: 'Good. Thank you, Roy.'

'Thank you, sir.' When well away from the room, Galloway said it louder: 'Thank you *very* much.'

'Hello, guv.' PC Litten grinned obsequiously. 'Keeping you busy, are they?'

Galloway brushed past him and clattered halfway down the stairs. 'Sergeant Cryer! I want to see you in my office. *Now!*'

Cryer kept him waiting. Deliberately: Galloway could be sure of that. He was in a mood to punch a fist into that beak when it finally came round the door.

'This is a bloody lumber, this one!'

Cryer stared. 'Got something on our mind, have we?'

31

'At least one of us has *got* a mind. Having to sort out the messes you lot get yourselves into.'

'Such as?'

'Such as this codswallop about restaurants and phone calls. Letting it drift on until I get lumbered with it. So. Just give me any details you've managed to trip over these last few weeks, and let me show you how to settle it. Fast.'

'Look,' said Bob Cryer, 'this isn't one of those jobs you can go into crash, bang, wallop. You have to sniff around. Use a bit of tact. But you wouldn't know what that means, would you?'

'I know what action means, and there's going to be some. Tact? Who've you been tactful with – and how far has it got you? Bloody idleness, more like.'

'You haven't got Solly Goldstein and Reggie Abrahams shouting at you from one side, and the chief super from the other.'

'But it's a prank,' yelled Galloway. 'Can't you see that?' His voice drew attentive glances from the next office. He got up and slammed the door. 'Look, I know Solly Goldstein. Believe me, if there was no PLO, he'd have invented it.'

'You do talk some bloody rubbish sometimes, you honestly do. You can't treat calls like that as a joke, you have to go through the procedures as if it was the real thing. Every time you have to treat it for real. There's no short cuts.'

'After three phone calls there must be some MO to follow up. *Something!*' Galloway waved at the door. 'All right, leave it with me. The CID will sort it all out, as per usual.'

Cryer paused at the door. 'One of these days, Roy Galloway, you're going to come tumbling off that high horse of yours, and no one's going to lift a finger – least, of all me.'

'Forget the violins, Robert. Tell you what' – Galloway took a ten-pound note from his wallet and slammed it on the desk – 'there you are, that says I'll crack it.'

Cryer stared down at the note. 'Two weeks?'

Galloway nudged the note an inch towards him. Cryer took out a tenner of his own and slapped it down to cover the other.

'Two weeks,' said Galloway, 'at the outside.'

Five

Maureen Galloway said: 'Don't answer it!'

The phone had begun to ring just as they came back into the house. They had been down the road for an Indian. It always had quite an effect on Maureen: something about a really first-rate Tandoori tickled her appetite – more than one of her appetites. She had been nuzzling her cheek against her husband's as they came up the path, and even without the food he would have got that same warm, glowing sensation inside.

But the phone was ringing.

'You're off duty,' she said. 'Let it ring.'

He put out a hand towards the hall table. She tugged away from him, then tried to catch his arm.

He said: 'It might be – '

'Whoever it might be, are they all that more important than me?'

Any second now the noise would stop. Galloway snatched up the receiver.

'Penny here, inspector. We've got another bomb hoax. I thought you'd want to know.'

'Where?'

'Dimitri's Greek and Continental nosh house. You know it?'

'I know it.'

'The area car's already round there with your Sergeant Roach. He thought you'd want to – '

'I'll be right with 'em.'

He turned to explain to Maureen and promise that he would be back in half an hour – well, no more than an hour anyway – but she was already storming up the stairs and giving him a look over the banisters which was not what you'd call inviting.

No sense of priorities, women.

Galloway knew all the back doubles and was at Dimitri's door within fifteen minutes. A 'Closed' sign dangled in the glass panel, but the door was open and at any rate one person was managing to snatch a quick snack: Sergeant Roach swallowed down a hasty mouthful and tried to look alert and dutiful as he scrambled to his feet.

'Inspector Galloway, my friend.' Dimitri's smile was wide, his arms were spread wide, he was offering the whole place on a plate – or in a glass. 'You would like a drink?' Without waiting for an answer he gestured to the man leaning behind the bar, and a triple-sized ouzo was set on the edge of the counter.

'Right. What's the form?'

It was the same pattern, just the same as the others. There had been a phone call to say that a bomb on the premises was due to go off any minute. Then the caller rang off, and customers were hustled out without more ado. Dimitri had called the police in right away, and the premises had been thoroughly cleared and searched. Then they were gone over again with a fine tooth-comb, taking no chances. If there had been a suspect package, the experts would have come in and padded round it very soft-shoe, breathing in that silent way they had.

There was nothing.

'I knew it was a hoax as soon as the man spoke,' said Dimitri. 'But you take no chances, no? I have to hurry everybody out. Only now I want to know. I want you to find out.'

'Right, Ted.' Galloway nodded at Roach, who was looking wistfully at a few shreds of kebab cooling on his abandoned plate. 'You and Mike call it a day. Take those uniformed bods down in the van with you, and I'll see you in the morning. Right?'

'You want me to put anything in the book?'

'I'll do it myself. Dimitri and I are going to go over everything, aren't we, Dimitri? Every little detail. Even if it takes all night.'

It had not occurred to him that such a corny phrase could come so close to the truth. He and Dimitri sat down, and ouzo was poured; and then, within surprisingly few minutes, more ouzo was poured. It did not appear to slow down Dimitri's explanations of what had happened, but after a while it began to slow down Galloway's comprehension.

Maybe, he thought muzzily, not a bad thing. In a sort of trance he began to reach for wisps of truth through a haze of speculation.

There were things in Dimitri's head which the volatile Cypriot did not even know he had absorbed. He talked about the phone call, talked about the rumours he had heard about bombs – hoaxes and the real thing – and tried several imitations of the caller's voice, all of them unconvincing and no two even resembling each other. It was quite some time, well into the fifth or sixth ouzo and the third dish of black olives, that he said something which penetrated Galloway's drowsy but dogged mind.

'Well,' he said plaintively after Galloway had sneered for the third time at his grotesque impersonations, 'it was not so easy, you know? I am supposed to pick up an accent with all that noise going on?'

'Shouldn't have so much noise in a high-class eaterie like this.'

'Not here. Behind this man, the one who talks to me. Roadworks.'

'Roadworks?'

'Behind him, you hear it, the drill, things going over a sheet of metal or something. You know how it is.'

'Roadworks?' Galloway repeated. 'On Friday night?'

Dimitri looked doubtful, then confident. 'Sound of a drill,' he said. 'Cars over a loose piece of sheet metal. I hear it just like that, you understand?'

'Can I use your phone?'

Dimitri waved a lordly hand.

Galloway rang first Solly Goldstein and then Reggie Abrahams. It was made clear to him that he had not chosen the most tactful time. The Jewish Sabbath was already under way, and Solly and Reggie were not best pleased to be interrupted with squalid weekday affairs at such an hour. But they were charitable men, and they told Galloway what he wanted to know. It was indeed what he wanted to know. They remembered, when nudged, that noise in the background, just the way Dimitri had said. Which narrowed it down. Somewhere on the patch, roadworks which went on through the evening – even a Friday evening.

Galloway felt pleased with himself. Lurching back from the phone, the waywardness of his lower limbs made him less pleased. But another ouzo from Dimitri restored the balance, even if only temporarily.

He went home with a great sensation of righteousness swilling around inside. It made quite a cocktail, added to the ouzo.

Home was not all that homely. The bed was empty. He swayed over it, swayed backwards, put a hand on the bedside lamp to stop it wobbling, and made a mental resolve to tell Maureen to get it fixed before it blew up, or fell apart, or did whatever else was in its evil mind.

Only where the hell was Maureen?

He contemplated the space from which two pillows had been removed, and considered going to the spare room to ask if she had a headache, or a bad cold, or something.

Then he decided against it.

He made an excursion to the bathroom, and did not much care for the results. He ought to have known better. As an acquaintance of Dimitri's all this time, he certainly ought to have known better. The trouble was, the ouzo had tasted so much smoother and friendlier then than it tasted now.

It was on his third visit to the bathroom, at some hour of the morning to which he would never have wished to testify in court, that things began to swim back into focus. Way down there in his subconscious was something that must have been nagging at him from earlier in the evening; or the night; or whenever.

A prank, he had told Brownlow. And Bob Cryer. And a prank it was.

Human nature, that's what it was: that old plague of all good policemen, plain-clothes or otherwise. Just look at it. If you were in a restaurant and the place was cleared because of a bomb threat, and you hadn't paid your bill, what

35

would you do? Honest blokes would go back next day, or put a cheque in the post, or at the very least fork out next time they went in. Particularly if the restaurant knew them.

Which of course was the point.

Galloway ran his tongue round his mouth and wondered why he was so irresistibly reminded of the bottom of a parrot's cage, when he hadn't been on speaking terms with a parrot since his grandmother's had been eaten by next door's tabby cat.

This had to be it. You narrowed down the field, and the pattern began to emerge. Right in the middle of that field, a right couple of scarecrows, were these two fellows. Solly hadn't said it in so many words, and Reggie Abrahams hadn't been sure enough to point the finger: but there were two shapes in there, and in Dimitri's place. Just suppose two jokers in each restaurant each time there was one of those bomb calls, and just suppose the calls came just when the bill had been presented: a bill that was never paid. And then there had to be the third party, the person who made the call . . .

From the same phone box.

Galloway crashed back into bed. There was not much to be done about it until Monday morning; but tomorrow, Sunday (or was it sliding well into Sunday already?), Ted Roach could get out on the manor and start asking around about two likely lads, and notifying restaurants, and jumping up and down on sheets of metal near telephone boxes if necessary.

He slept.

When he awoke, there were noises downstairs. Even from a distance they gave him a headache – or, rather, increased the pressure on the iron band round his forehead. Also there was a smell of bacon frying. It usually enticed him out of bed and down the stairs in a fine, hearty, greedy mood.

This morning he went yet again to the bathroom.

She was cruel. She must have known what she was doing. He was surprised she hadn't put garlic and onions with it, and set fire to the toast just to add to the general aroma.

He made a stab at getting dressed, and was tolerably proud of the results, even if he did have to put dark glasses on before picking up his pink striped shirt. There was no way, however, that he could get his cufflinks into the right holes. Each time he prodded the shank through one hole he either cut himself on the sharper link or got his thumb snarled up with a stray thread.

Finally he went downstairs and tried to kiss Maureen. He missed, and narrowly escaped falling across the kitchen table.

He held out his right arm, with the cufflink dangling. 'Could you . . . ?'

'It serves you right,' she said very quietly.

The bacon spat in the pan.

'Coffee?' he ventured.

'I fancy China tea right now.'

Heroin dealers weren't going to beat Roy Galloway. Shady little pranksters in restaurants weren't going to beat him. Nor was Bob Cryer. But there were times when he had to admit defeat. He left home without attempting that happy peck on the cheek which had become standard practice, and found his way to Sun Hill nick, where WPC Ackland smiled at him and then went pale, Ted Roach said, 'How did it go, guv?' and then decided not to pursue the matter, and young Dashwood showed his worthiness for promotion by scurrying about in search of black coffee and a supply of aspirins.

'Roadworks,' said Galloway when he had got his voice under some sort of control. 'On overtime. And a trench or a gap, or something, with a sheet of metal across it. Start looking.'

That was enough for starters. He groped for another helping of aspirin.

Six

Saturday turmoil in the streets was pretty much the same as any other day, but with some different faces, some faces missing, and not quite the same tempo. Jimmy Carver was getting used to the shifts and changes and differences of emphasis.

A lot of the riverside warehouses worked on Saturdays, but there were fewer delivery lorries and a lot more punters driving more slowly in their cars, looking for wine bargains or for snips in the street market.

He glanced sideways at PC Higgins to see what impact it was all making. Not much, from the look on Higgins's pale and rather disdainful face.

Sergeant Cryer had sounded a bit dubious earlier this morning before the two of them set out.

'I don't usually let new boys out with such inexperienced officers as Carver here. On the other hand, he hasn't learnt all of the bad habits yet, not like some of the reprobates you've been out with this week, Higgins.'

Was WPC Ackland smiling at Jimmy Carver, or snickering at him?

'Keep out of trouble,' said Cryer in that tone they were so used to that they could almost turn the volume right down and still get the message good and clear. 'And remember, anything you can't handle, straight on the blower.'

Carver sympathized with Higgins; or tried to. It seemed only yesterday that he himself had been thrown in at the deep end, just like this. They ought to have something in common. But Higgins was holding his head proudly back and staring ahead like some explorer who had just seen the promised land and was not much concerned with trivial things under his own nose. Not a matey sort, Higgins. Either he would go far or he'd get nowhere at all.

Carver said tentatively: 'What d'you make of it so far, then?'

'I expected to get more practical experience.' Higgins gave a contemptuous glance at three young yobbos mimicking his walk and the way he swung his arms. 'I thought I'd learn more this week in that respect, but nobody seems particularly keen to take me out, show me anything. I'm treated with suspicion.'

That, at any rate, Carver could remember. Of course they took their time sizing you up. You might have thought your probationary period was technically over, but there was still a trial period to be gone through with the other lads. He tried to explain: 'It's not because anybody's got anything personal against you, Higgins – '

'Derek.'

'Mm?'

'I've told everybody my name's Derek. But nobody wants to know.'

'Look, I went through all that, just the same way, in my first few weeks. All the lads who've been here any length of time, they've got places to go – you know, cups of tea here, cups of tea there, and all that. I mean, they don't want you knowing about their perks.'

'I wouldn't tell.'

'Ah, but you might just come back as a senior officer. Then where would they be, eh?'

Derek Higgins preened himself and looked away with a flutter of mock modesty. Oh, Higgins knew all right where he intended to go.

Then his wandering gaze settled. 'What's that?'

They stopped by a doorway into what on weekdays was a grotty arcade leading to seedy offices behind the blacked-out windows of what had once been equally seedy shops. On a Saturday there was nothing much doing in there: except that today a huddled shape was stacked against the wall some way in from the street.

Carver led the way. It looked as if they had come across a stray from a wedding or a football match. But at this time of a Saturday morning . . . ?

They stooped over the crumpled figure. The smell that wafted up was a mixture of whisky and damp: not whisky and water, just booze and damp. He must have been there quite some hours.

'Right. Come on up, sir. You all right?'

The feeble answering moan released another sickly stench into the atmosphere.

'He's light as a feather,' marvelled Higgins. 'All skin and bone.'

'Come on. Wheel him along the road.' Carver made himself sound brisk and authoritative.

Higgins obeyed, obviously no more impressed by this experience than by any of the other routine jobs he had so far encountered.

Sergeant Cryer looked far from overjoyed. His immediate, instinctive wince made it clear that this was no new phenomenon, and the tottering, wheezing creature was no stranger to him.

'Lampton! Legless Lampton himself.'

'Ah, my dear old trusted friend.' The drunk tried to hold out his hand, but swayed perilously and had to be steadied by Higgins. 'Always said so, always will.'

'Higgins. Carver. Witness the act. Flannel from an expert. File him away in your mind so you'll be ready for him next time. Freelance journalist, one-time Fleet Street, and it's no wonder it's one-time and not any longer.' When Lampton said nothing, Cryer went on bitterly: 'Come on, let's have the latest. Don't disappoint my lads.'

'Sergeant, do I really have to go to court over this? Couldn't you show just a little ben . . . bl . . . benevolence? A caution, maybe?'

Carver looked away, and saw that Higgins was doing the same. It was cruel to put this twitching wreck through this kind of thing.

But Cryer was inexorable. 'Cautions are over as far as you're concerned. Look, last week you nearly caused a bloody accident in the High Street. A few days before that, if it hadn't been for that special constable, you'd have been in the canal. So it's up before the beak on Monday morning, without fail. Carver!'

'Sarge?'

'Take him down to the pokey. When he sobers up, bail him.'

'A call, perhaps, at midday, officer? I'll be as right as rain then. And I'll promise, Scout's honour' – Lampton ventured an endearing grin – 'to be a good chap for the rest of the week.'

'I've heard your promises before. Go on, take him down.'

Carver and Higgins went through the ritual and were back on the street in ten minutes. It was an uneventful morning. Higgins complained again about the uselessness of it all. This wasn't going to do anything for his career. He had expected real action, expected to be plunged into real tough police work right away on a real tough manor, so he could distinguish himself, make his mark. Jimmy Carver nodded sagely with all the wisdom of several weeks on the beat behind him. Trouble was not something you needed to invite. It would come soon enough when it was good and ready, and Higgins might not like it when it did.

They returned to the station just as Lampton was making his way out of the side door. He clutched a brown paper bag to him, with a nearly empty whisky bottle in it. He was sober, but not looking as if he was enjoying it.

Carver squeezed back against the wall to let him pass.

'How are you feeling, sir?'

Lampton peered at them. 'You have me at a disadvantage, officer. Do we know each other?'

'Carver, sir. Higgins. We arrested you. Brought you in this morning.'

'So you did, yes. Thoughtful of you,' said Lampton sadly.

'You all right now, sir?'

'It's purely self-inflicted, young man. As your worthy sergeant so aptly puts it, it serves me bloody well right.'

Lampton went gingerly down the ramp. Higgins looked more and more disillusioned.

Jimmy Carver went on into the station and put his head round the door of the inner office. Taffy Edwards was sorting his way despairingly through a sheaf of crime sheets and making entries in his cramped handwriting. He hardly looked round when Carver spoke. No, he couldn't come for a drink right now. Yes, he knew there was only five minutes to go, but that wasn't the way Sergeant Cryer looked on it, and DI Galloway had been breathing down Cryer's neck just to make matters worse.

'Can I give you a hand?' Carver ventured.

'Yeah. Draw a firearm, put one up the spout, and just sort of wander into Galloway's office.'

'Well now, isn't that against the disciplinary code, PC Edwards?'

'What, shooting DIs?'

'No, drawing a firearm for private use.'

Taffy made a quick calculation. 'Look, Jim, I'll be about fifteen minutes. You go up the pub and I'll meet you there.'

Carver and Higgins changed and sauntered out into the street. It was a warm, sunny day. Carver drew a deep, appreciative breath and unzipped his black leather jacket, letting it swing loose. Great to think of Saturday afternoon all free and bright and sunny ahead.

He stopped by the door of the corner pub.

'Coming in for a quick one?'

Higgins looked uncomfortable. 'No, I don't think so. Got one or two things to do. I'll see you in the morning.'

Carver pushed the swing door and went in. A babble of voices seethed around him. Everybody else was feeling cheerful about Saturday, by the look of it. He fought his way to the counter.

'Two pints when you're ready, love.'

Sadie waved a buxom arm, uncapped three bottles of brown ale with three dexterous flicks of the wrist, and in minutes was heading towards him with two brimming, freshly pulled pints.

'Paid for,' she said.

'Oh, cheers, Sadie.'

'Not me, darling. The pain over there.'

40

Someone was writhing his way through the crowd. A flushed face came close to Carver's.

'My friend,' said Lampton. 'For a moment I thought I'd lost you.'

'Look, don't you think you've had enough of that stuff, Mr Lampton?' He watched the man sink a large whisky at one gulp and begin shoving the glass across the bar. 'I mean, I wouldn't like to see you being taken in again.'

'That stuff, as you so crudely put it, my friend, is inspiration. Ah, if only there were a reconciliation between my inspiration and my wayward pen!'

Taffy Edwards appeared at Carver's elbow and reached appreciatively for the full pint.

'Lovely. Cheers, Jim.'

'It was Mr Lampton bought you the drink, Taff.'

Edwards stared dubiously over the edge of his glass. In an undertone he said: 'That's not the drunk you nicked, is it?'

'Well, I – '

'Come on, Jim, time to go.'

'You've hardly started your drink yet, Taff.'

'Time to have it on your toes,' said Edwards loudly.

'While you two are arguing,' said Lampton, 'I'll just go and water the little feller.'

The moment he had lurched through the door at the end of the bar Edwards burst out: 'For God's sake, don't you know when to cut and run? It's a disciplinary offence to be associated with a man on bail, let alone bloody drink with him.'

'We can't just leave him like that.'

Sadie was edging her way through the crush, wiping sweat from her brow, gathering up empty glasses. 'Look, your friend's had enough. I want him out. I can't afford to lose my licence. Just get him out.'

'He's coming back,' said Edwards. 'I'm off. Don't catch me sticking my neck out for any old drunk.'

He had gone by the time Lampton staggered lovingly back to Carver's side. 'One for the road?'

'I think I'd better see you along that road right now, sir.'

'But I don't want to – '

'Just tell me where you live, and I'll see you get there.'

In spite of mumbled protests he succeeded in steering Lampton to the door. Sadie watched them go with a nod of relief.

They had got themselves organized, just the way it had been before with the chop house, and then the two Jewish places, and then the Greek one. Tasty bit of nosh, that Greek gear, though really they both preferred pie and mash down the market. But when you could get it all for free, and take the mickey and get away with it . . . well, it was good for a giggle, and somehow the food tasted better when you knew you weren't going to have to pay for it.

Tonight they were going to be down the disco with a couple of birds who'd expect to have money spent on them. So the food today was going to be early afternoon: save spending too much tonight. Hungry for something else tonight.

Matty and Frankie had it all worked out. They had given young Kevin Lee at the paper stall the number of the restaurant, Chinese this time just to make a change. He knew the routine by now: knew how long to give them, when to nip round to the telephone box, and what to say. Actually they were doing him a favour: he got one hell of a kick out of it.

It had worked without a hitch so far. It was going to work again. Chop suey and special fried rice, some chicken, and then the phone call, panic, and away through the doors. It couldn't fail.

It was a giggle, that's all it was.

'About half past two, right?'

'Whatever you say.' Kevin had been delighted.

'And mind what *you* say. Same as before and nothing else, and don't hang about.'

' "There's a bomb in the gaff," ' Kevin recited, ' "and it's goin' to go off any minute." '

'Good lad.'

The restaurant was up a narrow flight of stairs to the first floor, above a cycle shop and not too far from the street corner. Frankie made a quick assessment of the distance and the best direction. Wouldn't do to get held up by traffic near the junction. Then he sized up the staircase as they climbed to the first floor, noting which way the doors at top and bottom opened. No time to lose when the big bang threatened.

They had managed, the last couple of times, to get a table near the door, but here there were only two tables free, both of them in the middle of the room. They settled behind two large plastic-bound menus and covertly gauged the distance from here between other customers and the door, which opened inwards.

Right. No problem.

They ordered.

The service was quick and efficient. Too quick for comfort, really. To fill in time they had to order another couple of helpings – sweet and sour prawn balls, which dissolved like fluff in your mouth – and still there was a quarter of an hour to go before Kev set off the alarm.

Frankie gulped. He didn't go for the expression of that grave, dignified old fellow behind the little bar. Too much like some sinister mandarin out of a horror video.

'What'll you have?' asked Matty.

'I couldn't sink another thing, honest.'

'We can't hang about like a couple of prats, can we? We'd soon get sussed out.'

42

'I think the old geezer's already got his slant eyes on us.'

They tried to look away and pretend an interest in a silk picture of a placid riverside scene with a pagoda and bridge reflected in the water. It was a soothing picture; but they were not soothed.

Desperately Frankie ordered two coffees. The gaze of the proprietor behind the bar did not waver. The coffee was gone just as the clock behind his head showed half past two.

The phone did not ring.

Matty and Frankie watched the minute hand of the clock edge its way on. Still there was no sound.

Supposing the telephone box was being used, and Kevin couldn't get in? Or supposing it had been vandalized and he was dashing about looking for somewhere else?

'He's not going to ring,' breathed Matty. 'Better get some money out, see if we can pay up, and then get out of here.'

Frankie was stubborn. 'He's never let us down before.'

'We've got to do a runner.'

The phone rang. Frankie gasped and stared down, tense, into the dregs of his coffee. They were both poised, ready to move.

The man at the bar lifted the receiver; listened; stared straight at the two boys; then nodded to one of the waiters.

Frankie and Matty did not find out until later – much too late – that Kevin had been interrupted making the call from the local newsagent's, and had left the card with the phone number of the restaurant on it. But they knew, as one waiter positioned himself across the doorway to the toilets and another leaned back against the door to the stairs, that things were not going according to plan.

'Something's wrong,' said Matty. 'They've sussed us.'

'No. That must have been Kevin ringing. They don't know what to do, that's what it is. Give 'em time to sort themselves out.'

'They ain't going to empty the place. You can see that. You can see we're going to be grabbed.'

'Not if I can help it, we ain't.' Frankie shoved himself up on his feet and shouted across the room: 'Quick, there's a bomb! It'll go off any minute. Get moving, everybody out now! *Now!*'

There was a moment's pause, as if nobody had taken it in, or maybe nobody thought it was anything but a joke. Then it registered. A woman screamed, and began groping her way towards the door. The waiter there shook his head and refused to step out of the way. Two men from a table in the window shouted and ran to join her, pushing the waiter bodily aside.

At the same moment the door from the kitchen swung open. Two men erupted, brandishing huge kitchen knives. For a hysterical second Frankie wanted wildly to make a joke about not knowing you needed such large choppers to carve up bean sprouts. But then someone crashed across their path, a man's arm went up to protect himself, and there was a spurt of blood and a shout of agony. Then the two Chinese hit the two boys, and there was nothing to joke about.

Jimmy Carver heard the screaming as he steered Lampton warily round the street corner. He had been taking it easy, with half of his mind contemplating the free afternoon ahead. Other feet could plod this beat until tomorrow morning. Even so, it was impossible not to notice things from the corner of your eye. Once a copper, always a copper, even when you were off duty. You didn't walk along a street like anybody else, minding your own business and thinking your own thoughts while the world went by: instinctively you noticed a kid acting the fool on a bike – doing wheelies in the middle of the pavement with all those young mothers and their prams about! – and two men muttering in a doorway with their heads averted . . . hatching what bit of aggro? Not to mention playing guardian angel to this pathetic, drunken git.

Carver tried to quicken the pace once they were round the corner. Then came the screaming, above the rumble of traffic and the pounding of rock music from a record store. People were shoving and shouting and falling across the pavement right ahead.

'A bomb!'

'It's a hoax. They said it – '

'Oh, God, look at *him*.'

A man was collapsed at the foot of the Chinese restaurant stairs. Blood was gouting from his arm, over the shallow step and down on to the pavement.

Carver wrenched himself away from Lampton, leaving him to totter forward under his own steam. He elbowed his way through the crowd, dragging his jacket off.

'Put this under his head. *You* – phone an ambulance.'

The snap of command in his tone cut through any protest the bystander might have felt like making. He was on his way to the phone box as the welcome shapes of two uniformed officers hove into view – a PC and a WPC, both of them known to Carver but never appreciated as much as now. Messages went out; and from Sun Hill police station they came reassuringly back.

In a matter of minutes the ambulance rolled up. Plus another one for the mincemeat which the Chinese kitchen staff had made of the two moaning, shivering brothers.

And Detective Inspector Galloway: Galloway, looking pleased with himself and, for once, pleased with somebody else. As the blanketed figure of the injured customer was loaded into the first ambulance, Galloway thumped Carver's arm.

'Well done, lad. Probably saved that feller's life.'

'Thanks, sir. What about the other two, d'you reckon?'

'The Davis brothers?' Galloway allowed himself a vengeful leer. 'They'll live. Won't take the piss out of Chinamen again, though. As for you, my son,

I'd say you've done enough for one day. Go on, have it away on your toes before something else happens. See you tomorrow.'

Jimmy Carver walked away with his shoulders back and his head held high, as if he were in uniform, on the beat.

He was quite looking forward to tomorrow morning.

On that Sunday morning an unwelcome face showed up once more at the station. Sergeant Cryer was about to launch into a blistering tirade when Lampton, very sober and very correct on the other side of the counter, said:

'One of your officers has stolen my wallet, sergeant. Sixty-two pounds.'

Seven

Cryer leaned impatiently over June Ackland as she tried yet again to raise PC Carver on the blower.

'Here, let me try. Carver, are you receiving me? Carver. Are you receiving me? . . . Any other unit know where Carver is?'

'What's all the noise about?' Roy Galloway strolled across the office. 'Doesn't anyone know it's Sunday morning?'

WPC Ackland made a face. 'Trouble with a capital T.'

'My little bomb hoax firm haven't died in hospital, have they?'

'Worse than that.'

'Is there anybody out there?' Cryer bellowed, as if to use his own lungs rather than the miracles of modern science. 'What's Higgins' number . . . Edwards . . . ?'

Abruptly Carver's voice came through. 'Are you receiving me, sarge?'

'No, it was the jolly green giant! Carver, get yourself in here straight away.'

Galloway looked at their faces, trying to keep it joky but probing for something else. 'That tenner you owe me isn't worrying you, is it?'

'Don't talk to me about money. That drunken bastard Lampton's been here and alleged that Carver's nicked his wallet with sixty-two quid in it.'

'Carver? Never.'

Then Cryer told him the rest of it. Stupid young woodentop, drinking with the man in a pub down the road: drinking with a man on bail. Not only that, but he had walked Lampton back home, or started out that way, anyway, just before the bomb hoax, and then left him to go to the assistance of the injured man. All that good work gone to waste! Instead of a pat on the back, there was this: a nasty taste in the mouth, and a stigma that could follow Carver for the rest of his career – if he had any career left.

'We won't know which way it's going to jump until the chief super's finished interviewing Lampton.'

'You called the chief super out?' Galloway chuckled. 'On a Sunday morning?'

Cryer could not force an answering grin. He had known Lampton too long, and knew what he was like when he was sober. There was no way he was going to have Carver suspended for something he hadn't done, so he took a chance on Chief Superintendent Brownlow being able to sort it out before it all got out of hand. Lampton had said, and was probably saying it again upstairs right now, that he had had his wallet handed back to him when released from the police station, had certainly had it in the pub, and then had been with nobody else but PC Carver. The only way he could have mislaid it, he assured Cryer savagely, was if someone had hung him upside down and shaken him, hard. Yes, he did realize it was a serious matter, accusing a police officer; but who else could it have been? Carver had walked him most of the way home, hadn't he? And what motive had he had for doing that?

All they could hope was that Brownlow was hammering home to the little soak just what damage he might do with his crazy accusations – ruining a young man's career for what was probably his own drunken lapse of memory.

The trouble was, when he was sober Lampton denied his drunkenness and denied having a soggy memory, and quenched any little fits of remorse with bad temper and vicious remarks.

They heard the door at the top of the stairs open. There was deathly silence in the office as Brownlow escorted Lampton down to the foot of the flight.

'Whitewash,' Lampton was growling. 'A cover-up.'

'I assure you there'll be no cover-up,' Brownlow said very quietly and steadily. 'But I shall see PC Carver and some of his colleagues first. Then, if I'm satisfied that a crime has been committed, I'll call in the Complaints Division of Scotland Yard.'

'Whitewash.'

The chief superintendent looked stonily at Bob Cryer. 'Can I have a car to take Mr Lampton home, please.'

They had hardly got Lampton off the premises when Jimmy Carver came in from the street, with Higgins a few paces behind him.

'What's up, sarge?'

'You come with me. Higgins, stay here in the office.'

He led the bewildered Carver away; and told him what had happened; and watched bewilderment change to horror and utter disbelief. If ever he had seen an innocent man – and he had seen plenty, as well as plenty of the other kind –

this was one. But his voice hardened. He didn't want Carver to be under any misapprehensions. A rough time lay ahead in Chief Superintendent Brownlow's office, and the lad might as well be toughened up for it.

'But sarge, I never touched – '

'Just listen. The chief super's talking to Edwards, and to Higgins any minute now, and then it'll be your turn. When you get in there I don't want you being leary, right, just tell him the truth.'

'Sarge, I've never stolen anything in my life.'

'It's not what you've done,' said Cryer grimly, 'it's what they think you've done. All right, come on. Let's go up.'

For a moment Carver looked incapable of even setting foot on the stairs. Then, white-faced, he started upwards.

They stood on opposite sides of the corridor, outside the chief superintendent's office. Twice Carver attempted to say something, then licked his lips and tried again, only to shake his head despairingly.

Cryer let out a rasp of exasperation. 'I don't know what I'm going to do about you, Carver, straight I don't. I'm running out of bloody ideas.'

'Sarge, please believe me. You've got to. I've never in my life taken anything from anybody, honest.'

'If I thought for one moment you had, I wouldn't be standing here. I'll tell you one thing, though. Next time – if there *is* a next time – and you come across a drunk, you'll remember double quick that you're a policeman first and not a flaming social worker.'

'I felt sorry for him, that's all. He's got a problem.'

'No, Carver, you're the one with the bloody problem. Trouble is, you're bloody stupid enough to go and do the same thing again, aren't you?'

The office door opened. Taffy Edwards came out. He tried to give Carver a reassuring grin, and went down to relieve Higgins. When Higgins had been in to give his evidence and come out in his turn, he did not even try to smile. He looked as if someone had dirtied his hands and he wished he had never been involved in anything of this kind. It was all far too unsavoury for an ambitious young officer with a golden career ahead.

'Right, Carver,' said Cryer. 'It's all yours now. And remember what I said.'

When the door had closed again behind Carver, he could not bear the tension here any longer. They would know the outcome soon enough. He stamped downstairs.

Galloway was haranguing PC Higgins. Cryer sensed that, like himself, Galloway simply wanted to let off steam, to take it out on somebody because it was impossible simply to hang about, waiting in silence.

'Got a bit of experience under your belt now, then? Close quarters, eh?'

'Yes, thank you, sir.' Higgins was very stiff and correct. He would be.

'And when you get back to college you'll be able to write a nice little thesis on the police and relations with the public, won't you? And when it comes to malicious complaints and wasting police time . . .' He swung round as Cryer came into the office. 'What's the latest, Bob?'

'Carver's in there now.'

'You ask me, I think the super would have given Lampton one hell of a roasting. In a nice sort of way, of course.'

'That won't stop him giving Carver a roasting. And not so nicely.'

Somebody rapped on the counter, and a reedy, quavering woman's voice said: 'Excuse me, officer.'

'Yeah, just a minute, miss.' Cryer slammed his fist against the partition. 'I wouldn't be surprised if that bastard Lampton's just trying to have a go. Wouldn't put it past him.'

'Hm. Don't think so. Half the time he's too woozy to think up anything like that. Too thick.'

'Just like Carver's too thick to nick a wallet.'

'Cor strewth, ain't I gonna get no service round here?'

Cryer waved abstractedly towards the counter. 'Higgins, will you see to that lady, please.'

'I only want to 'and something in.'

'We just have to pray that when he finds the allegation's unfounded, the super won't go ahead with disciplinary charges.'

'I should bloody think not.'

'Look,' said the old woman, propping herself against the counter and staring up at Higgins, several inches above her, 'I found it in the gutter . . .'

'I mean,' said Galloway, 'after saving that bloke's life in Crayford Street?'

' . . . in Crayford Street. I couldn't bring it in before, I 'ad one of me turns, didn't I?'

'It's full of money.'

'Well, of course it is. I wouldn't bleedin' well nick it, now would I? Look, what 'appened was, I was coming along from the pub after dark and I found it, see . . .'

It began to ring simultaneously in Bob Cryer's and Roy Galloway's heads. They stared at each other, and at the old woman, and at the wallet lying open on the counter.

'In Crayford Street?' Cryer breathed.

'That's what I've been saying, isn't it?'

Cryer was not a sentimental man, but he thought he had never seen a sight so beautiful as that wallet, lying there.

He also quite enjoyed the sight of Carver's face when word had been taken in to Chief Superintendent Brownlow and, after a delay during which it seemed likely that some pretty straight talking had been done, Carver was finally allowed out. He was almost as pale as when he went in, but he smiled gratefully at Cryer; and if there were tears in his eyes, it would have been downright offensive to comment on them.

Galloway said: 'You look a bit more cheerful than you did earlier, my son.'

Cryer nodded. 'Looks like someone who's lost a quid and found a fiver.'

'Hey, that reminds me!' Galloway was jubilant. 'What about that tenner you owe me? "Crack it in a fortnight", remember.'

'Trust you not to forget.'

'Come on, let's see it.'

Cryer let him see it. He put the ten-pound note down on the desk. Unexpectedly Galloway took out one of his own and set it on top.

'Right,' he said. 'Now, Carver, I want you and Higgins to go down the market. I want one of those big hampers of food – you know, full of tins of ham, corned beef, chunks of pineapple.'

Carver was beginning to look bewildered again. 'Sorry, sir, I don't get you.'

Cryer felt exactly the same.

'Your fairy godmother, Carver,' snapped Galloway. 'The old dear who saved your skin. Brought that wallet in. You don't suppose she'll get a reward out of Lampton, do you? I bet she ain't got two pennies to run together, and not a bit of grub in the house.'

'I don't believe it,' Cryer marvelled.

'What's wrong?'

'I never thought to see the day. Detective Inspector Roy Galloway, social worker!'

'Oh, piss off.'

Eight

Another week was beginning, and another mixed bag of problems could be relied on to show up. What Sun Hill station could have done without was Jimmy Draper for starters.

Quite apart from a succession of villains, there were any number of small-time regulars of one kind and another, all sent to clutter the place up: that piss-artist Lampton for one, though with a bit of luck he would keep his head down for some time to come; the old tramp who obsessively gathered up waste paper from the pavements and gutters and stank so badly that he was always being thrown off buses he had tried to board; and the old dear down Prime Street who shared her favours between the police and the fire brigade when tracking down her wandering ginger tom-cat. There was Maggie, run in by every store detective in the district after 'mistakenly' dropping two or three tins of salmon into her shopping basket, and bobbing up smiling in court to be given reprimands, conditional discharges, to be bound over to keep the peace . . . and, probably, to get away with more tins of salmon than were ever traced.

Then there were the kids. Some of the little ones managed to get lost at least twice a week, even though they lived just round the corner. They ended up in the police station while the desk phoned their parents, or the parents phoned frantically in – or failed to phone in. Sometimes Bob Cryer wondered if some folk dumped their kids near the front steps of the nick before going off to work, hoping they'd secure some free nosh and warm surroundings for the day.

This was Jimmy Draper's third visit. He was clearly enjoying it. Clearly PC Edwards was not enjoying it. Trying to get through to Jimmy's mother on the phone, he had to try at the same time to elbow the little boy away from the message pad on which he was scribbling, and to avoid droplets from the can of Coke which had been provided. Getting lost wasn't a bad idea, the six-year-old had decided.

Sergeant Cryer watched from a distance, amused by Taffy Edwards' difficulties.

At last Taffy was through. 'Mrs Draper? Good. PC Edwards, Sun Hill police station. Yes, he's been found. Pushing a trolley round the supermarket.' He smiled; then stopped smiling. 'No, I'm sorry, Mrs Draper. Much as we'd like to, we can't hold on to him any longer. We don't have the facilities.'

Cryer nodded in mocking agreement. Jimmy, with happy abandon, eyed Edwards' pen and made a grab for it. Clutching the receiver with one hand, Taffy slapped the other one down over the pen.

'Gimme,' said Jimmy.

'I'm sorry, Mrs Draper,' pleaded Taffy Edwards, 'but aren't there any neighbours who could look after your other children while you . . .' He tugged at the pen. 'Yes, Mrs Draper, we'd appreciate that.' Having retrieved the pen, he gave Cryer a thumbs-up sign. One thumb, anyway. 'Yes. Twenty minutes, then. Yes, come straight to the front desk. Thank you.'

June Ackland edged past him on her way towards Sergeant Cryer, and smiled condescendingly.

Bob Cryer wiped the condescension off her face. 'Give Taff a break from that little monster for a while. Right?'

'Right, sarge.'

She looked confident and competent. Jimmy Draper looked hopeful.

The teleprinter started rattling away to itself in the corner. Edwards thankfully moved towards it, leaving WPC Ackland to deal with sticky fingers and potential juvenile delinquents.

'Not the paternal type,' Cryer winked at June Ackland.

'You can say that again.' She watched Jimmy's hand move suggestively towards her, not quite sure what he fancied collaring next. 'Hey, you! Sit down and behave yourself or you'll get a thick ear.'

The kid sized her up, and appeared to surrender. She sat down beside him with a shrug of accomplishment.

The teleprinter rang a summons at the end of its message. Edwards tore the sheet off and ambled towards Cryer, reading it as he came.

June Ackland winced. 'Listen, ugly – you kick me again and . . . don't say I didn't warn you.'

Jimmy grinned beatifically.

'Sarge!' Edwards flipped the teleprint in front of Cryer. 'How about this? We've got a prison escapee on the manor.'

He pointed to the last cluster of lines. 'A man on the run.'

Cryer skimmed down the page, then sniffed and began to laugh. Alfie Mullins, of all people: now that was a name that never stopped haunting him. Poor, hopeless little Alfie. Just one bloody marvellous skill that had never made up for his clodhopping clumsiness in everything else. Dangerous? They must be out of their tiny minds. Poor shrivelled-up little Alfie, cracksman, peterman, call it what you liked – but a dead loss. Serving a fifteen-year stretch, and by now getting close enough to the end of it to be allowed home leave as part of the rehabilitation scheme.

But a prison escapee? Not Alfie.

'Is he *that* dangerous, sarge?' asked Edwards.

'He's not an escapee,' said Cryer irritably, 'and he's far from being dangerous. These prison staff get the shits over nothing at all. Totally misleading in Alfie's case. He's simply a "failed to return" wallah. Probably had himself a juice-up last night instead of treading the path back to his porridge. A Monday morning hangover, that's about all it is.'

Edwards looked vaguely disappointed. It sounded a lot less dramatic that way.

Cryer looked down the details of the communication again. They ought not to put crap like that on messages. Some clever-clever little fusspot thought he would get the whole Met out on the streets to collect their poor little Alfie, wasting everybody's time while the screws took it easy and waited for the package to be returned to them.

Like hell. Cryer made a decision on the spot. He wanted no eager young copper blundering into the thing and having a punch-up just for the sake of the record. This one he would handle himself. It would be nice to get out on the old familiar patch; and he could guarantee Alfie Mullins would be back inside by tomorrow morning under his own steam.

The notion was strengthened by the arrival of Sergeant Penny. Cryer beamed. 'Just the man. Do me a favour. Relieve me for an hour?' He handed over the teleprinter message. 'I want to pop out and show young Edwards here there's more to police work than banging down doors and twisting people's arms up behind their backs.'

Penny studied the message and gave a reminiscent nod. 'Alfie, eh? We don't get that nice, shy little kind of crook any more, do we?'

'More's the pity.' Cryer jerked a thumb at PC Edwards, and they set off.

It was great outdoors. When you were pounding those perishing pavements, all you longed for was a cushy desk job: promotion, and a nice warm office and people jumping here and there when you snapped your fingers. But after long spells indoors, there was nothing like a stroll out into the sun and dust and stench of petrol, and the squad car rolling you through the streets in search of . . . well, whatever took your fancy.

They parked in a cul-de-sac on the edge of the street market. That was good, too: ambling through the market, in between fruit stalls and under the clamour of all the little shysters he knew so well – 'Look, darling, they've just fallen off the back of a lorry, and I'm not asking for a fortune . . . it's my birthday, I'm not asking one, I'm not asking two, I'm offering . . . Whoops, watch yourselves, here's the Ol' Bill.'

Stallholders waved, made a quick inspection of goods they had on display and goods they had shoved under the boxes, and yelled the usual things: 'Morning, Bob . . . how's your luck, sarge? . . . what happened to that West Ham on Saturday then, Bob? Hey?'

Cryer led the way out of the far side of the market and down a narrow lane on to a square surrounded by newish blocks of flats. They were not the depressing high-rise towers that disfigured the eastern end of the manor, but well-spaced little clusters of two- and three-storey terraces, with a few nicely angled to overlook them from six storeys up.

'This way,' said Cryer, waiting for Edwards to fall into step. 'He's expecting me.'

'Expecting you? How could he be?'

There were some things they could never be taught at Hendon. Nor would you find them in any police manual. It was something that came with experience; and experience got you angry when you read rubbish like that teleprint with its 'prison escapee' stuff and the hint that Alfie Mullins might be dangerous. Idiots like that never catered for people like Alfie. There was no in-between for them. It was either black or white; and Alfie, poor soul, was one of those grey areas. Yes, he'd be expecting Bob Cryer all right, but who else would know what they were talking about or how it came to be like that?

He remembered when he himself had first come on the manor, long before the likes of the Edwardses and Carvers and Higginses of the world came on the scene. Alfie Mullins had been a household name in those days. Brilliant: not a safe he couldn't open. Villains had queued up for his services. The only trouble was, he was tidy. His MO gave him away. He always tidied up after him: it didn't matter where he was, he always left the place as clean as a whistle. Taking a pride in his work, he got dragged into the nick every time, and usually before the shareout of the loot. The others got the money, and Alfie got nothing but the glory – and the porridge. Over and over again they tried to persuade him to shop the others, who were sitting pretty. But he never grassed and always pleaded guilty. The bigger the jobs and the bigger the rake-off for his pals, the bigger the sentence for Alfie.

This last stretch had really knocked him back, though. A fifteen, and he'd never had a penny out of any of it, contrary to what other people thought – including the judge. Nor was that the saddest part, thought Cryer philosophically as he turned across the patch of battered earth which had been laid out as a lawn but had suffered from the patter of little tiny feet too regularly and for too long. A year ago Alfie had been recommended for one of the pre-release schemes: weekends at home with the family, preparation for the big wide world. His first leave had come just before Christmas. He walked out of the Scrubs that morning with his obligatory brown paper parcel tucked under his arm, and what did he find? It wasn't what it used to be. None of it. The Old Bill were no longer going about their business in long capes, riding bicycles. Villains were now well into blaggings – armed robberies. No style, no subtlety. And nobody wanted to know Alfie. The days of the cracksman were over. Sticking sawn–off shotguns under bank clerks' noses was more fashionable and a lot more effective. It was a new world to Alfie: one he couldn't adjust to. By six o'clock that evening he was knocking on the prison door, begging to be let back in.

Behind the new flats was still a colony of old, yellowing brick tenements skilfully shielded by the corner towers. As they went up a flight of steps pitted and chipped around the edges, Edwards said:

'You reckon he's still here, then? Not done a bunk for good and all?'

'Alfie only comes home because he's forced to.'

Cryer knew that, and so did the prison authorities, which was why he had to fight down this seething anger against them. Bloody liars, the whole lot of them. They knew as well as he did that Alfie had to be literally thrown out of the nick to do his rehabilitation sentence. Psychologically he feared every moment, but of course he had to go through the charade of not wanting to go back, just to please his old woman.

'Sometimes,' Cryer confided, 'I'm part of a charade, just for the benefit of his missus.'

'You mean she – '

'I'm that cruel sergeant that comes banging on the door.'

'Sounds like Punch and Judy.'

Cryer smirked. 'Wait till you meet Mrs Mullins!'

They went along the landing with its rusted rail from which paint had been scaling for so long that its original colour had long been lost. The paint on the door of No. 15 wasn't so glossy, either. Bob Cryer raised his right hand, hesitated, and then banged on the door, standing back at once and waiting for the mock battle to commence. Edwards braced himself, not knowing what to expect.

Mrs Mullins was a plump woman in her late fifties who sometimes wore pink curlers, sometimes a pink silk head-scarf which might have dropped off the back of a lorry or out of a garment manufacturer's safe, and sometimes both. When she saw Cryer she showed no surprise, but gripped her flowered pinafore and stiffened as much of the flab as she was capable of stiffening. Cryer had been right: her expression confirmed that he was expected.

But the ritual had to be gone through. She said: 'All right, what do you want?'

'Morning, Eileen.' He sniffed. 'Cor! Is that eggs and bacon you've got going in there?'

'Mind your own business.'

She made a move to shut the door, but Cryer's foot was already wedged in it. 'Now, come on, Eileen. You know better than that. Don't mess me about, love.'

'Why can't you bloody leave him alone?' She made a halfhearted attempt at resistance as he shouldered his way in and past her, looking down the poky corridor. 'Cryer, you know what you are, don't you? You're nothing but a – '

'None of that. I've got a young 'un from the valleys here. Tender ears. Not used to your kind of language. Come on now, Eileen, me old darling.'

He paced along the passageway. Mrs Mullins followed, with Taffy Edwards warily bringing up the rear. Maybe he still believed his sergeant might be misguided this time, and there might be a potential killer lurking in the broom cupboard.

Very loudly and clearly, making sure each syllable carried, Mrs Mullins said: 'You're wasting your time anyway, Cryer. He's not here. He went back to the nick this morning, like he was supposed to.'

Cryer sniffed. 'Bacon smells good. Mind if we have a look around?'

'Why bother to ask? You're going to please your bloody selves anyway.'

There was not much room for her to push past Cryer, but she managed it, storming into the kitchen and starting to clatter plates and cutlery about. Edwards, catching Cryer's eye, opened a door off the passage and peered into a tiny bedroom. There was precious little space for anyone to hide in there. He stooped to look under the bed, then came out.

On the left was the living room, with the door slightly ajar. Light flickered pallidly within, and there was the boom of television voices. Cryer pushed the door wider and went in.

It wasn't much larger than the bedroom had been, but was crowded and untidy. Dominating it was a large sewing machine, a typical rag trade piece. It was plain that Mrs Mullins was doing outside work to make ends meet. Partly finished garments swathed in polythene were draped over a shabby sofa and two chair-backs.

The television was an old model, sputtering energetically away without any visible audience. Facing it, a fireside chair was empty save for a morning paper abandoned against the cushion. A coffee table between chair and television had a knife and fork laid out on it, with a neighbouring cigarette end still smouldering.

Edwards tugged at Cryer's sleeve. Cryer feigned interest in the screen. Edwards tugged again, mouthing silently in the direction of the long window curtains which were just not long enough to conceal the toes of a pair of carpet slippers.

Cryer raised his voice. 'Right then, Eileen. If you see him about, and I'm sure you will, mind you tell him nine o'clock tomorrow morning is the deadline. If he's not safely tucked up in the Scrubs by then, it's your door I'm going to keep knocking at. D'you hear me, Eileen?'

Mrs Mullins' head came round the door. She was wiping her hands on a teacloth, and had lit a cigarette for herself.

'Told yer, didn't I, he's back in the nick.'

'Not quite, but I'd like to think he's on his way. Don't want him losing remission, do we?'

'Come round here, threatening me. . . '

Cryer signalled to Edwards that they should leave. For a few seconds his hand rested on Mrs Mullins' shoulder. 'They're showing "The Blue Lamp" in the prison cinema again this week, Eileen.' He winked at Edwards. 'One of Alfie's favourites. Wouldn't want him to miss that, now would we?' Again he sniffed. 'D'you know, I think that's Alfie's bacon burning.'

They left under a shower of recriminations.

Back at the station, Cryer wasted no time. He put a call through to the prison, made his statement, and then listened to the sort of guff he could have predicted. He knew damn well that that oily Welsh git of a warder did not have to get the governor's permission. Yes, he knew regulations were regulations, but he knew as well that a man who had been twenty years in the prison service could organize or disorganize whatever he chose, within reason. Something could be worked out for poor old Alfie Mullins. Alfie was not a runner, and nobody thought he was.

'Yes, Mr Thomas-Llewellyn.' He played it as matey and understanding as he could bear. 'I know. It's more than my job's worth as well, but I guarantee Alfie Mullins will be back in your safekeeping by nine o'clock tomorrow morning. At the latest.' He waited, then nodded. Of course there would be a catch in it. Why did he stick his neck out on behalf of no-hopers like Alfie? It was going to cost him. 'Draw tickets?' he said resignedly. 'How many books? Blimey, you're a hard man, Thomas-Llewellyn. I hope it's a worthy cause.'

When he had put the receiver down, there was an unnatural silence. He looked around. Of course, that Draper kid had gone.

Edwards and June Ackland stared back at him.

Cryer said: 'Draw tickets! Look, how do you two fancy a weekend in Paris?'

Nine

Treffry Instruments Limited was a fair target. They had asked for it, and now they were going to get it. Colin Jackson had been nursing this notion along for some time, and tonight was the night. Redundant, they'd called him: he'd show them who was redundant. Wipe the smile off a few faces. Not a chance of getting them on the unfair dismissal line – he'd asked about that, and got nowhere – so this was the way it was going to be.

He carried three pints back from the bar and set them down on the table. Andy reached for his, and grimaced in Eddie's direction.

It was a pity about Eddie. Getting him away from that fruit machine was a big operation in itself. He went at the things with mindless determination, always managing to press the wrong 'hold', then feeding his tenpences in and getting it wrong again, until the money ran out. Whatever they got from tonight's little job, Eddie's share would be fed into this machine or one in some other pub. But he had to come along. They were mates, and it was Eddie who had put them on to that consignment of jeans in the market and tided them over for a couple of weeks. You couldn't very well leave him out.

The thumping and jangling of the one-armed bandit stopped. Eddie had run out of change. He looked hopefully back over his shoulder.

'Lend me a few ten-pees?'

'No,' said Colin. 'Come and sit down.'

Reluctantly Eddie joined them.

Andy said: 'It's on?'

'For tonight.'

'You want me to get a motor?'

'Don't need one. It's an office job – petty cash, nothing heavy. I know the place inside out.'

'Tools?' Andy was the reliable one, always able to get his hands on tools and gear of every kind.

'The way we're going in we won't need anything, but bring a jemmy anyway, just in case. There should be plenty of tools lying around inside – it's that kind of place. Oh . . . don't forget a couple of torches, though. We'd look a right load of wallies groping around with a box of Swan Vestas.'

'It's not alarmed, is it?'

'Would I take us into something that was wired up?'

Andy finished his pint and looked at the clock behind the bar. 'Half nine, then – here?'

'Couldn't we meet in the Bear and Crown?' Eddie suggested eagerly. 'They reckon there's a great new machine in the saloon there. Cops and robbers, pays out every other time.' He looked from one to the other, and his voice and grin faded. 'Oh, well. Sorry. Here, then?'

They kept it casual, leaving and coming back. Andy slouched into the bar in his usual way, looking bored out of his head, and bought a couple of packets of crisps as if to settle down for the evening. Colin noticed the bulge in the battered plastic bag he had tucked under the table, though.

Eddie, too, was his usual self. He nodded to them and went straight to the machine, taking out a fistful of coins.

They waited until he had got rid of them all. There was no way of getting him to concentrate until that was over.

Colin let half an hour go by before getting up, yawning and stretching, and saying: 'I'm off down the road. You coming, or not?'

'Might as well.'

The other two followed him indifferently to the door. Only Eddie looked back once, wistfully.

It was a walk Colin had once been used to: down towards the river, along a lane of uneven setts greasy in the dim light from a corner lamp, and then on the smarter concrete of an approach ramp. Once he had walked in through those red-painted gates every morning. Now he was redundant, and there was no way of going through the gates. He led the boys past a long wall and up a little alley which took a sharp left turn and concealed them from the road. Above were two blank walls, and one with a long window in it. Unless someone had repaired that dicey catch inside, it would be a walkover to open the upper half. He had stared at that metal frame and the bent catch God knows how many times while he stood there and peed.

'Give me a leg-up on to the sill.'

It was simple. No need for a jemmy. Nothing had been done to the fastening. One tug and he'd got it a few inches open; and then it was simple.

The three of them scrambled in and lowered themselves over the urinals to the floor. Colin moved confidently into the lead again. It was like old times, only usually there had been daylight from one end of the factory floor and strip lighting in the roof. Now only a faint hint of the sky's night glow came through the window and glass-panelled door of the office on the far side.

He moved round a silent lathe and opened the office door.

'Andy, get those curtains drawn. No cracks showing.'

He stabbed the beam of his torch towards the desk, and reached with a gloved hand for the top drawer. It was locked.

Andy muttered: 'They're not curtains, they're blinds.'

'I don't give a monkey's what they are – just get 'em over that window.'

There was the swish and rattle of the blind coming down, followed by a crash and a squeak of pain from outside the door. Colin groped for the desk lamp and switched it on, angling it towards Eddie as he limped in.

'D'you want to wake the whole bloody – '

'It's not my fault, is it? I didn't have a torch, did I?'

Colin thrust Andy's jemmy towards him. 'Here, let's see if you can do this little job without a bodge-up.' He nodded at the drawer.

It took only a few seconds. Two splintering cracks, and they tugged it open. Inside were four crumpled pound notes and a handful of change.

Andy grabbed the jemmy. 'Here, let me.' He went for the deeper bottom drawer, wrenching it out as far as it would go. It yielded up half a bottle of gin and a bottle of Scotch.

'We'd have been better off staying in the boozer till closing time,' whined Eddie.

'Why don't you stop moaning? You've been a jinx on this job right from the start.'

'Me? Now look, Mr Bleeding Big Shot –'

'You did promise, Col,' said Andy in what was meant to be a reasonable tone. 'Fifty nicker each, you said.'

'So I got it wrong. Didn't know they'd have emptied the place. Anyway, we're not finished yet.' He looked round the walls in search of inspiration.

Andy said: 'What's next door?'

Colin tried to remember. It was some kind of storeroom, he thought. Nothing big: just a small place where they kept office bills, papers and things. Or so he thought. It might have changed by now.

He flicked off the desk light and picked his way out with the torch beam raking ahead of him.

It was still a storeroom, all right; and the door was not locked. There was a smell of dust. Papers and bulging files were stacked up on metal shelving. The torchlight skimmed over them and came to rest on something square, dull and grey, but with a glint of brass here and there.

It was a sturdy old-fashioned safe.

'Cor blimey,' breathed Eddie appreciatively.

Colin checked that there were no windows, closed the door behind them, and found the light switch. They blinked against the harshness of an overhead bulb shielded only by a dusty green saucer-shaped metal shade.

'Right. Let's get that out.'

The safe was pushed well back under the lowest of a range of shelves. It was tricky to get out: Andy and Eddie had to go down on their knees at the sides, while Colin got his arms squeezed in between the shelf and the top of the safe, getting a painful grip on the back. They heaved, cursed, felt it move and heaved again. They were sweating and coughing by the time they had manhandled it out on to the floor.

Now Colin regretted not having asked Andy to bring a whole lot of tools. The jemmy was useless: it did not even scratch the paint on the old, heavy-weight safe. An exploration across the main workshop produced a couple of wrenches and some screwdrivers, but nothing even as hefty as a crowbar. Heavy stuff like that wasn't much needed around Treffry Instruments.

Andy poked one of the screwdrivers despondently into the lock. Then he noticed what Eddie was up to.

'Don't you think you'd better give that stuff the elbow for a while?'

Eddie took the Scotch bottle away from his lips and wiped them. The level had gone down several inches. He looked well pleased with himself, which was more than the other two were.

'You're getting to sound like Mr Big Shot,' he sneered.

'Cut it out.' Colin sagged against the shelves. 'Start coming up with some ideas or we'll be here all night.'

'I bet there's bugger-all in there anyway.'

'Listen, you berk, there's gotta be at least – '

'Don't call me a berk.' Eddie reached up and carefully set the whisky bottle alongside the gin bottle on a shelf above his head. The gin bottle was no longer even half full. He began pacing towards Colin.

'Firms don't have safes for nothing!' Colin growled. 'Get it into your thick skull – '

'I'll do you.'

Andy moved in between them. 'Look, Col's right. We could be just that much' – he held out his finger and thumb – 'from forty grand.'

'More like eighty,' said Colin with renewed hope.

'Get that! An hour ago it was a hundred and fifty all in, if we were lucky. Now it's bleeding eighty grand. Any advance on eighty, Col?'

Colin raised his right fist, but Andy was still set squarely between him and Eddie.

'Look,' said Andy, 'there's gotta be an answer to this. So let's work it out together, right? Like a team. Let's all have a drink' – he reached past Eddie for the whisky bottle – 'and then talk some sense. No arguments.'

They all had a drink. But when it came to talking sense there was nothing doing. They squatted around the safe, examining it from every angle, and all the time it just sat there and defied them.

Andy shivered. After all the heaving and hammering a little while back, it was getting chilly in here. He said thoughtfully: 'What if we take it with us? Cart it off and work on it in our own time.'

'Where?'

'My brother's lock-up is empty at the moment. Just the place.'

'And how do we do that without wheels?'

Silence descended again. Colin put his arm across the top of the safe and leaned on it. He tried to picture them manoeuvring the safe out of that lavatory window and down the alley to a waiting van. Fat chance. It would have to go out through the goods exit into the yard. That was easy enough, but there was still the little matter of getting the gates open.

Or getting the staff door in the wall open, a few feet away. That wouldn't be so difficult from inside.

Something was nagging at the back of his mind. Never mind about a motor. There was something else. Now he'd got it in focus. On the far side of the workshop, near a flight of stairs, the torchlight had fallen briefly on a large trolley. It ought to go through that outer doorway all right. Throw a blanket or something over it, keep to the back doubles, and who would notice at this time of night?

He put the proposition to the others.

'You're bonkers,' said Eddie without hesitation.

'We'd stick out like a sore thumb,' said Andy.

'If you've got any marvellous ideas of your own –'

'Hold it,' said Andy. 'Look, if we have to do it that way, then it's got to wait until the morning. Half four, five, when it's getting light. People moving about, on their way for the early shift down the road. We wouldn't look so sussie then.'

'Not bad. Not bad at all.'

'Yeah?' Eddie looked learily at the dregs in the bottle. 'And why don't we go and break Alfie Mullins out of nick to do the job for us, eh? Bleeding bonkers, you two.'

Andy was very still. 'Alfie Mullins,' he murmured.

'Who's Alfie Mullins when he's at home?' Colin demanded.

'That's it! He *is* at home. Out on home leave.'

'I still want to know who the hell – '

'Come on, Mr Big Shot.' Eddie was enjoying himself. 'You've never even heard of the great Alfie Mullins, the great cracksman, the wonder man of all time? Not a safe he can't open. And as it happens, I know him personally.'

Colin snorted, but Andy said: 'And know where he lives?'

'He might have moved, but I could find out. Only it'll take some time. I mean, you can't go knocking people up in the middle of the night, can you?'

It began at last to fit into place. Colin and Andy would get the safe on to the trolley, and when it got light would trundle it along the way to the lock-up. That would give Eddie plenty of time to find out where Alfie was living and bring him along. Always supposing, of course, that Alfie wanted to come.

Colin said: 'Offer him a twenty-five grand cut.'

They patted Eddie on the back, and handed him the bottle for a last celebratory swig.

Dawn was making a pretty seedy job of things when Eddie drifted in through the door of the all-night café under the shadow of the old buildings. It smelt of stale smoke and stale cooking fat. Eddie was hungry, but the sight of the sandwiches in their glass cabinet did not turn him on.

'Just a coffee,' he mumbled.

The proprietor poured him something hot and brown. At least it washed away some of the dry, sour taste of the whisky.

Eddie leaned on the counter and said, as casually as he could manage: 'Don't know where Alfie Mullins hangs out, do you? Know it's about here somewhere.'

'Next street.' The man did not even turn round. 'Top floor of the buildings.'

'What number, mate?'

'Take yer pick from twelve.'

Eddie forced himself to drink the coffee slowly and look as if the question hadn't meant very much and might just as well not have been asked. Then he turned away. Time to get down to business.

He hadn't noticed it when he came in – there, in the corner by the door, a one-armed bandit. He rummaged in his pocket. But of course he had got rid of all the loose stuff in the pub before they set out.

The café proprietor said: 'Don't you want your change?'

There it lay on the counter: change from the quid Eddie had handed over for his coffee.

He fed a coin into the machine; then another one; and there was that lovely, bloody marvellous rattling sound, and the money was spraying into the tray.

It took him ten minutes to get back where he had started, without a tenpenny piece in his pocket. Despondently he left.

The end of the buildings was tinged by watery sunshine, but the side with balconies and front doors still lay in shadow. Somewhere a baby was squawling, and a dog began to bark. Eddie stared upwards, wondering which door he was going to select when he got up there.

A milk float clanked past him, close to the pavement. He moved hurriedly away and came to a halt on the other side of the road.

Above, a door opened.

'And don't forget to write this time. D'ya hear me, Alfie Mullins?'

A small huddled shape began to edge down the stairs. When he reached the bottom, Eddie could see that he had his raincoat collar up as if to shut out the whole world, including his wife's voice. There was a brown paper parcel under his arm, tied with coarse string.

'Good-for-nothing ponce!' It was Mrs Mullins' fond farewell as she slammed the door.

The milkman was crossing the road to another flight of stairs. Eddie waited until he was well on his way, then began to trot after Alfie Mullins.

He lost him on the next corner. Where the hell could he have got to? The road ahead was empty save for a woman swilling down a doorstep. To the left was a churchyard with its population of tilting, dead stones. But something

61

moved between them. The path between the graves was a short cut to the nearest bus stop. Eddie broke into a run, and went in through the gate.

That hunched shape padded on ahead of him.

'Hey . . . Alfie!'

Looking neither to left nor right, Alfie Mullins wheezed his way towards the far gate. It was easy to catch him up. Years in prison had worn him down. Breath rasped in his throat with the mere effort of walking.

'Sorry to bother you, Alfie – er, Mr Mullins.' Eddie fell into step. 'You don't know me, but . . . look, you *are* Mr Mullins, aren't you?'

There was no reply. Alfie Mullins stared ahead as if needing all his concentration to get to that next gate and the steps down beside the bus stop.

'Course you are,' Eddie said breezily. 'Look, I'll come straight to the point. Me and a couple of pals, we got hold of this safe, see. Well, we can't open it. It's right up your street, Mr Mullins.' When there was still no response, he pulled the clincher. 'Thought you'd be interested for, say . . . um . . . twenty-five grand cut?'

He stopped, expecting Alfie to stop as well and face up to this terrific offer.

Alfie kept walking. Only a few yards to go now.

'What's the matter, then?' Eddie was fed up with being put down by everybody, fed up with trotting by this little zombie, fed up with every damn thing that had happened last night and this morning. 'Aren't me and my mates good enough for you, or something? Not your class, eh? Look, I'm talking to you, mister!'

He darted forward and swung to block the way. Alfie tried to nip round him to the right, but Eddie was there. Then the left, and Eddie was there again.

'Listen, Mr Has-been . . . you're coming with me whether you like it or not, see?'

Alfie Mullins did not see. He tried pushing Eddie out of the way, but there was just no way Eddie was going to stand for that. He caught the old man's sleeve, and tried to get him to shove his head up and look him straight in the eyes, just so he could see that this was business, real business.

The brown paper parcel went flying. Alfie groped vainly in mid-air for it, and slithered on the grassy verge of the path. Eddie went over with him, and jarred his arm against one of the gravestones. He heard the thud of something else – Alfie's head hitting the stone full on.

'You all right?' Eddie felt the dew seeping through the knees of his trousers. He scrambled up. 'Come on, Alfie . . . Mr Mullins . . . don't sod me about.'

Alfie Mullins was very still, with his head at an odd angle against the side of the gravestone.

Horror ran up from Eddie's damp, shaking knees to his head. It wasn't true. No way it could have happened like that. A little knock that wouldn't hurt anyone.

He stopped to touch Alfie; then straightened up again and began to run.

As he clattered down the steps, an elderly man came to a halt by the pavement and began to lug his bicycle up to the short cut. He glanced idly at Eddie. Must be some night-watchman on his way home. Eddie didn't know and didn't want to know. He kept moving while the man began to wheel the bike along the churchyard path.

Ten

The probationers' classroom on the second floor had been cleared, with desks pushed to one side and two long tables laid end to end below the blackboard. Sergeant Roach dumped a card index on one of the tables and glared at two sleepy detective constables who had appeared on the scene, one still rubbing his eyes, the other hastily running a battery shaver over his chin. A telephone engineer scuttled between them, crouching as he ran a wire from a junction box towards the tables.

DC Dashwood came into the incident room with a scribbled note. 'Found him, sarge. Inspector Galloway's going straight to the scene, meeting Sergeant Cryer there.'

'Forensic?'

'They're raising a fingerprint man. Haven't been able to sort out the SOCO.'

Litten bustled in, looking hopeful and important. This was the real thing. He was prepared to add his weight to that of the CID.

'Good,' Roach welcomed him. 'Want to make yourself useful, lad?'

'Yes, sarge. But I'll have to go on patrol in about –'

'Shouldn't have poked your nose in, then. Get that blackboard cleaned, and some decent chalk at the ready. Or you'll have to stay in after school.'

The whine of a car braking heavily filtered up from the street below. Footsteps pounded up the stairs. A uniformed constable who had just plonked a pack of stationery on the nearest desk to the door was pushed aside by Roy Galloway, dressed incongruously in a hired dress suit. Roach was tempted to ask how he had enjoyed the big fight last night, and the succeeding booze-up; but then thought better of it.

Behind came Bob Cryer, in civvies, ashen-faced and with his lips clamped thinly together.

The telephone engineer was mumbling something into the handset at the far end of the table. Roach tapped him on the shoulder.

'Get lost for half an hour, pal, would you.'

When the door had closed behind the man, Galloway propped himself against a desk and said: 'First of all, unless something like your wife's having a baby or your mother's died, there'll be no time off. I want you to get that straight, right from the start. No leave until this murder's solved. Any questions?' In the face of that tense glare there were no questions whatsoever. 'Good. We understand each other. Now, what I'm going to do is tell you briefly what we've got and what line of enquiry I want you to follow. Then you'll get out there and do your house-to-house or whatever assignment Sergeant Roach allocates to you. We'll meet back here again tonight at seven and see what we've come up with. Unless there's a bloody miracle and you fall over something earlier.' His thumb jerked towards the phone. 'I want that manned non-stop. And the other one, when it's fixed. Non-stop, you hear me? If you have to go to the can, get somebody to sit here and wait. Right.' The silk scarf slipped from his neck. His black tie was crooked. His mouth was angry and even more crooked. 'I'll start by telling you a little of Alfie Mullins' antecedents.'

Dashwood handed out small notebooks, and they all groped for their pens.

Galloway summed up curtly. Alfie Mullins had left home at five o'clock this morning to catch the early bus past the prison. His route was through a short cut used by everybody in that neighbourhood, across the churchyard – a short cut for Alfie in more ways than one. One witness had already come forward from a flat in St Andrew Street, just round the corner from the churchyard, saying he had been woken by a man's voice calling after 'Alfie'. It would be too much of a coincidence to suppose that it was anybody other than the Alfie they were talking about. The time fitted Alfie leaving home and the finding of the body.

Footprints in the churchyard suggested that somebody had followed him and then walked alongside him for some yards. At some stage there had been a struggle. The body had not been moved, and all the evidence pointed to the victim being thrown sideways, banging his head on a gravestone as he fell. The assailant then ran away, out of the churchyard gate, and came close to a night-watchman on his way home from work. The night-watchman had pushed his bicycle along the churchyard path, but luckily had not obscured the footprints. He found the body, and had the sense not to tamper with it.

Unfortunately the witness claimed to be as blind as a bat. Certainly he was unable to give a description of any kind – black or white, young or old.

'What we're doing right now,' Galloway concluded, 'is searching every inch of that churchyard. Anything we find, we'll let you know. And anything *you* find . . . on the wire right away, right into this room.'

Somebody coughed. 'Could it have been an accident, sir?'

Galloway offered him a withering glance. 'This, my old son, is a murder inquiry until proved otherwise. Now, as for a motive, I want you to be thinking along these lines when you're asking your questions.' Cryer shook his head, knowing what was coming and not agreeing with a word of it. 'There may be some around here who don't see it the way I do,' said Galloway heavily, 'but I've totted up the amount of money unrecovered from Alfie's past jobs. Not to be sniffed at, I'm telling you. I know it's a long time ago, but it comes to well over eighty thousand. My intuition tells me that this is what this business is all about.'

The pattern seemed likely enough. Somebody who was no stranger to Alfie had a good idea where some of that loot had been stashed, or at any rate an idea who could lead him to it. It was a motive far from unusual among criminals. Before Alfie went back inside, that somebody wanted a cut.

Cryer looked stony and disbelieving.

'Tonight at seven, then,' said Galloway. 'Good hunting, gents.'

He swung on his heel and went out into the corridor. Cryer was hard behind him.

'Roy, you're wrong. Completely wrong. I told you before and I'll tell you again. Alfie hasn't got a pot. Not a penny. D'you really think he'd still be living in those buildings if he had a few bob?'

'Oh, now, listen. Listen, sunshine.' Galloway's forefinger prodded Cryer in the chest. 'If you'd done your duty, Alfie would still have been around to spend those few bob, as you call them. Think about that.'

'You bastard.'

'And if I were you, *sergeant*, I'd go and get changed a bit smartish. You should have been on duty a couple of hours ago. Station officer – remember?'

He did not wait for a reply but swaggered off towards the stairs. Considering the way the poncey bastard himself was togged up, thought Bob Cryer, fuming, he was a fine one to be going on . . .

He counted up to ten and made sure Galloway was well out of sight and earshot before he clattered downstairs to pull on his uniform.

They all felt the lash of Cryer's tongue that morning. It was an unusually busy morning, which did not help. PC Carver found himself coping with two irate members of the public at one go, and had problems with the paperwork. June Ackland was handling calls at the switchboard as if caught up in some electronic game: only this was no game. A nervous PC Smith made an error in his report book, tried to alter it and made it worse, and was sent to the rest room to do it all over again, like some naughty schoolboy.

'Edwards!'

Taffy Edwards, who had hoped to slip through the office unnoticed, came to a halt.

'There's a break-in just gone in the crime book,' said Cryer. 'Round at Treffry Instruments – a factory on eight beat. The silent alarm went off last night, but there's no sign of a forcible entry. They've had a trolley nicked, of all things. I want you to deal.'

'But that's not on my beat, sarge.'

'With this murder inquiry running upstairs,' rasped Cryer, 'we've all got to be a bit flexible. Understand?'

Taffy understood. He jumped to it. The way things were today, it was no bad thing to be a good distance away from the nick anyway.

The facts at Treffry Instruments hardly seemed worth the effort. The manager, after a thorough search of the building, could report only two things missing: an old safe and a trolley. Nobody was much worried about the safe. It must have been a load of nincompoops who made off with it: there was nothing inside but a few old papers. The firm had ceased using it a good eight years ago when a new floor safe was fitted in the basement. Might just as well have thrown the old thing out while they were at it.

The trolley was a different matter. Its loss would be a nuisance to the men on the shop floor. The manager wanted the police to concentrate on getting that trolley back rather than waste time on the safe.

Edwards made polite noises and left. A load of nincompoops, the manager had said, and that seemed to figure: who else would go to the trouble of breaking into a factory just to help themselves to an empty safe and a trolley?

Colin and Andy had been hard at it for hours. But where the hell had Eddie got to?

It had proved trickier than they had expected to move that heavy trolley through the streets with its heavier load. Brute force was needed at every kerb. The wheels had a habit of slewing in awkward directions, and on one slope the whole thing had threatened to run away with them. At the end of an alley a policeman had stood with his back to them for what seemed a lifetime while they did not dare to go on or squeak back the way they had come; but not once did he look round. They were exhausted by the time they reached their destination, a service road behind a parade of shops with dilapidated lock-up garages on the other side.

The one belonging to Andy's brother was a bulging mess of rusty corrugated iron, pitted with holes. There was room inside for one car, with an array of old tyres and spare parts along each wall. The edge of the door shrieked over the ground as they pulled it shut behind them. Andy groped for the light switch, and they took the blanket off the safe.

There were plenty of tools to hand, though some of them could have done with a bit of oiling. None of them proved any more useful than the ones they had used in the factory. The handle came off a chisel, Colin managed to gash the back of his left hand and dripped blood over the floor and the safe, but the safe itself resisted every attack on it.

Andy sagged down on to the trolley with his head in his hands.

Colin flung a hammer against the wall. It answered with a deafening jangle, and flakes of rust descended from the roof.

'Where the hell *is* Eddie? He should have been here hours ago.'

'It's not like him. Perhaps he can't find Alfie.'

'Or perhaps he *has* found a bloody amusement arcade.' Colin slumped over the safe. 'We can't go on like this. I've hardly made an impression on the flaming thing.'

Andy got up and began rooting about in the shadows at the back of the garage. Hope was renewed. Wrapped up in an oily rag was an electric drill. It was nowhere near being the latest model, but there was a handful of bits, and although the power point near the ground wobbled the moment you touched it, something ought to be possible.

It ought to be, but it wasn't. The twist drill made a hideous screeching as it bored into the back of the safe, and then snapped. They tried again, with the same result. The place stank of hot metal, but the safe was still uncracked. They needed high-speed drills, not this grotty old stuff.

'And where the devil's Eddie?' Colin came back to the same disturbing theme.

'He should have found Alfie's drum by now.'

'I've got a funny feeling he's done a runner. You know him. Get a few ten-pees burning a hole in his pocket, and –'

'Burning!'

'Eh?'

'You said burning. That's an idea, Col.'

'What is?'

'That training scheme they put you on – that welding, right?'

'What about it?'

'You must know how to use oxy-acetylene.'

'Oh, yeah, and where are we going to get that kind of equipment this time of the morning, hey?'

Andy nodded his head wisely. 'Just so happens that there's a panel beater works two lock-ups away. Reg Atkins or something like that – got his name over the door. Fixed something for my brother once, I remember that.'

They had no trouble getting in. The hasp of the lock came away from the corrugated iron in a flurry of what looked like shreds of twisted brown paper. Andy kept a lookout, apprehensively checking upper storey windows over the backs of the shops, until Colin had lugged the equipment into the shelter of their work-place.

'Right,' said Andy. 'Now let's see what we've got.'

The torch blazed; and went out. Colin started it up again; and again it fizzled and died.

'What the hell did you do on that course?' moaned Andy.

'Well, I didn't finish it, did I? Different equipment, anyway, so don't blame me.'

'You could've told me before we nicked this gear. Somebody could have seen us. Somebody . . . '

His voice died to a whispering breath as they heard someone hurry towards the door and then stop. Andy's fists clenched. The door grated open. Eddie was framed in the opening.

'Where've you been?' snarled Colin.

Eddie shuffled forwards. In the bleak light of the overhead bulb he looked sallow and bedraggled. 'Sorry, fellers, I . . . look, I must have drunk too much in that place, remember? Woke up on a bench down the road.'

'Bleeding charming, ain't it! And what about Alfie Mullins, our saviour? I mean, that's what you went off for, wasn't it?'

'Did you find him, Eddie?' demanded Andy. 'Alfie – did you find him?'

'Took me ages.'

'Well?'

'He's . . . got a big job on. Couldn't spare the time.'

'Did you offer him a cut, like we said?'

'Didn't want to know.' Indignation put the colour back in Eddie's cheeks. 'I had to slap him about a bit. He got a bit naughty. I might've gone a bit strong,' he added weakly.

Colin threw his hands up. 'Well, that's bleeding well it, ain't it.'

'There's only one thing left if we're gonna get this safe open,' said Andy, 'and it's gonna cost. We'll need a motor.'

They stared at him in anticipation.

Edwards was in no mad hurry to get back to Sun Hill. Coming out of the factory gates he set himself a deliberate, measured pace which would get him back in reasonable time but not expose him too soon to whatever further wrath Sergeant Cryer had in store for his men.

A middle-aged man in a dirty boiler suit slewed his bicycle in to the kerb.

'Just the thing! Guv'nor, hey – just what I need. Somebody's broken into my lock-up. Nicked my welding equipment.'

'Where's your lock-up, then?'

'Behind the shops, off the parade. Bloody sods. That's my working tools they've nicked. How can I be expected to – '

'What number?' Edwards interrupted. 'Number of your lock-up?'

'Haven't got a number. Just Reg Atkins, panel beater. You can't miss the sign.'

Edwards quickened his pace. 'I'll follow you along. See you there in five minutes, Mr Atkins. Okay?'

There was nothing to go on. The idea of fingerprints on a shambles like that was just a bad joke. Edwards prodded about inside the lock-up, and duly noted the torn-off lock, but could do little more than enter it all up in his book. Atkins had no record of any registration number on the equipment, if there had ever been any: he had picked it up second-hand or maybe third- or fourth-hand, a couple of years ago. It was hardly worth nicking, really – but for himself it was something he couldn't do without.

Edwards made his way back to the station.

Somebody upstairs was shouting along the corridor. Two lots of feet went up two flights, and one came halfway down again.

He raised his eyebrows at June Ackland. 'Still a madhouse up there?'

'Too true. I'd turn round and creep out, if I were you. Cryer's got a surprise lined up.'

'For me?'

'For you.'

Edwards carried on into the front office.

He was greeted by a wide smile – a smile from the Draper kid who had got himself lost the previous day, and looked delighted to have got lost again. Someone had tried to keep him occupied with a Mars bar, but that was not going to last more than another ten seconds.

'Come you in, Edwards,' said Sergeant Cryer with malicious pleasure. 'Just the man I want to see.'

'I'd better do my crime book entries, sarge, while – '

'A word, Bob.' Galloway leaned in through the doorway.

His gaze took in young Jimmy Draper. The kid beamed. Galloway scowled. 'Can't you get rid of that kid? We're supposed to be running a murder enquiry in this place, not a bloody day nursery.'

Cryer nodded at Edwards. 'Take the kid home. Number seven, above the shops on the parade.'

Jimmy Draper pressed a sticky, chocolatey paw into PC Edwards' hand, stuck his tongue out at Galloway, and allowed himself to be led out into the street.

'And I've just *come* from there,' Edwards addressed an unfeeling fate.

An elderly woman beamed at the pair as they went along the pavement. Probably she was filled with nostalgia for the good old days when local bobbies saw old ladies across the road and walked hand in hand with adoring little boys. Two youngsters of a much later generation whistled, and dodged away down an alley.

Edwards went up the stairwell between two sections of the shopping parade. Jimmy still clutched him tightly, as if reluctant to be delivered back to his own front door.

Mrs Draper was an unkempt woman looking some ten years older than she most likely was, but she had a ready, engaging smile and a gushing voice which was impossible to dislike.

'Oh, isn't that nice of you to bring him home, officer,'

'We were thinking of adopting him, Mrs Draper,' said Edwards wryly, 'but the sergeant reckons we couldn't afford to keep him in chocolate.'

'You see, it's not all my fault.' She caught her son's free arm and dragged him in through the door, playfully smacking his bottom and chasing him off into a room opening out of the passage. 'You encourage him down there, that's what it is. You're a load of old softies, you lot.'

Edwards thought of Sergeant Cryer's face this morning, and refrained from comment. It was safer to venture a noncommittal smile.

'Don't stand there grinning like a Cheshire cat.' Mrs Draper's smile was decidedly arch. 'Come on in and have a cup of tea. I've just this minute made one.'

Sergeant Cryer's expression lingered, like the smile of the most celebrated of all Cheshire cats, on the air. Taffy Edwards told himself that he really ought to get back and really ought not to hang about here. But that face, and DI Galloway's face . . .

He tucked his helmet under his arm and walked in.

The kitchen was obviously the room where everything went on. An ironing board in one corner had not been folded up and put away, and cartons of breakfast cereal had simply been pushed to one corner of the dresser. Two toddlers were pushing each other about in a chipped play-pen. Along the window sill were some pot plants, a plastic container sprouting kitchen knives, and several matchboxes. At any rate it was a bright room, looking out over the service road and the roofs of a battered line of lock-up garages.

'Sit yourself down, young man. It's not often I get visitors now.'

Edwards took a chair to one side of the table. The sill was low enough for anyone to be able to look down on the decrepit doors across the way. Idly he watched as three youths came out of one garage. Inside was a trolley. That was all he saw before they banged the door shut.

'It's only since his father left home, you know, he's been wandering off like this,' Mrs Draper prattled on. 'We used to be a close-knit family, until *she* came along.'

There was the roar and splutter of a clapped-out car starting below the window. Still only half attentive, Edwards got up again, in time to see an old banger of a small red van drive away.

'Mrs Draper, do you know the three lads who've got the lock-up over there?'

'That one opposite?' She came to the window and stood beside him, teapot in hand. 'I don't, but I'd like to. Noisy beggars. Had me up since the early hours, they have, with their banging and drilling. Then with all those sparks flying about in there . . . Honest, what some of them get up to I just don't know.'

It dawned. Edwards said: 'You've got a phone?' Of course she had. The times they had tried to ring her and get her to come and fetch Jimmy! 'Where is it, please? Urgently!'

Detective Inspector Galloway took the call. His unwelcoming snarl turned abruptly into enthusiasm. 'A trolley? Drilling and cutting equipment? Hang on there, Edwards. Don't do anything until I get there. Five minutes. Good lad.'

In the background the familiar voice of Sergeant Cryer was saying: 'A trolley? Bet that safe'll be there too. Sounds like a job for Alfie, if he'd still been alive.'

The receiver was slammed down, and Edwards did not hear the reply, if any.

Galloway was as good as his word. A squad car was parked unobtrusively down a side street, and within another two minutes a team of them were inside Reg Atkins' lock-up. They had left the warped door slightly ajar, but even without that there would have been plenty of spy-holes in the fabric. Cryer, Jimmy Carver and Taffy Edwards were in uniform; Galloway and Dashwood in plain clothes; all of them poised, itching to go.

The three louts had to come back. The way they had left things, they had to be back here pretty soon. If not . . .

Galloway's breath hissed through his teeth like a draught under the twists of corrugated iron.

Jimmy Carver glanced at Taffy. Taffy was steamed up enough, but it was all he could do not to grin at Jimmy's expression. Oh, it was in the lad's blood all right. He just couldn't wait to race into action.

'Edwards!'

Galloway was gesturing him forward, closer to the gap in the door. That same red van was returning, bumping over the road towards the lock-up two doors away.

Edwards nodded. It was them all right.

The van pulled up. Two young men scrambled out of the front seats, a third pushed the rear doors open and jumped down. Past Galloway's shoulder Edwards could see a blurred picture of some old mattresses being hauled out, then the villains moving towards the nearby lock-up. Now they were inside, out of sight.

Galloway said in an undertone: 'Right. Get ready. We'll give them a moment to settle down inside. Then box them up, nice and neat. Remember, straight in, no messing about. We can't be sure exactly what they're up to, so get 'em fast before there's any mischief. Ready? Right . . . let's go!'

They erupted out of Atkins' cramped workshop. Galloway was in the lead, wrenching open the doors of the garage. Daylight spilled in to show two of the youths packing mattresses around a safe, with the third slapping a car tyre on top to hold them down. His head came round as the officers burst in, and he tried to hurl the tyre. Jimmy Carver launched himself, cannoned off the edge of the door, and bore his quarry down in a dusty crash. The other two tried to make a dash for it, but Edwards' truncheon picked one of them off, and Cryer got the second by the arm, forcing it up behind his back until he screamed.

'One for Alfie Mullins.'

'It wasn't me.' Another howl. 'It was Eddie, not me.'

Two police cars skidded to a halt outside. Galloway slapped handcuffs on to the one called Eddie with relish, and pushed him towards PC Carver.

'Take 'em away.'

It was all over so quickly. A couple of windows high up on the other side of the road opened, and curious faces peered out, still without much idea of why three youths were being bundled into cars and why two men in plain clothes were cautiously venturing into the garage.

Galloway drew back a couple of mattresses. There was the safe; and there was a small poultice of plastic explosive tamped down over the lock, a detonator inserted and attached to a crude transistorized receiver.

'Hm,' said Galloway, pleased. Then his eyes widened and he turned to DC Dashwood. 'It's remote control! Quick, get out there and tell them not to transmit on their personal radios, or they could set it off. *Quickly*, for God's sake!'

He began backing away as Dashwood raced out into the open.

'Hold it, you lot!'

One of the police car radios buzzed into life. A distant metallic voice said: 'PC Carver. Are you receiving? Carver, are you receiving? Over.'

'Don't use your radios!' Dashwood yelled. 'Don't transmit.'

He was too late. Jimmy Carver pressed his transmit button and began to answer: 'This is . . . '

He was cut short by a muffled explosion. Dashwood winced and spun round, starting to blunder back towards the lockup.

A great cloud of dust and fragments puffed out of the open doors and wafted across the road. Scrambling through it, a begrimed shape tottered to a standstill close to Bob Cryer, who began to laugh. Then laughed some more. It could have been a tragedy, but from where he was standing it was . . . well, it was enough to make Cryer double up and hug his stomach.

There were feathers in Galloway's hair, feathers all over his shoulders and clinging to his jacket, and feathers floating skittishly all about him.

'What bloody idiot did *that*?'

Dust and feathers settled gently, soothingly over the scene.

Eleven

Everything had been pinned on the south end of the High Street three days running. Two foot patrols had been diverted so that they could cross at an angle, and a car cruised within easy reach. Unfortunately the coverage had not worked. Twice in a row the muggers had picked the north end, hammered their victims hard, and got away with it. The third day they failed to show up, but it was unlikely that they had drifted off. The tally over the past fortnight was causing Sun Hill a lot of embarrassment: sixteen cases of mugging, and twelve handbag snatches, all in broad daylight and all on the same patch.

On top of that there had been a spate of armed robberies. These looked even more dangerous, and there was a lot more money involved. After successes at two building society offices, an off-licence and two garages, the little firm involved must be getting pretty cocky.

Sergeant Cryer was not pleased. He knew he would be even less pleased when reprimands and awkward questions began raining down from above. But he refused to be panicked into changing his tactics. Lightning had to stop striking the same place. Sooner or later the muggers would surely switch their operations and see what pickings there might be at the other end of the street.

In his usual place in the parade room, in front of the usual faces, he said: 'All right, I chose the wrong end of the High Street again yesterday. But that, as they say, is how the cookie crumbles. Despite that, we'll still continue our operation from the south end for today at least.'

Jimmy Carver held up a tentative hand. 'Isn't it possible, sarge, to get the foot patrols from beats 4 and 5 to include the north end as well? It'd take only two slight alterations to the route and then we'd get the degree of cover we need.'

'Not a point that had slipped my mind,' said Cryer hastily. 'We'll modify patrols for Bloom and Darling, Peterson and . . . let's see . . . Chilton, isn't it? And now we'll see about WPCs Ackland and Martela. Nervous, girls?'

'No, sarge,' came an indignant duet.

'Maybe our girls look a bit too hot to handle, sarge?' suggested Dave Litten. Before either of them could turn on him, he went on: 'I'm serious. Perhaps they don't look vulnerable enough, even when they're in civvies.'

It was quite a point, thought Cryer. 'Any ideas?'

'One or two.'

'And we all know what one of them might be,' said Taffy Edwards. 'Eh, Dave?'

June Ackland's lower lip grew more petulant.

'One more peep like that out of you, Edwards,' said Cryer, 'and you are in dead bother, chummy.' He nodded encouragingly at Litten. 'You come up with a good idea, and we'll see about it. Now, let's move on.'

Before he could say another word the door opened and Roy Galloway came in with a sheaf of photographs.

'Sorry to bust in, Bob, but if you're bending your mind towards those armed robberies – '

'Any minute now.'

Galloway fanned out the prints. They were black and white, in both senses

73

of the word – blurred pictures of a tall, rangy coloured man and a stunted little white youth who seemed to like looking at the ground or away in the opposite direction.

'Dashwood managed to get these. Thought they might give us a lead.'

'Not exactly Lord Lichfields, are they?'

'The best we can get so far. You reckon they're local?'

'Have to ask the lads. Here, pin 'em up on the board. Gather round, you lot.'

Chairs were pushed back as they gathered close to the board and craned their necks to look at the fuzzy prints.

'Have a good look,' said Cryer. 'If you remember seeing either of them, I want to know. Or if you see either of them from now on, I still want to know. Only be extra careful out there. We know one of 'em is armed with a small firearm, the other with a hammer. Unless they've thought of something even nastier. So watch it. Any questions?'

They all shook their heads.

'Right, then. On your way. The great British public is out there waiting for you.'

'God help 'em,' said Roy Galloway softly.

Galloway reached the door of his office as the phone began to ring. He lifted the receiver, then edged back a pace or two to kick the door shut.

It was Tombo Robinson.

'You were right.'

'It's Decker's?'

'Sure is. And a whole lot bigger than I'd have thought.'

Roy Galloway leaned back in his chair. It was good to feel that a guess had paid off and that now there was a good chance of getting his fingers on the strings and starting to pull them.

'When can we move in?'

Tombo was wary. He had been wary all along, getting himself accepted without raising any suspicion, until folk began to talk to him freely as one of themselves. You had to listen to a bit here, a bit there. What it added up to was that there was a buzz about a really big consignment coming in early next week. No, he couldn't say which day or what time. Not yet. But it was next week all right, and once Tombo was positive he'd be in touch, they'd have to meet somewhere, and he'd sketch out the layout of the place and tell Galloway anything he needed to know.

'We could make it tomorrow?'

'We make it,' said Tombo's deep voice, 'when I'm good and sure. I don't want no more meetings than is absolutely necessary.'

Dave Litten's face appeared at the glass partition, his fingers raised to rap on the door. Galloway waved to him to stand back and wait.

74

'All right,' he said into the phone. 'But tell me exactly when you'll be able to ring again. I don't want to be out.'

'Should know Friday morning. Ten o'clock?'

'I'll be here.'

Galloway put the receiver down and slapped his knee. The waiting was going to be the worst part. Now he was so close, he wanted it all over and done with.

Litten saw that he had put the phone down, and slid closer again.

'All right, Dave, come on in.'

'Hello, guv.' Litten swaggered a little, trying to be matey and respectful at the same time. 'How's it going, all right?'

'So so.' Galloway wondered what this was all about. 'How's yourself?'

'Oh, bearing up, guv. You know.'

'Well, what's on your mind?'

Litten leaned confidentially forward. 'Well, I think I may be able to help you out on this armed robbery number.'

Galloway felt a stir of distaste. He didn't like the smell of this. 'How come?'

'Well, I think I know him.'

'Which one, son?'

'Well, I'm not a hundred per cent certain, but I think I know that black bloke.'

'Have you told your skipper?' asked Galloway bluntly.

Litten retreated a pace or so, and shrugged. 'Well, no. I thought I'd come and have a word with you first, you know what I mean?'

Galloway thought sourly that he did indeed know exactly what Litten meant. But levelly he said: 'Right, hold on there a sec.' He reached for a pad and pencil. 'Okay, Dave, let's have his name.'

'Well, like I said, I ain't a hundred per cent' – Litten was getting uneasy about something in the atmosphere – 'but I think his name is Holt. Desmond Holt.'

Galloway wrote it down. Desmond Holt. 'Good,' he said. Then, ferociously: 'You didn't think you'd be scoring a few points by coming straight up here, did you?'

'No, guv, course not. I wouldn't – '

'Only it doesn't work like that.'

'I know that. I just – '

'You're out of order, son. I may not get on too well with your lot at times, but at the end of the day we're on the same side. There's a word called loyalty, and when and if you make the CID, it's a word you'll have to live with.' He looked up as another familiar shape swam across the glass, and there was a knock at the door. 'Just the man. Come in, Bob.'

Bob Cryer came in, giving Litten a sharp, puzzled look. 'What are you doing here?'

'Our friend here has something to tell you,' said Galloway smoothly. 'Now then, Dave, you tell your skipper what you just told me.'

'Well . . . '

'Hold it a second,' said Cryer. He jerked a thumb towards the door. 'I'll hear you later, lad.' When Litten had plodded sheepishly out, he said: 'Thought I'd break it to you quietly. Two gentlemen downstairs to see you. A Detective Chief Inspector Kirk, and a Detective Inspector Wheeler.'

Galloway felt winded. He had forgotten the possibility of this happening – had hoped it would go away, never come to anything.

'Thanks, Bob. Very tactful. Better get one of my lads out there to show them up.'

'Good luck.'

Roach, thought Galloway, was going to need all the luck that was going. He waited pessimistically for the two inquisitors to arrive and start the trouble rolling.

It was all so pathetic. Ted Roach's private life had often been a bit rough, especially in the months leading up to that messy divorce of his, but he had never yet let it interfere with his work. Now the wheels had started to grind just because of some stupid cow of a neighbour who didn't approve of the detective sergeant's lifestyle.

Why couldn't it just have been allowed to blow over? No one in his right mind could take that sort of thing seriously.

Galloway rose with weary politeness as the two men entered.

Detective Chief Inspector Kirk he had known and respected from way back. DI Wheeler was a different type. Where Kirk was bluff and friendly, steeped in the best old-time traditions and team spirit of the Force, Wheeler was younger and unrelaxed, showing a thin smile only when something was going wrong for some chosen victim. Together they probably made a good team for their particular job in the Complaints Division. Kirk would smooth over obvious sillinesses and put matters into sensible perspective, encouraging people to talk freely, while Wheeler waited to put the boot in the moment he saw a vulnerable spot.

'Hello, Roy,' said Kirk amiably. 'Long time no see. Sorry to be bothering you now.'

'Almost forgot you were coming. I'm up to my cobblers in it. You know how it is.'

Wheeler said coldly: 'Complaint against one of your sergeants – hardly a thing to forget. Always a serious matter, inspector.'

'There's nothing in this job that isn't serious. It's a question of priorities.'

'And you consider a complaint by a member of the public against one of your officers a low priority?'

'Not normally, but in this case it's almost laughable.'

'Laughable?'

'You know what I mean, guv'nor. The member of the public concerned has more complaints than a packet of aspirins. It's all so trivial.'

Kirk settled himself in a chair and tried to look comfortable and relaxed, though it was not really that sort of chair.

'Well, there's no doubt the neighbour is making a big thing out of this incident on the stairway.'

'She swears blind,' added Wheeler insidiously, 'that Sergeant Roach deliberately sets out to annoy her. Is there anything vindictive about him?'

'I wouldn't say so.' Galloway kept it very calm. 'He gets moody from time to time, but then who doesn't, in our line of work?'

Kirk laid some sheets of paper on the desk. 'According to this statement from this Mrs Taylor, Detective Sergeant Roach called her a nosey old cow, and told her to piss off out of it.' He allowed himself a faint, almost admiring smile. 'A very direct lad, by the sound of it.'

'He's a bloody good detective.'

'I can read. His record shows that. All we're asking is whether you have anything to add.' Kirk turned the sheets round to face Galloway. 'Read it – won't take a minute – and tell us anything we ought to take into consideration.'

Galloway had already heard the outline of the complaint when Ted Roach prepared a statement a fortnight ago. It was not going to be all that different from this bit of rubbish, no matter what slant the woman put on it. But he made a show of skimming over the declaration.

At the end he said: 'Nothing. Just that I'll say it again: he's a first-rate detective, and this has nothing to do with his work, or with relations with the public where it *counts*. This stupid slag is turning a silly incident into a major drama.'

Kirk nodded. 'We'll drop in on her and have a chat. Often that's as far as it goes. As long as they're being listened to and they feel something's being done, they're happy. Me and my oppo here, we're dab hands at smoothing over situations like this.'

'But,' said Wheeler, 'you might just tell him to be a little more diplomatic in the future. Especially where this Mrs Taylor is concerned.'

Roy Galloway felt a tingle of relief. They were going to sort it all out. You could trust Kirk. He got up and held out his hand.

'I'll tell him that. By God, I'll tell him a thing or two.'

At the door Wheeler paused and said with apparent casualness: 'Just one small point. I was checking the duty sheets on the day in question, and Sergeant Roach didn't book off until after five p.m.'

'Legitimate overtime,' Galloway improvised. 'That would've been the week when we were up to our necks in screwings. We hadn't done all the calls. Got a couple of nickings out of it, right after this silly business.'

'Nice to see overtime showing results. Well, I think that was all.'

June Ackland and Jimmy Carver were having a quiet morning. Apart from a newsagent complaining that at least ten Yorkie bars and one copy of *Penthouse* had disappeared while his back was turned, and two women with Yorkshire accents insisting that they had got out of the Tube at Oxford Circus and why wasn't this Oxford Circus, nothing had interrupted the steady tempo of their patrol. At one end of the route laid down by Sergeant Cryer they crossed the road, turned, and kept a row of shops under surveillance as they approached the junction. There was plenty of muggers' bait on the pavement over there, from two middle-aged women with massive handbags slung from their arms as they gossiped and stared into a supermarket window, to a young mother trying to stuff change into her purse while keeping control of a child tugging impatiently at her arm. No menace was immediately obvious, though.

As they resumed their plod along the High Street, June said: 'How do you pass the time when you're off duty, Jimmy?'

He looked surprised, and went faintly pink. 'Oh . . . you know, this and that. Don't have much scope, being in digs.'

'Scope for what?'

'Well' – he carefully did not look at her – 'listening to the hi-fi, or doing a spot of D.I.Y.'

'You can always swot for something or other?'

'Like Higgins.'

They both laughed companionably. At any rate the Sun Hill team were unanimous on that, relieved to have seen the back of the ambitious, humourless Higgins.

Through a gap in the traffic June saw, way ahead, a young couple peering into the window of Barry's Antiques. The name of the shop was a lot more posh than its contents. Sid Barry had one of the finest collections of second-hand junk in the district, but he liked to keep a few nice-looking pieces in his window, occasionally attracting the attention of some wandering expert who prided himself on discovering bargains in out-of-the-way places. The couple – the girl with long straw-coloured hair, leaning against the rakishly thin boy as if oblivious to the world around them – looked more like potential buyers of a cheap second-hand double bed. A bus blanked them out for a moment. Through the rumble of its passing, June heard a thin shriek.

It was louder, more hysterical, as the bus moved past. There on the far side of the High Street the couple had abruptly come to life, turning and flinging themselves on a young woman who had just emerged from a building society office. She flailed her handbag above her head. The girl made a wild snatch for it.

'Let go, you silly cow.'

The youth brought her down. His partner kicked their prey twice in the stomach. The handbag slid a few feet away. In a second it was grabbed up, and the two were racing for the corner.

Several bystanders shouted abuse after them; but nobody made a move to intervene.

June Ackland and Jimmy Carver went skipping and dodging through the traffic. The young woman was doubled up on the pavement, clutching her stomach and moaning with a rhythmic little hiccup of breath. As June knelt beside her, Jimmy Carver's radio began raising the alarm in Sun Hill station.

Too late.

Sergeant Cryer whistled up a patrol car. The hospital was alerted. In spite of the shock, the woman gallantly made a statement to WPC Ackland at her bedside. Things were not too serious: she had taken a nasty kick in the chest and another in the stomach, but there did not seem to be anything broken. She could talk, and she was willing to talk.

Not that it added up to a lot. There had already been sightings of the two muggers – young white male, young white female – but precious little in the way of positive identification. This time they had not made much of a killing. The woman had lost just over two pounds in cash and a cheque book, but she was one of the sensible ones, keeping her cheque card in her pocket, well away from the book.

'Thin pickings,' said Cryer. It was a fair bet that the animals would start again soon.

Ready to sign off, June Ackland found Jimmy Carver and Dave Litten arguing the toss over Saturday's football match. Litten was saying, 'All right, you buy me a drink on the way home, and I'll tell you just what's with the Hammers,' when Cryer's voice rang down the corridor: 'Dave – parade room, two minutes.'

The other two watched him go. He looked remarkably deflated.

'Well, now!' said June, not displeased.

'Do *you* fancy a drink?'

She studied Jimmy's earnest, apprehensive face for a few seconds, then smiled. 'Since you've been let down by your buddy – '

'Less of the buddy, if you don't mind.'

'I don't mind.'

They went out together; while Dave Litten went unhappily into the parade room and closed the door behind him.

Cryer said: 'You dropped one, didn't you?'

'Sarge?'

'Don't play the innocent with me, Dave. Look, we all know you can't wait to get out of the blue serge and start working with the superstars. But come on, why didn't you come to me about that villain?'

'I wasn't sure, sarge.'

'Cobblers. You were sure enough to go straight to Inspector Galloway.'

'I thought – '

'We know what you thought. Brownie points. Looks good on the record.'

'No, sarge.'

'Don't make it worse for yourself, son. What do you think we are, a load of old mugs or something? Loyalty, a team, all working together. That's what we're about.' As Litten wilted, Cryer let out a splutter of exasperation. 'All right, you can go. But here's something for you.' He held out an envelope which he had been holding behind his back, flicking it against his trouser-band.

'What is it?'

'Might be a cheque for your golden handshake. Or a copper handshake, more likely.'

'Sarge – '

'It's the result of your CID Board,' said Cryer, strolling off and leaving him to it.

Ten minutes later Dave Litten had tracked down the others in the pub. The two of them did not look exactly delighted to see him, but Jimmy Carver said: 'Hello, Dave, you having one?'

'I'll get them in.'

'It's my shout.'

'I said I'll get them in, all right? Bit of a celebration, you might say.'

Without asking June what she wanted, he brought her another half pint along with the pints for Jimmy and himself. When he was settled at the table he beamed at both of them, and raised his glass.

'You've had a result?' said Jimmy.

'That's right. Only the first stage, you know, but . . .' He shrugged. It was virtually in the bag. He knew the form. 'On secondment for a while, see how things work out. They always have to go through the motions.' He drank deeply and satisfyingly.

'Congratulations. That's great.'

Litten stared. 'You seem genuinely pleased.'

'Of course I am.'

'You baffle me, you know that? I mean, we ain't been exactly the best of pals' – he caught June Ackland's gaze and floundered – 'but . . . well, you live and learn.'

'Congratulations,' said Jimmy again, firmly.

Inspector Galloway and Ted Roach came in through the far door, looked across, and moved closer.

'All right, my son?' said Galloway. 'Happy now?'

'Yeah, well, it ain't sunk in yet.'

'Still a few hurdles to go.'

But Litten was already on his feet, trying not to make it too obvious that he was itching to desert June and Jimmy, and the whole uniform branch for that matter. As he moved away between Galloway and Roach, Roach glanced back and winked.

'He'll be unbearable now.' June Ackland's eyes looked darker and more bruised than ever.

'Give him a chance,' Jimmy protested. 'I hope he makes it. He'll make a good detective, he will.'

'Oh, yes. If being a bigot and a racist are qualifications for being a good detective, then Dave Litten's ideal.'

It rather spoilt the taste of the drink.

As she walked away alone, on her way to pick up something from the delicatessen but with her head down, brooding, June was conscious of the street noises only as a familiar, boring background. They didn't exactly hinder her thoughts, but they did nothing much to help, either. Maybe thinking was a rotten idea in the first place.

Suddenly, right ahead of her, there was a shout, the crash of a push-chair going over, and a flurry on the pavement.

'Give it up or else . . . '

Two figures had erupted from a doorway and thrown a woman to the ground. It was like a re-run – the same couple, the same pattern, tried and tested. A swift dash into action, a punch-up and a quick grab, and then away like the clappers.

Only not this time. June Ackland threw herself at the blonde and got a good lock round her neck. They crashed into the man and went down. He tried to kick June, but missed and nearly overbalanced.

The girl was cursing, spitting filth, as June wrestled her to the nearest shop frontage. The man turned on them; but then heard the shrill of a whistle and the pounding of feet. Still fighting to keep the struggling, spitting girl under control, June thankfully saw Taffy Edwards in uniform belting towards them.

The young man steadied himself, then was away.

Taffy shot past the woman.

'Police – stop!' He thrust a gaping bystander to one side. 'Out of the bloody way!'

The youth was fast. Also he knew his way around. When you planned the sort of caper he and his girlfriend carried out, you needed to be sharp on the getaway and know every gap and every side turning.

He wasn't going to make it, though. Taffy was gaining. They raced down an alley, spun round the bollard at the end, and across a street as a telecommunications van skidded to a halt. The sagging gateway of an abandoned factory yawned open before them. The man was through, racing up a creaking outer stairway, down a few steps, and across dusty, splintered floors. Taffy panted, and his shoulder bounced off a metal beam.

Somebody *had* to be there waiting on the other side. Word *had* to have gone out by now, rustling up support.

He was drawing close. Desperately the man leapt across a gap in the floor, slithered on uneven planks, and found himself at the head of a fire escape.

Taffy sprang. He came down heavily on the floor. It felt like blotting paper.

His legs were trying to run, but running on nothing. Everything came at him all at once from every angle, closing in, squeezing his ribs and lashing across his head as the floor dissolved beneath him and he went down into dust and darkness.

Twelve

Detective Sergeant Roach said: 'A sharpshooter from the Yard? What a load of old rigmarole. I'm grade A with firearms, you know.'

'Yes,' said Galloway bleakly. 'I know. But ever since that Baker Street cock-up, the people on the top floor have been playing it all very safe.'

'Baker Street was nothing to do with me.'

'No, old son. But it was very much to do with public relations. And anyway, the last thing I want is for you to have to tackle some headbanger at the wrong end of a shooter.'

'We don't even know yet if we can winkle him out.'

'No, we don't. So play it nice and cool. And while we're on the subject of public relations, it wouldn't do your career any harm to watch the way you go about your private relations. Know what I mean?'

'Yes, guv.' Roach's moustache seemed to pinch in round the ends of his lips. 'I know what you mean.'

'Right, then. And until our Wyatt Earp rolls up from the Yard, it's strictly observation as far as you're concerned. Tail this Desmond Holt character. See him sniffing around anywhere special, and I want to know. But we don't risk anything or anybody until we know what the score is, and where we can be sure of pinning him down. Him and his mate. Got it?'

'Got it,' said Roach glumly.

He was past the age when routine stuff was enough to pass the time. Sitting on street corners waiting for small-time con-men wore you down. Ted Roach was one for going in with both feet. Yet here, an hour and a half after what you could only laughingly call a briefing, he and Dashwood were tucked away in a car on a grotty street waiting for someone maybe to walk past. If the villain had any sense, he'd be holding up a bank in Edinburgh by now, or drinking himself mindless in some basement club down any one of a hundred flights of steps hereabouts.

It was all Dave Litten's idea. So bloody anxious to please, that great big prawn. Feeding the boss a name, any old name, and finding what he thought might just be an address, and then letting somebody else waste an hour, two hours, God knows how many hours before they got anywhere – if they ever did get anywhere.

Dashwood turned up the volume of the car radio. A disc jockey was so busy scratching his ego that he had forgotten to put a disc on the turntable.

'Nerves,' said Dashwood.

'What?'

'My old mum reckons it's nerves when somebody can't stop rabbiting on.'

'Hm.'

It wasn't the real villains who were your enemies. The villains were your opponents, and it gave you a great lift to defeat them. It was in the station itself, among your own lot, that you found the real trouble. Being lumbered with this sort of thing, for example.

If Dave Litten thought he was going to get any help during his secondment, that help was certainly not going to come from Edward Richard Roach.

'Hey,' said Dashwood, suddenly taut.

'What?'

'Let's see if I can get a better picture.' Dashwood's camera came up slowly and unobtrusively.

'Well, well, well,' said Roach appreciatively. 'And what have we here?'

The slim, slouching yet almost elegant Desmond Holt was sauntering out of a front door on to the pavement. On the scene as if popping up from one of the gutter gratings was a creepy little type who waved eagerly at Holt and then cringed, then grinned hopefully.

Dashwood said: 'Strewth. Didn't recognize him last time.' He took a picture, and another, and another. 'Known as Horse.'

'Because of his speed?' asked Roach sceptically.

'Because he's shit.'

'Don't let them see you.' Roach was growing worried about Dashwood's mounting enthusiasm for the pictures he was taking. 'Observation's no damn good if they know they're being observed.'

'Don't worry.'

'Hold it. Maybe you'd better get on the wire. Tell them we're on the move.'

The two, the short and the tall, had begun sauntering down the road. Little Horse fussed and fidgeted even when walking slowly. Desmond Holt had a lean, arrogant elegance. Following them was tricky, coasting along and hoping not to be noticed, or shooting past and maybe taking a wrong turning and losing them.

Two corners away was a little suburban grocery with a sub-post-office sign above the door and a pillar-box outside. The two men paused, stared at the sky and then at the shop, and silently consulted each other.

Dashwood muttered: 'Hey, you don't reckon they're gonna – '

'On the wire quick, like I said.'

'Uniform Oscar, this is DC Dashwood . . .'

The house in its dignified terrace had once been part of a prosperous group of middle-class merchants' homes, in those Victorian days when a five-storey building with mews for horse and carriage was both desirable and inexpensive, even allowing for the upkeep of half a dozen staff and their accommodation in basements and low-ceilinged attics. Six deep, wide steps led up to each front door between pillars which had once looked classical but were now peeling like blistered flesh. Each fanlight carried a gilded number, but beside the doors themselves the numbers had been subdivided down a panel of name tags and buttons, replacing the once ornate brass bell-pull.

Before pressing the button labelled A. Taylor, Detective Chief Inspector Kirk observed that two slots above it was the name of E. R. Roach.

There was a noticeable delay before Mrs Taylor appeared at the door. One glance, and it was clear that she was the sort of woman who would keep callers waiting as a matter of pride. She must have had her clothes and makeup all fixed a good hour ago, knowing they were coming, but at the last minute there would have been the obligatory glance in the glass, the little pat to a cushion on the couch, the flick of a finger down one strand of tinted and disciplined hair, and a deliberately slow progression to the door.

'Do please come in. This door. Do go right through to the lounge.'

Her voice was high and constricted, as improbably neat as her hair. Somebody must once have told her, or she had noticed for herself, that she had what used to be called rosebud lips. She had added a touch of puce to them, and must have had one little last-minute rehearsal of that pout of mingled roguishness and disapproval.

'Please take a seat.' She waved at the chairs, each with a cushion precisely centred, and the sofa, its three cushions lined up with the same admirable precision.

'I hope this isn't putting you out too much, Mrs Taylor.'

She sighed. 'When your office rang through this morning, chief inspector, I decided to cancel my plans for the rest of the day. I thought it best. The sooner you learn the facts about that sordid fellow, the better. Now some tea, or a little glass of sherry perhaps?'

'Tea will do just fine, thank you.'

She had been prepared for this. The tray was laid, the kettle must have been brought to the boil some minutes before they arrived. As an array of biscuits was pushed towards him, Kirk said: 'Now, this statement which you made, Mrs Taylor – you haven't had any second thoughts since? Any reservations?'

'Apart from being far too lenient to the dreadful person concerned, and not caring to put every sordid thing in writing, I stand by what I said.'

Wheeler looked down his copy of the complaint. 'And you're sure of the time?'

'Oh, yes, quite sure, chief inspector.' Mrs Taylor pointedly addressed Kirk. 'I'd just rushed home from the market because I wanted to see Connors versus McEnroe on the TV. It was being televised live – the French open.'

'Three-fifty p.m.?' said Wheeler knowledgeably.

'Give or take a minute, yes. Yes, it would be. I just arrived at my front door, when that man and his trollop were coming down the stairs. She, I might add, was nearly naked.' Mrs Taylor's nose wrinkled. 'Just a tiny little bikini bottom and a very thin see-through top. Quite disgraceful.'

Kirk and Wheeler exchanged covert glances over the rims of their cups. Kirk said: 'Can you tell us precisely what led to the argument?'

Mrs Taylor waved towards the window. The two men got up and looked out. Below, within a sheltering quadrangle of terraced houses, was a communal garden. A number of individual gates led in from individual blocks, and there was a larger gate opening on to a lane at the end. Flower beds and clusters of shrubs marked the perimeter, and a number of trees had been set with careful irregularity over the grass and near the central junction of two diagonal paths. It looked very tranquil, a pleasant oasis in the heart of busy streets, shops and run-down hotels.

'I have lived here a great number of years.' It had all the makings of a speech which Mrs Taylor had rehearsed any number of times. 'Fifteen years, in fact. All the tenants know me, and they all know how I am if I sit in the sun too long. It brings me out in a hideous rash. So I always have to sit in the one spot. It's the only shady spot in the whole garden.'

'Prickly heat,' commented Wheeler.

'I beg your pardon?'

'The rash, madam. It's called prickly heat.'

Mrs Taylor's nose wrinkled again, with growing distaste. 'Oh, no. No, indeed. This is something quite different.' She moved back, agitated, to the tea tray.

Kirk prompted: 'And Sergeant Roach made the mistake of occupying your chair one day?'

'Oh, no, chief inspector. Not your rude young sergeant, though I wouldn't have put it past him. It was his trollop. Lounging in my chair, flaunting herself. You do realize, of course, that they're not married?'

'Yes, madam, we are aware of the fact. What happened then?'

'Well, I went across and asked quite politely to have my chair back. You should have seen the look on that girl's face! She let me have my chair back, but I could tell she resented it. You only had to see the look in her eyes to know.'

'But nothing was said?' Wheeler interposed. 'No argument or anything?'

'No, there was not. But from that moment on your sergeant has done nothing but be rude to me. He takes every opportunity of deliberately upsetting me.' She leaned forward to command Kirk's attention. 'You realize he comes home all hours of the day and night?'

'Being a detective sergeant in the Met police, Mrs Taylor, he would. He has to work all sorts of strange hours.'

'But when he comes home at three o'clock in the morning and *deliberately* uses the toilet in the noisiest way possible . . .! I know it sounds silly, but he does, and he does it on purpose.'

Wheeler was intrigued. 'How do you mean, madam?'

'He lives directly above me.' She stopped, making a little *moue* and looking away at one of the plaster ducks on the wall, apparently preparing itself for a nose-dive into the illuminated fish tank.

'Please, Mrs Taylor,' said Kirk gently, 'you can tell us. No need to feel embarrassed.'

'Very well, if I must. When he . . . when he . . . pees, he does it right down the middle, right into the water. You can hear everything down here. Everything.'

Kirk preserved a suitably grave countenance. 'Most annoying, I'm sure. But now, getting back to the row on the staircase – what exactly happened?'

'Well, as I've explained, I'd just arrived home when they were coming down the stairs. And I might add that he was nearly as naked as she was. Just a tiny little pair of shorts. I merely asked him not to sit on my seat in the garden, that's all. Well, he got angry and started calling me names. He called me a . . . a silly cow, and when I said I'd complain he told me to . . . well, he swore at me.'

'Tell us what he said, please, madam,' said Wheeler.

'He told me to piss off,' said Mrs Taylor with sudden force. 'The man has a foul mouth.'

She looked triumphantly from one to the other. This, so far as she was concerned, was the clinching proof of the whole deplorable affair.

Kirk put his cup and saucer down on the lace runner lying across the tiny table beside him. 'Could you tell us why you asked him not to sit in your seat in the garden, Mrs Taylor?'

'I was thinking of sitting there myself, chief inspector. As I said, it's the only spot I can sit in with any comfort on a sunny day.'

'Do you have a portable television set?'

She blinked. 'Portable television? No. Why do you ask?'

Wheeler, who had seized the point, edged forward in his chair attentively.

'I thought you mentioned earlier that you'd rushed home from the shops in order to watch tennis,' said Kirk. 'Having a portable television set would have enabled you to do both. Sit in the garden *and* watch the tennis.'

Mrs Taylor wriggled uncomfortably. 'I see. Well, I intended going down after the tennis, straight after the match in fact.'

'I see.' Kirk began to get up. 'Thank you very much, Mrs Taylor.'

'That's all you want to ask?' She glanced round at all her tidy preparations, regretting that they had been on display for such a short time.

'I think that's all, thank you.'

'And something will be done?'

'I can assure you that we'll do all that is best in these distressing circumstances.'

Mrs Taylor's lips compressed into a satisfied blob.

Walking back down the steps to the street, Wheeler said with a certain dour satisfaction of his own: 'She's not going to let it drop, sir.'

'No, I can see that. And I can see why Roach doesn't get along with her. Don't see why we should feed her with her whole pound of flesh, though.'

'The trouble is, it's no longer just a matter of what *she* wants.' Wheeler glanced sideways at his colleague. 'There was something she said – '

'The time of day?' said Kirk sadly.

'That's right. Lined up against Roach's time sheets, I can't say I like the look of it.'

'Shame. Good man, good record.'

All the signs were that Holt and Horse meant business. A cheeky pair, you had to give them that, operating this close to their own doorstep. Now they sauntered into the post office, a few yards apart, not swapping another glance.

'Stay with the car.' Roach eased himself out.

'But look, sarge, if the two of them – '

'I'll send a recorded delivery postcard if I need you.'

Ted Roach crossed the road as casually as the two men had done. Desmond Holt, picking out a birthday card from the rack and putting it down again, looked warily at him as he entered the shop but made no other move.

An elderly man was shuffling away from the postal counter grille. Roach took his place. 'Er, could I have some . . . er . . . postal rates leaflets, please.' He waited, tense with the strain of not looking round, as the leaflets were handed over. 'Thanks. Oh, and while I'm at it, could I have . . . um . . . twenty-four first-class stamps as well, please.'

Holt's patience snapped. Suddenly he had crowded Roach out of the way, throwing him back towards Horse; and there was a gun in his hand, jabbed across the counter at the cowering man on the other side.

'Right.' The gun flicked towards Roach and flicked back again. 'You, keep quiet. *You* . . . pass the money over. All of it. And move it.'

'Do as he says' – Roach had his eye on the gun and Holt's panicky trigger-finger – 'for God's sake.'

'Shut up or you're dead,' snarled Holt. 'Just shut up.' With his left hand he hammered on the counter. 'You an' all, if you don't get a move on.'

Faintly, in the distance, Roach heard the mellow music of a police car siren. Was it coming this way, or heading for some other incident, somewhere else?

87

'The Bill!' squealed Horse.

Holt swung round to glare at the door. The man bending down, shaking, towards the safe made a suddenly wild, courageous gesture. His foot kicked out, and an alarm bell began jangling outside the building.

Holt cursed and raised his gun.

'Hold it,' said Roach. He fended Horse off with one elbow. 'Police officer.'

'That so? Then out of my way, man, or I'll top yer. I mean it.' Torn between the man now cowering on his knees behind the counter and Roach's burly shape, Holt advanced on Roach. 'You move, and you're dead.'

Horse made a run for it. He had reached the doorway when Dashwood came in fast. All at once there was a hammer in Horse's hand, lashing out and taking Dashwood on the shoulder. Roach went in low, catching Holt around the waist and flinging the two of them against a narrow display cabinet which rattled and tinkled like a job lot of door chimes. Holt began beating him about the head with the gun butt, and brought his knee up. A sharp corner of something solid and unyielding caught Roach across the corner of the mouth, but he made one last mighty heave and sent Holt sliding in one direction while the gun rattled away in the other.

Then the shop was full of uniformed officers. Two of them hauled Holt to his feet. Another looked down at Roach and Dashwood, slumped against the display rack, getting their breath back.

'You all right, guv?'

'We'll live.' Roach dabbed at something sticky and smeary on his chin, and found that blood was oozing from the side of his mouth. He edged himself a few inches to the left and groped for Holt's gun. Then he began to laugh helplessly. 'Bloody hell, would you believe it?'

'No need for that sharpshooter now,' said Dashwood admiringly.

'Never was.' Roach dangled the gun in front of him. 'Look at that. It's only a toy!'

Thirteen

First they laid two long metal ladders side by side across the surviving joists of the shattered floor, then began hauling lengths of rope along them, together with what looked to Bob Cryer like a bosun's chair. The fire officer in charge stooped over the hole with its pile of rubble and clicked his teeth ominously.

'There could be a ton of the stuff on top of him.' Straightening up, he glanced past the sergeant. 'That one of your lads back there?'

Jimmy Carver was standing well out of the way of the firemen as they cautiously tested the fringes of the floor and eased tackle into position.

'One of his mates,' said Cryer.

'He's looking pretty pale. May not be a pretty sight, when we scrape it out.'

Cryer stepped over a coil of rope and made his way to Carver's side. They watched as two firemen lowered themselves with infinite care over the jagged rim of the hole, testing beams that had sagged sideways, and guiding a grapple to the centre of the mess. Cryer longed to get in there with his bare hands, manhandling the muck out of the way while there was still a chance that Taffy Edwards might be breathing. It didn't seem likely, but those boys knew what they were doing and they were taking no chances.

Cryer said hoarsely: 'PC Carver, you can get back to the station and relieve Litten. Or the other way round. He can come and spell you.'

'I'd rather stay, sarge.'

'Look, lad, this may take hours, and it could be a bit nasty. For your own sake, I'm ordering you . . .' But he looked at Carver's face and let the order fade out.

'I'd rather stay, sarge.'

'Yes, I thought you would.'

Some splintered planking and a baulk of timber were heaved out and swung to one side. A hastily mounted light was dragged to a perilous angle above the hole, and a fireman with a heat-seeker probed through the rubble below for the evidence of Taffy's body.

'About there . . .'

Another man lowered himself over the edge, bracing himself against two splayed beams, and lifted, backbreakingly, a plank and then another one.

The brigade officer, as eager as Cryer to get his hands on something, to *do* something, grabbed one of the torches and shone it down past the gingerly working fireman.

Something sharply rectangular, dully gleaming, rested in an angle of grimy woodwork.

Cryer, venturing towards the edge, said: 'Oh, Christ.'

It was Edwards' radio.

'Hang on!'

The fireman shoved aside a thin but solid segment of boarding. It had been resting on two beams which had collided into a crosspiece, sheltering a small, unharmed space below. In the space, smaller than that of the smallest tent, lay Taffy Edwards. A few inches away, the crushed edge of what had once been his helmet protruded from a lethal tangle of bits and pieces. But Taffy was clear of any weight. As the light sought him out, the mask of filth on his face cracked and began to dissolve. He raised one arm, showering dust, and moaned.

'I'll be buggered!' said the brigade officer joyfully. 'Just look at that!'

Taffy opened one bleary eye, and began to cough.

'Anybody got a plaster?' he wheezed.

The return to Sun Hill was jubilant, and the reception there swelled into a double celebration. Roach and Dashwood, looking decidedly battered round the edges but strong enough to stand up to the fusillade of jokes, were knocking back tea in vast quantities and ready to cheer anybody and anything.

'Nice work . . .'

'What a day!'

'Hero of the hour!' Bob Cryer seized Roach's hand, and two of the WPCs began to cheer.

'Come on, come on,' groaned Roach. 'Shut up, you wallies. Routine stuff, and you know it.'

'Oh, hark at Mr Modest, eh?'

'Anyway, it wasn't a real shooter.'

Jimmy Carver, unable to stop smiling and tugging at his ear, and then laughing and fiddling with a button, bubbling over with joy, said: 'But you weren't to know that, were you, guv?'

'Of course I knew it. What do you think I am – silly?'

Roy Galloway came down from Chief Superintendent Brownlow's office to join in the general hubbub of mutual congratulation.

'The super wants a word with you in five minutes, Bob.'

'Probably about our friendly neighbourhood mugger.'

'You got him as well? In spite of Taffy –'

'We got him,' said Cryer. 'One minute later, to be precise. Found himself up against a nice big gate with a lot of wire mesh in his face.'

'Oho. Like that? Short riot?'

'Let's say he just got a slap.' Cryer decided it was time to restore order to the place. 'Right, what about showing some faces on the street? And Litten, don't you go scarpering off with your new chums until you've filled in those sheets in there – every last one of them.'

It took just twenty-four hours for the cloud to drift over that sunny sky. Reporting in next day with a sore mouth and a slightly sore head from an evening's celebration, Ted Roach was otherwise in a good mood. It was still good when Galloway said: 'Super wants to see us, Ted. At the double.'

'I was going to get my hair cut.'

'And say thank you nicely,' Bob Cryer suggested, 'when he pins the medal on.'

'I can hang it up with the other two, and my divorce papers. Oh, and the red letter from the mortgage company.'

He noticed that Roy Galloway was silent as they went upstairs, but for himself he had no forebodings. And it did start out pretty well. The moment they were in Brownlow's office, the chief superintendent said briskly: 'Sergeant Roach, I have just been reading the arrest report on Desmond Holt. Inspector Galloway has recommended you for a bravery commendation.'

It was no good joking about it. It did mean something. It meant a hell of a lot. 'Thank you very much, sir.'

'In the circumstances I can only say that I am going to endorse his recommendation. However, that is not the only reason for your presence in my office this morning.'

'Sir?'

Brownlow could not sit still. He got up and paced round his desk like an animal seething with a rage to spring. 'Sergeant Roach, are you aware that as a result of a complaint by one of your neighbours you've laid yourself open to a charge that's tantamount to stealing?'

Roach's stomach turned over. It was impossible. But from the corner of his eye he was aware of Galloway standing stiffly beside him; and Galloway's face was grimly set.

'Sir, I don't understand.'

'Don't you? Look, this complaint by that Mrs Taylor of yours – '

'She's certainly not mine, sir.'

'Shut up, sergeant,' growled Roy Galloway.

'In normal circumstances,' said Brownlow, 'this might be simply a case of smacking your wrists and telling you to watch your conduct in future. That's the way we'd like to handle it. But since Chief Inspector Kirk's enquiry it's no longer that simple.'

Roach wanted to speak, but decided not to.

'Since that enquiry,' Brownlow went on, 'there's every possibility that you could be suspended from duty and charged forthwith. As a result of your bloody stupidity you could have washed all the good work of twenty years down the drain – twenty years of loyal, dedicated service.'

'But what's this got to do with stealing, sir?' The room seemed to be spinning round. It couldn't be real. 'I haven't stolen anything.'

'You stole *time*, sergeant. Time is money. The taxpayer's and ratepayer's money. You still don't get what I'm talking about?'

'No, sir.'

'On the 31st of May you had a ruckus with your neighbour, Mrs Taylor, right?'

'Yes, sir, but I don't see – '

'We have Mrs Taylor's statement, and confirmation from two other neighbours who heard the altercation, that it took place on the staircase between three-fifty and four o'clock that afternoon. Also you were dressed in a manner which suggested that you were about to do a spot of sunbathing. So, too, was your young lady.'

The cloud darkened, but now Ted Roach began to see its outlines. Now he knew what the chief superintendent was talking about. It was worse than anything he could ever have expected.

'At the time of that argument, sergeant, the British ratepayer was paying you overtime. You were logged as being on the other side of the bloody district. You should not have been anywhere near home at the time in question. Do you understand *now*, Sergeant Roach?'

Roach hardly recognized his own voice. It scraped and rustled in his head. 'Yes, sir. I get it. I can only say, sir, that at the time I was under a great deal of stress.'

Galloway said: 'I'd like to confirm that, sir. We were at it every hour of the day and night, straight up. And we did get a result on all those break-and-enters.'

'I've made every allowance for that. It doesn't alter the fact that you cheated by making an entry for that afternoon which showed you booking off at five-thirteen.'

It was more than Roach could take. 'Look, sir what about all the hours I did do overtime and I never booked for them? God knows how many hours. What about *them?*'

'I am not interested in what has not been logged,' said Brownlow, 'only what has.' He spared one furious glance for Galloway. 'You've been a DI long enough, Roy – how the hell did this get past you?'

Familiar sounds welled up from the rooms and corridors below. Slamming of doors, a burst of laughter, a bell ringing somewhere. There was the reassuring swish of traffic outside, and a rumble in the wall which had something to do with the plumbing, and had been like that for at least five years now. Yet the room was suffocated by silence.

Roach stood quite still, waiting for the worst.

Brownlow leaned back against the edge of his desk. 'This is what saved you, Roach. The Complaints Division, having taken your full record into consideration, have decided to give you the benefit of the doubt. The matter of disciplinary proceedings has been left entirely in my hands. Consider yourself very lucky this is going to go no further.'

'Thank you, sir.' Roach just managed the words.

'You'll be informed in due course what disciplinary measures I do intend to take.'

'Sir. Thank you, sir,' said Roach again.

He and Galloway went down the stairs in bleak silence, almost as bad as the one that had clouded the office for an endless minute.

'Now that's over,' said Galloway in his most clipped tone, 'we'd better call in on your pop-gun pal.' In the office he stopped, half crouching in that predatory way he had. The mateyness, camaraderie, call it what the hell you liked, of the day before seemed to have been sucked up into that dark cloud hanging over Sun Hill. 'Sergeant Cryer!'

'Anything I can do to oblige?'

They were like two cats trying out their voices before they unsheathed their claws.

'Our friend from yesterday. Properly charged?'

'You know damn well he was.'

'Proper warnings?'

'We don't do it any other way.'

'And we can see him? Have a little encouraging word with him?'

'Wouldn't mind being there, just to check on it.'

Galloway thawed. 'Oh, come on, Bob. Let's go see, before he goes up. See if we can make the stupid sod see some sense.'

The three of them went into the interview room, and were waiting when Desmond Holt sidled in. A night in the cells had made little difference to his loping gait, and the constable who shepherded him along might just as well not have been there. Holt had his own image of himself, and it had not yet been shattered.

'Sit,' said Galloway.

Holt sat in the straight-backed chair as if it had belonged to him all his life. His dark eyes and dark lips were beautifully shaped – and contemptuous.

'Your so-called mate seems to have legged it,' Galloway proceeded. 'He's left you right in it.'

'Dumped you,' Roach contributed. He was in a right good mood to contribute anything, to work a lot of things out of his system.

'He's a shitbag.'

Holt favoured them with a drowsy, faraway smile. 'That's the way it goes, isn't it?'

'You're at a disadvantage.' Galloway hitched himself across a chair and leaned on its back, peering up at Holt in commiseration. 'Good-looking boy like you, I mean, really! Coloured, too.' He allowed himself a glance at Bob Cryer. 'He's on a loser or what?'

'Just a bit.'

'They don't have a special place to protect boys like him inside, do they?'

'Not that I've heard of.'

'All slim and lovely, eh? He won't come out the way he goes in, that's for sure.' Galloway scraped the chair round some forty-five degrees, and hit out: 'Now, I'm going to put something to you, and I'm only going to say it once, so you listen. And you listen good. You tell me where your mate's likely to have legged it to' – he tried a confidential wink and bob of the head – 'and maybe I'll have a little word with the beak for you tomorrow.'

'Yeah. Yeah, 'course you will.'

'Oh, come on,' Roach crashed in. 'You owe him nothing. He dumped you, left you to carry the can all on your own.'

They waited. Holt kept them waiting. When he raised his head, his liquid brown eyes were swimming with something that blended poison and defiance.

'I got nothing to say. I don't know where he'd be.'

'All right, my black friend, you want to play it that way, that's up to you.'

There was a tap at the door. Sergeant Penny came through with a message slip. Roy Galloway took it in at one glance, and then raised his head complacently.

Holt said: 'Don't try it on. I've seen cons before.'

'You have, son? Okay. Take him down, sergeant. You blew it, son. Blew a chance of having a friend in court tomorrow. Only now it's too late. Your pal Horse got picked up by the Essex police half an hour ago.'

'Like I said' – Holt's stubborn gaze did not waver – 'it's the way it goes, isn't it?'

Galloway nodded at Cryer. The sergeant and the officer propping up the door jamb moved in and stood on either side of Desmond Holt, whose limp indifference was an insolent challenge in itself.

He looked gloatingly at Ted Roach. 'The way it goes, eh?' Abruptly he brought his right hand up, two fingers projecting like a kid's fingers, playing cops and robbers. 'Bang, bang!'

Roach was halfway across the room before Galloway caught him. Bob Cryer raised an eyebrow, and shifted Holt out of the place at a rate of knots.

'Bastard!'

Galloway said: 'Temper, Ted! I'm beginning to feel a whole lot of sympathy for that poor Mrs . . . what was her name?'

'Mrs Bloody Taylor.'

'I wonder who christened her that?' As they left the room into the clean, dank, featureless corridor, Galloway added: 'Ted, what *were* you doing in that garden that day?'

A reminiscent gleam came into Ted Roach's eyes. 'It was a very warm day, guv'nor. Very warm indeed.'

Fourteen

Maggie was back. Murder and mayhem might come and go. Grotty little villains with lengths of lead piping and bits of bent wire to open car doors might put in an appearance and then disappear on to fresh patches. Maggie Drew came; and kept coming. The officers of Sun Hill police station felt that Maggie was likely to go on for ever.

This time it was WPC June Ackland who had made the arrest. Maggie had come bumbling out on to the pavement outside the supermarket, blinking in the sunlight and looking just like any of the rather vague, doddery old women who did their shopping along the street and tottered back to their cramped little rooms to sit in front of the telly or babble incessantly to the budgerigar. But she was not like all the others. Fate – and the store detective – had singled her out. Maggie had taken only a few steps away from the glass doors when a hard-jawed middle-aged woman caught up with her and brought her to a halt. As they argued, the store detective held up a peremptory arm, and June Ackland crossed the street to join them.

Maggie blinked owlishly from one to the other, shaking her head in pitiful disbelief.

Ackland said: 'Salmon?'

'Salmon,' said the store detective. She held out a cold, bony hand. 'Newnham, officer.'

'Miss Newnham – '

'Mrs.'

'Mrs Newnham, you're proposing to make a charge?'

'Not for the first time. For all the good it's done, the last few times,' added Mrs Newnham frostily.

'Come on, Maggie. You'd better come along to the station and tell us the tale. And you, Mrs Newnham, will you come and make a statement, please?'

'I'll be glad to.'

Maggie stood where she was, sucking her lips in and digging her right thumb into the handle of her shopping bag. Then she seemed to wake from her trance, and opened the bag to peer in.

'Well, I never!'

'But you did,' said Mrs Newnham. 'Over and over again.'

'Salmon!' marvelled Maggie. 'A tin of salmon! What must have happened, now I come to think about it . . . yes, that's it . . . I put the tin in my bag by mistake. My bag was in the trolley, see, and I wasn't looking where I put the tin. Now, that's a mistake anybody could have made. Couldn't they?' she appealed to them, with a sweetly reasonable smile.

'Anybody,' Ackland agreed. 'But not eight times in the last twelve months.'

Looking pathetically downtrodden under the harsh weight of the injustice which was being visited on her, Maggie was led away in the direction of Sun Hill. When the contents of her tatty shopping bag were tipped out on the desk, Sergeant Cryer looked almost as disbelieving as she was trying to do.

'Not salmon again?'

'Sergeant, I been trying to explain what an innocent mistake – '

'I bet you've got more tins of salmon at home than John West,' Cryer marvelled.

June Ackland tucked herself into a tiny cubicle with Mrs Newnham and began laboriously to write out the store detective's statement. There ought to be a duplicated version of it, she thought, with a few gaps for the necessary names, for in every other detail it was wearisomely the same as so many other shoplifting incidents. Store detective observes suspicious movement behind row of shelves; notices bulge in shopping bag before contents of trolley have been paid for and stowed in the bag; suspect leaves checkout point and proceeds to exit doors; is on her way out and along the street when challenged . . .

Cryer put his head round the door.

'Sarge, Mrs Newnham, store detective, Hartfield supermarket.'

'We do know each other.' Cryer was unusually curt. 'Your company prosecuting, are they?'

'Company policy. The way things are nowadays, we have no choice. No matter how little the value, or the circumstances of the offender.'

Cryer nodded at WPC Ackland. 'Add that to the end of the statement. All right?'

Mrs Newnham's austere features stiffened into those of a hanging judge. 'I can see you're not very happy about that.'

'I'm always happy, Mrs Newnham. Just that I want the magistrate, the public in the gallery, and the press . . . I want them all to know your company's policy.' June Ackland knew, if the other woman did not, that Cryer's tongue was firmly lodged in his cheek. 'A deterrent, you see.' As he began to close the door, he added: 'When you're ready come right out and I'll charge her.'

It presented quite a cosy scene when Ackland and Mrs Newnham did emerge. Cryer had a charge sheet and a cup of tea on the desk before him, while Maggie sat on the bench wrapping her fingers round a plastic cup and whimpering spasmodically at the heat.

'Why don't I get a cup and saucer no more? I remember the time when you could get a decent cup of tea in this nick.'

'Safety regulations, Maggie.'

'Safety? You don't think I'd try and do meself an injury, do you?'

'Not your safety, Maggie. Ours. Can't afford to have our cups and saucers disappearing into that bag of yours.'

As Mrs Newnham prepared to sign the charge sheet, June Ackland put the groceries one by one back into the bag. Maggie watched her tin of salmon with distant yearning.

Roy Galloway came clattering down the stairs. Maggie's face brightened immediately. 'It's Mr Galloway!'

Halted on his way to the outer door, Galloway looked at the desk. 'You again, Maggie? Not tins of salmon?'

'What else?' said Cryer.

'Cor, you must have more tins of salmon at home than – '

'She's already heard that one, Roy. Where are you off to in such a rush?'

Galloway imperceptibly shook his head, a warning not to push the conversation too far. 'Just a contact. I might have a job on tomorrow. Tell you what it's all about later.' He nodded at Ackland. 'Get the girls to bring in some civvies. Stuff they don't mind getting dirty. And Dave Litten as well.' As June Ackland raised her head over the shopping bag and lifted it from the desk, he added: 'A rehearsal for the station pantomime.'

'Shouldn't think your department would want any practice,' said Bob Cryer.

Galloway's lip curled, but he did not hang about to think up a retort.

Tombo Robinson had once done some training on his own account down on the running track of this local stadium and had made quite a reputation, even if it lasted for only a little while, in the 800 metres. Now younger and fitter lads were training down there. Tombo and a couple of friends from the Clayview estate still devoted some hours each week helping and encouraging the youngsters, and arranging a number of regular functions for them. He was a familiar figure on the ground and the stands, coming and going as he pleased, adding a darkly benevolent presence to the scene. Sometimes friends would be with him, sometimes he sauntered in alone to enjoy the spectacle. Today he was alone; but not for long.

Roy Galloway ambled down the aisle and worked his way along the row. When he sat down, Tombo kept him waiting while he rolled a cigarette. Then Tombo said:

'You didn't really know for sure, did you? About Decker's?'

'Not right at the start, no. Not one hundred per cent.'

'Oh, it's a hundred-per-cent set-up all right.' Tombo stared gloomily out over the stadium. 'They've got some real professionals backing them. People way up the line. Big time, big business, big money. Not your ordinary man on the street, Roy, pushing bits here, bits there. I'm telling you, man, this is the real McCoy.'

Galloway whistled faintly and thoughtfully between his teeth. 'If it's that big, d'you think I should hold off for a few days, keep it under surveillance, wait till we can be dead sure of making a killing?'

'Might suss you out. And me.' Tombo inhaled and stared unhappily ahead still, as if one glance at the detective inspector might let him in for more trouble. 'The sooner I'm out of that place, the better for my health. It hasn't been easy.'

He had made no great show of trying to get himself into the old, boarded-up cinema. It took an apparently chance meeting with one of his old cronies who had found himself a job as one of Decker's minders. Still not pushing it, Tombo had talked idly about the old days, and waited to be invited to try the new premises inside. He acted dumb, but let himself be coaxed – watched all the time by a white heavy, Pat Corcoran, who he could tell didn't trust him. But then, it took only a little time to discover that Corcoran trusted nobody. It wasn't his job or his nature to trust folk.

Inside, Tombo explained to Galloway, the auditorium was pretty much the way it had always been, but rooms and offices opening off the circle had been tarted up as plushy little hideaways where you could take a fix, smoke grass, or try anything else that took your fancy. Once you were there, Decker's boys could provide you with many a thing to take your fancy. The upstairs foyer had been converted into a bar, with reggae music part of the time and drowsy, insinuating stuff when the mood was right. And there was a corner bar where you bought not just what you wanted but what you just had to have, no matter what it cost. And, said Tombo, there was the old storeroom which had become a distribution centre for the country-wide trade.

'Big money,' said Tombo again. 'And behind it there's somebody a whole lot bigger than Harry Decker. You got to hit them fast, before they get their next consignment out on the streets.'

'You're sure there's one due in?'

'I might be wrong, but – '

'Come on, Tombo. You know. I can tell you do.'

'The way I heard it, a big delivery tomorrow morning. Late morning. Then they start sorting and packaging. You know. Could take some time.'

'What time do *you* reckon would be good for a visit?'

Tombo slumped down on the bench. 'It'll take careful planning.'

'What time, Tombo?'

'Hit it at half three. Tomorrow afternoon. That way they should be right in the middle of it.'

'Fine.' Galloway turned, and at last Tombo faced him, apprehensive. 'I'll need you in there, though.'

'That's what I've been dreading you'd say. Look, they'll kill me if they ever find out – and that, my white brother, is not a figure of speech!'

'All you have to do,' said Galloway soothingly, 'is be in there when we hit the place. You'll be my eyes and ears. Just point me in the right direction, the right places to look, and the right people to nick. No more.'

'Will I be arrested?'

'Of course. Got to make it look convincing, haven't we?'

'Then what?'

'Well, my old son,' Galloway smiled, 'have you ever heard the story about the one that gets away?'

He was impatient to get moving now. Everything had to be set up fast, but just right. He hurried downstairs to a payphone outside the stadium's changing rooms, and fretted while the bleeps went on and on for ever – did they have a siesta every day now at Sun Hill? – until he was through to Ted Roach.

The briefing was set up. Things to be said and done shuffled themselves and reshuffled in his head.

'And don't tell anybody *anything*,' he concluded.

'What're you talking about, guv?' came Roach's plaintive response. 'I don't *know* anything.'

They would all know soon enough.

The campaign began to take shape. In Roy Galloway's mind, for a start. He could visualize the dilapidated old cinema, looking so scruffy and abandoned from outside, but within those boards and padlocked doors so full of life – and the potential for death and drug-sodden despair.

He couldn't wait to get in there.

Ted Roach had been on early turn and ought to have left by the time Galloway got back. But he was hanging about, fidgeting, gnawing at a wisp of his moustache, dying to know what the hell this was all about.

'Who's on tonight?' Galloway demanded.

'I am,' said Dashwood.

Roach had to agree. 'He is.'

'Right, you can go, Ted.'

'Not if I'm going to miss anything, I'm not.'

'Haven't you got somebody waiting back there to offer you some health-giving crackling?'

'I don't mind hanging on, honest, guv.'

'Okay. There are some calls that have to be made. Share 'em out between you. Oh – and did you fix for the super to come back in?'

Roach grinned evilly. 'Like you said. And the way he reacted, I'd say you'd better come up with something hot.'

'I aim to do just that.'

'Tell you what, guv. Why not see him first, and cover for – '

'I'm not covering for anything or anybody. Not for more hours than I have to, any road. We get organized right here and now, and then you've got something to occupy your little minds while I go and spell it out for him.'

'It really is that hot?' Roach knew when the joking was over and the real thing was on its way.

'Scorch the pants off you. Right. This is what I want on standby for tomorrow.' He paused for a moment while Dashwood grabbed a scrap pad from his desk. 'All right? A couple of drugs dogs, but I don't want anyone else told about that for the time being. Two nondescript vans, one with ladders. The ladders are to be used, not for show. About ten lads from the crime squad – no, make that twenty. And remember, don't mention to them about the drugs dogs. Not until I say so. Some lamps, sledgehammers . . . yeah, I think that's about all for now.'

'Blimey.' Even Ted Roach was awestruck. 'What we gonna hit – Fort Knox?'

'Get it moving.' Galloway watched them both diving for their phones before he went up to face Chief Superintendent Brownlow.

Next morning, with encouragement and warnings ringing in both ears, like a stereo music centre gone on the blink, he was at the magistrates' court in the motley pile-up waiting for cases to be called, under the beady eye of a uniformed sergeant on a high stool, bolstered up by the legal power invested in him.

WPC Ackland, he noticed, was standing below the desk as Galloway entered. The jailer was saying: 'There's a warrant outstanding on Mrs Drew. Non-payment of fine. I've told the clerk.'

Maggie, close beside June Ackland, bridled. Ackland looked cross. 'The CRO didn't say anything about that.'

'Breakdown of communications. You know how it is.'

Galloway said: 'Looking for a couple of cheap tins of salmon, Bert?'

'Wouldn't get anything cheap off me, I can tell yer,' cried Maggie, uncharacteristically ferocious.

Galloway sidled closer to June Ackland. 'You got the message about the plain clothes this afternoon? Old jeans, scruffy old sweater, that kind of thing.'

Her brown eyes began to burn. 'Really something this time, sir?'

'Oh, really something. Wouldn't say no to a bulletproof bra, if I were you.' He glanced up at the lordly jailer. 'Who's on the bench?'

'Redmayne.'

Galloway allowed himself a happy click of the fingers. There wasn't going to be any legalistic needling and niggling, not with Redmayne. He slid unobtrusively into Court Number One.

'What I intend to do,' the magistrate was intoning, 'is to put this case back to later in the day, so that you may have a meaningful talk with the probation officer. This does not necessarily mean I'm going to place you on probation. Thank you. You may step down.'

Just as the clerk of the court was about to announce the next case, the court officer hastened forward. 'Would you take an application for a search warrant, sir? Inspector Galloway.'

From here on it all had to roll at top speed. One delay, one word out of place, one rumour snaking its well-oiled way round the grapevine, and the whole thing could fall apart. Galloway held himself ready, and felt a few beads of sweat prickle on the back of his neck and start leaking downwards. There was a nod of acceptance. He took the warrant and information forms from his inside pocket and handed them to the usher, who handed them to the clerk of the court. A polite gesture of the hand, and he was in the witness box with the card in front of him, taking the oath, declaring his name and official position, agreeing that his signature was in fact his signature, and testifying that the information he had offered was true to the best of his knowledge and belief.

It had happened so many times before. But this time it was somehow ten times more important. Those scum had to be done down. That housing estate had to be shielded from drugs and the drug peddlers and all the high-placed, high-priced bastards who made fortunes out of human misery.

This was when being a copper actually meant something. It was why you'd joined, why you'd slogged on, and why it had to be made to work.

One false step, one snag, and it was all blown.

The magistrate read quickly over the depositions, signed, and reached for the official stamp. At the last moment he seemed to have second thoughts. Galloway held his breath. Redmayne, the magistrate, tore off a small scrap of paper, scribbled on it, and attached it with a paper clip to the rest. Then he leaned forward and passed the warrant over.

Galloway quickened his pace round the edge of the court, not looking at the note until he was close to the door.

The brief scrawl said: 'Best of luck.'

Galloway paused and offered a grateful smile. The magistrate did not exactly smile in return, but over the edge of his bi-focals his eyebrows rose in what could only have been a semaphore of encouragement.

It was a good omen. Roy Galloway began to feel the adrenalin reaching parts other stimulants usually failed to reach.

Fifteen

Final briefing in the parade room was low key, yet as fraught with the awareness of danger as a wartime invasion briefing. Although they all knew the target building, squatting as it did in the middle of a run-down street with side alleys from which they regularly winkled out glue-sniffers and meths drinkers, only a few of them had ever been inside it. The lettering of its one-time name had cracked and distorted long ago, and three-ply boards masked spaces where posters had once invited audiences to queue for the latest all-star features. Harry Decker had never replaced the sign with anything to identify his illegal drinking club, but some longer-serving officers could remember visiting it nevertheless. They were the ones with key duties today.

Uniformed men mingled with men and women in a motley array of plain clothes, grabbing chairs where they could or leaning against the back wall of the room with a clear view of the blackboard. Galloway had gone over the route and the division of the attacking forces three times, word for word, as if afraid to reach zero hour and let them loose.

Chief Superintendent Brownlow broke in at last. 'Right, I think that's it. You all know what to do. I don't have to reiterate the importance of this raid.

If it's successful, it'll be a significant step forward in our fight against drug abuse. Unfortunately, this in turn will attract considerable publicity. Therefore I must impress on you that I don't want any cockups. Whether we win or lose, I want no cause for complaint. I want this operation carried out properly. And let me remind you . . . if there are no drugs found, then there are no drugs found. Understood? Rules and regulations, right on the line.'

He stood aside, leaving room for Roy Galloway to come forward again. 'Anything else you'd like to add?'

'Only what I've said before. When you go in, speed is the essence. As soon as we turn into that back street, make no mistake, the word'll be out. So when I give the off, don't hesitate – *go*!'

They all looked at the wall clock. That was all they wanted now – just to go.

'Ted, your group has got to get up those back stairs fast. You remember where they start, right inside the emergency door?'

'I remember, guv. Don't worry about us.'

'Sergeant Penny, steer your lot away from the edge of the circle. It may look a quick way from one side to the other, but some nasty person might chuck one or two of you over the edge. Right. Those of you with sledge-hammers, crowbars and the rest of it – don't leave them behind in the rush from wherever you're staked out. I don't want any last-minute problems getting into the place.'

'The lamps,' said Brownlow. 'I think you should mention them.'

'Yes, sir. Thanks. The lamps.' Galloway waved Sergeant Cryer forward. 'Sergeant Cryer is one of the few people who personally knows the layout of Decker's. He's been on two previous raids. Listen carefully.'

Bob Cryer said: 'As soon as they know we're hitting the place, the first thing they'll do is switch off the electricity at the mains. Now when that happens, whatever you're doing you'll stay put until those of you with lamps switch them on. Remember, there are no windows in those corridors. It'll be as black as hell. We don't want to be held up by any accidents or to start belting one another. It'll be my job to get those lights on again as soon as possible. But while I'm at it, the rest of you make sure each group's got a lamp with them.'

'Any other questions?' There was a reedy dryness in Galloway's throat.

One of the uniformed constables said: 'You mentioned an inside man. How will we recognize him?'

'You won't. I don't want this person to receive any special treatment. Could be more than his life's worth. So it's better that you don't know his or her identity.' His eyes narrowed. 'Right then, that's it. See you on the plot.'

'And good luck to all of you,' said Brownlow.

They moved out.

It was a quiet afternoon, and all the quieter on the approaches to the cinema. This end of the manor had declined since the modern High Street shopping

102

precinct was developed. Little shops which had once been as bright and busy as the cinema were shabby and, in several cases, gapingly empty. A few coloured boys sprawled on a doorstep. A road sweeper pushing his broom down the gutter from the main road along the side street was muttering under his breath as he made his way round a builder's lorry parked on double yellow lines. At the entrance to Decker's premises the two minders yawned and gazed unsuspiciously along the pavement. The black one, Ritt, was Tombo Robinson's old crony; Pat Corcoran, the mean-faced white, managed to look vicious even when he was bored.

A red van turned in from the main road, slowing as it drew closer to the parked lorry with its cargo of builders' ladders. It looked as if the driver was going to jump down and have an argument with the man blocking his way.

He did jump down. So, like shapes released from a suddenly exploding firework, did a dozen others. They burst out of the back of the van, two of them with dogs bounding across the pavement, others dragging the ladders into the road and swinging them up against the side wall of the cinema. The roadsweeper chucked his broom expertly into his little wheeled cart and snatched up a sledge-hammer. The ends of the streets were swiftly blocked off by a Panda car and a transit van.

Ritt let out a yell and turned to the dangling padlock on the door. Ted Roach went for him head down, and carried him hard against the wall. Corcoran ducked, wrenched the padlock aside, and went in, trying to kick the door shut behind him. They heard the rattle of a bar falling across it from inside.

Dashwood was halfway across the street with a sledge–hammer, wielding it like a battle-axe as he attacked the door. A great gash was torn down one panel. Then another, and another.

At the same time two plain-clothes men were shinning up a ladder propped under a small back window which Ted Roach had identified as the most likely one for entry to the passage by the projection room. Jimmy Carver and Taffy Edwards were halfway up the fire escape, making for the roof. WPCs Ackland and Martela were waved back by Galloway: they were too eager to hurl themselves inside the moment the doors collapsed. Their turn would come, when the drug-sodden women inside began to realize what was going on.

There was a satisfying, splintering crash. The bigger of the two doors was down. Galloway and Cryer went over the debris, leading the assault wave like troops going over the top of a trench.

The doors of the upstairs foyer must have swung open as Corcoran reached them. Above a murmur of music they heard his yell:

'The fuzz!'

Galloway and a uniformed constable pounded up the stairs, while Cryer hurried off along a side passage. The double doors to the foyer were still scraping together as Galloway flung himself at them. Then a chair leg was thrust towards the round glass windows, and slotted between the handles. Inside, people had been dancing drowsily in the crimson-lit foyer, but were now pulling apart. A man at the bar was bundling something into a suitcase.

'Get one of those hammers up here!'

Dashwood lumbered up behind him.

Inside, Decker was shouting: 'The lights, Pat – go and knock the lights off!'

Dashwood swung the sledge-hammer. His face glowed in the lurid light through the glass windows. He looked as if he was enjoying himself.

The doors shook. He braced himself, tried again. The second time glass shattered and tinkled about his feet. The third time, the improvised bolt cracked and the doors began to sag.

Then the lights went out.

At once a lamp went on behind Galloway and Dashwood.

There was no way that even the most skilled tactician could control events now. You couldn't be everywhere at once. It was every man for himself – just as it was for Decker and his pals. Galloway prayed that every separate group, every man and woman inside the building and outside, was functioning the way it had been laid down in advance.

Carver and Edwards ought to be on the roof, mopping up any fly character who knew of an escape route that way. Bob Cryer ought to be somewhere near the main switches by now – the nearer and sooner, the better. Junkies summoning up the energy to make a dash for it through the old front doors should be falling obligingly into the hands of two uniformed sergeants, Dave Litten and PC Smith.

While he himself and the wildly energetic, destructive Dashwood . . .

Galloway flung his shoulder against the doors, and was through. The beam of the powerful torch followed him, probing across the floor as phantom shapes scurried away through the far doors. A couple of abandoned knives shone in the stab of light. Three or four syringes had been dropped in the panic. And there was one man lying face down, near the door, with something dark shadowing his back and left hip.

The light picked him out and stayed on him, catching a glint from the blood-stained flick-knife a few inches away. Galloway went down on his knees and carefully turned the man's head.

It was Tombo Robinson. His lips moved, and for a second it seemed that his eyes had tried to open. But that might have been a trick of the light.

'Somebody get an ambulance!'

All at once the lights came on again. The mess strewn across the floor looked even worse. Tombo Robinson made a pleading, whining sound in his throat.

Corcoran and Harry Decker were halfway down the arc of the stairs when the lights glowed into life above them and below. Sergeant Penny and a constable stood by the bottom step, waiting. When they turned, Ted Roach and Dashwood were framed in the shattered doors of the upper foyer.

The dog-handlers came in, moving purposefully from one littered room to another, sniffing out a small trap-door behind the bar, growling gently as helpless groups of sagging, doped men and women were shepherded past them and settled on the edge of the desolate cinema balcony.

Bob Cryer reappeared at Galloway's side.

'Recognize any of 'em?' Galloway waved at the sullen faces and bowed heads.

'Not in this bloody light. Talk about psychedelic!'

'Decker's not amongst them. Or that other gorilla of his. Any news from downstairs?'

'Still sorting them out, but it didn't look like it. Could have slipped the net.'

'Shouldn't have. Not the way we've got this place sewn up. He'll be about here somewhere.'

'And what's this I hear about someone getting stabbed?'

The adrenalin which had driven Galloway at top speed through this last twenty minutes wasn't racing any more. He said dully: 'Still breathing, luckily.'

'Inside man, Roy?'

He could not bring himself to answer.

Feet shuffled closer. Sergeant Penny and one of his men were wheeling a couple of men in to join the others.

Bob Cryer breathed a sigh of congratulation. 'Like you said, Roy. About here somewhere.'

'Guv!' One of the dog-handlers was waving from a corner. 'Come and see this.'

It was a nice, neat little cache, tidily wrapped up and tidily awaiting collection. Galloway watched it being lifted out, and turned back to confront Harry Decker.

'Come on over here, you. Hold his hand, sergeant. Let him at least see what he's going to be nicked for.'

'Whatever it is, it's nothing to do with me. I've never seen it before.'

It was a relief, at last, to be able to laugh. A great laugh, not just at Harry Decker and Harry Decker's chances of getting away with that, but at the whole operation – a gusty laugh of achievement, triumph, sheer exuberance.

Behind the laughter, for Galloway, was the dark thought of Tombo Robinson.

He plodded down the stairs to supervise the loading of their prisoners and wrap up the last little detail. By now the streets outside looked a whole lot livelier, not just with police and captives but with curious onlookers who had crept out of the woodwork.

Sergeant Penny took charge of the invaluable suitcases. Both as goods and as evidence they formed a rich haul. Thousands of pounds worth of 'smack', and all of it a great weight on the shoulders of Decker and whoever his accomplices were. That would take some sorting out, but sorted out it was going to be.

Galloway watched an ambulance driving away.

If only . . .

June Ackland came hurrying along the pavement. 'Sir!'

'Later, love. Right now – '

'It's important, sir. Carver and Edwards have just been on the air. They chased a man who came out on the roof. He got over to that car park over the way. Tried to run them down in a car.'

'Did he get away?'

'Yes.'

'Stupid buggers.'

The radio crackled incessantly and argumentatively from the Panda car. A police transit van edged past it, and doors were thrown open. Prisoners were marshalled into it. Roach and Dashwood emerged into the open air and joined Galloway, looking pleased with themselves and yet a bit sorry that the short burst of excitement and violence was ended. You didn't often get such a chance to flex your muscles.

'Those weapons and things,' rapped Galloway. 'All that junk on the floor of the foyer. I want the whole lot photographed *in situ*, right? Mike, you can help the SOCO to package. I know it'll take a long time, but it's got to be done properly.'

'Right.'

'Ted' – this was the routine wrap-up, after all the punch-ups – 'you're to start questioning everyone up there. And what I want is a witness to the stabbing. Rules and regulations, remember. All according to the book. But somebody must have seen something.' He watched them set off back into the building, and turned his attention to June Ackland. 'That car – did they get the number?'

'Yes, sir.'

'That's something, anyway. Has it been circulated?'

'No.'

This was too much. 'Then *get* it circulated.'

'Sir . . . it's got CD plates on it!'

The corridor outside the charge room was milling with people like commuters at Charing Cross station learning that drivers had just started a work-to-rule. Doggedly Chief Superintendent Brownlow elbowed his way against the tide, fighting a way out to the freedom of the yard just as another van drew in and disgorged its dazed, dismal occupants. Quite a haul, it had to be admitted. This time a lot of the charges were going to stick. It was a warming thought. Maybe now the Clayview estate tenants would feel a bit warmer towards Sun Hill, too.

Roy Galloway ran a hand through his ruffled hair, tacky with sweat, and said: 'Sir. Glad to see you. I was just coming up to have a word with you. We've got trouble – a very interesting development.'

Behind him the Panda car reversed, tacked, and shot off again to collect more chunks of evidence.

'I know,' said Brownlow tightly. 'I've had two national dailies on the phone already, telling me I've had a raid. One insists I've recovered half a million's worth of heroin, and the other that a man's been stabbed. And both of them want to know if it's true an embassy car was involved.'

'Bloody hell. How did they find that out?'

'I don't know.' Brownlow's voice was drowned by the tumult as a transit van jolted to a halt and another load of prisoners came out, mumbling and swearing and shouting. 'Look, I think we'd better go up to my office. You'd better put me in the picture before the commissioner rings.'

The office was quieter, but there was still an intermittent throb from downstairs as doors opened and shut, and men and women were herded in from the yard to be questioned and, when the paperwork was completed, charged.

After the uproar of smashed doors and the chatter of excited radios and the complaints of junkies and the heavies who had found they were not as heavy as they had thought, this silence was not soothing. Roy Galloway, at any rate, did not find it soothing. He listened, pretending not to listen, while Brownlow put in three phone calls and made polite acknowledgements and sat back, having done everything according to the book; then, unable to stay still after all that had happened, he loosened his tie and began to pace up and down.

'Roy, for heavens' sake! We can't do a thing until Special Branch ring back.'

How long did it take Special Branch, then, to check on an embassy car? Galloway himself could have extracted the information they needed in seconds from the computer. But of course that was not the way hard-headed old diplomatic wheeler-dealers organized things way up there in their own protected stratosphere. Any minute now there might well be a sly hint that Carver and Edwards had imagined a Mercedes and a number-plate just because they had lost their man and needed a get-out. This was becoming a different ball game. Systems were laid down, and when it came to embassy cars you abided by a different code of instructions. Facts went out of the window: protocol was what counted, diplomatic bureaucracy was what called the tune. Galloway's stomach knotted up. They had come so close to cracking one of the biggest drug operations so far seen in this area, but instead of concentrating every last effort on the material right there in their hands they were hanging about on the end of a telephone at the whim of some pussyfooting civil servant.

Brownlow said: 'I know how frustrated you must feel, Roy, but it's out of our hands. What worries me more than anything at the moment, and should be worrying you, is Tombo Robinson.'

'He'll be all right. People like Tombo always survive.'

'What if he claims compensation? Have you thought about that? I was against involving outsiders right from the beginning, remember?'

Clearly Roy Galloway was not going to be allowed to forget. Brownlow, like everybody else in this racket, was armouring himself against any conceivable repercussion.

The phone rang. Galloway tensed. Brownlow answered, then held out the receiver.

Ted Roach said: 'I've got a witness, guv. That's the good news. He says the man we're looking for is a well-dressed feller. That ties in with what Taffy Edwards saw. He's the supplier, the top man. Very smart indeed. Just the type you'd expect to have a smart suitcase and an embassy car. And on top of that, he saw how that black got knifed – trying to get one of the doors unbarred so we could get in. Stabbed by that scum Corcoran.' There was the slightest hesitation, then: 'Your inside man, guv?'

'If that's the good news,' rasped Galloway, 'then what the hell's the bad news?'

'He won't give evidence. It's an "in confidence" deal.'

'Oh, the hell it is. Can't you put some pressure on him to give evidence?' He caught Chief Superintendent Brownlow's disapproving glare. 'All right, softly softly, if that's how it has to be. But keep at him. And listen, Ted . . . '

As he was talking, the other phone on the desk rang. Brownlow murmured into it, sat upright, and reached for a notepad. After a moment he scrawled a name and turned the pad towards Galloway. The name was that of Simbula. Could mean anything, so far as Roy Galloway was concerned. He shook his head. When both of them had put their receivers down, Brownlow said:

'Simbula. A West African state. Very important right now and very, very delicate.'

'Delicate?' Galloway exploded. 'Look, we've got a description of the car, we've got its number, we've got a pretty good description of the man from both Carver and Edwards, and by God I'll promise that we'll screw confirmation out of that witness Ted's got with him right now – '

'No description. Not the man, not the car. I told you, it's a very delicate situation. My instructions are to sit tight until someone from the Home Office rings.'

'The Home Office? And then maybe the Foreign Office. And then God knows what creepy little jerk who's being paid to fiddle the public relations image of some tinpot African state that happens to be in favour this week! Well, I'm not hanging around here waiting. Ted's hauling in that prisoner and I'm going to question him about the stabbing, and I'm just in the mood to do it.'

Before he could reach the door, the chief superintendent was commandingly on his feet. 'No, Roy. I'm not having you questioning anybody until you've cooled down. That's an order.'

'Then what am I supposed to do? Sit down and twiddle my thumbs?'

'What I would suggest, Roy, is that you go to the hospital and check on Robinson. That'll give you time to simmer down a little. By the time you get back we should be in a better position to know what steps to take in this matter.'

It was by no means a suggestion. Like the earlier bit, it was an order. Roy Galloway had to accept it, admitting it made sense. Somebody else had taken the responsibility, and he ought to be grateful for that. But he would sooner have taken the responsibility for everything and done it his own way. That way they might quite possibly have come out of this carve-up with some truth and justice. As if that had anything to do with it. Some Whitehall mandarin, he knew in his bones, was already making the real decisions.

He went down to the car and revved up with a loud snarl which was nowhere near as loud as he would have liked to make it.

A fussy little Greek car park attendant at the hospital screamed at him that he was not a doctor, he couldn't leave his car here, it would be towed away, he was to go off, go off now, get off these premises. Galloway shoved his warrant card close enough to the man's face to scratch his nose and make his eyes water, and trod on into the hospital.

Young PC Lewis was chatting to a girl behind a sliding glass window by the reception area. He made an attempt at standing to attention as Galloway approached.

'All right, son. What's happening?'

'He's in the operating theatre. Or was fifteen minutes ago.'

'Any news?'

'From what I can gather, internal bleeding. I don't know any more than that. Oh, except one thing, sir.'

'Yes?'

'His correct name. He gave a false name at first, but the doctor soon sorted him out. It's Robinson. Lives on the Clayview estate.'

Galloway tried to stop a muscle in his cheek twitching. 'Robinson, eh?' he said indifferently.

PC Lewis nodded past him. 'That's the doctor, sir. Coming through those swing doors.'

Galloway watched a rather scrawny, youngish middle-aged woman in a white coat let the doors swing shut behind her as she headed for a hot drinks dispenser. Her hand trembled as she touched the dispenser, stared unseeingly at it for a moment, then groped in her pocket for change.

'Her name's Bison,' Lewis supplied.

Galloway walked across and produced a fifty-pence piece.

'Doctor Bison, isn't it? I'm Inspector Galloway. Sun Hill police station. Coffee?'

'Thank you, inspector.'

He waited until the coffee had poured steaming into the cup, then took a deep breath. 'About . . . Robinson.'

'We lost him, I'm afraid.'

'Lost him?'

'He's dead,' she said, with a sort of pent-up inner fury.

'Nothing we could do. There were complications.'

'Nothing you could do,' said Galloway dully.

'We could have saved him in normal circumstances, but his inside was in such a state. His liver was inflamed, completely out of all proportion – an advanced form of serum hepatitis.'

'Hepatitis?' he echoed.

'It's a common disease amongst drug addicts. Usually transmitted by means of a contaminated syringe needle.'

'An addict?' Galloway fought to get it into perspective, and lost. This was the craziest thing of the whole grubby story. 'Robinson an addict?'

'A registered drug addict for some years.' The doctor's face was lean and sadly philosophical. To her, Tombo Robinson was just another case history, a sad and frustrating, lamentable but all too common slab of medical history. 'He was weaned off heroin,' she explained, 'to methadone and other substances. Then, like many others, he went back to heroin. The clinic dealing with him lost contact about . . . oh, somewhere around twelve months ago. Which usually means he was back to buying it on the streets. If we'd had his records available from the beginning we might just have saved him, but for some reason he started out giving a false name.' She waited for Galloway to make some comment. When he remained silent, choking down something sour and terrifying inside himself, she said: 'Will you be informing the next of kin?'

Galloway turned automatically towards the exit.

'Inspector . . . ?'

Near the door, PC Lewis stepped hurriedly forward. 'Sir, will I be relieved for grub?'

Galloway went down the steps towards his car.

In the passage outside the charge room, June Ackland patted her hair into some sort of order and said: 'Phew, I just want a shower. Just the thought of it! That place was absolutely filthy.'

'Sorry, love, you'll have to stick it out for a while.' Bob Cryer turned as Galloway came in and headed for the stairs. 'Oh, Roy, come and count the . . . '

Galloway went on his way. When he reached the chief superintendent's office he stormed in without knocking, to find himself faced not only by Brownlow but by two visitors, comfortably settled on chairs which must have been commandeered from another room. They were all holding whisky glasses, glowing amber in the light from the window.

'Ah, Roy.' Brownlow got up, lowering his right eyebrow in a warning frown. 'Do come in. Shut the door.'

Galloway shut the door and stood where he was, sizing up the two other men. One of them was an easily identifiable Whitehall product in a dark blue, pin-striped suit with an old school tie which Galloway did not recognize – not that it had ever been one of his hobbies to recognize old school ties.

'Let me introduce Mr North,' said Brownlow, 'from the Home Office.'

North favoured the detective inspector with an aloof nod, clearly categorizing him without hesitation and deciding just what helping of cool politeness to offer.

'And Mr Gilmoco,' said Brownlow, 'of the Simbulan embassy.'

Gilmoco was a smooth, almost glossy black. He had a rather noble hooked nose, lips which seemed ready to express amusement at the slightest provocation, and shrewdly watchful eyes. Unlike North, he half rose to his feet and held out his hand. The cuffs of a smart grey suit and matching shirt fell back from a gold bracelet as he did so.

Galloway ignored the gesture. Hastily the chief super waved him to a hardbacked chair beside the desk and dived into a bottom drawer for another glass. His eyes silently ordered Galloway to behave himself, play it cool.

He said: 'Mr Gilmoco has kindly furnished us with just the information we need to crack this case. We now have the full picture, Roy, and it's quite an interesting one.' He poured a generous measure of Scotch and pushed the glass towards the edge of the desk. 'I think you'll be pleased.'

You'd better be, said his gaze.

'Perhaps it would be more expedient if Mr Gilmoco explained to the inspector,' said North, almost deferential as he turned to offer the diplomat his cue.

'Thank you.' Gilmoco smiled agreeably at North and then, without any change of intensity, at Galloway. 'It's a matter of one of our embassy officials, inspector. A junior official, I might add.'

'Who will remain nameless,' offered North smoothly.

'Quite so. He has in fact been under close scrutiny for some time. We have not been happy, I assure you. He was suspected of bringing large quantities of heroin into Britain through the diplomatic bag. We could not be sure – these things are awkward and often very distressing – and his motive at first was not known and rather puzzling. Therefore – '

'There were sinister connotations, inspector,' North cut in. 'Security was of course the embassy's prime concern. And still is!'

'We thought it prudent to allow him to continue, so that we had a clear understanding . . . er . . . ' He had allowed himself to look straight at Galloway, and Galloway's stare threw him for a moment.

'Inspector Galloway fully appreciates the position you were in,' said Brownlow quickly.

'Perhaps you should get straight to the point, Mr Gilmoco.' You had to hand it to Whitehall: when moral support was needed, they could hand it out – but not always to the most moral types.

'Our man, inspector, was being blackmailed by a Mr Gavin. Some indiscretion concerning a young boy. The price for Gavin's silence was smuggling heroin into Britain.'

'How long have you known about the blackmail?' asked Galloway stonily.

'Only since the Foreign Office informed us our embassy car was involved in the incident. We did not waste time, inspector, you must grant us that. We immediately questioned the official concerned. He spoke with candour about his part in the affair.'

Galloway wondered how much that candour owed to remorse and how much to whatever methods they were accustomed to use within the embassy walls.

'I've already checked on Gavin, Roy,' contributed Brownlow. 'He's been involved in blackmail before, and the Drug Squad at the Yard has quite a file on him.'

'My official tells me the arrangement was always the same. He would put the suitcase of heroin into the embassy car and drive it to a rendezvous. Usually it was a public car park. Gavin would then use the embassy car to make his deliveries . . . '

So the story rolled on. Galloway registered every word yet was somehow not really hearing the thing all in one piece. Because there wasn't one whole piece. None of it bore any relation to what he knew in every fibre of his being to be the truth. But here was a well-dressed, well-educated Englishman obsequiously nodding at every one of Gilmoco's excuses, and Brownlow watching not Gilmoco but his own detective inspector, not wanting anything so embarrassing as talk about the truth.

Brownlow knew. Oh, Brownlow knew all right. But he was not going to say anything. You got promotion faster by not saying things than by saying them; and you kept where you were by keeping a civil tongue in your head, not asking too many questions – except when it came to asking questions of people who hadn't the power to slap you down. These two smoothies had the power, all right.

'Who'd think of stopping a car with CD plates?' said Brownlow.

'Precisely,' said North.

Galloway pushed the whisky glass away. 'Why are you telling me all this?'

'So that you will understand.'

'Understand what?'

'That the embassy official will be claiming diplomatic immunity,' said North. 'But he will be recalled.'

'And go free?'

'Roy!' said Brownlow warningly.

Gilmoco leaned forward, still playing the diplomatic line and exuding goodwill. 'No. He will be severely punished on his return to Simbula. This I can promise you, inspector.'

North cleared his throat and folded his arms across his chest to show that he regarded this as a good moment to close the discussion. Everything had been explained, so far as the Home Office was concerned. Everything had been done for the best.

'Inspector Galloway, Mr Gilmoco has gone out of his way to give you this information. It shows a co-operation between our two countries to stamp out the illegal traffic in heroin. Simbula does not wish to become a point in a new Golden Triangle.'

'It sounds nice and tidy. And what about Gavin?'

'That is surely a concern for our own authorities, not Simbula. Mr Brownlow tells me you have what I believe is called an "inside man". I don't have to tell you your job, inspector, but surely if this man is as good as Mr Brownlow says then he'll have no trouble infiltrating any new drugs ring Gavin may set up.'

'My inside man, eh? You think it'll be that easy?'

'I'm sure a substantial reward would be an incentive, don't you? Something could be arranged. Those sort of people – '

'Those sort of people!' Roy Galloway crashed to his feet. 'Let me tell you – '

'No, Roy!'

'I'm sorry, guv. I know I'm out of order, but there's some things have got to be said.' He pointed past North and Gilmoco towards the window. Automatically their heads turned. 'Out there,' raged Galloway, 'I've got parents at their wits' end, pouring their hearts out to me. Wanting to know what I'm doing, what any of us are doing, about heroin flooding on to their estate. Killing their kids. *Killing* them! And I have to listen to you talking about this job as if it's simply an embarrassment to some foreign embassy. Gentlemen, I've got an epidemic out there.'

North said: 'Let me assure you – '

'You can't assure me of anything, Mr North. You should be representing us . . . making the kinds of noise I'm making, not sitting there wet-nursing Mr Gilmoco. This is a Home Office problem and nothing to do with any foreign embassy. The problem is here at home, on this patch. And anyone who brings that muck on to this patch ought to be jumped on. Hard. Not shipped back home with a little slap on the wrist.'

'Inspector' – North's manner was getting a bit ragged round the edges – 'my department is deeply concerned about heroin abuse. There is in fact, at this very moment, a Home Office working party considering this tragic problem. But this particular matter is something entirely different. There are underlying complications which I cannot go into. Matters of which I cannot speak. I was hoping you would understand, Mr Galloway.'

'Oh, I understand all right. Only you try explaining to those parents out there. See if *they* understand!'

'I think you've said enough, Roy.' Brownlow had given up trying to control the situation by warning glances. 'You've made your point,' he said firmly and finally.

It was no good. Galloway was going to say it once and for all. 'A few moments ago, Mr North, you tried to tell me how to do my job. Well, let me tell you I'll crack this case with or without your help or the embassy's help. I'll have the evidence to convict Gavin. It may take more time than I would like, but I'll get there.' He stormed to the door. 'Oh, and by the way. My "inside man", for your information, was one of those parents. He's dead.'

It was like lashing a whip across Brownlow's face. All right, let him feel it.

'Dead,' Galloway repeated. 'Trying to help us pull off this job. But then you wouldn't understand that, would you? Good day, gentlemen.'

He slammed the door behind him, and left them to it.

Sixteen

Carver and Edwards had got there first, and hard on their heels was Sergeant Cryer. Dave Litten could see that DI Galloway was not best chuffed with this. They had driven at one hell of a lick through the streets, in a manner which did not increase Litten's respect for Galloway's driving, and at the end of it all the uniformed boys were there ahead of them. Litten tried to look as if he had worn plain clothes on the job for most of his career so far. Of course for the time being he was only on secondment, but the formalities would soon be over. He was at the detective inspector's side now, ready for anything, and that was how he was going to stay.

Not that he approved of Galloway's motives in rushing to the scene of the crime. Just because a real live lord was involved, did everybody from Sun Hill have to drop everything and run along to make respectful noises?

It looked like it. As they skidded to a halt there were already two cars at the kerb with their lights flashing, striking reflections from the brass knocker on the small but fashionably tarted-up Victorian terraced house. There were blue flowers in the window-boxes, and blue uniforms indoors.

PC Carver came down the steps as Galloway started up them. 'Where are you off to, lad, hey?'

'Doing a door to door, sir.'

'Better move your arse then, hadn't you?'

Jimmy Carver made a face at Dave Litten as he passed. 'What's wrong with him?'

Remembering the pork pie abandoned on the pub counter after the phone had rung, Litten grinned. 'Indigestion. Always the same after he's had a big meal.' He trotted loyally up the steps after his master.

The hallway retained traces of its nineteenth-century origin, some of them deliberately emphasized: the hatstand must have been bought somewhere along the King's Road, and although the florid wallpaper had the authentic atmosphere it was obviously new. But the combined bedroom and studio which occupied a large part of the first floor was a fine old mix of the impulses of its present owner.

He was tall and limp, with an inherited aristocratic face above scruffy denims. On the huge brass bedstead dominating the room was a girl with her knees drawn up under her chin, combining the waiflike charm of a little girl hardly out of her teens with the glazed expression of someone who had lived several decades too long and wondered when she would be allowed to pack up and have a long sleep.

Sergeant Cryer was saying: 'You can be sure, your lordship, that everything possible is . . . Ah.' He turned with a wickedly welcoming smile. 'Here is Inspector Galloway himself.'

Litten observed Galloway's shoulders stiffen and his chin go up as he paced to the centre of the room.

'Inspector Galloway . . . Lord Barstow-Smythe.' Bob Cryer made the introduction with a caricature of a bow.

Lord Barstow-Smythe was not interested in formalities. 'How long will it take you to recover my jewellery, inspector?' His voice had a dying fall to it, sad and weary – but ready to become spiteful and complaining.

Caught unawares, Galloway glanced desperately at Cryer, who obliged. 'His lordship's necklace in particular, inspector. I told his lordship you've already got things moving.'

'Quite right.' Galloway improvised with growing assurance. 'The moment we heard, we circulated the basic information throughout the Metropolitan Police district. And' – he turned to Dave Litten, who virtually sprang to attention – 'Constable Litten here has alerted Interpol.'

Litten nodded efficiently.

'It's not the money that matters. It's just that one particular piece of jewellery – sentimental value more than anything else. It was presented to the family by Her Royal Highness the – '

'A photograph?' Galloway cut in. 'And an insurance description of the items, anything like that?'

The girl slowly lifted her chin as if to contribute to the conversation. Then with infinite slowness she shifted into a cross-legged position but offered no other helpful response.

'Now you've mentioned it, inspector' – Barstow-Smythe appeared to have as much trouble as the girl in getting to grips with reality – 'it was all valued, not twelve months ago, at Sotheby's. And a photograph? Yes, I might . . . excuse me a moment, gentlemen, while I pop downstairs.'

In his absence Cryer and Galloway examined the room. Somebody had certainly turned it over, but without making the disgusting mess a lot of them went in for. There were some rooms you never wanted to live in again after they'd fouled them. This room, thought Dave Litten, wasn't one he'd have wanted to live in in the first place, but apart from a few drawers ripped out and a glass bottle on the dressing table smashed, it hadn't suffered a lot.

'Litten!'

'Sir?'

'Don't just stand there. Check downstairs, find out if there've been any callers. When PC Carver comes back, see if anyone's reported a frequent visitor, anyone sniffing around. And I noticed when I came in that there's a nosey cow on the first floor opposite. If anything's happened in this street she'd have seen it, you can bet your life.'

Cryer winked. 'You don't miss a trick, Roy.'

'That's what it's all about, sarge.'

They skirted the bed, glancing covertly at the girl in the middle of it. You definitely wouldn't have risked having her valued at Sotheby's.

It was established that the entry had been forced through a back window on the ground floor. The thief had touched nothing on his way up to the first floor, though if he had taken his time he could have found some quite choice items in two of the lower rooms. It must have been a nervy, spur-of-the-moment break-in, which would make it all the harder to sort out.

A SOCO, scenes of crime officer, was already at work on the window dusting for prints. There were distinct marks of a jemmy, but nothing in the way of dabs or even glove marks.

Galloway groaned. They had scores of cases like this every month; but this time there had to be a perishing peer involved, didn't there!

Lord Barstow-Smythe surfaced at last with a photograph of the necklace.

'What theories do you have at the moment, inspector?'

'Could have been some kids, I suppose. Then again it could have been someone wanting it to look like that.' He was unable to take his eyes off the girl on the bed, festooned with gear which might have been rejected by Oxfam. 'Dreamy Lil over there,' he ventured: 'she couldn't have nicked it, could she?'

Something boiled up slowly within Barstow-Smythe. Galloway looked pale. Dave Litten had a feeling the guv'nor had gone a bit too far this time.

Barstow-Smythe let go suddenly and loudly. 'Cynthia? She couldn't nick her own fanny.'

Which seemed to settle that aspect of the case.

Litten was glad to follow the detective inspector out, gingerly holding the photograph and slipping his notebook back into his pocket. He had scribbled diligently in the book, but was well aware that the scribbles amounted to nothing of any consequence.

'Inspector!' Barstow-Smythe posed imperiously at the head of the stairs. 'It's imperative I have that necklace returned by the weekend. My mother will simply die if . . .' He let it fade away, accompanied by a limp wave of the hand.

'We wouldn't want to upset your mother, would we? No, rest assured, your lordship, we'll leave no stone unturned.'

Galloway, to Litten's relief, drove towards Sun Hill more carefully than he had driven here. When they reached the station he did not get out, but motioned Litten to do so.

'All right, old son, now it's down to you.'

'To me, guv? Don't quite get it. I mean, shouldn't something like this be down to you?'

'I'm at court all day tomorrow, and there's someone I intend to see this very afternoon. Don't want any changes of plea or anyone getting washed down the sewers. So I've got to have someone doing the running about on *this* one, haven't I?' He wound his window down as Litten walked mournfully round the car. 'It's called delegating. You'll learn.'

'Thanks a lot, guv.'

'When I get back from court tomorrow I want to see those burglary reports on my desk, properly typed. Okay?'

Litten trudged on into the nick. He tried to persuade himself it was a good sign, him being given the responsibility of preparing all this. It showed what a good opinion the DI had of him. But typing was not his best point. He had looked forward to the CID as the branch where the action was, where the really complicated crimes got solved, and here he was filling in forms again.

The afternoon passed; his ashtray filled up with fag ends, and smoke curled round the filing cabinets; and still his typing showed no signs of improving. For the fourth time he crumpled up a sheet of paper and tossed it at the waste-paper basket – and missed.

Taffy Edwards stuck his head round the door some time in the early evening. 'How's the secondment to the superstars going, then?'

'I'm busy. Close the door behind you.'

'Nice piece of skirt at the front desk, boyo. Wants to see the man in charge. Told her Clouseau's gone home, I did, but his assistant, now . . . that, I said, is something else.'

Edwards made his escape before a ball of paper or even the whole waste-paper basket could be hurled at him.

Litten went out suspiciously to the desk. The smiling girl on the other side provided the most welcome diversion. She was the first good thing that had happened since his transfer. Dark hair brushed the shoulders of her grey trench coat, and there was an inviting fleck of green in her wide grey eyes. The touch of her hand was cool, and she did not seem to mind it lingering in his for a few extra seconds.

'Jennifer Crosby,' she identified herself, 'from the *Herald*. You're DC Litten?'

'Yes, that's me.' But it was better to hedge it a bit. 'Well, sort of *acting* DC. Dave to my friends,' he added hopefully.

117

'I was told you could fill me in with a few details about Lord Barstow-Smythe's robbery?'

For all the demure smile and engaging tone of voice, she was businesslike enough when she took out a shorthand pad and pen.

Litten leaned nonchalantly on the counter. 'Yeah, well, it's a little bit hot for anyone round here to handle. You know what I mean? With an insurance tag like that – forty grand, I mean! – and easily identifiable . . . Probably halfway to Saudi by now.'

'Is there anything I can put down . . . Dave? Something to make up a few lines.'

She nudged the pad a little way across the counter, so that her hair fell down one side of her face and she was close to Litten, smiling a charming little plea up at him.

'Well, mustn't give too much away, of course. But how about . . . um . . . we expect an early arrest?'

The smile hardened a bit. Jennifer Crosby put her pad away. 'And I bet you got that straight out of Galloway's box.'

'You know Galloway?'

'Oh, yes.' She swung her bag over her shoulder and turned away from the counter. 'I know galloping Galloway all right. I've got an editor just as mean.' At the door she said: 'If you get anything interesting, do give me a ring, Dave. I have been known to buy the Old Bill a drink once in a while.'

Regretfully he watched her go.

It came as a pleasant shock next morning to find what a glowing little piece she had managed to write about him in the local paper. Skimming down it by the kiosk outside the tube station, he felt a rush of pride. This was the real thing, this was. Things moving, people depending on you, hanging on your every word. Rolling the paper carefully so there would not be too many creases across the more important parts, he strode into Sun Hill police station.

Jimmy Carver and June Ackland were in a huddle over the desk. They looked up and greeted him with silly smirks as he made his way purposefully through the open flap.

'Who's got his name in the paper, then?' said Carver, closing a ledger with a thump.

'All part of the job, isn't it?'

'Litten of the Yard!' sniggered Ackland.

Disdainfully Litten went to the radio desk to pick up overnight messages from the CID bin. At least this was real police work, not like going round sticking tickets on everything that moved.

'And if I were you,' said Sergeant Cryer from the far corner, 'I'd start dusting my helmet. Because when Galloway finds out you've elbowed him out of the headlines, there'll be hell to pay. Officer in charge, indeed!'

They were jealous, that was all it was. Litten left them and shut himself away

118

contentedly in the CID office. He began to go through the messages and then, covertly, cast a glance at the folded newspaper; and unfolded it.

The phone rang.

The caller seemed a long way away, or might have been shielding his mouth with a paper, or half turning away from the mouthpiece. Throatily he said:

'Detective Constable Litten?'

'Litten speaking.'

'You don't know me, chief, but I've heard you're a fair man.'

'Who is this?'

'Never mind that, chief. Just listen a sec. How would you like to get your hands on that piece of tom from the Harvey Street job?'

'Too right I would. But who – '

'Meet me in the park, by the pond. Ten minutes, all right? But on your tod, or there's no deal.'

Before Litten could ask how he would recognize his informant, and even which park he was talking about, the dialling tone was ringing in his ear.

When he looked at the map on the wall there was little doubt about the park, anyway. There was only the one within a few minutes' walk. Still there was the matter of identifying the man when he got there, or of being identified. Then he got it. The newspaper lying on his desk – that must have given the man his name. Where else would he have picked it up?

Litten tucked the paper under his arm and dashed out of the office.

The park was almost deserted at this time of the morning. A few kids were playing and screeching in the distance, and the ducks on the pond were kicking up one hell of a fuss, but otherwise there was only one person in sight. Litten quickened his pace along the path which led to a rustic shelter and on down a brief slope to the water's edge. A man with a flat tweed cap crushed down over his ears and forehead was tossing pieces of bread to the clamorous ducks.

Litten halted beside him, uncertain. The man wore a pseudo-military raincoat over a blue blazer, with a badge on its pocket which implied a lot without actually saying anything. He did not acknowledge Litten's presence for a moment but went on tossing the last remaining crumbs into the pond. Then from the corner of his mouth he said:

'Come alone, did you, chief?'

'Just as you said.'

'Funny things, ducks.' The man dusted a few fragments off his hands. 'Only want you when there's something in it for them. Like people, I suppose.'

Without warning the stranger began to saunter along the path bordering the water. The ducks formed a flotilla to pursue him.

'The jewellery,' said Litten. 'You said on the phone you knew where it was.'

His companion shook his head. 'Oh, no, I didn't say that, son. You Old Bill, always wanting to put words into people's mouths.'

'But you did say – '

'Not me, son. What I *am* telling you is that I can find out. Now that's a different kettle of fish, isn't it?' just as Litten began to feel that this was a washout, the man went on: 'You're looking for a couple of youngsters.'

'We are?'

'Can't get rid of it. Nobody wants the aggro. Haven't got a clue, the silly little sods. Probably throw it in the canal, they will.' He looked genuinely shocked.

'You know who they are, where they hang out . . . anything?'

'Gotta be an earner in it for me, chief. Nothing for nothing, know what I mean? If I'm going to put myself out, I want some real money. Like today. Insurance money.'

Litten was out of his depth. But he remembered some of the training and some of the principles they had dinned into him. 'Insurance companies are a bit iffy on things like that. Pay out rewards on conviction only.'

'Want that bit of tom back, don't you? See those villains up before the beak, get your bit of glory. Detective Litten cracks it!'

'Yeah, but – '

'Look, insurance people are businessmen, aren't they? Lay out a grand, get forty back. Just you have a word with them, and you'll see.'

'I don't know,' said Litten wretchedly.

By the time the little man had finished instructing him, he did know. But it was not something he wanted to tackle on his own. Why did Galloway have to be in court this morning of all mornings? He made his way back to the nick half sizzling with the prospect of maybe pulling off something good, and half chilled by nerves.

Sergeant Roach was in his usual place by now, and Dashwood was bustling to and fro.

'Sarge,' said Litten thankfully, 'I need a – '

'You need a good kick up the arse. It's ten thirty and the messages haven't been filed, you haven't booked on, and the uniform's screaming for – '

'Look, sarge, I need your advice. Urgently. It's about an informant.'

Roach lit a cigarette and tilted back in his chair. 'Watch it, lad. Have you looked it up in the good book?'

Litten had no need to look it up. He knew. It had been plaguing him all the way back. The training manual was designed to cover every aspect of the game, and one of its unforgettable rules from Chapter 23 – Litten could even see the page in his mind's eye – was that an informant was a dangerous breed, to be treated with extreme caution.

'This is something different,' he begged. 'I'm asking for your help.'

'Nothing's ever different. If it is, you'll have to find your own help. You don't like the responsibility, you shouldn't have applied.'

It was clear that Sergeant Roach had either had another row with his neighbour, or was giving himself ulcers with the effort of not having a row with his neighbour.

Litten tried to grab Dashwood as he passed, but Dashwood was muttering feverishly to himself. 'Second time this week that bloody solicitor's changed the appointment.' The mutter became a roar. 'Do get out of the bloody way, will you?'

He was snatching up papers and a briefcase, and heading for the door.

Roach was on his feet. 'There's a few jobs down to you in the book, Litten. Better sort yourself out before Galloway gets back.'

Then Roach, too, was gone.

Dave Litten collapsed into his chair. The whole thing was in his lap. Either he could play it safe, doing the odd jobs he had been left by Sergeant Roach, and telling the informant when he rang that he would have to wait, or he could do what he had been advised to do. Nobody could blame him for stalling and doing it the first way. But if that meant losing the jewellery . . .

He had until midday. The man would be phoning then.

At eleven o'clock he gave in, and reached for the phone himself. According to the file on the case, the City and Global Insurance Company were responsible for covering Lord Barstow-Smythe's property – with the possible exception of Cynthia, thought Litten.

He was put through to a Mr Winstanley, and explained the position. It was not easy. Mr Winstanley sounded more hostile than anyone ought to sound when talking to the police. Litten tried to smooth it over, and to hurry a decision along. The company wanted to stall, just as he had thought of stalling. Of course it was against their company rules to pay out what was in effect a bribe to someone with criminal contacts, and to pay it out before they had even been assured of getting what they wanted in exchange. Equally, though, could you expect an informant to hang about waiting for maybe twelve months for a case to be wrapped up, the goods recovered (if they were lucky) and a conviction obtained?

'It's no skin off my nose, Mr Winstanley, if this geezer gets it into his head to ring his lordship direct.'

It came out more snappishly than he had meant, but it did the trick. He could almost sense Winstanley twitch. He began to feel optimistic and to forget his doubts. It was going to work. He'd show those snide uniform sniggerers out there a thing or two.

When the midday phone call came, right on the dot, he was ready for it.

'You've got yourself a deal,' he said in answer to that throaty voice.

'Right, chief. Now listen, I'll ring back within the next couple of hours. Maybe I can get back to you quicker than that. But you stay right there, and you'll be hearing from me.'

'I'd better.' Litten tried to assert some authority.

'I'll only say it once. The time and the place. Just once, get it? Then it's down to you.'

The time turned out to be two-thirty that afternoon. The place was a street of Victorian terraces which could have been as smart as Lord Barstow-Smythe and his neighbours' houses but had not yet been taken up by any fashionable set. Doors and windows had been boarded up, not smartened up. Bedraggled curtains still hung behind a few dusty panes. One whole segment had been marked for demolition. Some basement doors were secured by rusty padlocks. Others swung despondently on their hinges.

Litten, backed by two uniformed constables, trod carefully down a green-stained flight of basement steps. This was the place – unless it was all a hoax. That was what scared the daylights out of him.

There was a chink of metal inside, and a murmur of voices.

'Right.'

He thrust hard against the door, and it gave way before him. Light streaming in through the door and less brightly through the curtained window fell on two youths stretched out on a mattress – one reading a comic, the other beginning to open a sports bag and reach inside.

There was a jemmy in his hand and a bewildered expression on his pasty face as Litten triumphantly, mockingly said: "Allo, 'allo, 'allo. What 'ave we got 'ere, then?'

Seventeen

Pride of place in the charge room was given to the necklace, spread out for everyone's inspection on the desk. Dave Litten smiled graciously as compliments showered around his ears. Sergeant Cryer, dourly keeping his distance from all the jubilation, went at his usual methodical pace through the list of items taken from the less spectacular sports bag. It made a pretty imposing total: a black rubber torch, a pair of gloves, a jemmy, one hacksaw, one chisel.

'Look, sarge,' implored one of the two lads, shoulders sagging, 'I don't know what you dragged us in here for. That gear's got nothing to do with us.'

His mate was shivering. 'Honest, I don't believe this is happening. Look, can I at least go to the toilet?'

'Hoping to flush something down the loo?' suggested Taffy Edwards. 'I'm wise to all those tricks, boyo. Haven't spent all my life down the pits, you know.' He held the boy with his left hand and ran the right one exploratively down his thigh.

'Look, I'm going to wet myself in a minute if you don't stop messing about.'

Past the rest of them, Litten saw Detective Inspector Galloway come in from the outside world and survey the scene in wonderment.

'Hello, guv. Glad you got back.' Litten shouldered his way towards his boss. 'Tried to get in touch, but – '

'Had it off, then, Litten?'

'Had a bit of luck, as it happens, guv.'

Galloway looked at Cryer and the collection of tools, and at the gleaming necklace. He pursed his lips. 'Well, better come upstairs and tell me all about it, my son.'

They went through the outer office and on into Galloway's room. Without another word, Galloway tossed his raincoat over a spare chair and took off his jacket.

'Must have tried a million times to get through, guv,' said Litten placatingly.

'Close the door.'

'Did the best I could. Used my initiative, like you've always told me.' He didn't like Galloway's predatory expression, as if he were waiting for one little mistake he could pounce on. 'Put myself in your position, guv. Tried to think like well, you know what I mean . . . '

Galloway pointed a threatening finger, then grinned. 'It looks like you did well, my son.'

'Phew, guv. You really put the – '

'But I'd like to have been put in the picture a little earlier. I don't like to be the last to know. Remember that!'

'Yes, guv.'

'Now, make yourself comfy. And let's go right through it, right from the beginning. Right?'

Litten crossed his legs. Confidence was surging back through his veins. His judgement had been right. Galloway was in a mood to be pleased with results.

Airily he said: 'You know how it is, guv. Put the word out on the streets. Got in touch with a couple of my snouts. Word soon got round.'

'Snouts?' said Galloway dubiously. 'Didn't know you had any, Dave.'

'Well, I don't like to put it about. He's a bit sensitive. You know what I mean. Might not get on the blower if you don't . . .' He became uneasily aware that Galloway was not even looking at him, but staring past him, over his shoulder, at something beyond the glass partition. 'So anyway, I leaned on him a bit . . .'

Behind him the door opened. Dashwood's voice said: 'Excuse me, guv, there's a Mr – '

'Winstanley?' said Galloway very quietly.

'Yes, guv. Actually, he's here to see – '

'I know who he's here to see. Ask him to wait.' As the door clicked shut again, Galloway got up very slowly. Light through the venetian blinds behind his head gave him a sinister halo. Litten could hardly see his expression, and was not sure he wanted to. 'Listen, my old son,' said Galloway venomously, 'and listen

123

good. If you thought for one moment I was so naïve as to believe that load of – '

'Guv, I can explain.'

'Shut up and listen. One chance you've got, and one only. Now let's have it straight. No more of that crap you've been feeding me. Because if what's happened is what I think has happened, then you and that insurance man out there are in big trouble, believe me. *Tell me!*'

Litten gulped, and told him. Galloway nodded a couple of times, but it was not a nod of approval. When Litten had finished, he simply said:

'Let's go downstairs.'

A cell door was opened, and they were admitted to the stark little space where one of the two young men who had been arrested was sitting on a bench reading a comic, just as he had been when Litten led the raid on the basement.

'On your feet, son,' said Galloway. When there was no response, he stamped forward and shouted: 'I said, on your feet, son.'

The lad's eyes narrowed, and he half raised one arm as if to ward off a blow. Then he got up and stood in front of Galloway, staring defiantly.

Galloway said: 'There's only two ways you're gonna get out of here, my son. The choice is yours. It could be tomorrow morning by prison van, with so many charges round your neck they're going to throw away the key – understand? And that, sunshine, is when reality comes. When you meet all those other strong, silent types on remand, like yourself. Only they ain't silent any more. They're screaming the place down, protesting their innocence. Like you will be. But nobody listens. Nobody cares. Everybody's heard it all before, and it's too bloody late by then, my son. Too bloody late. D'you hear?'

The youth still tried to out-stare him, without a flicker; but he swallowed noisily.

Galloway dropped his voice. 'Now, listen. I know how you feel. You've been set up. I know that. But if you believe for one minute that there's honour amongst thieves, and it's up to you to stick by the rest of them, you're a mug. There's a lot of people out there doing time that'll tell you that – when it's too late.' He paused, and then said very gently: 'All I want, young man, is the truth. Nothing else.'

There was a long silence. Litten thought the DI would lose his temper and break into some sort of yelling match, but Galloway was holding off, waiting.

At last the youth said: 'The geezer said he wanted some decorating done. Said he 'ad a grant from the council.'

Bit by bit it came out. The stranger had come up to them in a café behind the buildings, and got into conversation. He wanted some work done on his old house – falling to bits, and there was a council grant, but only if he got started right away. He was getting on, had a bad back, couldn't tackle the job himself, but he was willing to pay out forty quid a day for someone who'd get cracking right away. They fell for it. He seemed straightforward enough. Gave them the address, told them to get round there and not be late, and he would bring the brushes and paint. The basement door was open, and the place certainly looked as if it needed doing up. They had settled down to wait for him, and then found that sports bag and wondered if there were some decorating materials in it . . . and then found the police on their necks.

'And that's the lot?' said Galloway.

'That's it.' The lad wasn't even expecting to be believed.

Galloway snatched the comic from his hand and led the way out, along the passage to the next cell.

The second lad looked up sullenly and said: 'Going to beat me to death with the *Beano*?'

Galloway showed every sign of doing just that. Instead, he leaned against the wall and tapped the comic rhythmically against his knee as he began to go through the same routine, the same threats and same coaxings, until the same story began to emerge.

Both versions were on the same lines; and both were convincing. Wretchedly, Litten found himself believing every humiliating word.

He was hustled back to the CID offices by Galloway, who hardly deigned to nod to the waiting, nonplussed Winstanley from City and Global. He went through to his inner office, waved Litten in, and slammed the door with enough force to raise a squeak of protest from one loose pane of glass. As Litten watched, fearing that the worst could only get worse, he tugged open the top drawer of the metal filing cabinet in the comer.

'Right.' A folder was tossed on the desk under Litten's eyes. 'Read that.'

Litten studied the name on the front. It meant nothing to him. James Roland O'Hara had never yet crossed his ken.

Or so he thought, until he began to read.

The photograph showed a youngish face, but even with the addition of a small moustache and a tweed cap tugged down over the forehead Litten had little difficulty in recognizing it. It was a knowing sort of face. The report beneath showed just how knowing. O'Hara was a dangerous informant. His special method was seeking out young, inexperienced officers, tendering bogus information, and then claiming insurance rewards by setting up innocent youngsters with stolen property he himself had been unable to place. There were several other names at the foot of the evidence: O'Hara had been variously known as Captain Rowlandson, John Jackson, and even Jacob van Riet from Amsterdam. The names changed, the technique was unvaried.

'Do you realize,' said Galloway, 'how close you are to conspiracy to pervert the course of justice – you and that insurance man out there? Oh, you could get your name in the papers, all right!'

Dave Litten surrendered as abjectly as the two lads down in the cells had done. 'Guv, you've got to do something. I wasn't to know he – '

'There's two things going for you, my son. One is, at least you got the gear back. The other is, I know O'Hara. I know how his mind works.' He glared mercilessly at Litten, then allowed himself a grin with just a fleeting touch of sympathy to it. 'All right. What time's the meet?'

'Four o'clock,' whispered Litten, 'in the park.'

'By the pond?'

'Yes, guv.'

Galloway nodded as if he could have predicted this and every other move in the game.

'I think it's time I renewed my acquaintance with Mr James Roland O'Hara.'

Litten kept his head low as they went downstairs and past the main office. Sergeant Cryer tried a cheery wave, but did not seem all that surprised when there was no response. Taffy Edwards, coming out of the washroom, was on the verge of saying something, but decided against it.

'Guv, if he gets a whiff of you being with me – '

'He's not going to get a whiff. Forget me. Pretend I don't exist – the way you've been doing from the start of this brilliant deal of yours, right?'

They took separate routes to the park. Litten had no idea just where and how Galloway would surface, but that was none of his business. He had been given his own instructions and did not have to deviate from them. It was a load off his mind. From now on, whatever happened would be none of his fault.

He tried to walk easily, loose-limbed, as if he was still in charge. If O'Hara was lurking somewhere along the way, checking on him as he approached, there should be no grounds for suspicion.

Somebody waved to him across the street. It was WPC Martela, escorting some old biddy of the headscarf-and-curlers brigade towards Sun Hill. Litten was conscious of a pang of envy. It was all right for that lot, wheeling in some tinpot shoplifter or fine-dodger, or listening politely to a tale of woe about a disappearing husband or a neighbour who kept stoking up a bonfire to ruin the washing, or happily leaning on a lorry driver whose tailboard had proved remarkably loose over the last few weeks. Child's play, provided you did it strictly according to the book. Money for jam.

He braced himself as he reached the park gate. In the distance, through the ornamental shrubbery and the knotted trunks supporting the rustic shelter, he saw a lone figure standing by the pond, feeding the ducks. Given the chance, he would happily have gone right up to O'Hara and pushed him in. But he followed orders, working his way inside the park railings towards a clump of bushes by one of the paths leading to the shelter.

Through the foliage he glimpsed O'Hara tossing away his last handful of crumbs and looking guardedly around.

Nothing moved.

O'Hara took a few steps up the slope and settled on one of the lumpy seats at the comer of the shelter, from which he could see across the pond and along the main pathway.

He could not see the branch path which came right up behind the timbered building. Litten, tensing, saw Galloway walk swiftly and silently along the path and lean over the back of the seat.

'Up to your old tricks again, Jimmy boy?'

O'Hara shot up from the seat. He hardly glanced at Galloway, but began to run. Galloway did not bother to pursue. He waited, hands in pockets, as O'Hara belted up the path towards the gate.

It was Dave Litten's chance of redemption. This at least he had to do properly. He waited until O'Hara was in range, then launched himself from the bushes. It was a perfect tackle. They slid off the path and along the grass, and finished up with Litten sitting astride the crumpled little man, reaching to pluck a primula from the border and waft it across O'Hara's nose.

Eighteen

Mopping up the tide of pornographic books and magazines was a job almost as unsavoury as the stuff itself. No copper worth his salt ever enjoyed posing as a member of the public and trying to con shifty dealers into digging something special out from the back room just in order to nick him. Of course the stuff was filthy and could turn your stomach when it didn't merely make you laugh, and there was a fair chance it did some damage to already diseased minds; but suppressing it was not the sort of thing that made you feel brave and virtuous.

So there was no great rejoicing when Jimmy Carver and June Ackland returned to Sun Hill with one Rodney Clements, on a six-month suspended sentence for stealing from cars and now caught doing that very same thing. His version of the story was that he had picked up a briefcase in the street and was on his way to Sun Hill to hand it in. In view of his remarkable turn of speed when he spotted the two of them, Carver and Ackland thought it more reasonable to suppose that he had lifted it from a parked car. The trouble was that the street in which they had intercepted him was jammed every day with commuters' and tradesmen's cars nose to tail along both kerbs. And another trouble was that Clements, on a 'suspended', was never going to admit to having even brushed against a parked vehicle. He stuck to his story: he had picked up the case in the street and hadn't the faintest idea what it contained.

When opened, it was shown to contain an expensive Nikon camera, a pocket calculator, a pair of sunglasses, and a dozen 'girlie' magazines. They were strong stuff, but not so strong as to involve the owner in any trouble – whoever the owner was.

Also, however, there was a small blue notebook.

Sergeant Roach took charge of that, flipped through some of the addresses, and compared them with one of his files. A pattern began to emerge. Several of the phone numbers were those of newsagents who went on the defensive the moment Roach rang them. Some were on the other side of town. One was continually engaged, another did not answer. But whatever the connection was, it could be more important than just the magazines in themselves. Until they had more to go on, though, it was difficult to think of the next move. Maybe there wouldn't be any next move, unless somebody else was the first to make it.

The somebody else announced himself at the desk as a Mr Greenfield. He had lost his briefcase, and was most impressed to learn that the police had already recovered it. His lean, sallow face did not change hue when the magazines were laid out before him by Sergeant Roach. They were his personal property, along with the camera and the sunglasses and the rest of it. Nothing to be ashamed of, so far as he was concerned. But his eyes covertly sought something else as Roach counted out the briefcase's contents item by item.

It was not going to be possible to stall for ever. The man might have a grubby mind and a slimy manner, but he had committed no offence. It might all be open and above board, after all.

'Now, Mr Greenfield – '

'Sampson!' It was Roy Galloway, coming down the stairs and stopping suddenly, accusingly.

The man turned colour this time, and not a particularly attractive one.

'Sampson?' Roach echoed, bemused.

'You aren't being taken in by this con man, Ted? Dear old Eric Sampson – still into the perversities and the mucky lucre, eh?'

'Mr Galloway, I've done nothing wrong. Those books are for my personal use, and – '

'D'you think I've just stepped off the boat or something? Let me tell you, old son. When Sergeant Roach has finished checking out all the names and telephone numbers in that little book of yours and they tell me what I want to know, I'll kick your arse all round the charge room for wasting police time. D'you hear me?'

'But Mr Galloway – '

'Carver,' barked Galloway, 'search him. Then bang him up. Don't miss a thing. Make sure he's carrying nothing. I don't want him committing suicide. That's too easy a way out for this man!'

Bob Cryer looked dubiously across the room. Galloway was going it far too strong. But there was no stopping him now.

'Can I have a glass of water?' whimpered Sampson.

'No. You tell me where you've stashed the bulk of those magazines, and where you've been getting them from, then we can talk about favours.'

'Look, all I did was buy some from a man in the street. How can I be expected to know – '

'Imports from Sweden. Illegal imports, on a bet. And you wouldn't be in it unless there was a lot of money.'

'I lay odds you wouldn't believe your own mother, Galloway.'

'I'll tell you why I don't believe *you*, Sampson! Four years ago, West London, a lot of ordinary people lost their life savings. And you lost nothing. Quite the opposite. Right, Carver – finished? Then bang him up.'

As Jimmy Carver led the protesting, trembling man away, Bob Cryer said dubiously: 'You had me worried, Roy. I thought at one stage you were going to jump across and grab him by the throat. And I'm not so sure about all the "Dirty Harry" act. He might call your bluff.'

'But I've got the advantage, you see.'

'How come?'

'He suffers from claustrophobia,' said Galloway icily, 'and he's never been banged up in a cell before.'

Cryer looked even less happy.

Maurice Cohen had nothing to be happy about. The day had started out well enough, with the latest consignment arriving on time without mishap, and young Gary setting to work shifting the boxes into gaps already made in the avenues of waste-paper bales. Everything going smoothly, just the way it had gone so many times before. The fork-lift truck lifted the boxes labelled as *Holiday Brochures* from the lorry and dumped them neatly, then lifted bales across to cover them again. It was like music, the way it went so sweetly.

Then the phone had rung.

It was Eric Sampson. His briefcase had been taken from the car. He had got back just in time to see some young thief clutching it and being jumped on by the police. And it had his notebook in it.

Cohen mopped his brow. The music was going sour on him.

'Maurice, are you there?'

'I'm having a coronary, that's all. They've got the samples – and the notebook?'

'Maurice, it's not my fault.'

'Next you'll be telling me they have this number.'

It was only a whisper in the receiver. 'Yes.'

Cohen wanted to pinch himself so that he could wake up. This couldn't be happening, not after things had been organized so nicely. Sampson was too

129

nervy for this kind of work, he'd always thought so. But he had to be stopped from panicking right now.

'Listen,' he said urgently. 'They don't know what they've got. And even if they suss it out, we've got maybe a couple of hours to move the consignment. So you go along there and reclaim that briefcase, and if they play awkward you demand your rights and ring our friend Sharman. Just stall long enough, right?'

Through the door into the warehouse he saw Gary scratching the angry red boil on his chin before manoeuvring the fork-lift into position again at the rear of the van.

'Hey! Start loading those boxes back on to the van, and move. It's a crisis.'

'But Mr Cohen, I'm halfway through getting 'em *off*.'

'When I say it's a crisis, it's a crisis. I'm paying you, ain't I?'

'You're driving me round the bend,' protested Gary, 'that's what you're doing.'

'Can't you work and complain at the same time? You're wasting precious time, and time I can't afford. So get moving.'

Gary swung the fork-lift angrily back towards the opening between bales. He went at it with such rage and frustration that one of the boxes swung out across the floor and burst against the jamb of the main doors out on to the street. Maurice Cohen squealed and ran forward, gathering the contents up in his hands and tossing them hysterically into the van. Not until the other boxes had been shovelled in any old how and Gary had heaved down the roller shutter did he feel he could breathe again.

'Right, Mr Cohen,' said Gary. '*Now* where do I take it?'

'To the police station.'

Gary stared. 'You don't mean you're going to hand over all that – '

'Hand it over? You think I give them presents, this time of year? Or any time of year? No, you park it outside, just the way I say. Listen . . . and listen good . . . '

Gary listened. At first he showed signs of wanting to cop out of this crazy idea. Then he laughed, and laughed a bit louder. 'Couldn't be much safer, could it? Until we're ready to collect.'

Even in the middle of this crisis, Maurice Cohen felt a spark of warmth towards anyone who could sound that admiring. Not that the kid wasn't right, of course.

He said: 'And when you're sure it *is* safe, you ring me, all right?'

It was a relief to see the van roll out on to the street and away towards the main road. It would be an even greater relief when he heard from Eric Sampson that the case and its contents had been safely removed from under the noses of Sun Hill police.

There was plenty of routine work to be done, but he was in no mood for it. The waiting was killing him. Maybe he should have stayed with the waste paper and steered clear of the glossy magazines.

No. It would come out all right. Everything had always come out all right

130

for Maurice Cohen; though there had been one or two narrow shaves, and one or two people he was in no hurry to meet again.

At last the phone rang.

It was Gary. 'Done what you said, Mr Cohen. Cleared it with the sergeant – told him I'll get a mechanic round before the day's out. Real nice he was!'

'All right, all right. So that's worked a treat. Like I told you.'

'But I've got some bad news, guv. They've nicked Mr Sampson.'

Cohen felt the receiver going damp and slippery in his hand. 'Nicked him? But what for – what charge?'

'Dunno. But from what I heard, he'd been given a right going over by someone called Galloway.'

'Galloway!' It came out as a sob.

Now Maurice Cohen knew he was in real trouble.

'Cohen?' cried Galloway. 'Maurice Cohen – running a waste paper warehouse?'

Ted Roach turned the open notebook towards him, and dropped a slip of paper on top of it, covered with his own scribbles.

Galloway was on his feet. The jerk of his thumb ordered Roach and Dashwood to shift. They clattered down the stairs. There was no squad car available, and Galloway wasn't going to whistle one in. He tugged open the doors of his own yellow peril – yellow once upon a time, before the strains and nodules of rust began to freckle it – and they all piled in. The engine coughed twice, and Galloway revved it mercilessly before reversing wildly out of the yard, narrowly missing a van parked at the kerb.

'There must be hundreds of Maurice Cohens,' observed Ted Roach when he had regained his balance. 'What makes this one so special?'

Galloway slowed for traffic lights, gunned the engine, cursed, and shot forward to the accompaniment of a shout from two women still a third of the way across a zebra crossing.

'I should have guessed. He's the slimiest, shrewdest con artist you'll come across. He's done me up like a kipper so many times. If I can get my hands on him this time, I'll . . . I'll . . .' The car faltered, jumped forward, and coughed again. 'But let me tell you, within half an hour of dragging that man into the nick there's always a bent brief on the doorstep demanding to see his client. He must send out radio signals or something.'

He cursed again. The clanging of a fire engine in the distance grew louder, and a policeman was standing at the junction ahead, holding up traffic. The engine rushed across, turning the way Galloway was waiting to turn.

The smoke was billowing out of a roof only half a mile down the road. Tongues of flame licked out and then shrivelled as jets of water lashed back, and foam began bubbling across the façade of the building. One engine was already there, giving all it had; the second juddered to a halt and began unreeling its hoses; onlookers appeared, as ever, from nowhere, gloating as if at a specially devised fireworks display.

'Tell me I'm dreaming.' Galloway crouched over the wheel and swung his car, hiccuping, in behind a fire tender. 'This isn't true?'

'Convenient,' said Dashwood.

'Convenient my arse! He's done me up again.'

He thundered on into the smoking, dripping mess of what had once theoretically been a waste paper warehouse. The heat and humidity would have brought anyone out in a dank sweat. Part of a ceiling had fissured, pouring water on to already saturated bales of ancient newspapers and packaging. Roach and Dashwood went squelching through the papery marshland in search of magazines, while Galloway concentrated on the fire brigade chief.

'Where d'you reckon the fire started – out here or in the office?'

'Right out here.'

'Arson?'

'Possibly.'

'Come on, chief. Something more definite. You found a can . . . anything?'

'I'd rather not say until Mr Cohen's here to say what he thinks might have happened.'

'Hans Andersen will have nothing on that!' said Galloway.

'It wasn't him that reported the fire, you know. Some woman going past saw the first puff of smoke and went to a phone-box. Public-spirited, you might say.'

Galloway grimaced. 'Must have been a shock to Cohen, all right. He expected the place to be burnt to the ground by the time you lot arrived – or me!' He padded over the mess, looking with disfavour at the partly charred, partly drowned mounds of newsprint. 'Tell me,' he probed, 'if there'd been a load of magazines stashed away here, hidden somewhere, would they have been completely burnt out? I mean, would they be charred to nothing by now?'

'No,' said the fire chief decisively. 'Have you ever tried to burn a magazine at home – on a bonfire, perhaps? To get rid of it completely you have to feed the fire page by page. Have a look – some of these bales round here are charred on the outside, but the centres are untouched, hardly scorched. If anything you're looking for was still here, it would be . . . well, still here. Most of it.' He wiped a spattering of rancid water from his ear. 'An insurance job, maybe?'

'You could say that. But not the kind of insurance you have in mind.'

Galloway went back to the car and waited for Ted Roach and DC Dashwood to finish their perambulation. None of it had offered much that he couldn't have guessed, if only he had started guessing a bit sooner. 'He's got more tricks up his sleeve than Paul Daniels,' he said with what might have been admiration if it had not been undiluted hatred.

Dashwood was sceptical. 'You mean he removed the magazines from the

132

warehouse and then set fire to all the other rubbish, just to put you off the scent? I mean, he wouldn't go to all that trouble, would he?'

'Yes, he would. That's the kind of man he is. He'd like me to believe they all went up in flames and there's damn-all evidence now, so we might as well give up trying. But those magazines are about all right, *somewhere*. And a lot more of Mr Cohen's sleazy imports, all illegal. I'm telling you.'

The car, having managed a mile and a half without a burp, began to produce some unsavoury spluttering noises.

'D'you notice, guv?' said Dashwood. 'Every time you mention Cohen, you get this sort of . . . well, I reckon the car must be on his side as well.'

As if to confirm this, the car lurched, slowed, jolted, and began an odd progression of leaps, pauses, and lurches. That was it so far as Galloway was concerned. He had had enough. Human beings were bad enough, malevolent enough. A maverick motor was inexcusable. Time to trade it in. Right this minute.

The car did a U-turn in the middle of the road, veered left, and went at an angle towards an open wired gateway.

Clinging to his arm-rest, Roach said: 'Bernie's?'

'Bernie's,' said Galloway vengefully.

Bernie was delighted to see him. Bernie had a whole range of spotless vehicles to offer the inspector. Bernie was known only for quality goods – or so Bernie told Galloway, who had heard most of it before but knew that if Bernie let him down there were ways of getting even. A deal was settled. A dark green Cavalier – a demo model, used only by an expert who'd known what he was doing – and such a pity the trade-in price for the inspector's old wreck could not be more handsome: but then, the car itself wasn't what you could honestly call handsome, was it?

Yes, Inspector Galloway would be back later. Yes, the Cavalier would be ready for him to drive away. No, it would not start having an epileptic fit every time he was on the verge of making an important arrest.

They limped back to Sun Hill, almost as worn out as the car, but buoyed up by the thought of what they could now bring to bear on the demoralized Eric Sampson. He was the weak link. Cunning and elusive as Cohen might be, his henchman was there, ripe to fall.

Galloway swung savagely round towards the yard and nearly hit the van that was still parked there. Swerving well out to avoid it, he nearly tangled with a sleek BMW pulling away from the police station. Mouthing an insult, he saw a face inside, and mouthed something much fouler. As soon as he had stopped the car he was out, up the ramp, along the passage.

'Who let that bastard out?'

Sergeant Cryer had obviously been ready for this for quite some little time. 'Rules and regulations. I had to bail him out, Roy.'

'My ace card? And you let him go, you let him walk out of that door!'

'His solicitor showed up. A Mr Sharman. All very correct, Roy. What could I do?'

'You could have held him for a few more hours, somehow. Any old how. Used any excuse.'

Cryer shook his head reproachfully. 'You know better than that. The man was going berserk, screaming the place down, slamming his head against the walls. And his brief in here demanding to see him. He hadn't been charged with anything, so there wasn't any way of keeping him. You're the man who put me on the spot – tell me what I could have done?'

Galloway's contemptuous glare suggested three or four possible answers, none of them complimentary; but he knew there had been no way of holding Eric Sampson once that Sharman character arrived on the premises. He remembered Mr Sidney Sharman. Remembered, too, one or two other clients of Mr Sharman's.

As Roach and Dashwood settled down into their chairs and looked around in the hope of some coffee appearing on the scene, Galloway said: 'So Sampson's away. And Cohen's done a bunk. When they get together, who d'you suppose will be offering them the best professional advice?'

Nineteen

Gilded lettering on a first floor window identified the offices of Sidney Sharman and Partners, Solicitors. There was no sign of movement within, but Galloway had no doubt whatsoever that a lot of talking and waving of arms was going on behind that window. He wouldn't have minded being a fly on it.

Ted Roach said: 'How can you be sure he's in there?'

'I can't.' Galloway hunched over the wheel, surly but sure. 'Let's just say I have to assume *something*.'

This was a reasonable enough assumption. Sharman and Sampson had left the nick only twenty minutes ago, just as the three of them got back from the fire. Sharman's BMW was round the corner, and right behind it was Sampson's Merc. They simply had to be in there, hatching a moody defence, and either Cohen was with them or they were waiting for him. Or maybe they'd soon be on their way to a rendezvous. Theirs was not the kind of business you talked over the trumpet.

From the back seat Dashwood leaned between Galloway and Roach. 'Is that him?'

Large and podgy as he was, Maurice Cohen could move swiftly and unobtrusively. He had emerged from a door below the solicitor's office and was halfway across the pavement, hailing a cab, before Galloway's attention was drawn to him. Without Dashwood, he might have missed him.

He turned the ignition key. The car whined, chugged to itself for a moment, and then faltered. Galloway gritted his teeth. Not this time, *please* not this time!

They were away. He kept the cab in sight with some difficulty. Traffic cut across his eyeline, lights changed and he had to make a risky dash across them, and all the time he had to hang far enough back to ensure Cohen did not spot him. They were heading in a familiar direction, though. Cohen lived only a few streets ahead. If he kept to his usual MO, the cab would drop him at any moment and he would walk the rest of the way down a narrow cutting. That was when they would lift him. Galloway felt a tightness in his throat. This time he was not going to miss.

The cab was slowing and pulling in to the kerb. Galloway braked sharply, and tucked his car in behind a parked truck, sticking out far enough for him to see the back of the cab. Dashwood, head rammed against the window, peered over his right shoulder.

Instead of getting out on the pavement and walking to the cut, Cohen appeared in the middle of the road, dodging between traffic.

'The devious git!' said Roach. 'He's crossing back again!'

Galloway pulled out desperately, and began to veer towards their quarry. 'Straight in and grab him – and don't let go! If he gets the chance, he'll run like hell. And he can run!'

Cohen glanced to one side as the car passed him, worried for a moment. Then it pulled up sharp ahead of him, and Roach and Dashwood tumbled out. Cohen saw he really had something to worry about. It was true he could run. But Galloway swung round in the middle of the road, to a blare of indignant horns, and coasted along the wrong side of the road, stopping Cohen from making a break for it. Roach caught up and seized Cohen's arm. Dashwood, grabbing the other, wrenched open the back door of the car, and they threw him bodily in.

'So suddenly the Metropolitan Police go in for kidnapping?' panted Cohen. He slumped back. 'Maybe you want to caution me, eh? Maybe you want to say "Maurice, you're not obliged to say anything" . . . ?'

Which was virtually what they did say to him when he was safely installed to everyone's satisfaction in the charge room. By then, even Cohen himself looked satisfied rather than frightened. He faced Galloway's questioning with a confidence born of long years of questioning and evasions, a sly knowledge of his rights and apparent innocence of any wrongs.

'You confuse me.' He looked genuinely hurt, yet anxious to help. 'You talk about fire. You talk about arson. You talk about burning the books, but what books? Are you talking about my VAT books, account books – '

'You know what books I'm talking about.' Galloway was unable to control himself. 'I'm talking about the ones you haven't burnt!'

'Maybe we are talking about library books? Ai, of course, I should forget so easily! No more than two weeks overdue, I promise you, inspector.'

Galloway saw red. Maurice Cohen certainly had something overdue, and he was going to rectify that. He seized him by the collar and began forcing that smug, moist face closer and closer to his own. Ted Roach shifted uneasily, moving his weight from one foot to the other.

'You're playing for time, you lousy little ponce. I'm warning you . . . '

The door opened and Sergeant Penny stuck his head round it. 'There's a Mr Sharman arrived. A solicitor. I've put him in the waiting room.'

'And let him bloody wait.'

But Maurice Cohen's face told him that this round was over, and the police had lost. You couldn't push things too far – not with a cunning brief like Sidney Sharman sitting out there counting off the minutes and framing more and more accusations against the CID and its methods. Galloway let go of the collar and stalked menacingly off to the waiting room, to be greeted by Mr Sharman's infinitely courteous, infinitely knowing smile.

'How is my client, inspector? Well, I trust?'

'Well trained.'

'That, I take it, means you're not getting very far with whatever it is you've trumped up against him?'

'You talk to me like that and . . . '

'And?'

'At the moment,' said Galloway stiffly, 'he's still helping police with their enquiries.'

'Come, come, inspector' – Sharman's smile broadened – 'you can do better than that.'

Galloway gave in. There was no point in prolonging the agony. 'All right, you can have him. But I want him and Sampson back here in a week, without fail.'

'You think by then you'll have enough evidence to lay charges? If not . . . '

Galloway knew well enough what that 'if not' implied. But to himself he swore he was going to have the evidence, and he would have them bang to rights, and there'd be no way Sharman was going to get them off. No way.

Cohen patted Galloway's arm as he left. It was a kind, consolatory pat. Galloway had half a mind to charge him with technical assault. But Roach and Dashwood were watching. They had already seen him nearly go over the top. It was not a good idea to create the impression that he was out of control, losing his grip.

Somebody was going to feel the strength of that grip any day now.

*

At any rate it was cheering, over an early breakfast, to be able to tell Maureen that today he was collecting a new car. She couldn't pretend she wasn't pleased: some of his worst outbreaks of temper had been due, these last few weeks, to breakdowns along the road and delays in getting home because the motor's temperament had been even more awful than his own.

He was in a tolerably good mood when he wheeled the old banger into Bernie's yard and took over the Cavalier. It did not cough, it did not stutter, and it didn't need revving ferociously every time you pulled away from traffic lights. Nice handling, nice turn of speed, nice steering. He swung with some dash into Sun Hill station yard, and narrowly missed the van that had been parked against the wall.

'Morning, guv,' said Litten cheerily. 'That's a right tasty-motor you've got there.'

Litten's cheerfulness was the sort that could put a damper on your own good mood at the drop of a helmet. Galloway glowered his way into the front office.

'Who stuck that van in the yard? One day it's bunging up the street, the next it's a death-trap right on our own premises.'

Sergeant Cryer grinned up from the night duty occurrence book, acknowledging the characteristic rasp.

'Broke down yesterday. The driver promised to shift it, but then he rang back to say he couldn't get the engine part until today.'

'Should have had it towed away. And why shove it in our yard, anyway?'

'I had the boys manhandle it in this morning, knowing you were taking delivery of your new crate. Didn't want you to graze it,' said Bob Cryer affably, 'as you came down the street.'

'Bloody near went head on into it, where it is now.'

'Give it an hour or two. If the lad's not round here with his spare part pretty sharpish, then it's off to the pound with it.'

Galloway grumbled his way up to the CID office, where Roach and Dashwood were tossing to decide who bought the tea. They looked peeved when Galloway squashed the whole idea of tea. There was serious thinking to be done. The obsession with Maurice Cohen was bubbling up in his mind again. Those bastards had to be screwed down. He needed a plan of campaign, but hadn't a clue where to start. Cohen and Sampson would be sitting tight and mute now. Without a word from their bent brief they would not venture a move. And if they made no move, what move could the CID possibly make against them? It was a waking nightmare which was going to give Galloway no peace.

The phone rang. Dashwood took the call, then handed the receiver to Galloway.

It was Bernie. At the sound of his voice, Galloway flinched. It was all too likely that Bernie was already regretting the exchange price he had allowed for the old car, and was going to start haggling and accusing him of pulling a fast one.

Bernie said: 'You lost anything?'

'What sort of thing?'

'Like the keys to hidden treasure. Didn't know the CID had special accounts like that.'

'What the hell are you talking about?'

'Better come and collect them,' said Bernie, 'when you're next passing.'

A flutter of suspicion jumped at the back of Galloway's mind. It did not amount to anything much yet, but it could be quite something. He needed a lead. This could be a false one, but he wasn't going to let it rest until, as Bernie put it, the next time he was passing.

'All right, have your tea then.' He grabbed his jacket from the chair and shrugged it on as he passed Ted Roach.

On the edge of Bernie's forecourt one coloured lad was busily polishing away at a mildly dented bumper, while another stuck large plastic numbers on the windscreen. Roy Galloway looked incredulously at the price that was being asked for his old vehicle. Now he knew who had ripped off whom.

Bernie came bustling out. 'Hey, turn round, Roy. Be fair. You ain't supposed to see that. That isn't what you call, in the motor trade, etiquette.'

'You've got to be kidding.'

'When it comes to kidding' – Bernie turned them both away to face the blank wall – 'what's this about, then?' He unobtrusively drew a small leather pouch from his pocket and handed it over. 'Your Porsche account, is it?'

Galloway opened the spring mouth of the pouch to reveal two keys clipped inside. 'All right, where did you find it?'

'One of my lads cleaning out your old motor. He found it tucked under the back seat.'

'What did you mean by a Porsche account?'

'Oh, come on now, Roy. One of these keys on its own don't mean a lot, but two at a time, like that – well, that's a different story.'

It was true. Galloway turned them over on his palm and then clipped the pouch shut again. These were safe deposit keys all right. And who had been squashed into the back seat of that car who would have been likely to have a well-guarded deposit? Not Ted Roach or Dashwood, that was for sure.

'You're a diamond, old son,' he said gratefully. 'You have just made my day. Now all I've got to find, is *where*.'

Bernie sidled another couple of inches closer. 'You wanna know what bank? Now, it's only an idea, and don't ask no questions.' He tapped the side of his nose. 'No questions, understand?'

The bank manager viewed his visitor with some qualms, put his glasses on and then took them off again, as if uncertain which put things in the best light.

'I'd like to help,' he said dubiously.

Galloway plunged in. 'What if . . . look, say you simply go out of the office for a few minutes and leave the book open on your desk at the appropriate page? A sly glance, that's all I'll need.'

'You're asking too much. It's a breach of confidence to which I could not be a party. But as I've said, if the matter is as serious as you claim, I would like to help.' He sounded a mite more positive this time.

'Look, all I'm asking for at this stage is a name.' Galloway dangled the pouch between his fingers. 'The name that goes with this key, nothing else.'

'But it doesn't end there, does it, inspector? Once you have the name then you'll obtain a warrant for the deposit box to be opened – *if* you can get it – and you'll be back again.'

'But all these things take time,' begged Galloway, exasperated. 'What I need is a short cut.'

The manager shook his head. 'It puts me in a difficult position. You must surely appreciate that. On the one hand, I don't wish to see this bank being used as a custodian for illegal . . . well, whatever it may be. On the other hand, it is strictly laid down as a matter of bank policy . . .' He stopped, wrestling with what Galloway supposed to be his conscience. Galloway sat very still. At last the manager said: 'You have an idea who the key belongs to?'

'A little more than an idea. Otherwise I wouldn't be taking up your time.'

The bank manager got up and turned his back, staring with apparent concentration out of the window, although the view must be wearisomely familiar to him by now.

'To save us both embarrassment, inspector, I'm going to tell you something strictly off the record.' It sounded dry and distant, almost impersonal.

Galloway tensed. 'Off the record,' he repeated.

'Early this morning one of our clients, who will remain nameless, reported the loss of his keys. We do not at this bank, for obvious reasons, have duplicate keys. In such circumstances we arrange for the deposit box to be forced open in the client's presence. In the particular case I am talking about, the client wishes to remove some important documents urgently.' His fingers tapped a quiet tattoo on the window ledge. 'If you happen to be, shall we say, discreetly outside the bank about midday, you may be able to confirm your suspicions, Mr Galloway.' He turned back and put his glasses on again.

'And you would, of course, have a clear conscience.'

'I think I could live with that, yes.'

They smiled politely at each other, and shook hands. Galloway could not wait to get to a phone.

Twenty

Once again they were sitting waiting for Maurice Cohen. This time, though, they were taking no chances. There were two cars. Whichever way he went, one of them ought to be after him at a moment's notice. All the same, Roy Galloway had a nasty prickling sensation at the back of his neck. He knew the cause. It was sheer, downright fear that Cohen might have spotted them and taken his own evasive action, laughing his fat, foul head off.

Galloway reached for his handset. 'You're not too close, are you, Ted?'

It was Dashwood who replied. 'Sergeant Roach is out on foot at the moment, guv, having a quick shufty round the plot.'

Galloway swore. He had wanted both of them in the car. If Ted Roach got sussed out, he would murder him.

Suddenly it was Dashwood again. 'Guv, hang on. Cohen's arrived. He's pulled up in a cab, about five cars in front of me.'

Galloway wished he could see through the towering office blocks which loomed above him, or have some camera in that other car picking up and transmitting every move.

'He's going towards the bank,' said Dashwood. 'Should be in your view any moment.'

Galloway slumped down in his seat, but not so far that he could not see the entrance to the bank and the corner of the street opposite. A bus blocked the way for a few seconds. When it had gone, there was Cohen waiting to cross the road. Silently Galloway urged him on – on across the road, across the pavement, up the steps, and on into the bank. He ought not to be in there long. Galloway tried in his mind to follow him to a counter, to wait for the bank manager to come and escort him, for the two of them to go down however many steps there were to the vaults, for the gates to open and the deposit box be lifted out . . .

Was there a back entrance? He knew there wasn't – they had checked that most carefully – but still there was the prickling at the back of his neck, and still the chance that Cohen had something up his sleeve.

'He's out!' He pressed the handset close to his mouth as if Cohen might somehow hear him through the constant throb of the traffic. 'Looking for a cab. Right, Ted. Take him . . . *now!*'

The car surged out of the side street and headed for Cohen, waddling along the pavement. Some sixth sense alerted Cohen. Without looking round he ceased waddling and set off at a spanking pace, crossing the road, unaware that he was heading straight for the second car.

Galloway got out and stood complacently waiting for him.

Cohen, swinging a supermarket carrier bag in his right hand, seemed to let its weight steer him in a different direction. He must have a radar system like a bat's. With no obvious effort he was smoothly off the pavement and into the front door of a little Italian snack bar tucked between a tobacconist's and a wine bar which relied for its profits on the earnest wheeling and dealing of city businessmen.

'Watch it, mate . . .'

'I say, do look where . . .'

Galloway went in after Cohen, with Ted Roach thumping after him. Tables rocked with the impact of their hips. The proprietor, cutting and stacking sandwiches, looked up indifferently as if this sort of thing were normal in the world of banks, brokers, and top-hatted messengers.

Cohen was out of the back door well ahead of them. He hardly faltered, scanning the cramped road between the great stacks of glass and concrete, before launching himself into the turmoil of traffic. Again those weird antennae of his seemed to function independently of the highway code. Somehow he was on the far side of the street before Mike Dashwood had raced round the corner, converging on Galloway and Roach.

They finally pinned him down at a corner near a modern statue which, stooping over a hole in its own belly, looked marginally less afflicted than Cohen himself, dramatically massaging his chest with his right hand.

Neither his right nor his left hand was any longer in possession of that bulging carrier bag.

He surrendered to the three CID men with a pitying smile and no word of argument. The argument was left to Mr Sidney Sharman, who appeared at Sun Hill with an alacrity Galloway had to admire, if with a tang of bitterness.

The bitterness was enough to give anyone ulcers. Roy Galloway battered his desk with his fists until the windows rattled, and Roach and Dashwood wondered what decibel level had to be reached before you could complain to the noise abatement folk. Galloway had once more been forced to let Maurice Cohen go. There was no charge that could be made to stick. That plastic bag must have contained enough documented evidence in the way of accounts, foreign names and addresses, papers going back to the days when corruption was first invented, to put the bastard away for a minimum of three hundred years. But it had vanished without trace. Roach, Dashwood and two uniform men had retraced every inch of the route between where they picked him up and the bank. And there was nothing. There surely couldn't have been an accomplice they hadn't noticed, ready to grab the evidence and make off with it? Cohen must have ditched it, tossed it in some passing truck or dust-cart, rather than be caught with it in his possession.

Dashwood ventured: 'Even so, guv, we're still in with a chance if we can find out where those magazines are. The whole load must be around somewhere – they have to be.'

'Yeah, sure.' Galloway was despondent. Maurice Cohen had slipped through his fingers a few infuriating times before, and obviously he had managed it again. 'What d'you reckon our chances are, then? Come on, you tell me.' He wanted to pace about the room and lay down the law, but the law wasn't in any helpful mood today. 'Those magazines,' he said, 'are placed some place we'd least expect them to be. A touch of the theatrical. Cohen's like that. Just to make us out to be bigger wallies than we already are.' He tried to blank it all out. 'Come on, let's go and have a cup of tea.'

They went glumly down to the canteen. At the desk, a young bloke in overalls was scratching a boil on his chin and saying unctuously: 'I'm sorry it took so long, sergeant. Can't tell you how grateful the boss'll be.'

'And you've got it started?'

'Like a dream, sergeant.'

'About time, too. Just get it out of the yard before I get into any more bother.'

The lad was digging into his back pocket. 'Can I put a quid in the poor box, or something?'

'The police orphans' box,' said Bob Cryer. 'And why not? It's the cheapest overnight parking you'll get anywhere round here!'

In the canteen, Roach and Dashwood collected their teas, and after a few sharp words about tea and milk slopped into his saucer, DI Galloway joined them. Roach winked and made a brief gesture towards a slumped figure alone at a table on the far side of the room. Dave Litten had his head down, either absorbed in contemplation or sunk in the depths of misery. With one accord they crept up on him. He had no warning until Mike Dashwood was sliding on to the chair beside him. Then he hastily dragged himself closer to the table.

Ted Roach's bushy eyebrows rose. 'What have you got there, Litten? Something you don't want us to see? Some promotional crib, or something?'

'Nothing, sarge. A magazine, that's all.' As Roach stuck out a searching hand, Litten blazed up. 'Leave it out, sarge. It's nothing to do with you.'

Roach grabbed the magazine and slung it down on the table. The cover was interesting, even at this time of day, even in this setting. From whichever angle they saw it, the three of them plus Litten, it was undeniably provocative: a girl up this way, another girl down that way, and a man with an expression which might have been greedy or just exhausted.

'Puts me off my digestive biscuit,' said Dashwood.

'I'm only browsing through it,' said Litten, going a fetching shade of pink. 'I'm over eighteen, aren't I?'

Galloway hunched over the cover as if to shield it from the delicate susceptibilities of two WPCs looking curiously across from their table. He said: 'You know better than to take anything out of the property store that's subject of an enquiry.'

'I didn't,' said Litten indignantly.

'Don't tell bloody lies,' said Roach.

Galloway took a mouthful of scorching tea. 'I'm not going to bollock you here, Litten. I want to see you, in my office.'

'I didn't take it from the property store.'

'Dropped off the back of a lorry, did it?'

'Funny you should say that, guv. I mean, it was like that, sort of. I . . . borrowed it from that van in the yard.'

'What van?' said Roach sceptically.

Galloway got that prickling sensation again, right the way down this time.

'The one that's broken down,' said Litten plaintively. 'I mean, there it was, sticking out – you know, trapped in the shutter as if . . . well, there it *was*. All I did was tug it out to have a look. Sort of.'

His mouth dropped open as Galloway, Roach and Dashwood deserted him with one accord. They went across the canteen like Olympic hurdlers, except that instead of leaping over the tables they knocked three of them aside and sprayed one wall with a bottle of tomato ketchup.

Galloway had been right. He had so often been right about Maurice Cohen, but it wasn't enough to be right about Cohen: you had to outguess him before he had even started to set up whatever it was he wanted to set up. And who would ever have thought that he'd have the nerve to try one on like this?

The three of them shot out of the side door as the van rocked through the back gate, slewed left, and accelerated down the street.

Sergeant Cryer had let this happen. Sergeant Bloody Cryer had played into the hands of Maurice Cohen and made a laughing stock of Detective Inspector Galloway. Cryer would pay for it. Cryer was never going to hear the last of this.

Bob Cryer said: 'Another pint, Roy? Good for the stomach lining, they tell me.'

'Only a brewer would tell you that. Alcohol's just a slow destruction of the human body.'

'Who's in a hurry?'

They meditated over their tankards, while a juke-box started blaring in one corner, a one-armed bandit rattled behind them, and two youngsters leaning on the bar began to mutter together so intensely that they gave off an aura of pure villainy. It was so pure that any professional would know they weren't villains, not in a million years.

Galloway brooded over the thin film of froth sparkling on the surface of his beer. 'D'you know something? This is a mug's game.'

'What – drinking?'

'No, you berk. The Force. The job. Must be easier ways of earning a crust.'

'I reckon there is.' Cryer eyed the pint. 'Fancy a Scotch to go with it?'

'No, I'll have a gold watch.'

'Not yet you won't.'

They looked on the day just gone, and the weeks and months and years gone by. And the days and weeks and months and years lying ahead wouldn't be all that different. Maggie would be back with her tins of salmon – unless she decided to switch to tinned peaches. Mrs Draper's kid would be back, until he was too old to bother, and by that time some other little urchin would fancy the idea of chocolate bars in the police station. Breaking and entering would go on at a faster rate than the sun could ever manage to rise and set, and people's homes would be defiled, pawed over, making you so sick you wouldn't want ever to set foot in the places again.

And the demos. They came round as regularly as bank holidays and rainy summers. Peace protesters would go on walking into the massed ranks of patriots with knuckle-dusters and lurid armbands. Yobboes would roll marbles under the feet of police horses and shove bottles into the faces of football fans down for the day. Prime ministers of places you'd never heard of would come for a state visit, and every road would have to be sealed off even if there was no remote chance of any of them ever wanting to see these seedy streets and seedy people.

And every year there'd be some raving loony wanting to stage a street carnival.

Dirty streets, dirty books, dirty habits, dirty deals on every corner and behind a hundred dirty windows. Lost cars, lost hopes, women screaming they had been raped and other women going for their husbands with kitchen knives or lethal kneecaps. Lost property, larceny, lost beliefs . . .

Roy Galloway said: 'You ever thought of jacking it in?'

'About as many times as you, I reckon.'

In the distance the siren of a police car began to wail imperiously. They pricked up their ears; but stayed where they were. It might mean work for them tomorrow. This evening it was somebody else's pigeon.

'One of these days I'll just tell them,' said Galloway earnestly. 'Tell them to stuff it.'

'Yeah, that would be good, wouldn't it. Me an' all. A great day that would be. Why don't you stuff your job right up your arse, eh?'

Bob Cryer laughed. Roy Galloway laughed. They were talking nonsense, talking far-flung fantasy; and they knew it.

THE BILL

2

One

Word had come down from on high that the newcomer was to get no special treatment. At the same time they were to go easy on him, and if there was any sign of discrimination there would be trouble. The instructions were as devious as so many others issued by Chief Superintendent Brownlow: no matter which way his subordinates got it wrong, he would have covered himself.

This was PC Abel Lyttleton's third posting in three and a half years. He seemed to have had a bit of a problem settling down. Of course everyone appreciated that it was not easy, being a minority within a minority, as it were. Or at least, a lot of people appreciated it. There would always be one or two who didn't care for the colour of that sort of minority. But, stressed the chief super, if he found Lyttleton being subjected to any form of internal racial bigotry then he would have the offenders out of Sun Hill in a flash. Everybody in the building had better understand the score. This station was going to succeed where the others had failed.

Sun Hill nick had acquired its first black police constable.

The day of his arrival was not a particularly auspicious one for a newcomer. Electricians were rewiring the building and a new telephone switchboard was waiting to be connected. The VDU had gone blank. Lights in the front office came on for ten minutes, went off for fifteen. Even when there was a temporary restoration of current this seemed to be mainly for the benefit of a man with a power drill intent on making one hell of a row and a lot of dust on his way through the ceiling. Upstairs Sergeant Roach in CID was bellowed at by his detective inspector. Downstairs Sergeant Cryer did his own share of bellowing at the electricians until there was a serious danger of them all walking out on strike. And all the time, outside, the various villains of Wapping went about their business only too happy that lights, computers and, in particular, the recharge rack for the Old Bill's personal radios should malfunction or pack up altogether.

Sergeant Cryer treated himself to a short recuperative spell by giving PC Lyttleton a conducted tour of the main building. It was interesting to see it through fresh eyes. Each time he found a new recruit on his hands he found also a new perspective on familiar surroundings. Every day he must have gone in and out of that door to the yard and garages at least a dozen times. Today he noticed its refusal to shut: always an inch open this way or that, creaking to and fro in a conflict of draughts. There was an oddly dry, tangy smell in the corridor, and what looked like a layer of fine dust on the stairs to the first floor – only it wasn't dust, but the worn texture of the concrete. The impersonal bleakness of the interview rooms made them suddenly as grim to Cryer as they must be to so many reluctant visitors. He glanced at Lyttleton, whose expression gave nothing away. He was two inches taller than the sergeant and held himself with a stiff dignity, yet managed to be attentive and deferential without making too much of a thing of it, looking and listening and nodding but offering no opinion of his own.

It was a relief to take him up to the comparative brightness of the canteen and hand him over to the colleagues he would have to work with. Half a dozen of them were at a corner table. Rattling off introductions, Cryer wondered what Lyttleton would make of them; and what they would make of him.

The two girls, WPCs Ackland and Martella, smiled a welcome. Jimmy Carver half got up and said, 'How d'you do, mate.' Taffy Edwards and Yorkie Smith edged their chairs aside to make room.

Pete Muswell edged his chair a few inches as well – as far towards the end of the table as he could get it, his expression making no secret of what he thought of a black face. Cryer said, 'That one feeding his face along there is Pete Muswell.' Muswell left his food half finished, got up, and went out.

Lyttleton nodded. His face was as impassive as the sergeant's. 'One out of six ain't bad.'

No internal racial bigotry, right? But no special treatment. Cryer went off and left them to it. It was not going to be easy. Sooner or later there would have to be decisions: routine decisions in the case of most young officers, but not simple routine in this case. Not when you had to work out duty rosters and know that sooner or later Muswell and Lyttleton would have to be sent out on patrol together.

Bob Cryer turned his attention back to the problems of live wires and dead light bulbs.

There was a bang which made an electrician drop his screwdriver. Instinctively Cryer ducked. There had already been one sputtering explosion and a shower of sparks this morning. Any minute now he was ready for a chunk of ceiling to come crashing down.

The crash proved to come from the door at the foot of the stairs. Detective Sergeant Roach came storming through, followed by an apprehensive Mike Dashwood.

'Just the man I want to see,' said Cryer.

'Not now, Bob,' Roach growled.

DC Dashwood scuttled off along the corridor to the yard, intent on reaching the car before anything else fizzed off around his earholes.

'You know the power's going off again?' Cryer warned.

Roach glowered. 'Not upstairs it's not.'

'I'm telling you. They're turning off the electricity altogether for about half an hour.'

'As far as I'm concerned they can turn it off forever.'

Cryer steered him away from the greedy ears of front office staff towards the corridor. 'You sound pissed off. What's up?'

'I'll give you one guess.'

'Not His Nibs again?'

'I can think of a better name for him than that.' Roach's cheeks were mottled with rage. 'Listen, I promise you, I'll lose my pension over him. One of these days I'm just gonna lose my rag and slap one right on his bloody jaw.'

'Hey now, hold on. Hold on.' Cryer glanced aside as PC Smith started upstairs. 'Yorkie, on your way tell 'em the power's going off for another half hour, will you?'

'Right, sarge.' Smith glanced inquisitively at Roach, caught the blaze of the DS's eyes, and hastily went on up the steps two at a time.

'I promise you I will, Bob.' Roach had lowered his voice but it was as fierce as ever. 'I mean, he's bloody impossible.'

'Look, Ted, if the super thinks he's good enough to let him get away with it – '

'The super? All he's interested in is a quiet life and keeping his eyes on the next rung for promotion.'

'All right, I know. And you know about Roy and what he's been going through. Give him time. He'll come to terms with it.'

'Come to terms? He's had three months, for God's sake. He's not the first policeman ever to have been divorced, you know.'

No, thought Cryer, but for Detective Inspector Galloway anything, big or little, that went wrong was a first time. Any setback was a personal affront. And this one was very personal. You didn't get over fifteen years of marriage in just three months.

He said soothingly: 'Now leave it, right?'

Ted Roach, clearly unsoothed, pursued Dashwood out into the yard. Cryer sighed. Somebody today was going to suffer. A lot of people, maybe. Galloway was suffering, so that had to be passed on to his DS; and Roach would take it out on his subordinate Dashwood . . . and what poor victim was going to be at the final receiving end of all this aggro? Cryer could only hope it was a really deserving villain rather than a helpless innocent. He comforted himself with the thought that you didn't get many helpless innocents around Wapping.

Back in the front office turmoil, he stared up at the electrician balancing on a ladder. 'We've got to have that recharger working. It's top priority.'

'Can't work miracles, chief.'

Galloway stamped across the office. 'Bob, I'm off out for an hour. Roach and Dashwood are bringing in a Danny Plummer. Put him in a cell till I get back.'

'Is he a sticker, or what?'

'No, just a questioning.'

'Well, what if he . . . '

Cryer's voice trailed away. When it came to a matter of questioning, there were a couple of practical questions he would have liked answered himself before shoving someone into a cell. But it was too late. Galloway had already rampaged off into the outside world. Clearly it was going to get even rougher for somebody out there.

Cryer took a pace towards one of the filing cabinets, trapped his foot in a cable snaking its way across the floor, and saved himself only by clinging to Viv Martella's shoulder. She giggled. 'Whoops, sarge!'

It was a madhouse. If ever there was a morning when he ought to have found an excuse for staying in bed, this was it.

The gloom in the office was relieved only by a torch propped near the switchboard. Out of the semi-darkness swam the darker face of PC Lyttleton. It offered an opportunity to escape for a few minutes.

'Haven't shown you the outside facilities yet, have I, lad? Or the guest suite. Come and make yourself familiar with the layout.'

They went out into the yard, into the garage, and back along the narrow corridor between the cells. Cryer spun it out. He was in no hurry to plunge back into the general upheaval. Let Sergeant Tom Penny have a dose of it for a while.

Again he was seeing the nick from a different viewpoint. Not that there were many surprises left after all these years, least of all along here. Even the characters locked away behind those doors were getting repetitive. You'd have sworn that the same half-dozen types kept coming back month after month, year after year, without ever getting any older or any wiser.

He tugged back a shutter and peered in.

'Look at that. We do get some charmers, don't we?'

Drunk last night, the occupant of the cell was presumably now sober, but looked little the better for it. Rhythmically he scratched his head like a monkey in a cage. When he saw Cryer looking in, he spat on the floor.

'So I see.' Lyttleton was still respectful and attentive.

In the background a shouting match began to build up. There were sounds of somebody thudding into a wall, kicking against a door. The noise grew louder. There was every indication that Sun Hill was on the verge of receiving another guest.

'Oh, come on, Ted,' Dashwood was panting. 'Give us a hand. Give us a . . .' He gasped, as if a fist or elbow had been skilfully planted in an uncomfortable spot.

Now Roach and Dashwood had manhandled their captive into the corridor, urging him towards a cell door. He was obviously reluctant to accept their hospitality. A squat man whose black singlet revealed broad shoulders and

150

muscular arms, he was evidently well practised in using both. From his wide grimace and the enthusiasm of his kicking and punching, you might almost have thought that he enjoyed the whole process of being arrested and lashing out until the last possible minute.

'Get off me.' He managed a mighty heave which slammed Dashwood's shoulder against the wall.

'Come on, Plummer, come on.' Roach, too, appeared to be working off some accumulation of savage energy.

Cryer stepped forward and obligingly opened the cell door. Having done so, he stepped much more smartly back to avoid anything Plummer might try on his way in.

'I hope you catch AIDS, you slags.'

'Having to handle you,' Dashwood puffed, 'I wouldn't be at all . . . here, go on, *in* you go.'

There was a final heave, the thud of the door. Roach mopped his brow.

'Bastards,' came a yell from within.

Cryer grinned. 'Pleased to see you, was he?'

'I used me charm on him,' said Roach.

'Lousy perverts!'

'Be a copper and see the world, they told me.'

'You stink, the lot of yer.' When no reply was forthcoming, Plummer let out another roar. 'Sodding tossers. I wanna see Galloway.'

'All in good time,' said Roach.

They all moved away to put a muffling distance between themselves and the solo recitation of abuse echoing round the cell, and made their way through the front office. It was an unwise thing to do, as Bob Cryer realized the moment he set foot in it. One of the workmen began earnestly to explain that they had set up a temporary line but it couldn't cover all the equipment and mustn't be overloaded. Sergeant Penny was getting suddenly puritanical, complaining that the place was like a pigsty and trying to stack papers neatly at one end of a shelf while a man with a drill was showering crumbs of plaster on the other. And Jimmy Carver, who had gone out only twenty minutes earlier, was coming back in off the street with that pale, earnest look of his which meant that he was on to something and would not let go until someone had eased the pressure on him.

'Sarge, I tried to call in but nothing here seems to be answering.' He held out a slip of paper on which he had scribbled a registration number. 'Any chance of getting comms to run a vehicle check on this?'

'I think that some time in the next fortnight we might manage that,' said Cryer weightily. 'Always assuming the resumption of normal services. Reason?'

'Well, it's a Ford transit open-backed, and the tax disc number doesn't correspond with the vehicle.'

'Whereabouts?'

'Outside a boarded-up shop front on Queen's Parade. You know the place – been plated up with metal sheeting and planks for a couple of months now. Don't know what they're up to in there, but Taffy and me reckon it'll most likely be another Indian takeaway.'

'I'll have it checked out and let you know.'

'Thanks, sarge.'

'Off you go before you get electrocuted.'

Looking round, Cryer found that Ted Roach had deserted him. Perhaps he had gone in search of a cup of tea, since at this time of day there was nothing stronger available. He debated whether or not to go in search of him and ask just what Roy Galloway was up to, tearing in and out, issuing instructions for wheeling suspects in and then neglecting to state what they were suspected of. Then he remembered the state Roach was in, all because of the state Galloway was in; and decided to leave well alone until there was some sign of calm being restored.

All the same, he did wonder exactly what Galloway was after. Up to his usual game of trying to score off the uniformed branch, not letting on until he had satisfied his vanity with a single-handed victory?

What was it going to be *this* time?

Two

The path below the railway embankment had once led to a local station. Years ago the branch line had been cut off to make way for high-rise blocks of flats and a road junction, but nobody had got round to demolishing the abandoned station. Buildings and platform had been left to decay of their own accord. It was something they showed quite a talent for. On one side of the district, brash new buildings were going up. On the other, old ones were being left to rot. The world in between often appeared to have no idea of its own true identity; but at least its confusions and conflicts were on a scale to keep the local police in full employment.

Plodding along the path, whose verges were now a mess of encroaching weed, Detective Inspector Roy Galloway began the ascent of a seamed, cracked slope which had once been the main pedestrian approach to the station. He reached what was left of the platform. Ugly holes gaped before his feet. A waiting-room window was only a yawning gap. Any ghost using that room must have had a long wait by now.

He scuffed his shoes along the platform. There was no voice, no sound of any other movement in response.

'If I'm in the wrong place, Conga,' he said, loudly enough to carry above the rattle of a train along the embankment which now curved fastidiously away from the overgrown branch, 'I'm gonna kick your arse. But then if I am, you won't be hearing me anyway, so it'll come as a nice surprise when I *do* find you.'

'Got a way with words, you have, Mr Galloway. How's your luck, then?'

'Plenty of it. All bad.' Galloway edged closer to a wide gap in the end of the main building, taking care not to brush his jacket sleeve against the encrusted brickwork. The smell hit him. 'This is a piss-hole.'

It was all too true. The space beyond had once been the station gents'. This was something else which had not been pulled down; and he doubted if it had ever been washed down before the place was abandoned.

'Nice and quiet, though,' said Conga. 'Step into the office?'

Galloway stayed where he was. 'You got something for me, or what?'

'Get the pound notes out, Mr Galloway. It's a right good 'un.'

'Let's hear it, then.'

Another train racketed past. A face appeared between two rotting props, like safety bars in a nursery window. Conga's loose yellow jacket was slimed with shadow or with something else: he had not bothered to keep himself at a distance from the smeared walls. That was the story of Conga's life. He was used to getting contaminated, and had ceased to notice the taste and smell of it.

'A tunnel job,' he said hoarsely, pouting his lips at Galloway. 'A bank. On your patch. Interested?'

Galloway tingled. It was like coming out in prickly heat all down your back. It had always been like this with him, ever since he had started to climb his way up through the Force. Once you got a tingle of the right thing it began to burn you up. Conga stank, but Conga liked money, and Conga knew a lot about other stinking folk and would sell that knowledge for what he could get. It made Galloway sick and exultant at one and the same time.

He kept his voice sour and noncommittal. 'Depends.'

'Aw, come on.'

'Don't feed me a load of crap, my old son, or you and I could fall out. Understand?'

'Oh, I understand, Mr Galloway.' Conga was half sneering, half wheedling. 'You know me by now. I wouldn't do that.'

'You'd do anything.'

'That's not nice. Not nice at all.'

'Are you coming across' – Galloway found no difficulty in letting the hard edge cut through his tone – 'or am I gonna have to do you for wasting my time?'

'All right. Two names, then. Frank Parry and Denny Lamb.'

'Where and when?'

'And the rest.' Conga could display his own bit of bravado. 'What about the rent? It's gotta be a good payer, a bank job.'

'You slimy git. What's the use of two names? Might as well expect a hand-out for telling me Marks & Spencer.'

'Oh, it's not Marks & Spencer, Mr Galloway. Like I told you, a bank. And like I told you, on your patch.'

'Come on, a lot more.'

They had played their ritual little duel, and now Conga told a lot more. It sounded plausible. It sounded better than plausible – or worse, as far as the bank was concerned, if it went ahead. Galloway knew the branch well enough and could see the logic of what Conga was telling him. Along Queen's Parade, right beside one of those derelict shops . . . oh, yes, that made good enough sense. And over this coming weekend? That made sense, too.

But he said: 'And why are you co-operating so nobly with the law this time, Conga?'

'Worth it, isn't it? You promised – '

'I haven't promised a single bloody note.'

'We've done useful business before, Mr Galloway. You wouldn't cheat on me this time, not when – '

'And just why are you cheating on your pals Parry and Lamb?'

'No pals of mine,' said Conga with sudden venom.

'Mm. This weekend?' said Galloway thoughtfully.

'That's the way I heard it.'

'This had better be kosher.'

'You'll see, Mr Galloway. And now, about the money – '

'Afterwards. When we've got 'em bang to rights.'

It was only as he walked away, quickening his pace down the path and across the road towards his car, that he wondered about Conga's readiness to trust him over the money. Usually they all wanted an immediate hand-out, and a big one. But maybe that was the difference between himself and Conga: Conga knew him and trusted him; while he himself knew the likes of Conga and trusted none of them. Results were all that counted, on either side. This time he had a hunch he was going to get a result.

On the way back to Sun Hill he took a route including Queen's Parade. At least Conga hadn't fed him a dud when it came to the scenery. There it was, sure enough – the bank, and right beside it a shop which was not so much shuttered as armour-plated against vandals, with one metal door in its grey façade. Nice cosy neighbours. Only this time there wasn't going to be a neighbourly chat over the garden fence but a lot of quiet activity under the floor.

154

Galloway stopped on a double yellow line on the far side of the street. He fished in the glove compartment for his camera, waited for a dawdling bus to gather speed and get out of the way, and then took a series of shots: the frontage of the bank, the half-obscured sheeting of the shop front, the estate agent's sign angled out from the first floor, and the Ford truck piled with rubble and splintered timbers which was doing the obscuring.

Dropping the film in at DHQ for processing, he went back to the nick. Cryer's head turned inquiringly like that of a hopeful vulture as he went through, but Galloway continued nonstop up the stairs and was reaching for the phone before he sat down.

The bank manager sounded wary. 'The police?'

'Yes, sir. Detective Inspector Galloway from Sun Hill police station. Firstly, could you look in your file and find this station's number and call me straight back, please?'

'I'm not sure I understand, inspector. Are the police running out of coins for call boxes now, or have you mislaid your own number?'

Galloway kept his voice tightly courteous. 'I could give you my number, sir, but I want you to be sure of my identity.'

'This is something serious?'

'It is, sir.'

As Galloway put the receiver down he was in a better humour than he had been all morning. He even managed an affable nod as Ted Roach came in.

'Right, Ted. Who's ready for a bit of excitement?'

'I think our Mr Plummer was enough excitement for one day, guv.'

'Come on, I warned you he likes a bit of a punch-up. You're getting a bit old, aren't you?'

'He's down in the cells. Not a happy chap.'

'My heart bleeds for him. Right,' Galloway went on briskly, 'forget about Plummer.'

'But guv, they want to know downstairs – '

'Something more urgent's come up.' He scribbled on his pad and tore off the sheet. 'I want you to get on to this firm of estate agents. Find out who's got the lease on the empty shop in Queen's Parade – around Number 20 or 22, I reckon it'll be – all right?'

'Right, guv. But what are we supposed to be looking for?'

'And then I want anything that Records can turn up on Frank Parry and Denny Lamb.' Before Roach could attempt any further questions the phone rang, and Galloway waved him away. 'Action. Right now.'

The door swung shut, but not before he had heard Roach snapping at Dashwood: 'How the hell does he expect us to work as a team when we don't know what the bloody hell's going on?'

The bank manager's voice was even more guarded than before. 'Detective Inspector . . . Galloway?'

'Thanks for getting back to me so quickly, sir. Now then . . .'

He got confirmation that the bank did indeed have those empty shop premises right next door. Yes, there was a party wall, with no intervening alley. No, the manager had not been aware of any unusual activity in the neighbouring basement. From the external appearance of the place and occasional movement outside he had assumed that new fitments were being installed, but could not say for what purpose: neither the previous tenant nor the agency handling the property were, he confided with some disdain, clients of his branch. He was a busy man. With so much to attend to in his own job, he had seen no reason to be concerned with what might be going on next door. Now, after a few questions and hints from Galloway, he began to feel very concerned; and very indignant.

When the conversation was over, Galloway beckoned to DC Dashwood through the glass partition.

'Get on to the Civil Engineer's Department at the Town Hall. I want a complete set of plans covering properties on Queen's Parade. Both sides of the road.'

'All right, guv.'

'And if they ask any questions, use your charm without giving anything away.'

'How can I give anything away, guv? I don't know what's going on.'

Galloway's fragile mood of elation began to cloud over. He did not like the smell of insubordination permeating the place. But as Dashwood went, Ted Roach came back and the demands of the job came back.

'Right, Ted, what've you got?'

There was not a lot. The property was up for let and had been on the market now for six months. The owner was a Mr Bryinski, but he was out of the country and had been so for some weeks. Nothing had been said about him leaving any instructions for builders, decorators, or anything like that, though the agents thought he could well have done so without necessarily notifying them.

'Listen, guv, with the greatest respect, where does Plummer come into all this?'

'Plummer?' Galloway stared blankly. 'Oh, him. He doesn't.'

'Then why the hell . . .'

Sergeant Cryer stood in the doorway, holding out a packet. 'Here we are, Roy. Just arrived by messenger from DHQ. Very urgent.'

'Great.' Galloway snatched the envelope of photographs from Cryer's hand.

'You been going round the back door again?'

'Ted, I want you, Chris and Jim ready for a briefing the minute Mike gets back. And call your wives and lovers, you're liable to be on overtime.'

'Cheers.' Roach shoved resentfully past Bob Cryer.

When he had gone, Cryer said: 'Anything we should know, Roy?'

156

'Thanks for the delivery, Robert.'

'Oh. So the Lone Ranger's alive and well and living in Sun Hill nick, is he?'

'You'll be informed, if and when.'

'Wonderful. By the way, what are you going to do about your Mr Plummer? We can't hold him much longer without a charge, you know.'

Galloway was impatiently slitting open the envelope, wanting to be alone with the contents. 'Well, he assaulted Detective Sergeant Roach, didn't he? Charge him with that for now.'

The briefing began the moment Mike Dashwood had pinned the photographs and the map to a pegboard, propped against the partition like a shield against prying eyes.

'We're assuming they're going to come in from the shop basement. Doesn't make sense any other way.' Galloway tapped the dark line between the bank and its neighbour. 'Once they're through this flank wall here, it's only a matter of digging through about twelve and a half feet of clay and they're directly below the vault floor. It's that simple. Any questions?'

'Do we know how they intend getting up through the vault floor?'

'I've received no direct information on that score,' said Galloway heavily. 'Making an educated guess, I'd say they'll attempt a series of small charges. Parry and Lamb seem to have a record of only petty stuff so far, but Frank Parry has form with explosives. Looks like he's ready to branch out.'

'Into the branch, you might say,' beamed Jim Ellis.

'I might, but I wouldn't.'

'When do we go in?' asked Roach.

This was the tricky one. Galloway had been mulling it over in his mind. Every instinct urged him to strike now and make a killing. But common sense advised otherwise. 'If we dive in too early our friends might duck any real charges. I think we've got to let them dig away until they're right under the money. It's ten to one they won't go for it until the weekend. Bank break-ins are nearly always weekend stuff.'

'The bank's been informed, guv?'

'It has. I'm having another meeting with the manager once we've drawn up our programme. But I'm not aiming to have every tinpot clerk there gawping out of the windows and playing Sherlock Holmes.'

'Do the uniform lads know the score yet?'

'No, they do not,' said Galloway fiercely. 'I'm not aiming to have a crowd of bloody woodentops trampling all over everything, either, and frightening our little firm away. For the moment I want this treated strictly as an obbo number. Observe, that's all. Everything has to stay the way it is, nice and normal, until I say otherwise.'

'Firearms, guv?' suggested Ellis.

'Not Parry and Lamb. Not from their record. That'd be way out of their line. Okay, that's it. Jim, clear this away and shift those pictures. Ted and Mike, take first turn as of now. Get down below, Mike. Ted, come and have a look at this.' Galloway took down the plan and spread it on the desk, indicating a side street at an angle from the bank. 'From what I've seen of the site I think the best place for you is here. And if Mike sits over *there*, you'll both have good views of the shop front. All right?'

Roach nodded dubiously. 'But we won't have a visual on each other.' He leaned over the map, probing. 'Now, if I sat here –'

'No, Ted. Look –'

'And Mike sits here. Much better.'

'Do it my way, all right?'

'With due respect, sir – '

'Look,' Galloway exploded, 'I haven't got time for a debate. Christ, what's up with you lately?'

'What's up with *me*? That's bloody marvellous, coming from you. Bloody marvellous, that is.'

'Now come on, what's all this about?'

'You really want me to tell you, inspector?'

'Oh, don't push it, Ted.'

'*Do* you want me to tell you? Really?'

They glared at each other until Roach turned abruptly and quit the room.

In the morning June Ackland was almost sent flying as DI Galloway went through the front office without uttering a good morning to Bob Cryer or even nodding when Tom Penny held the door at the foot of the stairs open for him. The two sergeants nodded at each other and shrugged. Lonely nights and an empty bed: none of it made for happy days.

Cryer looked cheerful enough, anyway. The VDU was working, the new switchboard was in good order, the lights were on. It was business as usual.

Including the inevitable first bit of trouble, as usual.

Taffy Edwards, at the switchboard, looked back over his shoulder. 'Woodclose Primary – that's not on your patch, is it, Yorkie?'

'Not for a couple of months now. I did go up there that once to do the "love your local bobby and don't talk to strangers" act. Do they want an encore?'

'It's the headmaster, Mr Davis. Says there's a kid gone missing. They're worried about her.'

'Gone missing?' said June Ackland. 'At this time of the morning? I wouldn't have thought they'd even have finished prayers yet.'

'If you run along quickly,' said Cryer, 'you might be in time for some spiritual uplift.'

'You mean you want *me* to go, sarge?'

'That was the general drift of it, yes.'

June sighed and reached for her cap.

It was a mild but gusty morning. Sunlight on the far pavement of Sun Hill suggested there might once have been some justification for its name before the warehouse, factory and police station walls rose to cast their long shadows. The brightness failed, though, to penetrate the playground of Woodclose Primary, a barracks of heavy brick in the same dour style as its neighbouring apartment blocks. All the school windows were barred on the outside, and as the headmaster led June up a flight of cracked steps he helped to haul himself up by clutching green-painted iron struts in the stair arches.

On the landing he stopped, his podgy chest heaving, and explained. Samantha Welsh was eight years old, very shy and not a girl for making melodramatic gestures. Plenty of Woodclose pupils played truant from time to time, and Mr Davis would not have been too distressed if some of them failed to show up ever again. But Samantha was not that type. She was an obedient child, with a very proper and watchful mother. When Samantha failed to show up this morning he had rung her home, and Mrs Welsh came round immediately.

'And the father?'

Davis paused with his hand on the knob of his study door. 'I don't know him so well. He doesn't come to the school very often, not even for parents' evenings. He's West Indian, a bus driver.'

'Any other children?'

'No.'

Davis opened the door. Mrs Welsh, sitting on the edge of a chair and twisting her fingers over the strap of her handbag, half got up, looked from one face to the other, and then untwisted the fingers of her right hand and dabbed helplessly at a loose strand of hair.

'Now, Mrs Welsh.' Davis spoke with well-meaning but rather unctuous benevolence. 'Don't be alarmed. I'm sure that with this young lady's help we can all . . . er . . . sort something out. Now, Miss . . . er . . . '

'Ackland. WPC Ackland.'

'Thank you, Miss . . . PC Ackland . . . Mrs Welsh.'

The woman stared challengingly at June, as if to say that anyone in that uniform, with hair that clean and crisp, ought to be just as crisp and official in settling everything on the spot.

June tried to sound direct and confident. 'Samantha left home this morning at the usual time?'

'Oh, I've already told Mr Davis that. Of course she did. I always make sure she's got everything ready the moment she gets up, so she doesn't cut things too fine. Always the same time, to the minute.'

'She enjoys coming to school?'

'Of course she does.'

'I can vouch for that,' said the headmaster. 'She's a quiet girl, but very conscientious.'

'She hasn't said anything about bullying, or anything of that sort?'

Mrs Welsh shook her head.

June took a deep breath. 'I'm sorry to have to ask you this, but has there been anything at home recently that could have upset her?'

Mrs Welsh bristled. 'Whatever do you mean?'

'Well, just if someone's been cross with her. Or if there's been any kind of trouble between you and your husband. If, as Mr Davis says, she's a quiet, sensitive sort of girl – '

'No.'

The answer was so sharp that June wanted to frame some more roundabout way of asking the same question so that she could get a more helpful line on things. But Mrs Welsh was getting up from the chair.

'I really ought to be getting back. I phoned the bus station for my husband to come home as soon as he could. He was going to have a look round on his way back. He might have had some luck. He . . . or Sammy might have come back while I've been here.'

It would be nice all round to have it tidied up that simply. June felt a chill of doubt in the air. All three of them were nodding now and trying to look cheerful and shrug it off and assure each other that this was how it was going to happen.

'Look, I'll pop in and see you later on,' she said. 'You know, pick up a photograph.'

That spoiled the atmosphere of optimism right away.

'Yes,' said Mrs Welsh hoarsely.

When the mother had gone, June looked glumly at the headmaster. Something was not quite right. On impulse she said, 'Is the kid really as . . . well, shy . . . conscientious, you said?'

'I wouldn't want to worry the mother unnecessarily until we have our end-of-term reports and parents' meeting.'

'So there's something else? Something to worry about?'

Reluctantly Davis opened the second drawer of his desk and sorted through a sheaf of papers. He offered one to June. 'Samantha has tended to be a bit slapdash in her written work this term,' he admitted. 'She ought to spend less time dreaming.'

'Hm. Any reason for the dreaming?'

'Nothing at all evident. Children do go through phases, you know, and we try not to jump to any cut-and-dried conclusions.'

June skimmed down the entries on the interim report. 'I see it says here that she has been having some problems with – what's this? – relationships within the group.'

Davis leaned over her. 'Ah, yes. Miss Horrocks. Probably means that Samantha doesn't talk enough in class. When she's spoken to, that is.' He attempted a watery smile.

'Does she seem lonely?'

The headmaster fidgeted. He was forever flicking an imaginary speck from his cardigan, rubbing his lower lip, or glancing from side to side in an appeal for help that refused to come.

'Well,' he said, 'she *has* struck up a friendship this term, so I suppose that ought to make her less lonely than before. A girl called Theresa O'Brien. Odd mixture, really. Irish family – one of eight.'

'Can I see her?'

'Naturally.' The headmaster looked momentarily smug. 'I've already arranged for her to come along. But I thought it best to have Mrs Welsh off the premises first.' As if on cue, there was a tap at the door. 'Come in.'

A thin woman with straw-coloured hair and aggrieved, straw-coloured eyes opened the door and ushered in a girl whose dark hair and deep-set eyes appeared all the darker in contrast.

'Thank you, Miss Horrocks.'

June would have liked a few minutes longer to assess the teacher who was apparently dissatisfied with Samantha's speechlessness in class; but Miss Horrocks fussed out and was gone.

'Right.' Davis pulled a chair forward. 'Come and sit down, Theresa.' His hand on her shoulder forced her gently on to the chair. 'Nothing to be frightened of. The police lady wants to ask you one or two questions, that's all.'

'I ain't done nothing.'

'We didn't think you had,' said June. 'I just want you to tell me a bit about Samantha. Now, Mr Davis says you're friends.'

The girl stared, mute.

'You walk to school together?'

Theresa shook her head. Her thumb found its way to the corner of her mouth.

'Go home together sometimes, then?'

At last there was a response. 'Part of the way.'

'And when you're on your way home, do you ever go off anywhere for a while?' Now it was a head shake again. 'Don't you nip into a playground, a park, anywhere like that? Do you have somewhere secret, just the two of you?' Another lowering, silent denial. 'Theresa . . . when you've been with Samantha, has anyone ever come up and talked to you? Offered you sweets, anything like that?'

The child kept solemnly shaking her head. The steadfast denial seemed genuine enough, yet there was an odd, calculating gleam in her eyes. When the headmaster had sent her back to her classroom he asked apprehensively:

'You think there's a possibility Samantha might have gone off with somebody?'

'We have to consider it, that's all. It's one in a million. Look, it's just that if you should hear of anyone hanging about – '

'Yes, yes, of course.' He cut her short, not wanting to hear. 'Yes, you may be sure.'

June drove round to the address she had been given on the Riverdale estate. The Elizabeth Garrett Anderson block was like a score of other blocks in this part of the world, where modernization had meant devastation. Somewhere a baby was crying forlornly. From an open window came the competition of a radio babbling out pop song titles in mounting hysteria. She picked her way over a morass of torn newspapers and crushed drink cans, and went up to the third landing in a lift scrawled over with obscenities.

She had hardly taken her thumb off the bell push when the door was flung open. The expectant look in Mrs Welsh's eyes faded, telling her that Samantha was not yet back.

'I've come to pick up the photograph.'

They went inside. June sat on a sofa with a pattern in mauve curlicues as Mrs Welsh leafed through an album, watched over by a large framed colour print on the sideboard. In all the pictures Samantha's creamy, coffee-coloured face with its deeper brown eyes looked demure, composed, but unsmiling.

June selected a head-and-shoulders picture, and a full-length one. Mrs Welsh watched them go from their usual place with a slight shiver, and reached for a cigarette.

'You've got a phone so you can call us if she turns up?'

'Not in here, no.'

'But you said something about ringing your husband.'

'From the box downstairs. On the ground floor, near the lift.'

'Well, I'll be back at the station if you've got anything to report. Any good news,' said June encouragingly. 'And we'll send out a call, see what we can do. Mr Welsh'll be back soon?'

Mrs Welsh shrugged. She was beginning to look as if she did not believe in anybody ever coming back.

June reported in, and the message went out to all units. Girl, half West Indian, missing, eight years old, hair tied back, wearing a pale blue anorak, green tartan skirt and white socks. answering to the name of Samantha Welsh. Last seen at her home . . .

It was less than an hour later when Mr Davis showed up at the desk with Theresa in tow. June Ackland was on her way to the canteen, but swung round as she saw Sergeant Penny leaning over the counter and beginning to ask questions.

'Mr Davis' – she hurried towards him ' – anything to report?'

'Oh, it's you. Good. It was you I wanted to see. Most urgently. Felt I had to come round, have a quiet word.'

'Sarge, is anyone using the interview room?'

Penny waved her towards the door along the corridor. Theresa, head down, let herself be shepherded through by the headmaster.

'Take a seat.' June offered Theresa a friendly smile. The girl looked down at her toes. 'Right, what seems to be the latest?'

'I'm afraid Theresa didn't tell you everything,' said Davis. 'She thought it might be a sin.'

Three

Galloway sat staring at the folded sheet of paper on his desk, willing himself not to open it and re-read it for the tenth time this morning. It was cold, clear and impersonal and it had come as no surprise; yet still, though he had been waiting for it, he did not want to believe it. One more glance, ten more glances, would only make it more and more believable.

He tried to drag his mind away and concentrate on the important issues of the moment. Roach and Dashwood had reported in on their observation during the night. None of it added up to anything exciting. The two targets had spent all evening in the Monk's Head pub, leaving only at closing time. Lamb had then dropped Parry off at his place around 11.45 and had got back to his own pad just after midnight. Both of them home to bed like good little boys: evidently they were not yet doing late-night shifts under the bank. Maybe that was being saved up for the weekend.

Galloway wanted action right now, but knew his decision yesterday just had to be the right one. Moving too soon would spoil everything.

His hand went out to that paper again. Then, as if acting entirely without his authority, it lifted the phone. He dialled the familiar number.

Something was sticking and aching in his stomach. He waited for Maureen to answer, as she had answered hundreds of times when he rang from this very office, this very phone – usually to tell her that he had got caught up in an urgent job and would be late home.

It was not Maureen who answered, but Julia.

The pain grew worse. Somehow it twisted itself over on itself, wrenching at him, before he could speak. 'Julia, it's me. It's dad.'

There was silence save for a faint singing note along the line, then: 'What do you want?'

'Well, just to say hello. You know. How are you?'

'Mum,' she was calling, 'it's dad on the phone.'

Maureen was the one he had been meaning to speak to, but now he wanted to postpone it. 'Julia, don't call your mum yet.'

Too late. 'Hello?' said Maureen, cold and very far away.

'Sorry to call you at this hour of the morning.'

'What do you want, Roy?'

'I . . . I just got the divorce papers through. I just thought we ought to talk.'

'Talk? You want to *talk*?' He could almost hear her silently reciting the catalogue of his iniquities, the late nights, the days when he had been too busy to get home for more than half an hour at a time, or too exhausted to be any kind of company.

He tried: 'Look, please – '

'You've left it just a little bit too late. About ten years too bloody late.'

She had smacked the receiver down. He clawed at the paper yet again, knowing nothing could wipe out those legal, formal words. He threw it across the office just as Bob Cryer came in.

'Sorry, Roy.' One look at his face, and Cryer was already turning away. 'I'll come back.'

'What is it?'

'Well, your Mr Plummer. We've got him banged up still. Been here all night, remember? Kept asking for you at breakfast time.'

'Did he, now?'

'Taffy Edwards asked whether he wanted you grilled or fried.'

'That must have gone down well.'

'He chucked the breakfast all over Taffy.'

Galloway could not even raise a smile. 'All right, I'll be down.'

'Cell or truth room?'

'What?'

'Do you want to interview him in the cell,' said Cryer patiently, 'or in an interview room?'

'Leave him to stew in the cell.'

'Fine.' Cryer paused in the doorway. 'You all right, mate?'

'Fine. Why shouldn't I be?'

Galloway gave himself a couple of minutes to stop his stomach heaving, then went down to confront Plummer.

'And about bloody well time, too.' Plummer swung his legs off the bunk and crouched forward as if ready to butt the DI in the stomach. 'Just what am I supposed to be here for?'

Cryer listened with some interest. The answer to this question was one for which he, too, had been kept waiting.

'You know what,' said Galloway. 'Roach must have told you in the vehicle.'

164

'Didn't tell me nothing. Ignorant git.'

'Armed robbery on the night of the eighteenth of April. How does that grab you?'

'Come off it. You must be joking.'

Galloway was in no joking mood. Neither was he any longer really interested. The whole business of Plummer had been a bit of a flyer, and he had known it all along. Right now he was a lot more concerned about what might be going on under Queen's Parade. But he was not prepared to let this greasy little villain get away scot-free.

'According to information received – '

'Stuff that. For *your* information, on the night of the eighteenth of April – and on the seventeenth and the twenty-first, come to think of it – I was spending some interesting hours with a lady of my acquaintance.'

'If you can't do better than that, you're in dead lumber.'

'You got me shivering in me boots, chief.' Plummer's evil little sneer goaded Galloway on.

'Who was she, this old slag you're supposed to have been knocking off?'

'Never mentioned old slag. No way. A lady, I said.'

'So on the night in question you were shacked up with a mystery. Okay. Who was she, what's her name?'

'Now come on, chief. Can't tell you that, now, can I? A married woman, see. Wouldn't be right if I told, know what I mean?'

Galloway snorted. 'And what would rubbish like you know about what's right, eh?'

'Be fair, chief, you know how it is. I mean' – Plummer leaned insinuatingly closer – 'it might well have been your own old woman I was humping.'

All the pain and rage came up from Galloway's heart and stomach. From his very guts. He hurled himself forward, dragged Plummer up to his feet and hurled him against the far wall of the cell.

'Leave it, Roy!'

Cryer was trying to get between them. Galloway elbowed him aside and began to smash his fist into Plummer's face, smashing that filthy bloody head back against the wall, again and again.

'Leave it. Enough, Roy!'

Cryer got his arm round Galloway's throat and dragged him away. They swayed together, panting.

Plummer was wiping his bloodied mouth. 'He's a nutter. A flaming nutter.'

'You shut it,' snarled Cryer.

'Bleeding nut. I'll have him nicked for that.'

'I said shut it.' Cryer hammered on the door to be let out. Galloway lurched out ahead of him and leaned against the cold wall of the corridor, waiting for the place to stop going red and blue and all the colours of the rainbow. He tried to make his heartbeat slow down. He still wanted – it was all he wanted –

to kill that stinking scum in there. He hardly heard what Cryer was growling at him. 'That was brilliant, Roy. That was really brilliant.'

He found words. 'Get rid of him.'

'What, Plummer? But you – '

'Chuck him out. While he's still alive.'

June Ackland tried it again, slowly and carefully. This was something you did not dare to get wrong.

'And you were with Samantha when you saw this man? But you didn't tell anybody about it – not even your mum?'

'No,' whispered Theresa.

'Can you tell me what the man looked like?' As the girl's head sank again and she looked sideways with that odd, sly expression of hers, June said more forcefully: 'Come on, my love. Samantha's your friend, isn't she? Hm?'

Theresa nodded.

'Well, I want you to think very hard, because we want to try and find her, don't we?'

Theresa considered this for what seemed an age. Even her eventual nod seemed equivocal. June was suddenly scared that the kid would freeze up – reluctant to come out with the full story in the first place, she had now said all she dared to say and was wishing she had kept quiet about it after all.

'How old was this man?' June probed. 'Some young feller, was it?'

'Oh, no.'

'How old, then?'

'Well, you know . . . quite old.'

'Older than . . . well, Mr Davis?'

'No.'

'Now, did he say anything to you when you saw him?'

Theresa was shaking her head again.

'What, then?'

'Well, like I told you.' The girl seemed to be thinking of something else, somewhere to the left of her left shoe. 'His mac, and all that.'

'He was wearing a mac? Not an overcoat, or a windcheater?'

'No.'

It was hard going. The whole wretched business was taking on a new dimension. Missing persons, missing kids, were one part of the job. There were dozens of reasons why people wandered off, and then got bored or frightened and wandered back again. Once it ceased to be a 'misper' and became a matter of real danger, of flashers and possible abductors, then it was a different game. And everybody at Sun Hill had to be in on it.

Galloway called in his obbo forces from Queen's Parade. The message to patrol units was repeated, but with a more sinister emphasis. Bob Cryer set up an emergency briefing in the parade room. Usually there were jokes, moans and groans. Before the meeting started, Taffy Edwards was grumbling about not getting away in time to catch a train to North Wales and the girl who would be waiting for him at the station, and Reg Hollis was complaining that his back trouble had got so much worse that he simply couldn't be expected to stand and listen to a procedural lecture for more than five minutes at most. Well within the five minutes they were all grimly silent and attentive. A runaway kid might have provoked snide remarks about parents and bloody schools and half-witted schoolmasters. Changed circumstances made for changed attitudes.

Galloway had taken charge. 'This misper is going to be treated as an abduction from now on. Which means that whatever's going on we have to get at it fast, and stop it. Bob, I'd like you and Martella to do house-to-house right through the flats. You both know that territory better than anyone. The rest of you . . .'

He assembled the programme with all his old, bitter commitment. If it had been his own daughter, his Julia, at that age – well no, he wasn't going to think of that; but it cleared his mind to think about somebody else, some other little girl who was still an abstract figure to all of them here but who was going to be saved and protected if he had anything to do with it. Lyttleton and Carver were assigned to the timber yard on the edge of Riverdale. And when they had finished turning that over, they could start along the dock road and look at every crumbling wharf, every little inlet. Hollis and Muswell were detailed to search the grounds and sheds, basements, boiler-rooms, rubbish dumps, anything whatever around the blocks of flats. Hollis flinched at the prospect. 'Look, sir, I'm still having treatment for my back, you know. If I have to do any heavy lifting, moving things aside, sort of . . .' Galloway ignored him. 'Ackland, you'll be liaison with the parents. Find out if their kid mentioned anything about this flasher.'

'Don't you think Mrs Welsh would have told me already?'

'Maybe, maybe not. Either way it's time to make sure they know the whole picture.'

Bob Cryer said: 'Look, Roy, you don't often get a flasher going in for abduction. It's two separate types. Flashers usually scuttle for cover the moment they've given themselves an airing. Of all the cases we've had on this manor – '

'I know, Bob. But Theresa whatsername has reported a flasher, and Samantha Welsh was there with her, and now Samantha's gone missing. Maybe this time we've got a nasty mixture – two different things both coming to the boil at once. So let's move, right?'

They moved. A dog-handler showed up in his van just as Lyttleton and Carver were piling into a panda car. Bob Cryer and Viv Martella began their wearying, watchful plod round the flats, up and down in the lifts, along every landing. Ted Roach and Mike Dashwood began riffling through lists of known sex offenders on the manor and beyond it, indulging in a few sour reminiscences and discarding one impossibility after another. Even some of the possibilities seemed improbable. There was still no helpful pattern. The trouble with this sort of exercise was that patterns took time to establish themselves, and by the time you'd got round to recognizing them it could be too late. Round up the culprit, fine; but not so fine for the injured, terrified kid who had had to suffer while you were working out the permutations.

June Ackland went back to the door which Mrs Welsh had hopefully and then despondently opened for her once before. Even before she reached it she could hear the yelling from within.

'Oh, it's always my bleeding fault, isn't it?' This was no longer the respectable Mrs Welsh so approvingly spoken of by the headmaster. 'I wish you'd go and do yourself a – '

'Shut up.'

'I just wish you were – '

'All right, what? You go right ahead, woman, you tell me what.'

June pressed the bell. There was an immediate hush, as if a radio had been abruptly switched off. Mrs Welsh opened the door. 'Oh.' She looked taken aback, then eager again. 'Any news?'

'No. It's just really to keep you in the picture.' When there was no reaction, June added casually: 'May I come in?'

'Oh. Oh, yes, sorry.'

'Is Mr Welsh back yet?' It hardly needed answering, but it was a tactful pretence.

'He's in the lounge.' Mrs Welsh prodded a stiff right arm towards the inner door. 'Please go through.'

Welsh was standing at the window, surveying the world below. He was slim and good-looking, almost graceful in his weariness. It was the weariness – an innate, sad sort of smothered resignation – which struck June at first sight. She had glimpsed it momentarily in PC Abe Lyttleton, the dark suspicion and the instinctive readiness to endure insults; but Abe had stuck his neck out and fought it by joining the police force – inviting all kinds of trouble rather than waiting for it to come at him.

'I see you have a search party.' Welsh did not even turn round to greet their visitor, but went on staring down. 'They're at the rubbish dump now.'

'Please don't,' whimpered Mrs Welsh. She was timid and shrunken again, now.

June Ackland kept her voice reassuring. 'It's normal procedure.'

'For you, maybe,' said Welsh.

It was difficult to know where to start; or, rather, where to pick up and start all over again. It was only by niggling away that there was a chance of something new being said, some fresh lead being given.

'Mr Welsh. Mrs Welsh. I'm sorry, but we do have to try . . . look, you're sure Samantha never mentioned any worries? Anything that could have upset her?

Mr Davis did suggest that her work had slipped a bit recently. Do you have any idea why?'

Welsh looked sullenly at his wife, who grew suddenly snappish. 'It's that Theresa, that's what. Look, I try to keep her away, but you can't. Not all the time, and not when they're in school anyhow.'

'You don't approve of Theresa?'

'She . . . puts her up to things. I can tell. *And* she even gave her the nits.'

'Her other school friends – does she ever go anywhere with them?'

'No.' Mrs Welsh was taut and self-righteous. 'She always comes straight home. I've always dinned that into her.'

June turned to Welsh, who had sat down for a moment but was unable to remain still. As she spoke he was already pushing up on to his feet again, drawn wretchedly to the window.

'Mr Welsh, what about places she might have been with you?'

His wife answered for him. 'She don't go to a lot of places, not really. Damon takes her out once in a while. On the buses, swimming baths, you know. Oh, and we went to that panto at Stratford last Christmas. We all three went.' For some reason she emphasized the last remark.

Brooding, Welsh left her to it. June tried to bring him into the conversation. 'Do you go anywhere particular on the buses?'

'Just usual places.'

'Such as?'

'Oh, the zoo.'

'Yes?' she prompted.

'Museums. Er . . . *Cutty Sark*.'

'That wasn't all that recent,' said his wife.

They were both quietly desperate yet could not bring themselves to dig down into the real facts and bring them out for display. June said: 'I know you're both naturally very anxious, and I don't want you to jump to conclusions. But we're having to consider every kind of possibility, however slight.'

Mrs Welsh was reaching for another cigarette. Ash already made a wispy trail down one side of her cardigan.

'Has Samantha ever mentioned a man to you?' June persevered.

She had at last got through to Welsh. 'What kind of man?'

'We've had a statement from . . . from one of the children that a man exposed himself to her and Samantha. Now, it could well be unconnected, but we're having to consider all the possibilities.'

'You keep saying that!'

She let it simmer for a moment, then said: 'Do you mind if I have a look in her room before I go?'

'Normal procedure?' said Welsh caustically.

'As a matter of fact, yes.'

For a moment she thought he was going to reach out and grab her, shake her, just to relieve his pent-up feelings. Then he jerked his head. 'The next room. Through there.'

It was the kind of room you would have expected to find: a kid's bedroom, with a few of her own blobby paintings pinned to a board, a scattering of toys, and a large brown rabbit on the bed, minus one ear.

'Benjamin Bunny,' said Welsh, tight-lipped.

'What happened to his ear? Mr Macgregor get him?'

He managed a smile. 'She chews it. Look, miss, I'm sorry if – '

'It's a lousy time for you.' She picked up a drawing on a crumpled sheet of white paper. 'The *Cutty Sark*?'

'No, that's meant to be St Katharine's Dock, last year. I promised to take her again, but . . . ' He hunched his shoulders defensively. 'You know how it is. The things you don't get round to.'

On the bedside locker was another picture with a touch of the sea and a distant boat in the background. This time it was no scrawl, but a bright and cheerful photograph. In the foreground were Welsh and his daughter. He had his arm round her shoulders, apparently trying to lift her off her feet, and she was smiling at the camera – one of the few unaffectedly smiling studies of her June had so far seen.

Welsh followed the direction of her gaze. 'Margate, last summer.'

'Your wife took it?'

'No, a photographer on the front. My wife was in hospital. You know, women's things.'

'But she's okay now?'

'Yes,' he said dourly. 'Perfectly all right.'

There was nothing more to be done here. June left, promising to be in touch as soon as there was any news. It was hard to decide who looked the more disbelieving: Welsh or his wife.

Dashwood had come up with two names. They were both local, and both on the loose right now. Terence Lowe, thirty-seven years of age, had raped a twelve-year-old and been given a life sentence. But he was out now, had been out just a month.

'Some bloody shrink, I suppose,' said Dashwood, 'giving him the all-clear to start all over again.'

'We're just checking up on him, Mike,' Ted Roach warned. 'No jumping to conclusions.'

Then there was Derek Hammond. His record was one of rather pathetic interferences, most of them bungled: no violence, no rape, just flashing and touching up little girls and then running away – until the law caught up with him. A short sentence, and a recommended course of psychiatric treatment. For his own good, naturally . . . if it worked.

Two likely ones, then. Find them and eliminate them; or clobber them.

Roach and Dashwood set off on the trail.

Muswell and Hollis clambering over rubbish tips, June Ackland asking the parents the same questions yet again in the hope of detecting one significant alteration in their story, Carver and Lyttleton pacing along dockside and towpath while divers went down into the choked waters of a canal, Roach and Dashwood pursuing men whose names just happened to be linked with the sort of crime this might or might not be: they couldn't all be on the right track. Maybe none of them was. Maybe while they were sieving evidence and suspicions in a dozen distinct ways, the real truth was somewhere else and nobody yet had even the beginnings of a relevant lead. It was simply a matter of covering every possibility and faint theory, saturating the area and then analysing the results in the hope that somewhere in the mess there was one nugget of truth.

Terence Lowe was not at home. His neighbour, a blonde with long legs and a very short white skirt, was languidly stretching out a long bare arm to paint a windowframe as Roach and Dashwood arrived. She seemed pleased by the diversion, alternately reaching up from the stepladder and leaning out from it to present some interesting viewpoints to the visitors. Her physical assets stimulated the imagination; but her spoken words were unhelpful. She was unable to offer any information about Mr Lowe except that he had gone away and asked her to cancel the milk. No, she had no idea where he had gone or how long he would be. It was not, she said archly, that they were all that *close*. Just good neighbours, that was all.

Driving slowly away, Roach radioed a request for the collator to put out a bulletin for the whereabouts of Terence Lowe. Reluctantly he stole one last glance at the blonde in his mirror, narrowly missed an oncoming truck, and forced himself to drive steadily and soberly to their next port of call.

'If it's Hammond,' he observed, 'the kid's in luck.'

'Luck, you call it?'

'He wouldn't hurt a fly.'

'Oh, no, he just takes little girls and – '

'I said *hurt*. Anyway, he's been out nearly two years and we haven't had word of any trouble. I think I'd have heard.'

'Why you in particular?'

'I was the one who nicked him.'

They drew up outside a block of modern council flats, clean but uninspiring, opposite a terrace of older houses sagging into dereliction.

Hammond was also not at home. He was out at work, his mother explained proudly. They weren't going to cause him trouble, were they, now that he'd got a job? It wouldn't be fair, not after all he'd been through and all the hard work he was doing now. Roach made reassuring noises. Dashwood looked sceptical and wrinkled his nose as if some nasty smell had reached it from along the landing.

Next call was the garage where Hammond was working. A quarter of an hour later he was in the Sun Hill interview room. He had whined protests all the way here in the car, and he was still protesting.

'It's nothing to do with me. Just because I've got previous. I haven't touched a kid since I've been out. Honest. You got no right to try and nail me just because – '

'Listen, my friend,' said Roach. 'We are not trying to nail you. We're trying to eliminate you from our enquiries. For your sake as well as ours. Now, you left for work this morning at eight fifteen, right?'

'I always do.'

'And you got to work about nine fifteen. Wasn't that rather a long time?'

'Now listen – '

'No. *You* listen. With a thing like this, and with your record, people are bound to point the finger. Eh? Now, answer my questions and then you're free to go.'

'You're not going to keep me here?'

'I don't want to have to.'

Roach was sure in his bones that Hammond was not guilty. He had to go through the procedure, but however little faith Hammond might have in his assurances, he genuinely wanted to eliminate the poor little freak and get him off the premises. The truth was somewhere else. He was sure of it.

He felt a twinge of complacency when Galloway called him out with a piece of news relayed from the national computer. Terence Lowe not only had the London house but rented two small flats over drinking clubs he managed: one in Brighton, one in Margate. The name of Margate had rung a bell with June Ackland. The kid's father had taken her there once, and it seemed to have been a place where she was happy. It might not have taken much to coax her back there.

With a bit of luck Lowe would be picked up in Margate. Or in Brighton – alone or otherwise. Maybe it could all be wrapped up neatly this very day. That was how DI Galloway certainly wanted it, so that he could put Roach and Dashwood back on full-time surveillance of that shop and bank before the weekend, before it was too late. That was how it seemed to be turning out.

Until Carver and Lyttleton, late in the afternoon, arrived with a witness and quite a different tale to tell, and quite different implications to be followed up.

They had drawn a blank in the timber yard and were crossing the road towards the channel between river and old dock when a Ford transit clattered past. Carver froze on the edge of the pavement as the vehicle careered round a boarded-up warehouse and was lost to view.

'I'd swear that was that dodgy numberplate job.'

'Not our job right this minute.'

'I'd still like to nab that one. When I get another look at Queen's Parade, if they're still – '

'Right this minute,' Abe Lyttleton insisted sombrely, 'we're looking for flesh and blood, not dodgy discs and plates.' As they fell into step he added: 'Got a couple of my own, round about that age.'

They paced along the water's edge, looking down but not wanting to find anything.

'Where were you born, then?' asked Jimmy Carver.

'The sunshine state of Hackney, my son.'

'Really. So what made you join the police force?'

'What's this, the first round of Mastermind?'

'Sorry.'

'It's all right.' Lyttleton slowed to study a tangle of weed trailing across the water, and dismissed it. 'I get asked that all the time. I joined because' – he ventured a self-deprecatory grin – 'I wanted to do something worthwhile. And you?'

Carver answered him grin for grin. 'More or less the same reason.'

They made their way down to the wide basin, derelict a few years ago but now beginning to glow with refurbished sheds and a number of brightly painted barges.

'Her father brought her to St Katharine's Dock last year,' said Carver. 'Could have walked her anywhere along here, or up that bank.'

'Talk about clutching at straws.' Lyttleton stared unhappily into the water. It was getting a hypnotic hold on him. 'They'll be sending the diving team down here too, any time now.'

The two of them stopped beside a gangplank. At its far end an elderly man with a matted yellow beard was propped at the top of the short companionway ladder. He held up a whisky bottle invitingly. When they did not respond he put it to his lips and swallowed greedily. When he paused to speak, his voice was harsh and shaky. 'Plenty more – better had be – down below.'

Lyttleton said, 'We're making enquiries, sir, about a child who went missing this morning.'

'Huh?'

'Little girl, wearing a blue anorak.'

'Relation of yours?'

Lyttleton tensed. 'What makes you ask that?'

'Oh, I dunno. All look the same to me, you lot.'

Lyttleton held out the photograph with which they had all been hurriedly issued.

'It's very muzzy.' The picture was indeed blurred, rushed through as it had been; but no more muzzy than the boat owner himself. As he leaned forward to get things in focus he lurched and almost fell overboard. 'No sea legs,' he mumbled. 'Not as young as I was.' He made a great effort, and all at once said clearly: 'Wearing a tartan skirt, wasn't she?'

Carver heard Abe Lyttleton's gasp, and moved in closer.

'What was that, sir?'

'That little girl, you booby. Black Watch. My old regiment. Awful lot of people seem to go round wearing it these days. Don't know where they think they've got the right . . .'

'I wonder if you would mind accompanying us to the station, sir? You could be most helpful.'

'Could I, now?' Under shaggy eyebrows there was a gleam of cunning. 'Anything there to wet my whistle, eh? Something to stop the old throat seizing up?'

He asked it again when he was sitting in the interview room, opposite DI Galloway.

'Coffee, that's all,' said Galloway curtly. 'Now, you remember this little girl was wearing a Black Watch tartan skirt, right?'

'Mm. Mmm, mmph.'

'And you saw her this morning?'

The boat owner appeared to be in danger of falling asleep. 'Isn't it tomorrow yet?'

'Not quite. Now, did you see her this morning?'

'That's what I told your two flat-footed friends. 'Course I saw her.'

'Good. Was she with anyone?'

A plastic cup of coffee was set in front of the witness. He peered unenthusiastically into it.

'Listen.' Galloway tried to keep his impatience in check. 'This is very important. That child's life could be in danger.'

'Can't I have a drink?'

'Only that. Now, please. You must be able to remember. Was the child on her own, or was she with somebody?'

The man gave a despairing tug at his beard, muttered into it, and surrendered. 'Well, I'm not sure if she was with anyone all the time. I mean, I don't know how long they'd been together.'

'*They?*'

'Her and this woman.'

'A woman?' said Galloway. 'Not a man?'

'Can't tell the difference sometimes, can you? These days, you never know. But this was a woman all right. Spotted coat. Might be leopard, or something.'

Four

It was well after dark when they began to cut down on some of the operations. The loudspeaker van touring the Riverdale estate and a neighbouring shopping area was recalled. Radio appeals continued to bring in a number of phone calls, none of them apparent hoaxes but none even remotely helpful. The door-to-door enquiries were suspended because there were precious few doors left to knock at. It hurt to mark time, now that the matter was clearly more serious than just a kid playing truant. Darkness was here, she had not come home, and it did not look as if she would do so now. So it was abduction – by a woman? Better than by a man. Or was it?

Perhaps during the night there would be a message from Margate or Brighton. Meanwhile patrols on night duty were ordered to intensify routine examinations of every alley and dustbin, every half-open door or splintered fence. But the ordinary public, the people who must sooner or later come up with a shred of useful memory, were by now mostly watching a late-night horror movie, or asleep.

Was Samantha Welsh asleep, or awake in terror?

First thing next morning, motorists over a wider and wider network of streets were stopped and asked if they had seen a little girl at this same time yesterday. Lyttleton, Muswell, Carver and Viv Martella had got so used to reeling off the description that they could probably have mouthed it in their sleep; would probably do just that for several nights to come. Divers tried another overgrown cut. A line of policemen fanned out over tracts of wasteland between dock buildings.

The radio again interrupted its music in homes and in cars stuck in traffic jams on the way to work. 'Black Watch type of skirt, white socks and brown sandal-type shoes. If anyone has any information, will they please contact the incident room at Sun Hill police station. The number to ring . . . '

Roy Galloway sat in his office, fuming and impotent. He had already spent half an hour pacing about, hovering irritably near the switchboard, and having another talk with the boat owner. There was nothing more to come from that source. Galloway sent the dismally sobered-up man back to his vessel after a breakfast more solid than he was used to.

The calls began to come in again, from Paddington and Bexleyheath and

175

Greenwich. Some of them made you wonder what point there was in giving out detailed descriptions: sightings were reported of a Chinese girl in a black raincoat, a toddler with glasses, a couple of twins lost outside a Clerkenwell convenience.

Something fidgeted in Galloway's mind. It was not anything even as solid as a hunch. Perhaps it was no more than a reflex action. There had to be action of *some* kind, and moving the pieces around on the board was better than sitting still and waiting for someone else to come up with a gambit.

He wanted WPC Ackland to go and have another word with Theresa O'Brien.

June Ackland phoned the headmaster, to learn that Theresa had not shown up at school this morning.

'Don't say *she's* been abducted.' It was too grotesque. Even the weirdest pervert rarely went in for collecting them two at a time.

June got the O'Briens' address from the school and drove there fast, half expecting to be confronted by another distraught pair of parents. The door was cautiously opened to her by Theresa. One glimpse of the policewoman's uniform, and she tried to close it again.

June put her foot in the opening. 'Hello. I came to see why you're not at school.'

Theresa clung to the door handle, looking down at her feet with that evasive expression with which June was becoming all too familiar.

'Mum or dad in?' she asked as lightly as possible.

Theresa shook her head.

'Oh. So they don't know you didn't go to school?' When there was no reply she went on more aggressively: 'Come on now, Theresa. Are you scared of something?'

'No.' It was little more than a whisper, and an unconvincing one at that.

'Why were you scared to go to school? Did you tell a fib?' Now June was really angry. 'Theresa, did you make up all that nasty stuff? All that stuff about that man? *Did* you?'

Theresa's face dissolved into tears. She coughed out a little whining noise and with an abrupt wild shove got June's foot out of the way and slammed the door. June rang the bell again. She could see the girl's shadowy outline through the glass panel, but Theresa was not moving, just standing there mute.

It would not look too good to break down that door and upset the child still further.

Back at the nick, she was in time to hear Sergeant Cryer taking a call from the Brighton police. They had picked up Terence Lowe. Cryer beamed, promised someone would come and fetch him, and grabbed the internal phone to report the good news to Roy Galloway. Only maybe it was no longer the good news they might once have considered it to be. June waited for

Galloway to come down and join them, and said: 'The O'Brien kid was at home.'

'Thank God for that. But why – '

'She didn't admit it outright, but I'm positive she's been lying. All that stuff about the flasher – she's been watching too much telly, if you ask me. It was invented. You could see it written all over her face.'

'You're positive?' Cryer snapped.

'Sarge, I know we still have to go on chasing up every possibility, but I'd swear this one's a non-starter.'

Galloway let out a shuddering breath. 'So it looks as if our little friend from Woodclose has been leading us up the garden path. The bloke we've been chasing after never existed?'

'Looks like it. Really, sir, I could be wrong, but – '

'I believe you,' said Galloway.

'You know something?' said Cryer wearily. 'I bet that kid's making sand castles on Margate beach right now. Any minute we'll get a phone call saying she's been taken in and given an ice cream and please will we come and collect her. Quite a little shuttle service we're running today.'

'Sarge.' Yorkie Smith, at the switchboard, indicated the phone on the nearest desk.

The call was not from Margate but from a small supermarket on the far side of Riverdale estate. The assistant had something to report about the little girl they had been hearing about on the radio – and about a woman who had been with her.

'A woman?' said Cryer. They all held their breath as he waited for more details. Then he looked across the desk and repeated slowly: 'In a leopard-skin mac. Yes, oh yes. We'll get someone over to the shop right away. And thank you very much indeed.'

Galloway said: 'So that old dipso wasn't just seeing things. I think I'll go and follow this one up. Address, Bob? Oh, and Ackland – you ought to be in on it, too. Let's go.'

The shop had a vast stock of goods crammed in on its shelves, behind glass under the counter, and piled up along the floor. It seemed to cater for every possible need on the estate: cans of food, a refrigerator full of fruit juices, rows of cigarette packets and sweets, teddy bears, jigsaw puzzles, newspapers and magazines, a rack of paperbacks, birthday cards, and coloured picture post-cards of Tower Bridge and the Prince and Princess of Wales.

Galloway showed the girl behind the counter a picture of Samantha Welsh.

She nodded at once. 'Yes, that's her all right. And she was wearing a blue anorak and that tartan, like they said.'

'And the woman? Can you describe her a bit more?'

'Well, sort of fair hair. Touched up quite a bit, I'd say. And wearing that mac, leopard spots, sort of.'

'Does she shop here often?'

'Can't say I've noticed her before. Unless she comes in when I'm off work – you could ask the boss, but he won't be in till this afternoon.'

'What did she buy?'

'Some food. Cakes, and a tub of ice cream. And a bottle of wine. Oh, and a bag of flour. And one of those little teddy bears, and a colouring book and some felt tips for the kid.'

'And the kid was all right?'

The assistant shrugged. 'Yeah.'

'Yeah?' Galloway echoed doubtfully.

'Well, I dunno, do I? I mean, I didn't take that much notice. You don't when you're serving a customer, you just serve them, and – '

'All right, all right.'

'Seemed happy enough so far's I could tell,' said the girl placatingly. 'I mean, nothing like a few presents, is there?'

Galloway silently consulted June Ackland. Where did they go from here? They were so close; there had to be a way of clinching it.

Off the cuff he asked: 'How did she pay?'

'Credit card.'

June Ackland smiled. Galloway felt a smile of his own coming all the way from deep inside. It was even better when the girl produced the counterfoil. A Smith or a Jones might have slowed things down a bit. But a name like Lubaczewska would surely not take too much locating.

'Have you got a phone book?'

There was no Lubaczewska in the area directory. From the car he called Sun Hill and spelled the name out carefully to Bob Cryer. The response came more quickly than he would have dared hope.

'Bit of luck, Roy. Yorkie Smith had dealings with a woman of that name just under a year ago. Married a Polish bloke who got killed in a hit and run. Yorkie was the one who had to go round and tell her, so it sticks in his mind. Number 5 Pickford Crescent, right?'

Galloway drove at a speed which made June Ackland cast two or three side-long glances at him. With any other man she might have thought he was trying to impress her. But Galloway was not the one to waste time impressing any-body. His mind was fiercely concentrated on reaching their destination as fast as possible just in case . . .

Neither of them wanted to pursue that 'just in case'.

June hazarded: 'She wouldn't have bought a colouring book for the kid if anything was . . . well, going to happen. Would she? I mean, why?'

They reached Pickford Crescent. Seeing the turn-off a few seconds too late, Galloway jammed on his brakes and backed screechingly up the side road.

'Number 5.' He was willing it to be the right address and the right conclusion.

The door was opened by a woman with a pale, narrow face whose bone structure preserved its beauty in spite of the melancholy in her eyes.

'Mrs Lubaczewska?'

'Yes.' The woman's oddly oblique, wide eyes widened even more as she saw the uniformed WPC Ackland behind him.

'I'm Detective Inspector Galloway. We're making enquiries into the – '

She tried to close the door, yelling 'No!' as June flung herself along the narrow passage to the kitchen at the back of the flat. 'No, please.' Tears sprang to her eyes and she stumbled aside and clung to the kitchen door as Galloway followed June Ackland. 'We're only having a tea party.'

Samantha Welsh was perched on a stool, contentedly rolling pastry. Her face was pallid with flour and there was a dab of jam in one corner of her mouth. She smiled at the three of them, puzzled by the intrusion but unworried.

June said: 'Samantha, we've come to take you home.'

In the cool and clinical atmosphere of the interview room Galloway said: 'You were widowed last year, I'm told?'

'Yes.'

'Any kids of your own?' When Mrs Lubaczewska shook her head he probed: 'What made you pick her?'

'I . . . I thought she was lost.'

'On her way to school?' he said sceptically.

'But she wasn't going to school, not when I saw her.'

'How could you tell where she was going?'

'She was by the boats. Not going anywhere. just watching the boats.'

'That was the first time you saw her?'

'At the dock,' Mrs Lubaczewska said dreamily. 'I like the docks. Especially in the summer. There are people to talk to.' Her eyes clouded over. 'Families,' she murmured.

The door opened. 'Oh, sorry, guv.'

'What is it, Ted?'

'Hammond, we're still holding him. The way things are now, wouldn't it be – '

'Let him go.' Galloway turned sympathetically back to the woman at the table. 'Look, the way I see it, you didn't mean any harm. But you must have known it was wrong. I mean, what about the kid's parents? They must have been worried sick, and there you were setting up little treats and parties and tucking her up in bed and all the rest of it. Didn't you ever think of the mother and father?'

'She never said anything about them.'

'Nothing?'

Her lips trembled, but she was not looking at him and no longer really hearing. Her misery came from the pain of loss, not from any awareness of wrongdoing or the existence of anybody else. As far as she was concerned, Samantha's parents had never existed.

Galloway wanted to be done with the emotionalism of it all. The facts had been verified; personal reverberations were none of his business. He was glad it was Ackland who had to hand the kid over, not himself. Tearfully ecstatic reunions, brimming over with a whole lot more emotion, were not his line.

June Ackland felt differently. She had gone through the bad bits, and now there was going to be the good bit. She looked forward to it. It was the sort of thing that made the job worthwhile. Holding Samantha's hand, she said: 'They won't half be pleased to see you.'

Samantha was silent and subdued. In her other hand she clutched the painting book, refusing to have it put in her school satchel or even to let go of it for a moment.

They went up in the lift and along the landing which June associated with bad news or depressing lack of news. Only now it was going to be a different story. There really were happy endings, every now and then.

She rang the bell and waited, smiling.

Mrs Welsh opened the door. She stared, then grabbed at Samantha.

'Sammy! What did I tell you, what *did* I . . . ?'

Samantha was dragged from June's grasp and thrown against the wall. She cried out just once before her mother, holding her with one hand, began to beat her about the head with the other.

Welsh came pounding along the passage. 'What d'you think you're doing, you stupid bitch?'

'Don't you call me bleeding names.'

June tried to say something but was drowned out by Welsh. 'You don't have to belt her about like that, you shouldn't, she – '

'She may well deserve it, thank you very much.'

'What d'you . . . ?'

The rest was lost as Mrs Welsh, fiercely active in her rage, kicked the door shut. June crumpled against the outside wall, putting her hand across her eyes to stop them blinking. Her fingers tightened across her forehead. Inside the flat the thudding went on, and now Samantha was beginning to scream.

June suppressed a sob in her throat. All in the day's work.

That's what she would be told if she lodged a complaint.

She headed for the lift.

'And now,' said Galloway, 'let's get back to the real villains. Ted, you and Mike get back on the job. Go and relieve Chris and Jim on Queen's Parade.'

'You're not still banking on that one, guv?'

'Banking might be the right word, Ted. Off you go.'

'I still get a creepy feeling you've been fed a – '

'Creep off, Ted. At the double.'

Roach bit back whatever it was he had it in mind to say, and went down-stairs. Galloway followed after a few minutes to check that Mrs Lubaczewska had read over her statement and signed it. He found the front office in uproar. Tom Penny and Bob Cryer were slanging each other and then taking it in turns to bellow accusations first at Hollis and then at Taffy Edwards.

'I'll have somebody's guts for garters,' Cryer was raging. 'We get through all that mess, everything out of order and now, on top of that, when we're sup-posed to be back to normal you . . . look, Tom, why the hell didn't you – '

'I gave the instructions,' retorted Penny, 'clearly enough. If some imbecile didn't pay attention to perfectly clear orders – '

'Nice and peaceful in here this morning,' observed Galloway. 'What's up?'

'The recharge unit's been out all night.'

'You mean, after all that switch-off chaos, nobody had the sense to switch on again?'

'We mean,' said Cryer, 'that all the radios over there are flat. And the ones that have been taken out on patrol must be just as flat, or with only a flicker left in them. So how the hell do we get in touch with anybody out there?'

'You'll just have to shout louder,' suggested Galloway.

He sorted out the last sad little details on Mrs Lubaczewska, and went back to his office for a call to the bank manager. No, there had been no apparent developments. No suspicious moves, or anyone showing any signs of acting strangely in or around the bank. Was the detective inspector quite sure . . . ?

Yes, in his own mind Galloway was quite sure. He was in no mood for doubts from Roach or the bank manager. Conga would have had no reason to feed him a load of lies – not if he expected to grab any reward, he wouldn't.

Towards the end of the morning Bob Cryer came into the office without knocking, and without preamble said: 'And what the hell are your lot doing along Queen's Parade without notifying us?'

Galloway gripped the edge of his desk. 'What do you know about Queen's Parade?'

'Only that Ted Roach has been on his car radio yelling his head off.'

'Why? What's gone wrong?'

He listened with mounting incredulity and fury as Bob Cryer spat it out.

Roach was clamouring for help. On an obbo job, he said, at Queen's Parade – and two bloody great flatfoots were about to blow the whole game. Couldn't somebody make contact and pull them out, quick? There they were, Carver and Lyttleton, prowling round a Ford transit and making themselves con-spicuous enough to frighten anybody off. From which Cryer assumed that the eager-beaver Jimmy Carver had rediscovered that transit where he had first spotted it, dodgy numberplate and tax disc and all, and was aiming to make a collar. Fair enough. But Roach wanted the two of them out of the way.

'So why don't you *get* them out of the way?' shouted Roy Galloway.

'Because their PR units are quite u.s., that's why. Dead. They can't hear us.'

'Your bloody great big clumsy woodentops – do you realize they're going to cock up a whole operation? What are you going to do about it? How are you going to get yourselves out of this bloody criminal mess you've made?'

'In the first place,' said Cryer, 'I've told your Ted Roach that we can't contact our two men, can't call 'em off, and he'll have to take whatever measures he thinks fit. And in the second place,' he said lethally, 'when it comes to a question of a cock-up, there wouldn't have been any such thing if you'd seen fit to put us in the picture.'

Galloway was seeing red. He had been so sure of making a killing, and now it was slipping through his fingers. 'Your mob has messed this up good and proper, Robert. There'll be hell to pay over this, I promise you.'

'Us? *We* messed it up? Now look here – '

'One more day,' ranted Galloway. 'That's all I needed, just one more day. It just *had* to be this weekend.'

'If you choose not to notify the uniformed branch of what you're up to, don't blame them for carrying out the duties they're supposed to be on. If you don't want your toes trodden on, at least give us some idea where you're planting those precious toes. Right now, inspector, if I read the tea leaves aright, the only thing you'll get out of whatever it is you're tailing will be a bent tax disc.'

Galloway thought feverishly of his next possible move. Before he could make any move at all, the message was relayed from downstairs, in the most formal language, that due to circumstances beyond their control Detective Sergeant Roach and Detective Constable Dashwood had been forced to move in and take two suspects into custody.

Two suspects and not much else, Roach reported when he got back to Sun Hill. Unless you counted some new shelving in the basement of the boarded-up shop, some rough-and-ready plastering and a built-in cupboard. It looked like a cheap refurbishing job being rushed through for the reopening of the shop. Nobody had been digging. No sign of tunnels or subterranean access to the bank vaults.

Galloway kept Roach standing there in front of the desk while he sat back, let the adrenalin really get circulating, and treated himself at last to a full-scale explosion. 'I just don't believe it. One more day, and we'd have had all we needed on them. I swear it.'

'I don't think so,' said Roach stubbornly. 'Looks like your snout gave you a bummer.'

'No chance. What d'you take me for? How the hell you and Dashwood could let a pair of flaming woodentops step in and blow it, I . . . no, I just don't believe it. I don't see it. A cock-up like that – '

'It was your cock-up, sir.' Roach was flushed and furious, the high colour in his cheeks getting higher and brighter. 'You run around shouting your head off and thinking you can lay down the law all on your own.'

'Ted – '

'Just who the bloody hell do you think you are?'

'I'm your governor, that's who I am.'

'Is that a fact? Well, let me tell you something, *guv'nor*. It's about time you learned a few home truths.'

'One more word from you, sergeant, and I'll have you on a report.'

'I don't give a monkey's what you have me on. Not any more. You have me up on whatever you like, sir. You cocked it up, not me. Not me, not Mike, and certainly not the boys in uniform. You wouldn't listen, you don't want to listen, you don't want to know.'

'Right.' Galloway was almost glad to have someone to take it all out on. Roach was for it this time. 'That does it,' he said.

'And you know something? You used to be a good copper. A bit on the flash side, but good. Now you're no more than a loud-mouthed bully-boy who stamps his feet when he doesn't get everything all his own way. You don't have a monopoly on being right, sir, whatever your rank.'

'Get out.'

Roach got out.

Roy Galloway sat gripping the arms of his chair as the denunciations built up in his mind and he framed just how he was going to word the final damning accusation against Roach. This time it had gone too far. This time Ted Roach was for the chop.

He felt sick: sick because of things going so wrong, and sick because of letting things reach this stage with Roach. There was no way he could back down now and still maintain respect.

Conga hadn't fed him a bummer. There was no way he was going to believe that. Whatever cover-ups Roach attempted, whatever rotten rubbish Bob Cryer spewed up about radios on the blink, woodentops on the plod, it made no difference: the truth was that he had been in reach of a great collar, and the rest of them had made a pig's ear out of it.

He was tired, hungry, thirsty. If he sat here at this desk five minutes longer, he'd start thinking about the divorce again and feeling sorry for himself, and counting back over the years and finding himself face to face with somebody else who'd had it in for him and would never listen to reason.

He went down Sun Hill to the corner pub.

Bob Cryer and Ted Roach were sitting at the far end of the bar. It was all too obvious that Roach had been bending Cryer's ear. Automatically Galloway drifted towards them; then stopped, and hauled himself on to a stool a good ten feet away.

Sadie, the barmaid, was saying: 'Hey, Bob, that bank job was a bit cheeky, wasn't it?'

Galloway felt a chill. He looked round. The door was shut, the artificial flames danced in the gas fire. He tried to stop himself twitching.

'What bank?' asked Cryer.

'Glasscock Street. Just been on the news.'

Ted Roach leaned across the bar, glum but responding instinctively to any hint of evildoing. 'Glasscock Street?'

'Reckon they must have been down there for days, and nobody any the wiser.'

'First we've heard of it,' said Cryer.

'Only dug right under the road, didn't they? Straight up the sewer, right into the vault.'

'I knew it,' said Roach very audibly to Cryer. 'I told him his snout sold him one.'

'Oh, I doubt it, Ted. Glasscock Street's not even on our ground.'

'Only just over the boundary. And don't tell me they wouldn't have been glad of a nice little diversion. Left them in peace to get on with things.'

Galloway's mouth was dry. He said harshly: 'Scotch, please.'

'Sorry, Roy. Didn't see you come in.' Sadie reached for a glass and swept it expertly up to the optic. 'Hey, you heard about – '

'Yes, I heard you.'

'Somebody dropped a clanger?'

Galloway looked along the bar. 'And whatever they're having along there.'

Bob Cryer favoured him with a dour half-smile, but pushed his glass forward. Ted Roach sat mute, refusing to turn his head.

'The usual, Ted?' said Sadie.

It was an almost imperceptible nod.

Galloway edged closer. 'Haven't been that bad, have I?'

It was Cryer who took it on himself to answer. 'Yes. Worse.'

They drank. Galloway's whisky took only a few seconds to go down. With an effort he said: 'Right, then. See you later, back at the nick . . . Ted. We'll go through everything we've got. Together. Straighten it out. Okay?'

Roach was still not looking at him. 'Okay, guv.'

'I'll see you.'

'See you, Roy,' said Cryer, into an infinity stretching behind the shelf of spirits.

Five

Some of the hard cases you had to deal with were often no better than animals. Animals: it had become a useful shorthand to describe a lot of them. The trouble was, a policeman's lot did not just involve human animals. Over the months and years Sun Hill officers had been caught up in the problems of several four-legged ones, not to mention a selection of birds, from parrots to thieving magpies. Yorkie Smith, on point duty, had once stuck out his arm to find it embracing a leg of lamb which had literally fallen off the back of a lorry. Valuable hours had been spent dealing with a rampaging goat which proved to have got high on cannabis growing wild among the weeds in a back garden. And now, right at the beginning of a working day, there was another matter of four-footed strays.

'Two of our pigs,' said a Mr Roger Philpot on the phone, 'are missing.'

WPC Martella repeated the message over her shoulder to Sergeant Cryer. He stared, suspecting a hoax. 'Since when did we have pigs on this manor?'

'Ask some of our admirers,' offered Muswell.

'The City Farm,' said Viv Martella. 'A break-in.'

Cryer checked the wall map. Taffy Edwards ought to be somewhere in the vicinity of that patch of green, most likely sneaking a second breakfast in that favourite café of his.

He sucked his lips in. On the whole they had a pretty good team here. Jimmy Carver, at first so soggy behind the ears, had settled in well. The newcomer, Abe Lyttleton, might not have made a go of his previous two postings but so far showed every sign of pulling his weight at Sun Hill. Yorkie Smith was a bit of a bouncing yokel in some ways, but utterly reliable. Hollis would always be a moaner, with an assortment of pains adding up to one great pain in the neck; but at least he had a knack with paperwork. Muswell . . . oh, Muswell was a sight too greedy, piling up the overtime during that miners' strike, and Cryer would not have put it past him to go moonlighting in off-duty hours – only God help him if it was ever proved. But in his own heavy way he was tough and resourceful.

As for the girls, Viv Martella looked too sleek and sultry to be a serious copper. It was a misleading impression, as many a petty crook had found to his cost. And June Ackland was . . . well, there was something about that slim, trim figure of hers and about . . . Cryer stopped himself. Talk about racism in the station: if they had known what he was thinking, there'd be a right royal outcry about sexism.

And so Cryer came back to PC Edwards. Getting slack. Too much time fretting about his days off and whether he could catch this or that train to North Wales; and too much time scrounging meals in that café, skiving on the job, waiting for radio instructions instead of pacing the beat to stop things before they happened.

Martella took another call at the switchboard. A man was ringing in about a pig trampling all over the back alley behind the bus station.

'Not far from Taffy's nosh bar,' observed Cryer. 'Get him out there. Keep the thing cornered, and we'll see about picking it up.'

They notified Mr Philpot, who sounded pleased, but not eager enough to go and collect his animal. The Land Rover was in for repair, he explained, and the only vehicle he had available was a Mini. And where, he demanded ungratefully, was the second pig?

'All right,' sighed Cryer. 'Who've we got? Muswell, you get out there in the Sherpa and I'll get Carver to meet you at' – his finger traced a route across a segment of the map – 'Pound Place.'

'The Sherpa's loaded up, sarge.'

'Well, get it unloaded. And hurry up.' Leaning over the switchboard, Cryer said: 'Get Jimmy for me. He's good with kids, he's probably good with animals.'

'Yeah, well,' protested Muswell, 'if it shits all over the van I'm not cleaning it out.'

'Oh yes, you are.'

As Muswell left, Hollis said: 'Rather them than me, sarge. Pigs can get very nasty, you know.' He swung his shoulders from side to side, and winced.

'Agony, is it, Reg?'

'Just catches me now and again, sarge,' said Hollis gallantly.

Martella glanced back at him. 'Only a prize wally would have hurt himself on a field training course.'

'Look, if I'd wanted to do PT I'd have joined the SAS, wouldn't I?'

'Yeah. He who dares, ricks his back.'

'Wait till they send the rest of you on it. It'll cripple half the Force.'

'Have you been to see the CMO recently?' Cryer demanded.

'Well, not since that time when he said I was to stay on light duties until – '

'I reckon it's time you had it checked again. A full physical. You never know, there might be something really wrong with you.'

'Look, sarge, I'm not swinging the lead,' said Hollis plaintively.

'Well, let's find out. Because if there's something wrong with you, you're no good to me and I'm getting you transferred.'

Hollis looked interested, vaguely hopeful. 'What, a job upstairs?'

'Yes. We'll have a lift put in.' Cryer turned his attention to the PR message coming in. 'You got that porker in your sights yet, Edwards?'

Taffy Edwards had in fact succeeded in cornering the pig, but was none too confident of his ability to hold out all that long. The animal was rooting contentedly along the cobbled alley, having overturned a dustbin and helped itself to the more savoury morsels, leaving the rest of the rubbish spread across the gutter. When it had finished, it was just as likely to charge out of the alley at the speed with which it had charged in. Taffy crouched in a position suggesting something halfway between a lion-tamer's coaxing stance and a bull-fighter's poised readiness.

'About bloody time,' he greeted the Sherpa as it came to a halt across the end of the alley.

The appreciative crowd of bystanders increased as Muswell and Carver joined Edwards. Jimmy Carver was self-consciously carrying a metal lasso, brought from the dog-handler's store, which looked more likely to inflict damage on the gaping audience than to snare the pig with brisk efficiency.

'Go on, Jimbo,' Muswell encouraged him. 'Get in there.'

'Pig,' said Carver entreatingly. 'Come on, piggy. Pig . . . pig . . . '

Their quarry grunted, and buried its snout in a stodgy mess of squashed food cartons. A few members of the crowd cheered it on.

'Take it easy.' Carver made a tentative jab with the metal ring, which the pig headed contemptuously aside. 'Hey, steady now. Steady.'

Muswell snorted almost as raucously as the animal. 'Go on, you great girl's blouse!'

Goaded, Carver made a wild lunge and at last succeeded in getting the metal round the pig's neck. It lashed out with its hind legs, but slithered on the débris and landed up against the wall, squealing in rage.

Muswell looked back at the van.

'How we going to get it in there?'

'I don't . . . ' Carver braced himself to keep his captive pinned against the wall. 'Look, that old door over there. On that tip at the end. Drag it out as a ramp or something.'

Together Muswell and Edwards hauled the door into place, and waved to Carver to bring his animal-training act to a triumphant conclusion. Half dragging, half steering the pig towards the van, he managed to get it to the foot of the ramp. It squealed and tried to lunge to the left. Members of the crowd scattered, regrouped, and cheered again. Muswell and Edwards closed in to either side, while Carver did not so much urge the pig into the van's interior as let it drag him along with it. When he had backed quickly out and Edwards had slammed the doors shut, Jimmy Carver said with some pride: 'Right, that's it. Over to you.'

'Yes, you can stop playing with your pet now. Back to the beat and some real work, eh?'

Carver paced off, not knowing whether the round of applause offered by the onlookers was genuine or ironic.

Muswell and Edwards drove to the City Farm, with their passenger thudding and honking a protest behind them. The farm was an unexpected little oasis at the end of a suburban street, with more rows of semi-detached houses on its far side. Roger Philpot was waiting for them, congratulatory but still slightly peevish about the absence of the second pig. Shepherding his retrieved animal towards its sty, he identified it. 'This is Plonk. So Pickle's still at large.'

'No sweat,' said Muswell. 'We'll put it out on all units. What's its reg number?' Then hastily, seeing that this had not gone down too well, he peered inside the van, wrinkled his nose, and added: 'You got a hose, sir? Taffy, go get the hose.'

'Oh, no, mate. You're the driver.'

'What are you moaning about? I thought you was brought up on a farm?'

'Yes, boyo. Welsh woollies, not English pigs. Now, Mr Philpot, we've not yet established how – '

'This has really thrown my egg deliveries this morning. Hold these for me, would you?' As if by magic a cardboard tray of eggs was put into Taffy's hands.

'Mr Philpot, please. We still have no idea how the pigs escaped. You talked about a break-in.'

'And that's what it was. No escape. Somebody let them out, deliberately. Come and look.'

Still balancing the tray of eggs, Edwards accompanied the farmer round the end of the sty to a stretch of wire fencing.

Philpot indicated a large ragged gash in the fence.

'The sty door had been opened,' he said. 'And as to the fence – well, pigs don't use wire cutters.'

'Vandals?'

'Animal Life League, I think. We've had a few letters lately – "Meat is murder," that kind of thing. You're not a vegetarian, are you?'

'Oh no, I'm Welsh, I eat anything.'

A flock of geese stormed across the path as they walked back. Edwards picked his way warily around the rackety gaggle and took the opportunity of handing the tray of eggs back to its owner.

'Pickle's still missing,' Philpot remarked with a heavy hint of accusation. 'You may not think it all that serious, but she's a very important member of our community.'

'It's not a question of what I think, sir. But we'll do all we can, depend on that.' Returning to the Sherpa, he walked round the side of the van to the open rear doors. 'You finished yet, Muzz?'

From inside came a last swish of stinking liquid as Muswell swept it vigorously out into the open. 'Gardez-loo! Oops.' He grinned down at the speckled mess over Taffy's trousers. 'All done, then?'

'No mate, you missed the top half.'

Muswell's lips twisted into false commiseration. 'Want a lift back to your beat?'

'Oh, thanks very much. You might at least say sorry.'

'Good stuff, that. Makes your toes curl.' Muswell shook the brush in the fresh air. 'How'd they get out, then?'

'The nutty brigade cut a hole in the fence. Least, that's what he reckons. Anyway, there's naff-all to go on.'

'Right. Let's leave it. Where do you want dropping off?'

'Larry's. I could do with a cup of tea.'

Edwards climbed into the van. Muswell, reaching for the ignition, said: 'Phew. Stick your feet outside, won't you?'

Taffy unbuttoned his jacket and flapped it in defiance.

Muswell drove fast, with the windows open, in a hurry to ditch him outside the café known to every man on this beat – better known to some than others.

'Not another breakfast already, Taff?' Larry, fat and hospitable in a greasy vest adorned with the splashes of a dozen earlier breakfasts, propped his top-heaviness against the counter.

'Elevenses,' said Edwards.

'What you been doing, then?'

'Arresting a pig, as it happens.'

'Saved a few rashers for us?'

'No, Larry. Look, I just want a cup of tea.' As Larry trundled behind the counter and stimulated the large urn into uttering a fine hiss of activity, he said: 'Here, you haven't got another runaway pig on the premises, have you?'

'Can't oblige, sorry. Plenty of dead flies, though.'

Taffy Edwards looked at the contents of an ashtray, the sandwiches in the glass case on the counter, and the consistency of the tea in his cup, and was prepared to believe every word of that.

Henry Talbot made a circuit of the Sun Hill corridors with a small clutch of memoranda in his left hand. With his right hand he doled them out like a philanthropist distributing largesse to the poor and underprivileged. He looked grave yet well content. As the chief superintendent's clerk he derived a certain relish from handing over instructions which he knew would be unpopular but for which he could at any crucial moment disclaim responsibility. Not that Talbot invariably wished to disclaim such responsibility: indeed, he took considerable pleasure in framing the memoranda himself, watching the chief super sign them, and watching the faces of those who found themselves landed with the result.

'Bullshit!' was Ted Roach's immediate reaction.

New overtime restrictions were to be imposed. These must not, however, be allowed to impair operational effectiveness. Although paperwork might in certain unspecified circumstances get held up, everyone must endeavour to be as efficient as possible in the issue of reports to whichever department was involved.

Roach glowered up at Talbot. 'You've read this crap you're carting about?'

'I drafted it.'

'Paperwork is the only bloody thing that *doesn't* get held up round here.'

'Perhaps if your CID brethren were to clock in promptly, there'd be less need for overtime.' Talbot grimaced meaningly at the empty chair behind Dashwood's desk.

'Mike's out on a job.'

'He's not booked out on the duty state. Or in,' said Talbot puritanically as he left the room.

'Pedantic little twat!' Roach hurled after him.

In Galloway's office the phone began to ring. Roach hurried through and lifted the receiver. The caller's name meant nothing to him.

'Barry Blades? Sorry, mate, what – '

'Immigration.'

Before Roach could pursue this, Roy Galloway came in and held out his hand to take the call. 'Hello, Barry. Sorry I didn't get back to you yesterday. What time you going to be here? Half-past eleven, fine. just see the duty sergeant if I'm not around, okay?'

'Immigration?' said Roach. 'And what would they be wanting of the likes of us?'

'Deporting the Irish. And you're first.'

Just to wipe the smile off his DI's face, Roach held out the memorandum which Talbot had delivered.

'Operational overtime?' Galloway read it out aloud. 'What's triggered all this off?'

'Maybe following up yesterday.'

'What yesterday?' Galloway looked round the office. 'And where's Mike?'

'Out checking on that con artist with the wardrobes. Checking on Miss Clark and the people who know her and who might have had a key to the flat.'

'Oh, that. Should have been wrapped up last night.'

'That's what I mean. The chief super told us no overtime, and Mike was on overtime, and not the only one. So now we get it all in writing.'

'Bloody ridiculous. Anyway, what are *you* up to this fine day, then?'

'That credit card job.'

'Any imminent danger of an arrest?' jibed Galloway. He went downstairs to arrange with Bob Cryer for Blades of Immigration to borrow three of his lads. Cryer was far from anxious to co-operate. He saw little reason why officers needed for nicking real villains should be commandeered to lean on a few poor sods who had been born in the wrong country and were now destined to be shipped back there. Routine policing encompassed enough dirty work of its own, without doing other people's dirty work for them. But in its way this too, officially, was routine. You had to go along with it, even when it turned your stomach.

PC Lyttleton was already on patrol in the area of the Caffrey Street sweatshop on which Blades had his eye. Carver and Muswell were detailed to take the van and join him at the junction with Commercial Street, following Blades and his sidekick in their car. The sidekick, Greg Swinton, was a quiet man but a deadly one: dark and withdrawn, he had the predatory look of a hunter who knew he could strike wherever he chose and always have the back-up of other officers' muscle.

Abe Lyttleton was waiting for them on the corner by a derelict chapel, its notice-board still holding shreds of waterlogged paper on which an indecipherable text had given up all hope of getting its message across. Muswell looked him up and down without favour. 'Hello, Snowball. You in on this?'

Blades, a dapper little man who made up for Swinton's shadowy introspection with a punchy intimation of going in and grabbing whatever there was to get without any argument, said: 'I want one of you at the front, one at the back, one in with us.' He stabbed a thumb at Lyttleton. 'You're the beat officer, right? So you'd best be the one inside. And remember, I'm not asking any of you to do anything. No rough stuff and no nonsense about acting on your own initiative, get it? You're just here to ensure there isn't a breach of the peace. Got that?'

They nodded morose assent.

Blades led the way down the street of decrepit brewery buildings split up into shabby factories and warehouses. Beside a door which could not have been repainted these past ten years was a notice-board advertising jobs available.

'We'll be doing the buggers a favour,' said Blades loudly. 'Most of em'd be better off back in Calcutta, anyway.'

Inside there was a whirr of machines. The floor creaked and thrummed under the pulse of the equipment, muffling the noise of the intruders' footsteps. An Indian in a shiny grey lounge suit saw them coming, and scuttled nervously from behind his glass partition.

'Mr Dev?' Blades expanded with the certainty of his own power. 'Immigration Department of the Home Office.'

'Yes,' said Mr Dev resignedly.

'I wonder if I could have a chat with some of your employees?'

Dev shrugged and stole a glance at Swinton, who had a glint of pleasurable anticipation in his eyes.

'Just the iffy ones, Greg,' said Blades. 'Straight down to the nick with 'em.'

Lyttleton stood a few paces back as Swinton approached a man stitching a jacket and began to talk quietly but incisively in Bengali. A white girl whose moist brow could well have illustrated the veracity of the term 'sweatshop' walked past, veering in close. 'Ain't you got nothing better to do?' Another appeared at Lyttleton's elbow. 'Leave the poor blighters alone.'

Blades was snapping his fingers for the passports of two dark, hunched women at one of the benches. When he had inspected them and found them in order, his expression was one of disgust rather than apology. 'Mrs Gupte and Mrs Chatterjee. Hm. There'll soon be more Chatterjees over here than Patels.'

He prowled round the room. Machines fell silent one after another. Heads bowed or tilted sideways. Uneasy eyes studied him; and studied Swinton, making his own soft-footed circuit but always alert for a command from his boss.

Blades stopped beside a man with a steam iron, whose regular movements slowed to a halt.

'Him, I think.'

Swinton resumed the questioning. He nodded with a show of sympathy, but the broadening of his smile confirmed that he had made a kill. As the man's shoulders slumped, Swinton turned to Blades. There was no need for words. They knew one another by now.

As Lyttleton led the man downstairs, a West Indian near the door said: 'You proud of yourself, black man?'

Out in the street, Abe waited for the others to join him. He kept a hand lightly on the defeated immigrant's arm, but the man was too dejected to make a run for it. 'Thanks for your help, son.' Blades emerged, waiting for Carver to come round the corner and Muswell to bring up the rear. He included them all in his thanks. 'Cheers, then. Maybe see you lads back at the nick. Well done.'

Swinton opened the rear door of the car and waved their captive in.

Muswell sneered as they drove off. 'Well done, chaps,' he mimicked. His gaze fell unfavourably on Abe Lyttleton. 'Another blow against the black economy, eh?'

Somebody from a side door spat.

Lyttleton moved away. Behind him, Muswell, about to cross the road to the van, said: 'Oh, Snowball, how many times have I told you to use a hanky?'

'What?'

'You've got gob all down your back. Here, Jimbo, take him in hand. Clean him up and change his loincloth.'

As Muswell disappeared round the far side of the van, Carver dug out a paper tissue and dabbed at Lyttleton's shoulder. 'Right, there you go. Fancy a drink after work?'

'What's this?' Lyttleton was taut with anger. 'Your community relations bit?'

Carver stared. 'All right, then. Piss off.'

It was the sort of thing to leave a nasty taste in your mouth. Unless, of course, you were a Swinton or a Muswell. They would both enjoy a scene like that, each in his own way.

Animals . . .

Sun Hill had not yet had its full quota of animals. Even before the pig incident had been satisfactorily rounded off, and only seconds after Jimmy Carver had got back to the station, the phone was clamouring about another batch of wild creatures – dead ones this time. There was a disturbance at the fur shop in Masson Row, apparently set up by Animal Life demonstrators. There were three of them in the shop, refusing to budge, and a few more outside: mostly women, according to the report from Simeon Logue, the owner.

'Masson Row,' said Sergeant Cryer. 'Taffy's beat again. Seems to be cut out for the world of wildlife. And who else can we raise?' He scanned the map and the duty roster. 'Yes, call up June, she should be pretty adjacent. Carver, you get down there in the van and go in with them. And be careful how you handle it.'

'Handle what, sarge?'

'It's Nutters-for-Nature flag day, Jimbo,' said Muswell cheerfully.

'And you go with him.'

'But sarge, we don't need that many . . . '

Cryer's nose swung towards him like a weather vane heralding a storm. Muswell bent to the wind, and set off once more with Carver.

June Ackland had reached the scene ahead of them. She was standing well back along the pavement, sizing up the situation and waiting for reinforcements. There was no sign of Taffy Edwards.

Outside the shop a group squatting on the pavement kept chanting monotonously: 'Fur traders out . . . fur traders out . . . '

Muswell looked as if he was ready to enjoy himself for the second time that day. 'You go at the dykes,' he said to June. 'We'll take the queers.'

'Fur traders out . . . '

Flanked by the two men, June edged her way into the shop. At the best of times there would be little space to spare in here. Right now the place was dominated by two women and a young man with long hair, drawn back into a wispy pigtail with a red ribbon. One of the women, dark-haired and determined, kept thrusting a leaflet at the shopkeeper. He snatched it from her and threw it over his shoulder. She began to wave another one to and fro in front of his face.

June reached the counter. 'Can I have a look at what you're handing out, please, madam?'

The woman ignored her and thrust the leaflet under Simeon Logue's nose yet again.

'I don't want to read your damned leaflet,' he yelled.

Carver and Muswell shouldered their way in. Muswell assumed his best official manner. 'Do you want these persons on your premises, sir?'

'Oh yes, they're very good for custom, very good for my business! Of course I don't want them on my premises. Or anywhere within a hundred miles.'

'Then we shall assist you to remove them.'

The young woman who had been flourishing the leaflet let herself crumple to the floor. She braced her feet against the counter. Obviously she had played this kind of drama before and knew how to be difficult. She was dressed in a black nylon blouse and skirt, and her hair and eyes were almost dark reflections of the clothes. She could have been attractive, if it were not for the shadowy gashes of impatience tugging the corners of her mouth down. She was well spoken, in a domineering way. 'We are only trying to put a point of view. Why do you have to come in here and – '

'Would you mind putting that point of view outside?' said Carver, bending to get his hands under her armpits.

'Yes, we do mind.'

'Now look, ladies – '

'Don't patronize us, you pig.' It was the other woman, getting one arm round a rack of furs. 'Fur traders out,' she began chanting again. 'Fur traders out.' The words were echoed by the supporters on the pavement outside.

'Either you leave under your own steam,' warned Muswell, 'or you get carried out.'

'Fur traders out!'

'Right. Let's clear the place.'

June Ackland made an abrupt swoop, dislodging the woman from the rack and throwing her neatly into Muswell's arms. He twisted her once and forced her out through the shop door. Jimmy Carver stooped to take over the dark woman more securely. She took some lifting. It was only when June came to his aid that they could heave her out to join her friends. The man was less trouble. He went on repeating their slogan in a thin voice but offered no resistance when Muswell came back in and bundled him towards the door.

In the doorway Carver said: 'Right, ladies, calm it. Anyone who tries to get back in gets nicked for a breach of the peace.'

'We'll do it again no matter how many times you lock us up.'

PC Edwards appeared on the fringe of the group just as the thin young man made an unexpected dive for the interior of the shop. Carver grabbed him.

'Better late than never, Taffy,' said Muswell.

'I only just got the call.'

'Oh, yeah?' Muswell went to open the back door of the van. The protesters were chanting yet again, but making no move to escape. They seemed to relish the idea of martyrdom. 'No point calling you while you was in Larry's, was there?'

'I wasn't in Larry's.'

'Breaking the habit of a lifetime.'

'I bloody wasn't.' Edwards turned his back on the protesters, who were beginning to look curiously at the two policemen. 'Look, I've been pounding the beat with pig shit on my trousers for the last two bloody hours because of you. Have you been dropping me in it with Cryer?' When Muswell ignored this and began urging one of the women towards the van, Taffy demanded: '*Have* you? Here, I'm bloody talking to you.'

'I don't need to, mate. He already knows you're a lazy git.'

Two of the group changed their tactics and tried to escape across the road, but were blocked by a slow-moving dustcart. The dark woman eyed the door of the shop as if contemplating a last defiant invasion. June Ackland and the other three closed in, herding them into the van like sheep. Made a change from pigs, anyway.

'Fur traders out!'

The raucous song went on and on as Muswell drove off towards Sun Hill.

Six

The newest housing estate near the main railway line was still a local show-piece. Tower blocks had ceased to be the favoured building style of housing authorities: tall monuments to misery, petty crime and ultimate dereliction, they thrust up from the fringes of the neighbourhood, but had made no inroads into the recent development. Town planners often made conducted tours of the tidy streets here, with their blocks of smart yellow-brick flats on a human scale and their trim little lawns. It was not suburbia, but it was not a potential slum. Or not yet, anyway.

Galloway did not like to comment aloud that even the criminals around here were smoother and more skilled than on other parts of the manor. The two ladies were already upset enough, and in no mood for flippant observations.

He looked from one smartly painted, unscratched front door to the other. The doors, like the window curtains and the narrow flowerbeds, were all of a piece with Mrs Dixon and Mrs Lambert and their remarkably unruffled hair-dos. Nobody would smash down doors like those, or go at the residents with an iron bar. Everything here was neater and more subtle.

'These men delivering the wardrobe,' he recapped, 'knocked on your door at nine thirty. That's right, Mrs Dixon?'

Mrs Dixon plucked at the string of her pinafore, a spotless pattern of corn-flowers matching the blue of her eyes. 'Two very nice polite men,' she said, as if to excuse them for whatever they might have done later. 'Mrs Lambert hadn't said she'd bought a new wardrobe, but she does buy lots of things from Bensham's, and . . . well, they seemed so natural. And I always do let people in for Beryl when she's out. You know, meter readers, television repairers and so on.'

Yes, Galloway could see all that. It was all so pat, good-neighbourly, part of the atmosphere. A sensitive villain with a sensitive nose would have no difficulty in smelling out the possibilities.

'Do other people know you've got the key to Mrs Lambert's place?'

'Well, I suppose some people could. They see us going to and fro a lot.'

'Mm. So, you came along with the men delivering the wardrobe to Mrs Lambert's, and you let them in.'

'They could hardly leave it in the street.' Mrs Dixon's eyes began to sparkle with a hint of tears.

Her friend put out a consoling hand. 'Please, Marian, nobody's blaming you.' Where Mrs Dixon was fluffy and agitated, with a repetitive note of self-pity in her voice, Mrs Lambert was spare and decisive, the austere cut of her grey suit matching her pleasantly authoritative manner. 'Perhaps you had better come in and see for yourself, inspector.'

She led the way through an unnaturally tidy sitting room to a combined breakfast room and kitchen. There was not a smear on the work surfaces, no pan was out of place, you felt that nothing would ever dare let itself be disturbed. A faint aroma of perfumed sink cleaner hung in the air. In the bedroom things were almost as orderly, yet not quite. A few undergarments had been tossed on the bed: normal enough if the owner was in a hurry to get out, but not normal for anyone as meticulous as Mrs Lambert. And the dressing table was not merely tidy: it was bare.

'If only I'd looked round properly when I let them out!' wailed Mrs Dixon. 'But I had to keep out of their way when they were carrying it through – I mean, I do always stay somewhere inside when I let people in for Beryl, only I wasn't to *know* . . . '

Mrs Lambert contemplated the room with distaste. 'It's just knowing somebody's been in here.' She reached towards the door of a fitted cupboard.

Galloway said quickly: 'I'd be grateful if you didn't touch anything until our scenes of crime officer has had a chance to look things over.' He turned back to Mrs Dixon. 'Did they get you to sign a delivery note or anything like that?'

'Yes,' she said eagerly. 'So they did.'

'Now, the letterhead – did you notice any name printed on it?'

'I'm afraid I didn't.' Mrs Dixon was despondent again. 'They just said they were from Bensham's, and they had this wardrobe to deliver. They only took a few minutes to get it in. I had no reason to suspect anything.'

'And when did they come back?'

'Oh, not more than three-quarters of an hour later. And they were very apologetic and said they'd made a mistake, the wardrobe wasn't for Mrs Lambert after all.'

'So you let them back in, and they took the wardrobe away.'

'But they were only here for a few seconds. I don't see how they could have stolen anything. I mean, I was right outside the door, and they just got the wardrobe and moved it out.' She looked dismally at her friend. 'Oh, dear. Perhaps I didn't lock the door properly when I let them out.'

'I'm sure you did, Mrs Dixon,' said Galloway. 'I think there was a man in the wardrobe.'

Driving back to the station, he was filled with reluctant admiration for the perpetrators of this theft. It had to be the same lot who had hit the Clarks, which Mike Dashwood was checking out right now. So cocky it wasn't true: the wardrobe in both cases. Even reference to the same store, Bensham's. It was odds on that some bent bloke in their despatch department was supplying the right names and addresses.

Someone must have seen those jokers and their van. They had been lucky once, they couldn't be allowed to get away with it twice. As for them having a third go – no, that was not on. There had to be extensive local enquiries made this very day.

In his office he rang the chief superintendent's office. Henry Talbot answered and smoothly asked if he could take a message.

'Yes, you can. I want Mr Brownlow to authorize some overtime.'

'Does it come within the terms?'

It would have been good to send a message back along the line that would wrap itself round Talbot's officious neck and strangle him.

'It's for enquiries into a firm of villains whom we'll lose unless we get a decent lead today.'

'I think Mr Brownlow wanted to see you this afternoon in any case, sir. I'll speak to him as soon as he's free, and let you know.'

In the doorway Mike Dashwood suppressed a smirk. He knew the effect Talbot always had on the DI. Galloway flung at him: 'All right, Mike. *You'll* be the one on overtime when I've fixed it.'

The name of Henry Talbot cropped up at about the same time in the front office. Reg Hollis, sidling up to Bob Cryer, said: 'Sarge, I've heard a rumour that Henry Talbot's thinking of retiring.'

'That's right,' Cryer grunted. 'We're holding a piss-up for him in a telephone kiosk.'

'Yes, well. I mean, how d'you see me, I was sort of wondering, as the . . . er . . . next chief superintendent's clerk?'

Cryer looked him up and down. 'I can honestly say I can't think of anyone more suitable at Sun Hill.'

'Oh, thank you, sarge.'

'Petty,' contributed Viv Martella from the switchboard. 'Bloody-minded. Sneaky. Oh, it fits.'

'Hey, look here. You don't know a thing about it. It's not an easy job. You have to be able to handle responsibility, take the load off the chief super, advise him, know all the rules and regs. Right, sarge?'

'Right,' said Cryer. 'The only problem is, it's not a job for an able-bodied copper.'

Hollis hesitated only a fraction of a second. 'No, well, exactly. Er, I mean, I'm not one to complain, right, but I've been wondering about whether my back's been – well, permanently damaged.'

'Match your brain then, won't it?' said Martella.

A sound of singing seethed up again as the door to the cell block swung open. 'Four little pigs in blue, lads, four little pigs in blue . . . '

'Do we have to put up with that row, sarge?'

'Until the court tomorrow, we do. No way I could give that lot bail. Right, where's the charge sheet? Come on, Carver. You're the one in the thick of it.'

They went along the corridor, as the chanting took another turn. 'On and on and on and on . . . '

'In the charge room with 'em. Muswell around? And June's up in the canteen. Get her down.'

The protesters redoubled the volume of their anthem as PC Carver began to read out his statement. 'At ten o'clock this morning I and the other officers here present were called to Premier Furs, a clothing shop on Masson Row.'

'Big brave boys in blue,' said the dark woman, her eyes smouldering hotter with hatred by the moment.

'In the shop were three persons who the proprietor, Mr Logue, confirmed were unwanted on the premises. We therefore assisted him to eject them.'

As the chanting threatened to drown Carver's voice, Cryer suddenly blew his top. 'Shut up!'

There was a surprising hush.

Carver gulped and went on: 'The prisoners were arrested while attempting to continue occupying the shop, and forcibly to re-enter it when once removed. Such an attempt amounted, in my opinion, to threatening behaviour likely to cause a breach of the peace.'

'Breach of the peace?' said one of the men. 'There was no breach of the peace till you lot barged in.'

Cryer scraped a chair along the floor and sat down, facing the huddle of men and women who had been offered chairs but preferred sitting on the floor or propping themselves against the wall. 'You heard what the officer said. Anything sensible you want to add to that?'

'Yes. You're a lot of bastards.'

Cryer turned to the woman, the one with undoubted style and intelligence. At least they ought to be able to discuss things rationally. 'What about you?' he invited her.

'Only that we'll do it again and again until the murder stops.'

Cryer gave up. The intellectual idealists were always the trickiest to deal with. They were often more grief than bank robbers. He said wearily: 'In that case I'm afraid we're going to have to look after your property while you stay with us. Do you mind turning out your pockets, please?' He waited, saddened but unpetrified by the woman's stony stare. 'Could you turn out your pockets?'

The woman who was so assuredly the centrepiece of the whole demonstration said very slowly and deliberately: 'No, we could not.'

Cryer winced inside, but refused to show it. Maybe there were some coppers who fitted the stereotype and loved throwing their weight about and pushing their legal powers as far as they would go. He wasn't one of them. But now it had come to it. You knew when it got bad, and now it was really that bad. He said: 'Ackland, take this lady down to one of the cells and search her. Muswell, take that other one down – oh, and her as well – and get Martella to give a hand.'

Muswell beamed with delight. June Ackland's inviting lips thinned and were sucked in, repelled and far from inviting.

The cell allocated was cold and clinical, enough to deter anyone who fancied putting on a great big act. What point in an act when there was only a trained policewoman to observe it and cope with it? But the woman was tingling with a sort of icily feverish ecstasy. In some way – June could sense it, and hated the sensation – this meant more than the squatting on pavements and wailing slogans in a grotty little furrier's shop.

She slipped on the plastic gloves and said: 'Look, I'm sorry, but if you won't take things off then I have to do something about it.'

'Then you'll have to do it, won't you?' The woman watched the sheathed hands until June swung her round to face the wall. 'Do you enjoy degrading your fellow women?'

'All you have to do is agree that – '

'I don't agree with pigs. Or sows like you. Go ahead and enjoy yourself.'

June went ahead; and did not enjoy herself.

It was a blessed relief to be released at last and sent out on the beat again, in the fresh air on a crisp, sunny afternoon. Viv Martella was still in the station, methodically and miserably doing a body search on two of the other women. One of the men had begun demanding his solicitor, had emptied his pockets of some useless bits and pieces, and then gone pale and thrown up all over the floor. Out here the sun was shining, the occasional bird sang – on the edge of a cemetery or above one of the dusty little council gardens with their vandalized benches and the bells were ringing.

Bells were ringing. June found herself drawn across the street to the railings of a church. It made a pretty picture, a load of sentimental nonsense, up the path to the church door. The bride in white, giggling and bumping suggestively into the laughing groom beside her, had a cheap little face and a cheap layer of lipstick on her mouth; but she was happy, and the friends throwing rice and confetti and some other unmentionable fragments were laughing and enjoying it all. It was sweet and silly. June felt a tug of envy. Without making it too obvious, she peered through the railings as the photographer positioned himself and began waving orders, directing bride and groom and the bridesmaids and the parents this way and that.

They were all having a marvellous time.

And then she got a good look at the bridegroom's face as he leered and postured for the benefit of the photographer.

She moved her PR close to her mouth. 'Sierra Oscar. Sierra Oscar from six-four-three. Receiving? Over.'

'Go ahead, June.' It was Viv Martella, back at the switchboard and sounding cheerful about it.

'Is Taffy around?'

'I think so. Hang on. Taff!' The shout nearly scorched June Ackland's eardrums. 'What's up?' Viv was asking. 'You found the other pig?'

Pig? She had forgotten the dramas of the early morning. 'Better than that,' she said.

Taffy Edwards came through. 'Hello, June.'

'What was the name of that bloke you were supposed to be in court with last week? You know, the firearms charge, the one who didn't show?'

'Er . . . hold it. Ricky Vassalo. Yes, that was it. Another wasted morning, that was. Why?'

June said blithely: 'I think I've found him.'

It was a pity, really. A dirty shame when they were all so pleased with themselves, and the bridegroom was so greedy for what came after, and the bride showed every sign of being in the mood once she had got rid of all the white trimmings. But the hunter's instinct overruled every other feeling. June was watching the family and the guests shuffling and nudging all over the church path, somehow unwilling to leave the solid old building and solid gravestones for the inevitable boozing and dirty jokes, when the panda car slid to a stop behind her.

Taffy Edwards was at her elbow. 'Oh, that's him all right, girl. Good for you.'

The two of them walked up the path towards the milling throng. Ricky Vassalo had one arm around his bride, another was reaching out for a girl who kept pouting at him and wiping her eyes with drunken insincerity. His father kept coming back and punching him on the shoulder, while the best man rubbed closer to the bride.

'Everyone say "suspended sentence"!' cried Mr Vassalo senior. They all howled uncontrollably. Heaven knows what it would be like at the reception – or would have been, if Edwards and WPC Ackland had not marched up the path and made their intentions clear.

Ricky was the first to see them. His boisterous swagger crumpled around him like a rainproof overcoat which had proved to be non-rainproof.

'Oh, shit.'

'Ricky!' said his bride with a reproving pout.

What had been planned as a procession of cars to the wedding reception became a procession to the police station. Trisha refused to abandon her new husband and was helped into the van beside him, ducking her head to avoid any disturbance to her blonde curls, and still clutching her bouquet as a talisman. Her father and mother insisted on coming along as well, in the best man's car. It couldn't take more than five minutes, the father kept reassuring them: it was just a formality, just a matter of charging Ricky and then they could all buzz along to the reception. Relations and friends, not wanting to miss out on anything, decided Ricky needed their moral support and joined the convoy. Some of them, fortified by drinks before the ceremony and inspired by music in the church, began to sing as they drove along. The singing stopped only at the station, overwhelmed by competition from the cell block. The animal rights protesters were hoarse by now, but unwilling to give up.

'I'm glad we didn't book that lot for the party,' said Ricky perkily.

He looked less perky when he faced Sergeant Cryer in the charge room and was ordered to empty his pockets. A bunch of keys clattered on to the table, followed by a tie, some shreds of confetti, a betting slip and a packet of contraceptives – unopened. Resentfully he added his gold watch and a ring.

'Right,' said Cryer. 'Richard Stephen Vassalo, you are charged that on a warrant granted at Thames Magistrates Court you did fail to appear on the thirteenth of May 1986. Do you wish to say anything?'

'Look, Mr Cryer, you know me, we don't have to go through all this – '

'Edwards, take him along.'

They emerged to a babble of gossip and complaint. Only Mrs Vassalo tried to get round Cryer and pretend it was all a nonsense, they were all having fun really. 'Bit of wedding cake, Mr Cryer?' She held out a slice from the cake which somebody was busy tearing apart with his hands in a corner of the corridor.

'Yeah, go on,' boomed her husband. 'Eat the evidence!'

'Come on, now.' Cryer planted himself in the middle of the heaving throng. 'I'm afraid you'll have to leave.'

'Oh, no, not when – '

'Did anybody bring a bottle?'

'I've asked you politely,' shouted Cryer. 'Now push off.'

Trisha pushed aside the exploring hand of the best man. 'But what about my Ricky?'

'You'll get him back tomorrow, if the magistrate says so.'

'But it's . . . it's our wedding night.'

The best man leered. 'You leave that to me, love.'

As if provoked by the transfer of police attention to other matters, the protesters began to chant even more loudly. Ricky, being led away by Taffy Edwards, said: 'Who's making all that bleeding row, anyway?'

'Animal rights campaigners.'

'Oh, nutters.'

'They don't believe in shedding blood. You tell them you're a butcher,' Taffy gloated, 'and they'll tear you limb from limb.' He opened a cell door. 'Give us your belt.'

'And supposing nobody ate meat? I'd be out of a job for a kick-off, wouldn't I? Anyway, wouldn't be healthy without meat.' He nudged Taffy hard in the ribs. 'Good for the old you-know-what an' all. Three pints of Guinness, couple of pounds of steak, and – '

'I brought you a bit of cake, Ricky.' It was Trisha, her hair beginning to get a bit shaggy and collapse over her shoulders.

He took the slab and looked at it without any apparent appetite. 'Ta. I'll sleep on it. Remind me of you.' Looking past her along the corridor, he raised his voice. 'And tell that bleeding Dennis to keep his hands off.'

When the uninvited visitors had been urged off the premises, Tom Penny and Bob Cryer took stock, glad of the breathing space. Breaches of the peace in cells three, five and six, Ricky Vassalo in four . . .

'And the illegal immigrant in two,' said Cryer.

'Oh, I'd forgotten about him.'

'Till court tomorrow.'

'Well, let's hope we don't get too busy tonight, then. Prisoners all been fed?'

'Taffy should be starting on his rounds now.'

In confirmation of this they heard a shriek of rage. Edwards, only recently decontaminated from his pig episode, was plastered over with a sticky mess again. This time it had reached his shirt and the tops of his trousers courtesy of the dark woman, who had given her name as Cronin, refusing to admit to either Mrs or Miss. He had offered her a vegetarian course – beans on toast – which she had rejected on the grounds that she was a vegan, and would have nothing to do with toast that had butter on it. Meat, she told Taffy, was murder. And to show how she detested murder and violence, she abruptly tipped up the tray and watched the beans trickle down his front.

'I'd like to see how a bloody vegan would make out on a Welsh hillside!' stormed Edwards, on his way to the washroom for the second time in a few hours.

'All things bright and beautiful,' the protesters began to sing triumphantly, 'all creatures great and small . . . '

Bob Cryer had had enough, more than enough, for one day.

He glanced gratefully at the clock and was on his way out when Shaw, at the switchboard, called out to stop him.

'Sarge – chief super wants you upstairs.'

'What, now?'

'Afraid so.'

Cryer groaned. 'All right, tell him I'm on my way up.'

Galloway could hardly restrain himself from leaning just that extra inch forward and pounding Brownlow's desk. 'Look, sir, I'm not asking for the Crown Jewels. Just three men to do four hours apiece this evening, that's all.'

'Sorry, Roy. I don't consider the seriousness of the offence warrants overtime.'

'But I'm going to lose them, sir. They'll be playing the same game on another manor in a couple of days.'

'Well, that's another manor's problem then, isn't it?' Chief Superintendent Brownlow looked pleased with this piece of reasoning.

'What d'you mean, another manor's problem? We're all trying to catch villains, aren't we?'

There was a tap at the door, and Sergeant Cryer arrived. Brownlow looked relieved. He was always happier addressing what might be called a meeting rather than discussing things man to man.

'Right, gentlemen. Now you're both here, I do want to refer you to my memo on operational overtime and make sure you understand it fully.'

'We understand it all right, sir.' Galloway did not even give Cryer time to settle in his chair. 'But I do wonder whether *you* understand – '

'I want it thoroughly understood' – Brownlow overrode him – 'that unless it's to investigate a major robbery, a rape, GBH, or a murder, foreseen overtime will not be authorized. But the message from on high is that the new cost limits will not reduce police effectiveness. And at Sun Hill I intend to see that the message gets through.'

'With respect, sir,' said Cryer with deceptive mildness, 'the message could come down from on high that shit doesn't stink, but that wouldn't make it a fact.'

'What *is* a fact, sergeant, is that we're working to a fixed budget, and I expect your co-operation in ensuring that we do live within it.'

'Yes, well, without that co-operation, sir, this place would have ground to a halt weeks ago. Look at the time. I'm supposed to be on overtime now.'

'I appreciate all that, Bob,' said Brownlow placatingly.

'Yeah, but do *they* appreciate it? We get all this bumf coming down the line – is there any bumf going up? I mean, do they know how pushed we really are here? Just lately it's all I can do to put one man out on foot patrol on the entire ground. The entire ground!'

Galloway took it up. 'We're being asked to do this job with both hands tied behind our backs. I've had two enquiries scuppered in the past twenty-four hours.'

'Please, Roy, don't give me all that crap.'

'It is not crap, sir,' said Galloway furiously. 'We have to face the fact that

203

just because we've reduced our overtime, that doesn't mean the villains are going to reduce theirs.'

'You're being so negative, man. If there's a cheaper, more effective way of doing our job we should find it. The more we streamline, the more money we save – '

'What are we, policemen or bloody accountants?'

'The more we save,' Brownlow persisted, 'the leaner and fitter the Force becomes. And the more resources we'll have in the future to give the public the sort of service they want. We have to look to the future, Roy. Have to be imaginative.'

'So what you're saying is that we're deliberately not solving crime now in order to solve it in the year 2000!'

'Roy, you really can be very obtuse.'

'But that is what you're saying, isn't it, sir?'

'No, it's not what I'm saying at all.' The chief super was getting very rattled.

'All right, then.' Galloway had the bit between his teeth. 'Let's take this Mrs Lambert case, the wardrobe business. She's not been banged on the head, she's not been raped. The things that have been nicked are all insured. So we just don't bother, right?'

'Nobody's saying that.'

'But you've just stopped me from pursuing enquiries.'

With a heavy show of long-suffering patience Brownlow said: 'It is simply that within the overall equation, certain enquiries are seen to be more cost-effective than others. The new guidelines merely take that into account.'

'So she goes to the bottom of the pile and she stays there. We're deliberately not solving a crime in order to save a few quid.'

'We are being realistic.'

'Then I think someone ought to tell Mrs Lambert that, and all the other poor sods who think the police are here to help them.'

'We are simply being asked to look at our work and sort out our priorities. To be pragmatic, right?'

'Pragmatic?' Galloway burst out. 'What's that supposed to mean?'

'Leave it, Roy,' said Cryer quietly.

Brownlow nodded. 'Right, Roy?'

Galloway fought down his contempt. 'Right, sir.'

'Good. Thank you. Bob . . . ?'

'Right, sir.'

'Right.' Brownlow stood up dismissively. 'Thank you very much, gentlemen.'

Galloway stormed down the stairs, not waiting for as much as a curse with Bob Cryer. At the foot of the flight Henry Talbot stood to one side, waiting to go up.

'How many prats in "pragmatic", Henry?'

'What?'

'Don't bother.' Galloway stamped past. 'I'll look it up myself.' He went on a few paces then, his temper almost spent, waited for Cryer to catch him up. 'What about murder?' he said in a seething undertone. 'What's the cost limits on that going to be, eh? Must have worked it out by now. Five grand . . . ten? What's the price of a life in this new brilliant cost-effective police force, eh?'

Bob Cryer found it wiser not to attempt an answer.

Seven

This was the worst. Deliberate violence was bad but it tended to happen on a small, calculated scale. Random death and injury like this was somehow more sickening. You picked your way through the carnage and wanted to throw up, but it was your job to put on a brave face. Some of the other faces were crumpled in shock. Others were pulped into what you could hardly call faces any more.

The driver of a Porsche belting along the road through the estate had been having a burn-up with a motorcycle. 'You'd have thought he was on the home straight at Brand's Hatch,' said a witness. Too late he had found that he had to pull out sharply to overtake a coach. The coach, full of residents from an old folks' home on a day's outing to Southend, had stopped to let a lorry out of a side turning. The Porsche failed to stop. Now the coach was on its side, the lorry was slanted across the splintered pavement in a tangled embrace with the Porsche; and a red Cortina was crushed against the overturned coach.

Sergeant Cryer and two of his men were tenderly easing dazed old men and women out through a shattered window and over the body of the coach, supporting them as they slid to the ground. There were others who would never move again.

'It's a bloody battlefield.'

Two ambulances homed in on the disaster. A doctor hurried into the heart of it. Sirens proclaimed the approach of the fire brigade. Lifting gear and cutting gear were organized with impersonal skill. It was better to treat it as a skilful exercise than to feel any personal involvement with some of the things that were staining the highway.

A couple of inquisitive boys scuttled across the road for a better look, kicking slivers of broken glass and a torn scarf out of the way.

'Get out of here!' Yorkie Smith showed every sign of murdering them if they came within range. Then he turned his attention back to the girl in the Cortina.

Blood was smeared down the inside of the driver's door, and the man's neck was twisted at an unnatural angle. WPC Ackland steadied the girl's head, not letting her look to either side, as the firemen began to cut their way through the buckled doorframe and the weight of bonnet and dashboard which had pushed inwards and down across her knees. She was a nice girl with a nice brave smile, trying not to wince or weep. She had been a pretty girl. It would be a long time before she was pretty again. One spinning wheel of the overturned coach must have raced briefly against the windscreen, mashing fragments of it into her face.

'Keep it coming there. Keep winching. Come on.' The fire chief waved a slow rhythm, and the Porsche was lifted gratingly out of the tangle.

The man working away at the Cortina looked in at the girl. 'Just keep nice and still.' June Ackland, half sprawled across the back seat, kept her hands gently but firmly in place. The doctor edged in beside her. They exchanged glances. She could see from his expression what the score was. Here and now the damage to neck and spine could not be accurately assessed, but the betting wasn't good; and glancing down at an angle, she wondered whose job it would be to tell the girl that she was unlikely to be able to use her left leg ever again.

'What's the time, please?' the girl whispered.

'Just after nine.'

She tried to look sideways at her companion in the driving seat, but June did not slacken her grip.

'I always have a cup of tea on his desk when he comes in for nine.'

'Who's that – your boss?'

The girl tried to nod, caught her breath, and went rigid. Then she managed: 'Lester, is *he* all right?'

'He's fine.' June wondered at the unwavering certainty in her own voice. 'Just a few cuts and bruises,' she lied. 'Now, do try and keep still. You're nearly out now.'

The driver's door was freed. He was lifted out, while June made sure that the girl did not turn her head to look.

Lester brought up the total of dead to six. So far.

Some of the older people, fussing more over handbags and holdalls than the shock they had suffered, were walking back the few hundred yards to their home. There was bound to be a cup of tea there. Some of them had gone through the Blitz, and there had always, in the end, been a cup of tea somewhere.

Cryer made a quick recce of the immediate neighbourhood. The injured were being driven away in the ambulances. A school round the comer would have to be used as a temporary mortuary.

Chief Superintendent Brownlow arrived on the scene and at once had to make objections. 'A school, Bob? Surely that's not on?'

'It's half term, there's no kids about.'

'I still don't think it's a good idea.'

Of course you could expect the chief super to cover his flanks in case of later complaints. Cryer said doggedly: 'It's the only place available.'

They watched as another corpse covered by a blanket was carried past. It shut Brownlow up for a bleak moment. But then he was summoned to the school itself, to brave the displeasure of the deputy headmistress. She made it clear that in her view it was against official policy to allow school premises to be used in this way. Once such a precedent had been set, there was no telling where it might lead. Her attitude was so hostile that the chief super instinctively aligned himself with Sergeant Cryer and decided that the school had to be commandeered. He did not put it as bluntly as that – his public relations bit was, Cryer had to admit, very smooth and practised – but it was clear that he was going to get his way. So long, she implied, as they did not leave any unpleasant souvenirs behind or expect any of the school staff to come in and help.

'It's only a temporary measure,' Brownlow assured her, oozing charm and respect. 'Only until we can find suitable mortuary space.'

'Very well.' But she was still unwilling to back away entirely. 'If I should want to get in touch with you . . . ?'

'I shall be here. I intend to remain on the premises and conduct the identification myself.'

'At least the headmaster will be relieved to hear that.'

When she had gone, Brownlow turned to Cryer. 'What's the situation on the driver of that Porsche? Is he going to be fit to make a statement, d'you suppose?'

'Came out of it better than a lot of them,' said Cryer grimly. 'Broken arm and collarbone, I'd say. Maybe a few other damages they'll find in hospital.'

'Was he able to talk?'

'Couldn't stop him. Quite hysterical he was. Name's Proctor. Kept saying he couldn't make sense of it, he's only had the car about four weeks and the brakes failed.'

'On a motor like that?'

'Doesn't sound too likely,' Cryer conceded.

He went back to the scene of carnage. The firemen were making it a lot tidier. The coach had been humped over on to its wheels again, and the lorry was parked almost conventionally at the kerb, though the shape of its cab was now far from conventional. The Porsche was set well apart, like a delinquent ashamed to mix with his victims. Sergeant Johnson, stooping in his bright yellow coat over the vehicle, straightened up as Cryer joined him.

'Driver wasn't kidding,' he said starkly.

'Eh? You don't mean – '

'Brakes have gone all right.'

'On a motor like this?' Cryer echoed the chief super's scepticism.

'Someone's been messing about with it. And it's not only the brakes. If I were you I'd get it on a low loader. Get it down the nick and call in the stolen car squad.'

'A ringer?'

'I reckon so. Registration plate obviously been changed recently. Nuts, bolts, screws, it's all new. Tell you what, Bob, I'll arrange for a C16 investigation if you like.'

'I'll buy that. And could you let Roy Galloway know as well? Our DI, you know. He hates being left out of anything like this.'

'Sarge,' Carver was calling, 'they're ready to bring her out.'

'Who?'

Then he saw the firemen lifting the final pieces away, and June Ackland beginning to slide the girl gently out of the Cortina. Another casualty to be added to the long dossier there was going to have to be on this affair.

'Someone take her head for me, please,' Ackland was pleading.

Sergeant Johnson's heavy frame humped across to the door. He was big, competent, and surprisingly tender. Jimmy Carver shuffled round beside him, and between them they lifted the girl towards the ambulance men waiting with a stretcher. She had gone ashen white by the time they laid her carefully down, all making soothing noises, willing her not to know what they already knew just by looking at her.

She forced words painfully out. 'How's Lester? Can I see him soon?'

'Let's get you sorted out first, shall we?' Cryer smiled down at her. When she had been carried away, he turned to Smith and Carver. 'Yorkie, I want you to go to the hospital and start taking statements from anyone who hasn't been seen yet. Jimmy, see if she's left anything in the Cortina, then get it carted away. And June, you come back to the nick with me.' He paused, looking long and hard at Smith. 'According to his little collection of credit cards and his driving licence, the bloke in the Cortina was a Lester Martin Simpson. When Mrs Simpson's been settled into the hospital and she's as comfy as she's likely to be, you know what you're going to have to tell her, don't you?'

'Me, sarge?'

'Yes, you, I'm afraid.'

'You mean tell her her husband's been killed?'

'Well, it's all part of the job.'

'But sarge, do I always have to be the one who gets lumbered? Remember Mrs Lubaczewska? And there was – '

'You'll be all right.'

Yorkie Smith departed, looking far from all right.

There were others to be told the same story. Muswell and Viv Martella went reluctantly on their rounds. Bloody pile-ups like the one this morning were bad enough. The aftermath was almost worse.

How do you ring a doorbell and tell a mother that her son has just been killed in a road accident?

What you do, as Martella wincingly discovered, is go in and talk too loudly, talk a load of old fanny about something else, anything else. And then you can't postpone it any longer, and it comes out. And then? Then the woman had acted as if it were a daily occurrence. She carried on polishing the table. When at last it hit her, she just sat down, still holding the cloth, and cried; and then asked Martella if she would like a cup of tea.

Muswell tried to brazen it out. What you did was come straight out with it, wallop, and make an end of it. That, at any rate, was what he said before he went gingerly into the hairdressing salon behind the post office and asked for Mrs Lockett. Her mother had been one of the victims from the old folks' home. It was simply a matter of breaking the news and leaving her to it.

Face to face with Mrs Lockett, he cleared his throat twice. 'Um . . . er . . . could I have a word with you?'

'Yes?' The woman's hair was a neatly cropped advertisement for her profession.

'In private.'

They went through a bead curtain to a little cubicle at the end of the salon.

'What's happened?' When Muswell shifted his weight from one foot to another and still could not get round to the inevitable words, Mrs Lockett said: 'There's been an accident?'

'I'm afraid so. It's your mother.'

'She's all right?'

'She's . . . er . . . in hospital.'

Mrs Lockett was beginning to shrug off her lightweight pink coat.

'How serious is it?'

'I, er, I think . . . ' Muswell very nearly choked, then blurted it out: 'Mrs Lockett, she's not at the hospital. She's dead.'

At the hospital itself, there was more bad news to be broken. Propped up in bed, with his left arm in a sling and a bandage swathing his left ear and half his forehead, Julian Proctor said aggrievedly: 'But I tell you, I only bought it a month ago.' He was a sallow man in young middle age, with the slack mouth of a spoiled child: not as young as he had been, but still anxious to present an active, macho image. If something had gone wrong, it had to be someone else's fault.

'Nevertheless,' said Ted Roach with a sort of savage relish, 'it's a ringer. Made up out of three vehicles, our expert Rigby thinks.'

'It's impossible.'

The young hospital technician in attendance at the other side of the bed, fitting up some apparatus whose purpose baffled even the observant Roach, looked as though he, too, was taking some warped satisfaction out of the saga. 'Had a mate bought a ringer once,' he contributed. 'Had no idea, went on running about in it for years.'

Roach ignored him and began spelling out the whole sad story to the Porsche's owner. Amongst other things, the letter on the vehicle identification denoting the year of the model did not match up to the year the licence plates were issued. Rigby had established not only that it had been put together out of three separate vehicles but that the putting together had been a skimped job. In normal circumstances it might have lasted a reasonable time. But it was amazing the things that came to light after a traffic accident. The stolen car boys were checking right now with the manufacturers, and from their own records. But in a long-running model like this, most of the parts were interchangeable. It was not going to be easy. Maybe it could be made a bit easier if Mr Proctor could produce documents – receipts, a guarantee. Hadn't the seller provided him with some sort of documentation on a pricey vehicle like that?

Proctor groped awkwardly for the bedside phone and rang his wife. He nodded at Roach, eager to please. 'She's gone to find it, sergeant. I'm certain Mr Regan's number and the address are on it.'

'Not too reliable, that,' said the technician happily. 'Not worth the paper it's written on. I once had a mate – '

'Do you mind?' snarled Roach.

'I'm only trying to be helpful, that's all.'

'Just get on with what you're supposed to be doing, and let me get on with *my* job.' Roach leaned on the bed. 'How did you pay this Regan – by cash or cheque?'

'For the Porsche? Well, it was ten thousand pounds by cheque, of course.'

'How did you get involved with Regan in the first place?'

'It was an ad in the evening paper.'

'Ten thousand quid? For something out of an evening newspaper? You must be out of your brain.'

'Quick sale,' suggested the young man in the white coat. 'Owner going abroad. That's what they usually say.'

'It was a telephone number I had to ring between seven and eight. Well, I rang, and Mr Regan brought the car round to the house.' A voice crackled in Proctor's ear, and he said into the phone: 'Yes, hold it a minute.' He looked over the receiver at Roach, who fished a notebook from his pocket and hastily flipped to a blank page. '47 Lower Poole Street.'

Roach repeated the address, wrote it down, and got to his feet.

'How was I to know it was bent?' said Proctor, letting indignation take over again.

'I'll tell you one thing, sir. Whether it was bent or not, the evidence we've got on the way you were driving is going to leave you with a lot to answer for.'

That was not all that the hospital enquiries divulged that morning. Bob Cryer could well believe everything that Rigby had discovered and Roach was verifying. But he was taken unawares by Yorkie Smith's call from the hospital foyer.

'Mrs Simpson,' said Yorkie, 'isn't Mrs Simpson.'

'I don't get you. Come again.'

'The Cortina driver who got killed. Name of Simpson, you said. And so does the girl. But *her* name's Crisp. His girlfriend, sarge. And Mrs Simpson knows nothing about it.'

'You're kidding.'

'No. He picks her up on his way to work every morning. They've been having an affair for about eighteen months now. The only man who ever meant anything in her life, she says. And his wife mustn't know.'

'Oh, you do complicate things, Yorkie. Honestly you do.'

'Sarge, it's not my fault. And sarge, I'm not sure I know how to handle this one.'

And that makes two of us, thought Cryer morosely.

Eight

Lower Poole Street was not in one of the more salubrious corners of the manor, such as they were. Ted Roach had half expected to find a sleazy car repair bay there, or even a scrap-yard. He was not prepared for the address to lead him through a narrow doorway with a sign identifying a nightclub, nor for the framed photographs within – a selection of girls not so much undressed as suggesting what was available when the flimsy dresses were off. After an appreciative glance at one especially lithe contortionist, he pushed open the inner door.

A man with a smart grey tint down the middle of his hair, and grey eyes that were smart in a much greedier way, was sitting at a table riffling through bills and what looked like a healthy cluster of bank-notes.

His welcome did not say much for the hospitality rating of his club.

'Who the hell are you? A rep?'

Roach studied the room, marvelling. 'We live and learn, don't we?'

'Listen, mister. I don't know who you are. And I don't see reps until late afternoon.'

'Oh, you'll see this one.' Roach flicked out his warrant card. 'I represent the Metropolitan Police.'

The man was transformed. He got to his feet and pulled out another chair, summoning up a broad smile. 'You should have said. Why didn't you say?'

'I just did. Roach – Sergeant Roach.'

'Sit down. You care for a coffee?'

'Sure.' As the man turned and bellowed a quite unidentifiable name into the shadows at the far end of the room, Roach said: 'I didn't catch your name.'

'Harold.' The man looked on the verge of bending over Roach and patting his hand. 'Harold Kaye. Now, what do you think of the place? I could see you were impressed, the moment you came in.'

'Very nice. Who's Mr Regan?'

'Do you take sugar? I'd better fix some if you do. I daren't touch it myself. I've got such a weight problem you wouldn't believe it.'

'Regan!'

Harold Kaye waited until a girl had brought a tray with two coffee cups and a silver sugar bowl, and when she had slouched away he said amiably: 'Oh, Regan. Yes, he took one of the short-let offices above the club.'

'Complete with resident bird?'

'Certainly not. Nothing of that kind round here. No, very nice accommodation, and I'm choosy about who I let in. Really nice guy, he was. Left about a fortnight ago. He only had it a month. I've got some Yorkshire geezer in there now. I can't understand a word he says.'

'Regan,' said Roach again. 'What business was he in?'

'Imports and exports.'

'Like what?'

'Sports cars.' Kaye said it lightly enough, then got a look at Roach's face. The warning bells began to ring. 'Oh, come on, no. The guy was straight.'

'He was?'

'Look, you haven't come here to . . . oh, no. Not him. I mean, would I buy a motor off a geezer if it wasn't kosher? I mean, would I?'

'Did you?' asked Roach commiseratingly.

'Look, just you come and have a look.'

They went out of the back door into a yard enclosed by a mixed lot of fencing – some wooden palings, a length of corrugated iron, and a further stretch of barbed wire. The background did not do justice to the sleek, low-slung black body of the Ferrari parked close to the wall of the building.

'Ain't she the business?' Kaye was ecstatic. 'Or ain't she the business?'

'A crumpet puller, all right.'

Kaye bent over his treasure. A reflection of the gold chain round his neck gleamed in the bonnet. 'This is some motor, I can tell you.'

'Are you a gambling man, Mr Kaye?'

'Harold, please. And am I a gambling man? You are looking at the biggest punter of all time. Why?'

'I bet you,' said Roach, 'that somewhere out there in the great wide world there's a Ferrari the same model, the same colour, same licence plates. The problem is, who's got the straight one?'

Dismayed, Kaye touched the bonnet. Just the feel of it gave him confidence. 'A ringer? It can't be.'

'And the plates from this are from a write-off.'

'You can't be sure of that, not just off the top of your head.'

'No. But as a betting man, Mr Kaye, what odds are you offering?'

Kaye's hand fell to his side. 'Mr Regan wouldn't do that to me.'

'Let's wheel it in,' Roach suggested, 'and let Rigby put your mind at rest.'

If any mind was put at rest by Rigby, it was not Harold Kaye's. There was little doubt that the Ferrari was yet another of Mr Regan's interesting constructions. And in its present condition, there was no way the police were going to let it out on the road again. Kaye's plea that he should be allowed to continue using it until they really needed it was brushed aside. Galloway, appearing on the scene, made the facetious suggestion that Kaye could apply in court for a custody hearing, then hastily withdrew it when he saw that the benighted man was halfway to taking it seriously.

And so to the common factor in the case: Regan.

Nobody knew Regan's whereabouts, but within a very short time it became evident that a fair number of people would very much like to know. He had not merely sold a number of clients some very dicey merchandise: he had left a number of unpaid bills around – all very straightforward in the sense that the bills were unpaid in his own name and not under some alias – and had also done his bank as well, to the tune of a ten grand overdraft.

Galloway enjoyed this item of news. Now he knew that they would get help. Banks were very reluctant to be taken for a ride, especially when the ride cost them ten thousand pounds. Of course they would be even more reluctant to admit that the ride had been taken, even when the enquirer was a detective inspector. But there were ways of overcoming their diffidence. Some people on Roy Galloway's list owed him a favour. They were not exactly employed by the bank, but a few – and Dave Collins was one of the first of the few – did security work after retiring early from the Force, and knew where to delve, where to ask the right questions and quote the right numbers.

Not that the numbers were all that spotlessly right as far as the bank was concerned. In two months a hundred and fifty grand had gone through Regan's account, not to mention the ten grand overdraft. The security officer, Dave Collins, recited it all to a spellbound Galloway and Roach in the pub round the corner: an ex-DS himself, he had become so security-conscious that he would not let them meet him on his own premises or anywhere he might be recognized. Roy Galloway got a whiff of a feeling that certain heads were in jeopardy over the name of that man Regan.

'What about Regan's references when he opened his account? Did you check them?'

'Somebody else's job at the time,' said Collins thankfully.

'They'll be as moody as the name Regan. I can tell you that for nothing.'

'Yes, well, before I start divulging any further confidential information, what's your interest? Nothing for nothing, if you know what I mean.'

A stripper began to perform on a platform in the corner of the bar. Roach's eyes widened. He was not likely to contribute much to the discussion in the next few minutes.

'Ringers,' said Galloway.

'Motors?'

'Porsches, Ferraris, that kind of gear. Nothing cheap and nasty.'

'Then he's using other names besides Regan,' said Dave Collins. 'You can only play that kind of game for a short time before you get tumbled.' He hesitated for a moment, then took out a slip of paper, wrote an address on it, and pushed it across the table.

Galloway rescued it from a puddle of beer, and read the address: H. Wilshire, Turbery Crescent. He raised an enquiring eyebrow.

'Regan wrote out a cheque to that man for two hundred pounds,' said Collins. 'It's the only cheque he wrote out to anyone other than for cash.'

'You know anything about this Mr Wilshire?'

'Nothing. I should think he was trying to avoid paying VAT. The cheque went through somebody's else's account. Conveniently he put his address on the back.'

Galloway said: 'Ted?'

'I'll have a gin and tonic, thanks, guv.' Roach did not take his eyes off the stripper's moving parts.

'You won't. You'll get round to this Mr Wilshire, right now.' A piece of pink chiffon curled in the air and drifted a few inches from Ted Roach's nose. Reluctantly he pretended not to notice, and turned to take the scrap of paper. Even more reluctantly he left the premises, inhaling one last whiff of pungent perfume and the equally pungent fumes of beer and cigarette smoke as he went.

There was a quite different smell on the premises of H. W. Wilshire, Joiner and Furniture Restorer. It was the clean tang of newly sawn wood. Trimmed lengths of planking were stacked against one wall, and on the other side of a partition there was the intermittent shriek of a saw spraying out a powder of sawdust to add to the atmosphere.

Mr Wilshire was a stooped little man, getting on in years but with all his wits about him. Wiping his hands on his leather apron as if to brush away remnants of one job before even beginning to discuss another, he had no difficulty in remembering Regan.

'He come in the door, same as you. Said he wanted a couple of sturdy wooden crates. Cash job.'

'Didn't say what he wanted them for, by any chance?'

'Second-hand motor spares to send abroad. Well, it's not my sort of work really, you know.' Wilshire looked around his workshop with a touch of hauteur. 'Making up bloody big crates. There's no skill in it, you see. Still, we've got to earn a living.'

'How big?'

'The crates?'

'Yes.'

'They were big. Gave me some measurements. I must have them somewhere in here. But big, anyway. Motor spares? Enough to build a whole motor, I'd say.'

'What about the cheque?'

'Well, he wanted to pay cash, but I charged him well over the odds. Took his breath away for the minute.' Wilshire dipped into his pocket for a pair of half-glasses, set them on his nose, and peered archly over them at Roach. He had the sceptical, calculating look of a cunning yet honest man. 'He didn't have enough readies on him, and I wasn't going to let him have the crates until I got paid. So we settled for half and half – half cash, half cheque. He wasn't too pleased about it.'

'I bet he wasn't,' said Roach. 'Listen, you didn't by any chance have to deliver them somewhere, did you?'

'No, he took them away on the back of a lorry.' Quite deliberately Wilshire kept the detective waiting, then added: 'Gary Sidgwick, Car Breakers.'

Roach almost laughed out loud. 'You sure?'

'Gary Sidgwick, Car Breakers. That was the name on the side of the lorry. I took special note of that. After all, supposing the cheque had bounced?'

Roach nodded appreciatively.

Even DI Galloway was capable of an appreciative nod when the news was brought back to him. A bit more research, a careful recce around the car-breaking site, and then there could be an excuse to spin the place. Galloway and Roach felt that excuses would not be hard to find.

Bob Cryer and June Ackland sat in the car in the shadow of a railway arch. Occasionally the radio crackled into life, as Hollis worked diligently at shifting responsibility for anything that went wrong in the station during the absence of so many officers. The cartographic expert had arrived to complete work on the plan of the accident area. Where should he be put? Cryer offered only the most restrained suggestions. And they were still trying to locate Mrs Simpson, the widow who still didn't know she was a widow: messages had been left everywhere, but of course they would keep on trying.

Then Galloway came on the air.

'Right, all units. Mike Dashwood and Jim Ellis are in place. All suspects present and correct. So let's go in!'

The viaduct bisecting the breaker's yard was one of many abandoned routes between the dock wharves and sidings which had long ago ceased to handle any traffic. Dashwood and Ellis were patrolling it from behind its low parapets, directly above a landscape of crushed cars and discarded tyres. Some of the viaduct arches gave access from one side of the property to the other; some had been filled in to make workshops and storerooms. Entrance to the whole straggling complex was between two corrugated iron palisades, jagged at the top not from design but from the ravages of rust. Galloway and Roach went in first, bumping over a sunken relic of railway line. Cryer kept close behind and stopped a few inches from the CID car. He made a gesture for June Ackland to stay in the vehicle while he followed Galloway and Roach through an opening into the semi-darkness of what might flatter itself as being the administrative area. Some empty packing cases were lined up against one curving wall. On top of one was a collapsed domino effect of box files, none of them looking very convincing or businesslike. Damp dripped from the roof. At the far end was a wooden cabin stacked up on old timbers, with a flight of rickety steps up to it. The inside of its impractical window was grimed with cigarette smoke, blurring the light from the office within.

Galloway and Roach went up the steps. Bob Cryer stood well back, ready for anyone who made a dash for the yard.

Nobody made a dash. As Galloway pushed the office door open, Cryer heard a shout from inside. 'What's all this about? I'm the owner of this place, you don't just bust in here and – '

'Show Mr Sidgwick the warrant,' Galloway said to Roach. 'Then spin the place.'

Then Cryer heard his gasp, and a curse and a rush of words abruptly cut off. A man appeared at the top of the steps, spraying a handful of playing cards over the rail, with Galloway right behind, looking good and ready to push him down the whole flight.

He reached the bottom under his own steam. The light was bad, but not bad enough to disguise those heavy jowls and thick eyebrows. Bob Cryer stared in disbelief. This face had never been one of his favourites. With the hatchet jaw of a custom-built bruiser and an aggressive manner to match, this slob looked a natural for any GBH charge you might care to throw at him – the heaviest of some villain's heavy mob. In fact he was Detective Sergeant Burnside, mercifully from another manor, but in the habit of getting his wires crossed with Sun Hill.

'Come over here, you.' Galloway was at the foot of the steps as well, grabbing

Burnside's arm and twisting him round against a baulk of timber. 'You bent bastard, what sort of payoff is it this time?'

Burnside tried to turn to face him. Galloway held him firm, threatening to push his face into the timber. 'Oh, guv'nor, you know what you've just done, don't you?'

Bob Cryer waved Muswell, standing in the entrance, to come and keep an eye on the other two men emerging warily from the office. At the same time Galloway waved the whole lot of them away, out of earshot. Cryer hustled Muswell and the two men against the far wall, but sauntered back and joined Ted Roach on the fringe of the argument. He was not going to miss this bit, whatever it might be.

Galloway dragged in a rage at Burnside's jacket. As it opened, a shirt button snapped. Inside, taped to the DS's stomach, was a microphone.

'What the – '

'That's what I'm telling you,' said Burnside. 'You've just fouled it up. You've just busted in on my job.'

'On my manor?'

'Guv'nor, there's a big ringing firm operating out of this yard. Stolen motors to the Continent. I've been on to it for months, and I was all set if you hadn't come – '

'On to it? Doing what?'

'Posing as a buyer. Getting myself well in.'

'Digging yourself well in, more like. Boozing with the boys, playing cards, waiting for whatever rakeoff – '

'Posing as a buyer,' Burnside repeated. 'As good as sewn up right this very day. Everything arranged to have a motor crated up and shipped out to my villa in Marbella.'

Galloway stared in loathing. Cryer felt much the same. But detestable as Burnside always had been, right now there was the galling probability that he was telling as much of the truth as he was capable of.

'Who are you dealing with?'

'A fellow calling himself Regan.'

Now they knew it had to be true.

'Only his name's most likely not Regan,' offered Ted Roach.

Obviously this was not news to Burnside. 'It's old man Galley's son, Mark.'

'Regan . . . Mark Galley . . . the rally driver?'

'That's how he's been financing his rallying.'

'Where is he?' demanded Galloway.

'Somewhere round the other side of those arches, putting the finishing touches on my motor. That is,' said Burnside malevolently, 'if you lot haven't frightened him off with all this commotion.'

'Bob! Ted! come on – come with me. At the double.'

As they began to run, Galloway shot a glance upwards and waved

Dashwood to keep an eye on the space below the far side of the viaduct. Then he led the way through one of the arches and paused by a half-open door. From inside came the flash and flare of a welding torch.

Galloway nodded to Roach, who kicked the door fully open.

'Right, Mr Regan. Or Galley. Or whatever. We're the – '

There were three of them. One of them had a shock of almost flaxen hair, ruffled in a style much doted on by admirers of the rally driving ace and much flaunted on television to the accompaniment of spurting champagne. Another, in a loose red jacket, was bending over the panel of a car with the welding torch in his hand.

As they burst in he straightened up. All at once the flame was licking out at Galloway, blistering his cheeks, forcing him back against the door jamb. He was trapped, and the flame kept coming on.

Ted Roach threw himself forward. The scorching tongue swept round wildly for a moment, then the man threw it full at Roach and threw himself clean through the doorway. As Galloway brushed an arm across his face and stumbled away from the side of the door, the man who called himself Regan ducked and sprinted in the opposite direction from his murderous torch-bearer. Ted Roach chose to set off after the latter. Bob Cryer was knocked aside by the other, who cannoned into Abe Lyttleton and then sent June Ackland flying as she leapt out of the car. She hit the edge of a half-demolished wall, and went down.

Bob Cryer stooped over her. 'You all right, June?'

'I'll be all right.' She tried groggily to push herself up off the ground.

'Stay where you are. Lie still for a minute.'

'I'm all right,' she mumbled. 'I'll be fine.'

'Do as you're told. Lie still for a minute.'

Ted Roach pounded over rubble and a tangle of netting, hearing his quarry beginning to pant and whine. Muswell came in at an angle. Passing both of them, Abe Lyttleton pounced, missed, and scrambled up again as Muswell closed in. The man stared wildly around, snatched up a rusty spanner, and made a crazy swing with it. Muswell ducked, hit him hard, and caught the spanner as it fell. He kicked the man once, twice, bashed his head down to the ground and lifted the spanner.

'Pete, that's enough!' Abe Lyttleton hauled him bodily aside. 'Enough, man!'

They looked around for anyone else. Another man had been splayed against a wire-netting fence by Yorkie Smith. Further away, Regan was shinning up a mountain of scrap metal and tyres to the rim of the viaduct. As he swung his legs over the parapet there was a jubilant whoop from Mike Dashwood. He and Ellis converged on Regan as Galloway hauled himself up in pursuit. Jimmy Carver was on his way to join them.

Backing warily away from Dashwood and making a swift calculation of the threat from behind, Regan came to an abrupt halt.

Yawning at his feet was a wide gap in the metalling of the viaduct. It was the only way out now. But it was a long drop.

'Go on, then,' Galloway taunted. 'Go ahead and kill yourself.'

'Yeah?'

Regan looked at them moving purposefully towards him; looked down; and jumped.

He landed on a heap of more old tyres, dumped in here out of the way. Bouncing and clawing his way over the hummock and out through the opening of the arch, he found himself beside one of the fitters' cars. As the fitter, already bewildered by the shouting and dashing about in which he had taken no part, yelled a protest, Regan slid in behind the wheel. The car spluttered, revved, and roared forward. Muswell jumped to one side just in time, and began to run after it, vainly swinging the spanner he was still clutching. Yorkie Smith tried to stand his ground, but Regan had no intention of swerving to avoid him. Yorkie left it until the last possible second, then nipped smartly back, grabbed a small trolley, and tossed it in a soaring arc. It went through the windscreen, spraying glass like a sparkling fountain.

The car stayed on course for a few feet, then went mad. It swerved at an impossible angle towards the wall, struck, tried to spin right round, and at last turned over on its side and slid along the ground in a shower of grit and more shards of glass.

'Get him out!' Muswell stooped by the driver's door and got his arm round Regan's shoulders, heaving him out.

Regan let out a yelp of agony. He tried to get up, then let himself curl up on the ground.

Ted Roach was on his knees beside him. 'Where's it hurt?'

'My leg. Christ, my leg.'

'Your leg, eh?' Roach thrust his face into Regan's. 'Six people have died because of your iffy motors. If I had my way you'd be number seven.'

His right fist was raised when Bob Cryer pushed his way in between them. 'All right, Ted, all right. Come on, the lot of you.'

Ted Roach was seething all the way back to the nick. If Cryer hadn't intervened at that moment, he would have throttled the bastard. He knew he could have done and would have done it.

But now it was all routine. Official mopping-up and filling in reports.

They were all winded, but still jubilant. In the information room Tom Penny fished out cans of beer and offered congratulations. He swore that he was sorry he had missed the fun; but then looked at a gash along Jimmy Carver's cheek, and the increasingly colourful bruise below June Ackland's left eye, and perhaps was not so sure.

'Sit down, Bob,' said Dashwood euphorically. 'Take the weight off your old legs.'

'Why not?' Cryer looked at Galloway. 'Better than having your eyebrows set alight, I suppose. Red hair's one thing, Roy. Flaming red hair's quite another, eh?'

Galloway was staring past him. Through the babble he muttered: 'That wally Burnside – he's not satisfied with creeping on to the manor and pulling strokes behind my back. Now he's trying to pull our crumpet.'

They sized up the couple by the map chest. June, propped against one corner, was thoughtfully sipping a glass of fruit juice. DS Burnside was making a big show of studying her bruise, and was reaching out to touch it when she knocked his hand aside.

'A touch of the Viking, you know,' said Dashwood. 'Rape and pillage and all that. Come to think of it, he does have a longboat moored up the river Lea.'

'What he needs,' said Cryer, 'is a longboat right up his arse.'

Burnside leaned closer to June and started to talk to her in an unusually subdued voice. Her expression did not suggest that his intimate communications were of any great interest.

'You know,' Roach was shouting, waving a can of beer until it frothed over the rim, 'I reckon after today I'm a pretty good candidate for the Robbery Squad. Best references, suitable for immediate promotion.'

'All that glamour, booze, loose women? It'd do you no good.' Cryer sighed, and put his can down. 'I don't know why we're having this piss-up. I'm in no mood for it.'

'Speak for yourself, mate.'

There was a further outburst of incoherent jokes and abusive shouts as Hollis put his head timidly round the door.

'Sergeant . . .'

'Which one?' came an answering bellow.

'Sergeant Cryer.' Hollis looked back at a woman standing close behind him. 'Sorry, sarge, but I couldn't get through from the switchboard, or anyway nobody seemed to hear me, and – '

'All right, Reg, all right.' Cryer moved past him. 'What can I do for you, madam?'

'I'm sorry to bother you, but you put a note in my letterbox.'

'Letterbox?'

'I'm Mrs Simpson.' While Cryer fumbled for words, she said apologetically: 'I went to a friend's yesterday and stayed the night. I didn't get back until – '

'I quite understand. It's all right, love. Let's go somewhere a bit quieter, shall we?'

She had a pleasant diffident smile. Her eyes were appealing – in both senses of the word. She was asking him something, a bit fearful but not yet expecting anything too terrible.

'I hope I'm not taking you away from anything. You seem to be enjoying yourself.'

Not much, thought Cryer. Not much, really.

The noise went on as he closed the door, fading into the background but still raucously there. It was one hell of a background for what he had to say. Yorkie Smith was not, after all, the one who was going to have to tell Mrs Simpson that her husband had been killed.

Nine

It was PC Abel Lyttleton's first big solo opportunity since joining the Sun Hill team. Here was a chance to star – to rise, quite literally, to dizzy heights. Unfortunately heights did make Lyttleton very dizzy. Now that it had come, he was not sure that he was up to it: not that far up.

He stood beside WPC Ackland, craning his neck and staring unhappily at the edge of the roof far above. Then, like other onlookers in the street, he dodged as two roof tiles came sailing down to smash themselves on the pavement.

One woman stood her ground. Her hair in curlers, she had come out for some urgent shopping and she intended to get it done. 'Look,' she yelled at an invisible figure on the roof, 'if you've got any more to drop, then drop 'em and be done with it. I need some bleach.'

'What's the problem?' Abe Lyttleton demanded.

'Stand over here,' advised a man cowering in the nearby pub doorway, 'or you'll be the problem.'

'Go up and get the silly sod down,' said the woman.

For once, it appeared, the general public believed that the police had their uses. But Lyttleton could not picture himself shinning up three storeys, even with the aid of a drainpipe. Nor did he even fancy finding a way up from inside. The mere thought of being out on a roof at that height turned his stomach.

'Hey, you up there!' June Ackland challenged. 'What d'you think you're doing?'

The man in the pub doorway peered out. 'He's on the Youth Opportunities Scheme, love. Creating jobs for roofing apprentices.'

Above them something moved. Lyttleton and Ackland stood back a few paces, to see a man's head appear above the guttering. He jabbed a thumb down at the street. 'See those tiles there?'

'I see them,' said June.

'Well, they're mine. I brought 'em up here, I fixed 'em up here, and now I'm stripping 'em down again.'

A balding man a few yards away from June Ackland let out a small cheer. 'Good for you, mate. Take 'em right down to the rafters.'

'Why *is* he up there?' asked June.

'No idea. But I'm all for encouraging people.'

June and Lyttleton went on staring upwards. The man on the roof edged back up the slope a bit, quite unconcerned about the height or the smoothness of the tiles. With a cheerful flourish he lifted two more of them from their setting and tossed them out in a wide arc. They split into a dozen lumps, skidding away towards the kerb. It was no good for anyone's morale, thought Lyttleton unhappily, just to stand here and stare upwards, waiting for the next batch.

June shared his view. 'I think we should call the brigade.'

'You think he means to strip the whole roof?'

'Why should he? Anyway, we won't give him the time.'

'He can do an awful lot of damage,' said Lyttleton, 'and the situation will have been severely aggravated.'

June Ackland wrenched her gaze away from the guttering above. ' "The situation will have been severely aggravated . . . "? Have you just joined the Tory Party, Abe?'

'They're too left-wing for me.'

A woman pushing a pram round the corner stopped just in time as a tile bounced down the roof, struck the head of a drainpipe at an angle, and came down edge-on a few inches before her.

'Right,' said June. 'You'd better get up there and arrest him.'

That was what Lyttleton had been telling himself from the moment the incident started; and then talking himself out of listening to himself.

'I suffer from vertigo.'

'I'm not that keen on Greek food myself,' said June heartlessly. 'Look, we have got to get up there.' As a tile struck the bumper of a stationary car, she shouted up once more. 'All right, all right. Now you've got everyone's attention, pack it in.'

'I'll stop when I get me money.'

'What money?'

'Ask that bastard inside there. I've been reasonable for months. Just you go and ask that bastard.'

An elderly woman who had been enjoying the spectacle until now was incensed by this. 'Watch your bloody language!'

June persevered. It was difficult to reason with somebody at the top of your voice, with an eager audience ready to pick on every word – and any sign of weakness. 'It's none of my business what you do to his roof, but what you're doing is a menace to the public. You're in trouble with the law. D'you get that?'

'Get me my money,' came the reply. 'Then we'll see. I give you ten minutes.'

'Ten minutes, love,' said the man in the doorway. 'Plenty of time to get the SAS down here.'

Abe Lyttleton decided to show some initiative. Without making too cowardly a dash for cover, he went to the door of the grocery shop directly below the roof demolisher, and tried to make a slow, authoritative entrance.

The owner's dark upper lip was dewy with sweat. His Pakistan accent made his protest a switchback of near-incoherence. 'What good if you stand about there, looking? He destroys my property . . . is mad . . . you let him go on with it, you do nothing . . . '

'Mr Mohammed, I get the impression that there is some question of money involved.'

'No question. No question at all.'

'He says they're his tiles.'

'Officer, it is *my* roof.'

'Nobody's disputing that, but – '

'How come they are his tiles if they are attached to my roof, eh?'

'Why is he pulling them off, then, and chucking them down?'

'He is breaking the law. You must stop him.'

In the doorway June Ackland said: 'We appear to have stopped him for a while, anyway. I still think we should call the brigade. He's only given us ten minutes.'

There was another crash out in the street.

'Correction,' said June. 'He hasn't given us ten minutes.'

As Mohammed held out his arms imploringly, Lyttleton said: 'Is there a reason why he's up there, or did he just pick you out of the phone book?'

It all fitted too predictably with what they could have pieced together from events outside, where the instigator of the trouble was reducing certain items to pieces. Mohammed had engaged the man, Brough, to provide him with a completely new roof in place of an existing one which had a nasty habit of letting in the wind and the rain. Parts of the old one had been dangerous, and tiles had fallen off from time to time – though not at the rate at which they were descending right now. The shopkeeper vowed that he had paid Brough in full. But the man was a crook. He had shown up and demanded more money. 'Money with menaces' – Mr Mohammed had picked the phrase up somewhere, and used it with great fervour. And the job was not very good anyway. 'What you call a cowboy' – another addition to his vocabulary. He was firm in his assertion that he had paid Brough in full even though the man did not deserve it. Brough, judging from a fresh series of impacts outside, took a different viewpoint.

Lyttleton and Ackland went out into the open again.

A little girl danced up and down on the far pavement. 'Go on, mister, one more!'

'Don't you start joining in.' Lyttleton shooed her away and said quietly: 'Well, we've landed ourselves in the middle of a financial dispute.'

'What's the matter with these people: don't they keep books, and receipts, and that sort of thing?'

The truth was, as they both irritably knew, that if Brough had not been throwing stuff all over the street, it would have been no concern of the police. Questions of financial contracts and standards of workmanship ought to be settled in the appropriate courts. The public highway was in no sense appropriate.

'How the hell did he get up there?' Abe Lyttleton speculated.

'By a ladder, I suppose.'

'What ladder? Where?'

'Well, I don't know. Round the back, maybe.'

'There isn't a back. I know the next street, and the way the houses are set against this lot, there's nowhere you could get a ladder in.'

'Skylight?'

'Can you see one?'

They backed away as far as they could to get a better view. The move was misinterpreted. The little girl, keeping her distance but not missing anything, jeered: 'They ain't going to do nothing. Hey, mister – they're not going to do a thing.'

'Do you want to get arrested?' June snapped.

'Me? What 'ave I done?'

'Inciting a riot and causing a civil disturbance. Now get lost!' She turned to Lyttleton. 'You know, we're going to have to get this road blocked off before someone gets hurt. Tell you what – you raise Sergeant Cryer and see who he can get along, and I'll go up to one of these flats on this side. Maybe I'll be able to get a better view of the scenery.'

The high-rise angle on the scenery was undoubtedly interesting, though a short distance could be an infinity when you thought of what lay so far below in the gap between one vantage point and another. June was leaning on the windowframe of a fifth-floor flat. Brough was propped unconcernedly against a chimneypiece only a few feet below her; but the void between them was unbridgeable. He saw her, and waved as if inviting her to join him.

She cried: 'Look, why don't you get down off there and talk it over, man to man? Be sensible.'

'I've been sensible for weeks. Where'd it get me?'

'What you're doing now, whatever way you look at it, isn't going to get you anywhere. The more problems you make for us, the worse it's going to be for you.'

He grinned at her and waved again. He was high on the roof and high on his own zest for revenge. 'I don't care what happens to me. But that bastard's going to get *his*. He's going to suffer, that I guarantee you.'

'I'm asking you one last time. Please go down.'

He reached between his spread-eagled legs, selected a tile, slid it free, and threw it at her almost as a love token. There was a howl of warning from that chasm between them as it went down and shattered. The answer was plain enough.

June changed tack. 'How d'you get up there, anyway?' She tried to sound admiring, a fellow professional admiring his expertise.

He smirked back. 'Helicopter.'

Basically there was such a short division between them, and if it had not been for the sickening depth of that division she might so easily have tugged her skirt straight, adjusted her cap, and walked over and wiped the smirk off his face and provoked a genuine smile. Somewhere inside him he must know that he was behaving like a spoiled kid. It was all there in his face – craggy, resentful without knowing exactly what he resented, yet with a sort of bloody-minded honesty which made June feel on his side rather than against him.

Which was all wrong.

They could have talked. Could have made a joke of it – a bad joke, but a joke. Only it was not her job to mediate: in this job, you played it according to the book.

'All right, you asked for it,' she said, leaving him sitting there while she went back to the ground floor and rejoined Abe Lyttleton. At least she had one bit of news in line with what she had gone up there for.

There was a skylight above the shop, masked by a neighbouring chimney-stack. Only there might be a certain overlap of premises, and it could just be that the skylight belonged to the shop next door. They asked Mr Mohammed. He knew nothing about the shop next door, and wanted to know nothing, and if they were assisting a trespasser on his roof and infringing his rights, was that not a simple matter for the police? Forbearing to tell him that it was no such thing, Lyttleton and Ackland hugged the wall along the shop fronts and went in through the next door.

An olive-skinned man standing behind the grille of a subpost-office counter at once lifted the flap and came out into the shop. Many of its goods seemed to be in direct competition with those of Mr Mohammed.

'Mr . . . ?'

'Patel. You have come to take my statement about this present regrettable disturbance?'

'Well, sort of. You see, from our observations it looks like the only way Brough – the man's name is Brough – '

'Yes,' said Mr Patel calmly.

'The only way he could have got up on to that roof is through your skylight.'

'Yes.'

'So we would like to go up there ourselves,' said Lyttleton, 'and have a word with him.' It was untrue. He had no wish whatsoever to go up there.

'Do you have a warrant?'

'Do we need one?'

Mr Patel smiled blandly. 'I don't know.'

'Look, sir. You're assisting the police in their line of duty. We don't have to have warrants to ask for the co-operation of the public.'

'I am not only a law-abiding man, I am also a fair man.'

'Yes, of course, it's just that – '

'I will not help you to arrest Mr Brough. Better he should strip all the tiles from the roof.'

June Ackland's eyebrows rose a fraction of an inch. 'Oh, so you know this roofer?'

'Yes.'

'How?'

'He has worked on my roof,' said Patel. 'He's done a lot of work around here, he is quite well known.'

Lyttleton was at a loss. 'But why did you let Brough go through your place and get up there? Didn't you realize it would lead to trouble?'

'I thought' – Patel was still calm, with the most tranquil smile imaginable – 'that once that unscrupulous bugger next door was desperate and that he was willing to – '

'Did Brough threaten you?'

'On the contrary, I invited him.'

'You invited him?'

June said: 'I don't want to get heavy, sir, but if you don't start co-operating you're going to be arrested for obstructing the police. And there'd be a little matter of aiding and abetting the commission of a felony.'

'On such an occasion it would be an honour.'

There was a shout from next door, and another clutch of missiles exploded on the pavement. June looked warily out. Mohammed was hopping up and down, shaking his fist upwards in impotent rage.

'Get inside!' June urged.

'Get him out of the way,' came a howl from above, 'or I'll kill him.'

'Will you go *in*!' When she was sure Mohammed had retreated, swearing and wailing to himself, she turned back to Abe Lyttleton. 'Look, vertigo or not, we've got to get up there.'

'I think you were right earlier on. Why don't we get the brigade?'

'By the time they get here, the whole roof could be in the street. Why don't you use Mr Patel's skylight, whether he likes it or not, and have a word with our friend?'

Lyttleton tried to croak a protest, but he knew that the moment had come. With a dry throat he went up the stairs pointed out by the reluctant Patel, up the three storeys to an attic where a ladder was propped against the rim of a half-open skylight. Obviously this was the ladder which Brough had used. Therefore, Abe Lyttleton silently assured himself, it must be safe. He set one foot on the lowest rung. The ladder wobbled. When he put his other foot on the higher rung and began to climb, the ladder let out a loud creak and he felt it bend under his hands.

It took a mighty effort to reach up and push the skylight fully open. Edging up another few rungs, he got his head and shoulders through the gap.

Brough, perched on the roof ridge, was engrossed in levering a further course of tiles free. When he sat back he became aware of the newcomer.

'Gawd! Sending sweeps up now! You've come up the wrong way, mate – the chimney's right behind you.'

Abe Lyttleton said: 'You are endangering human life down there.'

'Not if they keep their heads down, I'm not.'

'I am ordering you to come down.' He eased himself up another rung, and the ladder bent even more ominously, squealing against the skylight frame. 'Christ!'

'What's up ?'

'This ladder's not safe.'

'You're too 'eavy,' grinned Brough. 'Just keep still, now.'

Lyttleton gulped and steadied himself. 'Stop acting like a fool and come down. Pack it in before someone gets hurt.'

'I'm not budging from here till I get paid. I'll strip the whole thing. Why should he get away with, it?'

'I'm not getting involved in your financial affairs, but you're breaking the law and . . . and' – Abe clung to the lip of the frame – 'you're going to force me to take action. Then you'll have no money anyway, and you'll be up in front of a judge.'

'That's fine by me.'

Brough had a cheerful, crinkled, weatherbeaten face, and his voice was amiable enough. He was obviously used to being out in all weathers, sturdily coping with all conditions and technical problems, and working hard and fast at whatever job he was on. But he couldn't be allowed to go on with this one.

Grimly Abe Lyttleton hoisted himself out on to the roof. A grey expanse of slates stretched up to the angle where the more cheerful red tiles of the neighbouring roof began – those which Brough had not yet dealt with. Brough watched him coming, clearly welcoming the diversion.

Crouching, wavering from side to side, Lyttleton clawed his way up the slope. When he was almost in reach of the amused Brough, he looked to one side to judge his position; looked out over the rooftops.

It was a mistake. The world tilted. The block of flats immediately opposite showed every sign of swinging over and collapsing on him. And between them was a chasm deeper than he could ever have imagined. Far, far below June Ackland waved an encouraging hand. Lyttleton went down on his knees, and felt them sliding a few inches. The slates offered no grip, no hope.

Brough's grin faded. 'Hey, careful there. Careful!'

Abe got up to his feet, feeling his knees trembling, out of control. He made a wild lurch up the slope and spread his arms wide to embrace a chimney-stack.

Brough stood up, worried. 'Don't move.' He reached out and took Lyttleton's right hand, easing him round the chimney until he could sit on the ridge. 'Take it easy, now.' The skylight looked an infinity away. There was no way of ever getting back there. But Brough, catching his glance, chuckled and said: 'Time you got back on terra firma, mate. So let's go. Nice and easy . . . '

Lyttleton forced himself to move. He longed just to slide down the slates on his bottom, helping himself along with his hands, but Brough was standing up and urging him to stand.

'Don't tread on the cracks. It's unlucky.'

They slithered down, closer to that inviting, possibly just attainable gap. At last Lyttleton sagged against the edge of the raised skylight, and began to turn, reaching with his right foot for the elusive rungs. As he half hung over the edge, Brough said: 'Where you from? Sun Hill?'

'Yes.'

'New?'

'Few weeks.'

'Well, they know all about it there.'

Lyttleton felt, incredulously, both his feet on a rung each. The ladder creaked, but that was nothing: not now, not after those last few minutes. He whispered: 'Know all about what?'

'This, o'course. I went in this morning. Told 'em I was gonna try and get up 'ere. Said they were my tiles. Told 'em straight.'

Lyttleton felt even dizzier than before. 'Told who?'

'Young copper on the desk.'

'You told him about this?'

'Sure. Nothing to hide. Not so far as I'm concerned. I've got bills, receipts, materials and hourly rate, the lot. Look, I keep proper books.'

'What did he say, this young copper on the desk?' Abe Lyttleton was getting his voice back, and a fair helping of outrage boiled up in it.

'Not much. Didn't seem interested.'

'You say you've got receipts and so on. You've given receipts to Mr Mohammed for what he paid you?'

'Yep.'

'But you think he still owes you something?'

'I don't think so. I know so. Eighteen 'undred.'

Lyttleton nodded. It was time to go down. He looked back up the slope of slates, shuddered, and said: 'Thanks.'

Brough grinned again. 'I know you lot. The whole nick would've sworn I pushed you!'

By the time he got down and out into the street, still concentrating on keeping his feet moving in the right direction and his knees from going into the shakes, a police van was drawn up across the eastern end of the street, and two hundred yards to the west a constable whose face meant nothing to Lyttleton was erecting a temporary barrier. There was no sign of June Ackland.

'Looking for your girlfriend, dearie?' An elderly woman who must recently have arrived on the scene clucked her tongue commiseratingly. 'Had to dash off. Something they said to her on that walkie-talkie thing, you know, like that thing you've got.'

Lyttleton sent out a call from his own PR. Sergeant Cryer answered, greeting him with an unsympathetic demand as to how much bloody longer he was going to take over that roofer. No, June was not there: he had heard all her news, and sent her off to join Taffy Edwards on an urgent job. 'Urgent,' Cryer repeated, implying that he wouldn't mind some sense of urgency elsewhere.

Lyttleton said: 'Look, sarge, this fellow Brough says he went into Sun Hill this morning and told someone exactly what he intended doing. Told whoever was on the desk that he was going to strip the tiles because they were his.'

'He's winding you up, Abe.'

'Don't think so, sarge. He's got books, accounts, the lot. He seems a respectable kind of bloke. You ask me, I think he's had a raw deal.'

'We are not running a small claims court, Lyttleton! Bring him in. He's causing a disturbance, isn't he?'

'But he won't come off the roof. And it's very steep. We try anything, and he'll strip it down to the rafters.'

'Talk him down. Use some of that Irish blarney of yours.'

'It's not Irish blarney, sarge.' Lyttleton ventured a retort. 'It's Hackney charisma.'

'Whatever. Just use it.'

'Sarge, he's got to be got down. He's not going to come of his own accord. Somehow we call his bluff, or we put up a show of reinforcements, and somehow – '

'All right, Abe, all right. I'll get the brigade on its way.'

Abe Lyttleton had rarely heard music so enchanting as the distant sound of the fire engine siren, blasting its way closer and closer. The temporary barrier was hastily moved aside to let the engine through. The crowd on the far side began to cheer and squash closer.

A fireman sprang from the engine alongside Lyttleton.

'Cat in a tree?'

'Man on a roof.'

'Injured, threatening suicide?'

'No. He won't come down. He's unlawfully stripping the tiles off the roof.'

The fireman surveyed the littered street and nodded in understanding. 'Right, we'll get the ladder up. How long d'you reckon it'll take?'

'Soon as you bring him down, he's under arrest.'

The fireman's nod became a shake of the head. 'I can't bring him down. Physical impossibility.'

'Why?'

'It's not my job. No fire, no danger to life. Not my job to make the arrest.'

'Well, who's going up?'

'You are, mate.'

Lyttleton watched the ladder reaching swiftly and accurately up to the roof edge. The thought of going back up to that dreadful place was too much. Nobody could ask that. There was no way he could start back up. He burst out: 'I can't stand heights.'

'We're just providing the appliance, as instructions. Even if we did go up, we've got no authority. We tell him to come down, and if he doesn't want to come then that's it. No authority, you see.'

They were all watching him. The result of walking away would be more awful than starting up those metal steps. This equipment was safer than a rickety ladder. People's lives had depended on it more than once. It would be all right. This time he would be more in command.

In an undertone he appealed, so the onlookers could not hear: 'Will one of you come up with me?'

The fireman looked at one of his colleagues. 'What d'you say, Harry?'

'I don't know. I . . . oh, all right, I'll back him up.'

'There you are, constable. Your volunteer. Your lucky day. Must be the twinkle in your eye.'

There was no twinkle in PC Lyttleton's eye as he started off up the ladder. It looked reassuringly solid, but interminable. Beyond the top there was a great wash of sky. And beyond the top rung he could fall off into nothingness.

Behind him he could just feel the tread of the supporting fireman. There was no hesitating, no way of backing down.

He reached the top, held on until the metal bit into his skin, and looked up at Brough, who appeared to be taking a short breather before resuming his bombing raids.

'Right,' said Lyttleton firmly. 'You're under arrest.'

'Come and put the cuffs on, then.' Brough was as affable as ever. 'Come on, let's see you.'

'Are you refusing to comply with my request?'

'You could take it that way, yes. I'll see every tile on this roof is smashed before I leave it. You want to arrest me, you come over here. Try it.'

Lyttleton looked at the steep intersection of slopes, and beyond them to the reeling skyline. Below him, Harry coughed meaningly.

Defeated, Lyttleton said: 'Down.'

Brough's smile seemed to hang on the air above him as he descended. Then he had to pluck up the courage to radio in to Sergeant Cryer.

Cryer was not pleased. It could hardly have been expected that he would be. 'What on earth do you think you've achieved, Abe? I mean, just what are you doing round there?'

'Sarge, I think this has to be a talking-down situation. I'm doing my best, but it's going to take time and patience.'

'Time?' squawked Cryer. 'How much more of it are you going to need, for God's sake? Get it sorted out, Abe – as quick as you can.'

Lyttleton avoided the ironic gaze of the fireman, and put on an air of authority as he marched into Mohammed's shop. Mohammed was far noisier and more abusive than Cryer. Lyttleton took the full brunt of this further outburst of anger and impatience, and then suggested that it was time Mr Mohammed reached some kind of compromise. Brough felt himself wronged. Perhaps there was something in his complaint? Perhaps it was time to think back, and think over the financial implications, and if there had been any mistakes, any unfortunate misunderstandings . . .

When the storm had subsided, Lyttleton went all over it again. And the farce began again: out into the street once more, along to Mr Patel's shop once more, up Mr Patel's stairs and the creaking ladder to the skylight again. Was he doomed to go through the motions over and over again throughout eternity?

Brough was positively joyful as Lyttleton's head reappeared through the skylight. 'Hullo. The old jack-in-the-box popping out again, eh?'

'Look,' Lyttleton pleaded, 'what he's proposing is this: he'll give you twelve hundred.'

'How?'

'Cheque.'

'Scrap paper,' said Brough contemptuously.

'What about half cash, half cheque?'

'Has he offered that?'

'I'm offering it on his behalf. You accept it, I'll see what he says.'

Brough balanced a tile on the palm of his hand and contemplated the far scenery without any of Lyttleton's queasiness. 'I want it all in cash. I've come this far, I might as well go all the way.'

'You're going to need any money you can get, friend, with the fine you're going to have to pay.'

'Oh, and while we're at it,' said Brough, 'another six hundred for putting the tiles back.'

It was working. Brough still looked resolute, but something in his tone hinted that he, too, had really had enough of this. Basically he was the kind of man who would sooner do a creative job than a destructive one. When he put the loose tile regretfully back in place, Lyttleton knew they were within sight of the end.

He made the return trip to Mohammed's shop.

'If I pay, then I pay. All right. But I want to be certain that he will also

231

pay – the law will not let him go free after all this damage, this noise, every-thing.'

'He'll be charged, don't you worry,' said Lyttleton fervently.

'I must be absolutely certain that he gets the full weight of justice.'

'The full weight. Rely on it.'

Mohammed sighed. 'Very well. Thirteen hundred, and that's my final offer.'

Abe Lyttleton looked out into the street, up at the sky. Over his shoulder he said: 'Don't say "final", Mr Mohammed. It looks like rain.'

Sergeant Cryer was aware of PC Carver coming in off patrol and heading for the washroom, glancing happily at the clock as he went. Any minute now he would be off the premises.

Something occurred to Cryer. 'Jim.'

'Sarge?'

'Did some bloke come in here this morning, early – something about taking tiles off a roof?'

Jimmy Carver paused unwillingly. 'Well, a chap did come in and said he had materials on a site not paid for.'

'Materials on a . . . Didn't you ask him what he meant?'

'Well, not exactly, sarge, no.'

'So what did you say ?'

'Well, nothing.' Carver was anxious to brush it aside and be done with it, just as he had presumably brushed it aside this morning. 'It's nothing to do with us, is it?'

'Nothing to do with us? We've spent most of the day sorting this out.'

'Well, he just came in and – '

'Why didn't you get his particulars? Why didn't you call me?' Carver looked offended. 'I used my initiative, sarge. Didn't seem any reason to go into it. Not our cup of tea at all, as far as I could see.'

Cryer whistled thinly between his teeth. 'Well, lad, just you tell that to Abe Lyttleton next time you see him.'

Ten

It had been a depressing Sunday. Roy Galloway had felt a tightening in his chest as he picked his daughter up, and found it nearly impossible to make any sort of conversation with her on the way to the Zoo. Once they had got inside he said very brightly: 'Right, what's first, then?' And it began to drizzle. Not a deluge of rain, just a steady drizzle that drifted across your eyes and brought a damp smell out of the ground and the cages.

Julia had walked gravely beside him, accepting an ice cream when he offered one, eating lunch politely, and framing careful answers to his questions about school and her friends. Every now and then she would steal a quick, furtive glance at him as they walked along, but whenever he turned to smile or wait for whatever she might be about to say, she at once looked away again.

During the last half hour of their afternoon together he was tingling with a wretched, shameful desire to get away. And he was sure that Julia felt the same.

Only once did she come to life. As they stopped at traffic lights on the way home – her home now, no longer his – she let out a little squeak of excitement.

'What is it, love?'

She pointed to a large poster on a hoarding soaring above them. The contorted faces of four young men stared out, pugnacious and derisive. Galloway would have run the whole lot in as soon as look at them. But Julia was ecstatic.

'It's the Yellow Dogs. Daddy, they're fantastic.'

She was too young for those sort of performers. But nowadays kids seemed to be late teenagers before they had even been kids.

She went on: 'They're on up the road at the old Empire, a week on Friday.'

'You'd better stay well away.'

'My friends Sandra and Greta are going. They told me last week.'

'You'd better see what your mother says.'

'Oh, she thinks they're awful. She wouldn't let me go. And she wouldn't take me.'

'I'm sure your mum's right,' said Galloway flatly.

'Honest, daddy, they're just out of this world.'

They drew up outside the house. He knew this was wrong, but he said:

'Look, I'll have a word with mum. Maybe I can get away a week on Friday. I'll fix it.'

She looked at him in momentary adoration. 'Come in and ask her now!'

'I'd better not.' As the happiness faded from her eyes, he said: 'I'll ring her during the week. I promise.'

Julia gave him a quick peck of a kiss and slid out of the car. He watched her until she had opened the front door and was safely inside the house. One of the window curtains twitched, but he refused to spare it a glance.

The sad taste of it was still with him when he walked into Sun Hill next morning.

'So it's true?' Hollis was saying. 'Henry Talbot's really going?'

'All settled a week ago,' Sergeant Penny confirmed.

'Sarge, someone ought to have told me it was definite.'

'We all thought your ears were big enough to pick up the sound waves.'

'So if I get my application in right away – '

'You do that. Only mind you don't do your writing hand an injury. 'Morning, Roy.'

'Morning.'

Galloway was on his way towards the stairs when the boom of a draught along the passage signified that the door to the yard had opened and shut. He stopped and stared.

Bob Cryer was escorting two girls into the building. One had rumpled hair with a purple streak down the middle, though in fact the streak was beginning to stray from the middle as if she had been out in the rain all night. Her eyelashes were so heavily blackened that they obscured whatever the true colour of her eyes might be. The other girl was fair and very pale, apart from a glaring bruise high on her left cheek and an ugly scratch beside her mouth. Her cheap, skimpy, off-the-shoulder dress had been torn near the right armpit.

Galloway groaned inside. He knew real Monday morning trouble when he saw it.

'Roy.' Bob Cryer looked glad to see him and to see some chance of shifting the load. 'This young lady' – he put a sympathetic hand on the fair girl's arm, and she flinched immediately – 'is Miss Lindfield. She was assaulted by her boyfriend last night.'

'Shouldn't you be in hospital?' said Galloway.

'Silly girl, she walked out.'

'That casualty department was like Piccadilly Circus.' The dark girl had a harsh, pushy voice. 'Wait here, wait there, 'old this. Drive you up the bloody wall.'

Galloway was still looking at the victim's damaged face. 'So what are you going to do about this feller that's done this to you?'

'That's what we're here for,' her friend intervened again. 'Chris Garbett. She wants to charge him.'

'Sorry – who are you?'

'Sandra Morrison.'

Sandra. It was a common enough name nowadays. Galloway hoped his daughter's friend didn't look like this one.

'She stayed with Debbie – Miss Lindfield – at the hospital last night,' Cryer explained.

Debbie nodded, and went on nodding as if in a trance.

Galloway leaned over her. 'You realize you may have to go to court, give evidence, if we charge Garbett, don't you?'

'Of course she knows,' said Sandra Morrison.

'Oh, Pete.' Cryer waved across the office at Muswell. 'Take these girls and put them in the interview room. And stay with them until I send June along.'

As Muswell came closer, looking the girls up and down and getting an answering wriggle from Sandra, Galloway said: 'Debbie, do your parents know about this?'

'No,' said Sandra. 'She was supposed to be staying with me last night, her mum's not expecting her 'ome until this evening.'

Cryer and Galloway exchanged glances. The mother surely ought to be told. But until they had taken a statement and sorted out the truth behind it all, starting a panic and recriminations now might not be a good idea. Debbie was shivering intermittently. Better give her time to straighten herself out. As Muswell began to lead them towards the passage, Galloway said: 'I'll see you later on – right?'

When they had gone, Cryer scratched the side of his nose. 'I wonder what we're landed with?'

'To be on the safe side, don't make a move to nick her boyfriend until you've copped a statement from her. She might change her mind once it comes to putting things down on paper.'

'You're talking to an old sweat, Roy.'

'I know that, but there's something about this I don't like. The way that other one kept pushing in all the time, for starters.'

'June Ackland will sort her out.'

'Look, it might be an idea if you took the statement, Bob.' Cryer backed away. 'Oh, no. I've got more than enough to do.'

'She might open up to you more than she would to Ackland. Women are funny creatures.'

'You should know, Roy.'

Galloway prickled with a swift comeback, but held it in check. He simply nodded in the direction of the interview room – an appeal as much as an order.

Bob Cryer sighed, and went.

The story seemed brutally straightforward: crude, cheap, and obvious. The two girls had gone with Garbett to a disco the previous evening. They had danced, had a few drinks, and then Debbie and Garbett had left. They walked round the back of the building to some waste ground and stood in the fire exit doorway. Before getting all this down in writing, together with all the more unsavoury details, Cryer wanted to know that he was not wasting police time. He leaned on the table behind which Debbie and her friend Sandra were sitting – Debbie sagging, as if her forehead might at any moment drop and hit the table, while Sandra Morrison stared contemptuously at Cryer.

He said: 'Now, you know what all this will involve. Do you want to go ahead and press charges?'

'Yeah,' said Sandra, 'she wants to go through with it.'

'Please! Debbie's got a tongue. She can answer for herself.'

'I was only telling you – '

'If you interrupt again, I want you out of this room.'

Debbie jolted awake. 'No, please, don't send her away. I want her here with me.'

The door opened and Muswell came in with a tray of tea.

'That's better.' Cryer waited until the tea had been handed out, and Muswell had set himself against the wall, studying Sandra's legs. 'Now, where were we?'

'Behind the 'all,' said Sandra. 'That's where.'

'Debbie, would you rather talk to a woman police officer?' Debbie shook her head.

'I can easily arrange it for you. If you'd sooner tell it to – '

'We kissed and cuddled for a while,' Debbie began to speak, in a subdued monotone. 'It was . . . nice.'

Then she sank back into numbed silence.

'Go on, Debbie.' Cryer waited. 'Debbie,' he coaxed, 'I have to know. I have to satisfy myself there is enough evidence of an assault. Unless something else happened that you haven't told me yet.'

Sandra glared at Muswell. 'She ain't going to tell you with that moron standing there ready to work himself off.'

Cryer hesitated, then waved to Muswell to leave the interview room. When the door had closed, he said: 'You are not helping. With your continual interruptions, you're not helping your friend. I'm telling you for the last time – '

'Oh, but he was loving it, wasn't he, bogging at her like a dirty old man.'

'Shut up!'

Debbie said vaguely: 'He put his hand up my dress.'

'Go on, Debbie.'

'I pushed his hand away. I told him I wasn't that kind of girl.'

'Debbie, I've got to know. Now, this is important. Did he put his hand on your private parts? I have to – '

'Course he bloody did,' screeched Sandra. 'And when she pushed him away he beat 'er up and raped her. Yeah, bloody well raped 'er. That's what she's trying to tell you.'

236

The door opened. Half expecting Muswell back, Cryer was about to snap an order at him. Instead there were Roy Galloway and June Ackland.

'Sorry to break in, Bob,' said Galloway with unusual courtesy.

There was no need for apologies. Cryer was glad of the break.

'Debbie, I'm going to have you moved to another room,' said Galloway. 'A more comfortable one than this. Where you won't be disturbed, and where WPC Ackland here can take a more detailed statement.' Cryer wondered if Galloway had been listening at the door and had chosen that crucial moment to interrupt. 'Are you sure you're up to it?' the DS was continuing. 'I know it isn't very nice, but there are other procedures you're going to have to follow as well. I'm afraid it can't be helped. One is that you're going to have to be examined by a doctor.'

'She's already been examined by a doctor at the 'ospital.' Sandra was quick to move in again. 'Does she have to go through it all another time?'

'That will have been for a different reason,' said June quietly.

'They weren't aware of all the circumstances at the time,' Galloway added.

'And if it wasn't for me you wouldn't be aware either. Debbie wasn't going to tell anybody.'

'Are you sure you don't want your parents brought in, Debbie? What about your father?'

'He's dead,' said Sandra.

'Debbie, I do think we should inform your mother. She's bound to find out sooner or later. I think she should be here.'

'I wouldn't want *my* mum to know, I can tell you that. It's all right, Deb, *I'm* with you. It's got nothing to do with your mother.' Sandra got up as June Ackland took Debbie's arm and turned towards the door; but Galloway was blocking her path. 'Hey, what's going on?'

'I just want to have a little chat with you, Sandra.'

'Yeah, but I mean . . . ' The girl's sooty eyes tried to peer past him as Debbie and June went out of the room.

'A chat,' said Galloway. 'Right now.' As the girl tried to force her way past him, he fended her expertly off so that she collapsed on her chair again. 'Just stay there. Now you listen to me, young lady, and you listen good. That friend of yours has been through a horrific experience. One she might not get over. But while she's in this nick I'm going to do my best not to put any more pressure on her than is necessary.'

'Well, you don't think I'd want to do that, do you? Come off it – she's my best mate.'

'Then stop butting in when we're trying to create a sympathetic atmosphere.'

'I'm only trying to 'elp.'

'Then don't interfere, Sandra. You're only here because Debbie says she wants you here.'

Outside, Cryer said: 'About this examination she'll have to have – '

'I've fixed for the divisional surgeon to come in. You know, Louise Figg. I'm told she's good at rape.'

'Delighted to hear it, I'm sure.'

Then there was the real stomach-fuming bit. Galloway took it on himself to phone Mrs Lindfield. He made it sound as unalarming as possible, but it was a difficult trick to pull off. Tell the woman her daughter has been assaulted, but not to worry, just to trot down to the police station and have a chat. She was safe. Safe. On the phone Mrs Lindfield herself sounded some-how impersonal. If the news came as a shock, she coped: even went so far as to say in a matter-of-fact tone that she would bring Debbie a change of clothes.

Sandra Morrison was not pleased to hear that Debbie's mum was coming to join them. But Galloway was beginning to feel that anything that was bad for Sandra Morrison must in some devious way be good for Debbie Lindfield.

A change of clothing would certainly be no bad thing. Dr Figg was on her way, and having removed Debbie's soiled clothes for forensic examination, the best June Ackland had been able to offer was a blue denim coat with all the style and charm of a workman's overalls.

'Sorry for the delay,' said Galloway. 'But if you're feeling okay, perhaps you can help WPC Ackland here. Over to you, Ackland.'

The questioning took up where it had left off.

June made a preliminary note on the open page and said: 'Well, now. We got to the actual business of his hand on you. How did you react?'

'I . . . I think I screamed.'

'And when you say you screamed – '

'Miss . . . er, I don't know your name.'

'Sorry. It's June.'

'Could I have a shower or something, please, June?'

'I'm sorry, we can't do that, no.'

'A wash in a hand-basin would do.'

'Not until the doctor's examined you. I'm sorry.'

'That's a bit off, isn't it?' Sandra Morrison was back with her friend, and back in her old form.

'The doctor,' said June to Debbie, 'has to take . . . well, you might wash away evidence. Do you understand what I'm saying?'

'I think I understand,' said Debbie faintly.

''Ow long's this bloody doctor going to be, then?'

'You do want to see a woman doctor, don't you, Debbie?' June persevered. 'That's what we've fixed. But it means we have to wait just a little while.'

'You're getting a kick out of this, aren't you?' rasped Sandra.

'Please, Sandra, no . . . '

'Knickers damp yet?'

June got to her feet. 'I've just about had enough of you. We've all had enough of you. Now get out.' She twisted the girl's arm behind her back and thrust her towards the door.

'You can't do that. She wants me 'ere!'

'I don't give a damn. I don't want you in this room another minute. Now will you *go*!'

Before she could reach for the door it opened in front of them. Galloway said: 'What's going on in here?'

'This cow is trying to throw me out.'

'Sir' – June tried to keep it level and official – 'this girl is obstructing my investigation.'

'Deb wants me here. Don't you, Deb?'

'I . . . I don't know . . . I mean . . . '

Galloway stood to one side and gripped Sandra's free arm to speed her on the way out.

'I want my mum,' Debbie began to cry.

Galloway thrust his face close to Sandra's. 'I don't know what your game is, young lady, but you're going the right way to being nicked.'

'Sir.' Muswell put his head round the end of the corridor. 'The doctor's arrived. She's in the front office.'

'Good. Right, now take this young lady to the canteen and keep her there. Don't let her wander. She's a material witness.'

Muswell looked far from reluctant to accompany the girl to the canteen, sizing her up as he went.

Galloway steered Dr Figg, a maternal-looking woman with a no-nonsense smile and a clipped, reassuring voice, towards the room where June and Debbie were waiting. Then he issued instructions for Chris Garbett to be pulled in. They had plenty of back-up for an arrest now. Before he could escape to his own office, there was another message. Mrs Lindfield was in the waiting room. Well, let them keep coming fast. The faster the better: tie up all the ends, and be done with it.

Galloway hurried off. Through the glass panel he could see a plump, fretful woman talking to PC Carver, talking on and on. Even before he pushed the door ajar and heard her voice he knew the sort of plaintive, aggrieved voice it would be.

'I do hope I've brought the right trousers. She's very fussy about things like that. Wrong colour, I think, with these other . . . oh, well, I'm bound to be in trouble anyway.'

'We're sorry about what's happened to your daughter,'

Jimmy Carver was saying. 'It must have been a great shock to you.'

'I was going to bring the jeans and sweater, but then I realized the jeans were in the wash.'

'Inspector Galloway will be along just as soon as he can.'

'Why should he?' Mrs Lindfield unexpectedly changed tack. 'Debbie's just another case. Of the girl who brought it on herself. That's what you all think, isn't it?'

'No, it's not like that, Mrs Lindfield.'

'I know what the police are like.'

Galloway pushed the door open and went in. As the woman began to fuss to her feet he held out his hand. 'No, please, Mrs Lindfield. Carver, you can go now.'

'Sir.'

When they were alone together, Galloway said: 'I'm Inspector Galloway. I want you to feel that we're here to help you. And Debbie. We – '

'Please don't patronize me.' Mrs Lindfield was trying to take charge and show that she was more important than any policeman. She was the one who expected service from them, not the other way round. 'I'd like the truth,' she said, 'no matter how brutal or unsavoury.'

Very well. She had asked for it. Without dwelling on any of it too cruelly, Galloway gave her the truth. It came out with clinical exactitude.

'What if she's pregnant?' said her mother when he had finished.

'I know it's not much comfort to you, Mrs Lindfield, but I can arrange for Debbie to have a scan at the local hospital. And there are organizations, sincere people who give support to – '

'To victims!' she said with a grimace of disgust. 'I won't have her called a victim. But these organizations . . . if that man's diseased Debbie, will these nice sincere people castrate him for me? Tell me that.'

'Let's just say that he'll be punished. That I can promise you.'

She was on the verge of ranting on, and he would not have blamed her all that much. But all at once the wild flailing of helpless anger deserted her. 'I'm sorry,' she said in a defeated tone. 'Giving you a bad time. I seem to want to punish everybody. Except myself.'

'What makes you think it's your fault?' asked Galloway, alert. But it dawned on him that she was not really accusing herself, just indulging in maudlin phrases rather than sit dumb and bewildered. He said: 'This boy . . . that is . . . '

'Who raped her. It's all right, inspector. I'm getting used to the word now.'

'How long has Debbie been going out with him?'

'Debbie doesn't go out regularly, not with anyone. She hasn't ever been like that.'

'But she was with this feller last night.'

'I don't suppose she was with him to start with. Not unless she's been hiding an awful lot from me. She's never even mentioned a boyfriend, not even *mentioned* one.'

'Chris Garbett,' said Galloway casually. 'I think that's his name.'

Mrs Lindfield stared, outraged. 'Chris Garbett?'

'Do you know him?'

'Do I know him!' She was struggling to regain command and put him in his place. 'Chris Garbett's not my Debbie's boyfriend,' she said imperiously. 'Chris Garbett's that dreadful Sandra Morrison's boyfriend.'

Eleven

Sergeant Cryer had seated himself, facing Chris Garbett. Mike Dashwood leaned in a corner of the room, just far enough over to one side of the table for Garbett to have to twist his neck round uneasily whenever he wanted to check on what might be threatening him.

Chris Garbett was good-looking in a flashy, self-indulgent way. It was easy to visualize him swaggering up and down under the garish lights of a disco. He had a mass of fair hair, too rich in itself to need expensive styling, and a moody mouth which must, Cryer supposed, tempt a lot of girls. Not much taste or common sense, girls nowadays. Cryer, at any rate, was unmoved by the sulky self-admiration. It was quite something else that moved him.

'That poor girl shouldn't have to go through any more of this.' he said. 'It's not right. If you were any sort of man, Garbett, if you had any decency left, you'd plead on this.'

'There's nothing to plead. You don't catch me walking into that sort of thing.'

'Come on, give the girl a break.' When Garbett tilted his chair back, trying to preserve his aura of scornful indifference, Cryer went on: 'It's going to be a hard journey if you don't.'

'Why should I give that little prick-tease a break?' Garbett stared at the ceiling. 'Little liar.'

'A liar? Was she?'

'I'm telling you, it was nothing like the way you're making out. No way.'

'What *was* it like, then?'

'Look, you know what these birds are like when they've had a few.' He tipped the chair languidly back, shrugging, inviting them to share the wink and the nudge.

Cryer waited another long minute, then said: 'Rapists aren't the most popular people in the community, Chris. Oh, you're kidding yourself how strong you are, you'll survive, the hell with what people say. We've seen it before. Big

241

brave show on the outside, but inside . . . ah, you won't be able to come to terms with yourself. Seen it all before, haven't we, Mike?'

Mike Dashwood leaned across Garbett's line of vision, making a great show of opening a packet of cigarettes and offering one to Cryer.

Garbett took a quick, involuntary nibble at his right thumbnail. 'Can I have one?'

'Sure.' Dashwood turned the open packet towards him.

'Look.' Garbett's hand shook as he put the cigarette to his lips and Dashwood stooped to give him a light. 'All I'm going to say is, I didn't mean to do it. I was drunk.'

'Oh, so now *you're* the one who'd had a few?'

'She led me on. That's it.'

'A scared little scrap of a girl like that? It doesn't match up. Maybe,' said Cryer, 'you've got a sexual problem, picking one like that in the first place.'

'Don't be stupid.'

'Maybe you need some help.'

Garbett flushed. He could almost have been on the verge of crying. 'You winding me up, or what? There's nothing wrong with me. I don't need any help.'

'There's nothing to be embarrassed or ashamed about,' said Cryer equably.

'Having a sense of revulsion,' contributed Dashwood.

'What are you two talking about?'

'Well, there are people who specialize in your type of problem.'

'I don't have a problem.'

'All I've got to do,' Cryer went on, 'is pick up the phone and I can have someone here within the hour.'

'To do what?'

'Talk to you.'

'A doctor?'

'Yes.'

'Who you trying to kid, for gawd's sake?' Garbett raged. 'I ain't being examined by any doctor and that's that, all right?'

Cryer nodded. 'Your prerogative, Chris. Lock him up, Mike.'

Dashwood stood at Garbett's shoulder. 'Come on.'

'Hang about, wait a minute.' He looked hopelessly from one to the other. 'I want my own doctor,' he said at last, 'or there's no deal.'

'Now we're getting somewhere. Tell you what, I'll let your own doctor be present. How's that?'

'And while you're waiting,' suggested Dashwood, 'why don't you make a statement? Get it down on paper.'

'Never put anything down on paper.'

A head came round the door. There was a call for Sergeant Cryer. The implication was that it would be best for him to take it outside.

Roy Galloway wanted to know what progress he was making. Also he had a few scraps of information on Garbett. Not much: three findings of guilt, two other convictions, all of it criminal damage. There was nothing of a sexual nature. But he had something of his own to communicate. He still had Mrs Lindfield on the premises, and for Cryer's information, Sandra Morrison was Garbett's girlfriend.

'Is that right?' Cryer marvelled.

'Hell hath no fury, know what I mean? You'd better put it to him, Bob.'

'Can't trust anyone, can you?'

'Too true. See you soon.'

Cryer went at a slow, deliberate pace back into the room and sat down. He kept Garbett waiting until he could see that hand beginning to shake again, and then said:

'Sandra Morrison.'

'Who's she?'

'Your girlfriend.'

Garbett licked his lips. 'No. I don't know what you're talking about.'

Galloway went back to Mrs Lindfield and apologized for keeping her waiting. She acknowledged this with a fretful bob of the head.

'Now then,' he said, 'tell me more about the Morrison family. They live near you?'

'Family?' Mrs Lindfield snorted. 'Is that what you call them? I blame the mother for most of this.' Evidently she had now succeeded in dismissing her own suggestion that she might herself have been in some way responsible. 'I mean, look at them. Two brothers, three sisters. All latchkey kids. They've all gone the same way.'

'Which way is that?'

'Don't play games, Mr Galloway. You know what I mean.' He thought he could deduce it pretty well, but was not keen on floundering through too many generalizations. 'Tell me more about Sandra.'

'She's the worst. When she was fourteen, men used to pick her up in cars after school. She took them home, all hours of the morning, doing God knows what. And then sit down and write her own late note for school next day. Can you credit it?'

'Sandra and Debbie seem to be such poles apart,' said Galloway. 'That's what I find difficult to understand. They're complete opposites: what could they possibly have in common?' Mrs Lindfield pondered this. 'Well, they've no friends, don't you see?'

'No, I'm afraid I don't.'

'Look, Debbie's very shy. She finds it hard to make friends. And Sandra – well, everybody detests Sandra, she's such an objectionable little bitch.'

'Then why,' demanded Galloway, 'did you allow the friendship?'

Mrs Lindfield's attempts at haughtiness were fading. She looked lost and unable to cope. 'I couldn't stop it. Debbie was always being left out. Lonely. So I encouraged her to go out and meet people – go to discos, do something interesting, liven herself up a bit. I never thought it would turn out like this.' She had crumpled in on herself. 'Look, Mr Galloway, my Debbie . . . she . . . it's going to take a bit of time, isn't it? That medical business . . . all the . . . well . . . '

'You can be present at the examination or have a word with the doctor, if you like.'

Now Mrs Lindfield was almost panic-stricken. She wanted no responsibility, no unpleasantness. Which was perhaps how Debbie had got to where she was now. 'I'd rather wait at home than hang about here,' she babbled. 'It wouldn't be a very good example for my daughter, eh . . . a distraught mother? Mr Galloway . . . ?'

'When everything's finished,' he said, 'I'll give you a call. And I tell you what – I'll run Debbie home myself.'

Her thanks became effusive. He saw her off the premises, and turned his attention to the next stage. By now, in a vengeful mood, he had no doubt what that stage had to be.

Sandra Morrison was wheeled into his office. Muswell, who had set off with her to the canteen in gloatingly optimistic mood, now looked very glad to be rid of her. Whatever had happened between them, there were signs that the girl had got the better of him.

She was not going to get the better of Roy Galloway, though she started out with every intention of doing so. 'Don't you think I've been kept hanging about here long enough?' He stared implacably at her. She raised her voice to a shrill, piercing pitch. 'Well, say something. Don't keep bogging me like that. Don't 'appen to 'ave one of them dirty old raincoats with 'oles in the pockets, do you?'

Galloway said: 'Why didn't you tell me Chris Garbett was your boyfriend?'

'He's not.'

'Sandra, we've got him in custody.'

Her mouth twisted. 'He's lying.'

'Oh, no, he's not. He has to tell the truth, don't you understand? His future depends upon it. And so,' said Galloway viciously, 'does yours, young lady. So let's have it.'

She stared hatred. The blackness around her eyes had smudged even further, as if she had been crying and wiping the tears into the mess. But she was not the sort of girl to cry – not in front of Muswell, certainly, and not here in front of Galloway.

'I don't know what sort of rubbish he's been telling you.'

'Let's hear what *you've* got to tell us, Sandra.'

Her teeth showed momentarily between her lips. Then she closed her mouth tight. Galloway sat and waited. It took about thirty seconds before the words began to come.

'I didn't tell him to beat 'er up. To rape 'er. Did I? She's my friend.'

'Then what did happen?'

Sandra hesitated again. Galloway knew he could afford to let her take her own time now. And then it all came out.

'Debbie was always boasting about being a virgin. No man was ever going to touch 'er until she was married. That's how it all started.'

'You were jealous?'

'Me, jealous? I've got nothing to be jealous about. Just couldn't believe she was that innocent, that's all. Chris couldn't, either. She was a lying cow, he said. Anyway, while she was dancing . . .'

It was smoky in the disco and there had been plenty to drink. Debbie, probably befuddled very early on, danced with a few boys she didn't know and didn't seem to want to know again. Chris and Sandra had watched her from the bar. It was Sandra who first thought of the idea and made a kind of bet; only it wasn't really a bet, more of a dare. She challenged Chris, bet him he couldn't screw Debbie. He reckoned he was irresistible to any girl. 'He's only got to look at them,' said Sandra, half scornful and half admiring, 'and they drop their knickers.'

'I've got a few like that at this station,' said Galloway, 'except they don't go around raping young girls.'

'I didn't know he was going to do that. Not really. I swear it.'

'I'll need a bit more convincing than that.'

Sandra was totally caught up in her story now, whatever the consequences might be for her. Any shame she might have felt for her part in what had happened at that disco was washed away by memories of the way she had set things up and the way it had felt at the time. Or most of the time.

When Debbie came back to the bar, Chris had asked her to dance with him. They must have been on the floor for about half and hour, or maybe a little longer. Sandra could remember it was a long time because she had been left to buy her own vodkas and orange. That was funny, though. But it was not so funny when she recalled the way they had swayed around with their arms round each other. It was what she had meant to happen; but when it actually happened, and she was watching it and enjoying it . . . well, was she really enjoying it? It must have been one-ish when they left the hall, arms round each other. And all she had to do was wait and hear from Chris whether her dare had worked. When he came back. If he came back. She did not put that into so many words, but Galloway heard the pinching of her tone and quickening breath behind the story.

'Jealous,' he said again. 'Come on, Sandra, your boyfriend going out like that with your best mate. What if they clicked? What if it turned out to be a love job?'

245

'No,' she shot back at him. 'It wasn't like that.'

'It must have entered your head.'

'No!'

'Or perhaps up until that moment you though your charms were so great that in the end Chris Garbett wouldn't go through with it.'

'No,' she said again, crossing and uncrossing her knees. Muswell would perhaps have enjoyed that. Roy Galloway found the spectacle an unattractive one. 'No. There's plenty more where he came from.'

'Are there? Come on, Sandra – that was the turning point, wasn't it?'

'I don't know what you mean.'

'Spite, Sandra. First of all you want to dirty up your so-called friend Debbie. Then when it went along a bit too fast, you turned your spite from Debbie to Chris Garbett.'

'Debbie *is* my friend. And she didn't ask for all that. I could 'ave killed Chris.'

'You did incite him.'

'No.'

'And now you're after punishing him because he did exactly what you dared him to do.'

'I didn't dare him to rape her.' Now she was really in danger of crying, but from anger, not misery. 'He was going to screw her, not rape her. That's different.'

'Bit of a reckless dare on your behalf, wouldn't you say? I'm not entirely satisfied with your story, Sandra. I think you took a far more active part in this than you're letting on.'

Fear began to creep through her brash defences. 'Oh, now look. Would I have encouraged Debbie to press charges if that was true? Eh – would I?'

'You've got a twisted little mind, Sandra. And attack is the best form of defence. Up until now you've covered yourself pretty well, playing the role of the caring friend.'

'I've told you the truth.'

'Would you ever know the truth if you saw it?' Galloway raised a thumb to Ted Roach beyond the glass partition. As Ted obediently opened the door, he said: 'Get her down to the detention room until I make further enquiries.'

Now it was blind panic. 'No, you can't! I'm not going into any room. Not like that. You can't do that.' As Ted Roach reached for her she slashed out with her nails. 'Get off me . . . you, get *off* me!'

Roach held her with one hand and, with commendable style in the circumstances, waved a visitor in with the other. 'Doctor Figg.'

The doctor at least was professionally unshockable and detached, but she allowed herself the quizzical lift of an eyebrow. 'Do you always have that effect on young girls?'

Roy Galloway was not sure what effect he had on girls any longer, whatever age they might be. He had somehow not allowed himself much time to find out such things in recent years.

'What news have you got for me?' he asked. At the same time he delved into the bottom drawer of his desk and brought out a whisky bottle and two glasses.

Dr Figg offered him an appreciative smile. 'I never fail to get the finest hospitality at Sun Hill. It's my favourite nick, you know.' She lifted her glass. 'Cheers.'

'Cheers. So what are your findings?'

For some unfathomable reason she looked mildly amused. Galloway felt she had something up her sleeve. But then, medics were always like this: putting on their act, playing their professional game.

Not that detective inspectors were entirely immune from such temptations.

'Gynaecological examinations usually have their little snags in such circumstances,' said Dr Figg. 'But I have excellent forensic samples for you.'

'Good,' said Galloway, hoping to be spared the details.

'Blood,' said Dr Figg, 'saliva, semen stains, pubic hair. Swabs back and front – all good stuff, Roy.'

Galloway drowned a faint hint of nausea with a tincture of neat Scotch. 'I'll stick to being a policeman, if you don't mind.'

'But you do have a slight problem.' Her sparkle of amusement was positively glittering now. 'I'd take another swig of that, Roy, if I were you.'

'Now what? Go on – you won't shock me.'

'Won't I? Not even if I tell you that our Debbie is *virgo intacta?*'

'A virgin?' Galloway choked on his drink.

'Pure as the driven snow.'

'You must be joking.'

'I would say that the young man concerned was a young man in great haste.'

Galloway coughed and waited for the raw heat in his throat to cool off. He still found it hard to accept. But Dr Figg's knowing, tolerant smile was worth more than ten other people's loud affidavits and protestations.

'Big deal,' he muttered. 'All that, just for . . . well . . . '

'It's not unusual, Roy.'

This, he meditated, would certainly bruise Garbett's ego. And there was no doubt that Chris Garbett had an outsize ego. If nothing much else.

'A terrified girl in that situation,' said Dr Figg, 'wouldn't know what was happening. It's quite feasible, really it is.'

'I know that.' He wagged his head, still incredulous. 'But to actually believe you've been raped . . . '

'Certainly. Especially if you're a young girl with no sexual experience.'

'Hold it,' said Galloway. 'When it comes to sexual experience, what about Garbett? I mean, from what we've figured out about him – '

'Bull at a gate,' said Dr Figg bluntly.

'And Debbie has no idea?'

'That she's still a virgin? I thought I'd break the news to you first.'

Galloway raised his glass to her and drained the few drops from the bottom. 'Let's both go and tell her, shall we?'

They found Debbie Lindfield putting on a pair of shoes, lifting her feet to show them off to June Ackland.

'They're the first ones I bought myself. My mum usually buys everything for me out of the catalogue.'

'Your mum does a lot for you, doesn't she?' Debbie nodded eagerly.

Galloway led Dr Figg in, and the two of them stood over the girl, taking it easy, trying to convey the idea that the tension was off, nobody was forcing any issues.

'You feeling all right, Debbie?'

The girl's wan face showed in a timid smile how likeable it might be.

Dr Figg said: 'Debbie, this is going to come as a surprise to you. A pleasant one, I'm sure. You have not been raped, Debbie.'

Debbie, doing up the buttons of her recently laundered blouse, looked puzzled and vaguely offended, as if someone had been doubting her word. June Ackland shot a glance at Galloway, not offended but equally puzzled.

'You are still a virgin,' said Dr Figg decisively. She turned to the other two in the room. 'Perhaps it would be better if you both left while I have a chat with Debbie.'

They silently agreed on this. Outside, June shook her head and said: 'What a turn-up for the books! I'll be believing in fairy stories next. So what about the charges, sir?'

'I've got plenty of evidence for attempted rape. As long as Debbie comes up trumps in the statement. So when the doctor's finished, it's straight up to the top of the page for you and get that statement completed. And signed. Because without it we're snookered.'

'Where's Morrison?' asked June with undisguised distaste. 'What about her?'

'I'll push for conspiracy to rape.'

'Eh? Morrison was involved?'

'You don't cotton on to the full story, then?'

'No, I don't.'

Galloway told her, more succinctly than Sandra Morrison had told it to him. June listened motionless for the first half of the story, then began nodding in dreary acquiescence; then shook her head.

'Conspiracy's a bit thin, though. You'll have a hard time proving that, sir.'

'I haven't finished questioning her yet, have I? She might plead and turn Queen's evidence.'

'Fat chance.'

He had a nasty feeling June was right. Hastily he got the whole thing on to more general speculative topics. 'What I really don't understand, even now, is how any girl can send her boyfriend out to screw another girl.'

'Oh, I don't know.' June Ackland seemed to find no difficulty in understanding. There were times when that young but oddly world-weary face of hers hinted not just at the everyday disillusionment of her job but at some personal battering which she had never confided to anyone. 'I mean, she's probably never done it for love, only to keep some randy boyfriend. What else has she got going for her?'

Galloway had to admit that this was another way of looking at it: not so wildly different from some of his own suppositions, really.

'You see,' said June, 'I reckon Morrison regrets sleeping around, though she'd never allow herself to think any such thing. She can't turn the clock back, so she does the next best thing. She sets about bringing Debbie down to her level.'

'Could be.'

There was a moment of mutual respect between them, an odd drift of agreement that became almost personal. Other theories might be valid, other things might be said in the charge room or in court or on the local streets, but they shared a knowledge based on what they had seen and heard and felt. Only it wasn't really in any way personal. It was all part of the job, part of what made the system work.

'Men'll never get the hang of women and the way they think,' said June, in what might have been consolation.

'Thank God! Anyway, as soon as you finish that last bit of statement, bring Debbie in to me, all right?'

'Right . . . sir.'

But it was not all right. The pieces had slotted in so neatly together, and the rough edges had been smoothed off so professionally, that Galloway had been sure of the outcome. From now on it was tidy routine. All coherent, all wrapped up.

Except for Debbie refusing to complete her statement and refusing to sign anything. She had been told every last little detail of what they had wormed out of Sandra; had gone pale and tried to cover her eyes with her arm, blotting out filthy truths she did not want to know about; and then had said she'd had enough. She wanted to go home. That was all she wanted to do.

'But you're not going to give evidence at all?' Galloway pleaded.

'I can't. I've got nothing to say.'

'But Debbie –'

'They were my friends,' she said drearily. 'At least, Sandra was.'

'Conspiracy. Attempted rape.' Galloway hammered it at her. 'They're serious charges, Debbie. Without your evidence I don't have a case.'

'I want to forget the whole thing.'

'I can appreciate that. What worries me is, if I throw this case out, what'll your precious friend Sandra get up to next? And Garbett – he'll think he's got a licence to go out and try it on with some other poor girl, someone not as fortunate as you've been.'

'I couldn't give evidence,' she said numbly. 'Please don't force me to.'

'Will you at least think about it?'

'I'll think about it.' She said it just to get away and be done with the whole thing, not because she really meant to give it any consideration.

Galloway walked along the passage with her, stricken by the collapse of what he had painstakingly built up. 'Having to kiss this case goodbye, it really leaves a nasty taste in my mouth,' he said. 'It really hurts me.'

They reached the door. She looked at him with the first flicker of spirit, of a real inner self, she had shown so far. 'I don't think you're the one who's been really hurt,' she said. 'Are you?' She seemed to be gaining a bleak shield of self-possession by the minute. 'All this, like the doctor said to me, it's like I've been given a fresh start. It's important to me. I don't want to spoil it.'

Galloway gave in. 'I understand.'

'I don't want to relive that nightmare. Not ever. Not in a courtroom, least of all. I just couldn't.'

'It's all right,' he assured her. 'I understand. I really do. Now come on, I'll take you home.'

'No, please. I know the way all right.'

'Debbie, I promised your mum. Debbie, please . . . '

But with a new, frightening determination she had walked out and was gone.

Galloway turned back into the station.

Bob Cryer said, 'You look as if you need cheering up, Roy. A little celebration in the offing, right?'

'Celebration? Like hell.'

'A week Friday.'

A bell rang at the back of Galloway's mind. Julia. He was going to get tickets and take Julia to that godawful concert a week on Friday.

'What's all this about a celebration?'

'Henry Talbot's leaving,' said Cryer. 'Isn't that cause for a party? And it's all on the chief super. A fond farewell to his trusty creep.'

'Not Friday evening?'

'Friday evening. Everybody summoned to attend, unless on duty doing something vital – preferably not on overtime.'

'But I've got a date. Something very special. I can't break it now. She . . . '

'Oh, it's a she, is it? Knowing the number of times you've lectured Ted Roach about time-consuming habits in that direction –'

'Shut up. It's not like that.'

Cryer looked at him and got the glimmerings of the message. 'Sorry, Roy. But whatever it is, the chief super will be expecting you to get your priorities right.'

So, thought Roy Galloway as the echoes of past defections rang discordantly in his head, would his daughter.

Twelve

It sounded suspicious. In Roy Galloway's nostrils it produced a very unpleasant smell. The story itself was plausible enough, and the victim looked convincingly dazed and roughed-up and was making just the sort of noises you would expect anyone in that situation to make. When a couple of heavies bash into your office, beat you up, tie you up and make off with a truckload of sheepskin coats, you'd be expected to raise hell when the police showed up and released you. Too late, as usual. Always on the scene after the thieves have left it.

The trouble was, Galloway had heard it all before – and from the same source.

'Elkins?' he said, when Roach reported in. 'But this is the third time this last six months.'

'They do leave themselves wide open, guv, operating from that caravan. If they invested in decent premises –'

'Crawley and Elkins Transport,' mused Galloway. 'All set for another insurance claim, eh? And how much is it this time? Any idea?'

'Eight thousand quids' worth.'

'It stinks.'

The story as told by Fred Elkins was that he had been sorting out delivery notes in the caravan jacked up in one corner of the yard where he and his partner operated their transport business. Galloway knew the yard well enough from previous occasions. A board on the fence declared that the company undertook packing, storage and freighting on a national and international scale. Their two vans and one articulated lorry hardly looked capable of surviving a rough sea crossing, and barely sustained the occasional inspection by M1 motorway police; but Elkins and Crawley managed to survive, offering a cheap service to dealers and manufacturers anxious to cut down on every possible penny. Now, not for the first time, one of those vehicles had gone missing. This time, though, there was a variation on the theme. The previous incidents had been straight thefts of vehicles, lifted off the street and found minus their loads. This one was a tie-up job. The villains had rushed into the

251

caravan, grabbed Elkins, tied up his hands and feet and gagged him, then driven the van full of coats out of the yard.

What was strange was the phone call. After tying Elkins up and lifting the van keys, one of the men dialled 999 – went to the trouble of putting a hand-kerchief over the receiver and asking for the police.

Roach and Galloway shook their heads. No villain in his right mind was going to go to the trouble of making a 999 call on the spot like that. If he was worried about the victim because of the ropes maybe being too tight or some-thing, he would get well clear and then make the call from a public phone box – most likely after the stuff was safely stashed away.

'Unless they didn't have far to go,' Roach suggested. 'A calculated risk. By why take a risk at all?'

'Just to make it look good,' said Galloway. 'Make it different from last time, just to throw us. What about Crawley – where was he while all this was going on?'

'He's got a very good alibi. His accountant. He was there for over an hour.'

'That accountant's as bent as they are.'

The description of the van and its numberplate had been circulated, but it had contrived to disappear into thin air with remarkable skill. Mark you, thought Galloway, they'd had plenty of chances to develop that skill. If it *was* the two of them. And he was sure it was. Once a van dragger, always a van dragger. And the gear was customer's gear, not theirs, all covered by insurance.

He knew in his bones that it was true, but there was no way he could come out with a direct accusation. Instead he had to listen to Elkins bemoaning their loss, and the bad effect the news would have on their trade, and the likelihood of them going flat broke.

No line of enquiry was possible until that van was found. And then most probably it would be empty.

Galloway went downstairs to ask Bob Cryer if there had been any news from Muswell or Carver or Lyttleton, hunting for the missing vehicle. There was no point in badgering Cryer. If anyone had found it, Galloway would have been told soon enough, and he knew it. But he simply could not sit still.

Cryer was not in the office. In his place, Sergeant Peters was saying: 'And what gives you the impression that nobody wants to talk to you, Hollis?'

Hollis wore his familiar aggrieved expression, caused now by mental rather than physical pain. 'It's ever since I applied for the clerk's job with the chief super. I mean, I've got the qualifications, and it's more in my line. Won't make any difference to the way I behave.'

'Don't suppose it will.'

'I tell you, it's put me off going to this retirement party tonight.'

Peters glanced past him at Galloway. 'Won't be on your own.'

'And have you heard who's coming back for it? Dave Litten, of all people. Thought we'd got shot of him.'

'Bolshie bugger,' said Peters. At least on this they were agreed.

'No one'll want to talk to *him*, if they've got any sense. But why me, sarge?'

Peters winked at Galloway. 'Jealousy, that's what it is, Hollis. Touch of the old green eye. They see you as a flyer – you know, scrambled egg all over your shoulder.'

'Scrambled egg?'

'Well, the chief super started as a clerk, you know. Stood him in good stead. Never looked back.'

'Find yourself a niche, Hollis,' Galloway contributed. 'Study for promotion, that's my advice. Let mugs like us go chasing the villains.'

Hollis looked into a shimmering, beckoning future. He began to nod slowly. 'Speaking at conferences. Mm. Attending seminars.'

'Opening fêtes.'

'I think I could carry that off.'

'Some are born to greatness,' said Peters. 'Others have it thrust upon them.'

Galloway had had enough. Nothing was going to happen for a while yet, if at all. And that passing mention of tonight's party had been an added exasperation. Only worse than that. There was something he had to do. He had been delaying, hoping there would miraculously be some way out. But Chief Superintendent Brownlow had made it quite clear what he expected of all of them; and certainly officers in a position of authority like Detective Inspector Galloway had to be in attendance.

Back in his office, he picked up the phone and dialled that unforgettable number. When Maureen answered he said: 'Look, about this concert this evening – '

'You're not going to show up after all?'

'Something's happened. I wanted to get out of it, but you know what things are.'

'Oh yes, I know. Who better?'

'Look, I know you don't like that racket any more than I do, but it means a lot to Julia.'

'Glad you're aware of that.'

'Just for once you could put up with it. Right? I'll get the tickets round to you somehow, and next week I'll make quite sure of fixing something –'

She had hung up.

He was sitting rigid when Ted Roach came in.

'Guv, I've had a thought. That Elkins and Crawley team. Why don't I go on obbo tonight and see if they move the load?'

'No.'

'But guv, they could lead me to it, we could – '

'I know what you're thinking, Ted. But you're coming to that retirement party whether you like it or not.'

'Henry Talbot is a twenty-four carat prat.'

'What's that got to do with it?'

'The man is a prat,' Roach insisted. 'I don't even *like* him, let alone – '

'He's not exactly my blood brother, either.' Galloway was sure of one thing: if he had to attend that blasted party, then everyone else around him was going to have to suffer as well. Aloud he said: 'The chief super has said everyone's got to be there. So you'll be there, Ted.'

They usually enjoyed the moment when they pushed open the door of the saloon bar and walked into the pub on the corner. This evening it was different. Elbowing their way through the crowd to the bar, neither Cryer nor Galloway was in any hurry to go upstairs to the room where the party was officially being held. Cryer ordered two pints and surveyed the rest of the crowd.

It looked as if their sentiments were shared. Jimmy Carver and June Ackland had just arrived and were making no movement towards the flight of stairs at the end of the bar. June looked quite a different person, thought Galloway abstractedly, wearing a sleek khaki raincoat and with her hair like corn in sunshine – a breath of fresh air in this polluted atmosphere.

What the hell was he thinking about?

'I don't believe it,' said Bob Cryer, spluttering over his beer. 'See who's just walked in? Well, that's me off. I'm not staying here listening to him.' He began gulping the rest of his pint down.

'What are you on about?'

Then he saw. The insufferable DS Burnside had come in, looking about the bar as if he owned the place. As soon as he spotted Cryer and Galloway he came towards them as if expecting the most wonderful welcome in the world.

'Hello, guv. How's tricks?' He waved a large, meaty hand to embrace the whole scene. 'I see we've got the uniform pushing the boat out, then.'

'There's some nice boozers out in Epping,' said Cryer. 'Don't you know any?'

Galloway had thought nothing could get much worse. But Burnside's presence could make anything worse. 'What are you doing here anyway?'

'Just come to pay my respects to old Henry, of course.'

'Old Henry?' Cryer echoed mockingly. 'And who invited you?'

'I don't have to be invited. He's an old pal from way back. Know what I mean?'

'I know what you mean. Got a sniff of the free booze, didn't you?'

Burnside turned to Galloway for support. 'I don't have to take that off him, do I, guv?'

'Never mind all that. Where is it?'

'Where's what?'

'The bottle.'

'What bottle? I don't have to bring a bottle.'

'You don't get in, then,' said Galloway smugly.

'Who says so?'

'I say so.'

Burnside tried to face him out. Galloway preserved a stony stare until Burnside caved in and turned towards the counter.

'Oi, love, give us a bottle of Scotch. Cheapest brand you've got.'

Behind his back, Galloway gave Sadie a quick scowl and a shake of the head.

'Sorry, sir,' she said briskly. 'I'm not allowed to do off-sales. There's an off-licence up the High Street, about five minutes away.'

Burnside took another suspicious glance at Galloway and Cryer, still unsure; but he got no joy from them. After a moment's uncertainty he stumped off through the door and out into the street.

Cryer panted out a bottled-up laugh. 'Ought to be ashamed of yourself, telling porkies like that.'

'Didn't I do right?' Sadie was almost as fazed as Burnside.

'With any luck,' said Galloway, 'he'll have taken the hint.'

Cryer doubted it. 'He's too thick-skinned. If I know Burnside, he'll be back with a bottle of British sherry under his arm.'

The crowd was thinning out. Carver and June Ackland had already gone upstairs, and Ted Roach was beckoning from halfway up the flight. 'You'd better get along up, guv. The chief super's asking where you are.'

'Couldn't you tell him Roy's out getting a bottle?' Cryer suggested.

Roach looked blank. He hadn't been in on the joke. 'A bottle? I tell you, we should have waylaid some of the punters coming in here tonight. It's like a distillery up there. Bottles of Scotch all over the place.'

'I should charge corkage, maybe,' said Sadie.

Galloway finished his drink and headed for the stairs. One look at Roach's reddening face, and he paused on the top step. 'Go easy on the stuff, Ted.'

'I'm all right, guv. You know me.'

'I do indeed. Don't forget you've got a promotion board coming up soon. And the chief super doesn't miss a trick, my old son. So behave yourself.'

The noise hit them as soon as Galloway pushed open the door at the top of the flight. To boost up the babble of voices there was a background of steadily thudding music from massive speakers in one corner. Behind the bar across the end of the room, June Ackland had shed her raincoat to reveal a figure-hugging brown dress with splashes of coloured flowers wreathing and glowing all over it. It was not all she revealed as she bent over a firkin of beer. When it fizzed and spluttered, defying her attempts to pour a properly controlled pint, there were plenty of men only too glad to come round and offer assistance. Bursts of laughter and shouts of encouragement bellowed across the room.

Chief Superintendent Brownlow was not joining in any laughter. He came impatiently over to Roy Galloway. The party had been his own idea but he did not seem to be in party mood.

'Roy, who are those men over there?'

Galloway warmed with secret satisfaction. It was the chief super himself who had asked Roy to make up the numbers by inviting a representative selection of local folk. Good for community relations: that had been the implication.

'Local traders,' said Galloway.

'Look more like the Mafia to me. How did they get in here?'

'I invited them. On your orders, sir. A little local colour, I think, was the term used.'

Brownlow's beetling eyebrows descended a substantial fraction of an inch. His left shoulder jerked up and forward. It was a mannerism of his, most noticeable when he was about to get awkward.

'Look, Roy, I'm about to start the presentation. I hope for your sake they don't cause any trouble. There are other guests to be considered, you know.'

Oh, yes, Galloway knew that all right. He was not sure, though, that there was any great basic contrast between the two groups: the three local wide boys with their dark glasses and raucous laughs, and the men from Brownlow's golf club with their plump and far from quiet wives. There were brash ways of being a villain, and smooth ways of being a wheeler-dealer. The aims were roughly the same.

Viv Martella went past in a puce dress which jerked Sergeant Penny's head round. Even Brownlow spared her a briefly appreciative glance, but his gaze abruptly ceased to follow her.

'And Roy . . . you'd better keep your eyes on Roach. He's drinking far too much.'

'Yes, sir.'

As Brownlow headed for the shallow platform between the speakers, with a shrouded keyboard to one side, the door from the stairs slammed open. Burnside stood in the opening. Carver and Edwards, drinking from cans of lager on two uncomfortable chairs against the wall, grimaced as he passed them.

'Ladies and gentlemen . . . '

'Here we are, guv,' said Burnside loudly. 'I brought a bottle just like you said.' He held out something unidentifiable in a wrapping of rustling blue paper.

Chief Superintendent Brownlow glared over the heads between them. 'May I have your attention, please.'

Burnside was thrusting the bottle at Galloway.

'It gives me great pleasure, tinged with a little sadness . . .' Burnside tried to grip the bottle under his arm and applaud at the same time.

'Right.' Galloway whipped the bottle away and put it on a table near the door. 'Come on outside.'

' . . . that we're here today,' Brownlow went on implacably, 'to say goodbye to Harry Talbot. After twenty years of sterling service, I know we're all going to miss him very much.'

There was a ripple of laughter which pleased neither the chief super nor Henry Talbot, standing with his wife in a tight huddle on the minute platform.

'What's the problem, guv?' Burnside was muttering furiously. 'I mean, what have I done wrong?'

Galloway manhandled him through the door and out on to the landing.

'Now, what's your game, Burnside?'

'What are you talking about?'

'I want to know what you're doing on this manor, my son.'

'Nothing, guv. Honest.' Burnside spread his arms wide and nearly knocked over an elderly man with a white moustache who had arrived late and was fussing towards the door. 'I've just come to shake hands with old ... er, Henry ... Harry ... that's all.'

It was a load of crap, thought Galloway. Whatever his faults, Henry Talbot had always been too straight in his own mean-minded way to mix with any copper as bent as Burnside. 'You're up to something, and I want to know what.'

Burnside let his arms fall to his side. 'Look, it's not what you think, guv. I'm not up to anything. It's just a social call, seriously.'

'Codswallop!'

'On my life.'

Galloway produced the most contemptuous sound his throat was capable of.

'You've got it all wrong, guv,' said Burnside. His heavy, purplish lips were almost pouting. 'What it is ... but you'll only laugh.'

'Try me.'

'Well, you know how it is ...' But Burnside was still reluctant to take the plunge.

'Don't mess me about.'

'Well, to be honest,' said Burnside in a rush, 'I fancy June Ackland.'

Galloway nearly lost his footing on the tread of the stairs. 'You what?'

'There you go, y'see. I knew you'd take the mickey.'

'How could any bird in her right mind be interested in such an obnoxious git as you?'

The pout grew aggressive. 'Now keep it down, guv. Look, I've rung her a couple of times, but she's always given me the big E. Only I sort of thought, if I came along tonight ... I mean, everyone's going to be in a good mood tonight, eh ...?'

From inside came a sprinkling of applause. Galloway clung to the banister rail, beginning to shake with laughter. Burnside's face and Burnside's story – too bloody marvellous for words. It was all so absurd that it had to be true.

'Look, guv, you wouldn't tell anyone, would you?'

Galloway shook his head helplessly and lurched back into the room.

The chief superintendent was saying: 'We'd like to present you with this silver drinks tray, Henry, for all the loyalty and dedication you've shown to us at Sun Hill over the years.'

'Hope he drops it on his bloody toes.' Ted Roach's Belfast accent was all too audible.

It had not escaped Brownlow's attention. 'I might add' – he raised his voice meaningly – 'that it's not often realized what a difficult and indeed thankless task you've often had. Nor indeed what it entails.'

'Being a bloody snout!'

'Once again, Henry, we'd like to thank you for all your loyalty. We all know that without it there are times when Sun Hill police station would have ground to a halt. Have a long and very happy retirement.'

Everybody applauded vigorously, thankfully, as Talbot took the tray, and a bouquet of flowers was passed up to his wife. Somebody feebly struck up 'For he's a jolly good fellow', and with deadpan expressions Carver, Edwards and a number of others joined in.

'They'll be doing the hokey-cokey next,' said Burnside. Then he brightened up, making his way round the edge of the room until he finished up at one end of the bar.

June Ackland turned with a smile to serve him; and stopped smiling when she saw who it was. Her smile was not restored by the sudden appearance of Dave Litten. A lot of water might have flowed under a lot of Thames bridges since the day when Litten had been at Sun Hill and they had had a brief, stormy relationship, but old memories could still create a nasty jolt.

A cackling laugh from the three local traders started up the tide of noise again.

Litten stared at June, stared away. 'Well, I've done me loyalty bit. Good old Henry – I don't think! I'm glad I'm on night duty. Good excuse to get out of it soon.'

Burnside leaned across the bar towards June. 'You're not on night duty as well, are you, darling?'

She appraised him for a moment. He could not be sure whether she was laughing inside or whether it was a really inviting smile she was about to offer. 'Not tonight,' she said. 'Free and available.'

It might have been for Litten's benefit. She shot him a fleeting glance, and went to serve someone at the other end of the bar.

Burnside smacked his lips. 'Quite a tasty bird, ain't she?'

'Yeah, well, you can keep your eyes off there, skip.' Litten, too, was watching June. Something appeared to tickle his fancy. 'She's taken,' he said.

'Really?'

Burnside waited. Litten said no more, but very slowly nodded across the room. Galloway was standing with his back to them. Burnside gulped, said, 'Really?' again, and got Litten's grave nod of confirmation.

He drifted away, looking round for something to make the evening worthwhile. Chances were thin on the ground.

Others were drifting away now. Henry Talbot and his wife stood to one side of the room while a few men came over to shake their hands. Rather more dodged towards the door, not wanting to be seen anywhere near Talbot: even this late on, being friendly to him might arouse suspicions of having shared secrets with him. Carver and Edwards waited until Sergeant Cryer was off the premises, on his way back to night duty at the station. Hollis, having plucked up the courage to make a pass at Viv Martella and been slapped down for his pains, followed disconsolately into the night.

Ted Roach was still drinking and still talking, growing louder but more slurred.

Galloway took a sip from the whisky glass in his hand, coughed, and decided that if Roach was tipping back firewater of this calibre then it was high time he was stopped. He held the glass out to Mike Dashwood.

'Do me a favour. Take this over to the bar and discreetly water it down while I have a word with Ted.'

'Strong, is it?'

'If Ackland poured that, she doesn't know the meaning of the word "single".'

'D'you suppose she knows the meaning of – '

'On your way!'

Dashwood made his way through the dwindling groups of dogged drinkers, those stalwarts who would not be shifted until the last drop had been downed or a bossy voice told them categorically that it was time to go home. Viv Martella, her face almost the hue of her dress, bumped against Dashwood and peered into his face.

'What's a big, single, handsome hunk of man like you doing tonight, honey?'

Dashwood flinched. Whatever mixture of drinks she had been knocking back, it had certainly given her breath quite a punch.

'I . . . er . . . I've got a sick dog at home. Got to go home and look after it. I think it's on heat.' And not the only one, he thought.

'Thanks a lot, I'm sure.' Martella reeled on her way.

June Ackland grinned as Dashwood reached the bar.

'Here, top this up for me, will you. Water's not that expensive. Be a bit more generous with it.'

She reached for the water jug. 'Funny. I wouldn't reckon you for a Scotch drinker.'

'I'm not. It's Galloway's.'

She stooped and picked up a bottle. 'A bit of colour in the dose as well?'

'Hang on.' Dashwood put out a hand. 'Where did that come from?'

259

June turned the bottle round so that he could read the label. 'One of the guests brought it. There's another one down there. We haven't even opened it up yet.'

'Well, don't open it. Put it to one side.'

'Why?'

'Later.' Dashwood was turning back towards Galloway and Roach. As he reached them, Roach was grumbling vaguely on about Hollis, and what a snout he was, and what he would tell him the first time he tried acting up like Henry Talbot.

Galloway's right hand was out. 'Let's have your car keys, Ted.'

'Bloody little snout. I tell you, if he ever grasses on me the way –'

'You're your own worst enemy. Let's have your car keys. There's no way you're going to drive home tonight, Ted.'

'I'm all right, guv.' Roach swayed, and gripped Mike Dashwood's arm. 'Sober as a judge. Right, Mike?'

Dashwood said: 'Guv, I've got to have a word. Urgent.'

Ted Roach sniggered. 'What's the matter, Dashers? Something you can't handle, eh?'

Galloway said, 'Stay there, Ted. I want your car keys.'

He drew Dashwood to one side; and Dashwood explained. There had been a report two weeks ago on a theft of Scotch from a bonded warehouse on Limehouse section. All due for export.

No leads had turned up so far – until this evening. Two bottles of the stuff had turned up right here at this party. Galloway was momentarily apprehensive. It was just the sort of thing his three traders might have got up to. Brownlow would just love that.

'Couldn't have been Burnside, could it?' he said with little real hope.

'Only brought one bottle, and I don't suppose that was export quality.'

Galloway jerked his head, and the two of them went towards June Ackland. Burnside watched him with an odd expression. It did not appear that Burnside had made much headway this evening.

June confirmed that the bottles had been handed over by a guest. Not, to Galloway's relief, one of the types he had invited. Unobtrusively she indicated a man in a herring-bone jacket who was in the chief super's crowd. The chief super was still there, and they were still drinking Scotch. What was more, a couple of them had several times asked for it by name: real connoisseurs, or something.

Or something.

'Right,' said Galloway in an undertone. 'This is what you do. You keep pumping them with that Scotch. Don't let anyone else touch it. When the bottle's empty you put it to one side for me.'

'You want me to open the full bottle as well?'

'No. Put it to one side and I'll collect both bottles when the party's over.'

'Please tell me what this is all about, sir?'

'If it comes off, a rare coup,' said Galloway jubilantly. It took only a few seconds for the jubilation to fade. 'Hey – where's Roach?'

Ted Roach had taken the opportunity to leave.

He groped his way into the driver's seat and got the ignition key in at the third attempt. Bloody tired, that's what he was. And no bloody wonder, after a deadly evening like that, drinking cheap rubbish just in order to numb the pain of listening to hypocritical speeches about the worst hypocrite they had ever had at Sun Hill. And now there was the threat of a real disciple of Talbot's. If anyone could outdo Talbot in sneaking behind people's backs, it would be Hollis.

Roach roared the engine and in his head roared at Talbot and Hollis and every poxy little creep like them.

He switched the lights on. Four people crossing the road immediately ahead held their arms across their eyes in protest. Reaching for the heater, he turned the radio on full blast. A disc jockey began to rave up from under the dashboard.

Roach swung out of the side street on to the main road and headed for home. Sober as a judge. Hardly anybody about this time of night, nothing to worry about, and he couldn't anyway have spent another five minutes in that grotty room with those creeps.

He began to hum a song that bore no resemblance to the song erupting from the radio. Its steady rhythm kept him awake, kept him concentrating.

A motorcyclist almost blinded him with a dazzling single headlight. Roach swore. One wheel jarred against the kerb on a corner, and he swore again. All he wanted was to get home and get his head down and pass out.

Safest to stick to the back doubles. He knew every inch of the way. Past a half-demolished chapel, turn right by the pub knew it like the back of his hand – and down a quiet street of Edwardian terraces with small front gardens and white palings. The beam of his headlights flickered dizzyingly along the strip of fencing.

Shadows danced across the road. And suddenly one of them was the thick black shadow of a dog, bounding towards a doorstep.

Roach swore again and spun the wheel desperately. The house fronts swung towards him at an impossible angle, and all at once the white palings were ahead of him and not to one side. He stamped on the brake. There was a cracking, splintering screech, slats of wood twisted up in the air, and the bonnet of the car tilted downwards above a tiny basement window.

He reached for the door handle and tried to heave himself out, but was trapped. Then he realized he must have fastened his seat belt instinctively as he got in. By the time he had found the release and tottered out on to the patch of grass, light was flooding on to the path from an open front door.

'What's going on here?' A tall Jamaican with piercing eyes reflecting the light came down two steps. 'Hey, is this your car, man?'

'I . . . oh, God, what . . . '

Doors were opening all along the street.

'What's this doing in my garden, man?'

Roach made a run for it, towards the far, darker end of the street.

Thirteen

Bob Cryer inhaled several gulps of fresh air – or the nearest thing to it that the space between the pub and Sun Hill police station could provide – and eased himself thankfully back into the familiar atmosphere of slightly musty central heating, unpredictable draughts and the occasional waft of wet shoes and sweaty tunics. Even when the switchboard was going berserk and somebody was doing his nut in one of the cells, it was quieter here than in the boozy uproar he had just left.

Sergeant Peters looked up from the desk. 'Blimey, you're keen! Not half past nine yet.'

'Always raring to go,' said Cryer, who in fact was raring to sit down and go through the incident book and enjoy a bit of academic assessment.

'If it's excitement you want, this is definitely not the place to be. Quiet as a graveyard so far, Bob. Nothing happened at all. Not a dickie bird. Nothing in the book since . . . let's see . . .'

His meditation was broken into by a peremptory hammering on the counter. Peters had spoken too soon. A woman with a silk scarf knotted over her head was complaining, even before he was within a yard of her, about the noise up the road, the disgrace of it – 'I can't sleep, nobody can sleep.' Peters looked politely concerned. Cryer wondered who could get stroppy about not being allowed to sleep around nine-thirty in the evening.

'From up the road,' the woman declared over and over again.

'Up the road. The noise, it's a disgrace, that's what.'

'You can pinpoint the location, madam?'

'That pub on the corner. You know, up the road – down from here.'

Bob Cryer tried to work out the mathematics of this in his mind and then it dawned on him. This member of the public was making a complaint about the volume of the celebrations at the chief super's party. He contemplated intervening; then left it to Sergeant Peters.

'And they're starting up the *other* way,' the woman went on, outraged.

'What's the neighbourhood coming to, that's what I want to know.'

'Madam?'

'House on the other side, three doors down. Starting up a party, you can tell it's going to go on and on till God knows what hour of the morning.'

Bob Cryer looked at the clock, gladly accepted the routine that, compared with what was going on elsewhere, could only be described as tranquil, and went off on the dot to the parade room.

Carver and Edwards looked as relieved as himself at having finally escaped the party. Carver tugged his tunic straight. Edwards, for once, looked quite keen and attentive. The cool night air would do them good.

Cryer went down the list. That van-load of sheepskin coats had still not been located. Every eye should be kept open for the van, or even for any unlikely bunch of strollers wearing clothes of a quality to which they were not accustomed. Then, on three beat, the occupants of 43 Rampton Gardens were on holiday until the twentieth of the month. Casual attention was all that was called for: but casual as it might be, let it be attentive. Check on possible noise round the corner below a pub which should need no naming – but report back before making an issue of it, just in case there was a mix-up with late departures from the chief super's shindig. Another rave-up: a twenty-first birthday party in Vale View Gardens, going on till one. The householders had apologized in advance for any noise, and spoken to the neighbours. All the same, make sure it didn't get out of hand.

'But don't be tempted in,' Cryer warned, 'if you're invited. You're apt to lose your helmet at those kind of dos.'

'Or something else, sarge.' Yorkie Smith rolled his eyes.

Just for that, Cryer decreed that Smith could go down to Langham Sykes, the jewellers in the High Street, and relieve the late-turn PC. There was a broken window, the burglar alarm had been triggered off, and they had to wait until the keyholder turned up. It might involve a long wait.

'Oh, and all of you – have a look at the AS on the stolen sheepskin coats.' He took a note which Shaw had just brought in from the switchboard, and skimmed over it. 'Hm. Carver, you're on eight beat, right?'

'Right, sarge.' Carver waited for the worst.

'Number 14 Graceton Avenue. They've got a car in their front garden.'

Taffy Edwards grinned. 'Why don't they have little plastic gnomes like everybody else?'

'Take a panda down there,' said Cryer, 'and take the Welsh wit with you.' He waved at the rest of them. 'All right, off you go, all of you. Get out and terrorize the population.'

They went out into the night.

Yorkie Smith found himself the butt of jovial and not so jovial remarks from neighbours who regarded the frequently jangling burglar alarm as a bad joke in itself. Couldn't he shin up and stop it? Didn't he have some marvellous new electronic device that would silence it from a distance? Was it all right if they helped themselves through the gap in the window, or were those shutters electrified? He paced up and down on sentry-go, wondering when the hell Mr Sykes, or whoever, would summon up the energy to appear on the scene.

Plenty of people had appeared on the scene confronting Carver and Edwards as they turned into Graceton Avenue. A useful battery of lights from windows and open front doors illuminated the tableau of tilted vehicle and splintered palings. Neighbours of a variety of hues from pale white to gleaming black prodded their way round the car, leaning in the driver's door, peering under the twisted bonnet and trying to force it up.

Jimmy Carver moved in. 'Excuse me. Come on, sonny . . . excuse me, madam. Could you all move away from the car, please?'

A few of them edged a few paces towards their own houses, but no more than that. Two children stared solemnly up at the police officers, giggled suddenly, and scuttled round to the other side of the car.

'Could you go and stand on the other side of the road, please?' said Edwards authoritatively. 'Back there on the other pavement. Or back indoors. Please.' When there was a clear space around the car he spoke close to Carver's ear. 'God, you know whose car this is, don't you?'

'Officer!' A tall Jamaican stood on the pathway to the front door. 'Officer!'

'Is this your car, sir?'

'No, it's not, man.'

'Then you, sir, are . . .?'

'I'm the one who rang you. Had to dial 999 three times 'fore I could raise anybody.'

'Could I have your name, sir?'

'Name? Who needs my name? I live here, don't I? This is my house, man. Twenty years I've lived here.'

Edwards said soothingly: 'All my colleague wants to know is –'

'I'm a British citizen.' He drew himself up; a man of well over six feet. 'Ex Kingston Town policeman,' he said proudly. 'Acting –'

'Can I have your name, please, sir?'

'Samuel Winston O'Ryan.'

'Used to be a copper, did you, sir?'

'Yes, man. Acting sergeant first class.'

'Right, sir,' said Taffy Edwards, inspired. 'Let's see you get all those people out of here. It would be a big help to us. Then we'll see where we can go from here. All right?'

If it had been possible to draw himself any higher, the Jamaican would have done so. With majestic tread he advanced on his neighbours.

Edwards said again: 'You know whose car this is, don't you?'

Jimmy Carver stood back and studied it. 'It looks familiar.'

'It's DS Roach's.'

'Roach? It can't be.'

'I'm telling you. Look,' said Edwards, 'there's a public phone box round the corner. You go and phone Sergeant Cryer. He'll know what to do.' As Carver involuntarily touched his radio, Edwards said: 'Blast it all over the manor? The phone box, boyo. Do *not* transmit, right?'

He stared at the crumpled, motionless car. Roach's car all right; but where had the detective sergeant got to?

The phone box round the corner had been too close to the scene of the accident for Ted Roach's liking. He had stumbled, panting, another quarter of a mile before finding one near a badly lit bus stop. Words came out as confused as his thoughts.

'Hello, Linda. Listen.' Before she could get too far into questions as to where the hell he was, and how much longer before he got away from that perishing party and got back to bed, he pleaded: 'Don't say anything. Not now. just listen. I'm in a little bit of trouble. I've had a bang with the car.' The squawk in the earpiece did his headache no good at all. 'No, no, I'm all right. Only had a drop over the odds at that retirement party. I can't afford to be breathalyzed at the moment, that's all.' She started to tell him exactly what she thought of him. Not for the first time. He knew it all off by heart. 'Just *listen*, will you? I'm . . . going missing for a while. Until I've sobered up. All right? So if anyone calls you don't know where I am . . . and I haven't been in touch. Got it?'

As he hung up and forced the door painfully open, he had a feeling from her parting remark that she wouldn't be in that bed much longer. Same old story. She wouldn't be the first to walk out. He knew all that part of it, too, off by heart.

Trying to stay soberly upright, he looked along the street to get his bearings. Gratitude welled up inside as he saw the tattered awning of the Italian restaurant in whose corner he had settled, out of range of Galloway and other harassments, so often for so many plates of spaghetti and glasses of Valpolicella.

He made his way to the door, tugged at his jacket; and tripped over the mat inside.

'Sergeant Roach!' The welcome was warm and genuine, without a hint of any surprise at Roach's less than suave appearance, or his momentary unsteadiness. 'What a pleasure, we did not expect – '

'Luigi, listen.'

'I know, I know.' A friendly arm encircled Roach's shoulders. 'You forgot to book your table. Don't worry, is no problem.'

'Luigi, for God's sake listen. I've got to find a place where I can kip down for a while, out of sight . . . and no questions. You know what I mean?'

Luigi squeezed his shoulder. He knew, or could guess. Not all the details, of course, but enough to make a convincing scenario. And there would be no questions.

Leaving the waiter in charge of the restaurant, he led Roach out of the back door past a row of dustbins to a square of waste ground, appropriated by locals as a parking lot. Roach sagged thankfully into the passenger seat as Luigi drove the Fiat swiftly down a sequence of dark lanes to the riverside. A couple of container lorries were drawn up between warehouses and a freighter moored at the quay. Resting on the mud in a small, shallow basin was a cluster of houseboats in various stages of preservation or disrepair.

'There,' said Luigi fondly. 'This one. You sleep it off, yes?'

Roach peered down into the gloom. He could just make out the rusty skeleton of ladder plunging sheer down the greenslimed wall. It was the steepness, not the slime, which made him want to throw up.

'I won't forget you, Luigi,' he muttered abjectly.

Luigi slapped him on the back. It was almost fatal. Roach teetered on the edge, took a deep breath, and turned slowly and carefully so that he could descend to the deck.

'You sleep it off, yes?' said Luigi.

More likely stay awake till dawn, thought Roach as he clawed gingerly down, and sort things out. If ever there was a way of sorting this little lot out.

He found the deck, found his way into the cabin, and collapsed on the damp-smelling bunk. For a few seconds it felt as if the boat was spinning in a slow, sickening whirlpool. Then he slept.

The lights had not been put out, and no chairs or tables had been moved from their original positions, but somehow the room was beginning to look sleazy, sinking into a glum twilight. Sadie had sent a barman up to help shift the empty beer barrel and provide a fresh supply of tea towels. June Ackland was re-assembling some of the liqueur bottles behind the bar.

Roy Galloway, deriving increasing satisfaction from the sight of the chief super and his friends still dipping their noses into that particular brand of whisky, caught a movement across the room. The door at the head of the stairs was slightly ajar. Oddly framed in the crack was the face of Bob Cryer. Something in that face boded no good.

Chief Superintendent Brownlow was watching. Galloway sauntered towards the door as casually as possible.

Outside, he said: 'Something the matter?'

'Ted Roach.'

'Not another punch-up?'

'Unauthorized parking,' said Cryer drily.

'What was that?'

'Someone's front garden,' said Cryer. 'And he's done a runner, Roy.'

It had to be a joke. But Galloway knew it wasn't. 'Is he hurt?'

'Shouldn't think so, not the way he legged it from the scene.' Galloway pounded his fist into his forehead. This was going to be curtains for Roach if the chief super found out. There had been troubles before, but they had ironed themselves out or been ironed out. This time would be the last.

'Any idea where he is?'

'I phoned home. His missus – '

'Missus? Come off it, Bob. You know Roach.'

'Yes,' said Cryer regretfully. 'Well, whoever she is, she said she hasn't seen him. Doesn't have a clue where he is. Sounded awfully pat to me, Roy.'

'Well, he doesn't want to be breathalyzed, does he? Preparing the ground.'

'Yes, that's what I figured. And I suppose he'll come waltzing into the nick in the morning all nice and . . . '

The door was flung open. An elderly man with white hair and a very red face, supporting or supported by a woman with equally white hair of a somewhat less natural tint, blundered out on to the narrow landing.

'Steady!' said Galloway.

The man looked straight ahead. The woman, urging him towards the stairs, treated Galloway to a lofty smile. 'A lovely party,' she said condescendingly.

'Very nice.' The man began to thump his way down, step by step.

'One of the chief super's crowd,' Galloway murmured. When the door below had also crashed shut, he asked: 'And where's the car?'

'I'm having it towed in.'

'Much damage?'

'Superficial, front end, according to Carver. I've fixed for it to be parked nose against the wall so no one can see it.'

'And the people who saw it? I suppose somebody did see it?'

'A coloured bloke. It was right into his front patch. Might settle for a new fence, but it could be dodgy.'

'Can you square up that end,' said Galloway, 'if we manage to get Roach off the hook job-wise?'

'Oh, come on, Roy. I'm not sticking my neck out for some drunken CID officer, and that's straight.'

'Hey, come on, Robert. Remember . . . '

Cryer's mouth twisted wryly. 'I'll do what I can. But I warn you, if it gets iffy – '

'Good boys can't be bad boys? How many favours have I done your firm in the past?' Galloway demanded. 'How many times have I got your lads out of the proverbial, hey?'

'And what am I doing here right this minute?' Cryer retorted.

'Look, I'm not arguing with you, Roy. I'm just telling you so you know where you stand. I'll go as far as I can, and that's it.'

He turned and went back down the stairs. Galloway pushed his way back into the room, scowling; then tried to wipe his features clean of anything but a respectful smile as Brownlow came in his direction, saying goodbye to the last stragglers.

'I think that went off rather well, don't you, Roy?'

'Not at all bad, guv.'

'Yes.' Brownlow looked past Galloway at the door, as if expecting to find something that ought not to be there and that would need dealing with in no uncertain manner. 'Well, home to the little woman, I suppose. Perhaps you'd pop in tomorrow morning, Roy. There are a few things I'd like to discuss.'

'Right, guv.'

As he moved at a leisurely pace to where June Ackland had finished washing up a batch of glasses, Brownlow raised a quizzical eyebrow. Quite adept with his eyebrows, was the chief super. 'Hanging on, are we, Roy?'

'Er . . . um . . . I just wanted to see WPC Ackland gets away safely, that's all.'

'Oh, yes,' said Brownlow archly. 'Well, good night, Roy. Ackland.'

'Good night, sir,' they said in chorus.

Galloway waited a few minutes until he was sure Brownlow was clear, then put out a hand. 'Right, give me those bottles.'

June opened her eyes wide in mock astonishment. 'So you're not taking me home, then, sir?'

'I thought Burnside had that in mind. He seemed to go off the boil though.'

'Yes,' said June reflectively. 'Funny, that. Not that I much fancied the idea, mind you.'

'I should hope not.'

'Funny,' she said again. 'I got some impression that somebody warned him off. Something about me being bespoken, as you might say. Viv Martella seemed to be getting a laugh out of it, anyway, but she wasn't going to tell me what was so funny.'

She handed the bottles over to him in a plastic bag.

'You certainly wouldn't want me to take you home, would you?' said Galloway. 'I mean, some people might get the wrong idea.' He chuckled. 'Some might venture to think I'm this mystery man you're having it off with. And that would never do, would it?'

'No, perhaps you're right. It would never do.' She dried her hands, tugged her dress straight, and looked round for her raincoat. Her enticing little smile almost gave Galloway second thoughts; almost took his mind off the wonderful, exhilarating possibilities of those bottles in the plastic bag. But it was too late. 'I do have my reputation to think of,' said June. 'Don't I . . . *sir*?'

Fourteen

The piercing attack of the dentist's drill began to bite in an agonizing rhythm through his head. Only then it was no longer a drill but a skewer, screeching against his skull, torture without anaesthetic and without end. Ted Roach tried to fight it off. It only got worse, insistent, refusing to give up.

He opened his eyes. Bleak morning light splashed over an unfamiliar wall and a ceiling that was far too low. In the distance there was the throaty moan of a ship's siren. Much closer, his wristwatch alarm went bleeping on and on until he summoned up the energy and aim to cut it off.

There was blessed silence. Gradually the sounds of the outside world murmured their way into the cabin. A lorry trundled past, almost overhead. Somebody shouted something, his voice echoing between high walls.

Roach swung his legs off the bunk, sat up; and wished he hadn't.

He was still fully clothed, feeling sticky and rumpled and with a taste in his mouth which would have disgusted the least fastidious vulture. Blundering up on deck, he found the overcast sky far too bright. The uneven sheen along the wharf did nothing to help. Obviously there had been a steady drizzle overnight.

A truck splashed by and swung round the corner of one of the warehouses. Two hundred yards away a crane was starting to swing cargo aboard the freighter he had noticed the night before. The workers of the world were waking up and getting back on the job. Roach wished he could have postponed the whole business of waking up. He leaned against a wall until he could establish his balance. Cold bit into him. He thrust his hands in his pockets and tried to stop shivering.

A large lorry was drawn up behind a smaller van, tail to tail with only a small gap between them. Roach watched dully. Any minute now he had simply got to force himself to stand upright and walk away, back between those buildings and up the lanes to the main road; back, somehow or other, to Sun Hill and whatever was waiting for him there.

Two men came out from behind the van and stood talking by the cab. One of them laughed and rubbed his hands together, looking pleased rather than cold.

Now Roach was upright. He wiped his eyes, but the picture stayed clearly in focus. There was no mistake about it: the two men were Elkins and Crawley.

He made a cautious detour of the nearest warehouse and got a different angle down the lane. Framed in the opening was the open door of the van, partially masking the movements of a man reaching out to take something off another on the ground. It was a fair bet that sheepskin coats were involved in those movements.

Further along the row of warehouses was a phone box. Roach hugged the wall and made a dash for it.

The ringing tone seemed to go on for ever. Galloway surely couldn't have set off for the nick already – not after being kept late at that party? At last, just as he was about to hang up in despair, there came an answering snarl.

Roach said: 'Guv, I'm sorry to ring you at home at this hour, but –'

'Where the hell are you? Where've you been, you drunken berk? Do you realize just what you've let yourself in for?'

'Yes, all right, guv, all right. But listen. Elkins and Crawley. That's right. I've caught 'em red-handed. Coats and all, by the look of it. But we'll need some help.'

You could almost see Galloway dragging himself awake, scrambling out of bed in one of his killer moods, ready to organize the hunt and get going. Roach snapped out details and hung up so that the DI could start the round-up.

Now there was nothing to do for a while but wait.

Roach began to twitch with fear as the minutes ticked by – fear that the two men down there would be on their way, carrying all the evidence with them and spreading it through the markets before the Sun Hill lot could get here.

It was the most wonderful sight in the world, the Sierra nosing down the lane in search of him.

Galloway was first out. 'For your sake, Ted, I hope this isn't a load of old moody.'

'Look, I could have gone sick, missing – anything. I'm not asking for absolution, I'm just telling you. We've got a job. Believe me.'

'Let's have it, then. Where are they?'

'Down there. Right by those warehouse doors. They've got their van, they're liable to move off any time.'

Galloway led the way, with Roach limping behind him and Cryer, Mike Dashwood and Jimmy Carver crowding them as they turned the corner. There was a sudden shout, and someone ducked under the tail-bar of a lorry and was gone. Carver raced round the vehicle and took a few paces into the main store-room beyond. There was nobody there.

Outside, Sergeant Cryer stood baffled. All at once there was nobody in sight except for themselves.

'They must be around here somewhere. In among those lorries at the end?'

270

'You go that way, Bob.' Galloway waved to Carver to come out of the gloomy interior. 'You go with Sergeant Cryer. Mike, come with me.'

Ted Roach gritted his teeth. They had been within his grasp – he had been so sure of them – they couldn't just slip away into nowhere like that.

Suddenly he was knocked to one side. Dashwood, stooping between two trucks, tripped and came lurching out. He put his arms round Roach and came to a halt.

'Not now, Dashers!'

'Stop messing about, Ted,' snapped Galloway. 'Are you never going to learn?'

'Oi, you lot.'

A man in a stained duffel coat came out of another door. He looked suspiciously at the three men in plain clothes, then with a touch more respect at Cryer and Carver.

'Good morning, sir.' Cryer saluted smartly.

'What are you lot doing round here?'

'Looking for two villains.' Galloway was not going to be left out of this. 'Wouldn't be working with you, would they, sir?'

The man looked him up and down. He had a large head with a large nose and a smile that might turn humorous or ferocious according to his mood. Probably he was good to work for if you didn't cross him.

'Two men just went into my cold store,' he said, 'as the fork-lift truck came out.'

Cryer took a quick glance along the line of buildings. 'Is there any other way out?'

'No,' The manager jabbed his thumb towards one heavy steel door, opening to let out a hazy white breath as two men humped something in and came hastily out. 'That's it.'

'All right if we go in there?'

'I wouldn't bother. They won't be in there very long. It's well below freezing.'

'Um.' Galloway pondered this a moment, watching a van backing up close to the door. 'Have your lads had their breakfast yet?'

'Not for another half hour.'

'They . . . er . . . they couldn't take an earlier one today, could they?'

An appreciative smile broadened on the manager's broad face. 'I don't see why not.'

'Right.' As the man went off to rejoin his work force, Galloway turned to Cryer. 'Now we've got that lot banged up in there, why don't we turn Ted's fiasco into a success story?'

'No chance,' said Roach. 'You don't think I'm fool enough to believe that this Elkins and Crawley saga is going to save my skin?'

Cryer began to move back towards the Sierra. 'Look, I've sweetened your Kingston ambassador for you. All you've got to do is straighten him out for a new fence, right?'

'O'Ryan's not a bad bloke, sarge,' Carver added.

'Come on, Ted.' Cryer bent towards the car door. 'I'll drop you off on the way back to the nick.'

Galloway was jolted into protest. 'What d'you mean, on the way back to the nick?'

'Well, the early shifts have got to relieve us. Look, I don't mind standing around here for the love of it. Might even get a bit of cod to take home to Shirley' – he glanced at the door to the cold store, now firmly shut – 'but you know the chief super and his views on overtime.'

'Don't you worry about the early turn or the overtime. I'll sort that out. With any luck that'll be the least of the chief super's worries.'

Cryer looked at him doubtfully. 'Have you got something up your sleeve, or what?'

Galloway smirked. 'I think you could say that.'

'All right. I'll take Ted over to O'Ryan's, and I'll be straight back.'

Now it was Roach's turn to protest. 'But I want to be around when – '

'On your way,' said Galloway.

'All right, guv.'

As Cryer and Roach drove off, Galloway turned to Mike Dashwood. 'On your toes to the golf club. See if you can trace where that Scotch has come from. If they're not open, wake them up. Me and Carver'll sit it out here. All right?'

'Yeah, all right.'

'And Mike . . . be discreet.'

Jimmy Carver began to pace up and down within a few yards of the cold store entrance, as if he mistrusted the security of the door. Roy Galloway took a stroll to the edge of the quay and looked out across the dark, oily water.

Carver had been right about one thing, anyway: O'Ryan was not at all a bad bloke. He greeted Sergeant Roach as a long-lost friend rather than as the dangerous drunk who had smashed up his front fence. There was coffee on the kitchen table, and the offer of breakfast. Roach could not take his eyes off the large bottle of tomato ketchup; and managed to still his stomach's querulous reaction and politely refuse anything in addition to the coffee.

Equally politely he asked Mr O'Ryan to let him know as soon as possible what repairs to the fence would cost. No trouble about an estimate – just make whatever arrangement suited him best with some local contractor, and Roach would be glad to let Mr O'Ryan have the money fast.

'Not Mr O'Ryan,' his host protested. 'Samuel. Sam to my friends.'

Samuel Winston O'Ryan did seem remarkably friendly, and extraordinarily uninterested in the splintered mess across his front garden. It took Roach's befuddled brain a little while to cotton on to the fact that the conversation kept leaning towards the subject of the special constabulary. Memories of those days of authority in Jamaica had never faded. Sam wanted to play his part again. His new friend Ted Roach must surely be able to get him into the special constabulary?

'Look, it's not what you know, it's who you know.' Roach stalled. 'You have to realize that.'

'But you can put in a good word for me, Mr Ted?'

'Well, I've got to put myself about a bit. You know, grease a few palms, you understand what I mean?'

'I'm with you, man.'

'See what we can do, anyway.'

'It is nice there is folk a man can rely on.'

'And now,' said Roach, 'what about this fence, then? When'll you be able to get it fixed and let me – '

'What fence, Mr Ted?' Samuel Winston O'Ryan propped his elbows on the table and beamed matily.

Mr Wiggins gave Mike Dashwood a far from cordial reception. The golf club car park was deserted, the cleaner had just arrived to go through the club room, and Wiggins had been expecting the usual slow crank-up to the day. Answering awkward questions was a thing to be avoided at the best of times. Awkward questions at this time in the morning were unheard of. But he listened numbly as Dashwood identified himself and intimated that some queries had arisen over local supplies of spirits to a number of local outlets. The word itself appeared to pain Mr Wiggins: this was a very select golf club, not an outlet.

Just how select and expensive, he was at pains to show the detective. Leading Dashwood through the cellars, he managed to exude the conviction that nobody lower than the rank of superintendent ought, strictly speaking, to be allowed into these hallowed vaults. They were indeed very smart, with dark timbers, an arched roof and rack upon rack of wine bottles. The wine was presumably genuine; the rest of the décor was fake, but very stylishly fake.

'It's not the wine we're concerned with, sir,' said Dashwood. 'It's mainly a matter of whisky.'

'Could you be a little more specific?'

'I'm sure you'll find it's just a routine enquiry, sir,' Dashwood soothed him. 'Just that these fake brands, they're becoming a bit of a problem.'

Wiggins flicked an imaginary speck off the cuff of his blazer. 'Fake brands?' he said indignantly. 'I can assure you that all our spirits are purchased through reputable merchants. We buy nothing over the counter. No cheap offers.'

'Then we should be able to wrap this up without having to bother you any further.'

'So I should hope.' Conceding an inch or two, Wiggins asked: 'Was there some particular brand that you have grounds for investigating?'

'Monroe County. It's a malt.'

'There's a coincidence. The Monroe bonded warehouse is down in Lime-house. One of our members is a manager of the company.'

'Quite a coincidence,' Dashwood agreed. He turned back towards the foot of the cellar steps. 'Shall we go back to your office, Mr Wiggins?'

'I thought you were looking for – '

'Perhaps you can show me a bottle in the bar. I'm sure you have one there?'

'But of course.' Wiggins ventured a prickly laugh. 'We're always getting asked for it. Mr . . .' He stopped himself.

'Mr . . .?' Dashwood prompted.

'I'm sorry. It's outrageous to even imagine that any produce supplied to us through the good offices of one of our members could be . . . might in any way be . . .'

They reached the bar, with Wiggins' office through a door behind it. A sub-dued light cast colourful glints on to and off the array of bottles.

Dashwood said: 'You've got a members' book? Addresses, dates of joining and all that?'

'Of course. But I can't imagine why you should want to see that.'

'Can I have a look at it?'

'No. Oh, no. Quite irregular.'

Dashwood put one hand on the bar and leaned on it. 'Mr Wiggins, this is a licensed bar, isn't it?'

'Of course.'

'Which comes under police supervision?'

Wiggins tried to preserve a stance of wounded dignity; then gave way.

Galloway and Jimmy Carver stood in the manager's office, looking out at the deserted quayside – deserted because all the men had disappeared into the hut at the end for their breakfast. Galloway fidgeted. He could just get an angle on the door of the cold store, but he was still worried.

'You sure there's not another way out?'

'Quite sure. And there's no way they can open that door: I've cut the elec-tricity off at the end.'

Carver swayed. 'Do you think I could sit down, sir? I've been up all night.'

'Take a pew, son.' The manager shoved a chair forward. 'Would you gentlemen like a cup of coffee?'

Carver looked a shade more cheerful, but Galloway said: 'Don't get too comfortable there. You want to be out and about when they show themselves. Go and get a couple of those sheepskin coats. It must be brass monkeys in there.'

Reluctantly Carver left the office, just as Bob Cryer's car pulled in under the window.

'All set, then?' said the manager, patently looking forward to a bit of drama.

Galloway nodded. Time to go. The two of them went out and joined Cryer. Carver came tottering towards them, laden with sheepskin coats.

The manager gave a piercing whistle. One of his men drove a fork-lift truck towards them. 'All right, Fred. I'll do the driving. Just get that door open, will you?'

Well wrapped up, they clung on to the truck as the door swung back and they moved into the icy interior. Their bodies were warm enough, but the cold gnawed at their exposed faces. Gently the truck coasted along to the end of a huge four-tiered rack of food. It turned left and went along the end of the store while they peered down every aisle.

At last Cryer let out a whoop. 'There they are, the poor little buggers.'

Elkins and Crawley were huddled in a corner in search of warmth, or at least of something less cold. From their peaked expressions and the sound of their chattering teeth it did not appear that they were having much success.

'Now I know what they mean when they say "done up like a kipper",' observed Carver.

The truck slid in smoothly and stopped, blocking the way if the two men tried to make a run for it. Not that they showed much sign of being able to put one foot in front of the other.

Galloway leaned out from the truck. 'Could I interest you two gentlemen in a couple of bent sheepskin coats, eh?'

It was with considerable warmth, inside as well as outside, that they wheeled the wretched villains and the load of coats back to the nick. Half the men on duty took the chance of trying on the coats. 'Better than the old blue service, anyway.' Galloway watched indulgently. It was a good time. Knowing you'd got it right for once and sewn a whole case up neatly made you feel good. It had to. This would be one hell of a way to earn a living if you couldn't have the thrill of a triumph every now and then.

The door opened, and a chill swept through the room. Chief Superintendent Brownlow stood there for a moment; and it was a moment that cancelled out all the recent moments of pleasure.

'Inspector Galloway. I want to see you and Sergeant Roach in my office immediately.'

'I think Roach is out, sir. If there's anything I can – '

'Both of you,' said Brownlow. 'Immediately.'

The door slammed. Bob Cryer drew in a sad whistle. There was no mistaking the threat in the chief super's face. Galloway looked around the room, so silent all at once. Carver, too, had guessed, and looked sympathetic. Then there was Hollis . . .

And Galloway knew who had grassed. Hollis looked so innocent, not knowing anything that had happened or why the depression had fallen so suddenly on everyone else. But not nearly innocent enough. There was just that one telltale flicker of a self-satisfied grimace.

Galloway pushed past him and out into the corridor. June Ackland seemed to be having trouble with a stray dog. He said, 'When you've stopped messing about with that dog, get Sergeant Roach back here now. On the double.'

'He's back already, sir. Just gone up to the canteen. Oh, and sir' – as Galloway swung away – 'thank you for taking me home last night, sir.'

Galloway pounded up the stairs and lifted a finger to Ted Roach. Nobody seemed to need words any more. It was all in the air: Roach got to his feet, knowing what was about to hit him, and miserably plodded along behind his boss to the door of Brownlow's office.

The chief super had been building up a head of steam while he waited for them. The door was barely closed behind them when he blasted it all out.

'Your conduct last night, Roach, was unbecoming to any police officer, let alone a detective sergeant. It was a disgrace. Not only to the police force in general but to myself in particular.'

'Sir.'

'I took great exception to your vulgar behaviour at the party. An appalling exhibition, in front of my guests. But far worse than that, Roach, when you left the party you were in no state to drive a motor vehicle. It was obvious to everybody there that you had had too much to drink. And as for you, Inspector Galloway, standing by and allowing him to – '

'Sir, I must – '

'I shall be glad if you do not interrupt, inspector.' The intercom on his desk chose this moment to bleep a signal at him. He leaned angrily forward. 'I gave instructions that I was not to be disturbed.'

'It's for DI Galloway, sir.' It was June Ackland's voice. 'Says it's very urgent.'

Brownlow hesitated, then nodded at the handset. 'All right. Take it there. But it had *better* be urgent.' He sat back, fuming.

In the receiver Dashwood said: 'Guv, I've traced the Scotch connection. Sorry it took so long, but I've been going through the club's spirit receipts for the last quarter.'

'And . . . ?'

'And Richie Dicks, one of the chief super's guests last night, he's a manager of Monroe's bonded warehouse. Do you want me to go and pick him up?'

'What's the rest of it?'

'Sounds like a straight theft. Employee theft. He probably considers it one of the perks of the job. You know, lifting a couple of bottles now and again. Know what I mean?'

Galloway took a deep breath and tried to avoid the chief super's menacing stare. 'Don't,' he said forcefully. 'I repeat, *don't* take this matter any further.'

'But guv – '

'Return to the station, Dashwood, and we'll talk about it here. All right?'

'I'll be with you in about fifteen minutes. See you, guv.'

'Cheers.' And it was with dawning good cheer that Galloway now met Brownlow's gaze. 'A matter of great delicacy's come up, sir. I think we ought to talk alone. Could you leave us, Ted?'

'Inspector Galloway, I have not finished with Sergeant Roach yet.'

'No, sir. But just for a minute or two, could I have a word? Between ourselves.'

Ted Roach escaped. Brownlow watched him go with great displeasure. 'What are you up to, Galloway?'

'Last night, sir,' said Galloway, 'a Mr Richie Dicks, a guest of yours from the golf club, knowingly brought stolen bottles of Scotch to the party.'

Bob Cryer paced up and down the front office. Ted Roach watched him guiltily. It was long past Bob's time to knock off and go home, and after last night's party and this morning's burst of activity he looked dead tired. But like the rest of them he was hanging on, waiting to find out what had happened, hoping for a miracle.

Roach had given up hoping for a miracle. He'd had his promotion now. This was the end. All those wasted years studying. Or maybe that wasn't where the waste had been. Last night . . .

He had been remorseful so many times, the morning after. A fat lot of good it had been.

Hollis crossed the office almost on tiptoe. He was almost out of the door when Cryer said: 'You got in mighty early this morning, Hollis?'

'Couldn't sleep, sarge.'

'Guilty conscience?'

'Not me, sarge. *I've* got nothing to feel guilty about. Just that after that party, you know how it is . . . maybe something I ate.'

'Remembered to thank the chief super for his hospitality, did you?'

'Well, I did see him soon after I got in, sarge – '

'And had a word or two?'

Roach got the drift of it all right. He wanted to chuck himself right across the table between them and hammer the living bloody daylights out of that little creep. But he was in enough trouble already.

'Only in the line of duty,' Hollis was saying unctuously. 'You know, sarge, keeping my eyes open so I'll know how to cope when I get round to taking the new job over full-time.'

He was going to be a right one, was Reg Hollis: oh, a worthy successor to Henry Talbot. In spite of all the dangers, Roach felt tempted to go out in a blaze of glory by crushing that slimy face against the wall. Fortunately, or unfortunately, Hollis had gone.

It would have been a blaze of glory, too. Each and every one of the rest of them would have been on his side. He would at least have left them a happy memory to talk about for years to come. Leaving them . . . it was something he had not yet faced up to. Leaving them and missing the whole shower of them. Mike Dashwood and his infuriating habits, the bloody woodentops mucking things up over and over again . . . and now look at them, worrying much more about him than he had any right to expect.

It was the drink still making him maudlin. So he told himself, without believing it.

'Why don't you go home, sarge?' June Ackland asked Cryer quietly. 'You're dead beat.'

'I want to wait and see what's happened.'

'Well, I only hope when I'm in trouble, God forbid, that you'll be waiting in the wings ready to bail me out.'

Ted Roach could stand no more down here. He trailed off towards the stairs and the CID offices, knowing they would be watching him go and talking about him in muted tones.

Bloody woodentops.

Mike Dashwood was trying to swat a fly with a rolled-up newspaper.

'Stop prancing up and down,' growled Roach. 'You make me feel worse.'

Dashwood threw the paper in the waste basket. 'Are you sure it wasn't too late?'

'What?' So far as Roach was concerned, everything was too late.

'My phone call.'

'I wish I'd known about that stolen Scotch. I'm telling you, there'd have been no waiting around till the morning. I would well and truly have nicked Mr Dickie Dicks. Or I'd have been out there first thing, wheeling him in.'

'Then the guv'nor wouldn't have had anything to trade with, would he?' Dashwood pointed out.

Roach was not counting on much of a reward from that trade. Brownlow was ready to have him hung, drawn and quartered: there had been this brief reprieve, but any minute now he would be back in the office getting his final comeuppance. He knew it.

'That bloody retirement party,' he moaned. 'And all for someone I never could stand anyway. Should never have let myself be pressurized. Should have stuck to my principles and refused. Never again.'

The door opened with a swirl of air which lifted papers from the desk. Galloway was in the room, moving fast and pushy, his usual self, full of himself. 'Grab your coat, Mike. We're going for a meal.'

'We are?'

'Chief super says so. Orders. Take a break, have a meal.' Roach, incredulous, watched them turning back towards the open door. 'What's happening? What about me?'

'Didn't think you'd be interested,' said Galloway with a mocking sideways glance. 'Knowing how you hate being pressurized.'

They had paused and were waiting for him. Dashwood was laughing for no obvious reason other than sheer pleasure. Galloway tried to suppress his own grin of triumph.

Roach, shaky on his feet, tried to match Galloway's tone of voice. 'Well, if the chief super says you've got to go some place, you've got to go, haven't you?'

They made their way downstairs. Sergeant Cryer took one look, said nothing, and finally went home tired but content.

THE BILL

3

One

There were any number of bets and a lot of guesswork going the rounds of Sun Hill police station. A great deal of this spilled over into the neighbouring London streets, carried like an infectious itch by officers on patrol, in squad cars, in back alleys and in a number of cafés supposedly unknown to the superintendent and his sidekicks.

Who, for a start, was going to replace the irascible, sandy-haired and ruddy-tempered Detective Inspector Roy Galloway now that he had moved on to fresh (or fouler) fields of activity?

And what was the new uniformed inspector going to be like?

It all made for a tangier sauce in the canteen than the red and brown bottles which were such predictable features of the plastic-topped tables. No reasonably reliable aroma had yet filtered through the Sun Hill corridors about the first question, but this did not dull the appetite for wildly inventive speculation. As to the second, only one thing was known so far: the incoming inspector was a woman.

'I'm going to love watching you lot,' grinned WPC June Ackland. ' "Yes, ma'am, no, ma'am, three bags full, ma'am"!'

Reg Hollis sniffed. He was a dab hand at sniffing, was PC Hollis. 'I reckon it's all a PR job, meself. That's all the Force is, nowadays. All PR.' He brooded for a moment, then added: 'I ain't never worked under a woman before.'

'Under,' said June Ackland, 'or over.'

'But don't worry about it, Reg,' said PC Haynes. 'I mean, just think, it could be worse.'

'Worse than having to work under a female inspector, for gawdsakes?'

'She could've been black as well.'

They all laughed. They could laugh, and Malcolm Haynes could say it, because he was black.

June wrinkled her snub nose in a way which many men found irresistible. Those who failed to resist had all too often had their own noses squashed out of shape. 'That would really have blown their minds.' She savoured the idea. 'Mm, I like it.'

'It'll never happen.' Hollis spoke defiantly, but without a great deal of confidence.

'Ten years ago they were saying that about female inspectors.'

They tried to conjure up a picture of this threatening creature about to descend on them: a smart police college type, a tough old battleaxe who had learned the hard way in some savage inner city, or a glamour-puss to smarten up the Sun Hill image – a public relations gimmick, as Hollis had airily predicted?

Unwilling to pursue this matter too self-incriminatingly, Hollis edged his way towards firmer ground. 'Well . . . any more bets on the next bottom in Galloway's chair?'

There had been a rumour, about as reliable as a grass's whisper from outer space about con men in an orbital module, of some whizz-kid from north of Watford. Then there was talk of a shift from a mellower section of the Met of one DI Richards. Well thought of, well qualified – but a bit quiet after Roy Galloway. Maybe quietness was needed.

If not actually quiet in themselves, they were all a bit reluctant to name the one name which hung in the air. What about Ted Roach? Why not lay a bet on promotion, long overdue, for Detective Sergeant Roach, Galloway's harassed and harassing Number Two for so many years? They all felt it was Ted's due; yet nobody was eager to put money on it.

'Well, then?' Hollis pursued it. 'Put your money where your mouth is. Who do you fancy, any of you?'

'You do realize,' said Viv Martella, 'that what you're doing is illegal, and that as an officer of the law – '

'More money, please, and less mouth.'

'Charming!'

June Ackland said thoughtfully: 'What d'you suppose it's really like for Ted Roach, trying to go on as normal with this hanging over his head?'

Detective Sergeant – or, in the present, unsettled circumstances, Acting Detective Inspector – Ted Roach was, at that very moment, more worried about the hanging head of a certain CID man than about his own. DC Jimmy Carver did not look well. Head drooping over the edge of a Thames police launch, Carver was, indeed, very far from being the brisk, alert, ready-for-action man one needed in times of crisis. The only action he seemed ready for was that of throwing up his guts into the already-polluted river.

Undeniably, the water was choppy. The wind might have meant nothing to the hardened inhabitants of the Norfolk or Northumbrian coasts; but it was hard to stomach along the waterways below Wapping. Having thought that, Roach tried not to think of his stomach, or anybody else's stomach, for as long as possible. He clung to the wheelhouse and watched, with the nearest thing he could manage to professional detachment, as two of the river police officers leaned out over the side with long gaff poles, waiting as the launch slowed and swung gently to starboard. Jimmy Carver, close to the stern, was watching too; and gave no sign of enjoying what he could now see.

'Make ready, lads.'

The engines throbbed down to idling tempo. Roach floundered along to join Carver.

Something was bobbing, sliding in the water, edging above the surface and then slithering below it again, like a waterlogged raft about to make one last upthrust before disappearing forever. There was something on the raft, indistinguishable in the slime and ripples and the glints of uncertain sunlight: indistinguishable, that is, until the men expertly gaffed the object and began to claw it towards the edge of the launch.

Carver, finally ridding himself of a breakfast which had consisted of two eggs, a rasher of bacon and a greasy sausage, narrowly missed making an even nastier mess of the already smeared figure spread-eagled on the door which had served as its funeral carriage.

Through gritted teeth Roach said: 'Cabin class ain't what it used to be.'

Carver did not appear to find this a cheering restorative.

The river policemen were clearly accustomed to dragging all kinds of unsavoury objects out of the Thames which provided their living. They manoeuvred the door and its burden aboard, and with equal skill and calm, manhandled it ashore when the launch nudged in alongside the jetty. Roach, determined not to admit that his own digestive system was rapidly becoming as unreliable as Carver's, made a great point of stooping over the corpse and examining it without taking or expelling – breath.

There was a word carved crudely into the door, just above the dead man's head. It looked like *GRASS*.

Ted Roach straightened up. You could make a lot out of a word like that, and its probable ramifications. Especially if you had some clue about the identity of the corpse. The story was a pretty obvious one and would not take too much figuring out, once you had sorted out the names of a few of the main characters.

'Cor, dear. Ted Roach, would you believe? Long time no see, cocker.'

This, though, was a character you could do without. In no way would it improve the story. Roach groaned. In time of doubt and trouble, Detective Inspector Henry Dougan of Scotland Yard murder squad was far less welcome than the most putrid corpse, and certainly a lot noisier and pushier.

Roach said: 'This one's ours.'

'Oh, a messy one.' Dougan trod closer and nudged the body with his toes. 'Ta very much for dragging it out for us, anyway. I do hate that messy bit, myself.'

'Disappear in short, sharp, jerky movements. Our call, on our patch.'

'And our body,' said Dougan, as slimy as the object which lay between them. 'Terry Card. Part-time blagger, part-time snout. Now, how's that for good detective work, eh? On the scene for ten seconds, and already I know as much as you.'

'It's ours.'

'Oh, Teddy, you're out of your depth. Even more than poor young Terry got. This here body is a small part of a much bigger scene. Now be a good boy and disappear before my skipper arrives.'

Roach was beginning to seethe. 'I don't give a monkey's for your skipper, Dougan. This one is *our* baby.'

He had said it loud and clear – too loudly, as it proved. More quietly, but with impressive force, another voice said: 'I'll make out I didn't hear that remark, son.' Detective Chief Inspector Corrigan had arrived on the scene, without fuss but with considerable authority. 'Now, have it away on your toes before my hearing improves.' With an insultingly dismissive wave, he stepped past Roach and Carver and stood beside his DI. 'Right, what have we got, Henry?'

There was nothing to do but return to Sun Hill, without a result worth recording. Carver drove in silence. Roach fumed. Like a firm within a firm, that lot from the Yard: to them, the mere idea of teamwork, sharing out the load – and the credit – was just a bad joke. Let someone else do the dirty bit, then step in and pull rank. Send you away like a pair of snot-faced schoolboys. Roach was feeling sour and sick inside, in quite a different way from Jimmy Carver's sickness afloat. Something like savage indigestion, only worse, began to burn its way up through his system. It was ready to catch fire and explode as he stamped into the station and up the stairs to the CID office.

Beyond the glass partition, DC Mike Dashwood was slumped in what had been Roy Galloway's chair, swinging meditatively from side to side. Galloway's chair: the chair that ought, by rights, to be Ted Roach's now.

Dashwood saw his sergeant come in, and lurched up from the chair and through into the main office. Roach snatched up a fistful of papers from the desk without even looking at them, and began to shout: 'What about taking a gander at this little lot? *If* you can spare the time, of course. Nice fat selection of B and E's, muggings, thefts from cars, lead off church roofs – an in-tray full.' Full, he thought dourly, of crimes that fell in that grey area between CID and the woodentops. 'I'm getting well choked off,' he raged, 'with being lumbered with stuff nobody else wants to know about.'

'All right, Ted, keep your hair on. Things'll change just as soon as they give us another guv'nor.'

If Dashwood had meant this remark to be soothing, he had grievously miscalculated. Roach threw the papers down again and gestured furiously at the inner office. 'And what were you doin' in there, then? Trying out the seat for size?' He shoved Dashwood bodily out of the way, leaned over the desk and groped for the bottom drawer, opened it, and pulled out a small bottle of Scotch. The other two did not risk saying a word as he stormed past them on his way to the outer door and the stairs.

His pace did not slow as he reached the hallway, but he could not help catching the drift of a brief interchange between Sergeant Alec Peters, leaning in the doorway of the Communications and Display room, and Reg Hollis somewhere inside.

'Alan Boxwood's my tip. Take a fiver on it?'

'Sarge?'

'Oh, c'mon, son. I know what you're up to. What odds'll you give me on . . . ?' His voice trailed away as he saw Ted Roach.

They were all at it, each and every one of them. All sniggering, taking bets, taking it for granted that, after ten years as a DS, he was going to spend the rest of his life as a DS, while some oily little git was promoted over his head.

Roach, hand in his pocket gripping the bottle, looked straight ahead and did not stop until he was in the men's toilets and the door of one of the WC cubicles was firmly locked behind him.

In the CAD room the morning had been a quiet one so far, with Hollis spending more time taking bets than answering R/T calls. Sergeant Penny, motionless in front of one of the consoles, seemed to have gone off into a trance, his lips set and his eyes glazed. There was an unusual, uneasy silence. Even Reg Hollis's attention wandered for a moment from his calculations and scribblings, as if a cold hand had unexpectedly touched his shoulder.

'You all right, sarge?'

Penny's strange, rapt stare did not alter.

'Sarge?'

Penny started. 'Eh? What? Oh, yeah, of course I'm all right.' Before there could be any more awkward questions, the R/T crackled into life. Penny answered it with what looked like a mixture of relief and apprehension. 'Sierra Oscar. Go ahead, five-nine-five. Over.'

The request was for an ambulance at 396, Warrington Parade. A male person – PC Stamp was always one of the very correct and pedantic ones – in his mid-to-late sixties had been found unconscious on the pavement. Stamp and Taffy Edwards had been called upon, during their routine morning patrol, to assist the slumped figure outside a butcher's shop. Such collapses of the elderly were almost as routine as the patrol itself. Mugging suspected? No. Witnesses simply saw him collapse.

'Wilco, five-nine-five. Over.'

In fact there was not merely the unconscious man to be reckoned with, but a snapping, snarling little Yorkshire terrier which clearly regarded it as a matter of duty to keep curious onlookers well away from its master. Stamp had been glad to edge aside and make the call to the station, while Taffy Edwards endeavoured to look calm and in control of the situation. 'Stand back, please. Move along, there!' A few of the public showed signs of obeying. The dog showed no sign of any such thing. It glared menace through a tangle of wispy hair, and yelped piercingly through its yellow teeth. It had no intention of standing back or moving along.

'Little bleeder,' said Taffy in an undertone, advancing and then retracting his right foot. More loudly he added to Stamp: 'While you're at it, you'd better whistle up for a dog handler as well.'

'For a little mutt like that?'

'Well, *I'm* not going near it.'

A middle-aged woman with a shopping bag moved closer rather than away from the scene. 'Perhaps I can help, officer?' She had a wheedling voice, anxious that there should be a part for her in this scene, maybe the only bit of drama in her life all year. 'I don't know the poor old gentleman's name, but he does live down our road. I've stroked his little dog on the odd occasion.'

'Worth a try,' said Stamp. 'But please mind how you go, love. Okay?'

The woman rested her shopping bag carefully against the front of the shop and stooped, extending a hand. The whine in her voice grew more intense: more appealing, she clearly supposed.

'Come along then, my little angel. There. What a nice little . . . ' The terrier managed a remarkable vertical take-off from a standing start, and snapped with savage accuracy. 'Oh, you little git! My hand – the little swine bit me!'

Edwards raised an eyebrow at Stamp. Stamp twisted his mouth towards the R/T. 'Sierra Oscar five-nine-five to Sierra Oscar. Over.'

'Sierra Oscar. Go ahead, five-nine-five.'

'Yeah, er . . . sarge. Request a dog handler at same location, please.'

After a pause, Sergeant Penny, who seemed either not to have been concentrating or not to have heard aright said: 'Say again, five-nine-five.'

'A dog handler.' Stamp carefully enunciated each syllable. 'A dog handler required to attend situation at three-niner-six, Warrington Parade. Over.' When the request had been confirmed, Stamp shook his head at Edwards. 'We won't live this one down, y'know, Taffy.'

'Mm. Right, folks, show's over.' Taffy tried the masterful, authoritative touch again. 'Move along, please, you're blocking the way.'

Another woman, walking past, abruptly changed direction and came up to Stamp. She could hardly have been less like the whining dog-lover who had so swiftly been transformed into a dog-hater. In her mid-thirties, with smooth, short hair which from one angle looked sandy and then, as she turned her head, almost golden, she was dressed in a smart grey suit with a flicker of blue silk at her throat, and had a professional confidence that might have marked her out as a quietly successful businesswoman: but what sort of business could such a trim creature be involved in around a scruffy neighbourhood like this?

'Can I be of any help, officer?' There was the faintest burr of a Scots accent in her cool but amiable voice.

'Yes, love, you can help by just moving along and out of our way.' Stamp put a hand on her shoulder to ease her along the pavement. 'Do please move along.'

Her cool blue eyes became frosty. With the faintest slant of her head towards the hand on her shoulder, she made it clear that she did not like being treated in this way. Just that gaze was enough to make Stamp remove his hand.

'I might well be a doctor,' she said.

'And are you?'

'No, but – '

'Well, then. Actually it's a dog handler we need. So, please, be a good girl and move along.'

'As you wish.'

Taffy's gaze followed her as she walked off. 'A bit of all right, that one. Very tasty.'

'Huh. One of those bossy birds. Don't like bossy birds.'

As the woman stopped at the street corner, a van came round it and slewed in to the kerb. The terrier barked and then lowered its tone to a throbbing growl, as if summoning up the energy to make trouble for the dog handler who was purposefully approaching.

Taffy Edwards and Tony Stamp kept their distance. After all, they didn't want to impede a real professional in his work, did they?

The bottle of whisky was now a lot lighter than it had been when Ted Roach took it into the lavatory with him. God forbid that he should be expected to take a car out in a hurry today. But he couldn't stay here any longer. Sooner or later there was the outside world to be faced: meaning the sympathetic looks and, even worse, the non-looks and meaningless chat of Bob Cryer, Peters, Penny, the whole condescending lot of them.

The outer door of the toilets swung open and thumped shut again. Roach cursed below his breath. Whoever it was out there, he could do without any conversation right now.

There was a slight moan. Somebody humming to himself? Starting up some stupid, cheerful tune? No, it was no tune. The next note was the same as the first: a sort of humming, moaning sob.

Roach pulled the chain, opened the cubicle door, and stepped out.

Sergeant Tom Penny had been leaning over one of the hand-basins, stuffing a couple of pills into his mouth and washing them down with water clumsily sucked in from the tap. Caught unawares, he began trying to shove something into his top pocket, but his fingers were trembling, and in the end the bottle of pills fell to the floor. Roach went to pick them up. Penny stumbled forward and went down on his knees, trying to get there first and write the whole episode off. When he scrambled up his face was ashen, and there was a smear of cold sweat along his forehead.

Roach said: 'What the hell?'

'No need to stare like that. You as well.'

'Aw, come on, Tom. Just what the – '

'You're another one, aren't you? Think I'm past it. Light duties. Don't think I can hack it any more, right?'

'When did you ever hear me say anything like that?'

'Don't have to say it, do you?' Penny doubled up with pain, clutching his chest. Tears sprang to his eyes. 'Like all the rest of 'em, making stupid faces as if nothing was going on.'

Roach looked at the bottle of pills which Penny was still clumsily trying to push back into his pocket. It was pathetic. But then, didn't that make two of them?

He pulled the flask of Scotch from his pocket and looked at what was left. No point in wasting it. He took a long pull. Penny's head went down over the washbasin again, though all that his mouth could produce was a childish whimper. *What the hell?* This time Roach said it silently. He was in no mood to think there was some self-indulgent little woodentop worse off than himself. But it was there, in front of him; something wrong. Tom Penny was in a state about something, or an accumulation of something; a right old fellow victim.

Roach held out the bottle.

Tom Penny gazed blearily at what was left of the amber liquid in the bottom of it.

'It might help,' said Roach.

Penny shook his head. Then he reached out a shaking hand, took the bottle, raised it to his lips, and drank. And coughed and spluttered. He shook his head dismally, and laughed the saddest of laughs: 'Some job, eh?'

'Yeah,' Roach confirmed. 'Some job.'

Two

After all these years, Sergeant Bob Cryer had built up an information network second to none. It spread way beyond the confines of the Sun Hill manor, and way back into times when superintendents of today had been mere constables, and young villains had been no more than a gleam in some older villain's eye. This morning he had spent a good hour tracking down a number of old friends who simply had to know something about a certain newcomer's origins.

'What was she like as a WPC then, Len?' A few feet away, Alec Peters shuffled papers aimlessly, listening to every word. Cryer nodded, deliberately keeping him in suspense by saying nothing for a while in response to the stream of details being poured out from the other end. Then he nodded. 'Mm. Oh, really?' The rustle of paper ceased as Peters strained to make some sense of the tinny voice in the receiver. The lady, it was becoming clear to Bob Cryer, had quite a record, and quite a lot of bottle. Abruptly he asked: 'She straight or a dyke?'

Peters let out a thin whistle. 'Cor, subtle as ever, Bob.'

Cryer's contact assured him that the lady was good and tough, but certainly no dyke. Quite a sight for sore eyes, in fact: and he meant male eyes rather then female.

Cryer hung up. 'Everyone I've spoken to that knows her, says she's good.'

'No doubt we'll find out soon enough.'

It was a prophetic remark. Hollis's head came round the door. 'Sarge, she's here. Just walked in.'

Cryer was not prepared to give satisfaction to Hollis by any sharp reaction to such a blurted statement. 'And who might *she* be?'

'Inspector Frazer, sarge. She's putting gear into her office.'

'She's not due in till tomorrow,' said Peters.

'She's in civvies, sarge.'

Cryer pushed back his chair. 'Sit tight, Alec, I'm gonna have a gander.' Passing Hollis, he said: 'I've heard she's a looker, Reg. That right?'

Hollis smirked an oily smirk. 'Let's put it like this, sarge: I wouldn't climb over her to get at you.'

He scuttled past Cryer and was first into the CAD room with the news. Sergeant Penny, ashen-faced, and trying to rub his stomach without anyone noticing, looked as if news of any kind was something he could be doing without. Bob Cryer left them to it. Hollis, it had to be admitted, was like a murmur going round the court. Where there was smoke, there was fire; and where there was gossip, there was Hollis.

Once the fuse was lit, the news spread through Sun Hill without pause. The new inspector was in Brownlow's office. No, she wasn't: Brownlow was tied up with Ted Roach right at this moment, so she had dumped stuff in her own office and was chatting up DCI Conway. But then, who had shown her to her office anyway? Another whisper had it that she was changing into uniform in the ladies' toilet. Only, if she *was* doing that, how had Viv Martella managed to go in and out again without seeing a thing?

Along every corridor, outside every door, curious glances were taken round corners or through glass panels in the hope of a sighting. Trust Hollis to have managed it first!

Jimmy Carver and Mike Dashwood heard the rumour, but had no time for any personal verification. When Roach came back from seeing Superintendent Brownlow he would be in a bad mood, and all too ready to take it out on them if they had not come up with something on that Thames corpse. Not that it was any of their business. The Yard men had warned Ted that it was all part of a larger thing, and he was to stay clear. And Terry Card's file had been pulled from CRO. The message, clear enough in the first place, was reinforced: local police were to stay out of this.

'We shouldn't be messing about with it, Mike.'

Dashwood grimaced. 'Tell that to Ted.' He prodded a slip of paper into place on the top of the heap on his desk. 'Anyway, I gave an old friend of mine a bell at the Yard.'

'So much for not getting involved.'

'Seems our now-deceased Terry Card was linked with that big krugerrands job last year. They captured most of the gang, but only got half the loot back. Fingers were pointed at the investigating officer.'

'Wouldn't be the first time a lot of booty went amongst the missing during an investigation.'

Dashwood raised a hand in mock horror. 'Tut tut, Jimmy. Whose side are you on?'

'The law,' said Carver. 'Not bent coppers.'

'Speaking of which, there's something else I – '

He was interrupted by the swish of the door as Ted Roach marched in. If it had been possible to override the mechanism and slam it shut, Roach would obviously have done so.

'Well, what says the super?' asked Dashwood carefully.

'Load of old waffle.'

'Can't get a thing from CRO.' Carver began to excuse the lack of results before the detective sergeant pitched into them both.

Roach, surprisingly, was almost philosophical, though in a taut, coiled-up way. 'All right, I know. Yard robbery and murder squads working hand-in-glove on this one. "The last thing they need at this moment in time, sergeant," ' – he attempted an imitation of Superintendent Brownlow's most weightily pontifical manner – ' "is this third-party involvement." ' Roach allowed himself to kick a leg of the nearest desk. 'In plain English, back off and leave well alone.'

Dashwood said: 'Not that it matters now, but I did find out that Terry Card was a snout.'

Roach grunted. 'That didn't take much sussing out, Mike. I mean, when the word "grass" is carved out like that . . . '

'Ah, but I know who he belonged to.'

'Who?'

'You'll never guess.'

'Look, I've had enough of silly bloody games, what with the Yard and Brownlow and – '

'Burnside, ' said Dashwood hastily, but with a smug smile. 'DI Frank Burnside.'

For once, Roach was speechless. He stared, disbelieving.

'Before you say anything, ' Dashwood continued, 'my info is first rate. According to my contact, Terry Card dropped out of sight three weeks ago. Left his digs in Ilford and hasn't been seen since. Well, until this morning, that is.'

'Hold on a minute, ' Jimmy Carver looked up in a disbelief to match Ted Roach's. 'Did you just say *DI* Burnside?'

'Didn't you know? He was made up, three months ago. You never know – he might be a contender for here.'

Dashwood realized that in his desire to show off, he had again gone too far. He lowered his head and waited for another storm to break.

It broke. Ted thumped his foot against the desk again. 'Over my dead body! Burnside? Bent Burnside?' He looked round the office as if in search of something to smash. Then he made for the door, colliding with Bob Cryer just as he opened it.

'Have you seen her yet?' asked Cryer.

'Oh, naff off, Bob.'

But it was Roach who naffed off, leaving the sergeant staring after him and then turning to the two stunned detective constables.

'What's up with him?'

Carver told him. Cryer winced. The picture was as grim to him as it had been to Roach. Finally he shook his head. There was no way in which Burnside, whose dirty methods they had so often stumbled across this last year or two, could be brought into the Sun Hill team. Sooner or later Burnside had to be rumbled. The clean-up of Operation Countryman had somehow managed to miss him, but there were plenty of honest serving officers who knew that sooner or later he would be shown up in his true light. Preferably not on Sun Hill premises, though: there were some smells that really could not be allowed in this nick.

'A non-starter, ' said Cryer. 'Take my word for it. Not even on Hollis's list,' he added reassuringly. 'And if Reg Hollis's sensitive nose doesn't reckon anything on him, I don't think Ted needs to get too steamed-up.'

The snapping, snarling terrier had been safely shut away in the dog handler's van. The old man had been lifted on a stretcher into the ambulance. The few possessions he was carrying with him revealed nothing very helpful: a bunch of keys, six pounds fifty in change, and a large gold medallion on a chain. Taffy Edwards kept the keys but put the rest back in the unconscious man's pocket.

'If he comes round on the way to hospital, tell him not to worry about his keys.'

Then they checked on the address with the woman who, after a bout of moaning, grudgingly admitted that the dog's bite had not actually broken the skin of her wrist. Edwards rang in for permission to go to the house in Pope

Road and check that it was all safe and locked up. WPC Ackland, on patrol near St Mary's Hospital, was sent in to interview the old man as soon as he regained consciousness.

She did not have to wait long. He had already begun to struggle back to life as they transferred him from the ambulance to a bright but quiet, restful ward. He greeted the ward sister and June Ackland with a weak, apologetic smile. 'I feel like I've been out on the tiles all night.'

June laughed. 'You gave a few people quite a scare. And that dog of yours, from what I gather.'

'Donna.' His smile faded, and he pushed himself up against the pillows. 'Where's my Donna?'

June assured him that the dog was safely on its way to the kennels at Sun Hill police station. Flipping her notebook open, she got down to business.

'Now, then. We know where you live, because a passer-by said you were just up the road from her. What we don't know is your name. Apparently you're only known to your neighbours as the old man and the dog.'

'I keep meself to meself, ' he sniffed. 'Better that way.'

'Yes, until something like this happens.' She made it relaxed and friendly. 'And don't you think it would be a good idea to carry some identification on you?'

He sniffed again. 'Ain't never been necessary before.' He gave her a side-long, appraising glance. 'What happened to me?'

'High blood pressure, maybe. You passed out, right by the butcher's in Warrington Parade.'

'Never happened before.' He was reluctant to concede any weakness, but then slumped down deeper into the bed again. 'Must be getting too old.'

'Or overdoing things. Strain. Worry. Got any big worries?'

'Huh, who ain't?' Again he sounded defensive; and then, again, gave way. 'I tell you, my big worry is that lazy toe rag of a nephew. Ain't bothered to come 'ome for three nights.'

'Perhaps we can help there. But right now, what say we start with you giving me your name?'

It seemed plain sailing. A few minutes later she was exchanging details of Jack Randolph Card, of 14, Pope Road, E2, with the hospital registrar. They agreed that, in the absence of the inconsiderate nephew, a call to the social services might be a good move. It was all an uncomplicated process of tidying up: a matter of routine, just another everyday entry for the record. Only one last-minute query held her up as she moved briskly away from the reception desk, to be intercepted by the ward sister.

'Officer, will you be talking to the patient again at any time?'

'More likely social services will take over from now on.'

'Well, *somebody* ought to wag a finger at him for walking round with this on his person.' The sister held out a gold medallion dangling from a watch-chain.

294

'It's pretty valuable, you know. Solid gold krugerrand. We wouldn't like to see him back in here as a victim of a mugging.'

June inspected the heavy gold piece and nodded, making a mental note that when the door keys were returned to the old man, he would also get a warning word in his ear.

She returned to Sun Hill to join in the gossip about the still elusive Inspector Frazer, and to swap notes in the canteen with Edwards and Stamp. They confirmed that Sergeant Penny had the old man's keys and that the dog was safely shut away. If anyone doubted that, all they had to do was cross the yard and wait for the uproar to rattle the bars. June passed on the man's name and address. At the end of the table Jimmy Carver, engrossed in some private meditation which appeared to be giving him little comfort, suddenly looked up as she said: 'Jack Randolph Card.'

'Surname Card?' he snapped.

'That's right. Why?'

'Probably coincidence. But that was the name of a bloke we fished out of the Thames this morning.'

'How old was this corpse?'

'Hard to say, really. But I'd guess about twelve hours.'

'No, you wally. I mean how old . . . how *old*?'

'Oh, I'm with you. About twenty-five, twenty-six.'

June drew a deep breath. Stupid to jump to conclusions, but there was that little matter of old Mr Card's nephew who had moved in but hadn't been home for the past three nights.

'This bloke was a snout, ' Carver was going on. 'Linked to that krugerrand blagging last year.'

It was the magic word. June pushed her cup of tea away and stood up. 'The old man has a gold krugerrand on his watch-chain.'

Two minutes later she was being escorted into the CID office, and Ted Roach was rounding up Bob Cryer and PCs Stamp and Edwards to join them.

Roach was transformed. Outrage had given way to glee. He rubbed his hands together, and smacked his right palm down on a desk, not in anger but in jubilation. The killer instinct was fully awake again. He had been presented with a prey, in full view.

'Good girl, June. Now you get down to the hospital and get a full statement from the old boy. And take Jimmy with you.'

'In case Mr Card gets violent?'

'Just get moving, the two of you. Mike, you and me are going to look that house over.' He glanced at Bob Cryer. 'We do hold the keys?'

'Tom Penny's got 'em.'

Roach swung on Edwards and Stamp. 'You've already looked the place over, right?'

'All we did was make sure the old chap hadn't left fires going, ' said Taffy

Edwards. And, hurriedly forestalling criticism: 'We had no reason to do anything else, sarge.'

'I know that. I'm not having a pop at you, son. Right, let's all move.'

They crowded out into the corridor, Roach leading the way and itching to get his hands on the truth. A woman in a smart grey suit, approaching from the opposite direction, had to press herself against the wall to let the exuberant team pass.

'Excuse me, love.' Ted Roach gave her a briefly approving glance, but for once had something more important on his mind. Behind him, Bob Cryer said: 'Sorry, sweetheart.' June Ackland and Taffy Edwards did not even bother to spare her a glance. It was only Stamp, bringing up the rear, who slowed for a moment and, observing the niceties in that half pedantic, half familiar manner of his, looked into her face and said: 'Sorry, love.'

Her tolerant smile acquired a critical edge. She returned his gaze, nodded slightly, and said: 'I think the correct address is *ma'am*, constable.'

All at once Stamp recognized her, and knew that she had recognized him. He gulped, tried to speak; but she had taken advantage of the sudden emptiness of the corridor to proceed on her way. He dashed after the rest of the men, and tugged at Edwards's sleeve. 'Taffy, that bird . . . you remember the one who got snooty on Warrington Parade . . . ?'

'Come along, you lot, ' yelled Ted Roach. 'Sew this one up before closing time and I'll buy you all a pint across the road.'

For a while, they thought Roach was going to cheat on them. By a quarter-to-three they had, indeed, sewn it all up and were in the boozer – buying their own drinks, with no sign of the DS. It had been quick and efficient, the whole operation. Jimmy Carver and June Ackland were sorry for the bewildered Mr Card. The poor old soul hadn't got a clue. His nephew had arrived on the doorstep out of the blue a few weeks ago, and the uncle had agreed to put him up. It didn't take long for him to suspect that young Terry was up to no good, coming in and out at all hours of the day and night; but, 'I keep myself to myself, like I said, and I don't go round asking too many questions about other folk.' Perhaps the gift of the krugerrand, in lieu of rent, helped to keep him quiet. He didn't approve of Terry, least of all when he heard what he'd been up to. But the news of the young man's murder hit him hard. Even harder was the fact that the krugerrand with which he had been presented had been confiscated.

'Well, nobody can say we weren't on the ball, ' said Edwards.

'And nobody can say that a certain somebody doesn't owe us a pint.'

The door opened. They looked round hopefully. But it was only Bob Cryer and Alec Peters, heading for the bar, where one sergeant had already planted himself. A large Scotch and ice stood on the bar before him. Cryer took in the glass and Penny's distant, moody expression. He jabbed his beaky nose towards his colleague like a benevolent parrot, and although he tried to keep his voice down, it had something of a parrot's rasp. From their table, Carver and the rest heard the sharp comment: 'Bit early for the top shelf, Tom.'

Penny hitched himself away from the bar and went to sit at a table in the far corner. Cryer made to follow, but Peters caught his arm. Still on light duties after coping with a gunshot wound, Penny needed to be treated with kid gloves and not treated to any quantity of drink . . . or criticism.

Stamp was saying: 'Look, I've been trying to tell you, that bird we saw on the Parade on our way out – '

This time when the door swung open it was to admit a joyful Ted Roach, with Mike Dashwood hard at his heels. 'Right, drinks all round.' Roach leaned over the table and planted a smacking kiss on June's lips. 'You little darling!' Glad to take their minds off the brooding Sergeant Penny, Cryer and Peters ambled over for news of the final tally. It had proved to be a nice round figure: twenty-five grand's worth of krugerrands in a cardboard box under a bed.

'And the Yard boys are not what you'd call chuffed,' Roach rejoiced. 'They were gutted.' He moved to the bar and waved for the barmaid to fill up glasses.

'What about the actual murder enquiry?' asked Cryer.

'Oh, we were told to back off. So we're obliging. Us finding the loot's taken the cream off it for them – so let 'em dig down into the dregs.' He began to carry glasses back to the table. 'You know, for the first time, I'm in the super's good books.'

The pub was filling up as men came off duty and hurried in for a quick one before the bell went. Reg Hollis and Malcolm Haynes reached the bar counter. Hollis was quick to produce a congratulatory smile, for which he was rewarded with a free pint of lager.

Some came in; some left. Tom Penny, staggering slightly as he crossed an unevenness in the floor, was making his way to the door. As it was opened from the outside, he went straight on, pushing his way past a woman on her way in. She watched him go, and then thoughtfully made for the bar. As she hoisted herself on to a bar stool, she displayed a length of delightfully proportioned leg.

'That's her,' hissed Stamp. When they all looked uncomprehendingly from the newcomer to Stamp, he leaned between them and tried to hammer it home: '*Her*, I tell you.'

Roach, at any rate, was not bemused. He was more interested in the woman than in anything Stamp might have to say about her. It had been Ted Roach's lucky day so far. He saw no reason why his luck should not continue. Out of the corner of his eye, he noticed that Mike Dashwood was straightening his tie and making a surreptitious dab at his hair.

'Oh, no, you don't, Dashers. I saw her first.'

Roach did not worry about fiddling with tie or hair. He put on his best chat-up smile and headed down the bar. Stamp half rose, as if to call across and warn him, but Hollis came and stood by the table, grinning and waving him down.

Bob Cryer looked at all this and grew suspicious. 'What's up with you lot? just what's going on?'

'Trust me, sarge,' grinned Hollis.

'That'll be the day.'

'Sarge, that's her.'

It dawned. 'You don't mean – '

'I do.'

Hollis stood obligingly back so that the rest of them could have a full view. They saw Roach sidle into position and start his programme. His hand was already on the bar, sliding along towards hers. Suddenly it stopped; froze. She had spoken quietly. Roach, winded, coughed words out too violently to keep the volume down:

'I . . . beg your pardon . . . ma'am.'

Three

Inspector Christine Frazer realized that she had made a mistake in first presenting herself to so many of the Sun Hill team, of which she was to be an integral part from now on, in civvies. She had meant her first entry to be unobtrusive. It had worked out quite the opposite. Now, for a week or two, it might be advisable to keep a low profile, gradually picking up the threads and integrating herself more formally with the men on whom she had, carelessly, got off on the wrong foot.

The trouble was that Christine Frazer had never been used to working that way. Her career in the Force had not been built on diffidence and a contrived matiness. What she wanted, she went for. She would tread on any feet that came between her and success. She had learned in a hard school. Her father, crippled in the Second World War while serving with the Black Watch, had kept a stiff upper lip for some years and then become maudlin and peevish, lamenting the way old soldiers were treated, apologizing to his family for not being able to keep them as richly as he would like, and then demanding their continual attention and exposing them to interminable repetitions of his own misfortunes. Yet what she remembered best about him – and clung to – was his pride in taking her round the Black Watch museum, and the way he tried, in sudden unexpected bursts of defiance, to summon up the fortitude which had kept himself and his comrades going through the darkest and most horrific times.

Over the years, she willed herself to think rather of Balhousie Castle and the gallant echoes of its museum than of the maimed victim slowly degenerating in a dull back street in Perth.

He reminisced about men getting promoted on the battlefield, and sent his wife and daughter repeatedly to the library for books about nonentities who became heroes, implicitly drawing attention to his own missed opportunities. In due course, Christine doggedly pursued promotion on the battlefields of city streets, from Glasgow to Birmingham and ultimately to London: or, rather, pursued her dedicated cause and knew herself to be fully entitled to the promotion which came with it.

Now there was a fresh challenge. The moment the new job was confirmed, she had found herself a new house, not too far from Sun Hill, but far enough to be in a pleasant backwater, with a small garden and a view a lot more salubrious than that from her new office window. She knew she would have little leisure time for the house, or garden, for quite a while. Sun Hill was not going to accept her without question. Tough individualism or co-operation: which was the best line to pursue?

Inspector Frazer intended to keep wide awake until it was safe to relax; safe to accept and know she was accepted.

Warily she must learn when it might be acceptable to use a Christian name, and when it was best to keep things formal and official. That had its own problems: among them, the fact that, in spite of the recent installation of a load of modern gadgetry, Sun Hill station's basic construction dated from a time when police inspectors were such a rarity that separate facilities were not included. The newcomer was expected to share the sergeants' and inspectors' locker room with her male colleagues.

Perhaps that would have its compensations. Arriving one morning, she found Sergeant Peters standing on a chair with a milk bottle in his hand, watering two trays of tomato plants on top of his locker. He looked round as she came in, still not quite prepared for the appearance of a woman in these surroundings.

'Diversifying into horticulture, are we?' It came out on an accusing rather than chatty note. Tentatively she added: 'Alec.'

'Just a few plants from the allotment, ma'am.' Peters got down and tried a placatory smile. 'I bring 'em in every year for some of the lads.'

'An allotment? Time-honoured recreation of the off-duty copper.'

'Not many of us left now, ma'am. Most of 'em play golf.'

Inspector Frazer took her cap from the locker, glancing up at the plants. 'Healthy?'

'Not bad.'

'I was thinking of putting a few in this year myself,' she ventured, 'but those garden centres are so expensive.'

If she had meant it as a matey sort of appeal, the hint was not taken. 'I know, ma'am,' was all that Peters would say. 'That's why I grow my own.'

She followed him out into the corridor, and tried again, this time with more deliberation. 'Herbaceous borders. I don't suppose you – '

'No, ma'am. Strictly a veg man. You should try down the stall. Beaker Street market. Do you a tray of bedding plants for two quid, down there.'

She decided to give up before it all became fuel for some other gossip behind her back. She was sure there was still plenty of that. As Peters went into the CAD room, she pursued her way to her office, catching a few fragments of an incoming message through the open doorway.

'Sierra Oscar, one-zero-one. Just been called to an incident in Belgium Street. Assistance requested if . . . '

Taffy Edwards shouldered his way through shoppers on the pavement, heading for the supermarket. Somebody was shouting, and a number of people were milling to and fro, like the beginnings of a whirlpool that might get dangerous. Between two women pressing back from the kerb, screeching a protest, Edwards saw a number of yobs playing about in the middle of the road, holding up the traffic. Cars and vans sounded their horns, trying to weave round them, to be greeted by waves and two-fingered salutes.

Edwards forced his way to the edge of the pavement.

There were four men on the rampage. Three were in their late teens or early twenties, the fourth was a massive figure of a man who could have been in his thirties, but had the vacant expression of a retarded child. The younger ones seemed to be egging the older one on. Certainly, once he had planted himself threateningly in front of a Ford Fiesta driven by a middle-aged man, with his wife in the front passenger seat, there was no way the driver could risk going ahead or skirting round him. Horns began to bray more loudly. The man got out of his car as Edwards began to cross the congested, raucously resounding street.

The youngsters were crowing derisively, seeing a victim out of the protection of his vehicle.

'Bloody car drivers, you don't own the country.'

'This is a road, you know.' The man was small, bespectacled and almost bald, but what he lacked in stature he made up for in anger. 'There's a pedestrian crossing not more than – '

'We'll walk where we bleeding like, mate.'

'Well, if you get run over, that'll be your lookout.'

His wife was leaning out of the window. 'John please, it's not worth – '

'Why should we get out of your way, eh?' The leader of the yobbos was enjoying himself. He waved at his huge friend. 'Look here, Mickey. Look at this one, eh? Just 'cos he can afford a motor, he treats all the rest of us like dirt.'

'I'm not treating you like anything. All I'm saying is that – '

'Coulda killed us, Mickey. Look at him, couldn't give a toss.'

Three of them began to do a war dance, circling the car and yelling.

The slow, massive creature they had called Mickey began to build up a head of slow, single-minded fury, more frightening than any sudden outburst. 'Yeh, you coulda killed my mates.' He loomed above the driver and raised a fist to pound down on the top of the car. 'Bloody drivers. Look where you're going, can't yuh?'

His mates became aware of a policeman, almost upon them. Their triumphal dance stopped, and by the time Edwards reached the stationary car they had forced their way through the crowd and disappeared. Mickey did not see them go, and they made no attempt to warn him. He saw only the car and its owner, and shouted slowly and monotonously, 'Bloody car drivers, bloody car drivers, bloody drivers.' Lashing out with his right foot, he kicked the offside front tyre. 'You coulda killed my mates.' The man's wife began to sob. He edged away from Mickey and clawed his way back into the driver's seat. Mickey resumed hammering a fist on the roof of the car.

'Right, pal, that'll do.'

Edwards grabbed Mickey from behind and tried to pull him away from the car. One mighty shrug, and he had been thrown to one side. The car accelerated, while Mickey tried to keep pace, thumping the roof and then the rear wing. 'Bloody car drivers!' Thwarted by the first man's escape, he turned like a lumbering tank towards another car coming along the street and attacked its bonnet. Edwards made a further lunge, but found himself dragged helplessly along until Yorkie Smith appeared round the corner and came racing towards them.

'Cool it, mate. That's enough.' Yorkie added his voice and his efforts to Edwards', forcing Mickey laboriously back on to the pavement. 'Enough!'

They managed to pin him face first against a wall. At this range the curious bystanders began to have their doubts, and scurried nervously off.

'He tried to run us over. Bloody car drivers.' Mickey summoned up a new reserve of energy and tried to heave himself away from the wall. 'Think they own the country.'

Yorkie Smith took advantage of the flailing right arm to jerk Mickey's wrist into handcuffs. The touch of metal seemed to sober him down slightly. He sagged, and whimpered: 'Weren't doing no harm. Just walking.'

'Yes, well, now you're coming for a ride, ' said Smith flatly.

'Come on. Car's just round the corner.'

As they marched him along he was mumbling to himself about car drivers, about just wanting to walk and what was wrong with that, and did they think they owned the whole bloody country, those bloody car drivers?

Smith opened the doors of the Panda car. 'What's your name, pal?'

'Mickey.'

'So we heard, ' said Edwards grimly. 'But Mickey what?'

He giggled. 'Mickey nothing.'

Cautiously they bundled him into the rear seat. Edwards got in beside him, while Yorkie Smith took the wheel. Over his shoulder, Smith tried again. 'Where d'you live then, Mickey?'

'Nowhere. I don't live nowhere.' He turned a fixed, vacuous grin on Edwards, who was even more conscious than before of the vast bulk of the man.

'Come on, where d'you live, then?'

'In a house.' Mickey laughed uproariously, as if this was the most marvellous joke. 'I live in a house.'

Smith, moving away from the kerb, nodded briefly in Edwards' direction. Not quite the full shilling here, they silently agreed.

By the time they had returned to Sun Hill, Mickey had somehow sunk in on himself. His eyes were blank, and his face had gone as pale as flabby suet. As Smith opened the security door to let them in, Mickey did not hesitate: remote and docile, he plodded straight on, letting himself be steered along rather than manhandled.

It was a busy day for the custody area. Somebody, somewhere, must have made quite a haul, filling up the cells and provoking the arrival of a number of indignant solicitors, protesting the innocence of their clients before they had fully checked on the nature of the charge. In the middle of it all, Sergeant Penny looked a lot more active than he had done recently, but none the better-tempered for it.

'I don't care what his brief says, we have not got a Mr Lee Pen Woon here.'

'Lee Woon Pen, sarge,' said the hapless PC Frank.

'Him neither.' The arrival of Smith and Edwards provoked another on-slaught. 'That's all I need – Cagney and Lacey. And what bad news might you have to offer?'

'Didn't Viv let you know we were coming, sarge?'

'She did. I think. But how the hell I'm expected to remember every damn little . . . ' He was interrupted by the phone. Without mincing words, he in-formed the caller that, no, his client was not here, and no, that name was not on any list that he knew of, nor any name even remotely like it, while Edwards slipped slyly away, leaving Yorkie Smith to unfasten the handcuffs and indicate that Mickey should sit down. When Penny returned his attention to the two of them, he was still barking aggressively: 'Charge?'

'Well, I'm not sure, sarge. He's not quite . . . ' Smith tapped a finger to his head. 'You know. We brought him in for his own good, really.'

'How wonderfully altruistic of you, Smith.'

Yorkie explained the details as concisely as possible, while Sergeant Penny groaned a couple of times, rubbed his eyes, and then took a longer look at the dismal figure overlapping the edge of the bench. At last he showed a flicker of interest. 'Don't I know you, lad?'

'Name's Mickey,' Smith volunteered. 'That's all we could get out of him.'

'Mickey. Um. Mickey Cozens, isn't it?' When there was no reply, Penny said more harshly: 'Mickey Cozens?'

Mickey sagged a few inches further, staring down at the floor. But he produced a slow, sheepish nod.

Penny looked momentarily pleased, more with his own acumen than with the present situation. 'Bit of a ruck at a club in the High Road a couple of years ago, ' he condescended to explain. 'Cracked a bouncer's skull. Reg Hollis'll have the details on one of his little cards.' He got up, clutching a wad of custody sheets. 'Check it out. I think there's a father. Either way, he can't stay here.' Before Yorkie could protest, the tirade began again. 'In case you haven't noticed, Smith, I'm running a hotel for remand prisoners. Twenty-three vile bodies in eight cells, none of them nicked on our manor and none of them showing any sign of being removed. If our friend here is a danger to himself and others, I've got no suitable accommodation.'

'Yeh, but – '

Penny was on his way towards the cell corridor. 'If you can't find his own minder, you'll just have to section him and bung him off to the Royal.'

'But, sarge, they won't want to know, will they?'

'A psychiatric hospital is a place of safety under the act, Smith, just like a police station, ' said Penny in a patronizing sing-song. 'And they have doctors and social workers who can assess Mickey better than we can. Just do the paperwork and bung him off.'

Yorkie opted for tracing a possible minder first, and maybe saving the paperwork altogether. Hollis was the one who loved paperwork. Friends of the Earth might well have complained if they had realized how many forests had to be felled annually to cope with Hollis's passion for amassing, duplicating and triplicating documents and file cards. In his grudging way, making it all incredibly complicated, he was delighted, after earnest research, to produce the relevant material on Mickey Cozens.

It was all fairly predictable stuff. Up in court on two earlier occasions, Mickey had been referred for psychiatric tests and then released back into the community in the care of his father. Evidently the parental restraint hadn't lasted. With the mind of a seven-year-old in a hulking great body, Mickey had been wound up by his mates in the club episode, and let fly again. For some months after that he was subjected to regular visits by a social worker, but things had seemed to be going well, and surveillance had been withdrawn. It was a matter, now, of choosing between the social worker and the father. Yorkie studied the two addresses and phone numbers on the card, and decided on trying the father first. For one thing, he lived a lot closer.

Mr Cozens was at the station within fifteen minutes. He was a thin, stooped little man with a small head and a narrow, sad little mouth. It was absurd that he should have fathered such a gargantuan son. As Sergeant Cryer ushered him into the custody area, he was already making plaintive, helpless excuses. 'As far as I knew, he was just going to the sweet shop. I had absolutely no idea he was meeting up with those yobbos.' Only when he said 'yobbos' did some spirit and aggression come into his tone.

Yorkie Smith had been keeping his charge entertained by displaying the swivelling possibilities of his torch. The moment Mr Cozens appeared, Mickey dropped the torch and jumped up.

'Dad!' It was a cry of pure joy.

They flung their arms round each other. Dwarfed by his son, Cozens patted Mickey's back and began to speak soothingly, as if to a child, with a tearful tremor in his voice. 'It's all right, Mickey. All right. Nothing to worry about now. But what've you been up to, eh, you naughty boy?'

Yorkie and Bob Cryer exchanged glances, then looked away. It was embarrassing but touching, this welling-up of affection in these generally bleak, often quarrelsome surroundings.

Cryer intervened at last. 'Well, sir, now you're here I think you'd better sort things out with the duty inspector. Smith, perhaps you'll take them along.'

Inspector Frazer sat behind her desk. Her face was impassive as Smith outlined the details of the troubles which had led up to the arrest, but when she turned to the anxious father it was with a sympathetic smile, just enough to leaven the official staidness of her uniform.

'Your son does seem prone to creating public disturbances, Mr Cozens.'

'I can only assure you, inspector, that it won't happen again.' He might almost have been rehearsing it while Smith had been talking; or perhaps he was just desperately repeating what he had said last time, in a similar plight. 'Those lads are evil, that's the only word for it. It's them, not him. They egg him on. When he's away from them he's a placid, harmless . . . *loving* boy. He needs me. He has a good home, I understand him, he'd be totally lost if . . . ' It was something he could not bear to follow up. 'He's just a child, ' he pleaded, 'in his heart, in his head . . . '

'But not in size and strength, ' said Frazer judicially.

'I know. But this is the first time in two years.'

'Please.' The inspector raised her hand. 'I do understand.' She thought for a moment, not fidgeting with papers or a button on her uniform, and equally not making a big act of keeping the unfortunate Cozens in suspense: just sitting very still and balancing probabilities. At last she said: 'You and Mickey are free to go now.'

Cozens beamed at her and scrambled to his feet, tugging at Mickey's sleeve as if to get them both out of here before she changed her mind.

'But, ' said Inspector Frazer emphatically, 'you must understand that our responsibility is for the safety of the public. Whether your son *means* to hurt people is frankly not our concern. And I'm afraid that if you can't keep him out of harm's way in the future, you may find that the courts take a different view from the one they did two years ago.'

'Oh yes, inspector. Yes. I'm only too well aware of that. Thank you.'

He began to hurry Mickey out of the office.

'Do you have a car?' When Cozens shook his head ruefully, Frazer said: 'Smith, run them home, please.'

'Right, ma'am.'

Mickey, cheering up as he sensed that a weight had been lifted, gazed happily around while they walked towards the side door on to the yard. His father looked grimly ahead, indifferent to anything but the need to get out of the building and on their way home. As the door opened, Mickey had to squeeze past a man and woman coming in.

'Hey, sir – you can't come in that way.' Bob Cryer moved to block the newcomers.

'This is a police station, isn't it?'

'Yes, but the entrance is – '

'I've come to report a theft. Our garden has been stolen.'

'A *garden?*'

'Everything. Grass an' all.'

Yorkie Smith, opening the car doors for Cozens and his son to get into the back, was glad to feel that, just for once, he was moving away from trouble rather than towards it.

'Grass an' all, ' repeated the man who had given his name as Fairweather. 'We got back from holiday half-an-hour ago – '

'We've been to Spain, ' said his wife, dabbing at a spot on the end of her nose. 'The weather was awful.'

'And it'd gone. Whole garden. Flowers, grass, the lot.'

Jimmy Carver walked round the front desk and hesitated. It was fatal. Cryer seized on him. 'One for CID here, Jim. Couldn't spare a couple of minutes to speak to these good people, could you?' He smiled ingratiatingly at the Fairweathers. 'As they've taken the trouble to come in.'

There was no escape. Carver took over, and reluctantly led the couple towards the interview room.

The catalogue of theft was a lengthy one: two dwarf apple trees, one quince, one cherry, one pyracanthus, entire contents of a greenhouse, terra-cotta flowerpots full of geraniums – and, according to Mr Fairweather, one whole lawn.

'It wasn't really what you'd call a lawn, ' his wife jibbed.

'Oh yes it was.'

Jimmy Carver looked at his accumulation of notes, trying to make sense of them. 'How would it be if I came and had a look at the garden – or what's left of it?'

'What for?'

'Well, sir, I *am* a detective.'

Fairweather stared sceptically. 'You are?'

Carver drove in offended silence to the Fairweathers' house: silence on his part, though not on Mrs Fairweather's. She occupied the journey to the council estate by talking about the horrors of Spain and how they would have to find somewhere a lot better next year, or someone was going to hear about it.

The garden of the house did indeed look as if a plague had struck it. A remarkably tidy plague, though. The place had apparently been denuded by methodical experts rather than vandals. The difference was like that between a burglary carried out by neat professionals who knew what they were after, and a clumsy smash-up by impulsive amateurs.

It was only as they surveyed the plot, on which Mr Fairweather had worked so earnestly for so long, that he admitted having been the estate caretaker for the last sixteen years. And look what happened when his back was turned!

'Nobody even do the watering while you were away?' asked Carver keenly.

'Her-next-door said she would: Mrs Ingham. But she spends all day and night in front of the telly. They all do, round here. No good expecting anything from any of them.'

'There's not many keen gardeners on the estate, ' contributed Mrs Fairweather. 'You find it very therapeutic, though, don't you, Jack?'

Jack spotted one plastic flowerpot which had been overlooked, and kicked it violently across the bare earth.

Jimmy Carver decided it was time to interview a few witnesses, starting with the maligned neighbour.

Mrs Ingham was middle-aged and middling stout. She wore a very clean apron and an unwelcoming scowl. Indignantly she assured the detective constable that she had last watered the Fairweathers' garden the previous evening, and everything had been all right then. Yes, she had had a key, and yes, she was quite sure she had locked up behind her. And no, she didn't hear or see anything suspicious between then and this morning, and that was that, and it was the last time she tried to help anybody round here. To underline this, she shut the door in Carver's face.

So did two other women in the same street, one of them saying immediately that she wasn't going to buy any more insurance, so would he please get off her clean step. In contrast, one elderly man seemed to relish Carver's enquiries, and called happily through to his wife, 'The invisible man's had his plants nicked.' But when Carver asked for some elucidation of this, the man shook his head, laughed again, and closed the door – slowly and politely, though.

Christine Frazer, having despatched Smith with the father and son, joined WPC Martella and PC Haynes for half-an-hour on their patrol. She told them, honestly enough, that she wanted to familiarize herself with every inch of the territory, and it wasn't a minute too soon to start. They nodded respectful assent, but she could tell they were suspicious. Were they supposed to be helping her, or was she slyly sizing them up and forming the wrong opinions – or

306

maybe, uncomfortably, the right ones? They answered her questions, but volunteered very little on their own account.

At the corner of Beaker Street she glimpsed a long row of market stalls, some hundred yards down. It was as good a place as any to leave them. Their relief was not visible, but you did not have to be telepathic to sense it.

Frazer waited until they were out of sight before heading for a stall which sold tomato plants.

On her return to Sun Hill she approached the rear entrance to the station as briskly as possible, in the shadow of the neighbouring factory block. She managed to reach her office without comment, and was leaning against the door with her hands full, trying to operate the handle with her elbow, when Sergeant Peters erupted from the direction of the CAD room.

'Just passing the market and saw these, Alec.' Now they would all be told that she had gone shopping in the firm's time. 'Too good to miss.'

'Ma'am – '

'They need a drink, though.'

'Ma'am, Smith's been hijacked.'

'What?' She was leaning helplessly on the door, unable to move and unable to understand what on earth Peters was talking about.

'Yorkie Smith, ma'am. He's been hijacked.'

Four

The homeward drive had started in reassuring mood. Mickey had reclaimed Yorkie Smith's torch and was playing with it, laughing and shining it at the car window and up into his father's face.

'Seems happy enough,' Yorkie observed.

'His natural state,' said Cozens defensively.

'Has he got a mum?'

'Died when he was little. Nearly thirty years now, just him and me.'

It couldn't have been easy, Yorkie reflected, chaperoning that poor large lump of a permanent child around. It took guts. And a lot of love. In his mirror he caught a glimpse of Mickey leaning affectionately against his father. Somehow the man had done his best to make a go of it, and at least you couldn't say he'd got nothing in return.

Yorkie swung round a corner and began to accelerate along a street whose front gardens might once have been trim, but now were scruffy, no more than patches of earth or flagstones bordered by a low, crumbling wall. Three youths were sitting on one wall, swinging their legs and kicking their heels against the already-scarred brickwork. Yorkie recognized them at once.

So did Mickey. 'Dad, look! It's Steve – and Tel and Collie.'

As the police car passed and the three layabouts saw Mickey in it, they got to their feet, jeering at the driver and shoving their fingers insultingly in the air. Mickey laughed, taking all this as a sort of friendly greeting. 'Look – they're my mates.' He humped himself round to begin waving through the back window.

'They're not your mates. How many times do I have to tell you that, Mickey?' Cozens began to shake his bewildered son by the shoulders. 'They are *not your mates*!'

'Easy, Mr Cozens,' Yorkie warned.

'It *was*, Dad. It was Steve and Collie and – '

'They're just yobs, Mickey.' Cozens was suddenly wrenched by the strain of the day. It all came back to him in a rush. His voice cracked. 'They're just yobs, Mickey. They get you into trouble. Why can't you understand that one, simple thing? They don't like you, they don't care twopence for you, they use you – it's all a game to them. A game, Mickey: getting you into trouble, making you do stupid things.'

With relief Yorkie turned into a quiet residential cul-de-sac, no more grand than the street they had just left, but much better cared for.

'Mickey, please, I want you to promise me . . . '

'Number three, Mr Cozens?' said Yorkie Smith soothingly.

Mickey looked out and was pleased at the sight of home.

Yorkie reached back to open the door, and Mickey was lurching out at once.

'Mickey, I'm talking to you!' Cozens clawed across the seat and out, in pursuit of his son.

Mickey was already turning back towards the corner. 'Can I go and see Steve?'

Cozens grabbed his arm with such force that he actually swung him round. 'No, Mickey! No! Look, I'm telling you, I . . .' He was almost incoherent. 'If you ever go out with Steve or Tel or . . . or Collie . . . if you do, ever again . . . I tell you, you're going to end up in prison. In prison, Mickey! Behind bars. Locked away.' He was shouting now, so loudly that curtains in a neighbouring house were pulled aside; and Mickey, staggered, was staring, but only gradually beginning to take it all in.

Yorkie put a restraining hand on the distraught man's arm.

'Mr Cozens, please – '

'If you ever see them again' – Cozens was utterly beyond control now – 'you'll be taken away. You will! For ever. The police will come and take you away and lock you up for ever.'

Mickey let out a wild bellow and shook himself free. 'No!' He came face to face with Yorkie Smith, and the sight and threat of the uniform was, all at once, too much. He lashed out. The full force of his huge right hand caught Yorkie a blow on the side of the head. The car seemed to reel away out of Yorkie's vision, he heard Cozens cry something, and then it was all coming apart, and the pavement was at a crazy angle and he was falling towards it.

'What've you done . . .? Mickey, what've you done?'

Inspector Frazer marched into the CAD room, where PC Melvin and WPC Martella were both at the consoles, Viv Martella putting out a general call and Melvin repeatedly trying to raise some reply from Yorkie Smith.

'All right, exactly what's happened?'

Sergeant Peters said: 'We had a call from the Cozens' neighbour in Tolby Way, ma'am. She reckons she saw the lad wallop Smith, then father and son bundled him into the Panda and drove off.'

Hollis, eyes bright, fidgeted to and fro across the room, with no active part to play, but no intention of missing a moment of what was going on. 'Always said that mighty moron was too much of a risk. Should have been stuck away somewhere safe.'

Christine Frazer felt a prickly chill around the back of her neck. She was the one who had told Cozens he could take his son home, and told PC Smith to drive them there. It was right in her lap, this one.

'Occupants not known to be armed,' Martella was transmitting, 'but approach with caution.'

Frazer said: 'How long have they had?'

'Less than five minutes, ma'am.' Peters confirmed this with a nod at Melvin. 'Bob Cryer's on his way to check on the witness. She sounded genuine, though.'

'And not a word from Smith?'

They shook their heads.

Bob Cryer's voice came through, sharp-edged and definite. 'Have spoken to witness, Mrs Bannister. Her story's corroborated by her husband. No one's got a clue where they might have gone, though. No favourite haunts.'

'Straight into the river, if you ask me,' said Hollis with grisly relish. 'Kamikazi job.'

Frazer turned on him. 'Hollis, just get out.'

Hollis shrugged and sloped out. In the corridor, passing Mike Dashwood, he gave a more meaningful shrug which, in Hollis's easily-translatable language, meant *I told you so*. Her fault in the first place, he silently conveyed to anyone who cared to watch and interpret, and now she's in a funk.

They sent out messages; rang round; cars communicated with Sun Hill and with each other. No sighting. Hospitals had been tipped off, just in case, but so far there hadn't been a sausage. There was talk of radius nets, but how could you have a radius net if you had no idea of speed and direction?

'Yorkie's done this out of sheer spite,' said Taffy Edwards. 'You do realize that? Just because he knew I wanted to finish a bit sharp today. Now I suppose we'll be out till midnight, looking for him.' His annoyance was genuine; yet he did not really mean a word of it. He had been with Yorkie when they encountered that lumbering Mickey Cozens, and was sorry for Mickey; but, remembering Mickey's wayward fury when roused, and the sheer size of him, a lot sorrier for Yorkie, and a lot more worried about him. They all were.

Jimmy Carver plodded up to yet another front door and waited for yet another brush-off.

'No, mate, never heard or saw nuffink.'

'Thanks a lot.'

Hear no evil, see no evil, he thought as he went down the short path and headed for the neighbouring house. Nobody seemed much concerned about Fairweather's garden, and nobody wanted to admit having seen anything at all out of the way. It was a bit unusual; as a rule, a burglary or spot of aggro on an estate like this brought forth bitter complaints about police negligence and the sort of people who were allowed to get houses and flats here nowadays; but this time there was either indifference or a surreptitious grin. It made you wonder – made DC Carver wonder, anyway – if they were all, in some inexplicably secretive way, in it together.

A joint garden-grabbing venture? It made no sense.

He glumly rang at the next door. A young West Indian woman with twinkling brown eyes opened the door, smiled politely, and then lost the twinkle. 'Look, if you're another of them selling insurance –'

Having encountered this before, Jimmy Carver hastily produced his warrant card before she could peremptorily shut him out.

'I'm a police officer, madam. Your caretaker, Mr Fairweather, reports having had some gear stolen from his garden last night.'

Her smiled returned. It was an attractive, infectious smile. 'Is that so?'

'Yes. I was wondering – '

'Robbie!' It was like one previous interview, only this time Carver was not shut out. The girl seemed to enjoy the prospect of talking to him; or to her husband, who came to join her, frowning dubiously. 'The police,' she said, indicating Carver, not with the suspicion he had encountered all too frequently, but this time with chuckling approval. 'Guess what? Somebody did Fairweather's garden last night. Stole some gear.'

'Stole the lot, actually,' Carver amplified.

The man's sleek brown face ceased to be hostile. He grinned at their visitor as amiably as his wife had done.

'That so? Serve the old slag right.'

'Sir, if you have any information – '

'Information? Oh, I can give you a load of that, man. You know how long we been waiting for our side gate to be fixed? Eighteen months, that's what.'

'Well, I'm sorry about that, sir, but it's not really what I'm here to –'

'He spends all his time in that damn garden,' said the man's wife. Her smile grew prettier as she grew more contemptuous. 'You ask anybody in those flats over there how often the stairs get swept, or the rubbish cleared.'

A young white couple were passing, looking up to wave a casual salute.

'Hey, Colin, man – you heard the news? Somebody walked off with Fairweather's garden.'

'What's that?'

'All gone. All his plants nicked.'

'Fair enough. He nicked 'em from the council in the first place.'

Carver suddenly found himself surrounded with more cooperative witnesses than he'had anticipated. Remarks about the Fairweathers varied from 'lazy toerag' to 'sixteen years and his mop's as good as new' and 'the number of times I've complained to the rent office. . .' It was hopeless trying to explain to them that this was not exactly what he had come to investigate, or to ask if they could suggest who might have stripped the Fairweathers' patch bare. All of them in concert, maybe, working with vengeful enthusiasm after darkness fell on the estate?

He was saved by a toot on a car horn. Mike Dashwood was at the kerbside, engine running, waving at him. Jimmy Carver fled for a moment's respite. 'Looks like a poetic justice job here. This Fairweather's getting some right stick.'

'Forget it. You're missing all the fun. Yorkie Smith's been kidnapped. Briefing back at the nick. You'd better be getting your vehicle out of here.'

Whatever the prospects at the other end, Carver was glad to set about doing just that.

Those who were not on the road were crouched at the consoles, willing the cars to close in, willing somebody to break some news, give them a lead, give somebody, somewhere, a sighting. A police helicopter had been switched urgently from traffic duty over the M25 and was swooping over the network of streets in which Cozens and the stolen police car had to be snarled up, sooner or later. Sooner rather than later. Nobody knew what Cozens might be driven to, or drive to, in a panic. Or, worst of all, what Mickey Cozens might be capable of, already in a murderous panic.

Edwards and Ramsey looked up as the helicopter veered above them. Ramsey had always fancied that sort of job – you could make a fortune, surely, taking bird's-eye photos of your mates' houses while they were out on duty. He was about to make some crack along those lines to Taffy, knowing how recently he had been married and how twitchy he still was about his wife's demands on his time, and her Welsh tantrums, when the radio spluttered out information at last.

'All units, from Sierra Oscar. All units. We have a sighting of Panda BSH proceeding east along Taverell Road at speed. Drivers of non-pursuit vehicles are reminded – '

'Aw, shurrup!' Ramsey gave a whoop and accelerated away, to be chastened by an area car flying across his bows at a junction, siren screaming. Ignoring Taffy's whimper of protest, he pulled out after it.

Yorkie had to be somewhere within range, somewhere or other, in some state or other. Yorkie had to be found.

Those who had seen and heard Mickey Cozens in the flesh felt a cold terror at what Yorkie's state might actually be.

'One-four-eight,' Melvin went on transmitting, growing hoarse with the desperate repetition. 'One-four-eight, from Sierra Oscar. Receiving? Over.' Another pause, counting a few beats, and then again: 'One-four-eight. Over. You receiving me, Yorkie . . .?'

Yorkie Smith groaned, and heard himself groan, as he struggled up from a nightmare to the pulse of pain in his head. In a fuzzy distance he recognized Melvin's voice and tried to reply, but the words would not come and he could not work out where the hell the R/T had got to. And how could you operate it when you were crumpled up, getting over some forgotten hangover in the back seat of some car or other?

As he tried to get a grip on himself, or a grip on anything at all, he was flung to one side by the motion of the car. Some maniac was chucking it all over the road, cutting corners, increasing speed inexorably. And somebody was laughing and cheering, excited by the madness of it and by the sound of police sirens howling in from left and right. Now there was another one, somewhere up ahead. Yorkie braced himself against the inside of the door and got his head up, to see Cozens swinging the wheel as a police car loomed up ahead. The brakes screamed; the car spun to the right; they were in a side road, and Yorkie was half wedged down between the seat and the floor.

Then, for some reason, they had stopped. It was very quiet, until the sirens came ranging in again, encircling them and coming closer, only to fade away for a couple of minutes. A door opened. There was something large and heavy above Yorkie. He could not tell, through the splitting rhythmic agony in his head, whether Mickey had been beside him all along or had just clambered in.

'Oh, my God.' It was Cozens, faintly, from the driver's seat – a surrender, an utterly overwhelming misery.

Mickey said: 'I never meant to hit him. Is he dead?'

'I don't know.'

'Dad, what you gonna do?'

'I don't know.'

'Dad, can I come back and sit next to you?'

Yorkie heard the car creak, felt it lift as Mickey got out, and sag again as he went into the front. There was a long silence, until the baying of their pursuers came in closer again.

'I shall be locked away, Mickey.' Cozens was throaty, almost inaudible. 'Not you. Me. How will I live without you?' Now he was sobbing uncontrollably. Yorkie tried to say something, to calm him or finish him once and for all: he couldn't decide for himself what it would sound like when it came out. But he could not get it out anyway.

'One-four-eight from Sierra Oscar. . . '

'Shut up,' cried Cozens. 'Shut *up*.'

The car revved into life, backed away, skidded, and set off even more violently than before.

But the pursuers were rounding it up now. Cozens was not equipped for this kind of chase and was driving blindly, hopelessly, into any opening that presented itself, until there were no longer any more openings, and there was a police car across the road immediately ahead, one in each of the side turnings, and another one slewing in right alongside. The helicopter, satisfied, swung above them to inspect and confirm the certainty of the capture.

Cozens held his son in a tight embrace. It was hard to separate them as two constables heaved them out into the open. From the back, Yorkie Smith thankfully let himself be edged out and supported much more gently.

Sergeant Cryer was saying: 'Sierra Oscar from nine-two. Receiving? Over.'

'Receiving, nine-two.'

'Got him, Alec. Badly bruised, and I'd say he's been concussed. Hopefully, otherwise okay.'

'Ambulance on its way, Bob.'

It was there in under five minutes. As Yorkie was loaded aboard on a stretcher, Cryer looked round. 'Anybody going with him, then?'

Taffy Edwards feigned a sigh. 'I'll go. Mucked up my whole day, I might as well go. At least I'll get a word in edgeways for once.'

Cryer watched the ambulance go, and turned back towards his own car. Mickey was handcuffed, ready to be carted away. His father stood helplessly beside him, too shattered to need handcuffs, too shattered to ask for anything or be told anything. Fleetingly his eyes met the sergeant's. Bob Cryer passed him without stopping, but reached out a hand to pat him on the shoulder.

Not, he supposed, that it would help. Not that anything much could help the desolated Cozens and his son now.

Five

During the course of any one day it was not uncommon for officers of the Sun Hill complement, senior or otherwise, to dream of holidays. On the beat, on a sweltering day, mirages of cool foreign forests would flicker across the backdrop of scorching pavements, hot tar, supermarkets, pickpockets, drunks and traffic jams. In midwinter, the window of a travel agency conjuring up visions of sun-drenched beaches populated by scantily-clad blondes offered a far more alluring promise than anything suggested by the short-skirted blondes who lounged outside the coffee bars and amusement arcade not a quarter of a mile from the nick – more promise to the Dashwoods and Edwardses and Melvins, anyway, if not to WPCs Ackland and Martella, who had different daydreams.

Sergeant Tom Penny had brought a sheaf of brochures into the CAD room and was leafing through them, to a background of Melvin having an argument over the radio with Taffy Edwards. Penny's stomach twinges seemed to have been overcome for a while by the therapy of colourful pictures and even more colourful prose.

'It's always a false alarm,' Edwards was complaining. 'Anything sets it off: motorbikes, the wind, a bunk-up in the house next door.'

'Yes, Taff, but we *have* had this complaint, so if you could just take a look –'

'Total waste of police time.'

'Thanks, Taff.'

Penny was aware of a presence at his shoulder. Reg Hollis was leaning over him, shamelessly inquisitive. 'Going somewhere nice, sarge?'

Penny was none too pleased at this cloud over his sunny thoughts, but at the same time the chance of talking to somebody about his plans somehow made them more real. 'Thought I might give Corfu a bash, since you ask.'

Hollis took in a sharp, disapproving breath. 'Oh, no, I wouldn't do that.'

'Why, what's wrong with it?'

'Greek island, eh? You get sea urchins.'

'So? You don't have to eat them if you don't – '

'Tread on them, though, don't you? Millions of 'em, all over.'

'They're not that poisonous.'

'That's what they *say*. Painful enough if you step on one, though. I've still got the mark after two years. Here, I'll show you.'

Before Penny could object, Hollis was sitting down and starting to pull off his shoe and sock. 'The spikes break off under your skin, see, and there's no way of getting 'em out.' He extended his bare foot. 'The only thing that works is to pee on it.'

Penny viewed the flesh extended for his inspection. 'Pee on it? On the sole of your foot?'

'Yes,' said Hollis gravely. 'You have to get someone to do it *for* you, of course.'

'Of course. Well, I don't suppose that was too difficult in your case, Reg.'

Inspector Frazer put her head round the door. Hollis hurriedly tried to get his sock back on. She studied him with some distaste. 'Joined the masons, Hollis?' Before he could make any reply, she nodded at Penny. 'Tom, no calls for me from quarter-to-three, please. I'm looking after Miss Eveleigh.'

'Identification parade lined up all right, ma'am?'

'As right as it'll ever be. We just have to hope the poor old dear doesn't go to pieces.'

The poor old dear had been given a cup of tea and told that it would all be simple and painless, and she was not to be frightened. Nevertheless her hands were shaking, and there was a danger of the tea slopping over on to her lap. She had had her handbag wrenched from her in broad daylight, and indignation had driven her to the police and kept her going while she made a statement. Now she was scared of the whole atmosphere and the uncertainties which lay ahead, and was clearly wishing she had kept quiet about her loss.

Christine Frazer explained the whole procedure for the second time, patiently and reassuringly. The women would be lined up in the custody area. All Miss Eveleigh had to do was walk along the line at least twice, taking as much time as she liked. The women would each carry a number. If Miss Eveleigh recognized the one who had stolen her handbag, she was to identify her to the inspector afterwards by the number. She would be exposed to no risk whatever during or after the parade.

The elderly woman's attention span was as fragile as her thin, mottled wrists. She seemed to be nodding a vague comprehension of what she was being told, but all at once interrupted: 'What time is it, dear?'

'Just gone five to three.'

'Oh dear, my sister's meeting me from the four o'clock.'

'You'll be in plenty of time, don't you worry.' Frazer got up from her desk. 'Just one thing before we go in, though. I should explain that, although there is a suspect on this parade, there are also people who could not have been involved.'

Miss Eveleigh's unhappy frown showed that she had not grasped this. Before Frazer could explain further, there was a peremptory rap at the door and Acting DI Ted Roach came in.

'All set, Miss Eveleigh?'

'I think so, yes.'

'Whenever we're ready, then.' He held the door open invitingly.

Miss Eveleigh got up, flustered, and turned towards Frazer. 'When you say there are people who couldn't have been involved . . . I don't quite understand.'

'It's simply that the person who stole your handbag may or may not be on the parade, you see. I'm required to tell you that.'

'But why not?' She was more bewildered than ever. 'I mean, I thought you'd arrested somebody.'

'Yes,' Roach cut in, glaring at the inspector. 'We have arrested somebody, Miss Eveleigh, and we're certain – '

'We have arrested somebody,' said Frazer firmly, 'and there *is* a suspect on the parade. But there are also eight people who are definitely innocent. And the girl who actually robbed you may not necessarily be here.'

'You mean you think you may have arrested the wrong one?'

'No way,' growled Roach.

'Miss Eveleigh, all I'm saying is that you mustn't look at the parade under the impression that one of the girls is definitely the one who attacked you and stole your handbag. If you're certain you recognize her, that's fine. If you're not certain, say so. That's fine, too.' With a meaningful glance at Roach, she rounded off: 'I don't want you to feel pressurized into making a wrong identification, that's all. Okay? Let's go and have a look, shall we?'

Roach showed every sign of letting the door swing against Frazer as she passed him. She ignored his dark scowl. Ted Roach was far too anxious to get a conviction. After having one recent case thrown out by the judge because of what were described as 'irregularities in the conduct of the identification parade', he didn't want to lose another one; but the likelihood of his mending his ways was remote; and Frazer was not going to give him his head. This parade was going to be carried out strictly according to the book.

There were eight teenage girls in the custody area. One of them, Mandy Peake, had been roped in by Roach and Dashwood, but not by a flicker did she acknowledge Roach's presence. Hard as nails – surely she was so obviously the one that even the doddery Miss Eveleigh would pick her out at once?

The girl's solicitor stood watchfully in the charge room doorway. Frazer led the way out and gently steered Miss Eveleigh to one end of the line.

There was a long pause. One of the girls giggled nervously. Then they all stared straight ahead as Miss Eveleigh screwed up her courage and started along the line, too nervous and embarrassed to do more than glance at each girl. Reaching the end, she turned dismally back, then waved a trembling hand at the police officers waiting for her verdict.

'It's no use. I'm not sure.'

'Just take your time, Miss Eveleigh,' said Roach harshly. 'There's no rush. Have another look.'

'I really don't think it'll do any good.'

But she went slowly back along the line. This time she slowed, and paused in front of Mandy Peake. Frazer could feel Roach willing her to make the decision. Then she went slowly on again, reached the end, and shook her head. She was almost running as she left the line and headed for Frazer.

'No, it's no good. I'm sorry, I'm . . . just not certain.'

'It can't be helped, Miss Eveleigh. Really, you're not to feel upset.'

'Can we go out, please?'

As they went, the girls on the parade began to laugh and chatter. Mandy Peake's solicitor went across to his client, patting her on the shoulder. It was clear from Roach's taut, frustrated expression that he thought it a pity Miss Eveleigh couldn't have done that.

When the twittering, apologetic woman had been shown off the premises, Roach caught up with Inspector Frazer in the corridor. 'That was great, ma'am. Terrific. Thanks a lot.'

'I'm sorry if I cramped your style, sergeant.'

'Well, you certainly haven't cramped our Mandy's. That girl would mug her own shadow if it stood still long enough.'

'So that means we cut corners, does it? Even when we know it could get thrown. In court, one complaint – '

'No, no, by all means you go by the book.' Roach swung past her. 'I just wish you'd be a bit more careful how you read the damned thing.'

The burglar alarm was still ringing as the Panda car slid in to the kerb. Yorkie Smith, marked by the shadow of a bruise along his right temple where Mickey Cozens had laid into him, but otherwise fit and well, made for the open door of the off-licence. Inside he was met by a smart young woman in her late twenties, a lot cooler and more possessed than the man behind her, slumped into a chair on the other side of the counter.

'You all right, sir?'

'He's a bit shaken up,' said the woman. 'It's his first robbery.'

The alarm went on jangling. Somebody in the street outside shouted a curse at it. 'Can't you turn that thing off, now I'm here?' Yorkie demanded.

'Andrew, can you turn the alarm off?'

He looked incapable of even getting up from the chair. The woman walked past him. A welcome silence descended on the interior of the shop.

'Right,' said Yorkie. 'What'd they get?'

'About five thousand from the safe.' She jerked her head towards a security camera slanted above their heads. 'And the video from that.'

It was the turn of CID to move in. With some reluctance Yorkie handed over the slim Miss Chivers, assistant manager, to Mike Dashwood. Her white overall was no mere off-the-peg shop uniform, but smartly tailored to a figure which curved and tapered in all the right places. In spite of the recent shock, Paula Chivers' mouth was calm and gently provocative. It was a surprise that the robbers had not carted her off with their other loot.

She described them meticulously, in a faintly husky voice with a throbbing musical undertone. There had been two of them. One was white, in his mid-twenties, five-foot-six, wearing a red T-shirt, blue jeans and dirty trainers; and he had a flick knife. The other one had a sawn-off shot gun and was black, in his late twenties, six foot, very thin and lanky, wearing a navy blue sweat shirt and matching trousers, and clean white trainers. They had made Andrew Gibbs, the manager, lie on the floor. The man with the knife had stayed beside him while the black man got up and took the video, then asked Paula to open the safe. They had been very cool and polite. Once the money had been collected, they ran off through the back of the shop.

'All sounds very professional,' said Dashwood.

'Yes.' She sounded almost as if she approved of the whole episode. 'I said to the black guy, "You're very good at this," and he gave me a big smile. I'd know those teeth anywhere.'

Dashwood was taken aback. 'His teeth?'

'Yes. I used to be a dental nurse.'

Dashwood's hopes rose. 'Was there something peculiar about them, then?'

'No, they were in quite good nick, actually. But everyone's teeth are different, you know. A nice big smile's better than fingerprints.'

Her confidence was infectious. She made you feel that this was a case which was bound to be wrapped up in a very short time. All it needed was positive identification of a regular villain – for this had all the hallmarks of a regular, professional team.

Dashwood drove Paula Chivers back to Sun Hill to go through their collection of mugshots.

'I suppose,' he said as he offered her the chair behind his desk, 'there's a danger you'll remember me as well, is there?'

She crossed one leg over the other and let her right foot swing gently to and fro. He leaned closer across the desk, producing a wide, frozen smile. 'Yes,' she said with that same warm confidence. 'Your number three top right's slightly discoloured.'

The door opened, and Ted Roach stormed through to his office. 'Not in the firm's time, Mike.'

Dashwood straightened up. 'Miss Chivers is from the off–licence, guv. A key witness.'

Normally Ted Roach would have looked a girl like this up and down, and moved in and tried his own brand of appealing smile. Today he seemed hardly to notice her. All he could say was: 'Well, keep her away from Inspector Frazer, then.' Dashwood followed him through to the inner office, continuing his explanation.

'She recognizes people by their teeth. I was going to show her a few mugshots.'

'You don't see teeth in mugshots, Mike. People tend not to smile when they're banged up.'

'Yes, well, I just thought we might narrow the field a bit.'

'The grinning comes after the identification parade. Especially when Frazer's managed to cock it up. I tell you, the day I'm made up inspector, on equal terms . . .' Savagely he crammed papers into his brief-case. 'Anyway, there's probably something in PACE about it.'

'What, guv?'

Roach snapped the catch on his brief-case. 'Teeth. I expect they'll be inadmissible evidence under para 12, annexe B, section 38 of Home Office guidelines, or some such crap.'

He stormed out without even a glance at Paula Chivers. She pulled a questioning face at Dashwood.

'His fillings must be twingeing,' he said.

They spent the next half-hour going through a number of albums of glum or defiant faces. Ted Roach had been right: none of the subjects had been in a mood for smiling. But every now and then Paula herself smiled, struck by some amusing thought or by the weird expression of some unfortunate rogue; and her smile was worth watching. In no hurry to see her leave the premises, Mike Dashwood went off to fetch cups of coffee.

When she hesitated for a long time over one black man's face, he said: 'That the one?'

'Could be. I'd like him to open his mouth.'

'Even our best retouchers couldn't guarantee that. But he's a possible?'

'Oh, yes, very much so.'

In due course, they had noted four worthy of checking out. Mike felt it had been a good afternoon's work.

'If any of them are runners, we'll arrange a line-up or two and get them all to smile at you. Which won't be difficult,' he added ingratiatingly. 'Oh – have I got your phone number?'

He pushed his pad towards her. She reached for a pen and wrote a number. 'That's the shop.' Without looking at him, she was smiling covertly again, and writing again. 'And that's home.'

Definitely a rewarding afternoon.

Christine Frazer was driving back towards Sun Hill for a meeting, realizing she had cut it a bit fine, when things began to go wrong. There was a swathe of congested traffic at one junction; and not a policeman in sight to sort it out. Then she encountered a whole sequence of lights which all turned red as she approached. And to crown it all, as she swung off the main road down a side street in the hope of saving time, she found herself confronted by a huddle of rags swaying from side to side in the middle of the road. Frazer slowed and stopped a few feet away, sounding her horn. The female tramp paid no attention but continued to rock to and fro in a slow, steady rhythm. As she did so, an almost-empty brandy bottle detached itself from the muddle of carrier bags around her, and rolled gently towards the gutter.

When Frazer got out of the car, she realized there was a sound-track to this horror film. The woman was keening what even the most charitable listener could not have described as a melody.

'Come on, lovey, you can't sit there.' Frazer stooped over the ragged alcoholic lump, then stepped back as the stench hit her. 'Now, come on out of the road, love, or you'll get hurt.'

The woman showed no sign of seeing or hearing her. With a flare-up of impatience, Frazer took her arm and tried to drag her up and out of the road. Suddenly galvanized into activity, the tramp howled a protest and tried to shoulder the policewoman out of the way. She became aware of the bottle, coming to rest above a drain, and made a lunge for it.

'Don't be stupid!' Frazer grappled with her again, and floundered over the assortment of carrier bags. As one of them was kicked over, several full bottles of brandy toppled out. 'Where'd you get that lot from?' As the tramp struggled even more wildly, trying to free herself and collect up the bottles, Frazer saw there must be a good fifty pounds' worth there. 'Come on, where'd you get it?'

The woman thumped her, got away for a moment, and retrieved the nearly-empty bottle – only to hurl it and smash it against the side of the car. That was enough: more than enough. Inspector Frazer applied the sort of arm-lock she had learned in her early training but rarely had cause to use in recent years. In a matter of seconds the stinking bundle was ladled into the rear seat of the car, thrashing and moaning. Frazer threw the bags of food and clothes in after her, but kept the collection of brandy bottles for the front seat.

Her catch was not exactly welcomed at Sun Hill. Bob Cryer raised his nose, one of the best-equipped in the station for inhaling, and winced.

'Cor, what have you brought me?'

'D and D. Obstructing the highway. Assault, possible theft or handling.' Frazer swung the bag of bottles in her left hand, still holding her captive with her right.

'You've never brought her in the GP?'

'There wasn't any other transport. She was sitting right there in the middle of the road, Bob.'

'Phew. You can cross me off patrol next week, then.'

He accompanied the two of them through into the custody area, keeping his distance. The reactions of the others were predictable.

'God, she's alive!'

'She won't be if she drinks this lot.' Frazer dumped the bag inside the charge room doorway.

'I hope you've searched her,' said Cryer, 'cos I'm not going to.'

'Look, can you just stop whingeing? You're worse than Ted Roach.'

Cryer grinned. 'Give you some stick, did he?'

'I can stand it,' she said dismissively. 'I'll make commissioner before he does.

And *I'll* deal with this one, if your stomach's too delicate. just stick her in a cell for five minutes, I've got to see the chief.'

Disgusted, Bob Cryer took the cell keys from his belt.

Ted Roach had had a couple of frustrating hours and was in no mood for Dashwood's self-congratulation when he got back to the office.

'Four possibles for that off-licence robbery this lunchtime, guv.'

'Huh.' Roach threw his brief-case into a corner and went downstairs again. In the charge room, Bob Cryer was writing on a custody record, while Malcolm Haynes was marking up the cell information board. 'Edmondson,' snapped Roach. 'Cell 4, right?'

'Still looking for someone to shout at, Ted?' Cryer held out the keys to Haynes, but concentrated on winding Roach up. 'If looks could kill, I'd tell Madam Frazer to buy a flak jacket.'

Ted Roach chose to ignore that. Grimly he followed Haynes along the corridor. The smell in here seemed worse than usual. Stopping for a moment at a cell door, he identified the source.

'Who's in here, then?'

'Belongs to Inspector Frazer, fortunately.'

An unexpected flush of well-being rose from Roach's hitherto churned-up inside. 'Don't want to worry you,' he rejoiced, 'but she's started a bonfire,'

Smoke was beginning to billow out. In the middle of the cell floor the tramp had set her spare bags of clothes alight, and added most of what she was wearing. Clad only in a few shreds of filthy underwear, she was contentedly rocking to and fro, moaning a dirge to herself. Haynes flung the door open, hit the alarm button, and began to haul her out. Cryer, dashing to the scene, assessed the danger, not so much from the flames but from the thick, choking smoke.

'Get 'em all out!'

'No panic.' Roach was savouring every moment. 'I'll spit on it if you like.'

Haynes was off to fetch a fire extinguisher. Cryer seized it and managed to give Roach a squirt before turning it on the fire. Cell doors were flung open, and the occupants hustled out through the dark clouds to the open air of the station yard. There they presented an unexpected sight to Chief Inspector Conway and Inspector Frazer as they came out of their meeting.

'So what am I to say about Jasmine Allan estate, then? The truth, the whole truth – or what they want to hear?'

'You've got the crime figures, the analysis, it's up to them what they make of it. I don't see that we should bend over backwards . . . '

Frazer's voice trailed away as she surveyed a number of prisoners handcuffed to drainpipes and the bicycle stands.

Conway looked in disbelief at PC Haynes, on guard near the yard gate. 'I know we have an accommodation problem, Haynes, but is it really this bad?'

Haynes indicated the woman tramp, who had a rug over her shoulders to make up for what she had removed. 'This lady thought it was November the Fifth, sir.'

Frazer stared. An awful suspicion tugges at her. The tramp . . . the prisoner she had failed to search immediately on arrival . . .

As Conway went off, casting one dubious look backwards, she hurried in to the custody area and along the smoke-reeking corridor. Bob Cryer was standing with the fire extinguisher, surveying the interior of a cell with some satisfaction at his handiwork. The fire was out, the smoke was clearing. There was little of much substance left apart from a stout pair of men's brown boots.

Roach was waiting for Frazer to come within range. He wagged a mocking finger. 'Who's a naughty girl, then? I mean, *really,* inspector – failing to search your prisoner! Tut tut, and you always so careful about going by the book. God knows what the chief's going to say.'

Bob Cryer, moving away towards the charge room, said in a matter-of-fact tone: 'She did search her.'

Christine Frazer started, looking at Cryer in surprise. Her reaction was not lost on Roach.

'Matches in the old girl's boot.' Cryer held out a few Swan Vestas on his palm. '*You* wouldn't have found them, either.'

Roach laughed a sceptical laugh; but he knew when he was beaten. It was all in the game. 'I see – it's all girls together, is it?' He laughed again, good-humoured by now, and gave Frazer an outrageous wink. As he was leaving, he heard Frazer's flat, wry mutter to Bob Cryer: 'Thanks.'

In a pleasant mood of self-righteousness, he headed for the stairs. Dashwood, emerging from the collator's room, pounded up a couple of treads behind him. 'Guv, I've got a likely shotgun lad for the offry.'

'Nice to know we haven't all been wasting our time today.'

'The girl picked out four from the mugshots, and Reg reckons one of them is a real possibility. Worth a spin, in a discreet sort of way. Phil Kiley – that ring any bells?'

'Oh, Kiley's out again, is he? Wonderful thing, parole.'

They reached the CID office. Roach still felt cheerful. So did Mike Dashwood. 'He always used to drink at the Albion in Fozzard Street. I just thought you might fancy a swift half tonight?'

Acting Detective Inspector Roach could easily be persuaded to fancy a swift half, or a more leisurely pint, at any reasonable hour of the day or night. In this instance he was only too glad, for once, to accept advice from a subordinate. They both rolled up at the Albion in the middle of the evening, unobtrusively followed by two other plain-clothes officers. Everything had slotted into place so neatly all day, they could hardly be let down now. Unless Kiley had changed his drinking habits since he got out this time.

He had not changed his habits, drinking or otherwise. The moment they entered the bar they could see him in characteristic pose, leaning on the bar, casually dressed and casual in his manner, chatting up a girl without showing the slightest sign of effort or haste.

Roach ambled up to him. 'All right, Phil?'

Kiley turned lazily and smiled a wide, lazy grin of recognition. 'What do you want, man?'

Dashwood suppressed an instinctive groan. Phil Kiley's grin was utterly devoid of teeth.

Their streak of luck had given out on them.

Six

Garden sheds were not PC Ramsey's favourite venues for an evening's entertainment, least of all in the company of the slightly odd, unpredictable PC Melvin. But duty called; or, at any rate, duty in the person of Inspector Frazer, who had ordered the two of them to spend a whole row of consecutive evenings in such a shed. So Pete Ramsey and Ken Melvin, innocuous in civvies, strolled up the path of the Garwoods' semi-detached house and resigned themselves to more hours of probably futile surveillance.

Melvin rang the doorbell, expecting to be met by young Mrs Garwood's brown, shyly smiling features and lilting little voice. Instead he was faced by a much older West Indian woman with a tight, mistrustful mouth.

'Evening, love. Sun Hill boys, back again.'

'What is this Sun Hill?'

'Police, love,' said Ramsey chirpily, one foot planted on the step.

'You don't look like police. What you want here?'

Melvin spoke before Ramsey could have another go. His attitude was different, less chirpy. He was almost unctuous in his politeness and correctness.

'Is Mrs Garwood in, please?'

The courtesy made little impression. 'I'm her mother, Mrs Kirby. What do you want her for?'

Someone else hurried along the passage behind the woman and edged her aside. 'It's all right, Ma.' Mrs Garwood had a baby in one arm and looked flustered, but greeted the two men with her usual awkward, half-apologetic smile. 'Do come on through.'

'What you been doin', girl? They say they police.'

Reluctantly Mrs Kirby stood aside to let them follow Mrs Garwood down the hall and out of the back door. 'My mother,' she explained in an undertone. 'Paying us an unexpected visit. She doesn't know about all this.'

'Less she knows, the better,' said Ramsey.

'Ian's not home yet, I'm afraid.'

'No problem.'

Melvin knew the layout and marched straight to the bottom of the garden, ready to get set up. It was Ramsey's first assignment to this particular job, and he looked about the garden as he trod in his companion's footsteps. It was longer than one would have expected behind a compact little terrace like this, with an ill-kept vegetable patch and a stretch of grass which could hardly be called a lawn: much of it had been scraped and hardened by feet and toys, including a battered push-car which was rusting in one corner. A young coloured boy kicked a ball towards the car, looked shyly at the two men, and dodged away behind the back door.

'Andrew, get inside – you're to give up playing now.'

The boy's grandmother patted his head absently, and took a couple of steps into a patch of early evening sunlight slanting across the grit and gravel path. 'What they goin' to do in that shed?'

'Just take Richie, will you?' Mrs Garwood handed over the baby before re-joining Melvin and Ramsey.

'Any activity today?' asked Melvin.

'He went off to work, usual time, with the truck. Nothing since, though.'

Ramsey surveyed the interior of the shed without enthusiasm. The smell was not particularly offensive, but damp and stale; and the two folded garden chairs did not offer much prospect of comfort. If this was life at Sun Hill, he was even sorrier than before to have been gouged out of plain clothes and back on to woodentop penance. All because of a bit of trouble with cards and fellow officers, who had been keen enough to go along with the fun until they found how far young Ramsey could take them. Street-cred, Ramsey had in a big way. Back garden shed-cred was something he could do without.

Melvin, obviously in practice after previous sessions, was making himself philosophically at home. He edged his way round a lawn mower and a child's bicycle to get at the chairs, and began unfolding one. Ramsey went to the smeared window and looked out. This was the terrain they were supposed to be keeping vigil over; and pretty unprepossessing it was. Beyond the low fence where the gardens finished there was a cul-de-sac service road, flanked on the other side by a row of lock-up garages. The rusty door of one of them hung askew, and two or three youngsters were scrambling in and out, yelling. Another two raced bikes with stabilizers up and down the patch of rough roadway.

'It's still on for the rest of the week?' Mrs Garwood was asking.

'Roughly six till ten, every day.' Melvin took a two-way radio from his bag and set it on the cluttered workbench. 'That's what's been authorized so far.'

'So far?' She looked anxious to please, but not all that anxious to have them around much longer. Policemen at the bottom of the garden were not much approved of in this part of the world.

Turning back from the window, Ramsey said: 'Your old mum will be discreet, won't she?'

Mrs Garwood grinned wryly. She might well have said something about having to cope with too many visitors all at one time, but instead she shrugged, said, 'Sing out if there's anything you need,' and left them to it.

As they heard the faint sound of the house door closing, Ramsey grunted: 'What's with all this ethnic co-operation?'

'They're nice people.' Melvin took Ramsey's place at the window and began fixing an empty plastic sack over it, leaving only a small area of glass as a peephole from inside. 'No record, no trouble – and not related to our friend Tomson.' He gestured towards another piece of sacking. 'Hand us that, will you?'

'All this for one small-time shyster – '

'Tommo may be small-time, but lots of small bits make a mighty big heap.'

'You sound like flaming Frazer.' Ramsey thought this over. 'D'you suppose that's why she put me on this with you? So you'd be a reforming influence?' He leaned over his colleague's shoulder, squinting at the garage doors still in view. 'Which one is it, anyway?'

'Second in from this end. He usually gets back about six-thirty. But I think we ought to keep the noise down from now, don't you?'

Ramsey unfolded the other chair, to find that part of its seat was ripped away and it tilted to the left. He tried to adjust its unevenness to the unevenness of the floor. Now that he was here, he realized that he ought to have brought something with him to pass the time: food, for one thing, and something to read, for another. The crumpled copy of the *Sun* in his pocket wouldn't occupy him for more than ten minutes. If there *was* any chance of reading, now that the window was so effectively obscured.

He edged the chair round so that the light, such as it was, fell on to his left knee. 'Didn't think to bring a book, I suppose?'

Melvin handed him the carrier bag from which he had taken the radio. At the bottom was a black-bound book. Ramsey took out a Bible, stared in disgust, and dropped it back in again.

He tried to spin out his reading of the paper, which was made more difficult anyway as the sun sank and the light swung slowly over to the neighbouring garden. There was a faint gleam on one of the garage doors, but not on Tommo's. And, though half-past six came and went, there was no sign of Tommo himself.

Ramsey threw the paper on to the bench and got up for another look. Some older children were racketing up and down now on their BMX bikes. After a few minutes they swerved to one side to let a car through. A casually dressed black man in his mid-thirties got out to open the door of one of the lock-ups.

'Who's that?'

Melvin got up and took his place at the viewing slit. 'Mr Garwood.'

Ramsey watched Garwood stroll past and turn the corner at the end of the terrace. 'I suppose you get a lot of 'em at church, don't you? Blacks, I mean. I mean, that's the sort of church you go to, isn't it, from what they tell me? Hallelujah, sister, and all that old fanny?' When Melvin failed to rise to the bait, he went on: 'Not exactly full of missionary zeal, are you? Here am I, waiting to be saved, and you ain't said a word yet.'

'Keep your voice down. We're supposed to be doing a secret obbo, in case you've forgotten.'

'That the best you can offer?' Ramsey jeered.

Melvin kept it very quiet, either from an inner calmness or in obedience to his own warning. 'We can always go to the pub afterwards, if you really want to talk.'

'Oh, have to book an audience, do I?'

Melvin assumed an insufferably forgiving expression and reached for his Bible, crouching over it in the musty twilight of the shed. Impatiently Ramsey went back to the window yet again, like someone waiting for a long overdue bus, willing it to appear. Grown men, having to waste hours of their life like this! CID should be handling it, or a TSG. And in any case, since everyone was sure that Tomson was at it, nicking motorbikes and converting them, issuing ringers – dozens, maybe hundreds of them – it made better sense to move in and stop it dead. Never mind this piddling surveillance. Get a search warrant, go in and turn that lock-up of his over. As to evidence, once they were in there, it oughtn't to be too hard to *find* evidence. That was the whole point of a search warrant.

Inspector Frazer had methodically explained that it was not the job of the police to stitch villains up. It was their job to obtain evidence, make sure it was sound, and then go through the correct procedures. Ramsey snorted, hoping to make Melvin look up from his Bible; but Melvin went on reading, or meditating, or maybe both at once. It made no sense, sitting here. Why should villains go on forever because of rules and regulations that made it impossible to catch up with them? It was hardly in society's best interests: and wasn't protecting society's interests the job they were supposed to be doing? He glared at the garage door, longing to smash it down and find whatever there was to be found. Get Tommo on his own, too, when there was nobody to feed him lies and talk about his right to silence and right to a brief and right to everything he chose to fiddle. Even if they saw him drive up tonight with a truckload of stolen bikes, how many cases could they prove, over the years: how many would he have got away with, and continue to get away with? How well would he wriggle? How many lies would he tell? After a few years in the Force, you got to understand that truth and justice didn't have a lot in common.

Aloud he said: 'If our Tommo's not back by dark, I might just go and give his garage a spin myself. I've earned a bit of excitement.' He looked down on Melvin's bent head. 'Grass me up, would you?'

'Nope.'

'But don't you have to tell the truth? You're a Christian. Sort of.'

'I wouldn't grass you up. I'd just stop you.'

'Yeah? You mean you'd get violent, then?' When there was still no reaction, he squatted down directly in front of Melvin. 'I'm asking you: would you get violent? Holy Joe? Blessed are the meek, isn't that it? The wimps shall inherit the earth.'

He made a sudden snatch at the Bible. Melvin, equally suddenly, grabbed Ramsey's wrist tight and looked him straight in the eye. His voice was still very quiet. 'I'm not against minimum force.'

There was a taut silence, broken by a tap at the door. They both stood up, absurdly linked until Melvin relaxed his grip. Then Ramsey stumbled back irritably to the window, though eyeing the door as Melvin opened it. Garwood stood framed in the opening, smiling genially yet looking somewhat taut himself. Perhaps it had been a shock to him, coming happily home, to find his mother-in-law on the premises.

'All right, guys?' He stepped into the shed, looking round at his own property, somehow invaded and subtly altered in his absence. 'You okay in here? Like some coffee or something?'

'No thanks, sir,' said Melvin levelly. 'We're managing fine.'

Garwood joined Ramsey proprietorially at the window. 'No sign yet, then? That's good, you know. Late, means he's got some business.'

Ramsey fidgeted away from him. 'Not wanting to be rude, sir, but if you and your family could just keep away from the shed while we're here. Don't want to draw attention.'

Garwood raised an apologetic hand. 'Sure, sure. Sorry.'

He went out, with another slightly forced wave. Melvin smiled after him. Ramsey glowered. Somewhere, they could hear a police siren approaching and then fading away. Through an open window came the faint jangle of a radio pop programme. Other people were either on the move, seeing some action, or happily at home. Only mugs got lumbered with observation jobs like this. Only mugs accepted orders from the likes of Brownlow, Conway and Frazer. You didn't find chief supers or chief inspectors or even women inspectors trying this sort of thing out for themselves. Bags of talk about law and order, but not a lot of what they themselves rabbitted on about as active community participation.

Chief Inspector Conway was in fact, at that very moment, driving towards the council offices, with the prospect of a long discussion on those very subjects of law, order, and community participation ahead of him. He was not looking forward to it. Chief Superintendent Brownlow loved this sort of thing and was only too ready to display his addiction to the sound of his own voice; but Brownlow had dodged tonight's session. Brownlow was by now boozing his way up the Loire valley and beaming sociably at the natives, without a care in his head for the natives of certain London back streets and trouble-ridden housing estates. It was all up to Conway now, with the flimsy aid of some scribbled notes Brownlow had left, plus some much more direct comments from Inspector Christine Frazer. Frazer had not been long on the manor, but she had already assembled some very positive opinions. Conway agreed with a lot of them; but knew that directness was not always the way to win local approval. This evening had more to do with public relations than harsh facts.

One harsh fact was that he was three minutes late on arrival at the council offices. He covered this by striding in more purposefully than ever, implying a great wake of solved cases and physical hassle behind him. A security officer saluted, and hurried up the stairs ahead to open the door to the conference room. From inside came a buzz of voices, which rose to a turmoil as the chief inspector entered.

Most of the faces in the room he knew, some of them all too wearily well. Others he had seen before, but could not put a name to. A few were complete strangers so far as he was concerned. The expressions had a certain similarity, though: hostility was rarely below the surface; every little jack-in-office loved the chance of laying down the law to the police. As they talked among themselves, hushing the decibel level slightly as they grew aware of his presence but implicitly taking up battle positions, he made a quick appraisal of the group. A good twenty had attended this evening – a fair cross-section of the community, he had to admit. White councillors included the crusty George Hopkins with his inevitable pipe, which could choke any opposition by sheer pungency rather than verbal reasoning; and across the table was the articulate black councillor, Estelle Gambrill, left-wing and unquenchable, balanced by her virulently right-wing white opposite number in the local residents' association, Marion Moxon. A couple of youngish blacks, new to Conway, sat deferentially, yet poised for trouble, at one end of the table. He looked round the faces and smiled a greeting. Some smiled back. Some, like Councillor Thomas, looked nervously to either side to make sure whom the smile had been directed at, then produced the briefest response, in case he might find later that a friendly response caused him trouble with his more militant associates. Thomas, chairman of the Housing Committee and co-chair of the Police Committee, was not so much a thorn in the flesh of the local police as a burr which irritated persistently without ever causing a serious injury: a non-poisonous nuisance, but a nuisance just the same.

It was going to be quite an evening.

Patrick Roper, a self-important solicitor with all the time in the world and a lot of inclination for the niceties and not-so-niceties of local politics, had long ago become chairman of every significant group in the neighbourhood.

Hammering the end of the table for attention, he introduced Chief Inspector Derek Conway with a suitable flourish; and then went on to give much more emphasis to what he clearly regarded as a matter of greater significance.

'And welcome from all of us to Vincent Gomes and Bob Abrahams, our two new members from the JA Youth Association.'

There was a spattering of polite, if none too convinced, applause. Conway, shuffling his notes into order, was distracted by the possible importance of all this. The Jasmine Allan estate had been top priority in the notes which Frazer had sifted through for him. This was the trouble spot. Even discussing it was liable to be trouble, as Brownlow had found to his cost during earlier meetings. Conway ventured a tactful smile of approval at the two young Rastafarians, though nothing in their appearance filled him with any great hopes of a break-through in that neck of the woods.

Roper was proceeding, with oily self-satisfaction: 'The fact that JA Youth takes the membership of this Police Consultative Committee over the seventy mark clearly indicates to doubters, I'm sure you'll agree, that there's a tremendous willingness on the part of representative bodies of all kinds throughout the borough, both council-sponsored and independent, to come together and work together to create a better community.'

Yes, thought Conway with chilly detachment: so long as there was nothing worth watching on the telly . . . or nothing worth nicking off the back of a lorry. It would be marvellous to say something like that out loud, just once in a while. Provided you didn't mind forfeiting your job and your pension . . .

He noticed that all the members present had been prepared for his coming. In front of each of them was a copy of the local police leaflet on crime prevention. Studied and edited in the office, it had looked rather good and convincing. Now he watched sceptical eyes flicker over it and wondered what clangers its creators had dropped, what awful omissions they had managed to overlook. The two Rastafarians were not even deigning to read it. It would be nice to think that they had memorized it before showing up this evening; but Conway doubted it.

The chairman made a few complimentary remarks about the content of the leaflet and about police generosity in providing it for the community. Even as he spoke, three people drew in breath, ready to carve the whole project apart the moment he had finished.

Estelle Gambrill, her face shining against the pallid portrait of some long-departed alderman framed on the wall behind her, was the first to plunge in. 'Chair, I think I did point out at our last meeting that, although an Urdu translation of this new leaflet is necessary, versions in Gujerati and Bengali should also be published if we are to reach a substantial portion of the community. These citizens are just as susceptible to mugging and burglary as any others, and I feel we are discriminating against them by not making this advisory leaflet accessible.'

Hopkins struck a succession of matches and produced a great gout of smoke from his pipe. The prevailing draught drove it south-west down the conference table. 'They should learn English then, shouldn't they?'

Conway groaned inwardly. Starting the racist stuff this early on meant that everything was going to run late – and grow increasingly cantankerous as it proceeded.

The reaction was predictable. Jeremy Flack, a white community worker who shared Estelle Gambrill's views and felt it his duty always to oppose the most innocuous remark if it could possibly be misinterpreted, was pounding the table. 'Why should they be penalized because their mother tongue's different?'

'We don't publish it in Hebrew, do we? Or Greek, or Turkish, or Italian?' Hopkins, or his pipe, emitted a wet, seething, bubbling noise. 'There's thousands of people in London with them as their mother tongues, but we don't shove out translations by the yard for them, do we? This is England, not Urduland or Gujerat.'

Both Fleck and Gambrill clamoured for the chairman's attention. Hastily he said: 'Can we leave it that Chief Inspector Conway will investigate the possibility of a multilingual, as opposed to a bi-lingual, version of the leaflet and report back at our next meeting?'

Conway came to his rescue. 'Will do.' He made an ostentatious note on the top sheet of his papers.

'Be turning St Paul's into a mosque next.' Hopkins rattled his matchbox and set about rekindling the flame.

Councillor Thomas cleared his throat. 'We can really do without too much overt police propaganda, you know. It can be self-defeating. All these leaflets, are all very well in their own way, but . . . '

He went pink with embarrassment as a general wave of laughter rolled out. All at once his fellow committee members were on the same side. Thomas's addiction to leaflets was notorious. In his official capacity he was so keen on issuing leaflets to help the poor, the dispossessed, the homeless, the pregnant, and the pensioners, that he had been known to put his own address on several, for the use of urgent cases; only to discover that all the needy or the aggrieved felt that their cases were urgent.

'Next item,' said Roper, by no means displeased to have been helped back on to comparatively firm ground again. 'Crimestoppers. Derek?'

Before Conway could begin the declamation he had been rehearsing in the car on the way here, the door at the side of the room crashed open and a grim-faced tea lady pushed a rattling trolley towards the assembly. A couple of feet from the table she swung it sideways-on with a final clatter, and turned to march out again without a word.

Roper, slightly disconcerted, said, 'Oh . . . mm . . . yes, thank you,' by which time the door had slammed behind her. He looked round the table. 'Er, would you mind being mother, Alice?'

Mrs Askew, Age Concern representative, got up at once. She was white-haired, with spectacles which always seemed in danger of slipping off her nose to one side, and a squeaky voice which could set one's teeth on edge; but she was very committed to her good causes, and always eager to please.

Estelle Gambrill was at once raising a predictable objection.

'Why can't one of the men do it, for a change?'

'I don't mind, really.'

'Well, you should.'

'Why should she mind?' Hopkins bit the stem of his pipe aggressively. 'What's it got to do with you?'

Alice Askew had reached the tea trolley. 'Honestly, I'm quite all right.'

'If you don't want Alice to pour the tea,' growled Hopkins, 'then pour it yourself, while we get on with the meeting.'

There were murmurs of assent and dissent. Conway sensed all the makings of an ideological argument, but Roper was quick to suppress the babble. In doing so, he unwisely treated Gambrill to an admonitory look, which set her off again. Seeking fresh prey, she nodded across the table at Hopkins. 'And while we're on the subject of social rights, when are we going to get rid of that obnoxious thing?'

'Me?'

'No, your stinking pipe. It's high time these meetings were declared smoke-free.'

Before a mutter of approval and disapproval could again threaten something rowdier, Roper groped for a compromise. 'Perhaps you'd like to make a formal proposal at the end of the meeting, Estelle, and we could take a vote on it.'

The pipe still clenched implacably between his teeth, Hopkins grunted: 'I'd like to see you try.'

Roper turned quickly to Conway, who began his address to an accompaniment of rattling cups and saucers, and Mrs Askew's loudly whispered questions on the subject of sugar.

'Crimestoppers. It's a scheme that's working well in several areas already, and it has now been decided to give it a spin on our patch. Basically what happens is that each week we, the police, select a target crime – always a crime against the person, like attacks on the elderly, sex assaults on women and children – where enquiries have come to a halt owing to lack of information. Using media coverage, we seek to enlist the public's help in solving it. Absolute anonymity guaranteed. Anyone who can offer information just rings a special number. If their information leads to an arrest and subsequent charge, they can claim a specified reward.'

'So what we're aiming for is a nation of anonymous telltales who can point the finger at anyone, either for gain, out of spite, to settle a grudge, or just for fun?'

'Well, our problem, you see, Miss Gambrill – '

'Ms, if you don't mind.'

'Ms Gambrill,' said Conway smoothly, 'it's not always high-minded citizens like your good self who have the information we need. We have to use whatever sources are available. If, as a result of this scheme, we arrest someone responsible for a vicious crime, frankly I don't care why they've been shopped.'

'Or even if they're guilty, I suppose?'

'Oh, dear.' Mrs Askew, flustered, forgot to keep her voice down. 'She hasn't left us enough milk.'

Conway tried to look remote and dispassionate, ignoring Estelle Gambrill's insult and preparing to continue in the hope of getting a favourable response from one of the others. Hopkins, however, was occupied with his pipe; Councillor Thomas had criticized the police so often that he did not want to make up his mind yet as to whether they were now doing what he recommended or just the opposite; and Roper's polite nod was just that – the chairman's usual polite, bland punctuation mark to encourage the speaker. Mrs Askew fidgeted a plate of biscuits on to the table between them, managing to spill two as she did so. Conway could only hope that some of his men, somewhere, were making better use of the evening than he seemed to be doing.

Over the fence from the shed there was a boisterous game of football in progress. Every now and then the ball thumped against the fence, and Ramsey jumped irritably. Melvin watched the youngsters without any particular interest: it was one way of avoiding Ramsey's derisive probing.

But Ramsey could not let it rest. 'I just don't understand what you're doing in the police.'

'If I'd known it was going to bother you this much, I wouldn't have joined.'

'No, straight up, I just want to know how you can be a Christian *and* a copper.'

'No real difference between God's law and man's.'

'He doesn't have to walk the streets dealing with the crap we get faced with every day, though, does He?'

Melvin turned away from the window, serious and anxious to explain. 'Maybe you should put it the other way round then, Pete. How does anyone cope with the job *without* being a Christian – without God's help and peace?'

'Oh, I see. It's like a pair of rubber gloves: stops you getting infected.'

'It's more than that. With God's help you can be calm, and bring calm to others. Every call in this job is a chance to witness for Him.'

Ramsey mockingly clenched his fist. 'And give old Satan a right good hiding, eh? You do believe in Satan, don't you?'

'I believe in the power of evil, yes.'

'No, no.' Ramsey's voice was rising insistently. 'Not a "power". The Devil. Somebody real.'

'I don't think he's got horns and a tail, if that's what you mean.'

'What has he got, then?'

'Power, like I say. Power like God's, but used against us instead of – '

This time, the football did not smack into the fence but came through the shed window, showering glass over Melvin's shoulders and carrying an edge of plastic sacking with it to the floor. Ramsey, instinctively diving for cover, looked up from the shelter of the workbench as the shed door opened a crack and young Andrew peered curiously round it.

Seven

Mrs Kirby's voice, never gentle at the best of times, was raucous as she harangued the boys over the garden fence. 'Why you always play outside me daughter's house? Huh? Why you don't kick the ball through your own windows?'

Garwood, fixing the plastic sacks across the window again, while Melvin and Ramsey crouched out of sight, raised a weary eyebrow. When his mother-in-law appeared indignantly in the shed doorway, he heeled the football towards her.

'Here, give them the ball back, Ma.'

'Don't call me ma. I'm not your ma.' She peered past him into the gloom of a corner. 'Why that bicycle I gave Andrew out here gettin' dirty?'

'Because there isn't room in his bedroom. Now, will you just get back to – '

'What this Tomson man done to you, anyway?'

'Nothing.'

'Why you lettin' Babylon spy on him, then?'

'Because they think he's a thief,' said Garwood with barely-maintained patience. 'And I don't like thieves.' Since she had made no move towards the football, he picked it up and shouldered his way past her. 'Now, you coming for your dinner? Madeleine's dishing up right now.'

When the two had gone and Melvin had resumed his place at the window, Ramsey observed: 'Not much peace and love from the old black mamma. Or d'you reckon she's in the grip of Satan?'

'None of us are safe from that.'

'Not even you? When you're so on fire for the Lord?'

'You've got all the words, haven't you, Pete? You take the mick, but somewhere deep inside I think you're interested.'

Ramsey noticed that the Bible was lying on the chair where Melvin had left it. He picked it up and weighed it in his hand. 'Interested? All I'm interested in, brother, is your "minimum force". Try it again and I'll knock your head off.' He tossed the Bible over his shoulder and grinned a challenge at Melvin.

Melvin moved slowly past him and picked the Bible up from the floor, dusting it off. 'You really should come to one of our celebration services. Next one's on the fourteenth.'

The voices droned on. Asif Alam, from the Chamber of Commerce, presented a petition with some two hundred names on it, prepared by the owner of the corner shop on the Jasmine Allan estate, expressing total support for the current police operation against drug dealing in the neighbourhood. He handed it to Councillor Thomas, next to him, who glanced hurriedly down it and gave a non-committal nod and hastened to pass it further along the table in the direction of Roper and Conway. This, at any rate, was something to cheer Conway. Dealers who had hoped to settle in a big way on the local patch had been thwarted: largely, though he was not going to say this out loud, due to the response of individuals rather than self-important committees.

'It's very gratifying,' he said. That should keep it fairly uncontroversial for the time being.

'Rather less gratifying,' said Estelle Gambrill, 'for the hundred or so people who've been stopped and searched at random over the past month, wouldn't you say?'

'Hardly at random, Ms Gambrill. Of those hundred or so, sixty have consequently been charged with drug offences.'

'The operation is totally insensitive. The fact that someone produces a petition signed by two hundred Wasps doesn't mean it has the support of a local community numbering some five thousand.'

Hopkins, puzzled, looked at his neighbour on the right for enlightenment. 'Wasps?'

'White Anglo-Saxon Protestants,' said Jeremy Fleck tersely.

Conway said: 'Arresting people on or near Jasmine Allan estate isn't something we do lightly, believe me. I've had ten officers assaulted there since this whole drugs operation began – largely because there's a big vested interest in keeping us out.' He caught the flicker of a swiftly suppressed smile between the two Rastafarians, and felt a cold, hard certainty that their so-called JA Youth was nothing more than a cover: they had devised a plausible excuse to sit in on meetings, find out what was going on, and report back. He directed a sudden forceful plea at Estelle Gambrill. 'I think you have to be very careful not to let yourself be used by people who make allegations about police conduct simply to protect their criminal activities.'

'So everyone who complains is a drug pusher?'

'No,' said Conway, 'but nor is every copper a racist fascist with homicidal tendencies.'

'Well, you'd never know that, from some of the garbage pumped out by the town hall.' Marion Moxon of the local residents' association, who frequently and fervently proclaimed herself a keen supporter of law and order and the overworked police, was in effect as big a menace to police administration as any villain on the manor. Her vociferous partisanship was capable of setting otherwise reasonable people completely against ideas they would normally have supported. 'Has anyone else on the committee seen this little comic?' she demanded stridently.

Conway had indeed seen it. Sun Hill was already well aware of the existence of this pamphlet, advising young folk of their rights when stopped or spoken to by the police. It had been prepared by some rather over-zealous do-gooders, but there was nothing unduly prejudiced in its approach. It was not a subject he wanted to quarrel over this evening.

Hopkins, too, had evidently seen it. 'Why shouldn't coppers stop kids in the street? We were always getting stopped. Never scarred us for life.'

'You want to live on Jasmine Allan, man.' It was the first of the young Rastafarians, drawling but venomous. 'Just comin' out the front door enough to get you pulled.'

His companion nodded, more vigorous and a lot less laid back. 'People are not stupid. They are not fooled by this propaganda we gettin' about how *nice* Mr Policeman is nowadays. All this fund-raisin' for charity, this road safety, this five-a-side football. You live on Jasmine Allan or Dovey Road, you see that all crap, man. One hundred per cent crap.'

'Mr Gomes,' Roper intervened, 'may I just remind you that we're here to discuss, in a constructive way, the means of making our community a better place to live in.'

Marion Moxon was not prepared to let the initiative drift away from her. 'Give all policemen guns,' she asserted loudly. 'That would be a start.'

Gambrill was on her feet, protesting. Mrs Moxon waved contemptuously at her. 'Always using these meetings as a platform for anti-police propaganda . . . ' Jeremy Fleck was brought to his feet by this, and Gomes and his partner got up at a more leisurely pace, looking obscurely satisfied with the turn that proceedings had taken. Conway was surer than ever that their main object was disruption.

The Moxon woman was undoubtedly helping them. 'You and your cronies have no interest whatsoever in co-operating with anybody, least of all the police.'

As the protesters trooped out, Fleck turned at the door. 'Why don't you get into your bunker and nuke the lot of us.'

The door slammed. Red in the face, Marion Moxon turned self-righteously to the chairman. 'She was just looking for an excuse.'

'Well, you certainly gave it to her, Marion. How many times do I have to tell you that this committee is not a police fan club? It exists so that people of all – '

'Oh, well, if it's all my fault, I suppose I'd better leave, too.' She, too, was now on her feet, gathering up her handbag and a coat and a sheaf of papers. 'Banging my head on a brick wall in any case. It's perfectly obvious where the power lies.'

Councillor Thomas half rose, then sank back into his chair, smiling vaguely, in the hope of the chairman's approval.

'Well,' mused Conway, 'that's got rid of the moderates.'

Roper contemplated the unfinished agenda on the table before him, and the depleted resources around that table. He sighed. 'Can't really discuss that motion on ethnic recruitment when both sides are inadequately represented. And I was going to ask how the weapons amnesty was getting along.'

'Marvellous,' said Conway dryly. 'Opened our bin yesterday. We had two french letters and a piece of southern fried chicken.'

By eight-fifteen Ramsey was sure in his bones that nothing of any value was going to happen. Tommo's garage remained locked; Tommo had not put in an appearance; Tommo, if he had any sense, was in some boozer or club – or, just possibly, flogging some of his reconditioned write-offs to a sucker somewhere the far side of town.

Another couple of hours, and they could wrap up and hope somebody else would get the chore tomorrow and any other evening. Ramsey was bored already. He wasn't going to last another couple of hours without having a word with Lucy and making sure she would be ready when he got round there. By God, she'd better be ready: he was in the mood for some action, and in better surroundings than this grotty shack.

The Garwoods had a telephone. He could make it look official; and keep his voice down so that they wouldn't know what he was on about.

As he crept up the garden and in through the back door, he discovered there was going to be a little problem about being overheard. Garwood and Mrs Kirby were making enough noise between them to drown out a fire alarm. Through the half open door of the living room he could hear a slanging match that got noisier with every moment.

'Look' – Garwood was trying to knock some sense into the woman's stubborn head – 'Tomson runs a business, right? Motor-bike repairs. Only if a bike's a write-off . . . well, he's stealing *good* bikes, right? Stealing – you understand that? Bringing them back to his own garage out there and re-selling them with documents from the write-offs.'

'Can they prove it?'

'If they could prove it,' Garwood rasped, 'they wouldn't be watching him, would they? Now, you tell me what's wrong with letting them use my shed.'

Through the opening Ramsey could see Garwood pacing up and down, gradually quickening his pace, while Mrs Kirby sat stolidly in an armchair, not budging in her position or her opinions. 'Tomson's black and so are you,' she said, her lips pursed. 'That's what's wrong. You so desperate to be white? You buy a house like a white, you live like a white, and now you crawl like a white. You got no shame, man?'

Swinging on his heel, Garwood became aware of the newcomer. Ramsey moved briskly into full view as if he had just this moment arrived. 'Sorry. All right if I make a quick call?' He indicated the phone in the hallway. 'It's a bit urgent.'

'Sure.' Garwood had other things on his mind.

As Ramsey picked up the receiver, Mrs Garwood came down the stairs above him, managed a brief smile of recognition, and closed the living room door as she went in. The row was muffled now, but still Ramsey could make out every word. He paused before dialling, enjoying the free entertainment.

'Ma, what are you making all that fuss about now?'

'Don't know why you bother to come here,' said Garwood. 'Every single time you come into this house there's trouble.'

'Trouble? There was no trouble at all till you came along. And me grandsons – don't I have a right to see them? But one day I s'pose I get here to find them painted white.'

Garwood snatched the door open and headed for the stairs. He was too furious even to notice Ramsey this time. Mrs Garwood came out in pursuit. She was halfway up the stairs when a child's box of games was flung down, splitting open and showering bits on every tread. A chiming bell clattered out a mad carillon as it bounced from step to step.

'Ian, for God's sake!'

Ramsey put the phone down. From this angle he could see the two of them on the landing, Mrs Garwood trying to grab something from her husband before he could smash it against the banister rail. 'She give them this, too?' Whatever it was, it was flung down after the other pieces. Then Garwood himself followed it, two steps at a time, crunching fragments underfoot, heading for the back door and out into the garden. Mrs Garwood stumbled after him. Ramsey's enjoyment took on a sour tinge. Things showed signs of getting too rough.

He tried to calm her. 'No need to panic, love.'

Before she could even get out into the open, Garwood had reached the shed. He flung the door open, paying no heed to Melvin inside. Grabbing the bicycle, he charged out again, bellowing at the top of his voice: 'You can take this as well, voodoo woman!'

Ramsey made a grab to restrain him, and was knocked flying. Melvin, bewildered, emerged from the shed.

'What's going on?'

'Family conference.' Ramsey picked himself up, wondering how long the uproar would take to fizzle out. Then he realized that he had been right: it was going to get a lot rougher.

'No . . . help . . . *please* . . . !'

It was Mrs Garwood, screaming from the house. Melvin and Ramsey ran indoors. She met them with her right hand held piteously out, bleeding from a long gash. At the far end of the hall beyond, Mrs Kirby was pinned against the front door as Garwood advanced on her, holding a bread knife, blade first.

'Seven years I've taken it from you. But no more. So we're black, eh? Well, it doesn't matter if we're black or green or purple, you hear me. *Hear* me?' He stepped slowly, inexorably, closer until the blade was close to her chest. 'We make our own life, with our own children, in our own way. And you are *out*.'

Very steadily Melvin said: 'Mr Garwood.'

'Shut up.'

'Mr Garwood, Andrew's watching.'

It got through. Instinctively Garwood half turned, shocked, lowering the knife slightly. In the split second that it took him to realize there was no sign of Andrew, Melvin had hurled himself forward, carrying the two of them heavily to the floor. Mrs Garwood screamed again. Ramsey plunged to wrench the knife from Garwood's grasp. It had taken only a matter of seconds; and it was over. Garwood was not struggling. The fever had drained away, and he was emotionally and physically spent. Mrs Garwood tiptoed towards him as his head sank and he began to sob. Melvin released him, and his wife's arms went round him, holding him close.

Ramsey picked up the bicycle and propped it against the wall, then began silently to tidy up the toys strewn over the floor and stairs. Mrs Kirby moved away from the door, glared contemptuously at her son-in-law, and went back to resume her place in the living room armchair.

Melvin left Ramsey to the tidying up and returned to the shed, picking up the radio.

'Sierra Oscar from four-two-five. Receiving? Over.'

'Receiving, four-two-five.'

'Transport required, please. We've got a domestic that needs sorting out.'

'Domestic? What about Tommo?'

Behind the radio voice there was the clang of a garage door shutting. Melvin leaned forward to peer out through the observation slit. After all the noise and activity of the evening the cul-de-sac outside was empty, save for a black man in mechanic's overalls, locking the second garage in. He was whistling to himself, looking well-pleased.

Melvin let out a faint whistle of a less cheerful kind. 'Not tonight,' he said simply.

Eight

Councillor Philip Thomas rolled over in bed as the alarm began beeping its insistent, jarring note at him. He flung out his hand to stop it, and rolled back for just a few minutes. Instinctively his left arm went out towards Jenny. Only, of course, Jenny wasn't there. And there was no fitful bumping and scuttering about in the next bedroom as the kids woke early and started digging into their possessions and shoving them around until they were called down to breakfast. He wondered how long it would take him to get used to it. He didn't want to get used to it: he wanted them back, and soon. Jenny couldn't really have meant all those bitter things she had thrown at him just before they climbed into the taxi and went off.

It was no good lying here brooding about it. He swung out of bed. Not even six-thirty yet. He could almost hear what Jenny would have had to say about it, turning over and mumbling a 'Not *again*?' protest. And she was right, he had to admit it. Spending more time with other people's troubles than with her and the twins; coming and going at all hours of the day and night; sitting on committees, painstakingly writing up advice for pamphlets and community care handouts; and even now, after she had walked out on him, still getting up just to keep an eye on a police operation which no one would have blamed him for dodging.

Habits like this died hard. They could sneer, all of them. Lots of them did sneer, including a number of his colleagues who liked the pay and the power but didn't believe in voluntary overtime or too much commitment to good causes. It was too late for that to make any difference to Philip Thomas: he had his own dogged way to pursue.

On the table where he had left them the night before were the remaining pamphlets from the stack he had been distributing over the last week, taking them round by hand himself, giving his own address where people with housing problems could contact him in an emergency, when the town hall was closed, the council offices were closed, and nobody else would cope. That had been the last straw for Jenny. What sort of future did this have to offer? Always the phone ringing or people at the door; always her husband's attention distracted from his family by some unfortunate with no family, or else a troublesome family. Either way, it was Thomas they came to. 'They know a soft touch when they see one.' He could remember the despair in her voice as she rammed the kids' clothes into a couple of cases, refusing to look at him or listen to him. 'A soft touch for anyone except *us*.'

Beside the few spare pamphlets was the scribbled note he had made of the address for this morning's police raid. Nobody had told him officially about it: they simply could not be bothered to observe correct procedures in that slipshod office . . . any more than the police themselves could be relied on always to observe correct procedures. Thomas, numbering co-chairmanship of the Police Committee among his duties, was prepared to support the police when necessary, and to criticize when necessary. Today he would observe and decide which course was appropriate.

It was a bright, frosty morning. The sparkle of brittle whiteness along the terraces and on the grass patches below the tower blocks made the grass look less patchy and the pavements look as if some enthusiastic polisher had been at work well before dawn. The scene grew less attractive as he drove into the Melville estate. Some ground-floor windows were boarded up, and wherever there was a board there was a sprayed slogan, always aggressive and frequently obscene.

Parked close to the main door of a particularly seedy, run-down block was a police van. Sergeant Bob Cryer was leaning against it, surveying an upper floor through a pair of binoculars. As Thomas parked and approached, a man in plain clothes emerged from the other side of the van. Thomas had expected this would be the one: Jack Hunt, chief bailiff of the county court. He was efficient, and tough. That toughness, and the way the uniformed men backed it, was what had to be watched.

'Anything special we should know?' Cryer was asking.

'No, but watch out for the main man. Dennis Moynihan, known to his friends as Dennis the Menace. Not that he's got many friends. Built like the Kremlin and twice as cuddly. And Gnasher'll be there – vicious little animal.'

They became aware of Thomas's presence, and he could tell they were not in a mood to welcome it. That was just too bad. He decided to set the proper tone, right from the start.

'Sergeant Cryer.' He made it curt and authoritative. 'Mr Hunt.'

'Councillor.'

'Everything set, then?'

'Yes, sir. After Mr Hunt's served the order we'll stand by so the eviction can proceed quickly and smoothly.'

'Well, whatever you do, sergeant, I don't want any heavy-handed police pressure. Understood?'

'The reason we're here in the first place, sir,' said Cryer with studied patience, 'is because these squatters have a history of heavy-handedness of their own. Continual obstruction. A bunch of weekend revolutionaries, ignoring repeated notices to quit, and harassing the neighbours.'

'Just keep it low profile, right? After all, we are dealing with people who are homeless themselves. Or will be.'

'And is that through choice or circumstance, sir?' Cryer turned away and opened the back door of the van, to reveal three uniformed constables and a woman police constable. 'Right, we're on.' As they bundled out and grouped on the pavement, he said into the radio: 'Sierra Oscar four, this is Cryer here. We're going in.'

They went up the smelly, dark staircase, with Hunt and Cryer in the lead. Thomas positioned himself at the bottom, where he could hope to see and hear most of what was going on.

Jack Hunt rapped on a door. 'Open up, please. This is Chief Bailiff Hunt from the county court. I have a warrant of possession for these premises.' When there was no reply he repeated the words formally and slowly, at a much increased volume. After a long pause he stood well back and said: 'Right, I'm going to have this door broken down.'

The door opened. Thomas could just see a massive figure in the entrance, and heard a snarl, a 'Drop dead', and a sudden crisp order from Sergeant Cryer. Before Moynihan could close the door again, two of the men had flung themselves at it. They toppled through, with the other man and the woman after them. There was a crash, a sound of yelling, and suddenly a snapping, snarling dog was thrown down the stairs. Cryer was hauling Moynihan out and holding him twisted over the rail of the balcony.

From within, the squatters were screeching abuse. Thomas could not tell whether the police were using unreasonable force, and began to feel it would be better not to ask: certainly not right at this moment. There was a crash of broken glass, and he could just see one of the constables reeling out, his hand up to his face. Blood was seeping from somewhere.

Thomas turned instinctively away, in time to see another car arriving. He knew it all too well, even before the driver got out. Meadows was one of the least desirable journalists from the *Gazette*. Councillor Thomas had no wish to be interviewed on the spot, and probably misreported. It would be much better to go away and think calmly about the situation and its aftermath before forming an opinion and allowing himself to make a statement.

He made for his own car as Cryer and his men began bundling their haul of shouting, half-clad squatters down the stairs.

PCs Malcolm Haynes and Yorkie Smith climbed the broad steps towards the ornate nineteenth-century doors of the public library. It had only been open fifteen minutes this morning, but already they had been summoned to deal with a spot of bother. They were both curious: trouble in the hushed surroundings of a library was a rare occurrence. just possibly two ratepayers were having a punch-up over who was first in line for the new Catherine Cookson novel.

The librarian on duty was an elderly woman, with grey hair tightly scraped back from her forehead, and a precise little voice which could probably grow very acid when discussing fines on overdue books.

'I am so sorry to get you involved, but we do have to think of the wishes of other readers and borrowers.'

'If you could just tell us what – '

'The end of these stacks, down here.' The librarian led the way to the far end of the main room. 'Of course, one is sorry for them, but this is really not the place for them.'

Huddled in the remotest corner, under the shadow of laden shelves, was a shabby but clean woman, with two scruffy suitcases propped against the lowest row of books, and two small boys whom she was holding tightly against herself.

Haynes bent over her, patting one of the boys affably on the shoulder. 'Now, come on, we can't doss here, can we?'

The woman stared at the books closest to her as if determining to read every title from one end of the shelf to the other.

Yorkie Smith reinforced the warning with slightly more weight. 'Come on, love, play the game. You know you can't stay here.'

'Where'm I going to go, then?' Her voice was clear but dead. Her only remaining strength was in her arms, around her two children.

'What about home? Just tell us where it is.'

'Ain't got none,'

'Oh, now, there must be somewhere. With these two kids – '

'It were disgusting. I told him so, but he weren't listening.' A little animation came into her tone. 'Throw you out as soon as look at you.'

'And where was that?'

'Royalty. A fine name for a dump like that!'

'Isn't that one of those B-and-B places the council uses?'

'Disgusting it was. All that money they get – rip-off merchants, that's what. I'm not going back there, copper, and I got nowhere else. No money, neither.' Her shoulders slumped. One of the boys tried to wriggle free, and absently she slapped him. 'Wayne, stop it.'

'What's your name, love?'

'Marie.'

'Marie what?'

'What difference does it make?'

'What about the social, Marie?' Haynes suggested. 'Or the council. You must be a priority case.'

She shook her head sceptically.

'Well, you can't stay here. Come on.' Reluctantly Yorkie bent down to get an arm around her hunched shoulders and heave her up.

Marie was not going to suffer that indignity. She scrambled to her feet of her own accord, not letting go of the two little boys.

'All I want is me own little place. For the kiddies, like.'

The librarian, who had gone off to attend to a borrower at the desk, came back with a leaflet from the rack. 'Is this of any help? It's a council leaflet about temporary shelter.'

Haynes scanned it with approval and handed it on to Marie. 'Just the job. Tells you where to go, the lot.'

'No use. It's in Pleydell Street. Ain't got the bus fare.'

Young Wayne was struggling again. She hit him again, wearily and without real force.

Haynes dug into his pocket and produced a pound. Anything for a quiet life.

When they reported in at Sun Hill again, they found that at least they had had a quieter time than some of the others. In the canteen, Pete Ramsey was drinking from a cup tilted awkwardly in his left hand, with his bandaged right hand resting on the table. June Ackland, with a swelling bruise close to her left eye, winced every time she moved her head. 'Like having a hangover, without the fun of being drunk the night before,' she moaned in answer to a sympathetic question from Yorkie. To make it worse, they had just witnessed a procession of their captives leaving the station. All bona fide members of the property-owning classes, Hollis confirmed: parents had come flocking in to reclaim their fun-loving offspring, and the bail forms were covered with expensive Hampstead addresses. Quite a contrast to Marie, thought Smith: well-heeled squatters who did not even need to squat.

'Haynes . . . Smith.' Sergeant Cryer was crooking a finger in the doorway. 'Inspector Frazer wants you downstairs. At the double.'

'Oh, and what were you two up to while we were getting beaten up by the upper-classes, then?' June shook her head in flippant reproof, and immediately regretted it.

The two followed Cryer down to the front office, where the inspector was talking to a slim, earnest young woman at the desk. 'But, Miss Bloomfield, it's only been a couple of hours. Aren't you being a bit hasty?'

'As a social worker, I know what mood my clients are likely to be in. And I'm worried about Marie Tucker. And about her children – Wayne and Sammy.'

'You think their safety is at risk?'

'Oh, no. Not them. She wouldn't harm a hair on their heads.'

Inspector Frazer turned to the two constables. 'Sergeant Cryer tells me you've reported moving a woman and two children from the public library.'

'That's right, ma'am. Called herself Marie. That's all she would tell us. And one of the kids was called Wayne.'

Miss Bloomfield looked half relieved, but still half apprehensive. 'Where did you send her?'

'Gave her a leaflet for that centre in Pleydell Street.'

'She hasn't shown up there. It's the first place I checked.'

'She wouldn't have gone to some friends?' Frazer suggested. 'Or some place she's familiar with? I mean, as I said, it's not all that long, and they might just be wandering round the park or – '

'I don't think you understand,' said Miss Bloomfield tensely. 'I'm afraid she might be suicidal.'

Philip Thomas did not usually call in at home around the middle of the day. There were far too many demands on his time. But he had come out this morning before the post arrived, and the thought had kept nagging at him that there might be a letter from Jenny. There had to be a phone call or a letter, sooner or later, and as he was out so often she was more likely to write a letter than try to ring him. It made little difference whether he read it first thing when it arrived or picked it off the mat when he got back in the evening; but as the hours wore on it became an obsession, and there was only one way to deal with it. He drove home.

The front door was open. He started up the path angrily, then slowed. There was no telling who was inside. He had no wish to run straight into a couple of thugs who would smash his head in. Typical that there wasn't a policeman in sight.

There were voices inside: a woman's, crying, and a man's voice saying something which made no sense: 'Do you need a hand with that, love?'

From closer range Thomas saw that there were two uniformed policemen in his hallway, staring up the stairs. At the top of the stairs was a woman struggling with two suitcases, and behind her two children, peering down at the policemen. One of the officers, a coloured man, began cautiously to climb the stairs. 'Come on now, Marie.' His voice was warm and reassuring. 'You know you don't belong here.'

'Not here, either?' she screamed back at him. 'Don't belong anywhere, that's it, isn't it?' In a sudden panic she bundled the children through the bathroom door behind her.

Thomas heard the key turn in the lock as he stepped into the hall – his own hallway, invaded by strangers. 'Just what the hell is going on?'

The constable at the foot of the staircase swung round. 'Mr Thomas – Councillor Thomas?'

'That's right. And this is my house, and I'd very much like to know what – '

'PC Smith, sir. And PC Haynes, up there. We've been sent here on information that this Mrs Tucker was likely to be on your premises.'

'Why the blazes should she be?'

'Homeless, sir. She was advised to go to the emergency shelter advice centre, but your name and address were on the leaflet as well, and her social worker thought she might be planning to throw herself on your mercy, if you see what I mean.'

Haynes was tapping softly on the bathroom door. 'Marie?' When there was no reply, he rapped more forcefully. 'Come on, love.'

'You mean to tell me,' Thomas burst out, 'that you charged in here like a couple of characters from . . . from Starsky and Hutch . . . put the fear of God into that poor woman . . . and now she's holed up in my bathroom. Marvellous. Really marvellous.'

Haynes was coming back downstairs, shaking his head despondently.

Smith said: 'Sir, perhaps if we broke the door down – '

'Are you out of your mind? I don't want any dramatics in my home. You've done enough damage already, if you ask me. Oh, no, we're going to talk her out. You said her social worker sent you. Sonja Bloomfield, would that be?'

'I did gather her name was Bloomfield, yes, sir. She'll still be at the station, I reckon, waiting to hear from us.'

'A pity you didn't notify her before setting about that poor creature.' Thomas stormed into the sitting room and picked up the phone. When he had finished the call he looked witheringly at the two constables just outside the door. 'It's as well for you that she *was* still there. Now we'll get somebody who does know how to handle the situation.'

He tugged the sideboard door open and helped himself to a large Scotch. The police officers remained sheepishly in the hall, though both of them looked up the stairs every now and then, as if wondering whether to make another attempt at getting through to Marie Tucker. There was no sound from above, other than a faint tinkle as if someone had dropped a bottle to the floor; then stillness. Not dropping his own bottle, Thomas poured himself another whisky.

It took Sonja Bloomfield no more than five minutes to reach the house, with Inspector Frazer driving. As they came in she was saying 'She knows me. Perhaps if I have a word first . . . '

Thomas stood in the hall beside Inspector Frazer. With the two of them and the two large policemen, the narrow space was pretty crowded. Sonja Bloomfield went steadily up the flight and picked her way over the suitcases.

'Marie . . . ?'

In an undertone Frazer said: 'Miss Bloomfield was explaining to me on the way here that Marie has been in that rather unfortunate bed-and-breakfast place for a year. Ever since she left her husband.'

'So there's a husband. Do we know anything – '

'He was drunk half the time. And violent.'

'A familiar combination,' said Thomas knowledgeably. 'And I suppose she blamed herself: "I married him, I must be what's made him change from the man I loved into a monster." '

Frazer looked at him with a faint tinge of respect. 'Just about the way Miss Bloomfield sums it up. And that's when Marie made her first try.'

'Try?'

'At suicide.'

'Oh, God, no. Not here.' Seeing the look of respect fading, he added hastily: 'Or anywhere, of course.'

345

'Marie? It's Sonja here. Sonja Bloomfield.'

Faintly they heard a boy's voice. 'Mummy, it's the nice lady what sees us . . . '

'Hello, Wayne. How are you, love?'

There was an answering giggle. 'I'm in a bath with Sammy.'

'Wayne, tell your mummy I've come to say hello, eh? I've come to take you home.'

At last Marie herself spoke. 'Ain't got none.'

'She's still alive, anyway,' breathed Thomas.

'If you call that living,' said Frazer. 'One of the world's walking wounded. Coping on her own, without anything to look forward to.'

'These bed-and-breakfast places do their best, I'm sure.'

'Not according to her social worker. I wouldn't get her started on that subject, if I were you.'

'Marie,' Sonja Bloomfield was persevering, 'locking yourself in there isn't going to help. Why don't you open the door, and then we can have a chat about things.'

'We're always bloody chatting about things. And it don't change nothing.'

'Be reasonable, Marie.'

Glass of some kind was hurled and smashed against the door. 'Just go away, right? Just get out.'

Frazer glanced ruefully at Thomas. 'I hope you didn't have anything valuable in the bathroom.'

'Just a vase my wife gave me.' He hoped it was not that; became edgy at the thought that it almost certainly was, and another part of Jenny and their life together had been shattered.

The social worker had edged a few steps back to whisper over the rail. 'She's never been like this before.'

'Well, what are you going to do about it?' Thomas felt himself surrounded, crushed by all these intruders. He went back to the whisky bottle and splashed more into his glass. 'Stand by – ' he rejoined them – 'and let her smash up my bathroom? Was she in the habit of doing that in her previous accommodation? No wonder she – '

'The place was a tip,' said Miss Bloomfield in a fierce whisper. 'Anyone in their right mind . . . ' She drew a shuddering breath. 'We've got a government that slaps spending restrictions on councils so they can't build or maintain homes for people to live in, yet allows B-and-B's to charge what they like. A seventh of your budget, Councillor, going into the hands of – '

'Break down the door.' Flushed by the whisky, Thomas had changed his mind. 'Inspector, I'm asking you to break down the door and get her out, before there's any more damage.'

'Give her a chance,' Sonja Bloomfield pleaded, 'and she'll come out by herself, I know it.'

'Break it down.'

'There are children in there.'

Thomas stumbled towards the stairs, grabbing PC Smith's arm and trying to force him upwards. 'Go on, break it down!'

'Smith.' Inspector Frazer was terse and commanding. 'Ask Councillor Thomas to show you the kitchen. And make us all a cup of tea.' She looked up at the bathroom door and called: 'You'd like a nice cup of tea, wouldn't you, Marie?'

'Don't want no tea and sympathy.' Then, contritely: 'Mr Thomas, I'm sorry about your pot. I'll pay you back for it.' This was followed by a shaky, mirthless laugh. In Smith's grip, Thomas tugged back to listen. 'Or I'll try. Only, you see, there was your name on that leaflet and the back door was open and we sat in the kitchen for a warm, and I thought I'd talk to you when you got back.'

'Yes. Er, yes.' There was nothing much else to say.

'Lovely bathroom you've got here. Lovely. In the hotel, we had to share. Fifteen of us. Broken seat, no paper, no flush even. People would shove anything down the bog. And me bedroom – damp in that corner, over there, rotting bit there and roaches all bloody over.' She was beginning to sob. 'And the kids. Stuck inside that room, they've been getting so I can't keep control. Like Jim. I can see Jim in them. It's no life for them.'

Sonja Bloomfield was cautiously returning to the door. 'Don't upset yourself, Marie.'

'They'll be better off without me.' It was a dwindling mumble, barely audible.

Thomas saw both Inspector Frazer and the other woman stiffen. Sonja put her ear to the door, then straightened up in alarm. 'We've got to get her out. Get her *out*!'

'Smith: Haynes.' Frazer stood back and urged them past. 'Break down that door!'

There was not much space for a good charge, but Smith's hefty shoulder and Haynes' boot made a powerful combination. At the second lunge they had splintered a panel, and Smith could grope inside for the key. Frazer took a careful look, then made way for Sonja Bloomfield.

Marie lay motionless on the bathroom floor. The two boys were sitting in the bath, Sammy beginning to cry.

Wayne peered over the edge. 'Mummy's gone sleep.'

Dazed, Thomas looked helplessly at Frazer. She said: 'Do you keep any drugs in the bathroom?'

His antidepressants, of course. It was only recently that he had persuaded his doctor to prescribe them; and they certainly had not worked. But they had worked for Marie. The bottle was empty, cast aside on the floor. Now he remembered the sound of it dropping. She must have taken the lot, right after shutting herself in there.

'You get the children out,' Frazer said to Haynes. 'Smith, resus.' She was on her way to the phone, summoning an ambulance, before returning to see how Smith was getting on.

Thomas plodded upstairs and into the bedroom across the landing. The two children, with Haynes standing protectively close, were sitting on the edge of one of the beds, and Sammy was playing with a woolly rabbit which had been left behind in Jenny's rush to get away. After an eternity, Frazer appeared in the doorway. She looked at the children and at Thomas. She was not going to say anything in front of Wayne and Sammy; and she did not need to put the news into words for Thomas's benefit. Her defeated expression was enough.

In the distance, coming closer, was the wail of an ambulance siren. Too late.

Philip Thomas went to the window and looked down on his neat back garden. It had suddenly become a bleak, unfamiliar place. Strangers' voices murmured in his bathroom. A stranger was clumping downstairs and back up again. A strange woman lay dead in his house. The reason he had gone into local politics was to try and help people like Marie Tucker. He had worked and sacrificed a lot for those ideals, including his marriage. He had made a lot of mistakes, but he had done his best. And what did it all amount to? You ended up running round in circles, looking over your shoulder, dashing from one meeting to another and issuing one directive after another, and along the way failing the very people you most wanted to help: people like Marie.

Behind him there was a faint plopping sound. Sammy had dropped the woolly toy and was staring down at it, unsure as to whether he ought to slide off the bed. Thomas stooped, picked the rabbit up, and handed it back. He stroked the boy's head for a moment and Sammy smiled timidly.

The ambulance was at the door.

Nine

Jasmine Allan estate was suddenly back in the news; or on the Sun Hill airways, at any rate. A woman's agitated call from the Telgar Road high-rise block reported noises from her rubbish chute. It was probably a cat that had got stuck, but investigation was recommended. Pete Ramsey, driving towards the estate, cursed himself as he went, disliking cats as a breed and their owners as a type. Little tibby-wibby, stuck in the rubbish, chasing mice down the chute – and the police, with naff-all else to do, had to go and make soothing noises to any neurotic female with all the time and warped imagination in the world on her hands. Swinging round a corner below the offending block, he practised noises that were far from soothing.

Mrs Turville was a disappointment insofar as she was not obviously neurotic, nor the standard, soppy cat-worshipping figure. In her mid-thirties, smartly dressed if a trifle worn about the eyes and round the mouth, she forestalled any of Ramsey's grumbles by apologizing at once: 'I hope I'm not wasting your time.'

She did not wait for an answer, but briskly led the way past the foot of the stair-well and into a large chamber where the chute from floors above emptied into a series of huge containers. 'I was just emptying the kitchen bin before going to work, and I heard it.'

'You reckon it's a cat?'

'I thought so at first, but now I'm not sure.'

The large container positioned below the chute, was almost full. The floor was also piled high with refuse of one kind and another, some in bags, some spilling all over the place.

Ramsey wrinkled his nose as he picked his way over the débris towards the chute. Undoubtedly there was a thin, feeble noise coming from the bin below it.

'Sounds like a cat,' he agreed. 'I should fetch the caretaker.'

'We haven't got one,' said Mrs Turville unhappily. 'And I don't think it's a cat anyway. I think it sounds human, don't you?'

There was nothing for it but to start rooting in the unsavoury mess. Clambering on to a pile of rubble so that he could peer over the edge into the bin, Ramsey reluctantly prodded tins and bags and assorted slimy masses to one side and another. After a few handfuls had been squashed against one edge, he saw a plastic carrier bag, cleaner than the rest. Inside, wrapped in a towel, barely visible but more clearly audible now, was a tiny baby.

Ramsey stared, aghast. Young, middle-aged or ageing villains he could cope with. A new-born baby was new to his experience, and he could remember no discussions of the subject during his training or in recent briefings. He reached in and hauled the package out, hearing Mrs Turville's squeak of horror. Handing it gingerly down to her, he groped for his radio.

Sergeant Penny's response was quick enough, though his voice did rise half an octave as he heard the news. 'A new baby? My God, get it over to the General, quick.' There was a brief, muttered consultation with somebody in the background, and then Penny was saying: 'Don't unwrap it or anything. Just keep it as warm as you can, and get going. Right? I'll let them know you're on your way.'

Ramsey eased himself back from the edge of the bin. Just as his head was out of the way, a consignment of bottles came clattering down the chute. Maybe that was how the baby had been despatched in the first place. He stepped clear of the accumulated gunge and tried to brush a streak of grease from his tunic, but only made it worse.

'Poor little thing,' Mrs Turville was crooning anxiously over her wailing armful.

Ramsey said: 'You don't know anybody on the upper floors who might've –'

'Goodness, no. I simply can't imagine it.'

'Have to check on them all later.' He hurried towards the car and put the carrier bag on the back seat, well back, covered with a blanket. The baby started bleating, more vigorously than before. That was no bad thing. Let it keep crying, and not go and die on him.

He wove his way through the back streets as quickly as he could, without risking any jolts or sudden braking. His only near mishap was the appearance of a milk float, emerging from a narrow street right across his path. Slamming on the anchors, he spoke comfortingly over his shoulder. 'Don't panic, we're nearly there.'

Mrs Turville had said she couldn't imagine it. Neither could Pete Ramsey. His contacts with infants had been few and uninstructive. On the whole he placed them in the same unfavourable category as cats. But it would never have occurred to him that anybody could dump a human being this new and fragile; not in this fashion, anyway. Leaving babies in baskets or on doorsteps or in telephone booths seemed to be a common occurrence, judging from the newspapers; but throwing them out with the garbage was a new, nasty one. Maybe the mother had been on drugs, or mentally disordered, or a wino. But even then, would she just give birth, wrap her baby up neatly in a carrier bag, and stick it down a chute? Or if she wasn't a junkie, it could have been that she was scared stiff of her parents. Ramsey doubted it. Even from his own limited observation, he thought it unlikely that a mother and father would not have noticed a blind thing for nine months.

There were a lot of questions to be asked in that block of flats once the top priority matter had been dealt with.

With a sickening twist in his stomach he realized that the baby had stopped crying. 'Wake up, you stupid little nit. Start yelling.' As he pulled up outside the casualty entrance to the hospital, two nurses and a doctor were already hurrying out towards him. The doctor felt briefly in the bag, then hurried back inside. A glass-topped trolley was waiting. The moment the baby was settled into it, still and silent, one of the nurses began to wheel it away.

Ramsey, uninvited, kept pace. 'Is it gonna be all right?'

They provided him with a polystyrene cup of tea and sat him down in an alcove, out of harm's way. He watched people bustling to and fro, wondering which of them were concerned with the baby and which with other emergencies. An old man in a dressing-gown limped past and looked at him with a quiver of amusement. In his plain-clothes days, Ramsey supposed he could well have been mistaken for an expectant father: improbable then, the way he operated, and crazy now. He sipped his tea, scalding his upper lip.

A door swung open and one of the nurses who had met him at the entrance came out. She had a pert nose and wide, humorous eyes. If she was overworked, like the rest of them, she seemed to be enjoying it. When Ramsey waved to attract her attention, she stopped and smiled.

'Still waiting for her to make a statement?'

'Oh, it's a girl, is it?'

'Can't you tell the difference?'

'I never look unless I'm asked.'

She ignored his rash grin, but let herself sink down companionably on to the seat beside him. When she said nothing, he began to feel alarmed. 'She is going to be okay, though, isn't she?'

The girl shrugged. 'Poorly, but stable at the moment. In an incubator. But she's a good weight – six-and-a-half pounds.'

'Oh. They tell me I was only five.' As she looked him incredulously up and down, he ventured: 'My name's Pete. Ever go out with coppers, do you?'

'Not till Christmas.' She yawned. 'I'm on double shifts.'

Malcolm Haynes leaned back from the console. 'A brass eagle's gone missing,' he announced, 'from St Mark's church.'

'Sure it's not a stork?' said Penny. He looked up at the roster on the wall. 'Edwards and Melvin should be cruising around that region. Try and raise them. Give 'em something to do instead of arguing religion.'

'How d'you know they're arguing religion, sarge?'

'You ever been out with Melvin?'

'Not so far.'

'Your turn next,' said Penny with gloomy relish. 'I'll see to that.'

Taffy Edwards, in fact, was the one to bring up the dangerous subject. As he responded to the call and changed course for St Mark's church, he said indignantly: 'Well, I do think that's well out of order, thieving from churches.'

'All thieving's out of order, isn't it?' said Ken Melvin.

'You know what I mean. I mean, *more* out of order.'

'Than mugging old ladies?'

Taffy scowled. 'Yeh. I mean, no. No, just not . . . well, not *right*. Like vandalizing graves.'

'A violation,' said Melvin. 'Sacrilege.'

'That's it. Sacrilege.'

'D'you go to church, then, Taff?'

'Me? Not likely.'

'Chapel?'

'Only when I was a kid, because I had to. We all had to.'

'D'you believe in God?'

Edwards began to get intimations of what he had let himself in for. 'I dunno. Well, no, I don't think I do, as it happens. Not any more.'

'So what's specially wrong with stealing from churches? Why do you

351

think it's worse than stealing from a factory or some old age pensioner's pocket?'

Edwards was beginning to get peeved. 'I don't know why I think it's worse than stealing from a factory. I just do. Everybody thinks it's worse than stealing from a factory, don't they?'

'Superstition, then,' said Melvin with lofty irony, as the van pulled up outside the church.

St Mark's was a Victorian building, in what had once been red brick patterned with yellow brick coigns and lozenge patterns, but was now an overall murky ochre, with just a hint of pitted red, like smoky embers, underneath. Its spire had been patched up after bomb damage during the Second World War, and bulged in such a way as to give the impression that it was about to collapse outwards and come down in shreds. A path up to the door in the tower was scattered with soggy lumps of confetti left over from a recent wedding. Edwards strode up and seized the heavy iron ring in the door, turning it and pushing.

The door was locked. Melvin caught up with him as he went round a cluster of gravestones towards the linking path up to the south porch. There was something just too damned pious in the way that Melvin walked and kept glancing at his companion. Needled, Edwards said: 'What about you, then? Do you go to church?'

'I do, actually, when I can.' Melvin peered up at the rusting bars over the stained glass window. 'Not this sort, though. House groups. Charismatic.'

Edwards stopped under the carved arch of the porch. 'You? A born-again Christian?'

'When my shifts allow, yes.'

Before Taffy Edwards could pursue this, they saw a man and woman approaching from a small gate which presumably led to the vicarage. The Reverend Hugh Ford was in his late thirties and sported a dark brown beard, whose drooping strands suggested there was not much of a chin to support it underneath. He wore a leather jacket over his clerical vest and collar. Even at this hour of a weekday morning his wife looked more formal, in a neat blue dress with a thin belt and tight cuffs. Her mouth, too, was thin and tight.

'Mr Ford?'

The vicar hastened to shake hands, overdoing a firm grip which lasted a few seconds longer than was absolutely necessary, and then making an all-inclusive gesture towards the woman at his side. 'My wife, Cath.' Edwards felt that Mrs Ford would rather have been introduced as Catherine. Or, even better, as Mrs Ford.

'Well, sir. How did these folk get in?'

The vicar took his arm and led him under the shadow of a buttress. A small window under its angle with the wall had been broken.

'Cath noticed it,' said Ford admiringly, 'when she was walking the dog.'

'It's getting beyond a joke.' Mrs Ford was sharp and peremptory. 'We're the fourth church in the last three weeks.'

'We're aware of that, madam.' Edwards bowed his head politely.

The vicar took keys from his pocket and led them into the interior. His wife came to a halt near the font and stood there with her arms folded, as if to ensure that their visitors did not remove anything else from the premises. The other three walked up the aisle towards the pulpit. On the floor near the chancel steps, a patch of clean tile stood out in sharp contrast to the faded expanse around it. Here, the vicar explained, had once stood their lectern with its mighty eagle. Solid brass and, he admitted, as ugly as sin.

'Worth a few bob, though, even melted down?' suggested Edwards.

Ford shrugged. 'Not much, I shouldn't have thought.'

'Nothing else gone?'

'We keep everything else locked up,' said Mrs Ford in clarion tones.

Ford gave Edwards and Melvin a slight, man-to-man smile. 'Cath and my PCC are great ones for locking things up.'

'We wouldn't get insurance otherwise, would we, *dear*?'

Melvin stooped over the chancel steps and turned to look down the aisle. There were marks on a patch of carpet, and a wavy line had been scoured along part of the tiling. Something heavy had obviously been dragged up to the north door.

'That was locked, was it, sir?'

'Yes, but the key's always in the door.'

'Possibly an inside job, then – I mean, knowing about the key?'

The Reverend Ford looked incredulous. 'Officer, the average age of my congregation is a hundred and eight. All six of them together wouldn't have shifted that monstrosity.' Sadly he surveyed the ranks of pews. 'The way things are going, I soon won't be allowed to open the church even on Sundays.'

'We'll just have another look outside before we go,' said Edwards. 'If you could keep away from that door though, please, till the Scene-of-Crime Officer's been round. CID will want a look as well.'

He and Melvin made for the door. Behind them, Mrs Ford was talking in a throttled-down voice that, by its very nature, was too thrusting to be discreet. 'When are you going to grow up, Hugh?'

'Cath, this is a house of prayer, a *sanctury*. I resent turning it into a fortress.'

'It's hardly that. Goodness knows what the premium's going to be next year.'

'Would Jesus put up a burglar alarm?'

'Oh, don't be so – '

'No, go on, tell me. Would he?'

Edwards and Melvin made their escape before they were lumbered with what was building up to a 'domestic'. Taffy had a premonition that Ken Melvin was all too likely to take up that last question of the vicar's and use it to trigger off further theological discussion. He could do without it.

Any likelihood of an immediate resumption of Melvin's evangelism was swiftly demolished. The moment Edwards had finished reporting in on the church robbery, Sergeant Penny was saying: 'While you're out there, get along to Coates Crescent. Number Eleven. There's a Mrs Kennedy whose son says he was talking to her on the phone earlier this morning and got cut off. Couldn't get through again, and he's a bit worried. See if she's all right.'

It sounded simple enough. The street was a quiet residential one, and the front of Number Eleven looked clean, recently painted, and respectable. But that did not necessarily mean that an old lady couldn't have dropped dead behind the neatly looped curtains.

Melvin stayed in the van while Edwards went to ring the doorbell. He began to feel apprehensive when, after several attempts, there was no reply and not a hint of a sound from within. Perhaps the bell was out of order. He began to pound on the door with his fist.

A door opened; but it was the neighbour's front door. An elderly woman looked out crossly. 'Who d'ye want?' She had a strong, unmistakable Irish accent.

'Does a Mrs Kennedy live here, madam?'

'Why would ye be wanting to know?'

Edwards explained about the phone call. 'The son's a bit concerned, so he – '

'Concerned?' She laughed contemptuously. 'Him, concerned?'

Edwards remained patient and courteous. 'Do you happen to know if Mrs Kennedy's in, madam?'

'Of course she's not. She's not back from Mass yet. Spends half her time round there, praying for that heathen brat of hers.'

'I see. Oh, well, then – '

'And how often does he come over to see her? The young are all the same nowadays, all the world over, that they are. Turning their back on God and the family – '

'Yes, well.' Edwards turned to make his way back to the van. 'Perhaps you'd be good enough to tell Mrs Kennedy we called.'

'That I will not.' The woman was clearly affronted. 'We don't speak.' She slammed her front door.

Taffy climbed back into the van, silently vowing mayhem if Melvin dared say another word about religion. There seemed to have been a lot of it about this morning; and none of it had created much in the way of sweetness and light.

Ramsey tore himself away from the hospital with the greatest reluctance. The reluctance owed less to the charm of that nurse, even though she was a bird of some class and he was sure he could have found some way of luring her out before Christmas, than to the thought of leaving that baby in there, not knowing, not being close at hand.

As he went back into Sun Hill through the front entrance, Sergeant Peters and Reg Hollis were coming along the corridor from the washrooms. 'It's true, you know, sarge.' Hollis was on one of his hobby-horses. 'This shift work, it's killing us all. Cocking up our circadian rhythms.'

'That's not what worries me,' said Peters. 'What gets me is the number of old mates who retire and drop dead in a month. Waste of the superann and everything. Not to mention the retirement parties and the presents: more like a wake in advance, some of them.'

'But that's it, don't you see – '

'Poor old Stan,' Peters reminisced. 'One of the best farewell booze-ups ever. And then he was gone in no time.'

'You know what did for him?'

'Yes. Scotch and bitter.'

'No, sarge, you've got to realize that – '

'Ramsey!' Peters was glad to change the subject. 'Here comes our little angel of mercy. All right, lad?'

'Oh, terrific, sarge. I shall never be able to look a carrier bag in the face again.'

'Yes, well, don't go into post-shock trauma. You're on house-to-house next.'

'But, sarge – '

'Inspector Frazer wants you to report the moment you're back. She wants you and Ackland and Martella out there knocking on doors.' In the doorway of front office, Peters stopped for a moment and asked, with genuine interest: 'How's the baby, anyway?'

'Fifty-fifty, when I left.'

Ramsey was furious with the shakiness of his own voice. He would sooner have had an indoor job for some hours, or as long as it took for better news to come through from the hospital. But at least there was some purpose in going out with June and Viv. Somewhere there was a mother who ought to be found, and soon.

He did not know whether, when they found her, he would feel sorry for her or hate her guts.

Ten

Nobody in the Telgar Road block of flats, or in any of the lower ranges along the street, had seen or heard anything which could lead to the mother of the discarded baby. No local girl had been noticeably pregnant, and none had mysteriously gone missing for any period of time worthy of gossip. Of course, Viv Martella learned, there had been that slut, Shirleen, and the three randy rovers she had been knocking around with those couple of years and got knocked up by twice; but then she had married that half-baked kid from the newsagent's who believed every word she told him, and if there'd been another kid she would have been the first to flaunt it, having a name to put on it for the first time in history. There had been squatters, both sexes, and other things besides, but they had been chucked out before that package could have been dumped in the chute. Nobody had moved out in a hurry. Nobody had gone into hospital with some excuse about a holiday virus or cystitis or a, 'Well, you know, one of those . . . just a check-up, nothing to it, she'll be out in a few days.'

Except that one woman mentioned casually to WPC Ackland that they hadn't heard a word from the Johnsons since they left a month ago. Mrs Johnson and her niece – an odd pair, both of them – had moved to a plushier flat over by the Memorial Park at very short notice, and mark her words, there must have been some fiddle with someone in the housing department to fix that one, but don't ask her what sort of favours had been given or received because it wasn't up to her to guess at goings-on of that sort.

It could all have been idle malice, but June radioed through in the hope that someone over that side of the manor could follow it up; only to be told that Ramsey and Martella should continue combing the Telgar Road vicinity while she herself followed up this new lead. Haynes was just dropping Yorkie Smith off to wrap up some unsavoury details at the Cutler's Arms pub on the edge of the estate, and could pick her up and take her across the park on his way back.

The lead did not sound wildly promising, especially as the girl and her aunt had been gone for a month and would hardly have taken the trouble of returning just to dispose of some unwanted extras, but it would make a change from going along these unappetizing landings asking the same old questions of a lot of people who resented giving the police any answers whatsoever. The resentment might be no different, but at least there would be a change of scenery.

Malcolm Haynes got out of the Panda car and opened the door for her with a sweeping flourish. 'The posh side of the park, ma'am?' he intoned.

'Quite right, Haynes. And don't spare the horses.'

They had managed no more than a quarter of a mile in the direction of the park when Penny's voice groaned into life, or an approximation of it, on the radio. 'Two-nine-four from Sierra Oscar. Are you receiving?'

'Yes, sarge.'

'Disturbance in progress at Southend Road bus depot. You anywhere near?'

'Well, sarge, actually we're on our way to – '

'Thought you might be close. Get there, before we get the blame for not protecting the next westbound convoy.'

WPC Martella reached the end of the highest balcony, asked the same question for the last time and got a blank denial, and thankfully made her way down the stairs. There was a lift, but she felt choked enough already without getting into that claustrophobic box. Her difficulty in breathing had got worse: she had thought her sinuses were completely blocked up, but somewhere along the way she had managed to inhale something which smelt dry and harsh and made everything ten times worse. Surreptitiously she studied the landscape. June had been driven off. Pete Ramsey had disappeared, and you could hardly blame him. Nobody was looking or checking on her movements.

Viv Martella snuffled, tried to breathe in, and stumbled off towards the corner and eventually on to the main road.

Of course there had to be a queue in the chemist's. Some middle-aged woman was arguing about a prescription she ought to have had, but which the doctor had forgotten to provide, only she knew exactly what it was she wanted and she was entitled to it, but she couldn't be absolutely sure of the name. It was for her usual trouble; they would understand, she was sure. Martella balanced a number of cold cures and a decongestant in her left hand while groping for her handkerchief with the right and vainly trying to blow into it. The noise provoked a distasteful look from the girl ahead of her, but Martella felt irrationally cheered: the girl's perfume was so penetrating that she could actually smell it. Maybe the fog was lifting.

She got another glance, this time a mistrustful one. A man's voice was speaking from the radio jutting out of her top pocket, hoarse and swaying in and out. The message was breaking up. The only way to receive it clearly was to get out of the shop into the open. Martella dumped the various medicines she had collected and fled to the street.

'Viv?'

'Yes, sarge.'

'Where the hell have you been?' Before she had time to fumble for an excuse, Sergeant Penny was continuing: 'The estate's not all that far from Slade Lane market, is it?'

'Actually, I'm standing in the middle of it, sarge.'

'What are you doing *there*?' Again, before she could frame some reply, he went on: 'Look, this sounds an urgent one. Pop in and see a Mrs Simmons at the Caricola Café. Car-reecola – got it? Apparently she has a problem with a corpse.'

Martella looked longingly at the chemist's shop. Two other people had already gone in, presumably to add themselves to the end of the queue. Nobody had come out. She resigned herself to the fact that she would have to sniff and rub her eyes for a bit longer.

'On my way, sarge.'

The café was only four doors away. It had a drab frontage, enlivened by a couple of metal advertising plaques, and in the window were a fading handwritten menu and a more legibly chalked blackboard announcing dishes of the day. Viv Martella had passed it scores of times before.

A woman clearing away a table straightened up with evident relief at the sight of a police uniform. That made a change, anyway, from earlier experiences today. It was nice to know that, just once in a blue moon, you were welcome though it usually foretold worse trouble than usual.

'Mrs Simmons?'

'If you wouldn't mind coming upstairs.' The woman wiped her hands on a flowered apron, glanced at a customer tucking into a plate of bacon and sausage, and led the way to a flight of stairs behind a bead curtain. 'I wouldn't have rung, but today of all days they ain't turned up.'

'Who hasn't turned up?'

'Them. The owners.' Mrs Simmons, leading the way up to a narrow landing, made even narrower by a heap of food cartons, pushed irritably at strands of hair working loose from a slide in the shape of a bent butterfly. She was a permanently harassed type: probably, Martella assessed with a practised eye, married to a poorly paid husband and with two or three kids, too young to bring any money in but too old to do as they were told any longer. 'I only work here,' complained Mrs Simmons. 'And their father's lying up here, dead.'

She pushed open the door to a tatty bedroom. On the bed lay a man, fully dressed, staring at the wall with eyes which would never again see the peeling wallpaper, or anything else. Beside him sat a woman with dark hair and dark eyes, one hand clamped over his lifeless wrist, crying quietly to herself.

Martella blew her nose, not in emotional sympathy but in physical desperation.

Next to the bedroom was a tiny living room with a gas fire in it, unlit. Martella had a look in, and went back to the bedroom. The woman did not even look at her, but went on sobbing in almost ritual fashion, still clinging to the dead man on the bed.

'Come on, love. Let's go and light the fire and sit down and talk this over.'

'She won't move,' said Mrs Simmons. 'I've tried.'

'But it's freezing in here.'

'That's Giorgio. He's a tight little git. Never let his old man have the heating on or nothing. I mean, it ain't fair, is it, not for an Italian. They feel the cold.'

Martella decided it would be tactful to lead Mrs Simmons out on to the landing and pursue a hushed conversation there. 'So who's Giorgio?'

'Nasty piece of meat, that's what. Son of him in there. There's a daughter as well, called Isabella, and she ain't much better. They're supposed to run this place but they ain't never here. Me and the old man do it . . . used to do it, that is.'

'And that's the mother with him?'

'No, their auntie, I think. A Mrs Borenno. Only turned up a couple of days ago. Don't speak a word of English.'

'Janet,' a customer was calling from downstairs. 'You retired or something?'

'I'd better go.'

As Mrs Simmons started down the stairs, Martella asked hopefully: 'Have they got a family doctor?'

'No idea. I kept out of their private life.'

It was time to report in. Martella moved close to the landing window and battled to open it, in the hope of avoiding too much breaking-up on the radio. When she had freed it from the stickiness and swelling that held it in place, she drew a breath of comparatively fresh air, and contacted Sun Hill.

'It's a sudden death all right. No suspicious circumstances. Could I have the divisional surgeon to confirm it, please?'

Either the transmission was worse than usual or Sergeant Penny was going through one of his despondent spells, for she had to repeat it and then, in desperation, climb out on to the rickety fire escape and try again. Penny glumly acknowledged receipt, but tried to avoid having to take any action from his end. 'Haven't they got their own GP?'

'Doesn't look like it, sarge. Oh, and you couldn't try and raise an Italian-speaking doctor, could you?'

Penny's sigh transmitted clearly enough. 'It's the middle of morning surgery and you want me to find an Italian-speaking GP? I drink water, Martella, I don't walk on it.' There was a mumble in the background, and Martella said, 'What was that?' and Penny said, 'Wait a minute, can't you?' and then: 'Bob Cryer thinks he knows one. You'd better stay put until we've got somebody along to you.'

Viv Martella clambered back in and reluctantly went into the bedroom. Mrs Borenno had stopped crying but was still holding her brother's wrist, her head bent over him. There was no use trying to say anything to her; no use doing anything but wait, and hope the wait would not be too long.

Martella blew her nose. Mrs Borenno looked up fleetingly and offered an understanding nod of emotional companionship.

Southend Road bus depot had a wide forecourt in front of its huge open doors. The inside looked like an aircraft hangar, and as the car with Haynes and June Ackland approached, there was a man standing, dwarfed, in the centre of the opening, waving his arms frantically like somebody flagging a plane in. The Panda slid to a halt, and even before they were out of it he was ranting in high-pitched anguish with a wailing Irish accent and starting to walk away, waving for them to follow him into the depot.

'Come on, get a move on. Took you long enough to get here. You'd better take a good look at what he's done.'

'Who?'

'Gore. Ian Gore. Didn't they tell you? I gave them all the details over the phone.'

'Well, why don't you tell us again, Mr – er – '

'Didn't they tell you that either? Deegan.'

'Right, Mr Deegan.'

They passed a couple of bus crews, leaning against the side of a red bus which could have done with a wash. One of the men looked at June and shaped his lips into a soundless whistle. Another looked Malcolm Haynes up and down and muttered something about the sunburn you could get along Wapping High Street these days.

'Ian Gore,' Deegan snarled out. 'One of my drivers, and he's a damned nuisance. Came on duty yesterday absolutely rat-arsed. I had to suspend him. Even the union bloke didn't complain. Turns up this morning still drunk – and how the hell he could be drunk at that time of day, I don't know. But in he comes, shouting his mouth off, thundering great sledgehammer in his hands, and starts smashing up the crew room. It's going to cost thousands to repair.'

Haynes stopped. Deegan's own agitation carried him a few steps further before he realized he was on his own. He swung back querulously.

'This Mr Gore's running amuck with a sledgehammer, is he?' said Haynes, thoughtful.

'I've just told you he is.' Deegan attempted an important clearing of the throat. 'Would have tackled him myself, tried to calm him down, you know. But I thought I'd better call in the professionals.' He hesitated. 'I didn't expect a woman, though.'

'Not his day, is it?' said Haynes quietly to June. 'A spade and a mere woman.'

Deegan waved towards a low-roofed office like a building site cabin, tucked into the rear corner of the depot. 'That's the crew room.'

No noise was coming out. Perhaps Gore had run out of things to smash. Before they could get closer, the door opened. Only a woman bus conductor came out. 'He's gone,' she announced. 'And a right mess he's made of my locker.' Behind her they could see what appeared to be a pile of jagged waste timber heaped in the middle of the floor. Lockers tilted at unnatural angles. June Ackland made a move to go in and investigate, when there came a mighty yell from far across the shed.

'You slag, Deegan. Can you hear me?'

What they could not fail to hear was the sound of splintering glass. The off-duty men, who had been leaning against the bus and listening to Deegan with mild amusement, leapt away as the windscreen shattered into pieces, spraying across the floor.

Deegan whimpered, but it was more in horror at the destruction than fear. There was, however, plenty to fear, as Ackland and Haynes discovered when they edged round the rear of the bus and saw Ian Gore for the first time. He was a massive, muscle-bound hulk of a man. It was a wonder he ever managed to get himself into a driving seat. At the moment he was standing by the closed doors near the front of the doubledecker, bracing himself to swing his sledge-hammer up and around, smashing through one of the windows.

June Ackland waited for a lull in the noise, and shouted: 'Come off it, Ian! Just calm down. Give it a rest.'

He laughed and swung the hammer again. Slivers of glass rang against the side of the depot. A small crowd of curious bystanders was forming on the fore-court, waiting to see how the police would cope. They were delighted by another crash; another shower of fragments. 'Maybe,' said Haynes, 'he's just a frustrated glazier.'

The two of them stalked along the hitherto undamaged side of the bus, keeping pace with the destructive Gore on the other. It was hard to assess what to do for the best. When they met him at the end, the two of them would be no match for that rogue elephant with his murderous plaything.

Ackland tried again. 'Ian, this is a bit silly.'

'Ain't got nothing to do with you lot.'

'It has if you're going to go around smashing up buses. Look, Ian, you haven't hurt anyone yet. Why don't you give it a rest now, before someone does get injured.'

'Do you want to be the first, lovie?' Gore unexpectedly turned back, before smashing the last bit of glass still in place on his side of the vehicle. He heaved himself up into the driver's seat and waved contemptuously at Haynes. 'And take your monkey with you.'

Haynes accepted this in good part. He had heard it all before. As he used his radio to report the situation and plead with Sun Hill for back-up, June Ackland, flushed with anger and far less forgiving, walked recklessly round the front of the bus. The engine sprang into life, and for a moment she thought Gore was going to slam it into gear and drive straight at her. Instead, he leaned out of the window and pointed to a scar on his cheek. 'See that, love? That's a stanley knife did that. A stanley knife, right?' He pointed at Deegan, who was fuming but keeping his distance. 'He wants me to go back on nights, so they can do it again. Well, I'll show you what I think of that, you Irish moron.'

Haynes edged closer to Ackland. 'No shields, no back-up, no one for miles.'

'Just us and our slings, against Goliath Gore?'

Suspicious of their subdued exchange, Deegan demanded: 'Are you ever going to do anything? It may interest you to know that every one of those win-dows costs eighty-five pounds, and that doesn't include the VAT.'

'You see this, sir?' Haynes tapped his chest. 'This is a valuable piece of property as well, and it isn't about to take on a sledgehammer with . . . with a stick of wood.' He thrust his truncheon forward, so that Deegan took an in-voluntary step backwards.

At the same time there was a roar from the bus engine, clamorously am-plified by the echoing fabric of the depot. Gore drove forward, scattering Deegan, three of the lounging crew members, and a handful of onlookers who sprang clear just in time. As the bus lurched on to the road, the sledgehammer was hurled out of the open doors and bounced across the forecourt.

'Did you get a look at his destination indicator?' asked Haynes mildly.

Yorkie Smith turned the corner of Granville Street for the second time on this tour of duty and plodded along the familiar pavement, past the terraced council houses with the familiar punctuation of boarded-up windows. He was not in the best of moods. Next week was his AQR interview with Inspector Frazer, and he knew too well what one of her first comments was going to be. He hadn't had a result in months. He was craving for a bit of action, even if it did mean getting clouted over the head or roughed up in some way that had not been tried on him yet. But how was he expected to come up with heroics or daring collars on a beat through the least troublesome streets in the district?

The front door of Number 17 was open and a builder's truck was parked at the kerb. Somebody was getting round to tidying up parts of the neglected property at last. Maybe Councillor Thomas had been listened to, for a change. It was typical of the council, though, to use cheap labour: the truck was a battered old pick-up with a home-made corrugated cover fitted over the back, just the sort of clapped-out old wreck some cowboy builder and decorator would muddle along with until the wheels fell off, or some officer of the law insisted on inspecting the tyre treads. Yorkie was tempted. But he needed a more dramatic result than just a report on bald tyres. He trudged on.

There was an urgent tapping noise close to his right ear. He caught the flickering of curtains in the front window of Number 19, and saw the face of an elderly woman pressed against the glass. She pointed towards her front door. When Yorkie hesitated, she waved and pointed more insistently. He walked to the door and waited.

A door key on a piece of string was pushed through the letterbox. 'Let yourself in,' said a croaky little voice from inside.

'Can't you open the door yourself?'

'I . . . I'm not well.'

Mystified, and none too confident about the outcome, Yorkie cautiously put the key in the lock and turned it. When he stepped into a minute parlour, straight from the street without any hallway and with only a shabby curtain to keep out draughts, he found the old lady already backing away from him. She was the one who had invited him in; yet now she seemed to be having second thoughts, and he would not have been surprised if she had told him to get out right away.

But she said: 'Shut the door quickly and come in.' She lowered her voice, 'Before they see you.'

'Before who sees me, love?'

'Them two next door.'

He checked that the door could perfectly well be opened from the inside.

Although the old lady looked very fragile and probably suffered from wandering notions and a limited attention span, she was surely capable of opening her own front door.

'Well now, Mrs . . . ?'

'Mrs Allison. Only do call me Daisy. Everybody does. Only there aren't many left nowadays, not the folk I used to know – not what you'd call *everybody*.'

'Right, Mrs Allison. just what is the problem with your door?'

'The problem isn't with the door.' She managed a brittle, shaky laugh. 'The problem's me, I suppose. I'm sure you'll think I'm just a silly old woman.'

Yorkie was prepared to reserve judgment on that for a while, but as she picked at the back of a chair cover and looked at the window and quickly looked away again, he felt it was one he might very well reach in the not-too-distant future. Tactfully he said: 'You should put a chain on here, you know.'

'There's no need. I never open it.'

'But you must open it to go out sometimes.'

'No. I never do go out.' She turned her back on the window and the lace-shrouded view of the street outside. 'Oh, it's silly, really. It's a "condition", you see; that's what they've told me. I don't like going outside, you see. And I don't open the door.'

'Not even to go to the corner shop?' A possible explanation for her behaviour struck him. 'Is that it – you want me to nip along to the corner shop for you?'

Her faded blue eyes blinked in an uneven rhythm, and she shook her head repeatedly. 'No, oh no. I've got a home help twice a week for all that sort of thing.' She ambled aimlessly round the chair, found herself face-to-face with a laden teatray on a low table, and let out a squeak of dismay. 'Oh, look at me! Forgetting my manners. Would you like some tea?'

Yorkie Smith was tempted. Granville Street and its neighbours, indistinguishable one from another, boasted as few chipfat-smelling cafés of the shopping street variety as they did indications of promotion-winning crime incidents. This was his only opportunity for sneaking in a crafty cup. 'I should be getting on,' he said feebly.

'Please, I don't think I can remember the last time I had a nice young man to tea.' Without waiting for a reply she scurried out for a few seconds and returned with another cup and saucer.

Yorkie Smith had the benevolent feeling that he was doing the old dear a good turn simply by being here. Good community policing, that's what it was. 'So when was the last time you went out, then?' he asked chattily.

'About four years. Oh, some days are better than others. I force myself to stand in the window sometimes.' A tear sparkled in her left eye and rolled slowly down her cheek. 'I'm so stupid. A silly old bag, that's what I am. No wonder you didn't believe me about them two next door.'

'You haven't told me about them two next door, Daisy.'

'I thought I had.'

'Not yet.'

'I think they're burgling the place,' she said flatly.

'Who are?'

'Them.' She sounded remarkably matter-of-fact. 'You see, they knocked on the door at about half-past-eight and asked for the key to next door. They said she'd told them I'd have the key, but she'd never leave the key with me. She knows I can't answer the door. Scared me half to death, they did. I just shouted at them to go away.'

Smith put his cup and saucer down and went to the window, standing well to one side of the lace curtains. It was a dull, ordinary, uneventful street. The blue pick-up truck still stood there, but nothing and nobody moved.

'Perhaps they'd just got the wrong side of the street,' he suggested.

She looked at him with unexpected shrewdness. 'They might have. But I heard what they said next. One of them was peeking in through the letterbox at me, and he saw the key on the string, and he told the other one. And he said' – she struggled to recall the exact words – 'to forget it, because there was bound to be an empty one somewhere else.'

'That doesn't sound much like a builder, does it?'

'That's what I thought. I thought to myself, they're up to no good.'

Through the gap between the curtain and the window, Yorkie got a slanting view on the rear of the truck. Somebody was moving at last, coming round it with a black plastic bag slung over his shoulder. It was a square-shaped bag, and looked nothing like builder's rubble. As to the man, he was shaped and looked remarkably like a certain Mark Bright, one of two brothers who usually operated in somewhat less cosy neighbourhoods than this. Yorkie Smith was conscious of a tingle of sheer delight.

'If that's who I think it is, Daisy,' he said gratefully, 'you could be very right.'

Viv Martella decided she could afford to leave Mrs Borenno alone with her dead brother for just a few minutes. Perhaps there would even be time to nip a few doors along the street and see if the chemist's was not too crowded.

Janet Simmons was busy at the counter, washing up a stack of greasy plates. 'How you getting on with her?'

'The language thing doesn't help. It'd simplify things if I could get hold of the son and daughter.'

Mrs Simmons' face screwed up disparagingly. 'You wouldn't say that if they turned up, believe me. Especially Giorgio. He's a law unto himself, and coppers don't exactly come top of his favourite people list.'

'I've still got to find him.'

Mrs Simmons' grip on her tea-towel tightened. 'Your lucky day, then.'

The door of the Caricola Café opened, and a man and woman came in. He was swarthy, with thick black hair sleeked up into a glistening coxcomb, looking about thirty years of age but trying to put on a youthful swagger. He wore a black leather jacket and sported two rings, large enough to be knuckle-dusters. The girl with him, younger, had the same eyes and heavy, surly mouth, and could hardly be anyone but his sister.

'What do *you* want?' Giorgio circled Martella like an animal calculating the right moment to pounce.

Janet Simmons gulped and said: 'I rang 'em, Mr Caricola.'

'Well, that's a novel way to hand your notice in.'

Martella made it as calm but firm as possible. 'Mr Caricola, I wonder if we could – '

'Ain't nothing round here we don't sort out for ourselves, right? And you're making the place look like a pigsty, if you know what I mean.' His voice was the coarsest sort of London snarl, with only a faint trace of Italian accent. 'So on your way.'

'Told you he was a little charmer.' Mrs Simmons had untied her apron and was tossing it across the counter.

Steadily Martella said: 'Mr Caricola, I'd appreciate it if you'd just come up-stairs. What I've got to tell you, you don't want to hear down here.'

He glared, and she thought he was capable, no matter what the consequen-ces, of chucking her bodily off the premises. But it dawned on him that the customers at the café tables were all drinking in every word, along with their tea and fried tomatoes. Without another word he stamped towards the stairs, with Martella between him and his sister, who watchfully brought up the rear. Before Martella could reach the landing and begin her explanation, Giorgio had marched in through the open bedroom door.

Mrs Borenno, who had been so crushed and quiet until now, erupted in a fit of fury. The mere sight of her nephew set her off screaming, and he began to scream back. By the time Martella had entered the room, the two of them were lashing out at each other, with nails and fists as well as words.

Martella tried to radio in, but got only a spluttering, distorted response. Abandoning this for a moment, she tried to thrust herself between Giorgio and Mrs Borenno. Blows rained on her shoulders.

'Look, just what is this all – '

'Woman, you either shift,' raged Giorgio, 'or I'll do the both of you.'

'Just calm down.'

'I ain't in the mood for this.' He tried to heave her aside, but Martella had got a grip on his left arm. 'I'm telling you,' he screeched, full into her face, 'move, or I'll stripe you.'

In his right hand there was a flick knife.

Martella reeled backwards, grappling with the radio again. 'Two-two-seven, urgent assistance.' But she was in a blind spot, and just got feedback.

Giorgio ignored her now, and turned his attentions back to Mrs Borenno. The older woman, fired with the inhuman energy of utter hatred, clawed and spat simultaneously. His knee came up, and she panted out a choked groan of pain. Martella saw there was nothing she could achieve against the two of them, enraged and beyond rational argument. She stumbled back to the window and the fire escape.

'Two-two-seven, urgent assistance. Caricola Café, Slade Lane market. Urgent assistance!'

Eleven

Slade Lane market was a long-established feature for locals, a picturesque sight to the occasional visitor venturing off the beaten tourist track, and in several different ways a nuisance to the police. Today its stalls and delivery vans were causing a worse traffic snarl-up than usual. Bob Cryer, driving the van with a new and nervous constable beside him, slammed his fist against the dashboard in frustration. God knew what sort of a fix Martella was in by now, while here they were, stuck, with no chance of easing a way through.

'Come on,' he decided. 'Time for a run.'

'What about the van, sarge?'

'Lock it and leave it. And get moving.'

Heads turned, jokes were sniggered, as the two of them pounded past towards the Caricola Café. Cryer was in no mood for jokes or even for an attempt at answering. He led the way into the café to find a dark young Italian woman trying to block his way. 'Out of the way, love. Where's it at, then?' The question was hardly necessary. There was an outbreak of shouting and a thumping of feet on the floor above. Cryer raced up the stairs, leaving the young PC to try what delaying tactics he could on the woman.

Martella greeted him with a moan of relief. She was holding on grimly to a man with a flick knife who seemed anxious to carve a piece out of an older woman. Since the older woman was equally determined in her attempts to claw chunks out of his face, Cryer wasted no time on deciding an allocation of sympathies. He grabbed the man's wrist and began to twist it, trying to force him to drop the knife.

'What you doing to my brother? Get off him! Get off my Giorgio!'

The constable had failed to restrain the younger woman, who came up the stairs like an avenging fury and set upon Cryer from the back. Viv Martella let go of Giorgio and got a handful of the girl's hair. There was plenty of it, more than enough to provide a good grip. The PC came up, panting, to redeem himself. He simply threw all his weight on Giorgio, toppling him over on to the floor. Cryer had the handcuffs on in three seconds flat.

They were all breathing hard, except for Mrs Borenno and the girl, who continued to exchange insults with unwearying fervour, when a slim, middle-aged woman with a bland, professional smile put her head round the door and surveyed the bizarre scene.

'Hello. Did someone here ask for an Italian-speaking doctor?'

Cryer nodded to Martella. 'Take this lady into the bedroom. And you'd better take *that* lady with you, to explain what the hell has been going on. As for you . . . ' He turned to the girl, who tried to make a lunge at the older woman as she went past.

'Her name's Isabella,' supplied Martella as she shepherded Mrs Borenno and the doctor towards the bedroom door.

'Right, Isabella. Let's find somewhere to park you for a minute or two.'

'You can't treat us like this. It ain't allowed. She assaulted me, that old – '

'You don't need an interpreter, anyway. That's something.'

'I tell you – '

'And *I'm* telling you, copper' – Giorgio was safely immobilized but still uncowed – 'you're going to be looking over your shoulder for the rest of your natural after this.'

'You trembling?' Cryer asked the constable, who had moved fast and effectively and could do with a comradely nod.

'Like a jelly, sarge.'

Martella appeared in the doorway, indicating to Cryer that he should come out. The doctor had emerged from the bedroom and was going thoughtfully to the end of the landing, out of earshot of the others. She waited for Cryer to reach her, and then said quietly: 'You know what this argument seems to be about, sergeant?'

'You must be joking! We've been too busy trying to stop 'em killing each other.'

'Well, whether she's to be believed or not I don't know, but the old woman in there is accusing her nephew of killing his father. Or him and the girl together. Says they've removed some vital heart pills.'

'Is she serious?'

The doctor laughed dourly. 'I'm afraid that's as far as my interpreting goes, sergeant. I can confirm life extinct here. The detective work's up to you.'

She moved back towards the stairs. Cryer accompanied her to the front door of the café, ignoring a splutter of eager questions from inquisitive customers who were in no hurry to leave the food congealing on their plates. Out in the open, it was easier to get through to Sun Hill and call for the CID circus to come and lend a hand. Now it was a matter of waiting until their work could be done and the Caricolas carted off in the van.

He went back inside. Martella was fidgeting at the top of the stairs, trumpeting throttled noises into her handkerchief.

Cryer said: 'Hope you're not doing anything for the rest of the day.'

'Well, I was planning a little time off to be seriously ill.' Her voice was nasal and miserable.

'With this little lot! We could be stuck here for hours. And the paper work's going to take days, Martella, we are talking days.'

'In that case, sarge, if we're going to be stuck here for hours, can I nip out for a few minutes?'

'What the hell for?'

'I need to go to the chemist.' She put on her most appealing, distressed look.

'Why?' said Cryer obtusely.

She looked away. 'You know, sarge. Ladies' problems.'

'Oh. I, er . . . right . . . yes, all right. Of course. But don't be long!'

Martella shed some of her wretchedness and conjured up a winning smile. 'Cheers, sarge.'

Isabella Caricola came to the boil again. 'You cannot do this. This is our café, you cannot just come in here and do these things. You – '

'Shut up,' said Sergeant Cryer.

Whatever his alcoholic intake and however uncontrollable his rage, it had to be admitted that Ian Gore was a very competent bus-driver. He knew every crossroads, every set of lights, every awkward corner and likely hazard, and how to use every half-inch of road space. By the time Haynes and Ackland had scrambled back into their Panda car and set off after him, Gore had put several hundred yards of crawling traffic between the double-decker and his pursuers. A bus on a more conventional route, crossing their path, set the two police constables back even further. June Ackland's jaw set. It was a matter of honour, now, to prove that she could overtake that runaway. And then what: surround it?

Ahead, over the roofs of the intervening cars, she saw the red top deck slowing. Then it turned abruptly left, down what was surely too narrow a street for any regular run. Taking a chance, she swung the car down an alley running parallel, and then jerked right to intercept the bus. She missed it by a matter of yards. It racketed past, shedding a few fragments of glass as it went. Gore went careering on, driving a terrified motorist up on to the kerb, and slewed around another turning in the warren of back streets. It would be easier now. There was little traffic, and the panda began to overhaul the bus. Maybe Gore was getting tired, or the drink and raging adrenalin were taking their toll, for he grew careless. Misjudging a corner, he mounted the pavement and charged straight through the privet hedge of a small front garden, coming to a halt only a few inches from the front doorstep.

Before the police car could pull in alongside, Gore was out and running off down an alley between two terraces of houses. Haynes went after him in a fierce sprint. But Gore, for all his weight, could run. Like a loaded lorry, going downhill, once he had got going the sheer inertia added to his speed. At the end of the alley, Haynes emerged, to find an empty street: nobody in sight in either direction. There was no way Gore could have doubled back; but after a fruitless exploration in both directions he went back to the car, where June was finishing a call in to Sun Hill.

She wound her window down. 'Don't tell me you let him run out on you?'

'Just disappeared. Got his trainers on – and look at all the rubbish I'm wearing, weighing me down.'

She shook her head reprovingly. 'Too many biscuits in the canteen, that's what it is, Malcolm.'

He thought it would be a good thing to change the subject without delay. Taking a few steps along the pavement, he patted the rump of the bus. 'What we going to do about this thing, then?'

'I've just passed on the news. Our friend Mr Deegan's been asked to come and collect it.'

'Oh, great. Give him the chance to tell us how much the towing truck's going to cost him.'

'Hey!' cried June. 'Hide-and-seek, now!'

She was pointing down the alley. At the other end, Ian Gore stood for a moment grinning, then jumped over a fence with an agility which showed he was far from worn out. Haynes set off again, while June Ackland roared the car away round the corner in an attempt to cut Gore off.

Reg Hollis's voice over the radio spoke of his continuing pride in his filing system. Yorkie Smith did not interrupt. If Hollis could provide the facts, that was what he was there for, and facts were very much needed at this moment. They did seem to fit. Mark and Grant Bright were out on bail, for an affray in the Hope and Anchor. Hollis sounded injured by the mere thought of allowing those two out on the streets. Yorkie was none too pleased either at such leniency, remembering how, once before, they had slipped through his fingers and made a fool of him under the very eyes of Ted Roach. But at least the fact that they were out and about gave him a chance to add a few merit points to his somewhat sparse record. This time, with a bit of luck, it was going to be a different story.

'But watch it, Yorkie,' Hollis was warning. 'If you're thinking of nicking those two, be careful. They've got a string of violent crimes down here that makes the Kray brothers look like social workers.'

Daisy Allison had been watching in fascination as Yorkie made his call, and had enjoyed listening to the exchange, though little of it made coherent sense to her. It was undoubtedly a high spot in her secluded life. Admiringly she asked: 'Are you going to try to arrest them?'

'Not until I'm sure. I'm going to have a little nose round first.'

'You be careful, then.' Daisy lifted the teapot, found it empty, and clicked her tongue against her teeth. 'I still don't understand,' she said vaguely, 'why they came here for the key in the first place.'

'I don't think they did, Daisy.' Yorkie tried very slowly to explain. 'They must have thought your place was empty. It was just something they said when they realized you were in. So they decided to try next door while they were at it.' He tugged disapprovingly at the key on its string, dangling inside the front door. 'You really ought to have a chain here, you know. I think we'll have to come back and sort you out, eh, Daisy?'

'Oh, will you?' She brightened at once. 'I could have a proper tea ready for you next time. Would you really come back?'

'Um . . . er . . . well, next time I'm on this beat. Better not make any promises, eh?'

Her brightness was dimmed. 'No. It was just a thought.'

'Tell you what, though. I can definitely ask the Crime Prevention Officer to come and help you.'

'Can you really? Do you think he'd like to stay for tea?'

'Probably jump at the chance,' Yorkie assured her. 'In the meantime, I'd better start checking out these two likely lads next door. Can you let me out the back way – and leave it unbolted for a bit, in case I have to nip back in?'

With a mixture of apprehension and excitement, Daisy opened the door to her back yard, into which she herself had obviously not ventured for a long time. It was unkempt and heavily overgrown, with weeds thrusting up through cracks in an uneven patch of concrete. The fence to his left was clean and solid, obviously renewed in recent times by the neighbour on that side. On the right, it was rotting and sagging.

Yorkie Smith eased himself on to a pile of rubbish, to peer through one of the widening gaps.

The Bright brothers were putting a compact disc player into a large black plastic waste bag. It was obviously one in a series: they had been methodically stripping the house of its valuables and carrying them out to the truck as building rubbish. Grant, with a broken nose and one eye permanently half-shut because of an altercation with a razor some years ago, heaved the bag up on to his shoulder. In his labourer's overalls he would have looked almost like a real builder's mate if it had not been for those souvenirs of past activities: workers in the building trade often suffered injuries, but not quite of that kind.

For Yorkie Smith it was a very pretty sight. 'Jackpot!' he whispered to himself.

He retreated to the house and, under Daisy's adoring gaze, called up Sun Hill again, asking for assistance – and fast, because he reckoned the Bright brothers were about ready to leave. 'Fast as you can, sarge,' he implored, peering through the curtains. An elderly Allegro had drawn up close to the truck, and for a moment he thought there were going to be some additions to the team.

But the driver got out, locked his vehicle, and went into a house across the street. Mark Bright appeared again, this time loading some genuine building equipment on to the truck, all part of the act.

Daisy said breathlessly: 'Why don't you get on the back of the truck?'

It was quite a bright idea. Smith patted her on the head, and she giggled. He waited to make sure the two of them had gone back to collect their last bits and pieces, and scuttled out into the road, crouching behind the providentially parked car. Carefully poking his head round the side, he could see a reasonable space immediately inside the improvised corrugated iron cover on the truck. If he could make it into there, they would not be able to see him from the cab.

The two brothers came out, slung a bag of tools and a roll of felt on to the back, and went round to climb into the front. Taking a deep breath, Yorkie ran along the pavement side of the Allegro and got a grip on the rear of the truck, glancing back to see if anyone was watching. Daisy had drawn her curtains and was waving encouragingly. Frantically he waved back, gesturing that she should disappear.

The engine coughed into life, and a gout of dark fumes spewed up around Yorkie from the exhaust. As the truck began to move, he swung himself up and rolled under the cover.

It was a rackety old banger, and he was glad of it: the noise would cover the sound of his radio. June Ackland was there suddenly, saying, 'Six-four-three, I got that, sarge. We're just around the corner. What's the score, Yorkie?'

He put his mouth close to the radio. 'I'm on the back of a truck.'

'You're *what?*'

'On the back of a truck, moving north on Padgate Road.'

'Got you. If they keep on course, we'll have 'em.'

'Just remember,' said Yorkie, 'this is *my* bag, right?'

He heard June laugh, and then he stopped listening: whichever of the brothers was driving had swung round a corner close enough to clip the pavement, bouncing the contents of the back of the truck up and down and sideways, including PC Smith.

They were in a shopping street. Any minute now, the passers-by would notice the substantial shape of the policeman tucked uncomfortably on the back of the truck.

As if to confirm this, June Ackland was coming through again. 'We can see you, Yorkie. Any minute now.' The truck slowed for traffic lights, and eased past a police car. Haynes was leaning languidly against the bonnet, apparently paying no attention to the pick-up. Yorkie got his handcuffs from his pocket and waved them, praying that the lights were going to stay red for just long enough to stop the truck and allow Haynes and Ackland to jump the Bright brothers. The two of them had stepped into the street now and were sauntering unobtrusively behind the truck.

It stopped.

Smith slid off the back. Haynes and Ackland dashed round to the front. Haynes took the passenger side, reached in and got the cuff on Mark Bright before he had the faintest idea of what was happening. On the driver's side, Ackland had to open the door – which gave Grant Bright, the brawnier and more lethal of the two, a chance to throw himself out. Smith arrived just in time to help shovel him back inside. Ackland handcuffed herself to him. On the other side of the cab, Haynes was not doing too well. He had successfully handcuffed himself to Mark Bright through the open window, but now, when Mark half opened the door and started rocking it to and fro, slamming it into his captor, Haynes found himself taking a lot of punishment without being able to retreat and get his breath back. As he sagged down against the door, Mark began to slide himself out through the window opening.

Yorkie Smith had just managed to handcuff Grant Bright's free arm to the steering wheel, and now clambered across to tackle the man's brother. Mark was hauled back in. Haynes put his weight against the door and closed it.

The job was almost done. The three officers grinned at each other. All that remained was to manhandle the brothers back to the police car, still hand-cuffed to Haynes and Ackland and, by now, too despondent to attempt any last-minute scuffles. Yorkie Smith held the car doors open, feeling very pro-prietorial about the whole thing.

'Hey!' said Ackland tensely. 'Don't look now, Malcolm, but our mate's back.'

Yorkie glanced round, uncomprehending. On the edge of the crowd which had immediately collected, was a man taller and heftier even than Grant Bright.

'Gore!' Haynes exploded.

The man was laughing, mocking the two of them, attached to their captives and unable to get away and deal with him. He began to stroll off with insulting casualness.

'Yorkie – get after him! Nick him!'

'What's he done?'

'We'll tell you when you catch him. Get moving.'

Gore realized that one of the team was mobile. He broke into a trot. Yorkie Smith went pounding after him. Gore began to run faster. Yorkie quickened his pace, and felt twinges down his right leg where it had been crumpled awkwardly under him on the back of the truck.

The watching crowd was in no hurry to run, or even to disperse in a leisurely way. It was not often that such a free treat was provided by the local consta-bulary.

It seemed such a short time ago, thought PC Smith confusedly as he began to overhaul his quarry, that he had been lamenting the lack of action in his life.

Twelve

News from the hospital was that the baby found in a bag by PC Ramsey was improving and the chances were now a lot better than fifty-fifty. News about the identity and whereabouts of the mother was still non-existent. Continuing enquiries were time-wasting, when there were so many more important crimes to be pursued and cleared up; but a mixture of compassion and irritation seemed to have infiltrated the atmosphere of Sun Hill nick, like a virus from the air conditioning system.

Detective Constable Dashwood, sifting through a list of stolen ecclesiastical property, kept his gaze well down as he heard Acting Detective Inspector Roach on the phone, using a tone of voice he only adopted when speaking to Inspector Frazer: half respectful, half needling.

'We are all very concerned, ma'am. But if the baby's alive . . . y'know, if we're not talking murder or manslaughter, then . . . well, as you know, we're very short-staffed up here at the moment. A lot of stuff on our plate.'

'Including,' said Dashwood under his breath, 'three plates, one font cover, a lectern, and now a statue and four candlesticks.' You might have thought that the dedicated, specialist robbers were in the business of setting up a full-scale religious denomination of their own.

'I mean,' Roach concluded, 'don't get me wrong, I'm all for co-operation, but right now I think it would be better if the uniformed branch could continue basic enquiries, and bring us in when there's really some solid evidence worth pursuing. Right, ma'am? Thanks a lot.' He put the phone down with a touch of complacency, implying if not an out-and-out victory at least a commendable defensive manoeuvre, and came through to the outer office rubbing his hands. 'Right, Dashers, you'd better be on your way to Streatham.'

Their opposite numbers at Streatham had reported finding a quantity of church furnishings in a local antique shop and removing it for further examination, since its resemblance to items notified by Sun Hill appeared to be worthy of detailed investigation. Dashwood had no objections to spending an hour or two examining and collecting the material, before something more harassing and possibly dangerous reared its ugly head.

'Coming along, guv?'

'I've got more important things to attend to,' said Acting DI Roach irascibly. 'I'm going to see the clerk. They've paid me as a mere sergeant again this month.'

Dashwood felt that it would, indeed, be less hassle to deal with inanimate objects from the tranquil ambience of a church than to be around when the far from inanimate Ted Roach returned from an argumentative session about his present status and salary. He soon felt a more positive glow of satisfaction, when comparison of the individual pieces at Streatham tallied so nicely and neatly with various entries on his own list. It was not the right time of year for any guiding stars in the east, but the trail of ecclesiastical objects was certainly leading in a useful direction.

His next port of call was at a shop whose façade was lettered in olde-worlde characters, proclaiming its stock-in-trade as *Antiques*. Above the entrance, in less archaic style, was the name of the proprietor: Edwin G. Staples.

The contents of the shop were less impressive than its outward claims. Dashwood was no expert on the finer points of classic English furniture, glass or silver; but he had a suspicion that most of the stuff was secondhand rather than antique, and that it had been acquired from less reputable sources than a sale at some stately home. Through an open door behind the cluttered counter he could see a man bent over a workbench: possibly inserting, with incomparable craftsmanship, eighteenth-century wormholes into a middle-twentieth-century reproduction sideboard.

Dashwood rapped a knuckle gently on the counter. The man in the room beyond looked round and came out, head to one side like an obsequious parrot. He was about thirty, had not shaved that day, and spoke with a tang of West Country burr.

'And what could I interest you in, sir?'

'In some candlesticks and a statue, for starters, Mr Staples. It *is* Mr Staples, I presume?'

The obsequiousness faded: 'And who might you be?'

Dashwood held out his warrant card. 'Sun Hill police, sir. I've just collected some property from Streatham, including a pair of candlesticks and a statue stolen from a church on our patch. I understand they turned up here in your shop . . . initially?'

'Look, I told the other lot all about it. I bought them off a guy who came in last week.' Staples spread his hands philosophically. 'Occupational hazard. I'm a pine chest man, really. I did give a description of the guy to your mates from Streatham.'

Dashwood was already aware of that. The man had been white, in his early fifties, slight build, thinning hair, grey trousers and a grubby fawn cardigan. Staples was at least possessed of a keen and retentive eye, probably essential in his business. Add a Cockney accent and 'a nervous, shifty look'. Such a frank assessment did not seem to have deterred Staples from acquiring the contents of the black plastic sack the man had brought with him.

'Sort of person you usually do business with, Mr Staples?'

'I buy artefacts, not character references.'

'And the price was right.' Dashwood had speedily formed his opinion of Staples' own character.

'Twenty quid for the candlesticks, thirty for the statue. They're worth ten times that.'

'I thought you were just a pine chest man?'

'You pick up a bit as you go along. Can't be too specialized, nowadays. Can't be too choosey.'

'Well, I should be a bit more choosey what you pick up in future, Mr Staples, or you could find yourself done for receiving.'

'Yes, sir.' Staples smiled and offered a mock salute. 'Yes, major. As you say, sir.'

Dashwood left. There was nothing worth pursuing here. As long as there were people like Staples, there would be petty thieves of every kind; and as long as there were petty thieves, there would be people like Staples. It was not so much a vicious circle as a vicious yo-yo.

He returned to Sun Hill with his booty. In the CAD room, Reg Hollis was in full flow, still obsessed with his circadian rhythms, and adding even more gloom to Sergeant Penny's already murky clouds of depression. 'You just can't tell your body it's night-time when it's not, and vice versa. It's still trying to do things the right way round whether you're on earlies, lates or nights. We're abusing our bodies all the time.'

'What d'you mean *we* are? You've been on permanent days for heaven knows how long now, Hollis.'

'Too late, now. I'm irreparably damaged. As for the rest of you . . . I mean, over a hundred shift changes in a year, it's no wonder coppers drop dead when it all stops. It's like winding a clock arse-about-face for thirty years, then flinging it at a wall. The spring goes, doesn't it.' He produced a graph which he had been preparing, obviously with the greatest dedication. 'Now, if you look at this comparison between our system and the one they're adopting in the USA, sarge, you'll find that out of two thousand and sixty-eight annual working hours, they only have twenty shift changes – '

'Excuse me, Reg.' Dashwood had not specifically aimed to relieve Sergeant Penny from Hollis's barrage, but Penny's expression was nevertheless one of devout gratitude.

Caught in mid-sentence, Hollis was off balance for a moment. 'If you want more money on DI Richardson, forget it. He's off to make a fortune in Hong Kong. Surprised Galloway didn't see the chances there. So if you want a good tip . . . ' He became aware of the candlesticks and the statue of the Virgin Mary which Dashwood had brought in. 'What's all this?'

'All right if I leave these in the collator's room?' Before Hollis could frame a plausible objection, Dashwood said briskly: 'Just in case I'm out. I'm phoning the vicar to come and identify them, and then cart them off.'

'Well, I suppose so. But I don't want it to be seen as setting a precedent.'

Dashwood made himself scarce. As he left, he heard Haynes at a console, reporting a burglary in progress in Vinchella Road. At this time of day: in broad daylight? Mike Dashwood's curiosity was aroused. He sent it to sleep again. That sort of incident was strictly for the woodentops.

'The burglar,' he heard faintly as he headed for the stairs, 'is apparently a woman.'

'A woman?' said Taffy Edwards, receiving the message in his van. 'It's getting to be a shameful old world, isn't it?'

'As I've told you already,' said Ken Melvin piously. 'But the greatest shame is in despair.'

'Number forty-one, Vinchella Road,' Edwards repeated dutifully into the radio. As he cut down a side street he turned his attention back to Melvin. 'So what do you actually do at these house groups, then?'

'Read the Bible,' said Melvin. 'Sing. Discuss things.'

'Like, if there's a God; and if there is, what's he doing while people are stuffing babies down rubbish chutes and women are breaking and entering and coveting their neighbour's goods?'

'You do seem to remember a few moral issues, Taff.'

'You haven't answered the question.'

'We know there's a God,' said Melvin, 'and we know there's suffering.' He glanced at his companion as Edwards accelerated impetuously and then had to slow down for an elderly couple making a moral issue of crossing the road in the middle of the traffic rather than walking twenty yards to the nearest pedestrian crossing. 'But there's joy as well, you know.'

'Oh, good. That takes a load off my mind.'

They had been weaving their way through a labyrinth of grimy back streets, which gave way to a new development into which aspiring yuppies and middling successful, middle-aged City middlemen had moved in recent years. At first inspection the address they had been given yielded nothing of any interest. Then, as Melvin stationed himself at the front door and Edwards moved along the side of the house, a woman began lowering herself unhurriedly from a ground floor window which had clearly been forced open previously. Before she was even aware of his presence, Edwards moved closer and took her arm.

'Need any help, love?'

She was quite unperturbed. Shrugging off his hand, she set foot on the ground unaided, an expensive-looking holdall dangling from her left arm.

Edwards said: 'Is this your house, madam?'

'I don't live here, if that's what you mean.' She was coolly belligerent.

'Would you mind if I had a look in the bag, then, please?'

'Yes, I would mind, frankly. It's none of your business.'

'Well, perhaps you could tell me why you appear to have broken into – '

'I have every right to force an entry. My solicitor said so.'

Edwards had heard some good stories in his career so far. This was a new one. He laughed. 'Really?'

'These are my things, not his.' The woman was in her thirties, self-possessed and attractive in a rather hard, pushy sort of way; and even more attractive as the smooth skin of her throat coloured and her hazel eyes grew angrier. 'He may own the house, but he doesn't own my belongings, any more than he owns me.' She tried to walk away, as if her affairs could be of no possible concern to this mere police constable, but was brought to a halt by Melvin blocking the way. 'Oh, for God's sake, do I look like a burglar?'

'You're saying this is your husband's house, madam?' said Edwards. 'So you used to live here yourself, then?'

'Until I couldn't stand it any more, yes. Not that it's any concern of yours.'

'Can you prove it? Have you any documentation on you?'

'No, I don't have any documentation.'

'Perhaps the neighbours could verify – '

'I very much doubt it. I never had anything to do with any of them. Look, this is disgraceful. I will not be treated like a criminal.'

She made another attempt to push past Melvin. The two men moved after her. 'Please, madam,' said Edwards as civilly as possible, 'don't make things worse. If you'll just come with us, back to the station, I'm sure we can sort it out.'

Now she lost her temper well and truly. 'I shall sue you for this. Do you hear me? I'll sue you.' Possibly half the street could have heard her. But it was not that sort of street. In a residential area such as this, nobody was brash enough to show curiosity, to tug aside a curtain, or to admit to hearing anything whatsoever.

By the time the woman reached Sun Hill police station she had summoned up additional energy to promise that Sergeant Cryer would also be sued, especially after he had tipped out the contents of her holdall on to his desk in the charge room. Stolen jewellery and suchlike were no strangers to this table, but it was rare to see, in addition, quite such expensive underwear. Edwards, standing guard beside his captive, kept a straight face and tried not to let his imagination run away with him. It took a good five minutes to persuade her that if she wanted to prove the truth of her story, she would need to give her name: and, Bob Cryer intimated to the accompaniment of a further outbreak of threats, it had better be the correct name.

She was a Mrs Saunders: Wendy Saunders. Her solicitor was a Mr Hewitt of Peakirk, Pelham and Hewitt. He would soon put these meddling flatfeet right. Cryer telephoned the firm's office, to find that Mr Hewitt was out and the time of his return was uncertain, but that, of course, an urgent message would be left for him. The promise was given in such a dreary voice that Cryer suspected urgency was a frequent word but an infrequent reaction in that organization. He braced himself for further questioning of Mrs Saunders.

'While we're waiting for Mr Hewitt, what about your husband? At least he could verify your story.'

'He's out of the country. And if he were in it, he's the last person I'd ask a favour of.'

'Isn't there anybody else who could – '

'It's nobody else's business.'

'Mrs Saunders, if you'd just give us your new address.'

'And *that's* none of *your* business.'

She was quite prepared to be stubborn. It was difficult to know what question to ask next. In the face of such lack of cooperation from a burglar caught red-handed, the usual thing would be to bung the suspect into a cell while waiting for further evidence to come in. But in this present case, Cryer had an uneasy feeling that such procedures would rebound on his head later. Disobliging she might be; but there was the ring of truth in what she said.

'Get the lady a cup of tea, Edwards.' Gathering up the custody sheets, Cryer was saved from any immediate decision by WPC Brind putting her head round the door. 'Sarge, Trinity church have got a couple of visitors. One fits the description of our candlesticks man.'

'Great. I'll go over there myself.'

'It's all right, sarge. Sergeant Peters is dealing with it.'

'Then why – '

'He's asked someone to organize back-up at short notice, if needed. I notified DC Dashwood, and he asked me to contact you as well.'

'I'll be right out.' This was a lot more straightforward than coping with the aftermath of a broken marriage.

Trinity church was neither architecturally distinguished nor fashionable, but it had a clean, flowery smell about it, and the atmosphere of being used regularly by a fair-sized, appreciative congregation. Some of the brightness could be attributed to Mrs Morris, the elderly cleaner who was waiting for Sergeant Peters in the porch, filling in the time by polishing the large, already gleaming handle of the inner door.

'Two of them,' she started the moment he appeared. 'There was two of them, wandered in while I was hoovering.' She opened the door and began to lead him down the south aisle. 'I mean, they weren't doing any harm, just looking around. You *should* be able to just walk into a church, shouldn't you? But – '

Alec Peters interrupted the flow. 'And when you came back from the phone, they'd gone?'

'Well, I felt I had to go and ring you because . . . well, there was something funny and . . . but nothing seems to be missing. It just shows you,' said Mrs Morris apologetically, 'how quick we are to draw the wrong conclusions nowadays.'

Peters looked around. Nobody stirred. Light shone on the glowing mahogany of the chancel rail. A bird momentarily beat its wings against the window, high above the vestry door, and then was gone.

'Have you checked in there, Mrs Morris?' He nodded towards the vestry.
'No, I haven't.'

He put a finger to his lips and motioned her to stay where she was. Moving silently towards the door, he opened it with a quick thrust and looked inside. In here there was the same silence as in the body of the church. But something had been happening, and not so very long ago. On the far side of the room was a stout wooden chest with fresh gashes along the edge of its lid. Somebody had clearly been trying to force it open. Peters took a couple of steps towards the chest, then was distracted by a faint movement to his right. One of a row of choir cassocks and surplices seemed to have been stirred by a faint breeze. Only there was no breeze. Peters reached out and parted two of the garments. Between them stood a man looking sheepish – and looking, to Peters' delighted eye, very familiar.

'Brignell! Joined the choir, have you?'

Gus Brignell had looked self-conscious and vaguely injured during earlier collars. This time he looked simply dejected as he emerged from hiding.

Peters said: 'All right, where's your mate?'
'What mate?'

Peters took his arm and guided him firmly out of the vestry. As he exhibited his catch to a spellbound Mrs Morris, the south door opened and DC Jimmy Carver strode in.

'Mike Dashwood told me you might need a bit of – '

Mrs Morris emitted an outraged scream. 'Look! He's got my hoover!'

A large man in his early forties had sprung out from behind the screen of a small chapel and was heading for the south door to the porch, clutching the vacuum cleaner: Tony Leech – Peters identified him in a flash – always worked a double act with Gus Brignell. Carver spun on his heel to get back to the door and cut him off. Leech got there first. He pulled open the inner door and charged out into the porch; to find his way blocked by a young mother with a pram and a couple of toddlers.

Leech looked wildly around. He backed away a few feet, and saw the flight of steps curving tightly upwards to the bellringers' chamber. Before Carver could lunge at him, he was dashing up the stone stairs, emerging on the narrow balcony leading to the studded door of the chamber. Then he looked down.

He was higher up than he had thought; the stonework underfoot was worn away at a dizzying camber; and there was nothing but a flimsy rail between him and the drop to the aisle below.

'All right,' he yelled as Jimmy Carver came panting up behind him. 'All right, just get me down. Get me down, that's all.'

Peters and Carver returned in triumph to Sun Hill. Bob Cryer, still waiting for confirmation or otherwise from Mrs Saunders' solicitor, relished the opportunity of sitting down and dealing with the paperwork for tried-and-true petty criminals.

'Right, Gus, what's all this about churches? Hardly your style, is it?'

'I've got a conscience, Mr Cryer, that's the trouble.' Brignell lowered his eyes mournfully.

'Oh yeh? With twenty-seven previous convictions?'

'Well, that's it, innit?' Brignell seemed to mean what he was saying. 'I mean, think of all the upset I've caused over the years, nicking people's money and pension books and videos and stuff. It worries me, y'know. But churches is different. Don't do nobody no harm nicking from churches, does it?' When Cryer conspicuously failed to be impressed by the logic of this, he went on plaintively: 'Anyway, Tony says they're supposed to give to the poor, and we ain't got naff-all, have we, Tone?'

Tony Leech could not summon up even the energy to shake his head. Cryer made up for it by shaking his head in wonder at Sergeant Peters.

'Nobody ever said thieves had to be clever,' said Peters tolerantly.

Cryer consulted the list at his elbow. 'What about this lectern, then?'

This time Brignell had the grace to look rueful. 'Bit off more'n we could chew with that thing, didn't we, Tone, eh?'

'So where is it?'

Brignell nodded at Leech. 'In his back yard.'

Cryer leaned back in his chair and called over his shoulder. 'Melvin, job for you and Edwards.'

Half-an-hour later, Reg Hollis was presented with proof that he ought not to have allowed anyone, in his own words, to set a precedent. In the middle of the collator's room stood the lectern, with its huge brass eagle spreading its wings as if to envelop anyone who dared come close. Indignantly Hollis stormed through the door of the CAD room.

'Sarge, who the bleedin' hell . . . ?'

Sergeant Peters waved him imperiously to silence, winked at PC Frank at one of the consoles, then turned to Sergeant Penny, who was bent over a sheaf of papers which did not appear to be improving his spirits. 'Here, Tom, you seen what Hollis has taken under his wing?'

Tom Penny got up doubtfully. When he saw what was in the collator's room, his face lit up with his first grin in a long while. 'Ah, the eagle has landed.'

Peters thrust out a hand towards Frank. 'Five quid.'

'What?' said Penny blankly.

Peters beamed as Frank reluctantly handed over a note. 'I bet him five quid that'd be the first thing you said.'

Penny descended into gloom again. 'Oh. Oh, really.' He stalked back into the CAD room. 'Sorry to be so predictable, Frank.'

Hope of finding the abandoned baby's mother had been virtually given up. Wherever she was, whatever condition she was in, she was not calling for help, or asking about her baby, or giving anybody the slightest clue. It was one of those irritating loose ends that would continue to fret away at the minds of the Sun Hill team. For weeks yet, they would be instinctively on the lookout, waiting for a nudge, a whisper, a sudden flash of inspiration. But gradually the unanswered questions would fade into nothing more than a blurred memory of failure.

At least the questions about the baby's welfare were getting some reassuring answers. At his console in the CAD room, Haynes reported the latest message from the hospital: six to four on, and improving all the time.

He saved one special item of news for Pete Ramsey. 'And the very sexy-sounding nurse who phones *does* go out with coppers, she *can* change her shifts, and I'm meeting her Saturday lunchtime.' Before Ramsey could protest, Haynes added: 'Oh, and they're calling the little girl Petra, after the sweet guy who brought her in.'

'You . . . you toerag.'

In the surge of laughter around the room, nobody had noticed the arrival of Inspector Frazer. She looked across at the blushing constable, and said blandly:

'Could be worse, Ramsey. You might've been christened Wilfred.'

Thirteen

After several weeks at Sun Hill, Inspector Frazer knew better than to expect utter tranquillity to be reigning when she arrived; but this Wednesday morning even she was startled by the turmoil which met her as she passed the front office desk and walked along the corridor. Two constables pushed past each other, one dashing upstairs and one down. Voices from the Communications and Display room overlapped in confusion, until Chief Superintendent

Brownlow's all too recognizable boom reduced them to order. His holiday in France had not, by the sound of it, mellowed his temper. PC Reg Hollis shot across her path waving a sheaf of documents, and Sergeant Cryer emerged more slowly, also with a fistful of paperwork.

'Morning, Bob. Has the Third World War started, or something?'

'Morning, ma'am. There's been an attempted armed robbery at Leyton's. Two of 'em.'

'At this time of day?'

'Traffic are screaming blue murder. We've got every available mobile unit dashing about the manor. Chief super's in there,' he jerked his head unnecessarily in the direction of the CAD room, 'directing operations.'

'Thanks, Bob.' She went on her way, then paused. 'Oh, don't forget we've got those two DCs coming up from Somerset to pick up Blakelynn today.'

'Mm, yeh.' Cryer looked uneasy. 'You do know Ted Roach is looking to hold him for another twelve hours?'

'Oh, come on, Bob. He knows the crack. He's had the man in custody for over twenty-eight hours as it is, and not a thing to show for it.'

'I know, ma'am. Custody officer's not very happy.'

'I bet he's not. Is Ted Roach about?'

'Out chasing the bandits.'

That was something he could hardly be criticized for. Frazer dumped her briefcase in her office and made her way back to the CAD room. 'Good morning, sir.'

Chief Superintendent Brownlow, standing at the wall map, glanced across at her. 'A good one it isn't, inspector.' He went on prodding various points on the map and barking out instructions. Foot patrols on beats six and seven were to be alerted: one man was on the run, reportedly without a firearm, but should be approached with caution; the other had driven off in a stolen car, was armed, and with the traffic at this time of day would probably be using the back doubles. In either case, patrols were to observe and report only.

It appeared that after the raid the robbers' own getaway vehicle, a BMW, had taken a corner too fast, crashed against a wall, and bounced back, to lie sideways across the road. One man had legged it across a nearby car park; the other, still carrying a firearm, up the street. The bad news was that the one with the shooter had hijacked a blue Sierra, registration Delta Four-Five-Nine, Charlie-Golf-Uniform. Worse news was that he had taken its owner, a woman, along with him.

Frazer noticed that Sergeant Penny's brow was moist with sweat. Blood had drained away from his face at the mere mention of a firearm. Things with Penny were getting too bad, and too obvious. This was a problem which would have to be tackled before much longer.

Brownlow snapped out orders for mobile units to cover crucial junctions. And the car with Smith and Ackland in was to cut across to Lamont Street nick, where three armed TSG officers were waiting to be picked up. With all that action going on somewhere out there, in dangerous streets where dangerous men moved or hid, Christine Frazer felt almost superfluous when the only task allotted to her by Brownlow turned out to be that of dealing with the Somerset men when they got here. She went off moodily towards her office.

Bob Cryer and Alec Peters had just left the custody area and were walking down the corridor with their backs to her. She heard Peters, on duty as custody officer, lamenting: 'Why is it always Ted Roach's collars I have trouble with, eh? This system was devised to give protection to us, as well as the public.'

'If it's any consolation, the Somerset lads are on their way to pick chummy up.'

'And not before time.' Peters slowed. 'How's Tom Penny holding up?'

'Bit twitchy, but he's holding it together. Shooters always did give him a migraine.'

'Just between you and me, Bob, you noticed the bottle in his locker?'

'First chance I get, I'm going to have a word with him.'

Frazer caught up with them. 'I'd appreciate that very much, Bob.' Before the men could start conjuring up excuses or denials, she added: 'Look, off the record, I realize Tom Penny's had a tough time. Family problems as well, just before I got here – so I've heard.' She waited for the faintest of nods in acknowledgment, but Cryer and Peters remained stony-faced. 'However, I can't go on turning a blind eye. He's no good to us or himself with a drink problem.'

'I'll talk to him, ma'am,' said Cryer stiffly.

'And as quickly as possible, please.' She changed the subject smartly. 'Right, Alec. On prisoner Blakelynn, you go strictly by the book. If the Somerset people's paperwork is in order, sign him across.'

'Yes, ma'am. But if I do it by the book, ma'am,' said Peters with a sly smile, 'I have to check that our lads here are finished.'

She knew what he meant, and could almost see the threatening wraith of Ted Roach at his shoulder. 'By the book, Alec,' she repeated. 'By the book.'

Fifteen minutes later she was notified that two detective constables, Willis and Hawtrey, had arrived as planned. Cryer showed them into the canteen while Frazer studied the Blakelynn file in Jimmy Carver's keeping. Carver was far from happy at seeing her with it, or at seeing Peters' anxiety to be done with Blakelynn. Frazer felt a flicker of blended amusement and sympathy. He would be the first to bear the brunt of his boss's rage when Roach got back and found his bird had been removed from its cage.

It might soften that rage if Ted Roach managed to snare some of the wild life that was running extra wild out there in the streets right now.

The three men lined up on the Lamont Street pavement could well have posed as three heavies waiting to go into the police station yard for an identity parade:

in which case, the suspect must himself have been a pretty alarming sight. Wasting no time, June Ackland was already opening the back door as Yorkie Smith swung the Cavalier in beside the kerb.

'We've had a sighting,' she said eagerly.

The three men squeezed themselves into the back seat, looking ineffably bored. 'Fall about in my back yard,' said the largest of them contemptuously. As Smith drove off again, he added with even less interest: 'You can call me Alfie. Lenny on my left. Dick on my right.'

They slumped down into the seat.

The radio was chattering non-stop. Car park sealed off, but no sign of runaway. Contact had been lost with the stolen Sierra for an agonizing forty seconds, but was swiftly reestablished. 'Turning left and proceeding north along Grape Street.'

Smith slowed for a T-junction; and Ackland realized they were actually in Grape Street. Before she could draw a breath, a blue Sierra sped across their bows. Smith needed no prompting. He swung to the left and accelerated. June reached for the handset and began to provide Sun Hill with a running commentary. They were closing in, turning right, then left again, now proceeding north along Globe Road at a speed of fifty-six miles an hour. Smith closed in, then slackened off: they were getting dangerously close.

From the seat behind, Alfie, interested now, said: 'Get right up his end, son.'

'I'm sorry, but our brief is to – '

'Listen, son, you've got the three wise monkeys in the back here. We see everything, hear everything, and we do everything. And when I say *do*, I mean – '

'With all due respect,' Ackland attempted to intervene, 'our super – '

'Get up on him. We can't do sweet FA, poncing about back here. Put your foot down and get up his pipe.'

Resentfully Smith shoved the Cavalier forward faster, weaving past a clutter of parked cars, assessing the situation at the next corner.

'Come on, son, closer,' urged Lenny.

The Sierra swung violently right. Smith was halfway round when he glimpsed the dead-end traffic sign. It was too late to change course. He braked hard, and slithered to a stop only a few yards from the stolen Sierra, now at an angle across the narrow cul-de-sac. The front door of the Sierra was opening and a man was getting out, levelling a shotgun at them. After the pace of the pursuit and then the shock of the sudden halt, everything now seemed to take place in slow motion. The gun puffed lazily. Ackland, crouching down, was taking all the time in the world.

There was a tooth-rasping screech as a large hole appeared in the centre of the police car's windscreen, followed by a dull thud from the rear seat. The bullet had torn into the back of the seat through a two-inch gap between the shoulders of two of the armed officers.

Smith struggled to find reverse gear. The gunman sauntered round the rear of the Sierra, crouched against it, and fired again. This time the shot tore through the driver's door and into the side of the seat, missing Smith by a fraction of an inch.

There were yells of anguish from the back seat. The three men had not been hit, but were trapped, immobilized. The rear doors of the police car, designed to keep prisoners in, could not be unlocked from the inside: Alfie, Lenny and Dick were sitting ducks. Alfie was cursing. 'Open the bloody doors!' June Ackland craned her neck round to see if she could manage it through her open window, without getting out fully into the gunman's sights. While she struggled vainly, praying she would not get a bullet in her arm, Yorkie Smith found reverse and gunned the Cavalier backwards. Another shot thumped into the door jamb. At the same moment there was a louder, shuddering crash. As Smith backed away towards the corner, another squad car came racketing round in answer to June's earlier location messages, and piled into their rear bumper.

Dick was hammering on a rear window with his gun. As he succeeded in smashing it so that he could grope through for the outer handle, Smith got his driver's door open, ducking behind it for protection. A fourth shot made a second hole through the panel, again missing him by a hair's-breadth and screaming up the metal frame of the seat to make a ragged exit through the roof.

June Ackland had opened her door and sprawled out on to the ground. She clawed up at an angle to turn the handle of the rear door on that side.

The gunman took a few seconds to look around and size up his surroundings. He backed away towards a low wall with a footpath beyond it, leading between raw new blocks of flats. Dick's arm, still groping vainly for his door handle, was too great a temptation. It provoked one last shot, which missed Dick but made a neat hole in the driver's side window and continued through the window of the door June was trying to open. There was a vicious shower of glass about her head and neck. She screamed, cowering down on to the ground. When she put out a hand to steady herself, her palm landed on a scattering of sharp, glassy slivers and needles.

The sheer physical size of the three men in the back was impeding their attempts to release themselves. There was not just Dick's weight against the door he was trying to open, but the weight of his two struggling, cursing companions. It was not his grip which finally turned the handle outside, but Yorkie Smith's. The sudden release was good for neither of them. The door flew open with Dick full against it, and smacked Smith a swinging blow across his right shoulder and head. He was sent rolling across the road. Dick tumbled sideways out of the Cavalier with such force that his head hit the tarmac. He was not only knocked unconscious, but his large frame became wedged into the door space. It would have been farcical if it had not been so fraught with immediate terror.

On the other side, Lenny had slid out of his door and was shoving himself up, his hands shaking with undisciplined fear and ferocity. The impotence of those moments imprisoned in the back of the car had wrecked all the principles of his training. 'You bastard!' Against all the rules that had been dinned into him, he tried to train his gun on the fast disappearing target. 'Bastard!'

Just as he squeezed off a shot across the roof of the police Cavalier, Smith tottered to his feet, dazed. For the third time a bullet narrowly missed him. This one skidded against a lamp standard some fifteen yards up the pavement. Lenny, quivering, saw what he had nearly done, and let fly with a stream of invective.

'Look, you . . .' Yorkie Smith had felt the breath of the bullet whistle past him, and was in no mood for the breath of his attacker's bullying excuses.

'You stupid sod!' Lenny yelled. 'I told you to stay down.'

He had told none of them any such thing. Had been beyond telling anybody, even himself, anything worth listening to. And he knew it. He staggered round to the rear of the Cavalier and drooped over the tangle between the Cavalier's bumper and the car that had run into it from behind.

Smith was white, with an anger fuelled by a fright far worse than Lenny's. He paced in uneven, lurching steps across the narrow street, and came to a halt a few feet away from Lenny.

Without thinking about it, without thinking about the consequences, without anything but the immediate need to let it all go, all in one accumulation of raving anger, he hit out – hit Lenny in the guts, and as he began to crumple hit him again on the chin.

Lenny's fingers let go of his gun. He went down; and stayed down.

'A shambles!' Chief Superintendent Brownlow stamped along the corridor with Chief Inspector Conway and Inspector Frazer in close but unhappy pursuit, led the way into his office, and slammed the door. 'A fiasco! It's a miracle we're not filling body bags.'

'Sir,' ventured Conway, 'we don't know the full details yet.' 'We know that those lunatic cowboys out there did their damnedest to turn our patch of London into a fair semblance of Dodge City. I specifically called the TSG team in to avoid having to issue firearms to our own people, and where has it got us?'

'It was a difficult situation, sir.' Frazer felt she had to back Conway up in his attempt to defuse the spluttering crisis. 'You do get an accumulation of accidents and wrong reactions on the spur of the moment. We don't know – '

'Christine, I can do without all this rubbish about not knowing. We know enough. We know that an armed man discharged a firearm four or more times at police officers, and that armed police officers I'd called in to be given instructions were somehow there on the spot instead of here . . . and seem to have contributed nothing whatsoever. Why in God's name did they get so close, and then fluff it? What *did* happen out there?'

Conway said hopefully: 'We're pretty sure we've got the second man boxed in at the back of the park, sir. It's only a matter of time.'

'Time!' breathed Brownlow as if it was the dirtiest word in his vocabulary. He reached for the phone. 'There are going to be questions about this from every civic busybody in the business, from Councillor Perishing Thomas upwards – not to mention the Commissioner – and I'm the one who's going to be in the hot seat answering them. So I shall want some convincing answers. For starters, I want PC Smith, WPC Ackland, the three TSG officers, and you two, here half an hour from now. Understood?'

'Sir.'

'Sir.' Frazer went out, mopping her brow as she reached the end of the corridor. She could almost begin to feel a kinship with the sweatings and miseries of Sergeant Penny.

She went in search of Smith and Ackland, and found them in the canteen. Smith's hands, she saw at once, were as shaky as Penny's had frequently been. He was having difficulty in raising a cup of tea to his lips. As he got it into position, his eyes met those of one of the TSG men, sitting at a table quite some distance away and the cup clattered down again. 'He nigh shot me head off.' Or that, to Frazer, was what it sounded like.

Smith became aware of her, and tried to get to his feet. She put a hand on his shoulder and forced him gently back on to his chair. 'Stay put, constable. No rush.' To WPC Ackland, on the other side of the table, she said: 'What you might call a bitch of a morning, eh?'

Ackland was in a worse state than Smith, though trying not to show it. She could not summon up a reply. Biting her lower lip, she fought back tears and at last managed a nod. Frazer looked around the canteen. The TSG men, obviously not in good odour with the rest of the occupants of the canteen, were muttering together, one of them dabbing at his lip with a wad of cotton wool. Without drawing too much attention, Frazer said quietly and authoritatively: 'Come with me, please, WPC Ackland.'

June Ackland, already shaken, looked up uncomprehendingly. Surely there couldn't be anything even worse in store? Without her own volition, surrendering to the inspector's firm hand on her arm, she got up and drifted across the room in a trance. Frazer steered her down the stairs and along the corridor to the ladies' toilets. Inside, she made a quick check to ensure that all the cubicles were empty. Her voice ceased to be crisp and official.

'Right, let it go, June.'

June Ackland went on staring, shaking from head to foot but still refusing to surrender.

'Let it go.' It was partly an order, partly the insistence of a dispassionate expert who knew what was needed and intended to coax it out. 'No men in here.'

For another half-minute Ackland tried to fight it, then seemed to collapse inside and bend over, hugging herself. Frazer waited, saying no more, not putting out a hand in support because it had gone beyond that sort of gesture. At last June Ackland let out a wail that had been pent up there for too long. She began to cry and gag in a convulsive hiccup, and made a dash into one of the cubicles, weeping and vomiting at the same time.

Frazer pulled the cubicle door shut. 'And don't worry, I'll not let a soul in here for five minutes.'

Fourteen

After watching June Ackland leave the canteen, Alfie slowly got up from the group of TSG men and joined Yorkie Smith at his table. Yorkie's pent-up wrath was all too ready to boil over.

'What's next, then? Missed shooting me – going to drop poison in my tea?'

'Look, son, you belted a brother officer,' growled Alfie. 'You'll get done.'

'You saw what he did. Even I know the rules for you lot. You don't discharge a firearm at a target moving away.'

'You don't need to tell me, son.' Alfie glanced back at Lenny, hunched over his table. 'Nor *him*, now. Look, we're trained up for most types of situation, but what we all went through this morning ain't in no manual.'

'He could've hit a civilian,' Yorkie persisted. 'And he didn't give any warning.'

'All right, all right. I know that. The whole thing was a major cock-up. But what about you, son? I mean, did you give the prisoner locks a thought? Well, did you?'

'If we had kept our distance as ordered – '

'Our job is to catch up with armed villains, not let them get clean away. Why do you think we were called in – just to phone up your chief super every time we wanted to put a bullet up the spout?' Alfie tilted his chair back and studied Yorkie thoughtfully. 'But whatever way it went, you assaulted a fellow officer. How do you get round that?'

'He's lucky he didn't get my boot in his face,' said Yorkie with a dismal attempt at bravado.

'Tell you what, son. I'll square that away with your guv'nor, that's a promise. Now, you keep shtum about Lenny's little indiscretion, and we'll put his fat lip and that blue mark on his chin down to a fall. Right?'

Yorkie Smith looked doubtfully towards Lenny. His own future was bleak if he didn't go along with this suggestion; but he was still trembling with the memory of that near miss, and he didn't see why the man should get away without another word being said. Punching a fellow officer was a sight less serious than blasting away at one with a shooter.

'Look,' said Alfie tensely, 'Lenny's a twenty-year man. He's a good copper. If this comes out, it'll blow him out of the job.'

'He gets off scot-free?' said Yorkie dubiously.

'Not quite, son. I'm his skipper. I promise you he'll have me to answer to when the dust settles.' He tapped one meaty finger in a funereal rhythm on the table. 'I'll not let him forget this in a hurry.'

Yorkie Smith had still not really made up his mind when they were summoned to Chief Superintendent Brownlow's office and faced by Brownlow, Conway and Frazer, sitting round one end of the table. Brownlow waved them to chairs set at the far end. June Ackland joined them a few moments later, still pale but holding her head up and clenching her fists to stop her hands shaking.

Alfie summed up the details of the incident in a formalized, unemotional language in which he was obviously well-versed. It took the heat out of the whole thing, making it sound like an everyday occurrence on a rather uneventful patrol. Even the fact that their prey had got away seemed as predictable a matter of routine as a traffic offence in the High Street. Concluding, he said: 'And may I add, sir, that all concerned showed exemplary conduct under the most extreme conditions. Sir.'

Brownlow looked at the faces of the others. 'Anybody got anything to add to that?'

Yorkie Smith and June Ackland exchanged the briefest of looks; but shook their heads.

'Right. Thank you.' Brownlow got up. 'I realize how you must all be feeling. However, I must ask for all your reports to be on my desk by the end of this relief. That's all.'

As they left, Alfie favoured Smith and Ackland with an almost imperceptible nod of thanks.

In the CAD room, Sergeant Tom Penny was staring at a custody sheet without taking in one word of it. Sweat kept breaking out on his forehead and dripping into his eyes, but he made no move to mop it away. Melvin took occasional furtive looks at him, with growing concern. Even Hollis was disturbed, and tried to cover up by chattering away at an even faster rate than usual.

'I've closed the book on DI Richards. I mean, he's got to be the man. Poor old Roach.'

'I keep hearing Burnside's name coming up.'

'Now, that's really being an alarmist. Burnside? No chance. A non-starter, eh, sarge?'

The R/T spilled a cheerful message into the room. 'Sierra Oscar eight-seven to Sierra Oscar. For your information, suspect in Victoria Park now in custody. Over.'

Tom Penny shuddered. He lowered his head as if flinching away from the walls and ceiling closing in on him. All at once he slid away from the desk and made a sprint for the door. Bob Cryer, on his way in, stood aside. 'Oh, Tom, I wonder if you've . . . Tom . . . ?'

He stared as Penny headed unsteadily for the sergeants' locker room.

'We've collared the suspect in the park, sarge.'

'Good,' said Cryer abstractedly. 'Fine.'

He hesitated a few seconds, then followed Penny. Outside the door of the locker room he hesitated again. It was slightly ajar, and from within came a low-pitched but hysterical mumble.

'All right, all right now. Done. Finished. Look, no guns . . . can't shoot you . . . all right.' Penny seemed to be pacing up and down, his voice alternately rising and fading. Then there was a clatter as he dropped keys on the floor; and the rattle as he retrieved them and began to open his locker.

Bob Cryer walked in.

'Come on, mate, that's not the answer.' Penny swung round, his eyes full of tears. 'They had guns, Bob. Shooters.'

'I know, Tom. But you weren't out there, so – '

'Next time. There'll be a next time, and – '

'Come on, mate, let's have a sit down.' He eased Penny away from the locker and down on to the low bench. 'That's it, mate. Nice and easy with the breathing.'

Penny took great shuddering gulps of air. 'What's happening to me?' He leaned forward, his head sinking into his hands, and began to sob loudly.

Cryer moved round and crouched in front of him. 'You're all right, mate. It'll go, don't you worry. You're going to be all right.'

Penny sagged forward, put his arms round Cryer's neck, and let the sobs take possession. Bob Cryer stayed in that awkward, back-aching position until Penny had cried it all out and was simply breathing in and out, panting, gradually becoming aware of the room around him and where he was sitting.

'That's better.' Cryer stood up. 'All right?'

'Bob, I – '

'Fine.' Cryer looked meaningfully at the locker. 'Sure you're all right now?'

Penny forced a pitifully meagre grin. 'Don't worry, Bob. It's safe to leave me. I'll just . . . have a wash. Wake myself up.'

Cryer clapped him on the shoulder and went out.

Ted Roach was storming through front office and along the corridor.

'You bloody lot! Raving bloody idiots.'

'Had a good morning, Ted?'

'I knew I should never have turned my back. Signing away bloody Blakelynn

390

just when I was going to have the whole thing sewn up. What raving lunatic authorized that?'

'Better have a quiet word with Inspector Frazer,' Cryer suggested. 'If you know any quiet words, that is:'

Roach crashed through the door into the locker room.

Tom Penny was coming out of one of the cubicles. His eyes were red, but Roach was in no mood to worry about the colour of other people's eyes. His own were still blazing with anger. He pulled out his hip flask and took a long swig, then thrust it towards Penny.

'God protect us from wet-behind-the-ears coppers.'

Tom Penny looked long and hard at the flask.

'And them that can't keep away from the booze,' he murmured, pushing the flask away.

'And what's come over *you* all of a sudden?'

Penny made no reply, but left the locker room with a shaky determination in his stride.

Ted Roach pounded up the stairs to his office. Somebody was going to suffer for this. Mike Dashwood followed at a wary distance.

Jimmy Carver was pecking inaccurately at a report whose typing errors would puzzle his superiors almost as much as the incident itself. Roach started in at once.

'Did Alec Peters come up and check with you about Blakelynn?'

'Er, well, yes . . . in a manner of speaking.'

'What d'you mean, "in a manner of speaking"? Either he did or he didn't, son.'

Knowing he was on to a hiding for nothing, Carver gave up. 'All right, sarge. First there was Inspector Frazer, and then Sergeant Peters came up and went through the motions. Okay? I mean, what could I do under the circs?'

Roach thrust his face into Carver's and yelled at him from a few inches away. 'You could have stalled them, that's what.'

'Listen, sarge.' Carver's voice was taut, ready to snap. 'Next time you want me to fight what amounts to a rearguard action on your behalf, at least leave me some bullets for the gun.'

'Don't you get leary with me, son.'

'Leary? You reckon I'm leary?' Carver's long, pale face was etched with livid lines. He got to his feet and snatched the file of Blakelynn material from Roach's desk. 'Well, I tell you what, sarge: if that's what you think, how about me telling you what I think *you* are?' He opened the file and thrust it so violently at Roach that the DS automatically grabbed it and tried to balance it so that sheets did not spill out. 'Have a gander,' breathed Carver. 'Go on, have a gander at that.'

'I don't need to.'

'No, of course you don't. You already know that after having that body banged up for nigh on thirty hours you've got sweet FA in there.'

'All right, Jimmy.' Dashwood, startled, made a clumsy attempt to pour oil on troubled tempers. 'You've made your point.'

'Oh, have I?'

Ted Roach said acidly: 'All right then, son, get it off your chest.'

'When are you going to understand that it's a damned sight more productive all around to work with the system than it is to bend it? I mean, surely you must have learned that lesson from Galloway's mistakes?'

Mike Dashwood closed his eyes in anticipation of the coming explosion. There was a long pause. Ted Roach went on staring into Carver's face, at a loss for what to say. At last he produced a convulsive twist of the shoulders and strode out of the room.

It was perhaps not the wisest move he could have made. Inspector Frazer, at the foot of the stairs, said: 'Ah, Sergeant Roach. Just the man I was looking for. Can you spare me a moment?'

Roach felt he could spare her a lot more than that. If he was just the man she had been looking for, he would give her just what she had been asking for.

Following her into her office, he let fly at once. 'Thanks for making a free gift of something I was just about to wrap up for our own benefit rather than for our country cousins, ma'am.'

'You had the man in custody for over thirty hours, sergeant.'

'I know that, and given another – '

'What you don't seem to realize, sergeant, is that you placed the custody officer in a situation that was, to say the least, an unhealthy one.'

'It wasn't my fault we got called out on the ground on this other business.'

'Nor was it the prisoner's,' said Frazer with infuriating reasonableness. 'Look, sergeant, so far you and I have had little time to get to know how each one of us works.'

'I work the way I work, and I get results. *Ma'am.*'

Inspector Frazer folded her arms and continued to look smugly sure of herself. The note of sweet reason grew quite insufferable. 'Okay, Sergeant Roach, I think I know the score.'

'Ma'am?'

'And *I* work the way *I* work, sergeant. And these' – she touched her shoulder pips – 'tell me my way is better than yours.'

Roach shrugged contemptuously. He had had enough of this pretentious rubbish. She had nothing to offer but generalizations, official dogma. Moving towards the door, he looked back just once. 'They can tell you what they like, ma'am. When you were working the angles, picking up rank, I was working the streets, picking off villains.'

'Sergeant,' she was still smiling and unruffled. 'I'm sure your new DI will be most interested in your views.' He flinched. That one was really below the belt, and she knew it. She picked up a piece of paper from her desk. 'I do in fact think you know him.'

She kept him waiting a full malicious minute before she told him.

Jimmy Carver headed for the canteen, then decided he could not face the rest of them right now. He turned into the recreation room for a brief spell, to get himself under control again. It ought to be deserted at this time of day. But Sergeant Cryer was making a note about some gear in the far corner. Perhaps that was no bad thing. Carver was in a mood to pour out his woes to someone, and Cryer was probably the best person to consult.

'Hello, Jim. Come to skim through the papers and learn what a dangerous lot of bullies the police are turning into?' Then he appraised Carver's expression, and said: 'Oh, I know that look. Problems?'

'Sarge, I think going into CID was a big mistake for me.'

'Oh, really. And what's brought all this on, then?'

Carver tugged at a button on his jacket. An impulsive outburst was one thing; logical explanation quite another.

'I just don't think I'm fly enough,' he confessed lamely.

'Fly? Hold it a sec . . . I know what it is. Ted Roach did his crust at you over the Blakelynn business, right?'

It was the way it had always been. Cryer always seemed to know. He was not nosy, not forever pushing and prying like Reg Hollis: he just knew, and that was it.

'Something like that,' Carver sighed.

'So you got a rollocking, so what? Ain't the first, won't be the last.'

'Only this time I didn't just stand there and take it, sarge. I said a few things of me own. From now on I'm going to have to watch my back.'

'Do what?' Cryer's bluff good humour vanished. 'Watch your back? Now you listen, sunshine, and listen good. I've known Ted Roach for a lot of years, and the one thing he ain't is a back-stabber.'

It was bad enough having Roach sounding off at him. Now Cryer was putting him through it. 'I . . . I didn't mean it like that, sarge.' By now he was even less sure of what he did mean.

'If you thought you were right and stood your ground,' said Cryer, 'you've got nothing to fear from Ted Roach.'

'I more or less told him to stop trying to work against the system, though, sarge.'

Cryer's sunny tolerance began to seep back. 'I've been telling him that for years.'

'Yes, but I'm just a DC, sarge.'

'So what? Listen, son: Ted's the first bloke to acknowledge that rank hasn't the monopoly on being right.' Cryer grinned widely. 'It just seems that way, that's all.'

As Jimmy Carver continued his progress in the direction of the canteen, he heard Cryer chuckling behind him. That was something else he could not decide: whether it was worse to be yelled at or chuckled at.

In the canteen, he spotted June Ackland and Yorkie Smith sitting at a table together, both looking very pale. They had been close mates once, when he was a raw recruit. For all his growing pains in those early days, there had been something special about being in the uniformed branch. Then he remembered what he had recently heard about the ordeal the two of them had gone through today, and had his doubts. And in a far corner, being studiously, compassionately avoided by the rest, Sergeant Penny sat alone, looking no more cheerful than Ackland and Smith.

As if in some mutual, silent communication of kinship, Ackland and Smith suddenly got up from their table and moved across to Penny. He looked up with red-rimmed, lacklustre eyes as they scraped chairs back and sat down. Then June Ackland put her hand over his and grinned, and Yorkie nodded; Tom Penny was managing a smile, and some of the tenseness began to drain slowly, very slowly, out of him.

Behind Carver, Taffy Edwards and Malcolm Haynes hurried along the corridor and tried to push impatiently past him into the canteen. On their heels, Reg Hollis was holding forth in his shrillest, most insistent know-all manner.

'But I tell you it's true.'

'Likely bloody story.'

'I'm *telling* you. Galloway's replacement. It's Burnside.'

Now, at least, he could be assured of a hushed, attentive audience for once. Heads turned. All other conversation stopped.

'Burnside.' Hollis sounded as if he could hardly believe it himself. 'Frank Burnside.'

Taffy Edwards said what was in all their minds: 'If that's true, Ted Roach'll do his crust.'

Within ten minutes everyone in the station had heard. Within another ten minutes Reg Hollis's indignant assurances of his own infallibility on such matters were officially confirmed. Burnside, of all people. It was true. Trying to have any kind of conversation during the next few days with Ted Roach, still Detective Sergeant Roach, was going to be a risky business.

Fifteen

They had all had a bellyful of 'in-depth' television programmes and lofty government pronouncements. Cocooned in safe studios or safe offices far from the football terraces, earnest or indignant interviewers and junior ministers held forth interminably on the evils of soccer hooliganism and the increased efforts needed from the police. Somehow it always came back to the police. Some commentators blamed the basic problem on deprivation in the inner cities. Others asserted that it was a phenomenon of the young overpaid rather than the young underpaid, and went hand in hand with a reviving National Front seeking the next best thing to outright war. But both factions agreed that, in the actual field, it all came down to the police. They ought to be handling things better. Either they were mounting too heavy a presence; or they were not sufficiently in evidence when trouble broke out between opposing gangs.

Two Sun Hill constables who had been called in at the start of the season to control rioters outside the local ground were still recuperating two months later from a fractured skull and a smashed hand, trampled on by a gleeful drunk, who was arrested and then discharged because of lack of witnesses. Another man, called in with a group of reinforcements to an international match, nearly lost the sight of his left eye. In all such cases the routine, official post-mortem – which one day might well be a literal post-mortem – was unable to resolve the questions being flung at the forces of law and order by press and television reporters: had the police underestimated the scale of the likely events that day, or overestimated them? Responded too brutally with provocative moves and threats, or been too supine?

There had been days, long past, when it had been a pleasure to be on duty at a football match: the equivalent of a free ticket, and always with a commanding view of the pitch. Now it was a task to be dreaded.

The Home Office issued a series of instructions, framed with suitable vagueness so that its interpreters could always be blamed for unforeseen consequences. Then it was announced that the Prime Minister was 'taking personal charge' of the matter. A number of hearts sank, especially among football club managers. For a while the heat was off the police, while the experts and commentators swapped views on falling attendances if compulsory identity cards were introduced, the impossibility of checking every ticket-holder at every match, the aggro there was likely to be as queues grew impatient, the ease with which cards could be forged, and the still crucial matter of alcohol drinking on trains, around the grounds, and, despite every precaution, on the terraces themselves. But when all the dust of theorizing and pontification had settled, the control of those queues and the rounding-up of suspected troublemakers would still come down to the police once more. And whichever way it went, there would inevitably be more blame than praise. It was one of the things you learned to live with; but it never ceased to rankle.

A directive, unpublicized, went out that prevention rather than cure was to be the order of the day. Identities of leading hooligans and their well-organized gangs were known, even if it was often heartbreakingly difficult to prove such things in court. The thing was, to pool knowledge acquired by different branches and regions, keep an eye on forthcoming fixtures, and apply every possible resource to breaking up the hooligans' plans before they could be put into action.

Few of the Sun Hill personnel had even a hint that they had been allocated a part in such a sweep until every last little detail had been agreed by their superiors. Nevertheless there had been a strange tingle in the air for some days before a large contingent was notified of an important briefing in the squad room at four o'clock on a dark Friday morning. Duty rosters and days off had been adjusted. Something was very definitely going to happen.

There was a hubbub of speculation which died away to fraught expectancy when Chief Superintendent Brownlow came into the room with Chief Inspector Conway and Inspector Frazer. He wasted no time. 'Good morning. The signal for the operation in which you will all be involved over the next few hours is "Red Card". I don't know if that gives any of you a hint as to the nature of what's involved.'

Taffy Edwards, who was regarded as one of the lucky ones because last season he had suffered only two thick ears two weeks running, ventured: 'Soccer, sir?'

'Right. We are to take part in the final phase of a very tricky operation.' Brownlow permitted himself a wintry smile. 'The fact that this is a surprise to you all speaks volumes for the security that has been necessary in conducting this operation. I can now reveal to you that for the past month two officers have been working undercover in what can only be described as the most hazardous conditions. The secrecy has been vital to the safety and well-being of those two undercover officers. We wouldn't have got this far without their infiltration. Now, for detailed briefing I'll hand you over to Chief Inspector Conway.'

He stood aside for Conway to take his place.

Conway glanced at his watch, and continued the explanation. Two officers had wormed their way into the notorious group known as 'Front Line'. This brought a subdued whistle from several personnel in the room. The public knew about Front Line from lurid stories in the papers which never quite named names or offered solutions to its activities. The police knew – even knew a few names – but had never been able to pin the ringleaders down. Their violent followers appeared in force, without warning, in football grounds all over England and Scotland, in Belgium and Germany and Italy, but were skilled at dispersing and playing innocent if any of them were pursued by the police of this or any other country. Their tactics were skilfully predetermined: they were murderous, semi-military campaigns rather than spontaneous outbreaks of anger. Sudden outbursts and fist fights after the fans' disappointment at a poor result by their own team had been a sporadic feature of matches from way back. But the supplying of weapons designed to inflict injury, and the plotting of the timing and deployment of thugs even before a match had started, were a phenomenon of recent years. Front Line, boastful of its prowess if not of its individual members' names, had increased its activities over those years; and had introduced murder into what had once been sporting occasions. It was now time for them to be put out of business.

Conway slowly spelled out three addresses and allocated personnel to each one of them. He waited while the sergeants attached to each contingent made a note of the exact position and confirmed it, so that there should be no slip-ups. So far, nothing had been written down. Now, with zero hour approaching, it was all going to come out in the open.

'We will be entering all three premises in coordinated raids at precisely O-six-hundred hours.' Conway paused, and leaned forward to say, slowly and emphatically: 'At this point I must warn you that our two undercover officers are still *in situ*. They will not identify themselves to you. They will be rounded up and arrested along with the rest of this gang, and for the sake of future operations of this nature it is imperative that no hint of their identity should leak out. For the sake of form, they will more than likely put up a pretty rough show of resisting arrest. In the event of your knowing either of them, you must not – repeat, *not* – show any signs of recognition. We do not want this group to know they have been infiltrated. Now, any questions?'

The machinery began to tick into motion. Sergeant Peters wiped the prisoner board clear. In a few hours' time this area was going to be the busiest in the whole nick.

Sergeant Cryer came in with two mugs of tea, yawning. 'I'm getting past these early mornings.'

'Me, too. How many bodies do you suppose we can expect?'

'From what her ladyship tells me, a dozen or more.'

Peters sipped his tea. 'Oh, marvellous. Terrific. I need that like a goldfish needs a pushbike.'

'Mm. It's going to be a long and silly day. Today of all days, on top of everything else.'

397

'What makes today any different from any other day?' Bob Cryer stared. 'Alec, I know it's early, but wake up. Today is a sad day for the nick – a sad day for the whole of the Met, in fact.'

'What you going on about?'

'Today,' said Cryer wearily, 'is the day that that prize toerag, Burnside, takes over CID here.'

'I forgot all about that.' Peters looked at Cryer over the edge of his tea mug. 'I gather you don't like him.'

'Has Pinocchio got a wooden whatsit . . . ?'

As six o'clock approached, Cryer strolled to the open door of the CAD room. Tom Penny, chewing his lip, was gazing hypnotically at the wall clock. Viv Martella sat at a console, willing it to speak. Even Reg Hollis was silent, attentive, keyed-up.

'I wish I could be out there with them,' said Martella.

This, at any rate, provoked a knee-jerk response from Hollis. 'Stuff that for a game of tin soldiers. Those Front Line blokes are sick in the head. They won't come along like good little boys. Right, sarge?'

Penny looked sick. 'You're better off in here, Viv.' His gaze did not waver from the clock. 'Right, stand by.'

Hollis gnawed at the corner of a thumbnail.

The R/T came on, remarkably calm and casual. 'Four-eight to control. Commencing with Operation Red Card. Over.'

'Received, four-eight.' Martella sounded a lot less calm.

Hollis was singing softly: 'Here we go, here we go, here we go . . .'

One of the targets was a terraced house, into which Mike Dashwood led two uniformed officers, one of them wielding a sledgehammer. They were wasting no time on niceties such as ringing the front doorbell. A larger one was a semi–detached house a mile away, in what, on the surface, was a more well-to-do residential area, but which, underneath its prosperous respectability, sheltered as good a proportion of disreputable characters as anywhere on the manor. Ted Roach and Jimmy Carver led the assault on this: or did so until the last minute, when Roach pulled Carver to one side and let half-a-dozen uniformed men dash past and set about the front door.

'First rule on one of these jobs, son, is to let the wallies steam in first.' Roach tapped his head and winked. 'Stick with yer old Uncle Ted!' As the door gave way, he confirmed in his R/T: 'Three-nine to control. Red Card. Over.'

They followed the others into the house.

As the first of the uniformed officers reached the first-floor landing, a bedroom door opened and a skinhead, wearing nothing but underpants, blinked astonished, sleep-filled eyes at them. Before he could protest, two burly coppers bundled him backwards into the bedroom. Another wave reached the landing and began wrenching other bedroom doors open.

'Pigs!' It was an all too familiar cry.

Ted Roach ambled up the stairs, unhurried. In a wild fit of enthusiasm, Carver had decided to join the main attack, and threw himself through one of the open doors. Roach shook his head and sighed. He propped himself against a wall and listened to the shouting and hollering, and the intermittent thuds as coppers thumped their captives, or vice versa.

Without warning, Jimmy Carver emerged backwards from the room he had brashly entered. He was moving at a fair speed until he hit the opposite wall and went sprawling on to the threadbare carpet. He was followed at a slower pace by two constables keeping tight hold of another man sporting the current fashion for underpants, and in addition a fine display of tattoos on both arms and across his chest. He was almost as burly as his captors, and was doing his best to break free, kicking and struggling and yelling a selection of abuse which Roach had to admire. 'No-good slags' and 'pigs' were among the mildest of his epithets.

As he was more firmly armlocked and heaved towards the stairs; he turned and spat into Roach's face. Instinctively Roach, twisting aside, headbutted him, cutting off another imprecation in mid-syllable.

'Get that scum out of here.'

Others were being heaved out of the various rooms. Jimmy Carver tried to get his legs out of their way and haul himself upright. Halfway up the wall, he went rigid, staring past Roach.

'You all right, Jimmy?'

'Yes, I . . . I'm all right.'

Carver gulped. Roach followed the direction of his gaze; and felt as if he, too, had been hurled painfully across a landing to have all the breath knocked out of him.

The man being dragged from a bedroom by two policemen was dark-featured, heavy-jawed, surly, snarling and struggling, as crooked and repulsive a character as you could expect to meet. And Roach had met him more than once. In the view of most of the officers at Sun Hill nick, they didn't come any rougher or more bent than this one.

It was the loathsome Frank Burnside – one-time Detective Sergeant, now Detective Inspector.

At the same instant, a man of similar build was kicking and cursing as two officers dragged him bodily out of the neighbouring room. He caught the expressions on the faces of Roach and Carver; and twisted between the arms of the constables to look at Burnside.

'You . . . you filth! I knew there was a bad smell about you.'

'Get 'em out of here.' Roach tried to recover himself. 'Both of 'em, get 'em downstairs and off the – '

'No-good slag. You're the filth. You no-good, conning sod.'

He was hustled towards the staircase, still trying to wrench his head round and yell abuse.

Burnside's face was evil, his thick lips moist with all the things he wanted to spew out. 'Right smart pair, you two, eh?' He tried to pull clear of the two men restraining him. 'All right, turn it in.' When they ignored him and tried to shove him towards the stairs in the wake of the others, he bellowed: 'I said, turn it in, you dim gits. I'm blown out.'

'All right, lads,' said Roach wretchedly. 'He's on our side.'

When he had been released, Burnside turned on the two uniformed officers. 'Right. Start turning this gaff over. And if you miss so much as a nail file, I'll have your nuts in a tin.' Now it was the turn of the shattered Roach and Carver. 'You two ain't exactly bursting with A-levels, are you?'

'Well, how the hell were we to know?' Roach demanded.

Very quietly and venomously, Burnside prompted him: '*Sir*.'

Ted Roach held his breath and shuddered. It took him an age to manage it. 'Sir.'

By a quarter-past-six the detachment under the chief superintendent's personal supervision had cleared its allotted house and was shepherding sullen or vengeful characters towards the paddy wagon. Taffy Edwards, who had escaped even a minor scratch in this encounter, surveyed the scene with considerable satisfaction as he made his way towards Brownlow.

'That's it, sir. Nobody left on the premises.'

'Good. Start the search.'

As Edwards was turning away, a milk float coasted to a halt nearby. The milkman looked at the assembly of policemen and vehicles, and scratched his head. Automatically he reached for two bottles from a crate, then decided to let them clink back into place. 'I take it leaving milk'd be a waste of time today, guv'nor?'

'And for the foreseeable future, I hope,' said Brownlow.

'But what about me money, for gawd's sake? They owe me for three weeks.'

'It's a hard life.' Brownlow offered him a philosophical smile and followed Edwards indoors.

On the first floor a PC new to the job, excited over the whole cloak-and-dagger atmosphere, was rooting assiduously through a suitcase he had pulled out from under a bed. Whatever he had expected to find, its actual contents puzzled him, and he waved Edwards closer.

'Have a gander at this lot.'

Taffy Edwards peered in. 'What the hell are they?'

Brownlow edged past them and stooped over the open case. 'CS gas bombs, son.' He picked one out and examined its markings. 'Made in France.'

'But that's madness! Utter madness! What the hell do they think they're doing, this lot? I mean, what do they get out of it?'

Brownlow put the canister back. 'I have no idea, son. None whatsoever.'

Yorkie Smith was just coming out of the adjoining room, carrying a polished box in his outstretched arms. He headed for the chief super, and raised the lid to display a Verey pistol.

'Absolutely right,' sighed Brownlow. 'That's what it is, Edwards – utter madness.'

There were two more boxes and a cluster of sketches on graph paper, which meant nothing at the moment, but would surely yield something on analysis. There were also clothes to be retrieved from wardrobes or from the backs of chairs where they had been carelessly slung. Everything was going to be sieved through once it was carted back to Sun Hill and subjected to detailed, unhurried attention. The exhilaration of the wild rush and heat of the successful raids was over. Now came the painstaking, analytical part.

The custody area at Sun Hill did not immediately suggest that the pandemonium was as good as over and would soon be replaced by a spell of contemplation. The prisoners were not standing meekly in line waiting to be interviewed. Some of them kept up a constant chant of obscenities, and others struggled and pushed, goading their attendant policemen in the hope of managing one last, brief punch-up to prove what stuff they were made of.

'Pigs!' The police station seemed to have acquired an unquenchable echo. 'Pigs!'

Bob Cryer and Alec Peters were working at a desk each, rattling off the standard formula and not even flinching at some of the replies. In front of Cryer's desk, a sneering man in his late twenties was manhandled into position by Mike Dashwood and Malcolm Haynes.

Cryer recited the charge for the fourth time in a row. 'Conspiracy to cause a breach of the peace. Do you understand?'

'Shove it.'

'Whatever you say, sunshine. Right . . . name?'

'Dick Turpin.'

'Oh. Occupation?'

The man leered. 'Stage-coach robber.'

'I'll make a note of that. And you're also going to be charged with armed robbery. Next.'

'You can't do that.'

'I just have,' said Cryer, unruffled. 'Come on, don't keep us waiting. Next!'

At Peters' table, another prisoner was trying his hand at the same sort of cocky humour, giving his name as Lord Lucan. Whatever that missing peer's reputed misdeeds, he had surely never looked as vicious and scruffy as this.

Ted Roach and Jimmy Carver crossed the custody area like warriors home from a foray into hostile territory. In a momentary lull, Cryer watched them with a satisfaction he assumed they must share. Roach was carrying a crossbow; Carver had a large holdall stuffed with knives, metal bars, chains and martial arts nasties. As Mike Dashwood returned from delivering his charge to the cell block, Roach shoved the crossbow towards him. 'Whoever's collecting

401

this junk, Mike?' He did not wait for anything further, but went on his way with a face like an impending thunderstorm.

Dashwood raised an eyebrow at Carver. 'What's up with him this time? Thought everyone'd be bursting with goodwill. Job satisfaction, they call it.'

'You ready to hear it?'

'Oh no: what's he done this time?'

Before Carver could embark on a blow-by-blow account, Detective Inspector Frank Burnside came in. His warped grin made it clear to Cryer's equally practised eye that Burnside had at once sussed what the two of them were about to discuss. He winked knowingly at Dashwood, then scowled at Carver with his load of weapons.

'Listen, old son, if I were you I'd get that lot out of here a bit rapid. Out of reach of these lunatics.'

'Yes, guv.' Carver was only too glad to beat a retreat.

Burnside said: 'Well, Mike, how's it going?'

'Er, fine. Fine, guv.'

'Good. Oh, I want to see you, Ted Roach and young Carver up in CID as soon as you've got clear of this little lot down here.'

'Okay, guv. I'll let the others know.'

'You do that.' Burnside sauntered towards Bob Cryer's desk, just as another prisoner was set before it. Cryer concentrated on the job in hand rather than offer Burnside even a token greeting.

This one had had a coat thrown round his shoulders from somewhere, but was still displaying a pageant of tattoos across his chest. Cryer looked at the whorls and curlicues without finding them worthy of artistic commendation; but at least they were more shapely than the man's face, which could never have been lovely at the best of times and was now in no way enhanced by two swollen, purpling lips.

'Name?'

'Get stuffed.'

Deliberately laborious, Cryer wrote this down on the form. 'That's with two fs, Mr Stuffed?'

Burnside laughed. 'Good to see you still got a sense of humour, Bob.'

Cryer hoped he could succeed in keeping the contempt out of his face and voice as he raised his head and acknowledged the DI's presence. 'Mr Burnside.'

The hatred he felt was matched in every way by the prisoner's. The man was staring murderously at Burnside. 'You're one of those filth, then. I should have seen it. Filth.'

Without even taking his bland smirk off Cryer, Burnside lashed out sideways with his right hand and slapped the man hard enough across the face to send him sagging back between his police escorts.

'Mind your manners, old son.'

Bob Cryer got to his feet. 'Won't be a moment,' he said to the escorts. 'A word, please, Mr Burnside.'

'Of course, Bob.'

As the two of them left the room for an empty office two doors away, a jeering squawk followed: 'Tosser!'

Burnside, hands in pockets, said: 'How's tricks then, Bob?'

'Mr Burnside.' Bob Cryer closed the office door. His eyes were bleak and unyielding. 'May I remind you that as one of the custody officers of this relief, I am forbidden to allow my prisoners to be slapped around.'

Burnside rocked to and fro on his heels, snorting happily. 'It was only a slap.'

'I could have you done for it.'

The smugness began to evaporate from Burnside's face. He stopped swaying, and stood very still. 'You try it, old son.' The snarl was much more the old Burnside they all remembered; and all detested. 'You just try it. You'll come well unstuck.'

Cryer said steadily: 'Just don't ever breeze into my area and expect to get away with that kind of thing again.'

'All right, sergeant. All right.' Burnside looked him up and down, trying to reassert his superiority. 'Just what is it with you, eh? Getting all uppity so fast.'

'I don't like you. I don't like your methods. I don't suppose I ever will.'

'Hey, we're among friends here, aren't we? Don't beat about the bush. Let's know where we stand, and why.'

Cryer knew he ought to have dropped the whole thing, but the words simply had to come. The thought of Sun Hill being lumbered with this creature, after all he had done to them in the past and all they knew about him, was too much. 'I don't know how you ever became a DI,' he blurted out. 'And how they missed you with Operation Countryman, *nobody* can ever figure that out.'

'You're out of order, sergeant,' said Burnside lethally.

'Like I said' – the only sensible thing to do was to get back to the desk and get on with the real job – 'there's two fs in stuffed.'

He wrapped up two more prisoners in double-quick time and, still trembling every time the thought of Burnside crossed his mind, went off to see how the boys and girls in the exhibits room were getting on.

The haul was an impressive one. Three large tables had been set up against one of the walls, with address labels pinned above them to identify the source of each object. Inspector Frazer was logging each item as June Ackland labelled them and laid them out. The crossbow was among the largest exhibits, but not necessarily the most lethal. In a football stadium, or at close quarters in the alleys outside, the ten-inch Bowie knife and a few of the pronged knuckle-dusters and martial arts star pieces could inflict hideous damage in a matter of seconds. 'So much for an amnesty,' observed Inspector Frazer, contemplating the frightening array of hardware.

Ted Roach came in. Wherever he had been, he seemed to have recovered some of his usual brash, provocative manner, and eyed Frazer shamelessly up and down in a way which made her fidget without being able to decide whether or not his gaze came under the heading of insolence and merited a reprimand.

Carver was digging out some more material from his holdall. 'Albury Street, this lot.' He unloaded it where June Ackland was indicating.

Roach edged closer to Frazer, who froze. Before he could try on whatever it was he had in mind, Mike Dashwood came in search of him.

'Excuse me, ma'am. Ted, the guv'nor wants to meet with me, you and Jimmy up in ours, as soon as we're clear.'

'Guv'nor?' Roach's concentration had been elsewhere, and it took a moment to re-focus it.

'Burnside. Inspector Burnside, that is.'

Frazer turned. 'Oh, is Frank . . . the inspector's arrived, has he?'

Ted Roach reacted to that 'Frank'. His good humour was immediately on the wane again. Something was maybe even worse than any of them could have predicted. Old pals' act between two newcomers to the patch – no, it was not a pretty prospect.

'Caught us all on the hop,' said Dashwood ingratiatingly.

'Yes.' She was laughing, looking absurdly relaxed and cheerful. 'That's typical of . . . Inspector Burnside.'

Roach said: 'You know him, then, ma'am.'

'Yes, from way back. A good copper is Frank.'

With a noise in his throat which was hard to categorize, Ted Roach turned and left the room, passing Bob Cryer without even appearing to notice him.

Inspector Frazer frowned inquiringly at Mike Dashwood. 'Obviously Sergeant Roach doesn't agree.'

'No, ma'am. I think I'm safe in saying that Mr Burnside is not the most popular man in this nick.'

That, at least, wiped the last vestiges of a reminiscent smile off her face.

Sixteen

The turmoil of processing the prisoners and trying to relate each address to its group and their armoury grew worse as a flock of solicitors and welfare workers came buzzing indignantly in. One woman solicitor who had not yet even been in to see her client was already suggesting that the police must have planted a number of items on the innocent, persecuted sports fan, whose only interest was a good, clean game. A probation officer was vainly seeking someone he had been told was here by what must be a terrible mistake, but whose name was not on Cryer's or Peters' lists. He haughtily denied the likelihood of the misguided chap having given a false name; but went on to say if that was in fact what had happened, it could only have been because of police intimidation.

Bob Cryer at last found himself with no further customers awaiting his scrutiny. The papers on his desk represented a long, exhausting session; but now it looked as though the documentation had reached its peak, and the pace was likely to slacken off.

Tom Penny came to join him, apparently on the verge of confiding something personal. Then he changed his mind, gave Cryer an awkward half-smile, and said with something of his old, easygoing matiness: 'How's it going, Bob?'

'Not too bad. All over bar the shouting.' Cryer indicated a cluster of solicitors queueing for entrance to the cell block and conference with their clients, who had been quick to assert their rights and send out alarm calls. 'And there's going to be lots of that, I reckon.'

'So what's new?' said Penny lightly. Less lightly, he asked in an undertone: 'You seen the man yet?'

'If, by "the man" you mean Burnside, yes, I've seen him.'

'Y'know, Bob, it might just be worth giving the bloke a chance.'

Bob Cryer did not keep his own opinions to an undertone. It came out with the force of a flame-thrower: 'Tom, I don't give bent coppers any chance.'

'What did you say, sergeant?'

Neither of them had been aware of Inspector Christine Frazer coming along the side of the custody area, avoiding any grabbing for attention by the legal vultures. Cryer got up hurriedly. 'Ma'am.'

Her face was bleached with anger. 'Did I hear you correctly, Sergeant Cryer?'

Penny, his relaxed mood rudely shattered, was clearly praying for any interruption from anywhere at all. Cryer fumbled for a moment, then said with utter conviction: 'Yes, ma'am. In my considered opinion –'

'I do not share or care for your opinion, sergeant. And I will not tolerate malicious gossip or ill-founded insinuations about other officers. Do I make myself clear, sergeant?'

'Yes, ma'am,' said Cryer tightly.

'Good.'

Frazer turned and strode off. Penny revived sufficiently to watch her legs appreciatively. Bob Cryer appreciated neither her legs nor her manner, and thought even less of her dismissal of his views on DI Burnside as mere gossip. He had been around this manor many a year longer then Frazer and knew its ins and outs and twists and turns; and nothing was going to alter his views on Burnside.

Mike Dashwood was beginning to regret that he had not been on the same assault wave as Jimmy Carver and Ted Roach. It must have been one of the great treats of an eventful day. Just hearing the story of Burnside's appearance, a stage demon turning out to be the fairy queen, was no substitute for what the real thing must have been like.

'I bet your faces were pictures.'

'They still should have told us about it.' Roach found it less funny. Roach was not finding anything very funny right now.

'Oh, come on, Ted,' said Dashwood, 'you've been under-cover before.'

Roach headed for the inner office, then remembered the bitter facts and turned back to the sergeant's desk he had been tied to for so long. 'Fat lot of good that's done me, an' all.'

'That's not the point. The less the people who are in the know, the better.'

'We're not just people, Mike.'

From the doorway, Burnside said amiably: 'That's right, Ted. You ain't just people. Not any old people.' He sauntered towards the inner doorway and leaned on it, looking possessively down on them. 'You're *my* people now. Mine.' Studying Roach's reaction with needling complacency, he let this simmer for a few seconds before pushing himself back into the room and perching on the edge of the sergeant's desk. 'I know you don't like that a lot, old son, but that's the way it is. Right, sergeant?'

'Sir.'

Burnside savoured that, then got up and resumed his prowling, flicking at a map whose edges were peeling off the display board, shaking Carver's pending tray as if to judge its weight, and running a finger along a filing cabinet like a housewife looking for signs of dust.

'Right, let's get one or two things straight. I know a lot of people in this nick don't like me very much. And as it happens, I don't give a toss. I ain't here to win a popularity contest.'

'Just as well.' Roach could not restrain it.

Dashwood and Carver sat rigid in expectation. But DI Burnside simply grinned and carried on. 'I am what you might call thick-skinned. It makes no odds to me if people like me or not. All I'm interested in is getting the job done.' He was enjoying every minute of this, and enjoying the fact that the rest of them were not. 'Whatever you as individuals might think about me, you gotta be honest, I do get the job done. I'm good, ain't I?' He was directing it straight at Roach, daring him to argue. 'Now look, you little lot.' He waved towards the inner office. 'That door's open, right? And it's always gonna be open, and provided you all do your jobs and don't try me on as some old mug, I'll back you up all the way. And that applies even to you, Ted.'

'I'll manage,' growled Roach. Then, under the silent pressure of Burnside's gaze: 'Sir.'

The pressure was lifted by the arrival of Brownlow and Conway. Brownlow stuck out his hand. 'Welcome aboard, inspector.'

406

'Thanks, guv'nor.'

They shook hands. Conway and Burnside shook hands. Ted Roach watched, numb.

'And thank you,' said Brownlow warmly, 'for a job well done. A fine achievement to mark your arrival, eh? Thanks to you and DS Trimlett, Operation Red Card has been an astounding success.'

'Nobby Trimlett did most of the graft.'

Roach started at such an uncharacteristic remark. He longed to swap a cynical glance with Carver, but did not dare risk it.

'The DAC is well pleased, inspector, and so am I. Just a pity your cover was blown. It makes life more difficult for future operations.'

This time, Roach and Carver could not restrain themselves. They looked fleetingly at each other; and each took a deep breath. Here it came . . .

Burnside seemed, all of a sudden, to be in the business of exchanging glances with them, too. But he kept them waiting, until at last he said: 'A shame about that, guv, but couldn't be helped.' He paused, kept it dangling just a little while longer. 'Was my own fault. I just reacted all wrong when I saw DS Roach and young Jimmy here. That Lennox louse was always the fly one. Had me tumbled straight off. Sorry, guv.'

Roach was stunned. Brownlow, apparently unaware of the mental communications and non-communications in the office, was still in congratulatory mood. 'Compared with the results of the operation overall, I think we can weather one minor misfortune.'

'On that point, what about your friend Trimlett?' asked Chief Inspector Conway.

'He's still safe, skip. We'll get him dropped out on a technicality in a day or so.'

Again there was an orgy of shaking hands.

'We all hope you'll be happy here at Sun Hill, inspector.' Burnside's smile was almost a gloat. 'I'm sure I will be.' He was still smiling when Brownlow and Conway had left and he was alone again with his reluctant team. 'Right, then. Let's have a gander at the case load.' It sounded innocuous enough, until he reached his inner office and again paused in the doorway. 'By the way, Ted, you ain't out of the woods yet.'

'Eh?'

'One of the prisoners is yelling police brutality,' said Burnside, dwelling on it. 'Claims you head-butted him.'

'And *did* you head-butt the bloke, Ted?' asked Bob Cryer, sipping tea and welcoming its soothing warmth through his vocal chords, overworked asking the same formal questions again and again this morning.

'Suppose.'

'What d'you mean, suppose? For gawdsakes, either you did or – '

'All right, all right, so I did. The scumbag gobbed all over me.'

Cryer set his cup down and contemplated his old colleague. When was Ted Roach ever going to wake up to the full realities of life and the law? It was no good lecturing him: advice and warnings flowed off Ted Roach's rumpled head like water off a duck's back – or, more appropriately, like whisky under a greedy palate.

'Well, what's the SP then?' he asked resignedly. 'What's going to happen?'

Roach peered glumly into his cup. There were no tea-leaves at the bottom; and if there had been, they would hardly have offered any very optimistic predictions. 'I can tell you what,' he said. 'Burnside'll hang this one over my head for as long as he can. He got me and Jimmy off a hook this morning, only because he knew he had something better to hit me with. I was supposed to sit there and say, thank you, sir, three bags full, sir, and aren't you a kind new guv'nor, sir. Well, stuff that.'

There was no need for Roach's vehemence. He was preaching, as he should have known by now, to the converted. Bob Cryer had nothing to add or take away. Then a pleasant little fancy dawned on him. 'Hold on a minute.'

'Huh?'

'I just might be able to help you out, mate.'

'How come?'

Cryer tapped the side of his nose. There was plenty of it to tap. 'I think a quiet little word in Burnside's ear might just do the trick.'

He got up from the table, waving Roach to stay where he was and cool down. At a table near the door, he grinned congratulations to Edwards, Smith and Haynes, who had been joined by an envious Ackland and Martella.

Viv Martella was pursuing one of her obsessive themes. 'I don't see why we can't go out on real jobs like that.'

'Oh, come on, Viv.' Taffy Edwards leaned back, still glowing with recollections of glory. 'I'm all for women's lib and all that, but even you have got to realize that raids like this morning's are better left to male officers.'

If June Ackland's already crisp curls could have bristled, they would have bristled. 'I don't agree.'

'It was no picnic, June,' Yorkie Smith contributed. 'You just don't get the picture. Most of them blokes were right headbangers. If you could have seen the gear we found in their gaffs – '

'I've spent all morning,' Ackland pointed out resentfully, 'labelling it all up.'

Reg Hollis was rash enough to put in an appearance, still exuding self-satisfaction over being the first to break the bad news about Burnside. Martella welcomed him with unusual fervour.

'So there you are. I've got a bone to pick with you, Reg.'

'I'll have you know I'm very fussy who I pick my bones with.'

'When you started running the book on Galloway's replacement, you said half of any of the profits would go into the Widows' and Orphans' Fund.'

'Did I say that?'

'Yes, you did,' June Ackland confirmed. 'Any sign of the actual breakdown yet – apart from your own permanent breakdown?'

Haynes added his grievances. 'I still haven't been paid out for winning. I was the one who had a tenner on Burnside, if you remember.'

He ought not to have spoken so resonantly. From the far side of the room, Ted Roach was fixing him with a convincing imitation of the evil eye. This revelation of ultimate treachery within the camp would not be forgotten in a hurry.

'Don't worry,' Hollis said, in a minor flap. 'You'll get your wedge.'

'I'd better, Mr Bookmaker, or else . . .'

Cryer made himself scarce, before he was forced to listen to threats of indiscipline which might have demanded his official attention.

He found Frank Burnside strolling down one of the corridors, sizing up his new quarters like a cat staking out its territory. It would not have surprised Cryer if he had detected Burnside peeing on crucial bits of the perimeter.

'A word, Mr Burnside?'

'Another one, Bob? Already?'

Cryer opened the door of the nearest interview room.

Burnside swaggered in, full of himself and the joy of being here.

'I'd like to talk to you off the record,' said Cryer.

'All right. What's your problem, old son?'

Cryer weighed his words carefully. This had to be done right, or the trouble might get a whole lot worse. 'It's about Ted Roach.' He took the plunge. 'I gather he's in a bit of trouble over head-butting one of those Front Line tossers.'

'What's that got to do with you, old son?'

'Ted's a good copper, and – '

'Good coppers don't go around head-butting prisoners.'

'But it's all right to give 'em a little slap, is it, Mr Burnside?' Burnside thought this one over, seeing where it was all leading. 'So that's it. You reckon I should be worried about what I did?'

'All I'm trying to say, Mr Burnside, is that if Ted Roach cops it in the neck for what he did – '

'You'll suddenly feel duty bound to report me for slapping the same geezer? 'Cos it was the same geezer, as a matter of interest.'

Bob Cryer began to feel uneasy. A chill instinct warned him that something, somehow, was leading off in the wrong direction. But he was committed now. 'Something like that,' he grunted.

'I see.' Burnside's smile was increasingly ominous. 'I assume you've already had a little chat with the prisoner about all this?'

'No, Mr Burnside. I thought it best all round to speak to you first.'

The DI walked to the door as though intending to walk out on the whole affair. 'Well,' he mused, 'as it happens I've been wanting to have a word with him myself. So while we're at it, old son, what say to me and you and Roach all having a word with him?'

Bob Cryer groaned inwardly. Not knowing what the sequel to this was going to be, but scenting disaster, he hurried after Burnside, who was lit up with a desire to fire off instructions right, left and centre. He caught a passing Mike Dashwood by the arm and ordered him to get Sergeant Roach to the custody area, and fast; and in the area itself, began chatting up Alec Peters, who looked diffident in Cryer's presence and then relaxed and started putting on a friendly act. It was enough to make any decent, hard-working Sun Hill regular throw up.

Ted Roach appeared, apprehensive. 'You wanted me, Mr Burnside?'

Burnside offered no greeting, but led the way towards the cells. 'Number five, I think, Sergeant Peters.' Alec Peters grabbed the keys and deferentially edged past to open the door.

The tattooed man sprawled on the bunk within propped himself up on one elbow and turned a menacing gaze on his visitors. In his whole lazy, waiting posture there was a threat of imminent mayhem.

'All right, chummy,' snapped Cryer, taking charge of the territory to which he was well accustomed. 'Up on your feet.'

'Go get stuffed.'

Cryer was about to advance on the prisoner when Burnside put a restraining hand on his arm.

'Yes, ta very much, sergeant. Now close the door.'

Cryer hesitated; but there was no mistaking that this was an order. He pushed the door shut and watched, bewildered, as Burnside ambled across the cell and flopped down on the edge of the bunk.

'Right, then, old son.' He surveyed the occupant benevolently. 'I hear tell you're well choked with me 'cos I gave you a slap.'

The man made a cautious assessment of Burnside and his companions. When he spoke, the ferocious rasp had gone. He was mild, almost apologetic, but with an odd undercurrent of slyness. 'What you going on about, Frank?'

The terrible truth began to dawn on Bob Cryer, just before Burnside took up the conversation again.

'Gentlemen, meet DS Nobby Trimlett.'

'I don't believe it,' Roach whispered.

Cryer silently seconded that. But the truth was that he did believe it, and saw how everything was shaping up against Ted Roach and himself.

Burnside was making the most of it. 'How d'you feel now, Bobby, old son?'

At the same time Trimlett was on his feet, looming over Ted Roach. 'Well, who's been a naughty little copper, then?'

Roach tried to face him out. Trimlett was silent, waiting. And Burnside was waiting for someone else to make a certain move.

'I'm sorry,' said Roach at last. 'I'm not in the habit of hitting prisoners.'

'Glad to hear it, mate.'

Trimlett was smiling, seeming genuinely matey. Roach risked a sheepish grin in return. Without warning, the detective sergeant ducked and faked a head-butt at him. Burnside evidently thought this was uproariously funny; Roach did not.

Trimlett said, with a savage edge more like the character he had been playing up till now: 'If it hadn't been for your guv'nor here, I was gonna have you on offer.' He patted Roach's cheek, virtually daring him to flinch away. 'He talked me out of it. Now, if I were you, I'd take him round to the first available boozer and buy him a nice big drink. Know what I mean?'

Inspector Christine Frazer had seen enough lethal weapons and enough vicious faces to last her for the rest of the year and quite a while beyond. She had listened to too many whines from solicitors of dubious integrity, and heard too much foul language from the direction of the cells. But once the grubbiness had been scraped away, there was a considerable sense of achievement. Sun Hill had done rather well for itself. The men on the operation had pulled off their coup without anything going up in smoke too soon; and you couldn't fault the composure and professional expertise of the men processing the catch as it was trawled in through the doors. It was on occasions like this that you knew you were in the right job. She felt part of the team, and was glad to be one of them. Even alongside Bob Cryer, a good man, but one with harmful limitations.

She would have to put Sergeant Cryer right before long, if he failed to put himself right. They could not afford the teamwork they had seen today to be impeded by old enmities and misunderstandings. Or, she thought ruefully, by old passions and misunderstandings of a different kind.

Christine Frazer paused at the foot of the stairs to the first floor. If anyone had a right to disapprove of Frank Burnside, surely she was the one. But that had nothing to do with the job; and since that crazy time, long ago, and yet somehow only yesterday, she had concentrated singlemindedly on the job. Whatever its dangers and frustrations, the inner hurt was a lot less.

She told herself she was glad Frank had come here. She would be glad to work with him. He would be good for the place. She was positive of that, even if few of the rest of them saw it that way yet. As for herself, whether his presence would be good for her . . . that was something to be decided. And she was the one who would do the deciding.

The confrontation had to be faced sooner rather then later. Resolutely she climbed the stairs and went into the CID office. Finding Dashwood and Carver in the outer office, she almost snatched at the excuse to utter a few platitudes and make her escape. But that would only be postponing it. Through the partition she saw Frank Burnside at his desk, taking it over just by sitting there, as he had taken over so many things in his time by just being there. She went through, trusting she looked more trim and official then she felt, and closed the door behind her.

411

'Hello, you sexy bit of prime beef.'

It was the typical exaggerated old language, the typical coarse, suggestive smile. But she had to smile back. That had always been the trouble.

'Hello, Frank.' She shook hands formally, unsure whether Dashwood and Carver were covertly watching. 'Welcome to the farm.'

He waved her to a chair. She hesitated. But there was no reason why she should not sit down to discuss official business; no reason why there should ever again be anything between them but official business.

'Cuppa?' he invited.

In spite of what she had told herself, she somehow did not want these few moments to be interrupted by Carver or anyone else fussing in and out with tea and trimmings.

'No, thanks.' She studied him across the desk. 'So here you are, a DI at last.'

'Good, isn't it? But no less than I deserve, sweetheart.'

'Modest as ever.'

'Modesty was never one of my faults. You of all people should know that, Chrissy.'

Yes, she of all people did know that. But she felt a tremor inside. It was a long time since anybody had called her Chrissy.

'I still think about you, Chrissy,' he went on, his expression giving nothing away to anybody who might be looking through the partition, but his voice ready to suggest giving a lot.

'Frank, please.'

'Well, I do.' For once he sounded unsure of himself. 'I'm divorced now, you know.'

'Yes, I heard.' It was time to change the subject and really talk sense – official sense. 'Look, Frank, there's something I ought to say to you. I do think you should mark a few people's cards about the Countryman business.'

'Oh. Like who?'

'Ted Roach, for one. And Bob Cryer.'

'Stuff them.'

'Frank, I don't believe you understand what they're thinking.'

That familiar stubborn expression was settling into place.

'Darling, I don't give a toss what they think. They can think whatever they like.'

'So, if you don't mind one way or the other, why not tell them anyway?'

He shook his head. 'No way. If Ted Roach don't like me, that's his problem.'

Frazer got to her feet. 'I don't think you're being fair. Ted can only go by what he –'

'Ted?' he echoed meaningly. 'So it's "Ted" already, is it? Now don't tell me you and him . . . ?'

'Certainly not.' Her voice rose, but she throttled it back. 'That is not the situation. A ridiculous idea. I just think it would be better all round if you let

412

them into the whole picture, so that you can all start over again, from scratch.'

'I don't mind starting over again with you,' he leered.

'Frank –'

'Nope. I don't have to explain me, or my past, to no bastard. Especially a pair of wets like Roach and Cryer.'

'What did I ever see in you?' She had her hand on the catch of the door. 'You really don't care, do you?'

'I care about you, Chrissy.'

With a disillusioned shake of her head she went out, hoping that neither Carver nor Dashwood could lip-read.

After she had changed into her own clothes and was heading out, with the prospect of a solitary afternoon and evening in the house ahead of her, tidying up yet again, watering the plants, considering a change of colour scheme in the sitting room, or leafing vainly through the televison journals in the hope of finding something tolerable to fill in the odd hour or so, she passed Alec Peters, Tom Penny and Bob Cryer coming out of the men's locker room. They, at any rate, had something to occupy their minds: they were in the middle of a heated argument about a footballer whose tactics as a striker, from what little she could catch, bore a remarkable resemblance to those of the hooligans so forcefully rounded up this very day.

Interrupting a graphic description by Peters of a goal-mouth collision and subsequent colourful injuries, she said: 'Got a minute before you knock off, Bob?'

'Of course, ma'am.' Cryer glanced at his watch. 'See you over there, you two. And mine's a pint.'

When the other two had gone out into the street and the door had swung behind them, Frazer said: 'Bob, there's something I think you should know.'

His reaction was immediately prickly. 'If it's about what I said earlier, ma'am – '

'It is.'

He could look as stubborn as Frank Burnside. With Ted Roach thrown in for good measure, a fine working trio they were going to make! 'I'll not mention it again, ma'am,' he said stonily, 'but that still don't change how I feel and what I know.'

'And what do you know, Bob? Come on, tell me.'

After a sombre pause, Cryer said: 'I was around when Operation Country-man was under way, ma'am. There were some nasty smells and some nasty people, and it was a stinking time for everyone. But when it came to the real ripest stink . . . well, how they missed *him*, I don't know.'

She was not sure Frank Burnside would approve of her coming out with the truth. Contemptuous of everyone else's opinion, he would most likely be furious if he discovered she had blabbed. He had as good as told her that. But she had her own stubborn streak.

413

'You don't know?' she said quietly. 'Well, I do. Frank Burnside was an actual, integral part of Countryman. A very important part of it, as it happens. Just as he was of Operation Red Card these last few months. And a lot of people like you wouldn't have known about *that* one if Ted Roach hadn't given it away, would they? Or believed it, if they'd been told?'

'Countryman?' whispered Cryer. 'Burnside was in the thing, not . . .?'

He looked in danger of banging his head against the wall, involuntarily, or maybe deliberately.

She said: 'Right, I've marked your card. See you in the morning.'

At the bar of the pub, Mike Dashwood stood close to his new boss, flannelling away for all he was worth, recalling odd tales of Burnside's past adventures and glossing over the unsavoury bits to leave a shimmer of admiration. Carver, not to be outdone, contributed: 'You know the guv'nor here done me up like a kipper on me first real collar, don't you, Mike?'

Dashwood was far from happy at being interrupted. 'Jimmy, if I've heard that story from you once, I've heard it a dozen times.'

The fawning enthusiasm was damped down as the door swung open. Although nobody wanted to make any kind of an issue of it, pretending that everything was going on sociably as normal, just the way it ought to do in the bright atmosphere of any pub, it was impossible to avoid a sudden hiatus, like a sustained rest in the middle of a piece of rowdy music, when Ted Roach came gallantly in and made for his usual place at the bar counter.

Alec Peters began to talk more loudly about some football complexities. Tom Penny seemed all at once to find something worthy of examination floating in his beer.

Burnside greeted Roach with that slash of a smile. 'Right, what are you having, old son?'

Roach did a swift rundown of all the familiar regular faces, and ended up with the face that was going to rule his life from now on. 'Well, if it's all the same to you,' he said stoically, 'I'd like to buy you the first one . . . guv'nor.'

Burnside's smile was all-encompassing now. Nobody would have called it attractive, but for once it appeared to pack in some genuine goodwill. 'You just called me guv'nor. That's good enough for me, old son.' He held out his hand. 'So, like I said, what you having?'

Ted Roach surrendered with a lopsided grin of his own, and shook hands. There was an audible sigh of relief around the bar. Any outbreak of hostilities had been averted; or, at the least, postponed.

'A pint of the best, ta, guv'nor.'

'And another one of the same for me, darling.' DI Burnside was sketching a commanding gesture at the barmaid when he spotted Sergeant Cryer pushing through the corner door from the street. Cryer swerved towards the far end of the bar, but Burnside kept his finger raised and added his strident voice to it. 'Well, Bobby, old son. Drink?'

'Thanks a lot, but the lads have got me one in down there.'

'Please yourself.'

Cryer wavered, then changed course and approached the DI. A drink might have lubricated what he had to say, but he made an effort to manage without it. 'It seems I owe you an apology, Mr Burnside.'

Burnside rolled this round his mouth and his mind, savouring the flavour. 'Well, Bobby, old son, if you can't accept my drink, I don't see how I can accept your – '

'This is hard enough as it is, Mr Burnside.' Bob Cryer's teeth grated against one another like fingernails scraping the bottom of an enamel bowl. 'I've said I'm apologizing. I've been in the wrong. I was out of order this morning.'

Burnside reached for his glass and raised it in a mocking salute. 'So shall you reap.'

'That's how it has to be,' Cryer accepted. But he could not restrain one last defensive thrust. 'I still don't like you that much.'

'I won't lose any kip.'

'No, nor me.' Bob Cryer found himself echoing the shamefaced grins of Ted Roach and his underlings. 'All right, then. I'll have a pint, thanks very much.'

'Well, it's a start, isn't it, old son?'

So it was a start. There had to be a fresh start on the Sun Hill patch. That had been obvious from the day that Roy Galloway's departure was announced. What it would lead to next week, next month, and all the months from then on, nobody as yet would risk predicting.